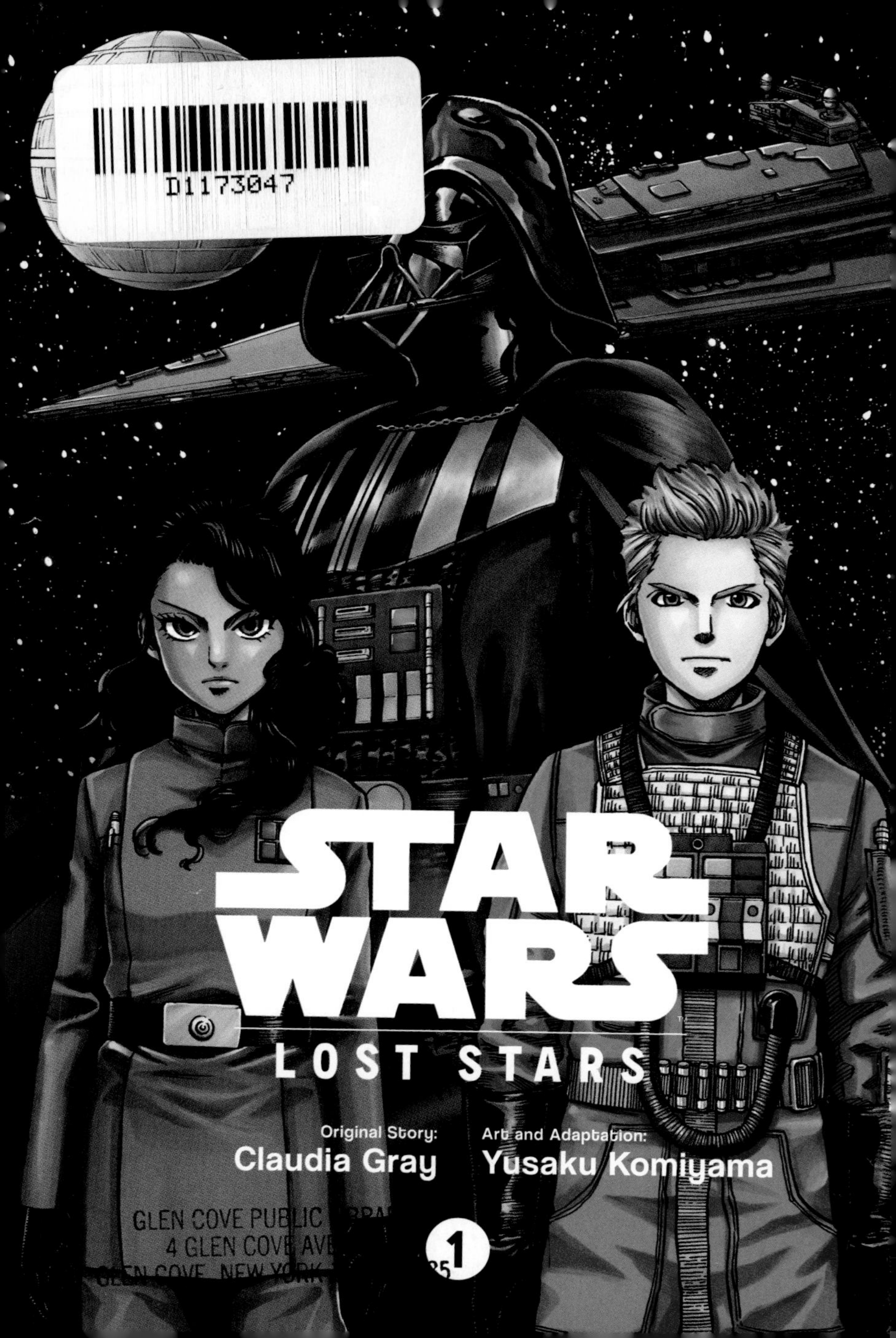

STAR WARS
LOST STARS

Original Story:
Claudia Gray

Art and Adaptation:
Yusaku Komiyama

1

STAR WARS  LOST STARS

VOLUME 1 CONTENTS

Chapter. 01
003

Chapter. 02
059

Chapter. 03
131

Chapter. 04
163

Chapter. 05
185

Chapter. 06
223

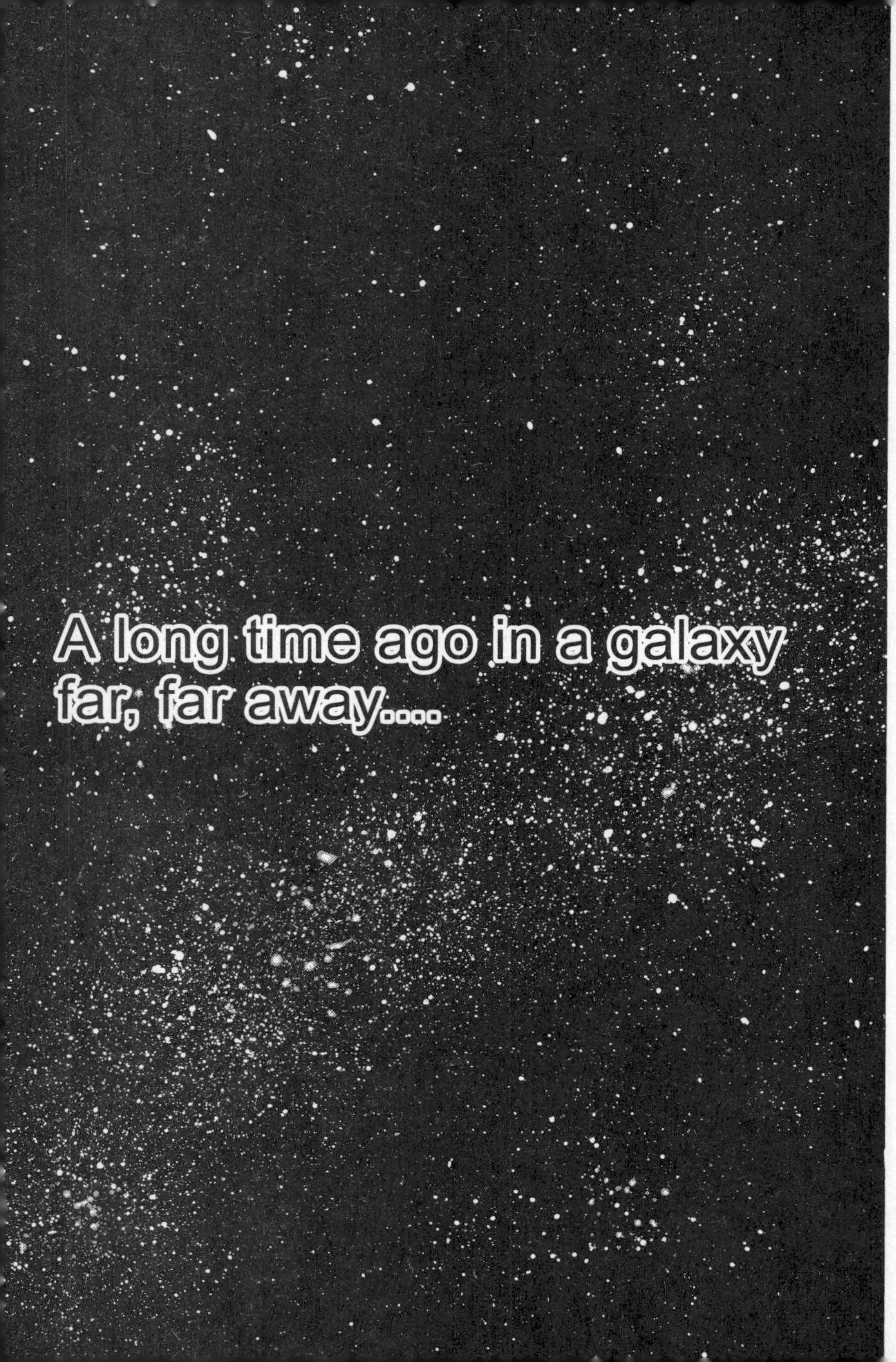
A long time ago in a galaxy far, far away....

Chapter. 01

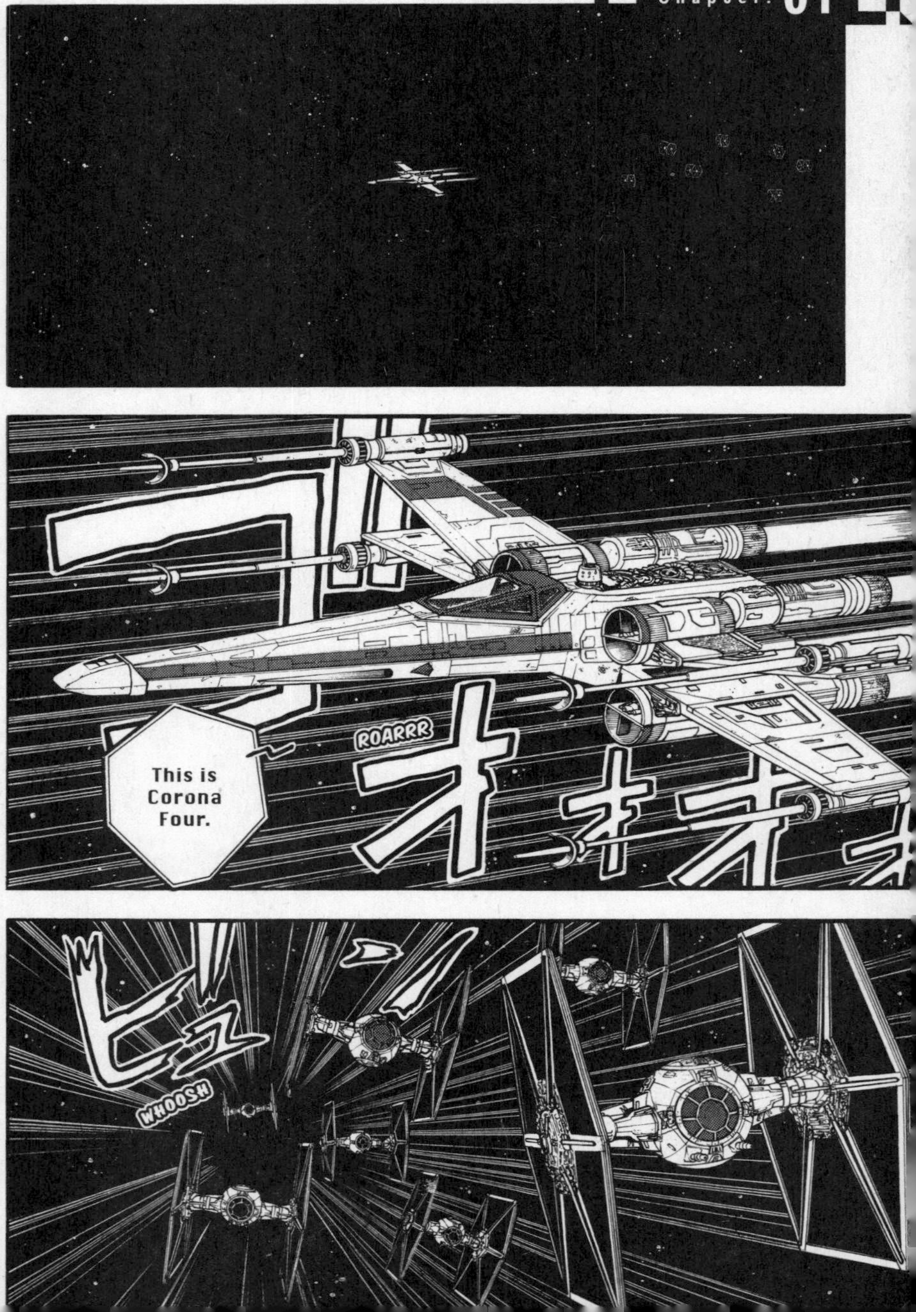
ROARRR
This is Corona Four.
WHOOSH

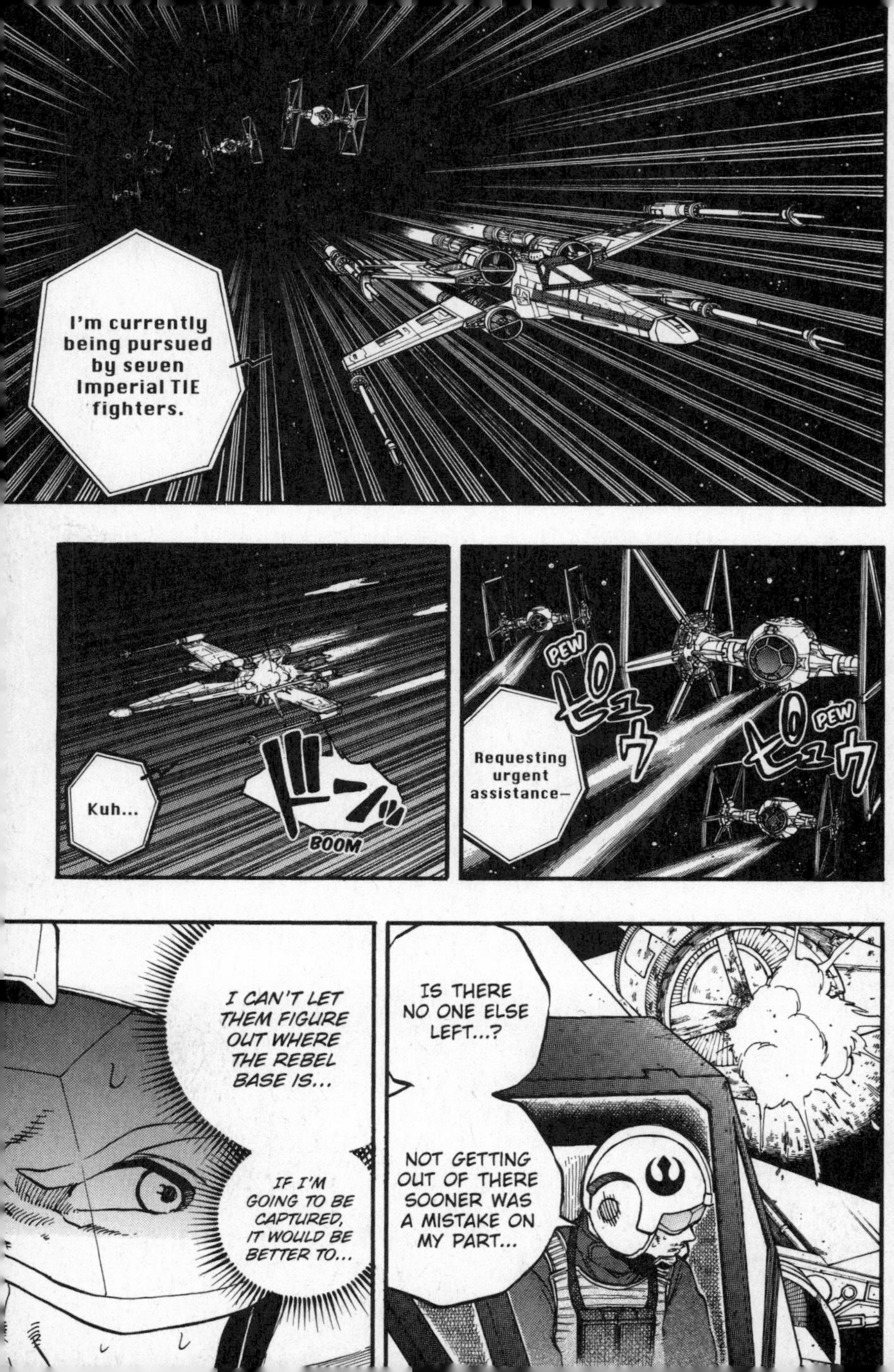
I'm currently being pursued by seven Imperial TIE fighters.
PEW
ピュウ
Requesting urgent assistance—
PEW
ピュウ
ドーッ
BOOM
Kuh...
IS THERE NO ONE ELSE LEFT...?
NOT GETTING OUT OF THERE SOONER WAS A MISTAKE ON MY PART...
I CAN'T LET THEM FIGURE OUT WHERE THE REBEL BASE IS...
IF I'M GOING TO BE CAPTURED, IT WOULD BE BETTER TO...

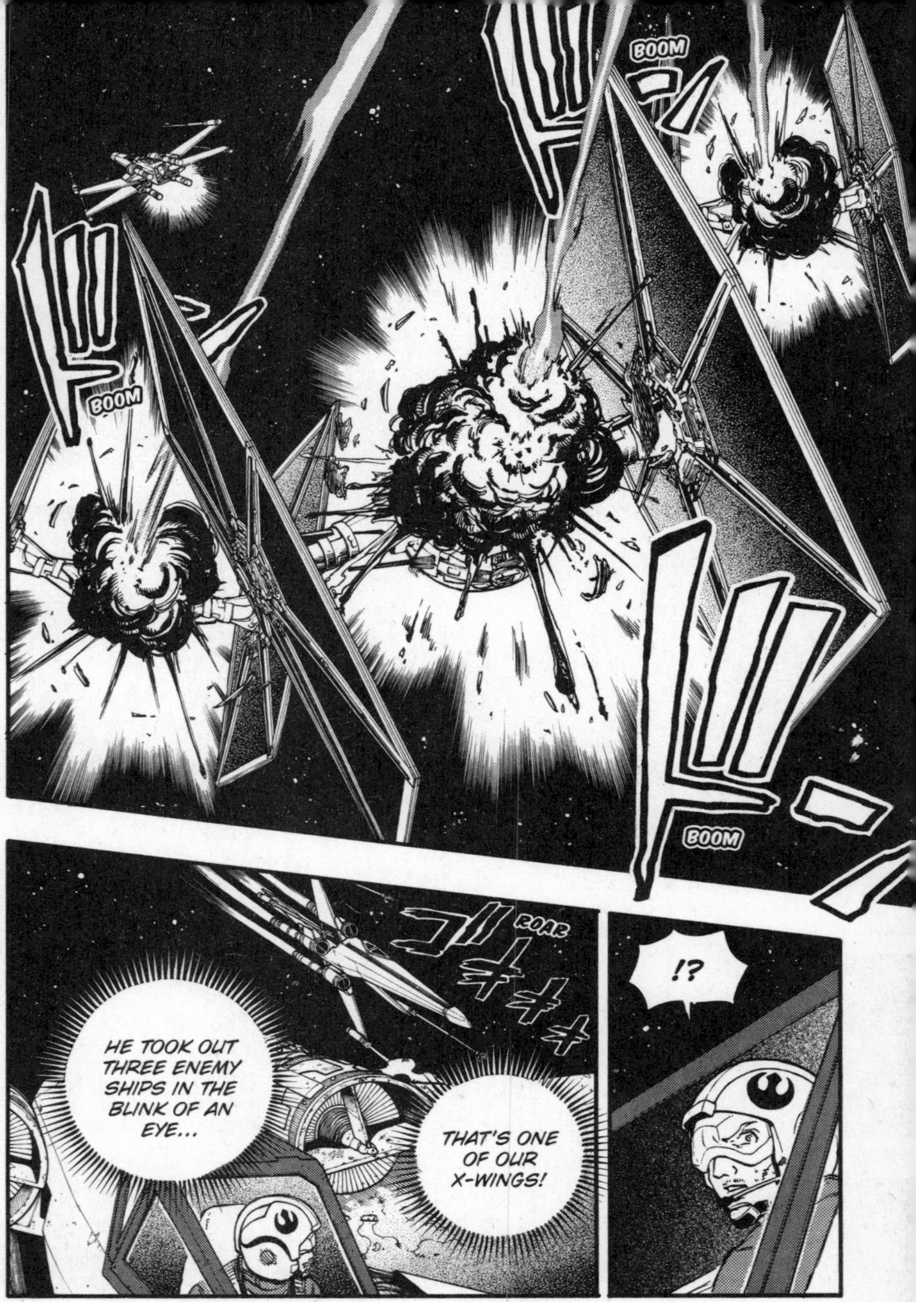
BOOM
BOOM
BOOM
!?
ROAR
THAT'S ONE OF OUR X-WINGS!
HE TOOK OUT THREE ENEMY SHIPS IN THE BLINK OF AN EYE...

PEW
PEW
VWMM
WHIRL

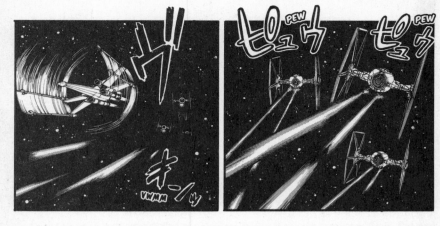

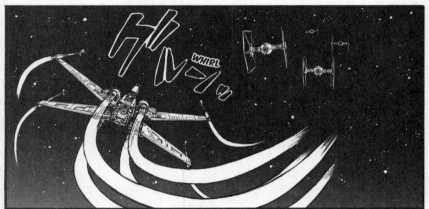

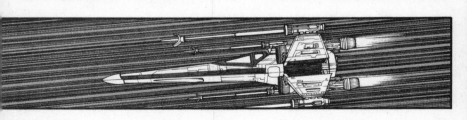

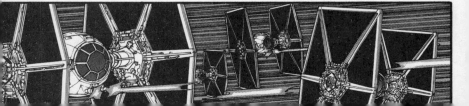

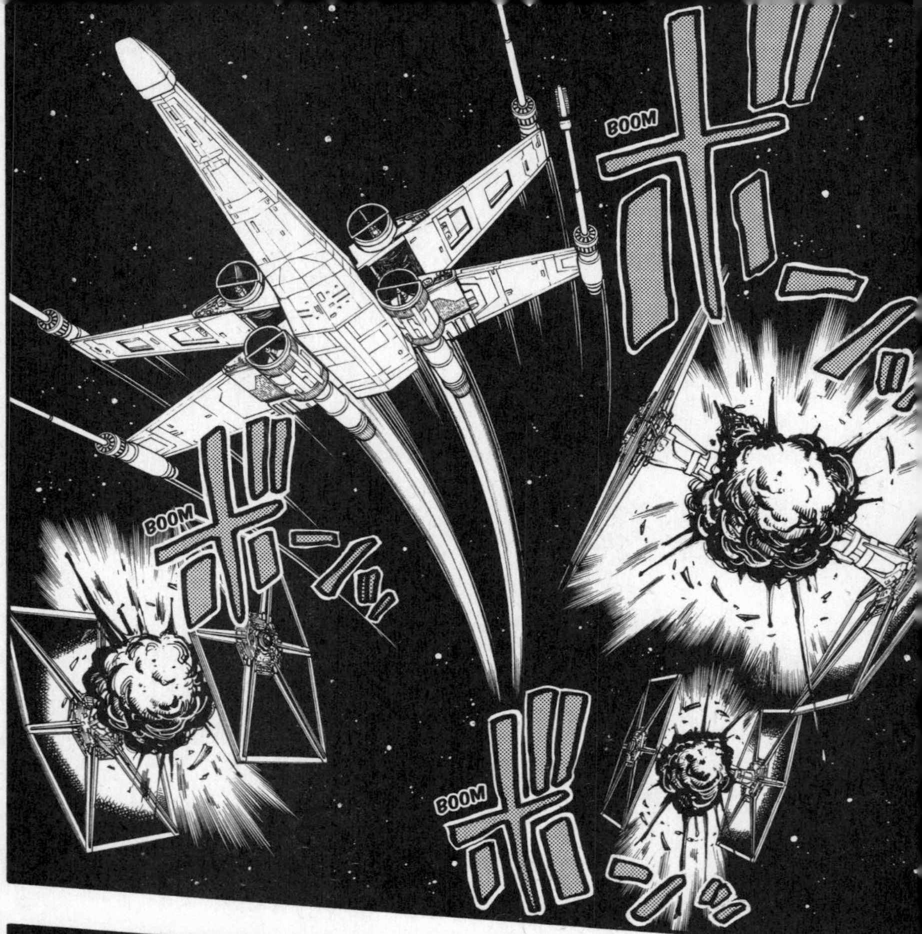
BOOM
BOOM
BOOM

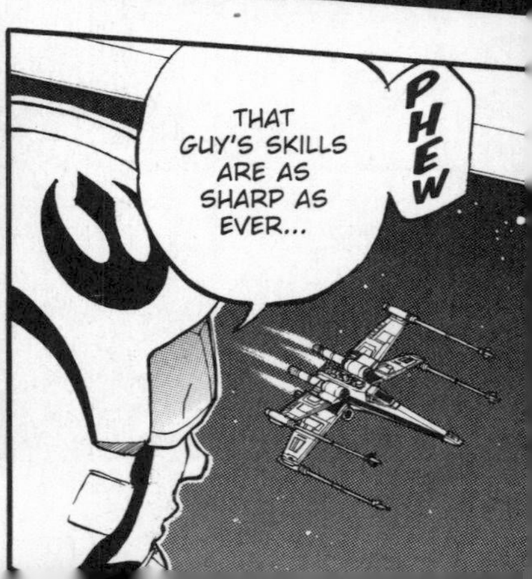
PHEW
THAT GUY'S SKILLS ARE AS SHARP AS EVER...

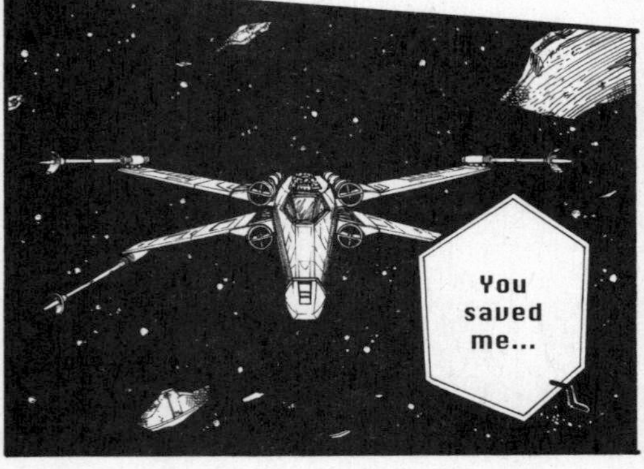
You saved me...

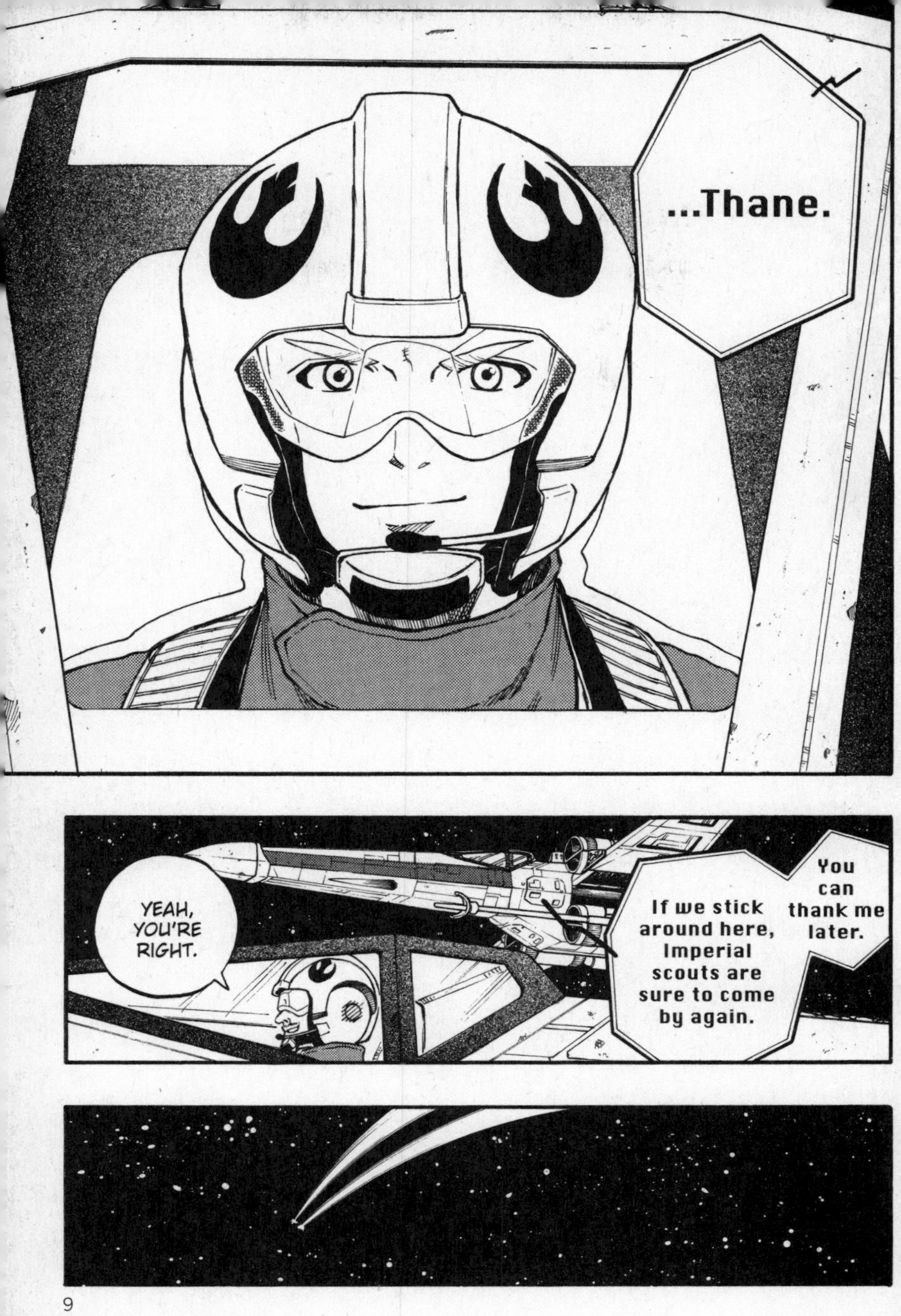
...Thane.
You can thank me later.
If we stick around here, Imperial scouts are sure to come by again.
YEAH, YOU'RE RIGHT.

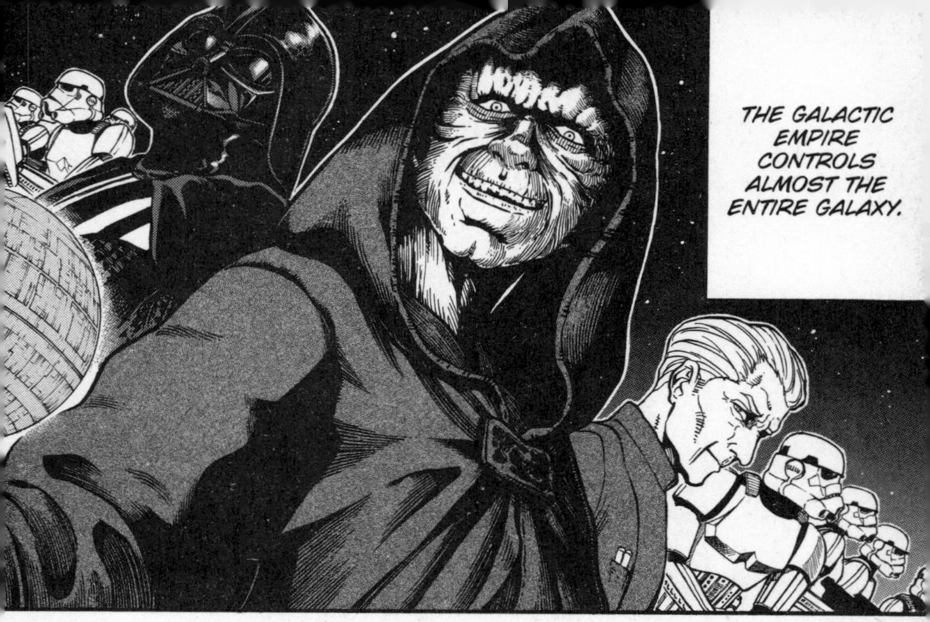
THE GALACTIC EMPIRE CONTROLS ALMOST THE ENTIRE GALAXY.
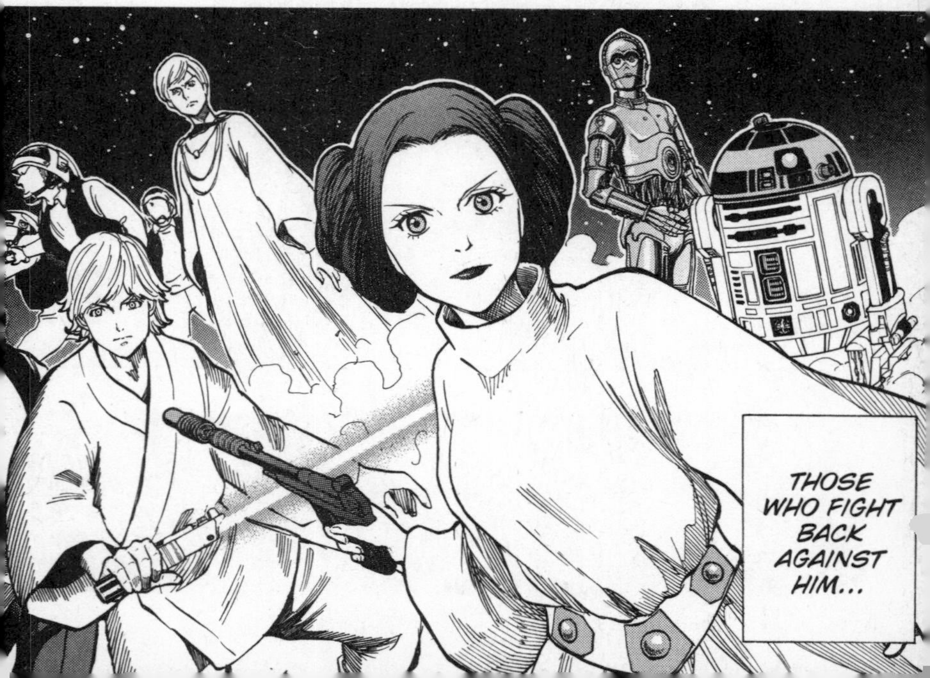
THOSE WHO FIGHT BACK AGAINST HIM...

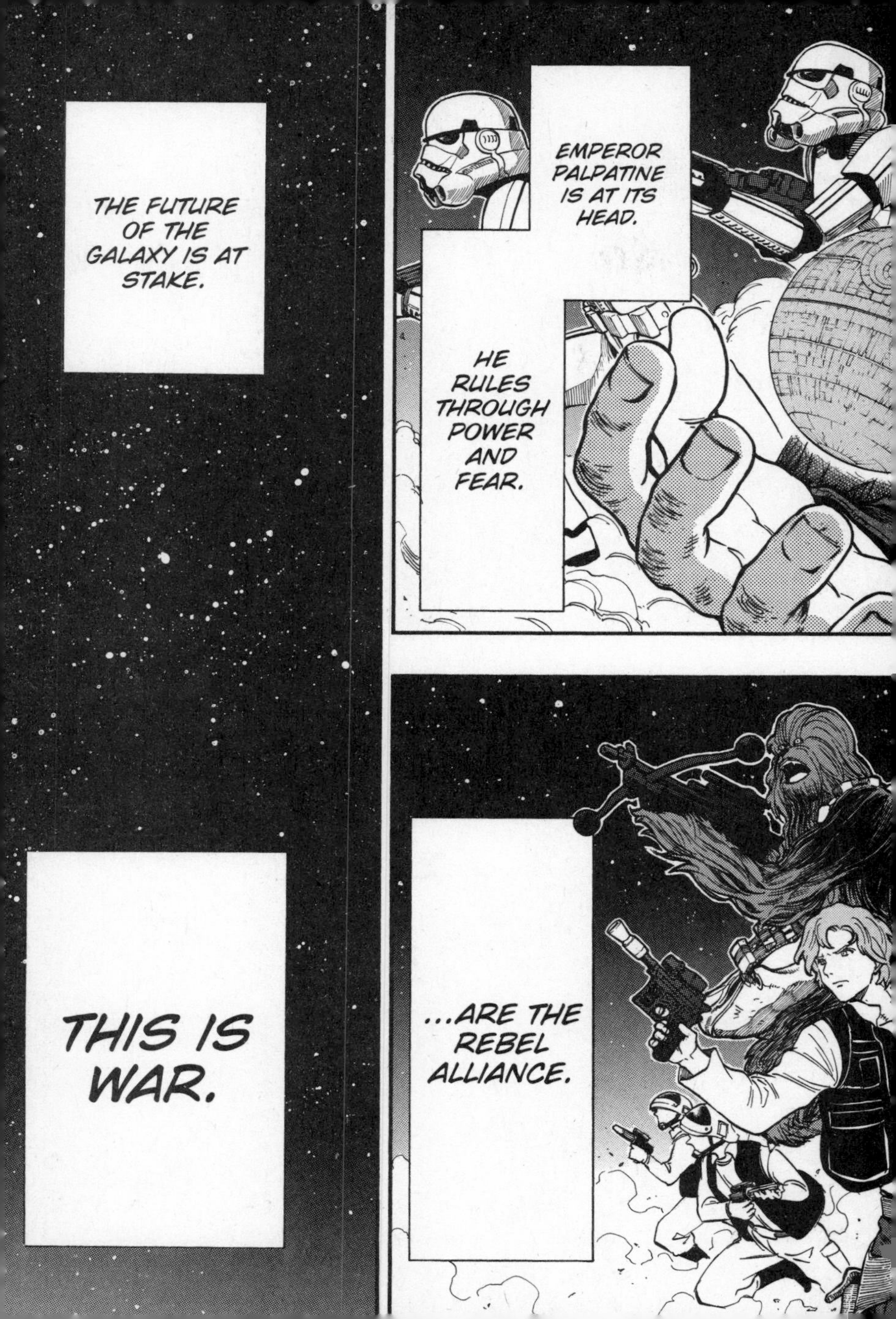
EMPEROR PALPATINE IS AT ITS HEAD.
HE RULES THROUGH POWER AND FEAR.
...ARE THE REBEL ALLIANCE.
THE FUTURE OF THE GALAXY IS AT STAKE.
THIS IS WAR.

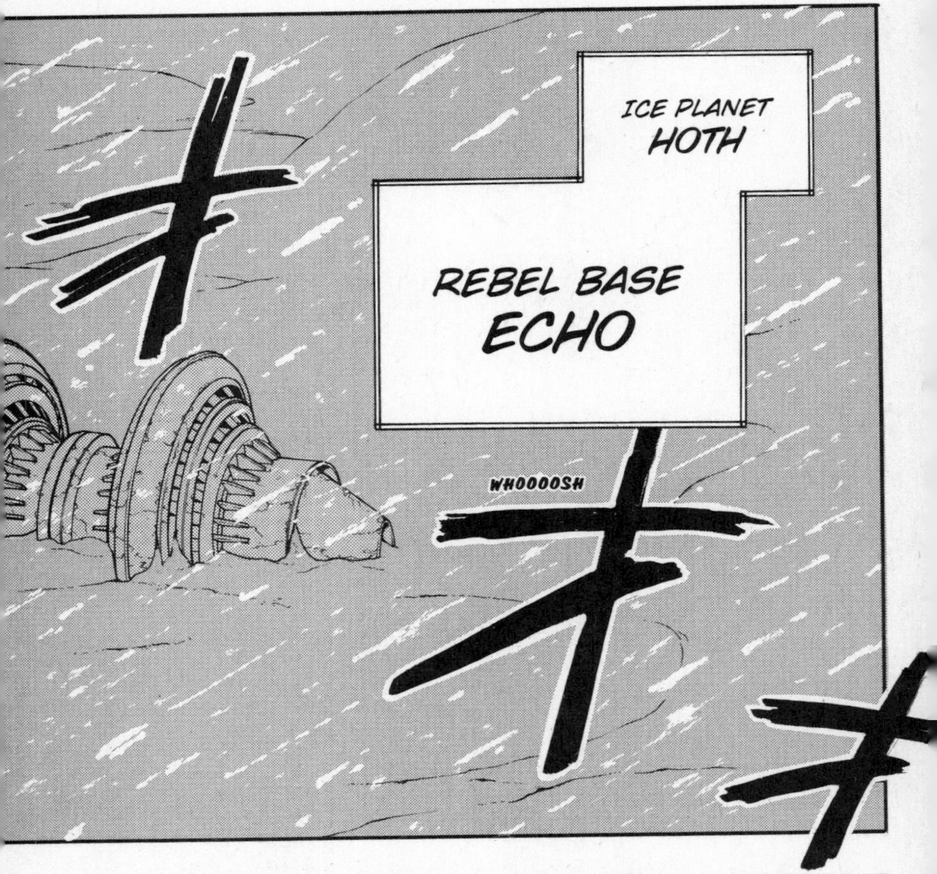
ICE PLANET HOTH
REBEL BASE ECHO
WHOOOOSH

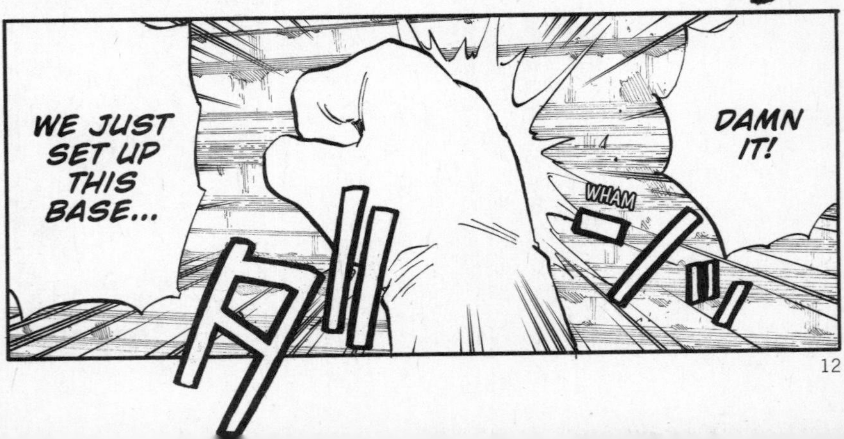
DAMN IT!
WHAM
WE JUST SET UP THIS BASE...

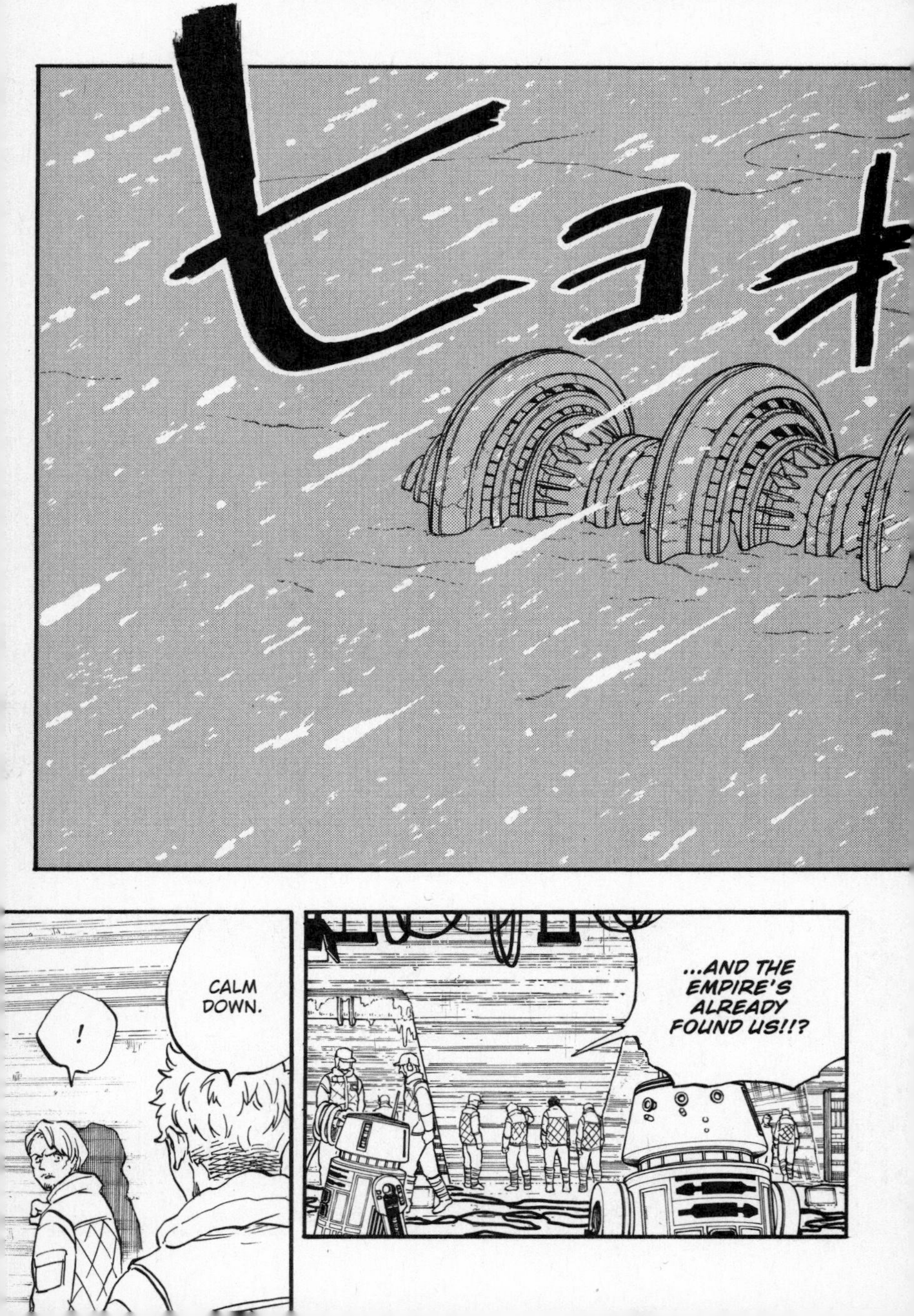
ヒョオ
...AND THE EMPIRE'S ALREADY FOUND US!!?
CALM DOWN.
!

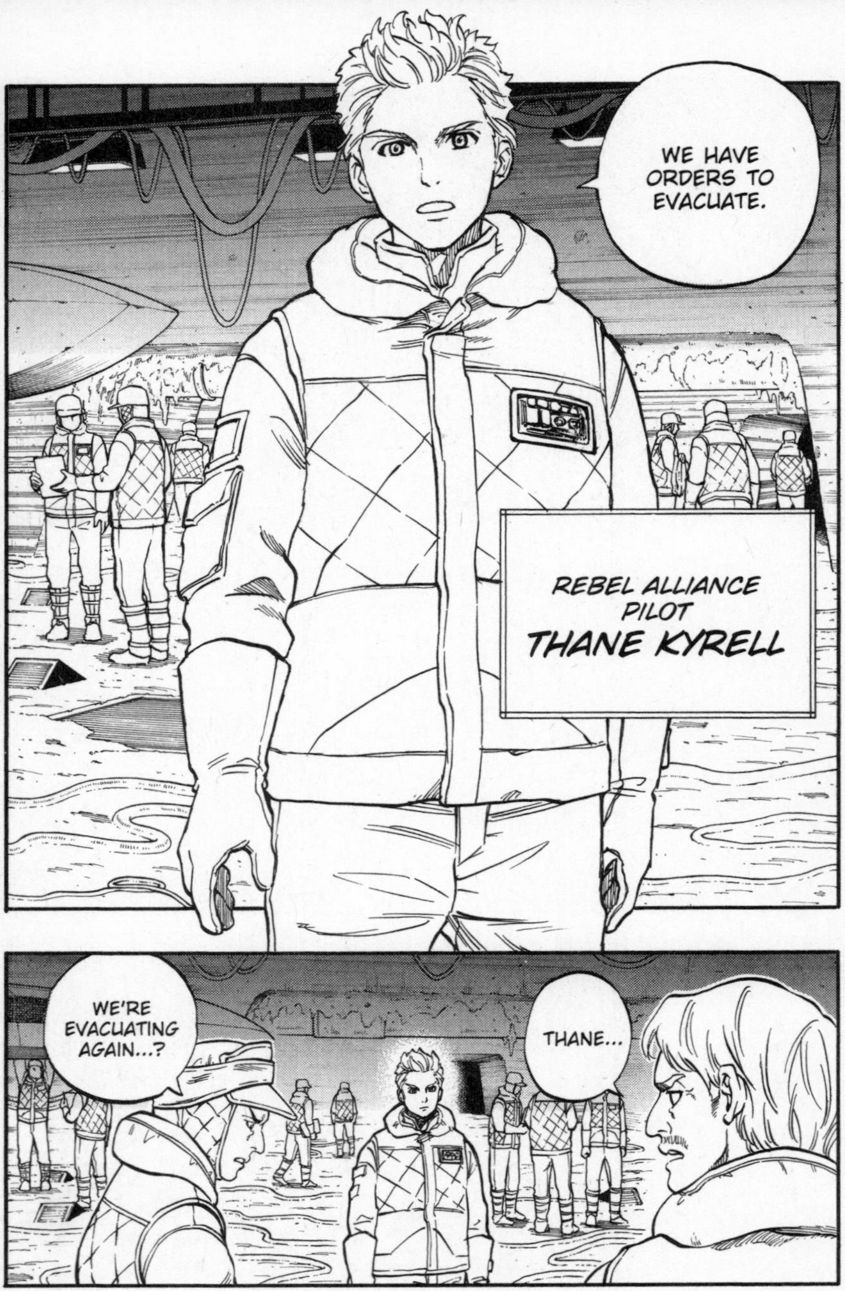
WE HAVE ORDERS TO EVACUATE.
REBEL ALLIANCE PILOT THANE KYRELL
THANE...
WE'RE EVACUATING AGAIN...?

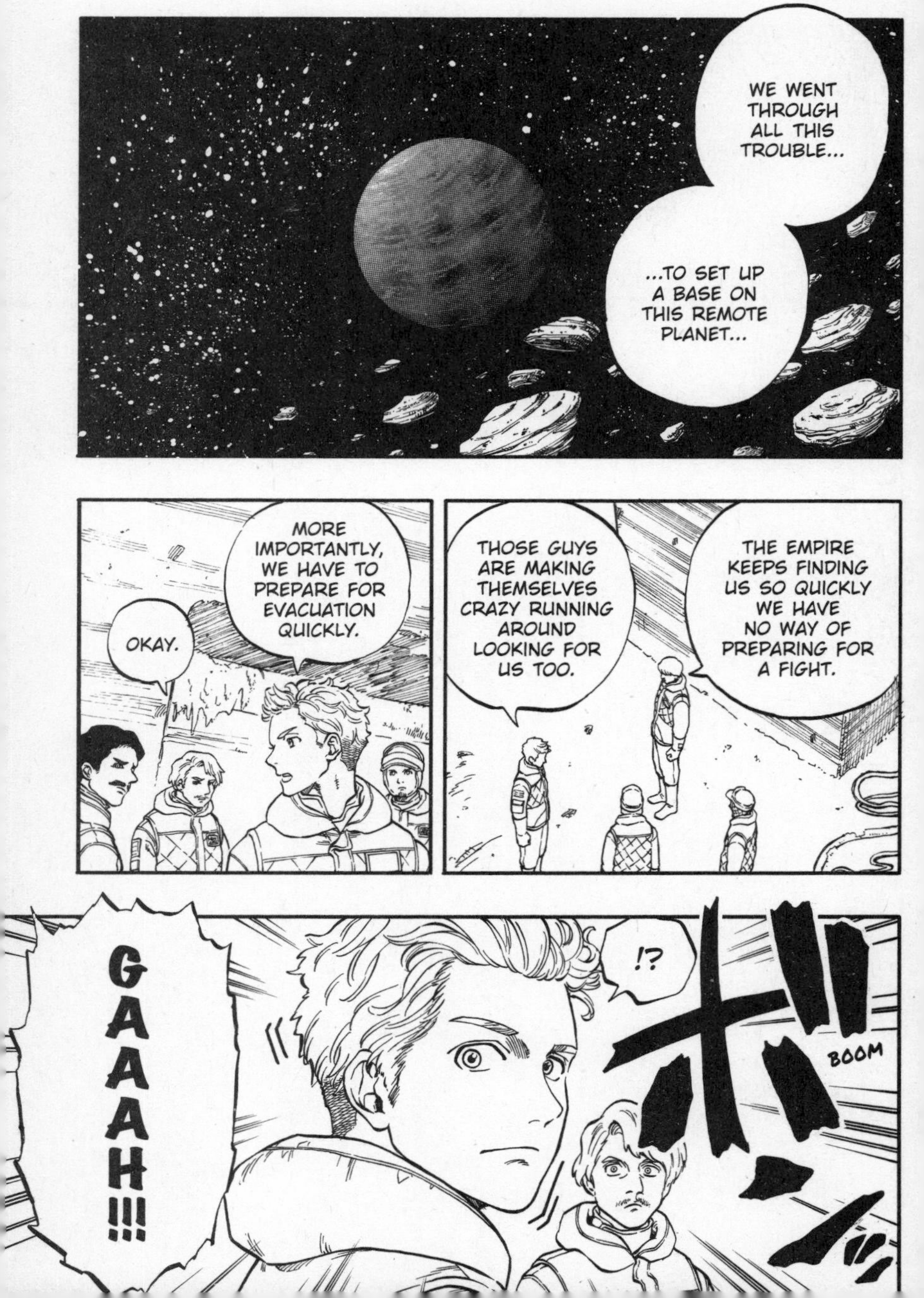
WE WENT THROUGH ALL THIS TROUBLE...
...TO SET UP A BASE ON THIS REMOTE PLANET...
THE EMPIRE KEEPS FINDING US SO QUICKLY WE HAVE NO WAY OF PREPARING FOR A FIGHT.
THOSE GUYS ARE MAKING THEMSELVES CRAZY RUNNING AROUND LOOKING FOR US TOO.
MORE IMPORTANTLY, WE HAVE TO PREPARE FOR EVACUATION QUICKLY.
OKAY.
ボッ
BOOM
!?
GAAAH!!!

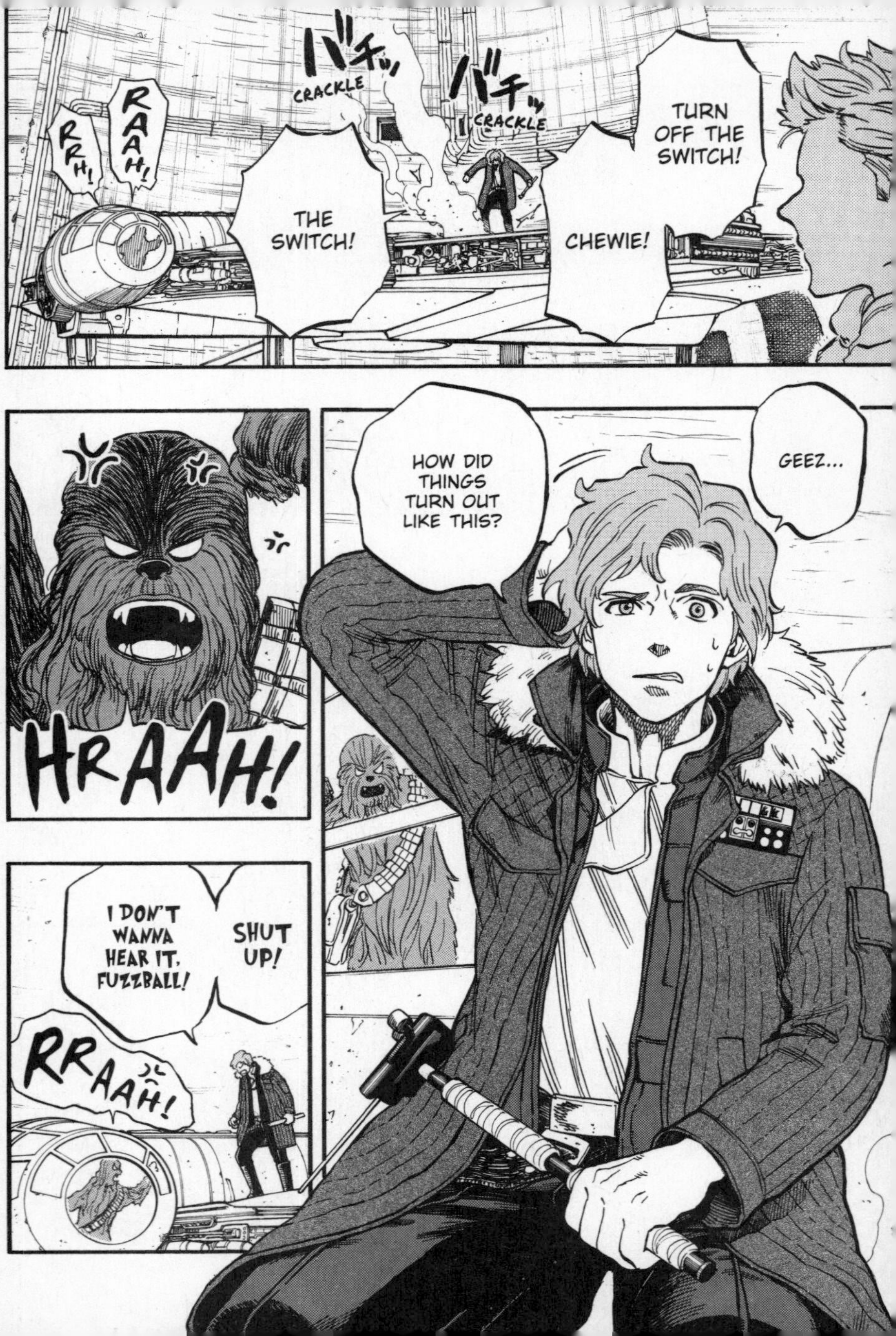
TURN OFF THE SWITCH!
CHEWIE!
バチッ
CRACKLE
バチッ
CRACKLE
THE SWITCH!
RAAAH!
RRH!
GEEZ...
HOW DID THINGS TURN OUT LIKE THIS?
HRAAH!
SHUT UP!
I DON'T WANNA HEAR IT, FUZZBALL!
RRAAH!

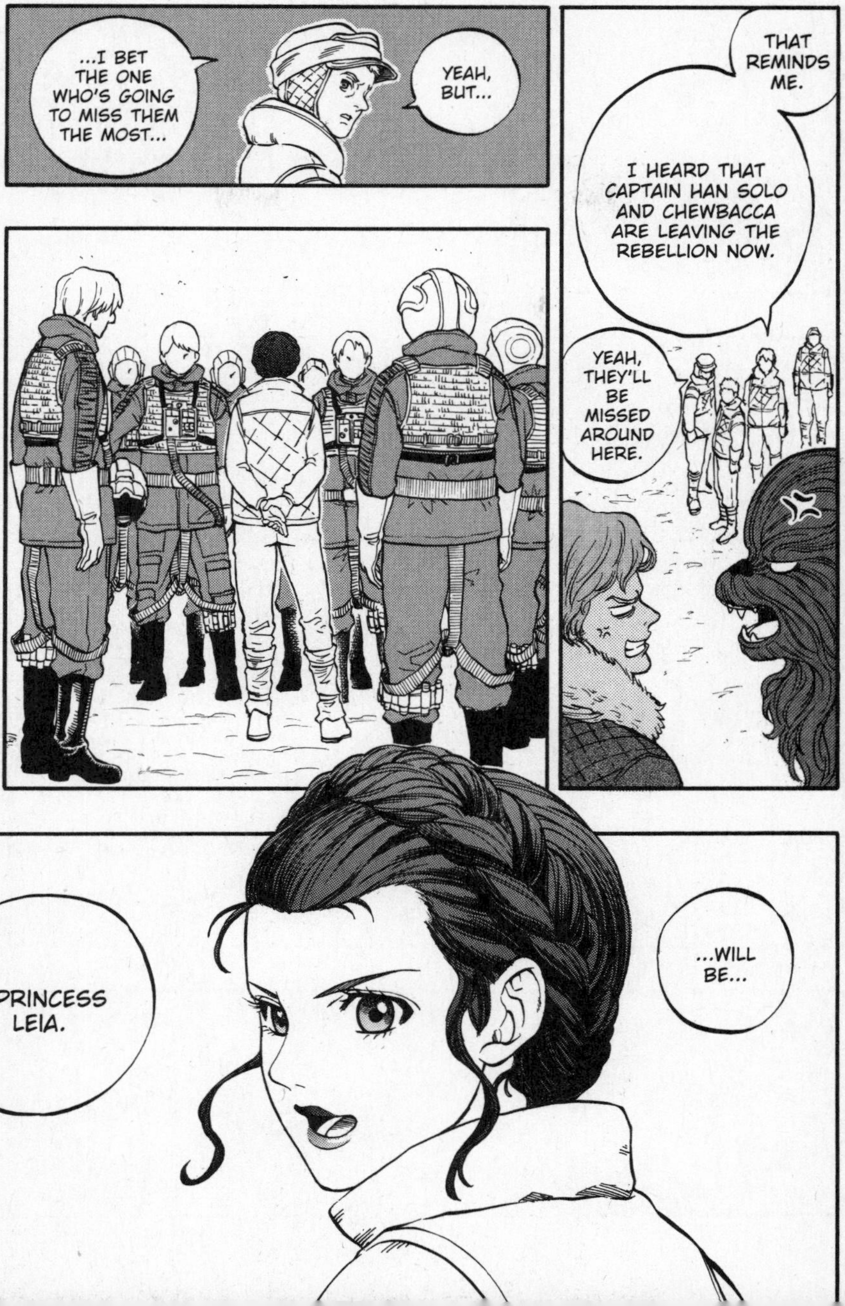
THAT REMINDS ME.
I HEARD THAT CAPTAIN HAN SOLO AND CHEWBACCA ARE LEAVING THE REBELLION NOW.
YEAH, THEY'LL BE MISSED AROUND HERE.
YEAH, BUT...
...I BET THE ONE WHO'S GOING TO MISS THEM THE MOST...
...WILL BE...
...PRINCESS LEIA.

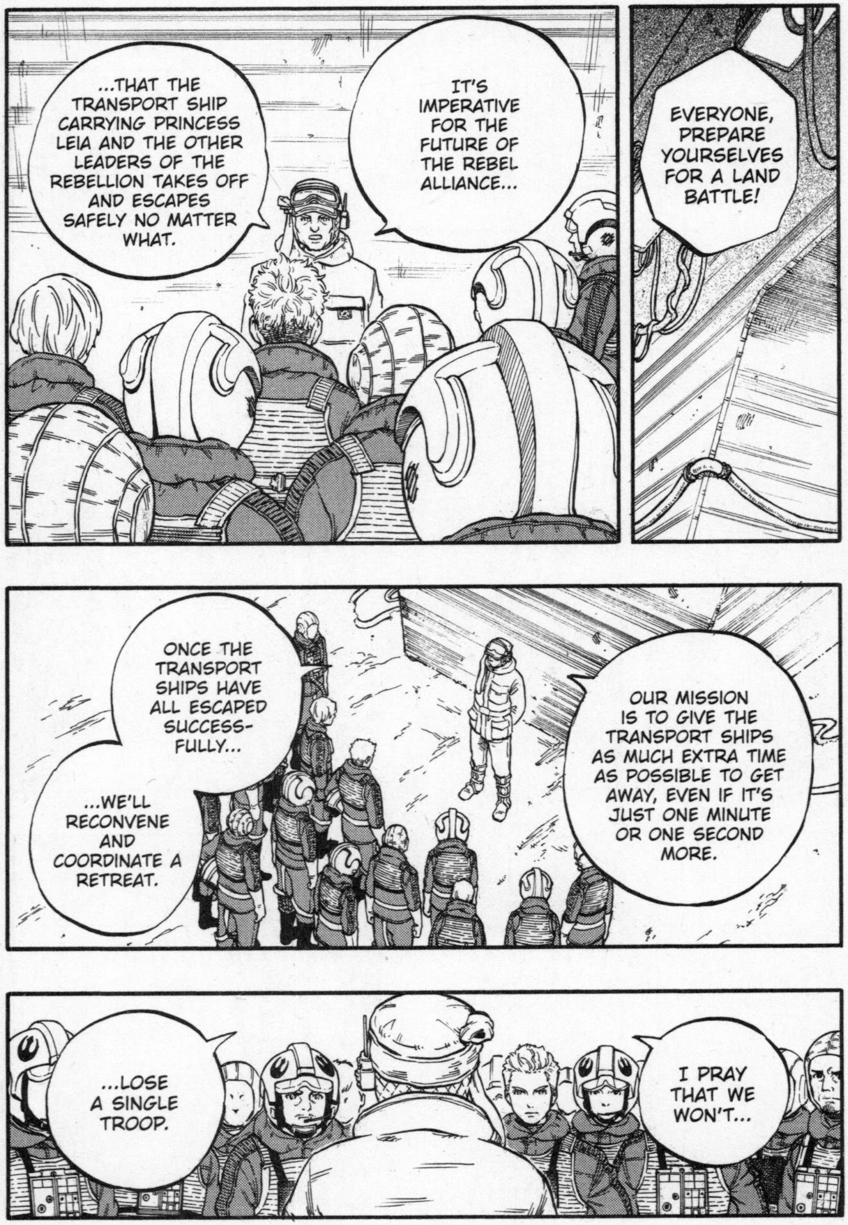
EVERYONE, PREPARE YOURSELVES FOR A LAND BATTLE!
IT'S IMPERATIVE FOR THE FUTURE OF THE REBEL ALLIANCE...
...THAT THE TRANSPORT SHIP CARRYING PRINCESS LEIA AND THE OTHER LEADERS OF THE REBELLION TAKES OFF AND ESCAPES SAFELY NO MATTER WHAT.
OUR MISSION IS TO GIVE THE TRANSPORT SHIPS AS MUCH EXTRA TIME AS POSSIBLE TO GET AWAY, EVEN IF IT'S JUST ONE MINUTE OR ONE SECOND MORE.
ONCE THE TRANSPORT SHIPS HAVE ALL ESCAPED SUCCESS-FULLY...
...WE'LL RECONVENE AND COORDINATE A RETREAT.
I PRAY THAT WE WON'T...
...LOSE A SINGLE TROOP.

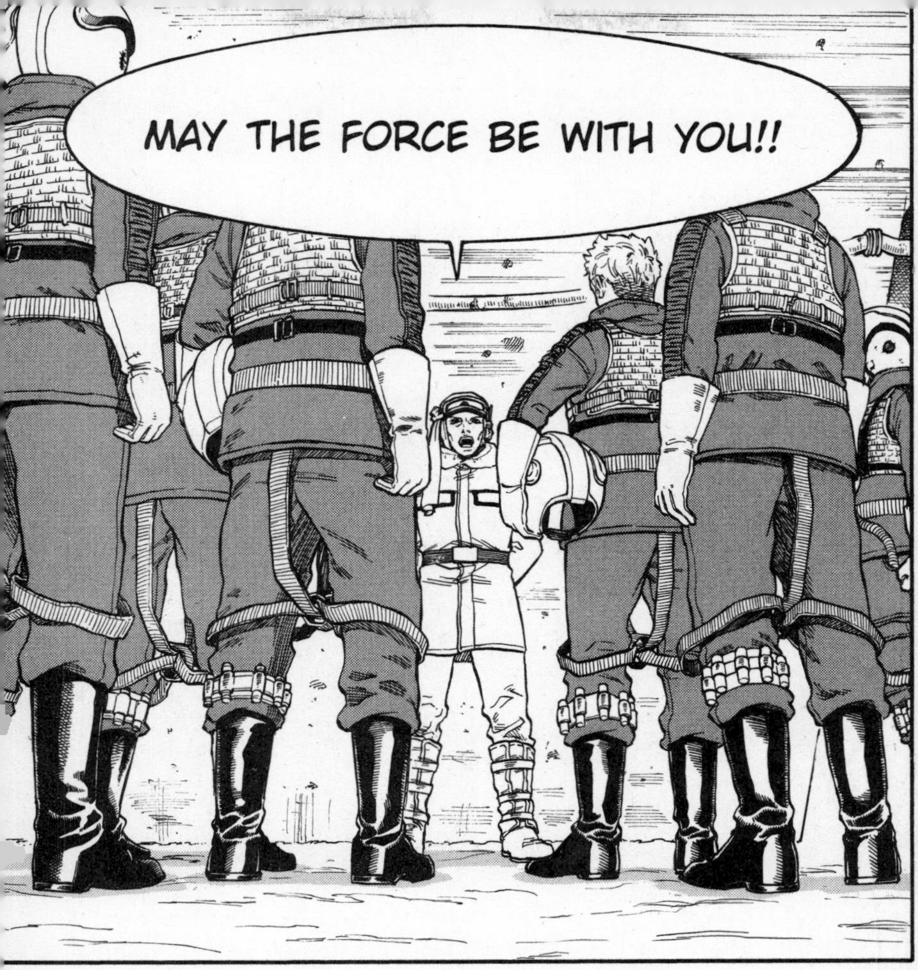
MAY THE FORCE BE WITH YOU!!
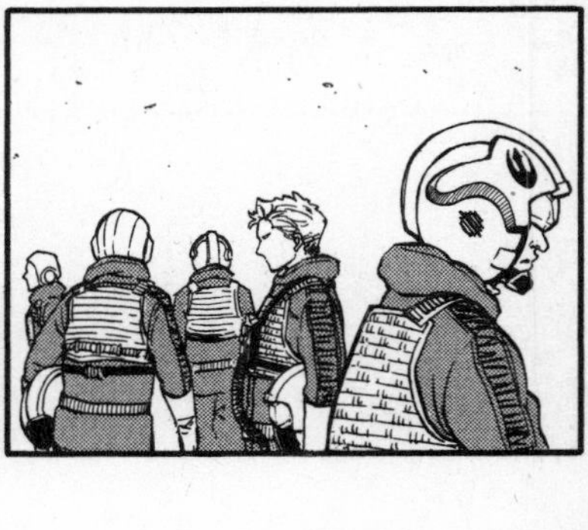
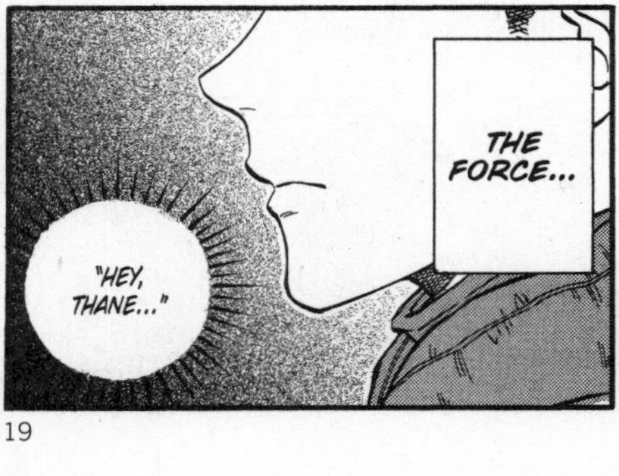
THE FORCE...
"HEY, THANE..."

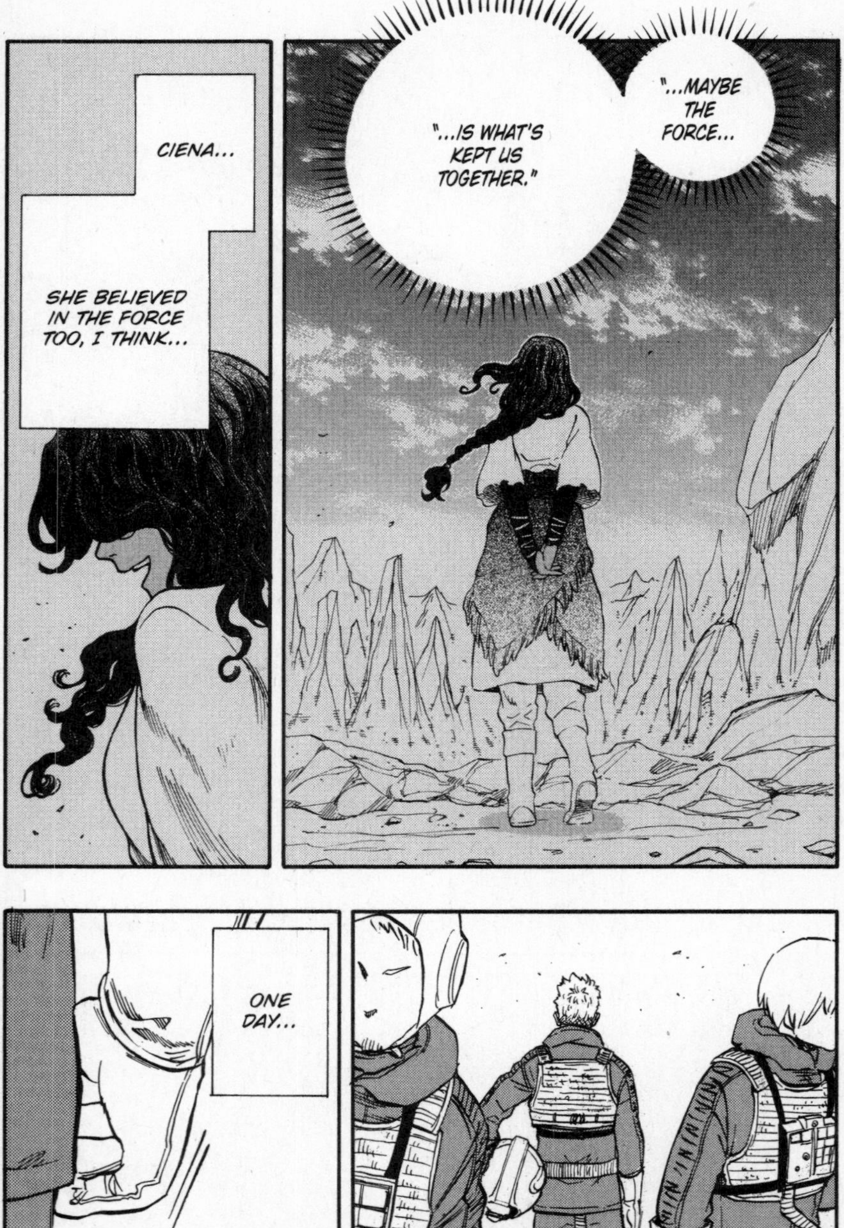
"...MAYBE THE FORCE...
"...IS WHAT'S KEPT US TOGETHER."
CIENA...
SHE BELIEVED IN THE FORCE TOO, I THINK...
ONE DAY...

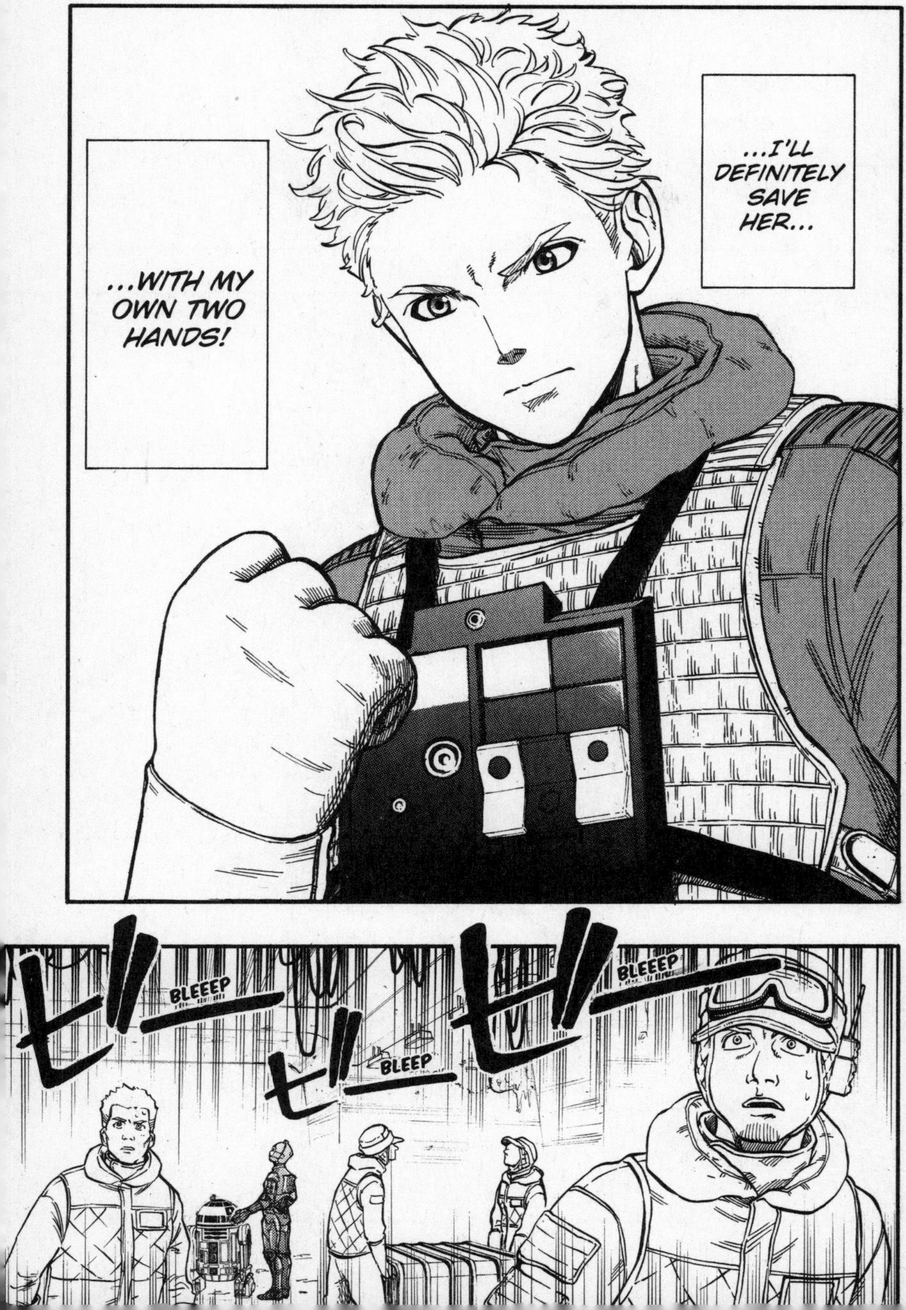
...I'LL DEFINITELY SAVE HER...
...WITH MY OWN TWO HANDS!
ビー
BLEEEP
ビー
BLEEP
ビー
BLEEEP

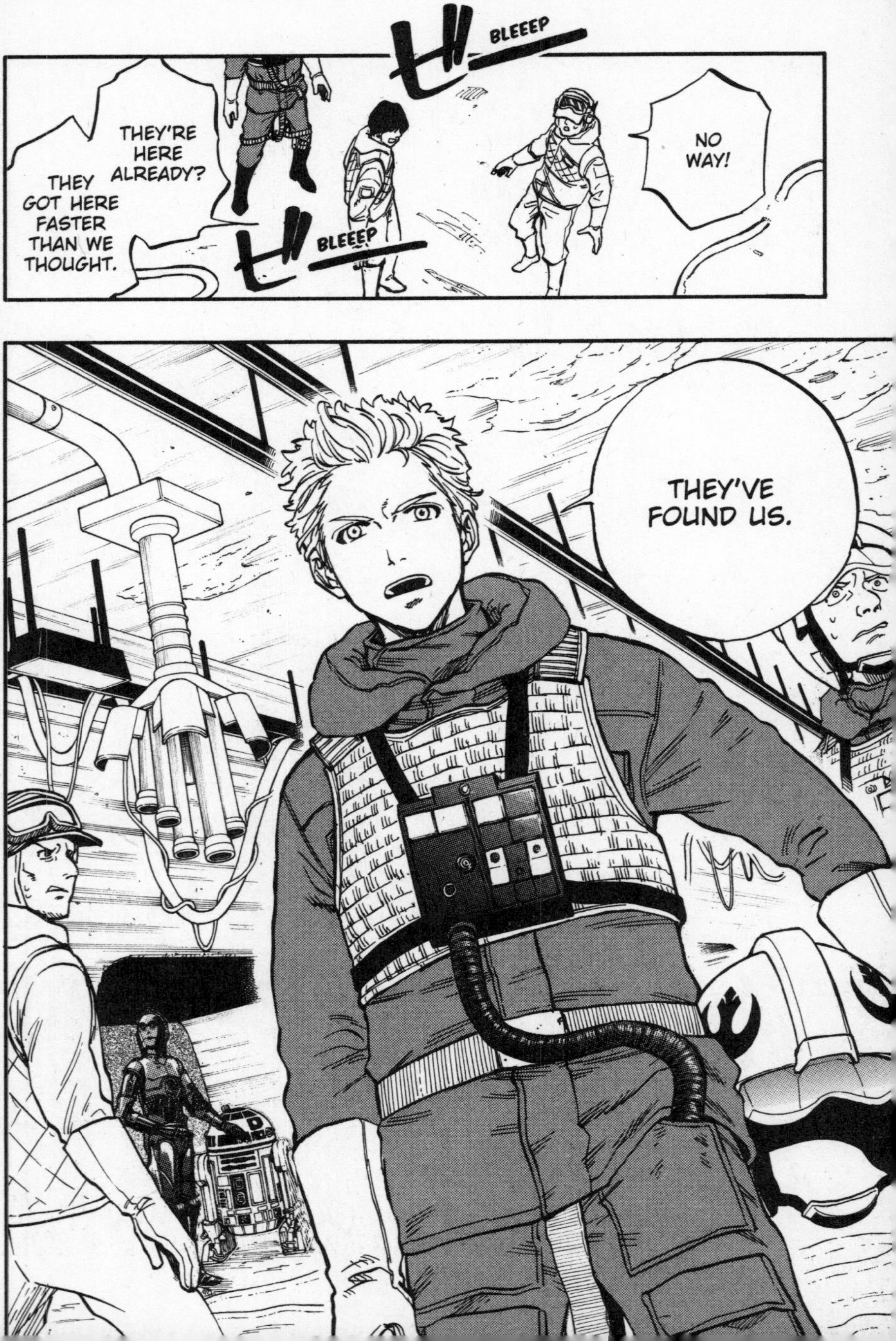
BLEEEP
NO WAY!
THEY'RE HERE ALREADY?
BLEEEP
THEY GOT HERE FASTER THAN WE THOUGHT.
THEY'VE FOUND US.

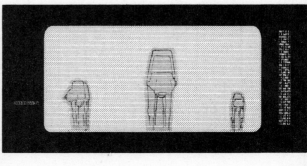

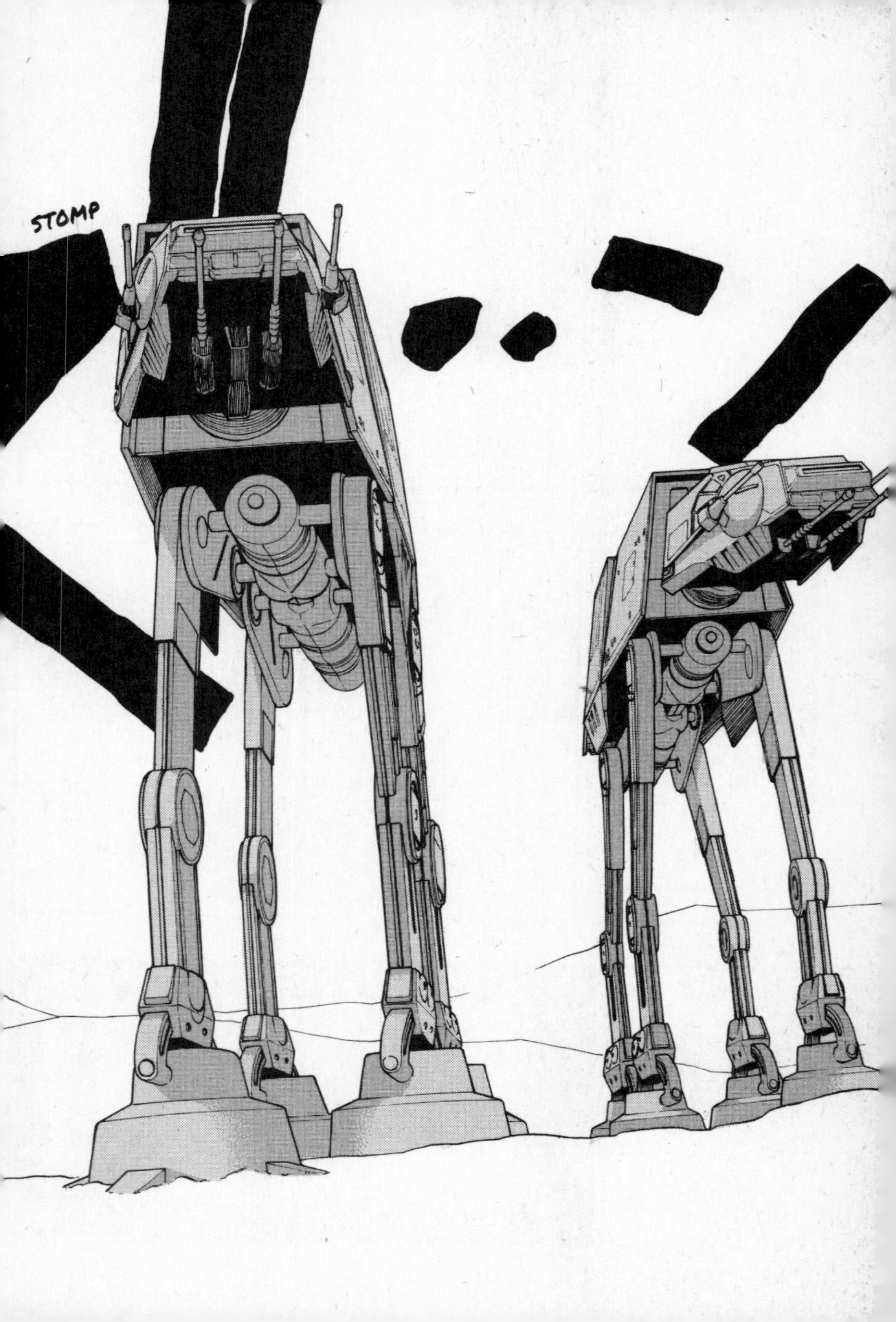
STOMP

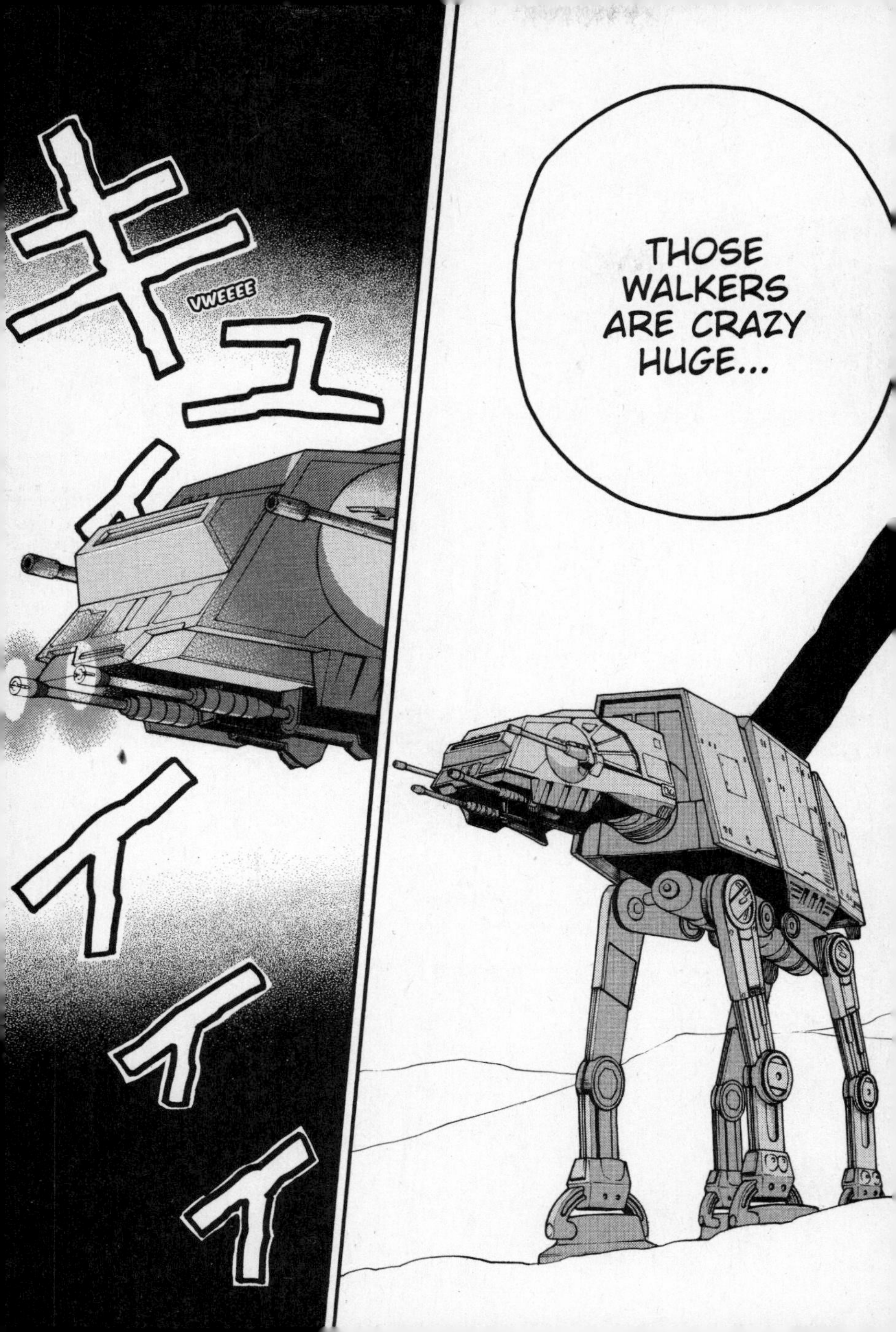
THOSE WALKERS ARE CRAZY HUGE...
キュイイイ
VWEEEE

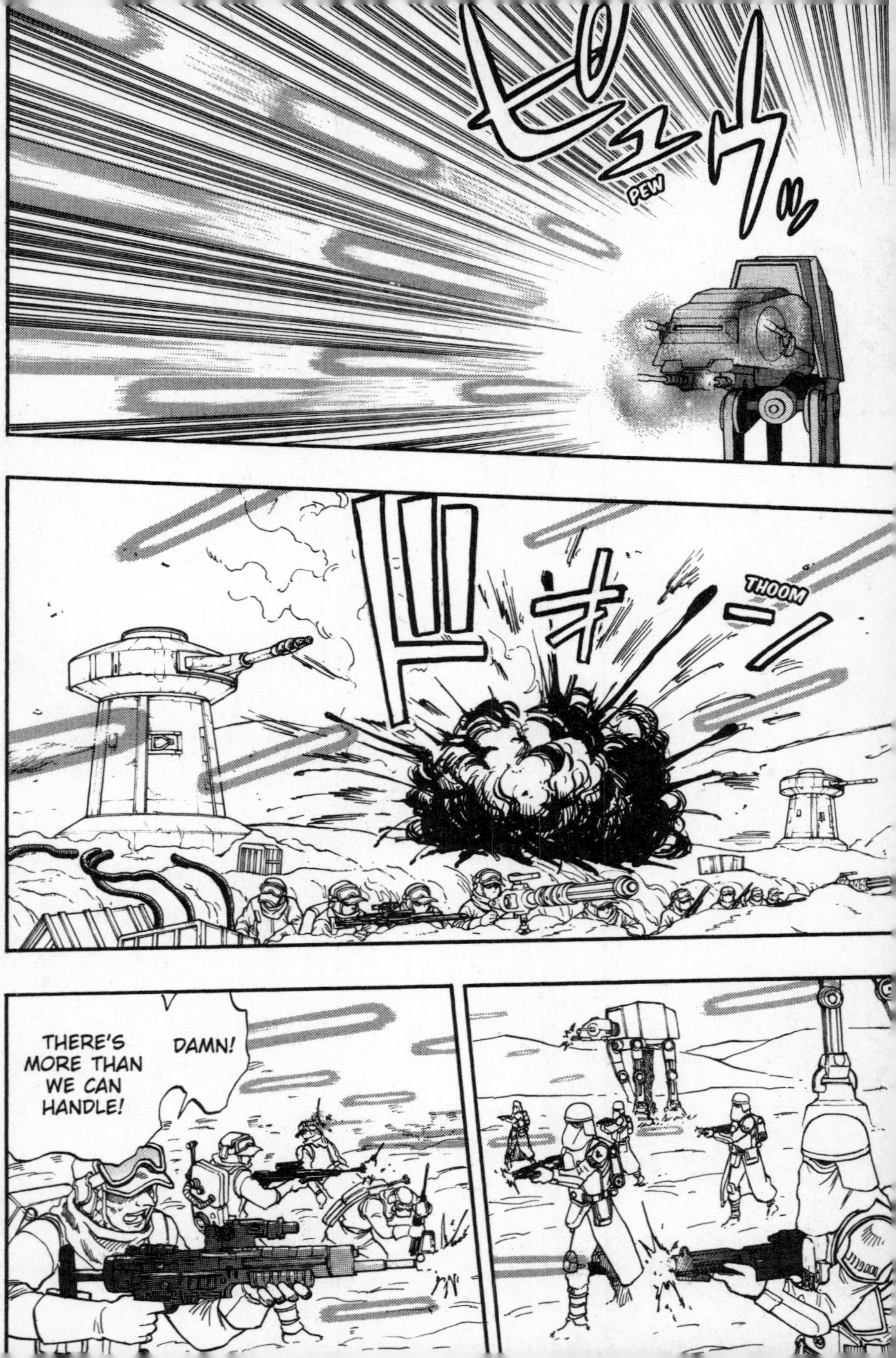
ビュウ
PEW
ドォーン
THOOM
DAMN!
THERE'S MORE THAN WE CAN HANDLE!

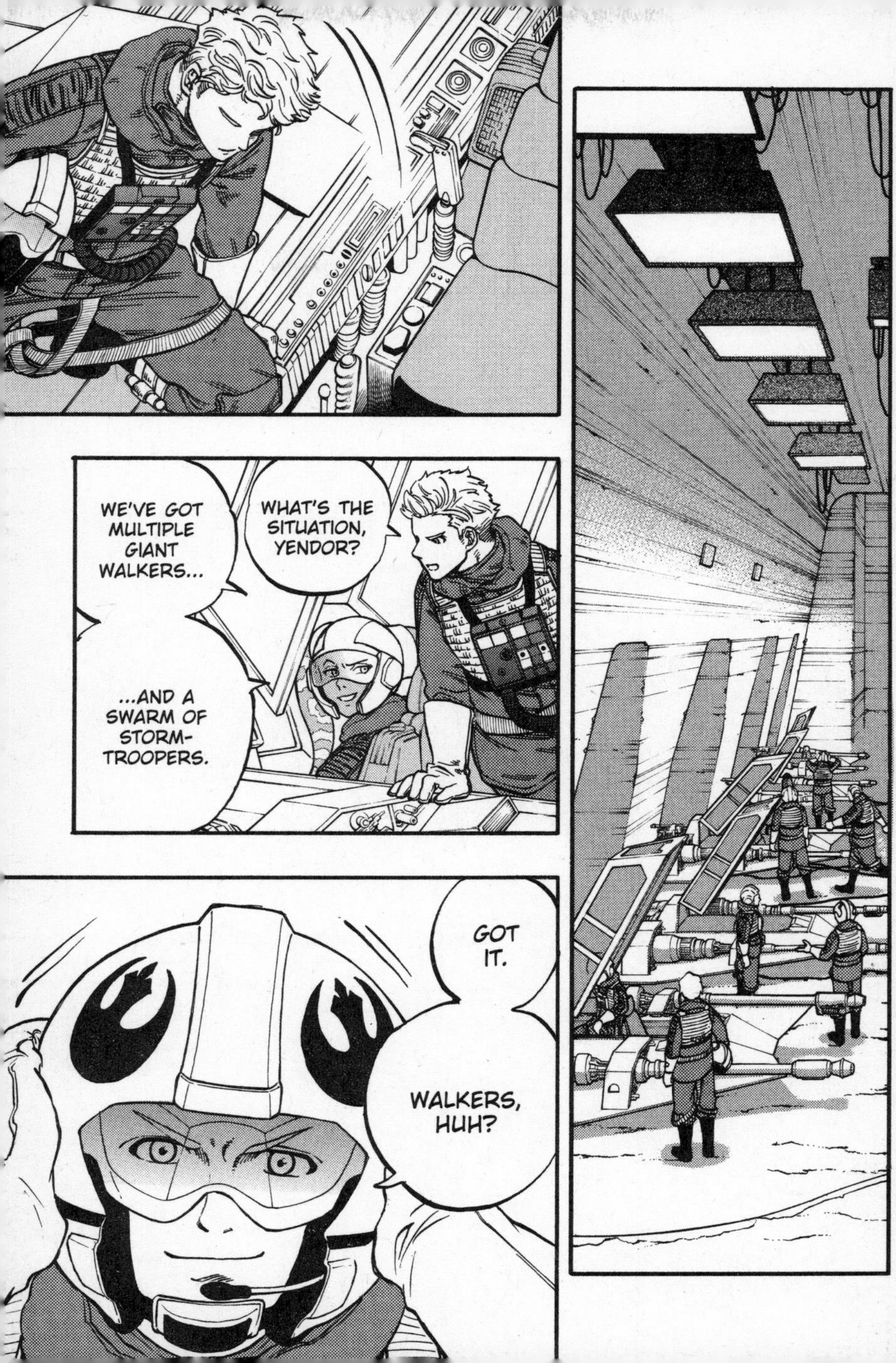
WHAT'S THE SITUATION, YENDOR?
WE'VE GOT MULTIPLE GIANT WALKERS...
...AND A SWARM OF STORM-TROOPERS.
GOT IT.
WALKERS, HUH?

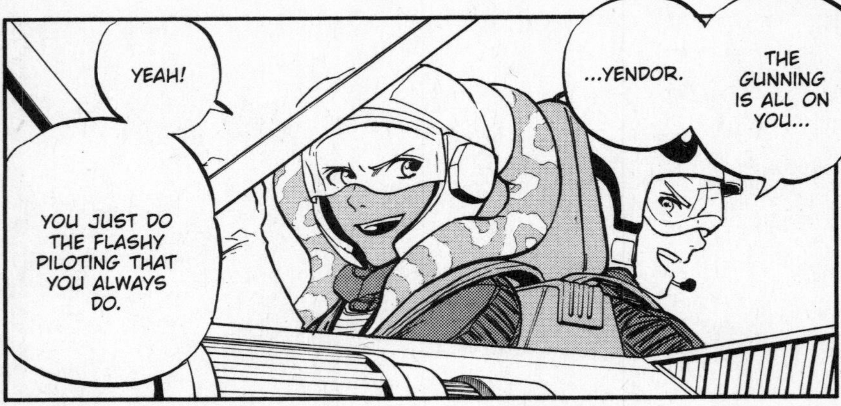
THE GUNNING IS ALL ON YOU...
...YENDOR.
YEAH!
YOU JUST DO THE FLASHY PILOTING THAT YOU ALWAYS DO.
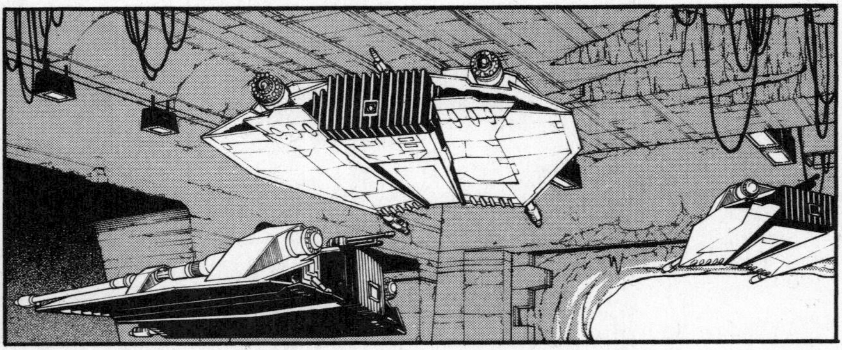
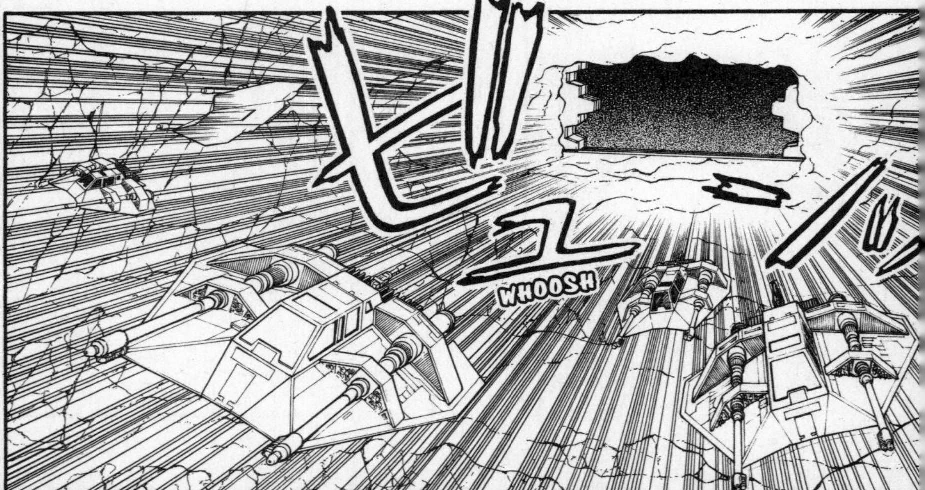
WHOOSH

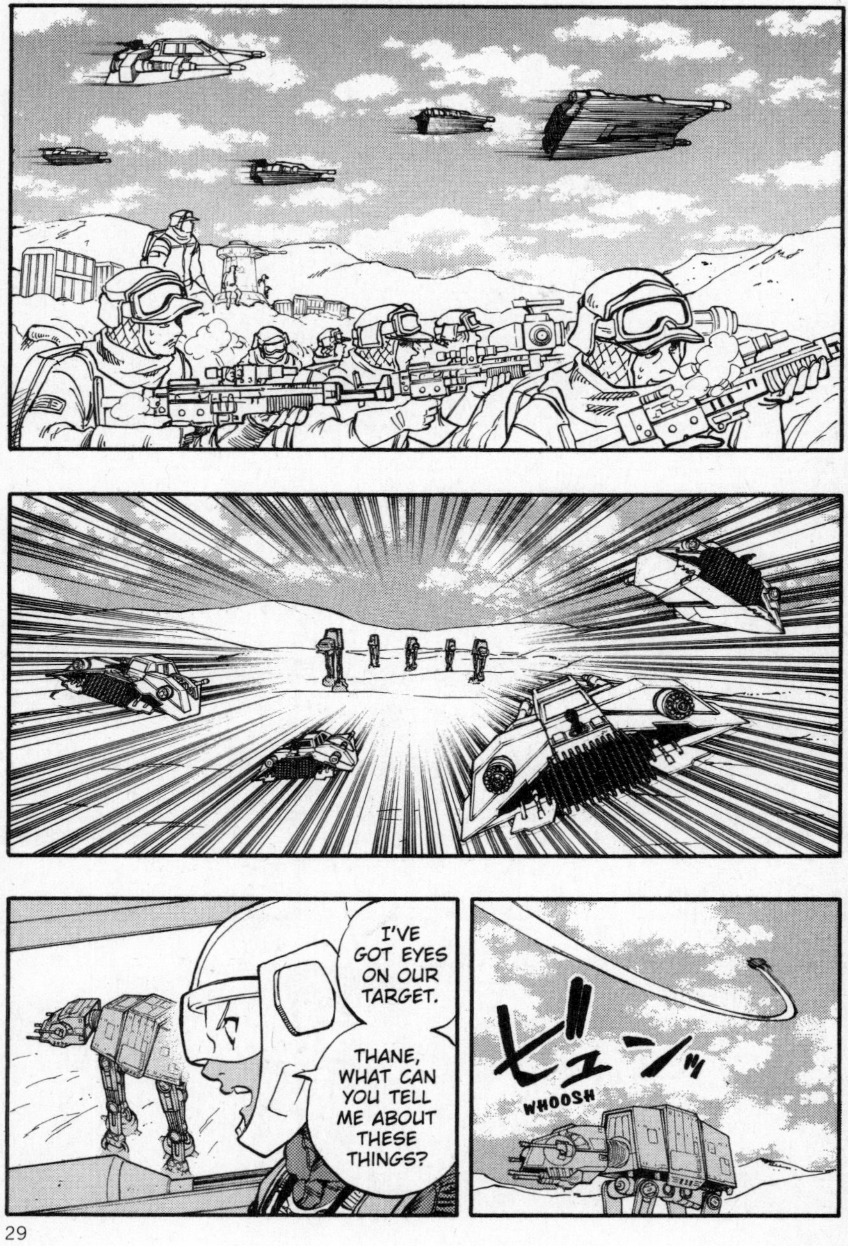
WHOOSH
I'VE GOT EYES ON OUR TARGET.
THANE, WHAT CAN YOU TELL ME ABOUT THESE THINGS?

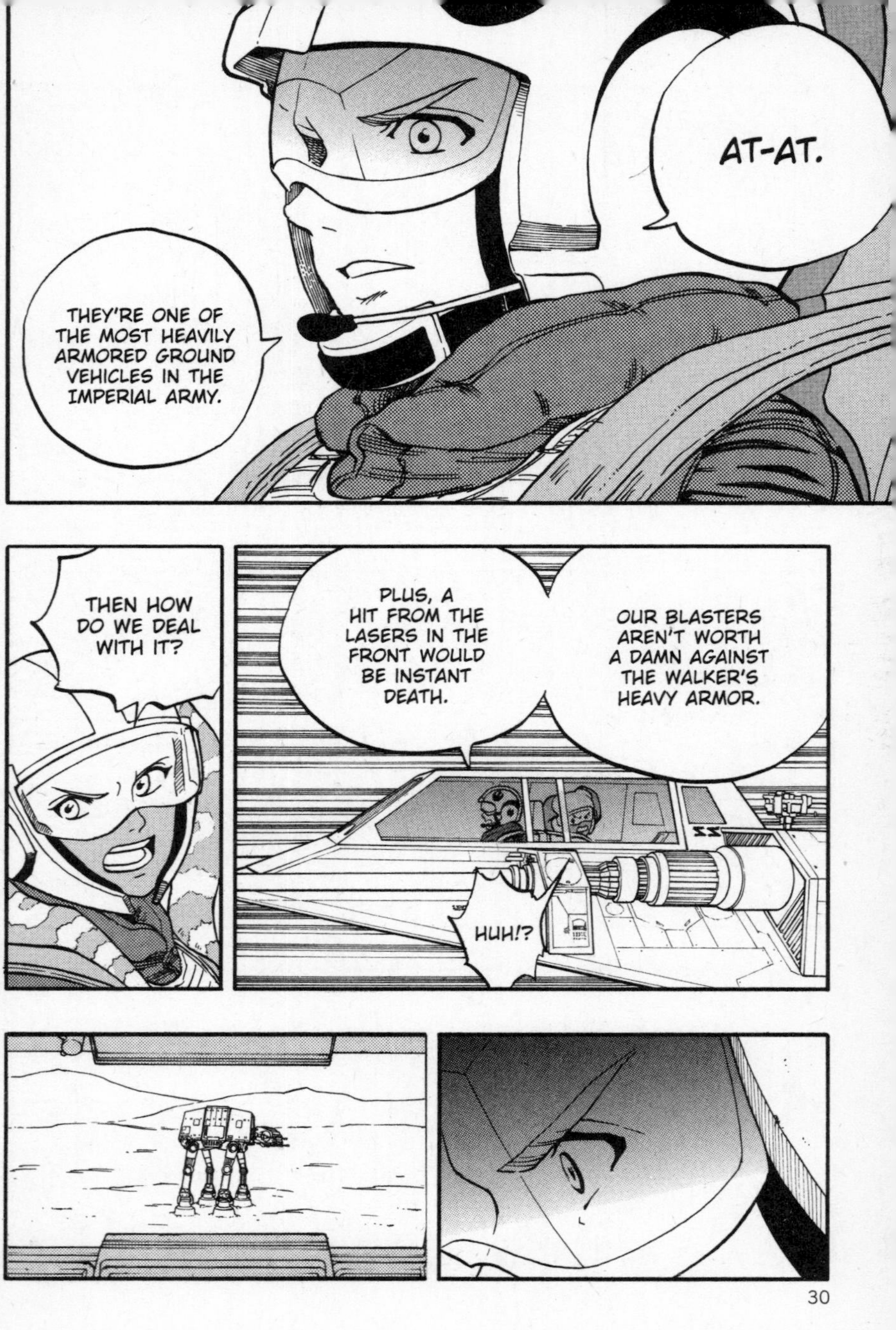
AT-AT.
THEY'RE ONE OF THE MOST HEAVILY ARMORED GROUND VEHICLES IN THE IMPERIAL ARMY.
OUR BLASTERS AREN'T WORTH A DAMN AGAINST THE WALKER'S HEAVY ARMOR.
PLUS, A HIT FROM THE LASERS IN THE FRONT WOULD BE INSTANT DEATH.
HUH!?
THEN HOW DO WE DEAL WITH IT?

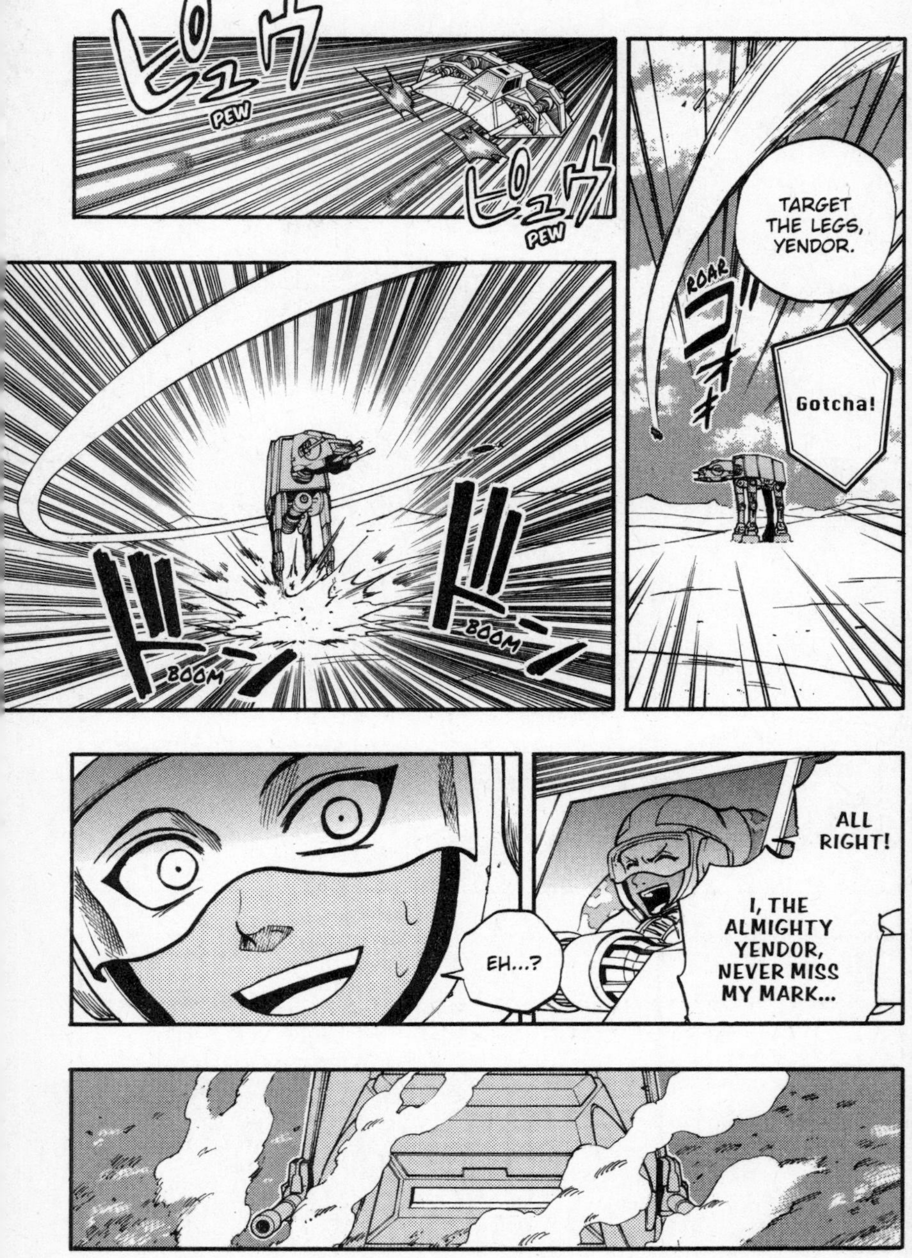
TARGET THE LEGS, YENDOR.
ROAR
Gotcha!
ピュウ
PEW
ピュウ
PEW
BOOM
BOOM
ALL RIGHT!
I, THE ALMIGHTY YENDOR, NEVER MISS MY MARK...
EH...?

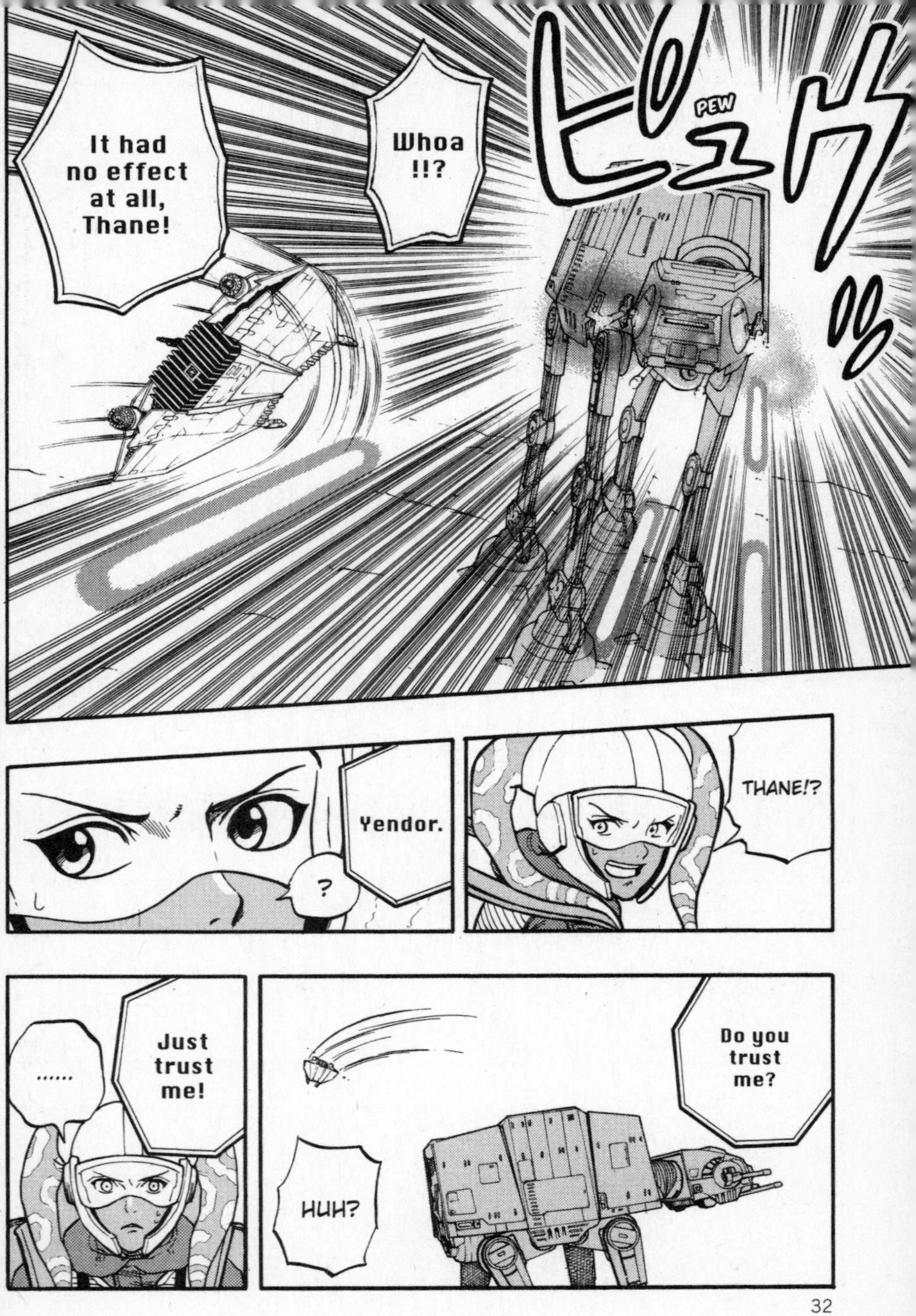

ヒュウ
PEW
Whoa !!?
It had no effect at all, Thane!
THANE!?
Yendor.
?
Do you trust me?
HUH?
Just trust me!
......

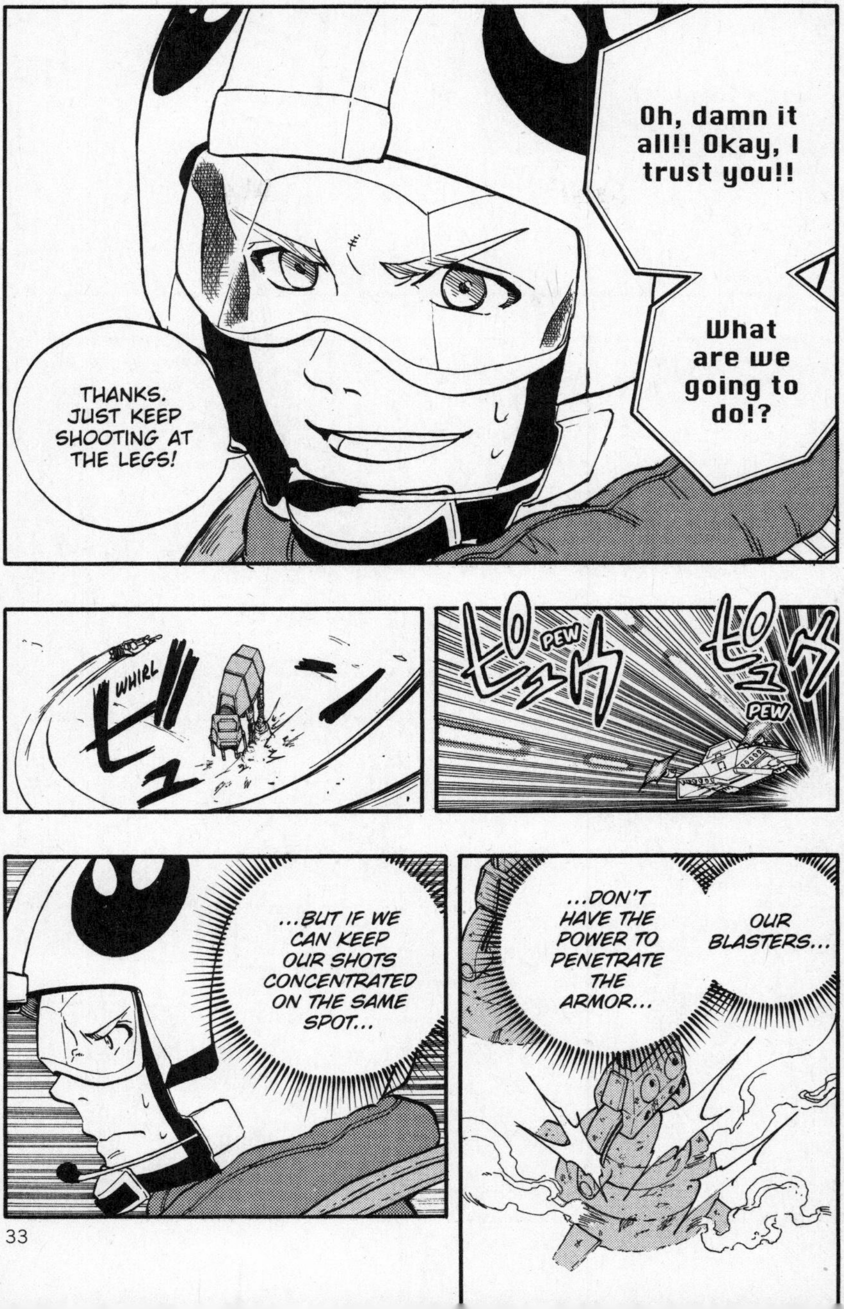

Oh, damn it all!! Okay, I trust you!!
What are we going to do!?
THANKS. JUST KEEP SHOOTING AT THE LEGS!
PEW
PEW
WHIRL
OUR BLASTERS...
...DON'T HAVE THE POWER TO PENETRATE THE ARMOR...
...BUT IF WE CAN KEEP OUR SHOTS CONCENTRATED ON THE SAME SPOT...

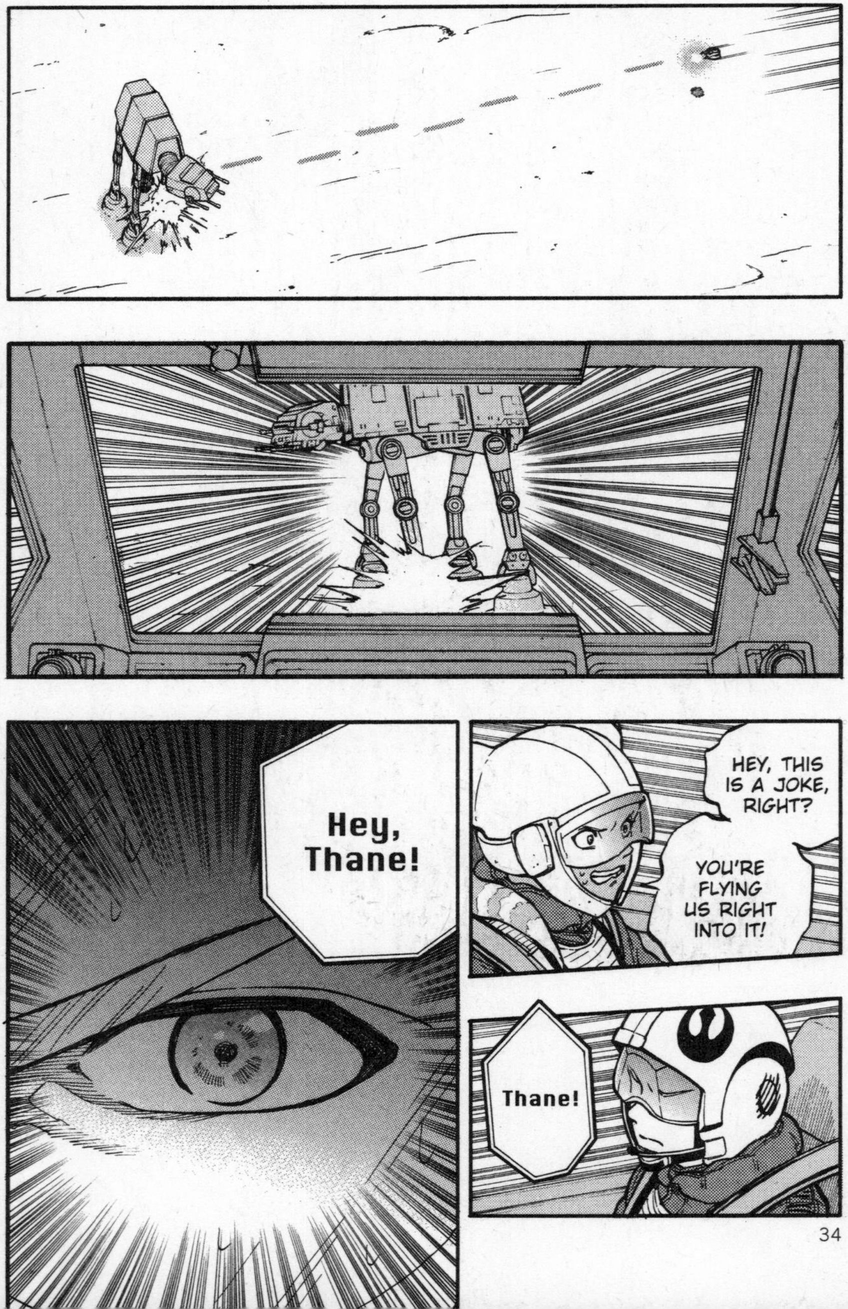
HEY, THIS IS A JOKE, RIGHT?
YOU'RE FLYING US RIGHT INTO IT!
Thane!
Hey, Thane!

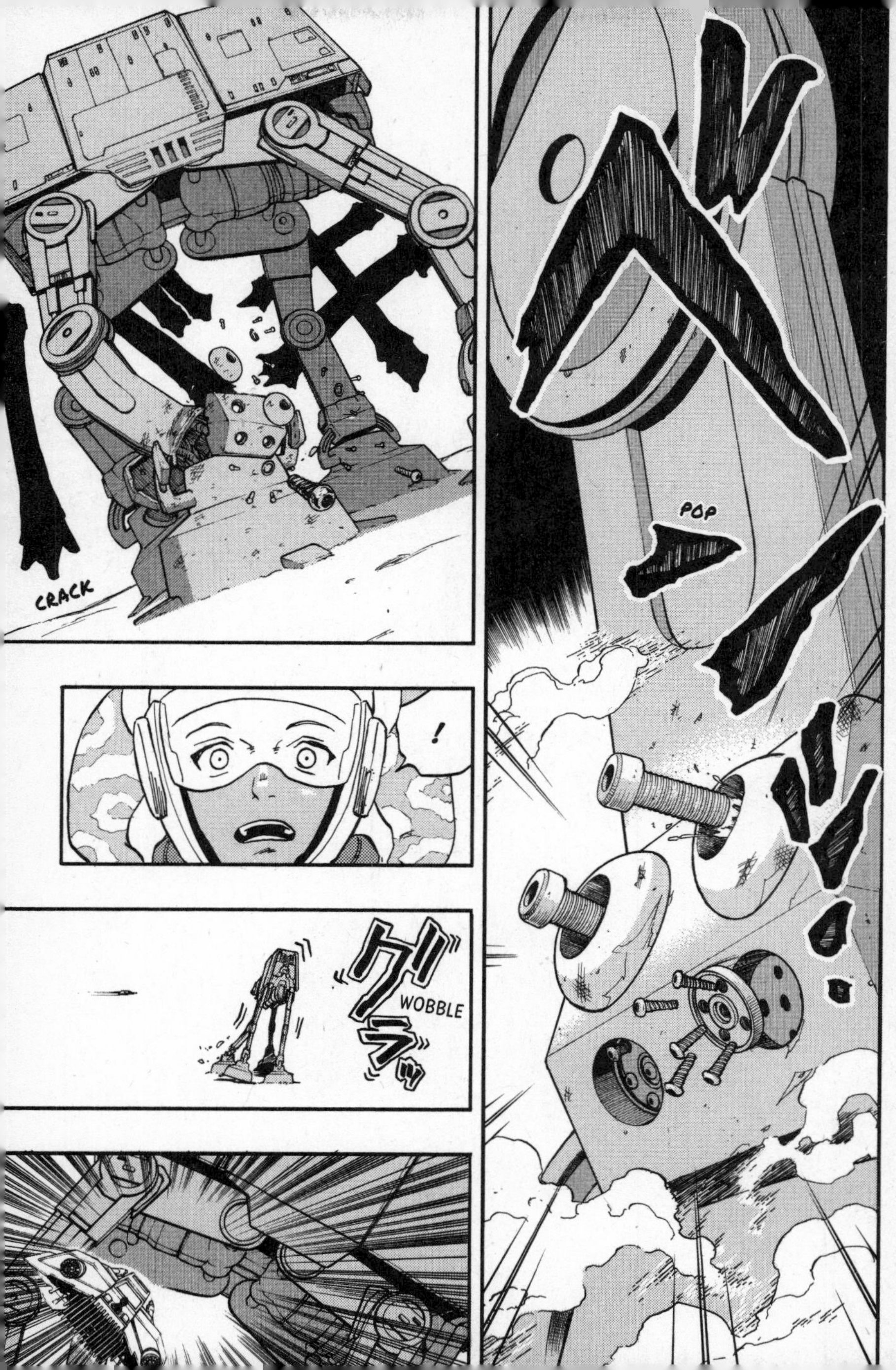
POP
CRACK
!
グラッ
WOBBLE

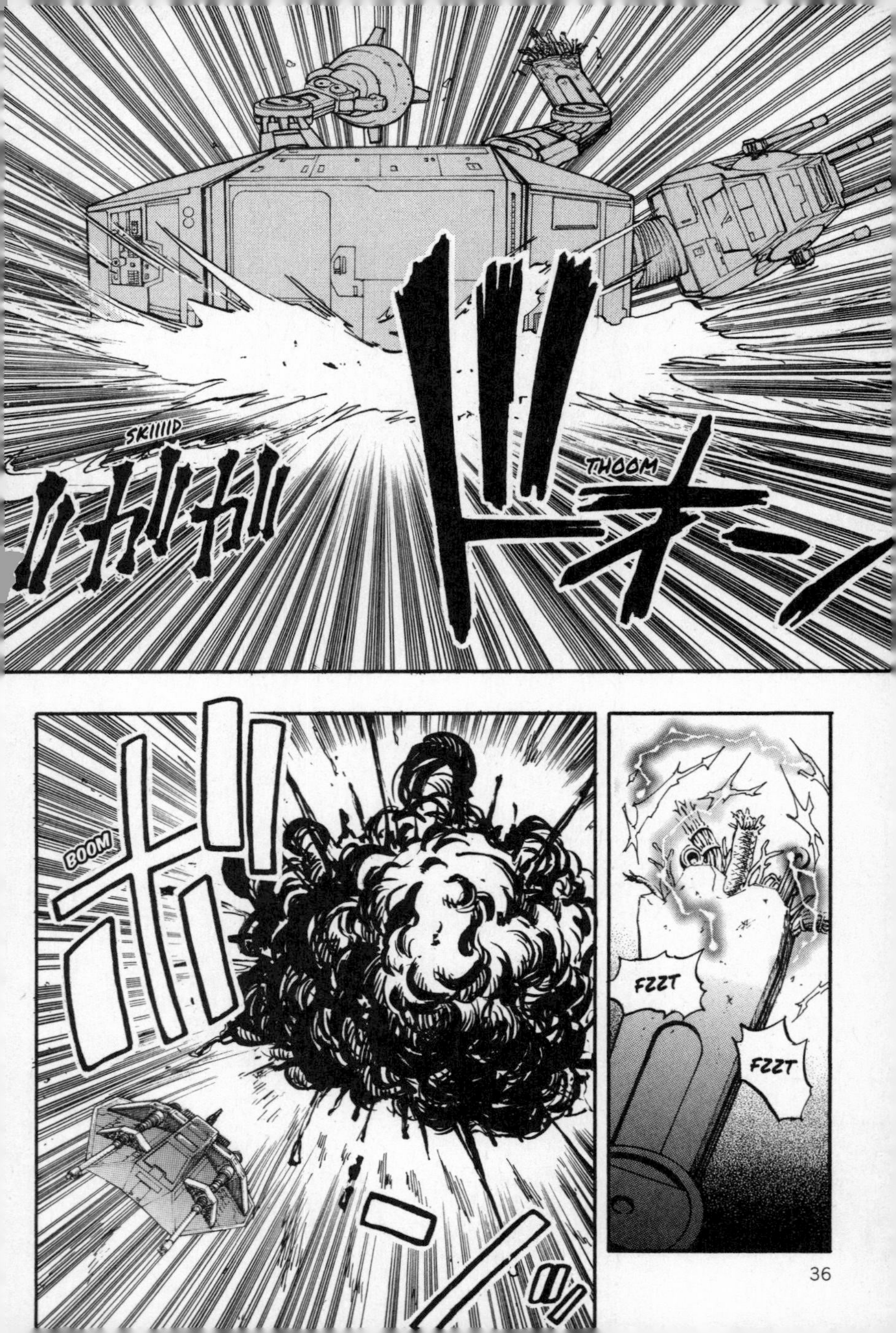
THOOM
SKIIIID
FZZT
FZZT
BOOM

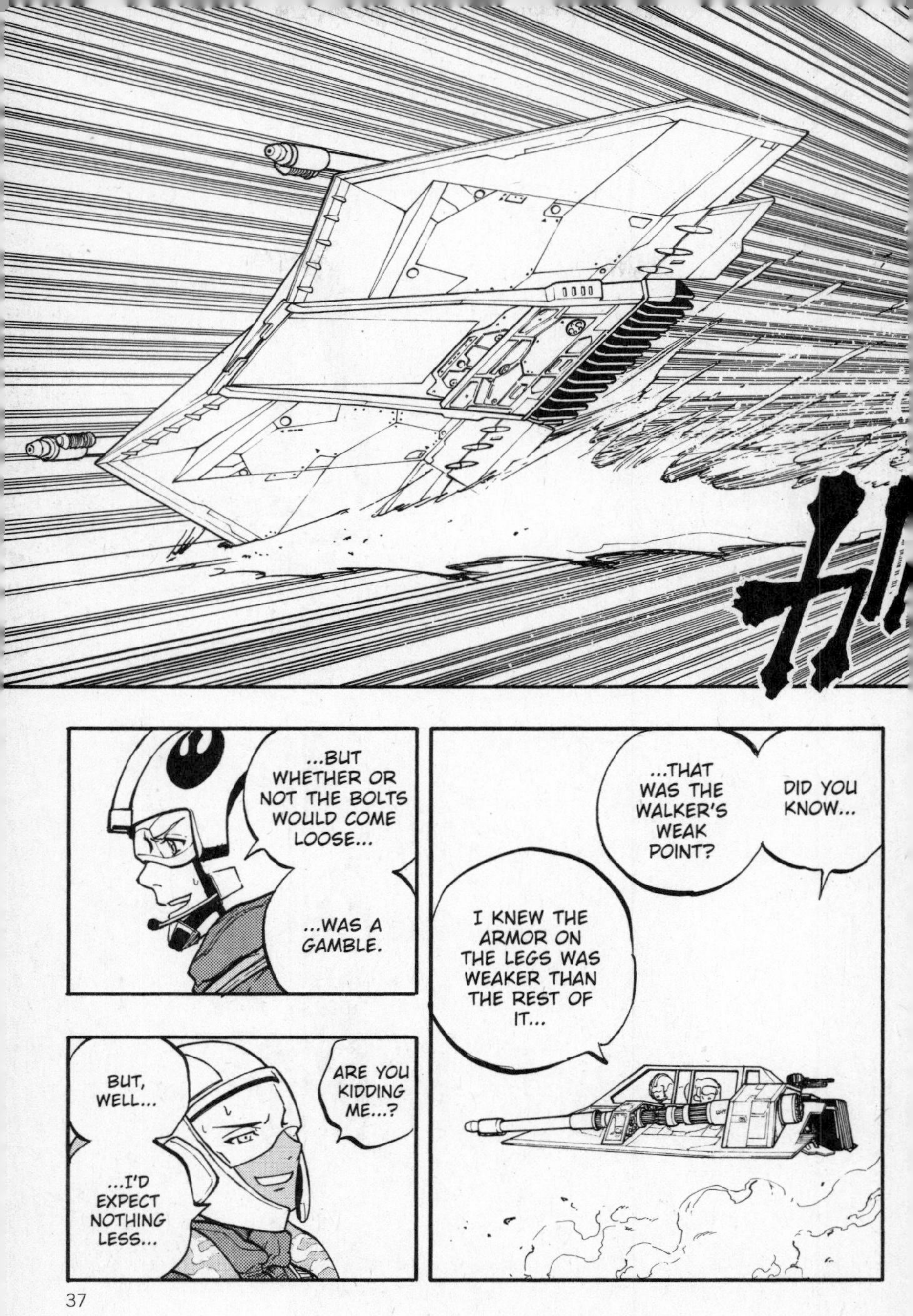
DID YOU KNOW...
...THAT WAS THE WALKER'S WEAK POINT?
I KNEW THE ARMOR ON THE LEGS WAS WEAKER THAN THE REST OF IT...
...BUT WHETHER OR NOT THE BOLTS WOULD COME LOOSE...
...WAS A GAMBLE.
ARE YOU KIDDING ME...?
BUT, WELL...
...I'D EXPECT NOTHING LESS...

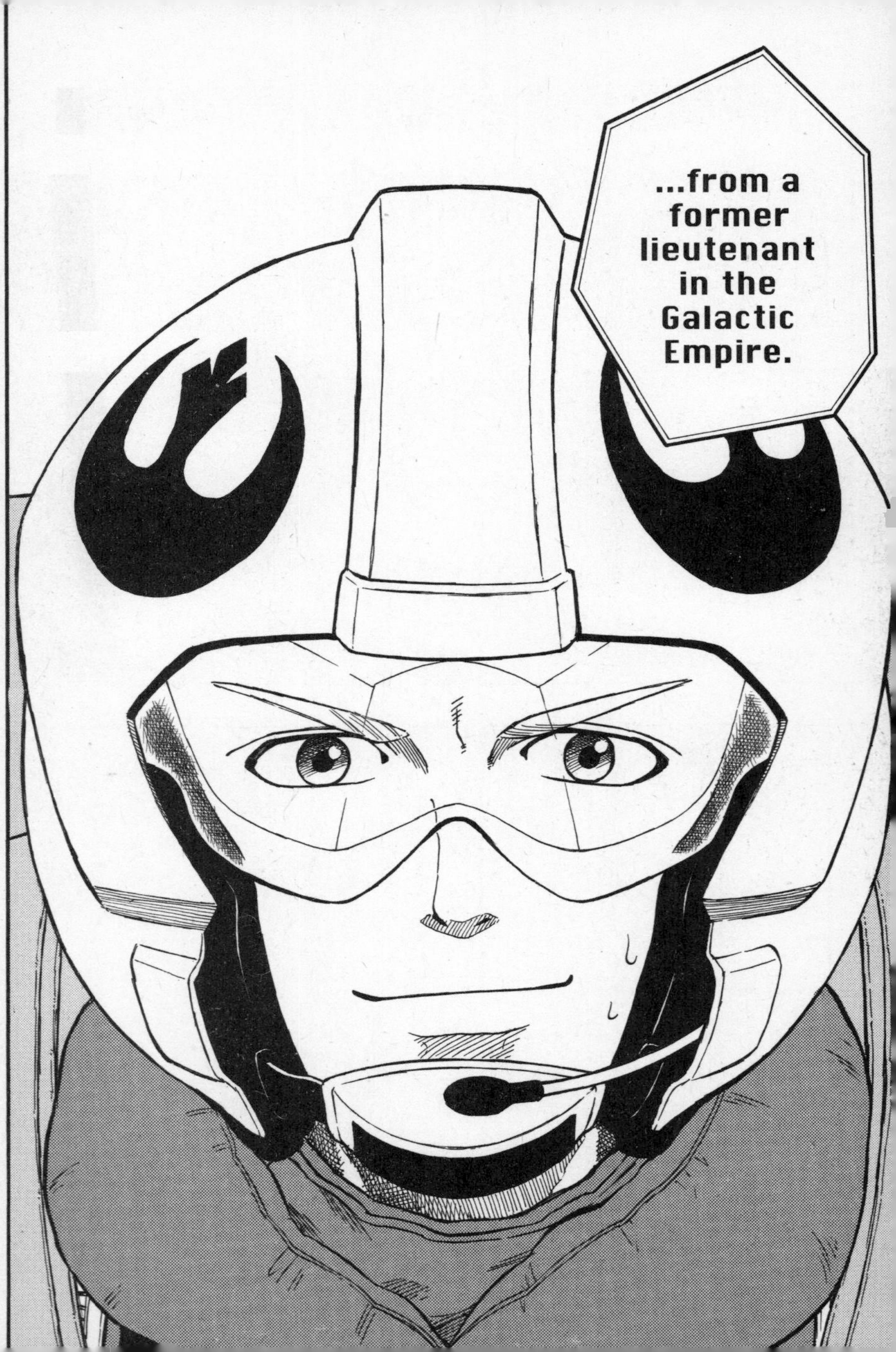
...from a former lieutenant in the Galactic Empire.

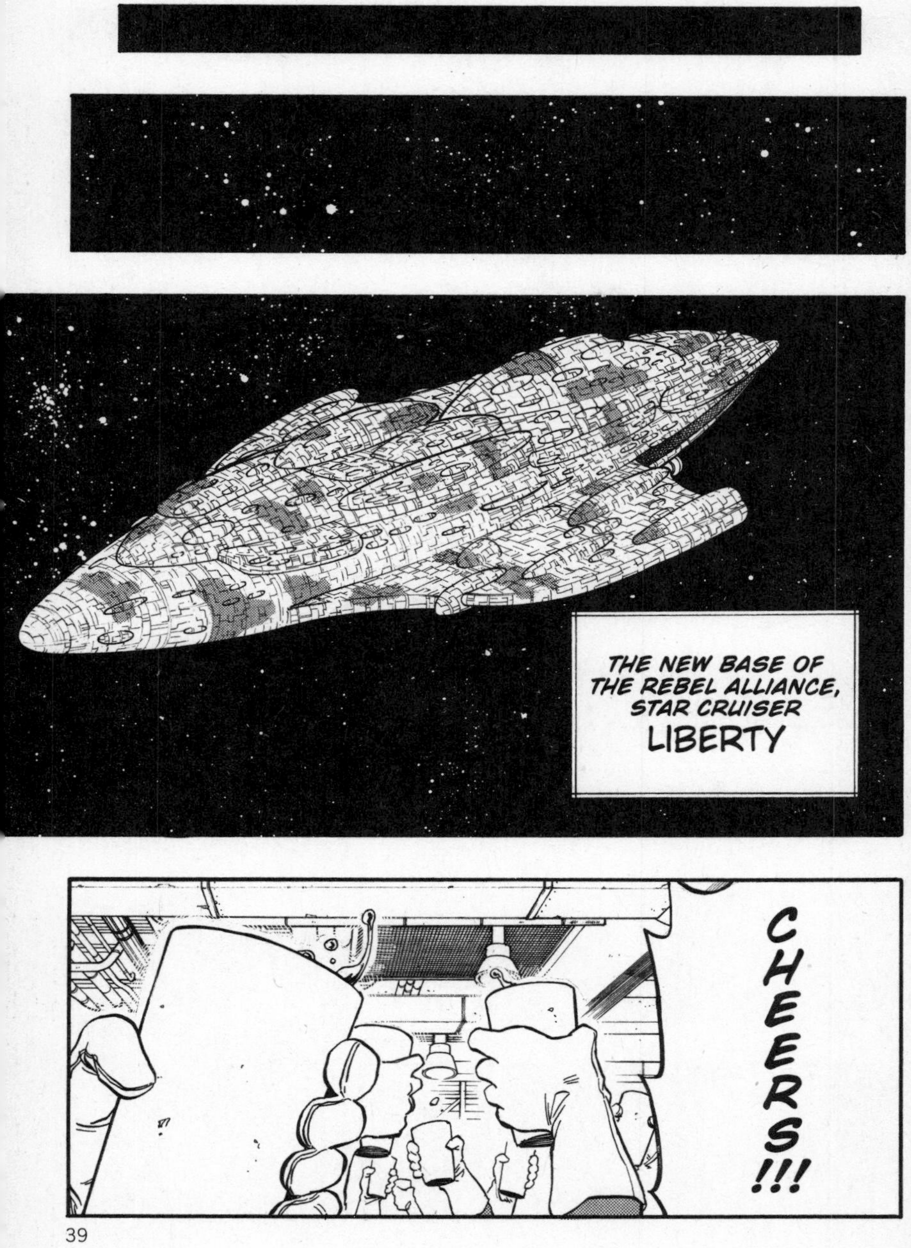
THE NEW BASE OF THE REBEL ALLIANCE, STAR CRUISER LIBERTY
CHEERS!!!

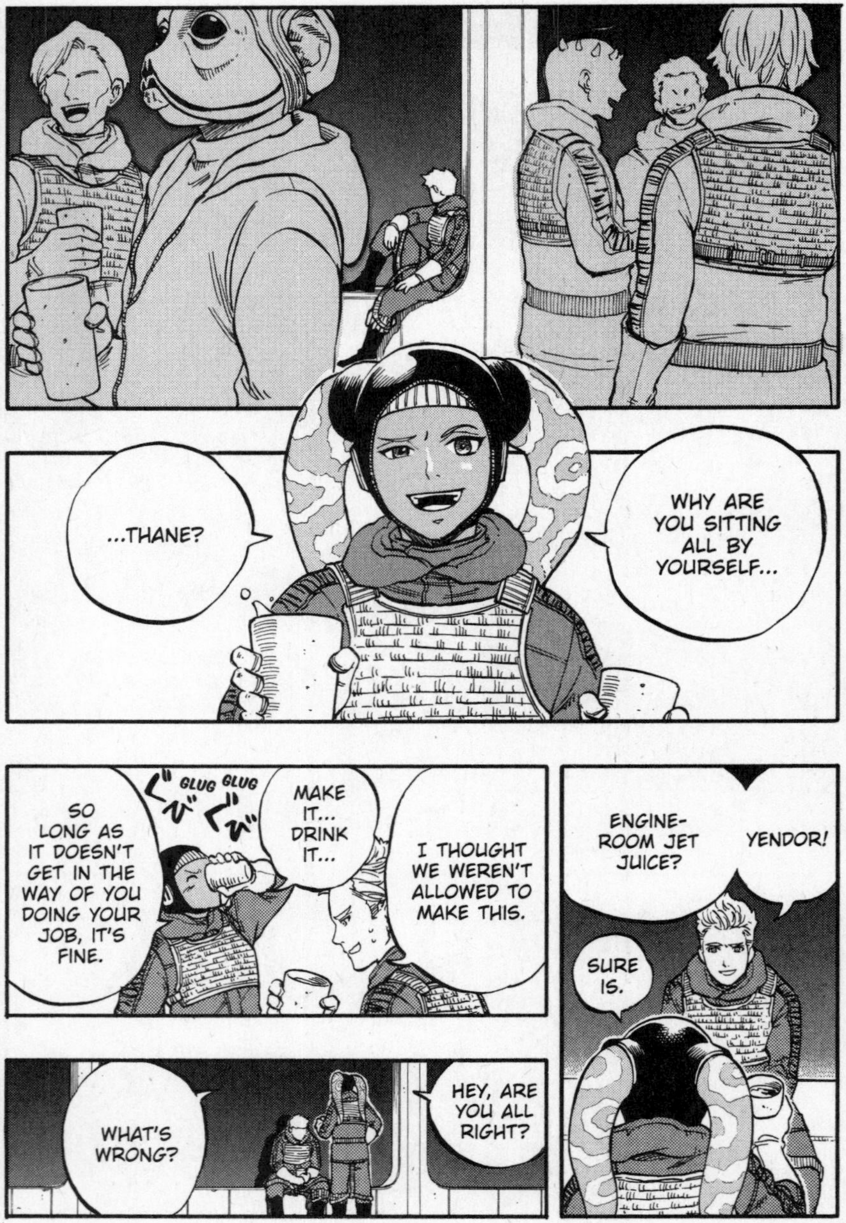
WHY ARE YOU SITTING ALL BY YOURSELF...
...THANE?
YENDOR!
ENGINE-ROOM JET JUICE?
SURE IS.
I THOUGHT WE WEREN'T ALLOWED TO MAKE THIS.
MAKE IT... DRINK IT...
GLUG GLUG
SO LONG AS IT DOESN'T GET IN THE WAY OF YOU DOING YOUR JOB, IT'S FINE.
HEY, ARE YOU ALL RIGHT?
WHAT'S WRONG?

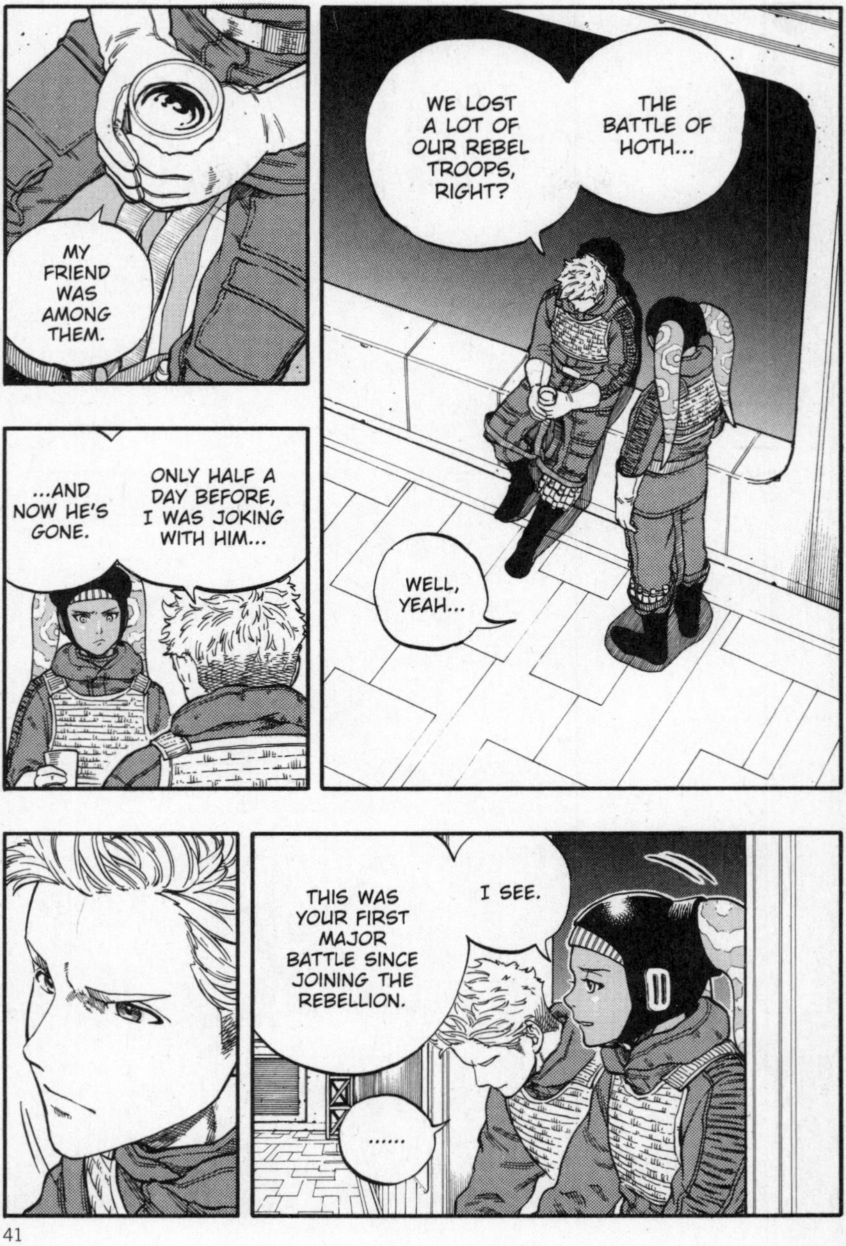
THE BATTLE OF HOTH...
WE LOST A LOT OF OUR REBEL TROOPS, RIGHT?
WELL, YEAH...
MY FRIEND WAS AMONG THEM.
ONLY HALF A DAY BEFORE, I WAS JOKING WITH HIM...
...AND NOW HE'S GONE.
I SEE.
THIS WAS YOUR FIRST MAJOR BATTLE SINCE JOINING THE REBELLION.
......

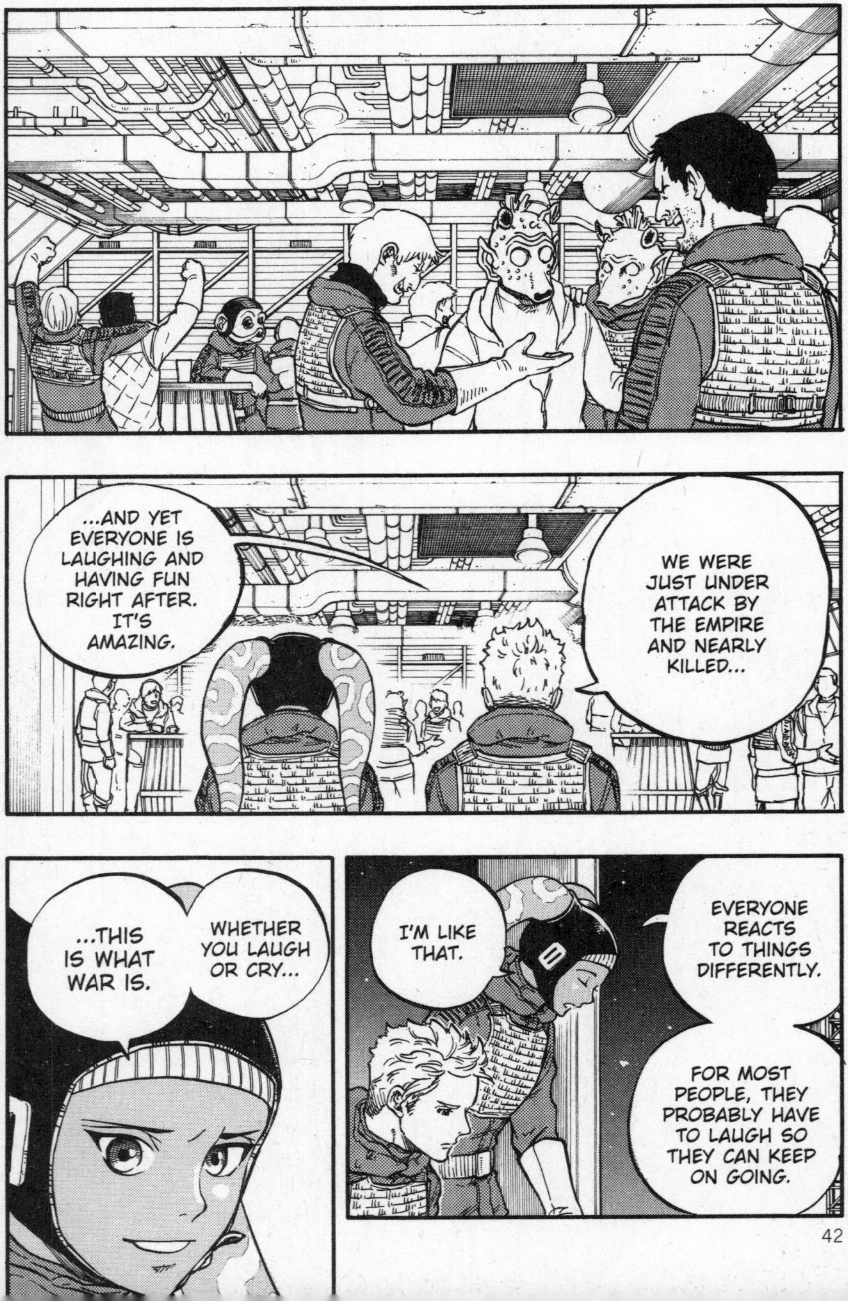
WE WERE JUST UNDER ATTACK BY THE EMPIRE AND NEARLY KILLED...
...AND YET EVERYONE IS LAUGHING AND HAVING FUN RIGHT AFTER. IT'S AMAZING.
EVERYONE REACTS TO THINGS DIFFERENTLY.
I'M LIKE THAT.
FOR MOST PEOPLE, THEY PROBABLY HAVE TO LAUGH SO THEY CAN KEEP ON GOING.
WHETHER YOU LAUGH OR CRY...
...THIS IS WHAT WAR IS.

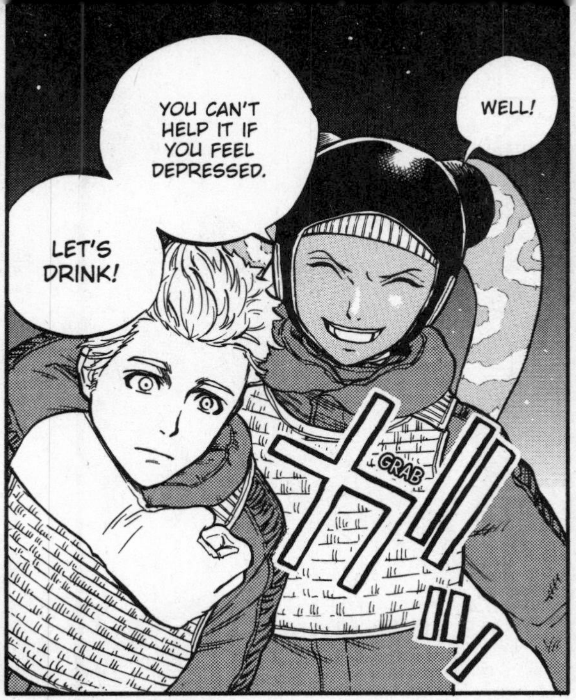
WELL!
YOU CAN'T HELP IT IF YOU FEEL DEPRESSED.
LET'S DRINK!
GRAB

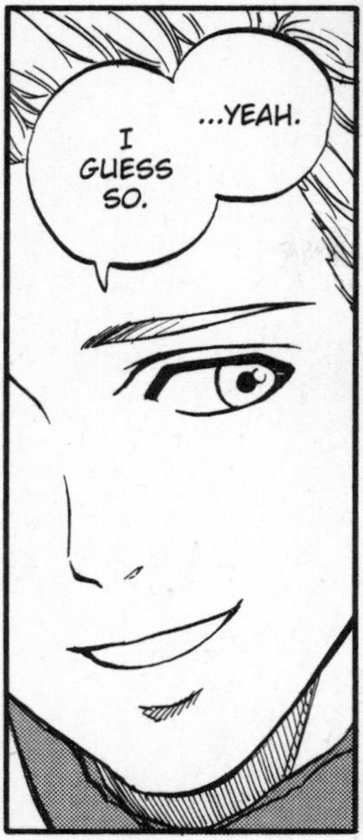
...YEAH.
I GUESS SO.

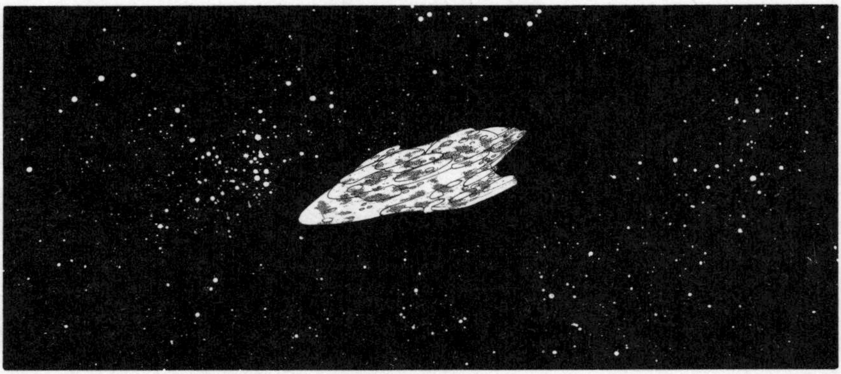

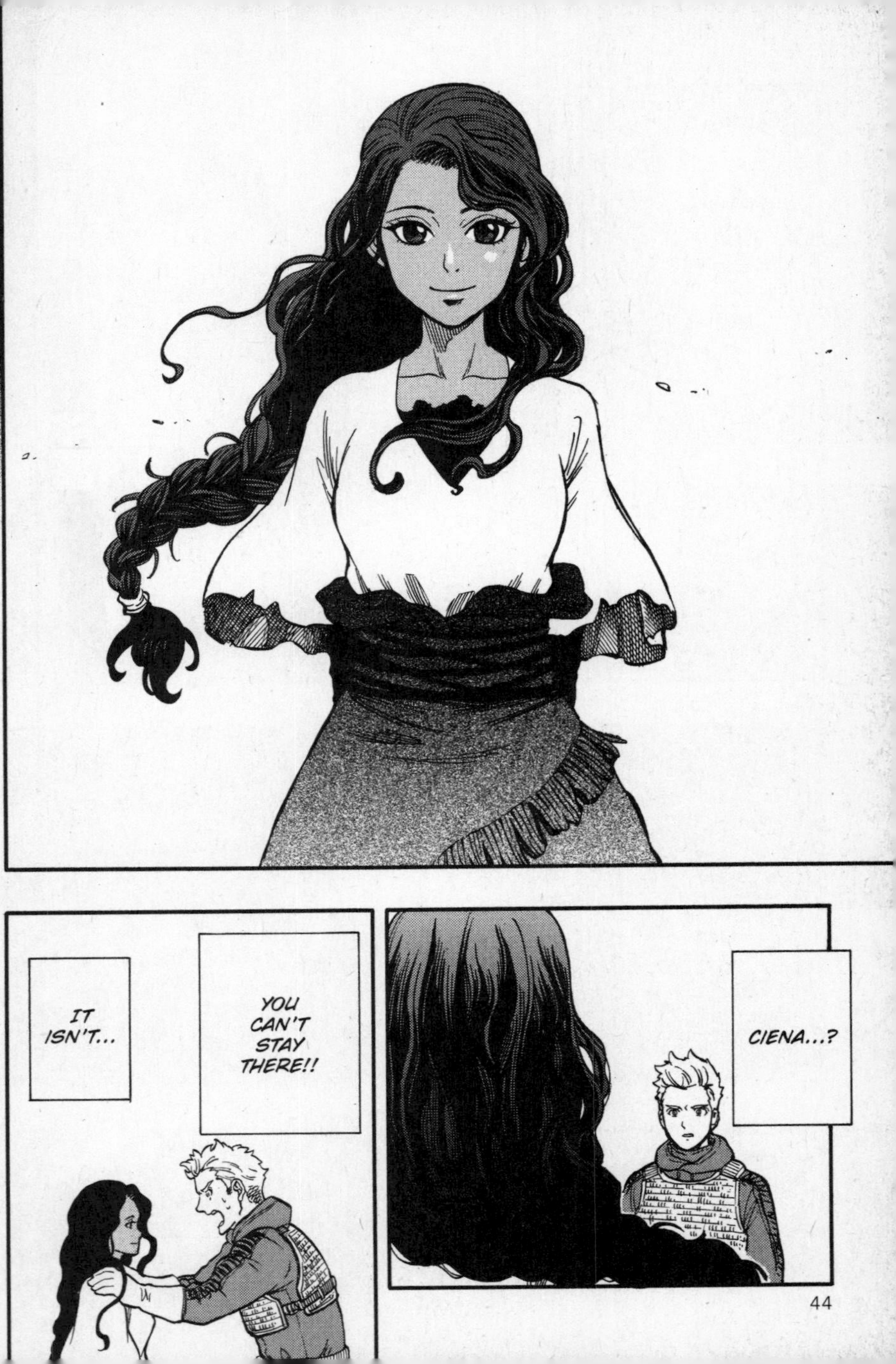
CIENA...?
YOU CAN'T STAY THERE!!
IT ISN'T...

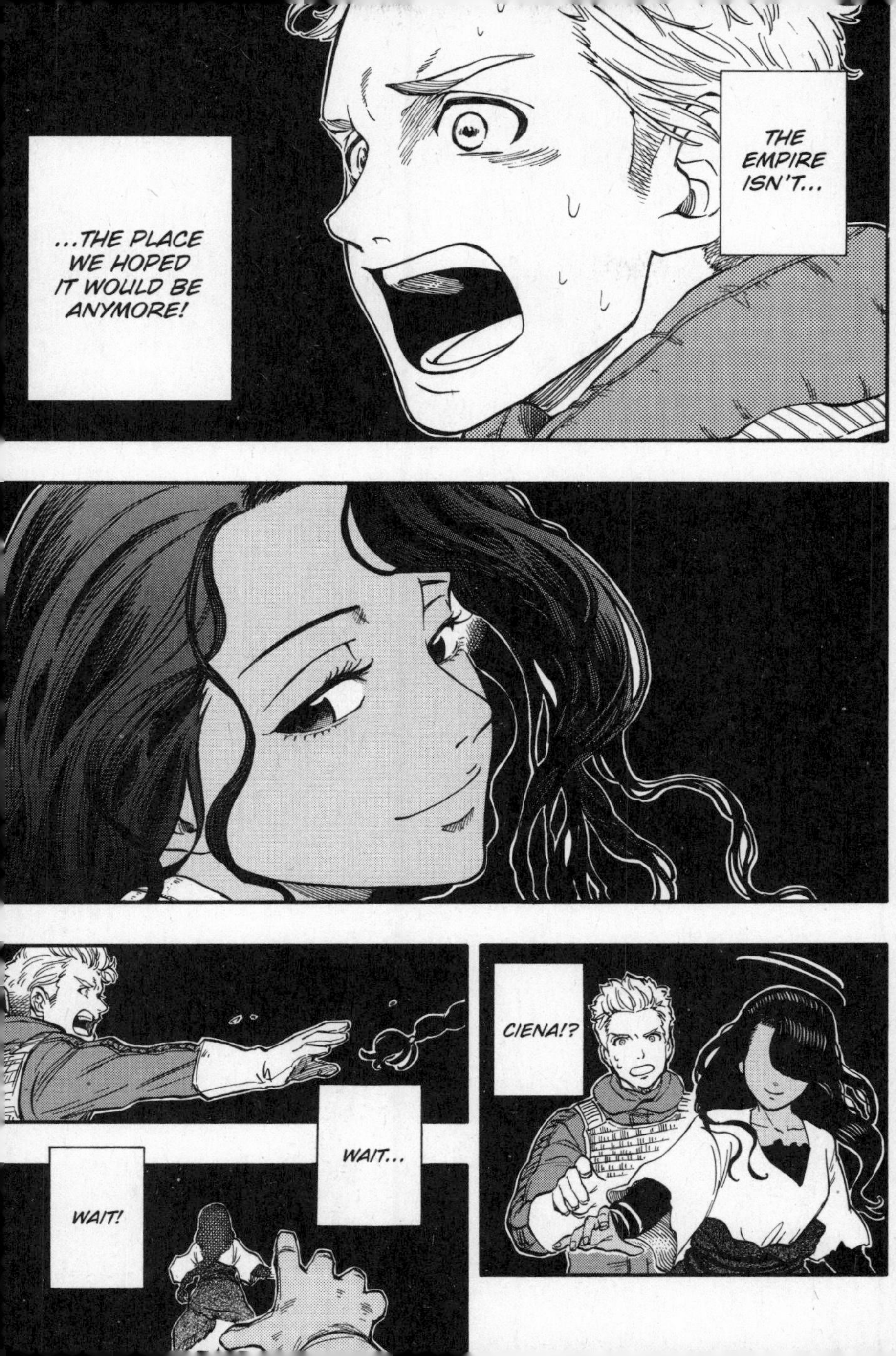
THE EMPIRE ISN'T...
...THE PLACE WE HOPED IT WOULD BE ANYMORE!
CIENA!?
WAIT...
WAIT!

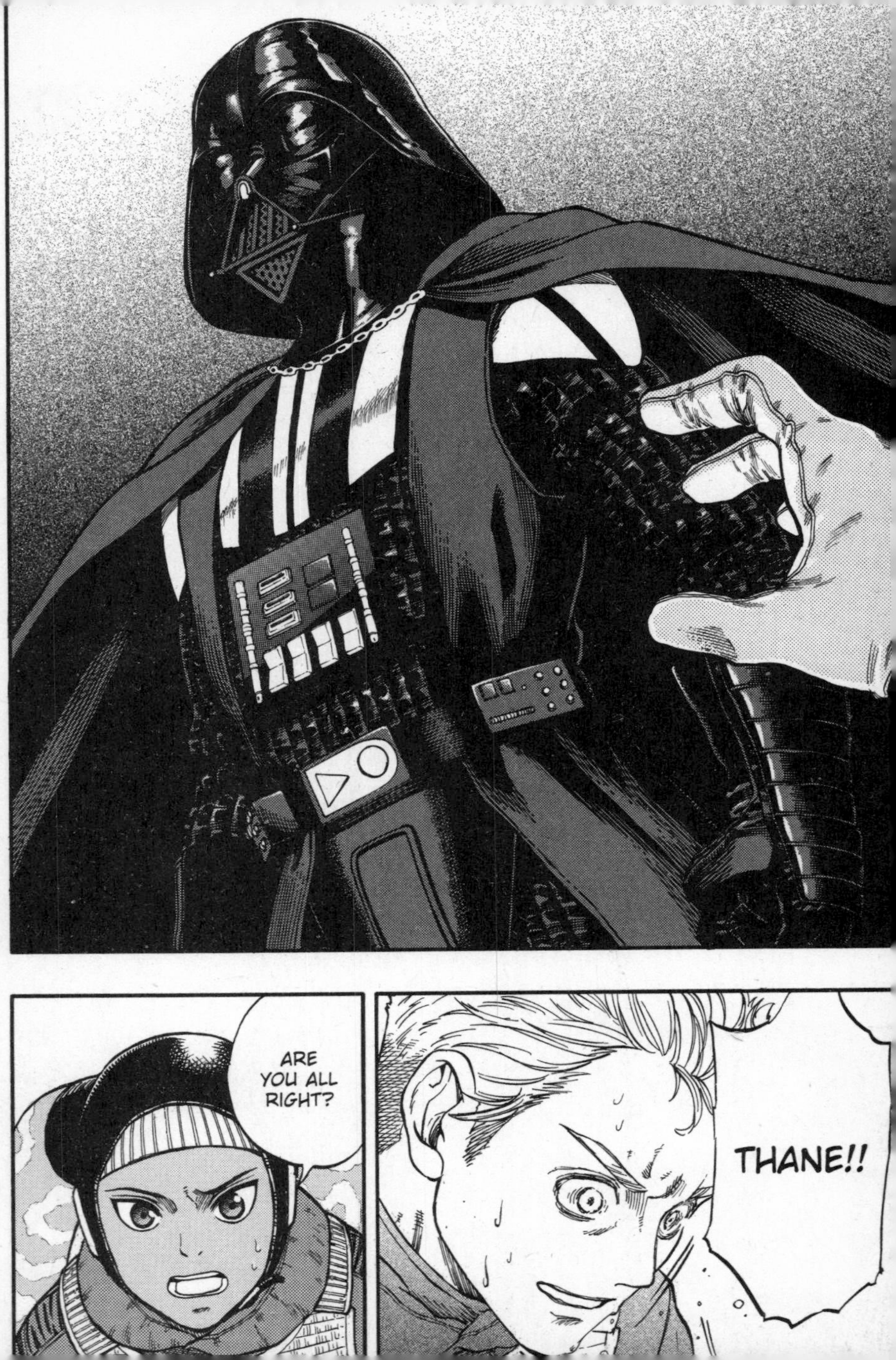
THANE!!
ARE YOU ALL RIGHT?

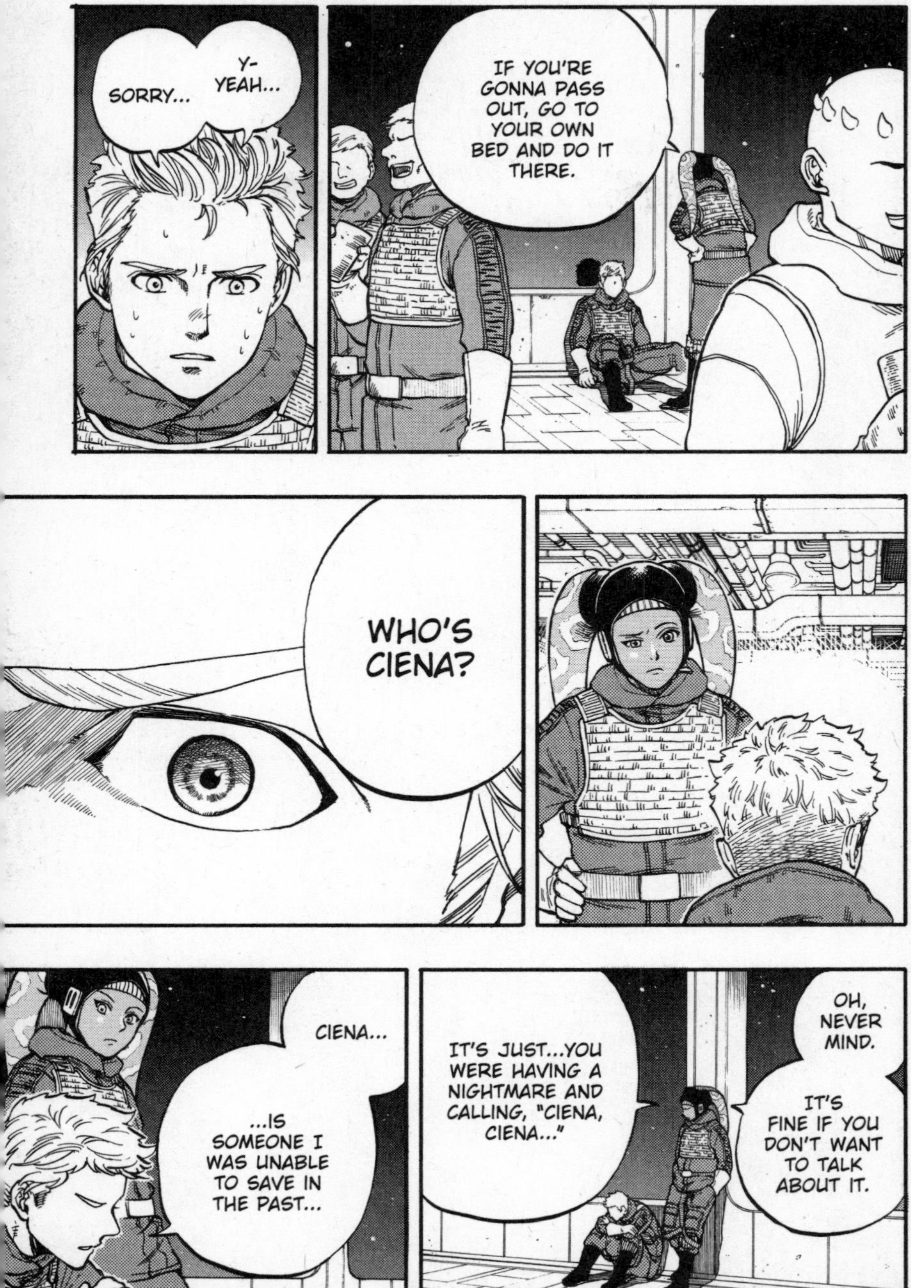
IF YOU'RE GONNA PASS OUT, GO TO YOUR OWN BED AND DO IT THERE.
Y-YEAH...
SORRY...
WHO'S CIENA?
IT'S JUST...YOU WERE HAVING A NIGHTMARE AND CALLING, "CIENA, CIENA..."
OH, NEVER MIND.
IT'S FINE IF YOU DON'T WANT TO TALK ABOUT IT.
CIENA...
...IS SOMEONE I WAS UNABLE TO SAVE IN THE PAST...

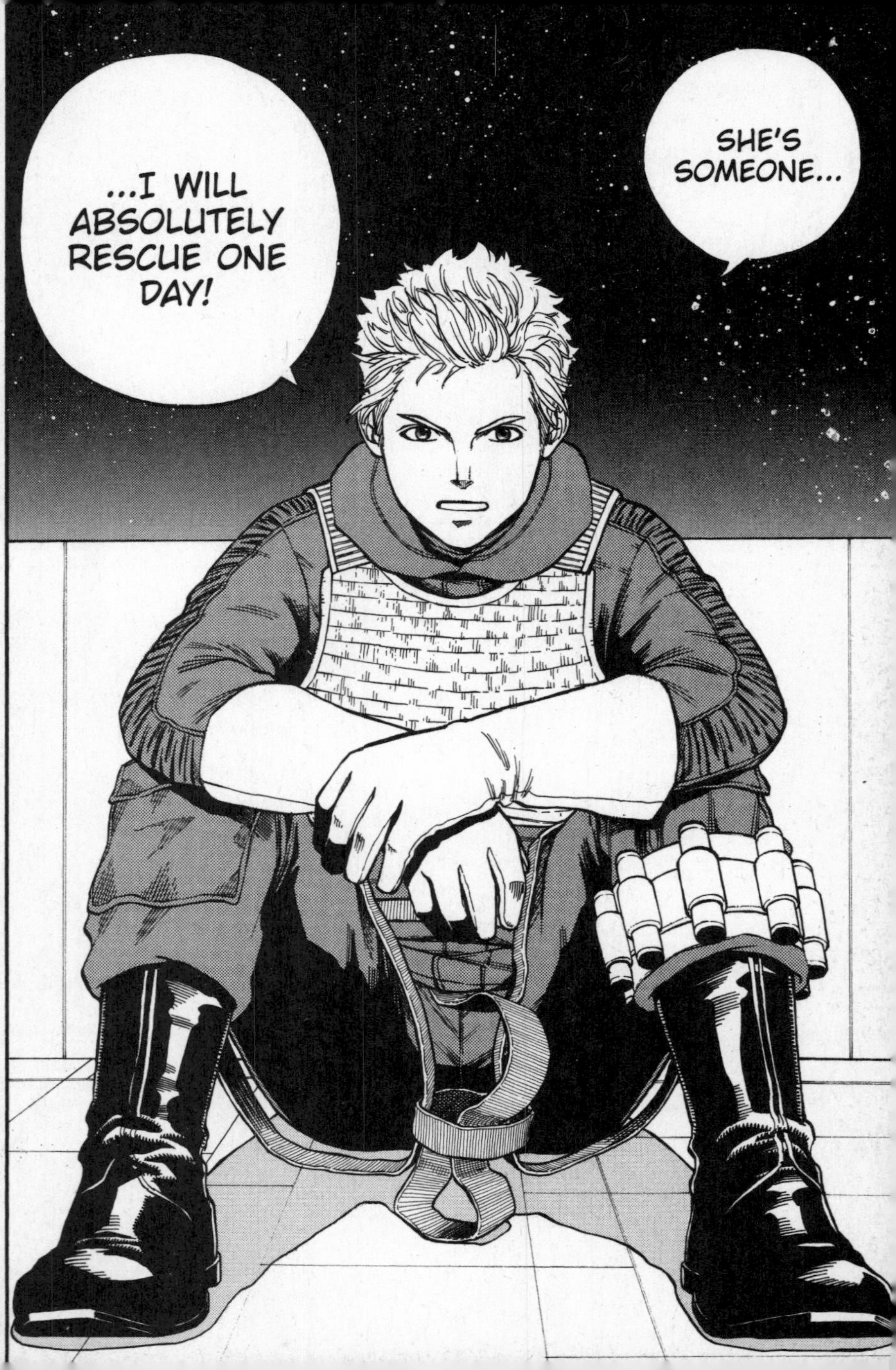
SHE'S SOMEONE...
...I WILL ABSOLUTELY RESCUE ONE DAY!

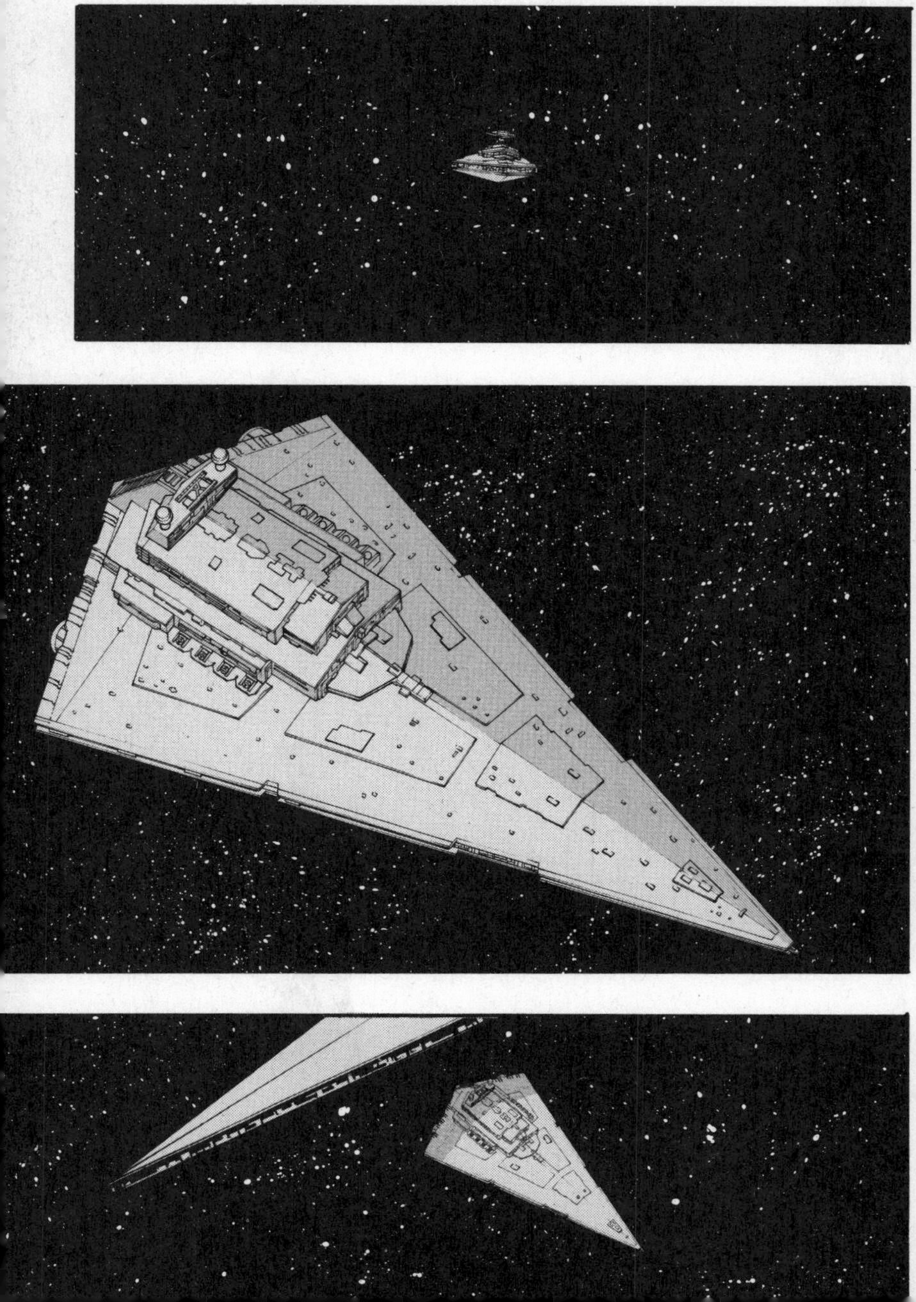

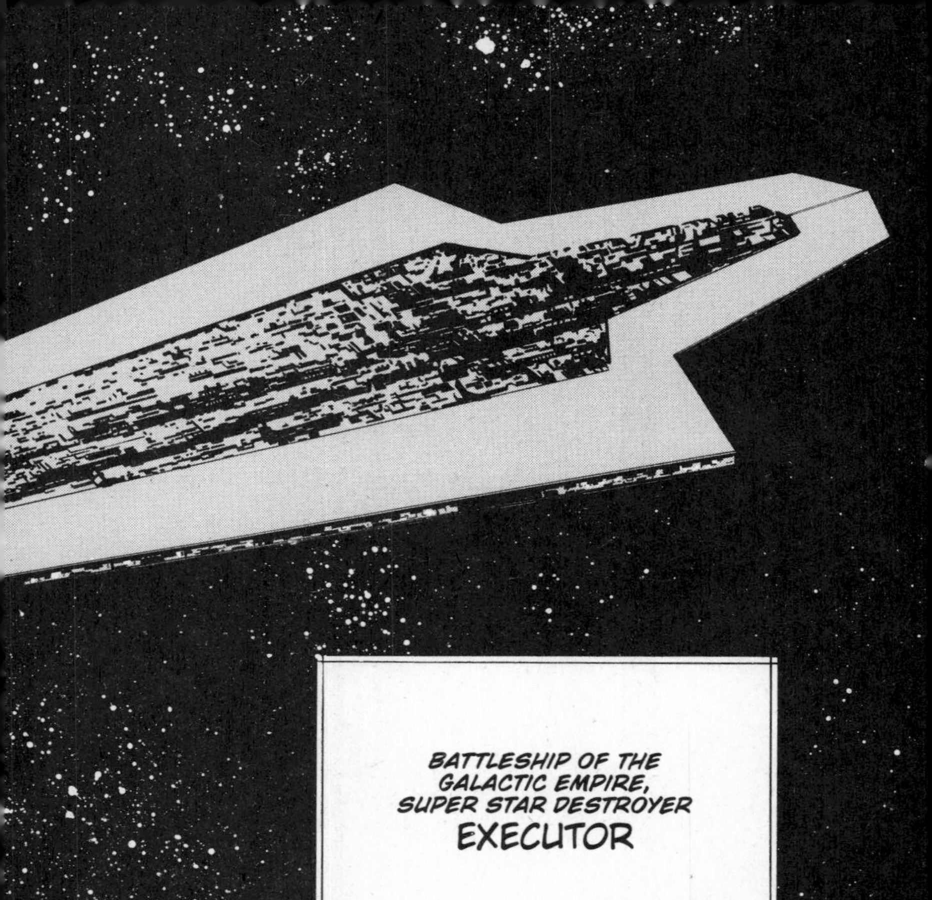
BATTLESHIP OF THE GALACTIC EMPIRE, SUPER STAR DESTROYER
EXECUTOR
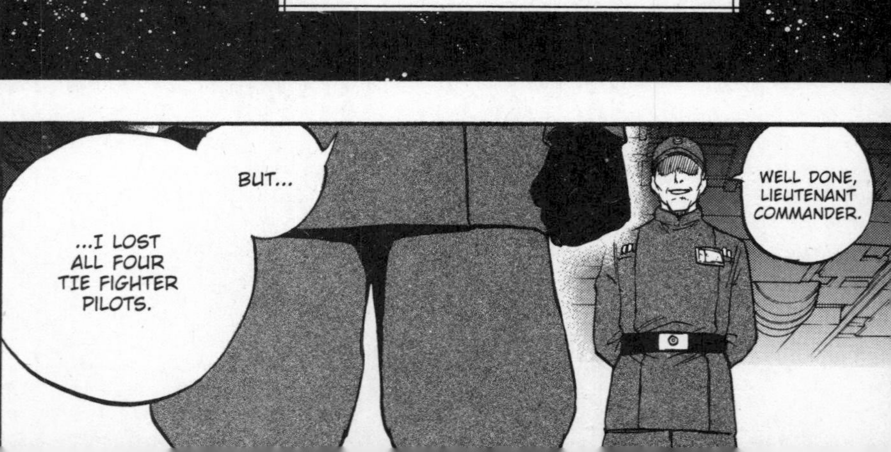
WELL DONE, LIEUTENANT COMMANDER.
BUT...
...I LOST ALL FOUR TIE FIGHTER PILOTS.

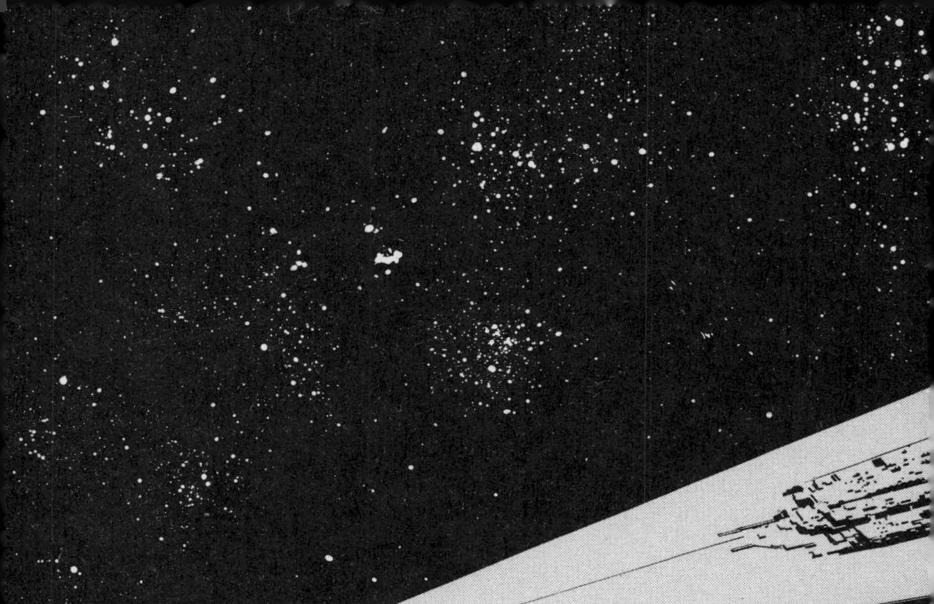

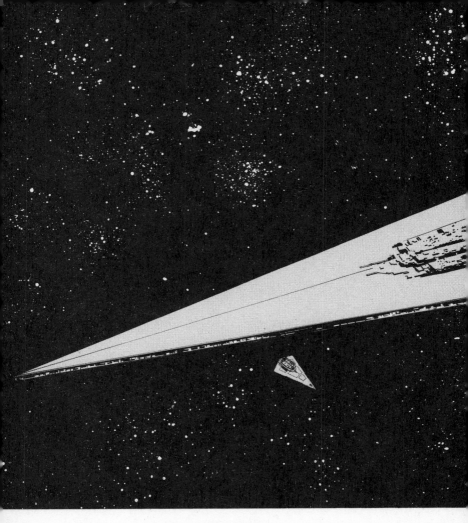

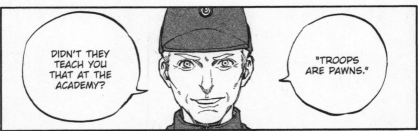

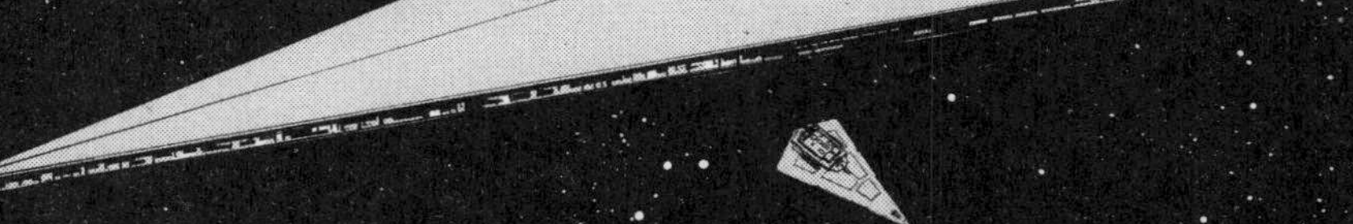
"TROOPS ARE PAWNS."
DIDN'T THEY TEACH YOU THAT AT THE ACADEMY?

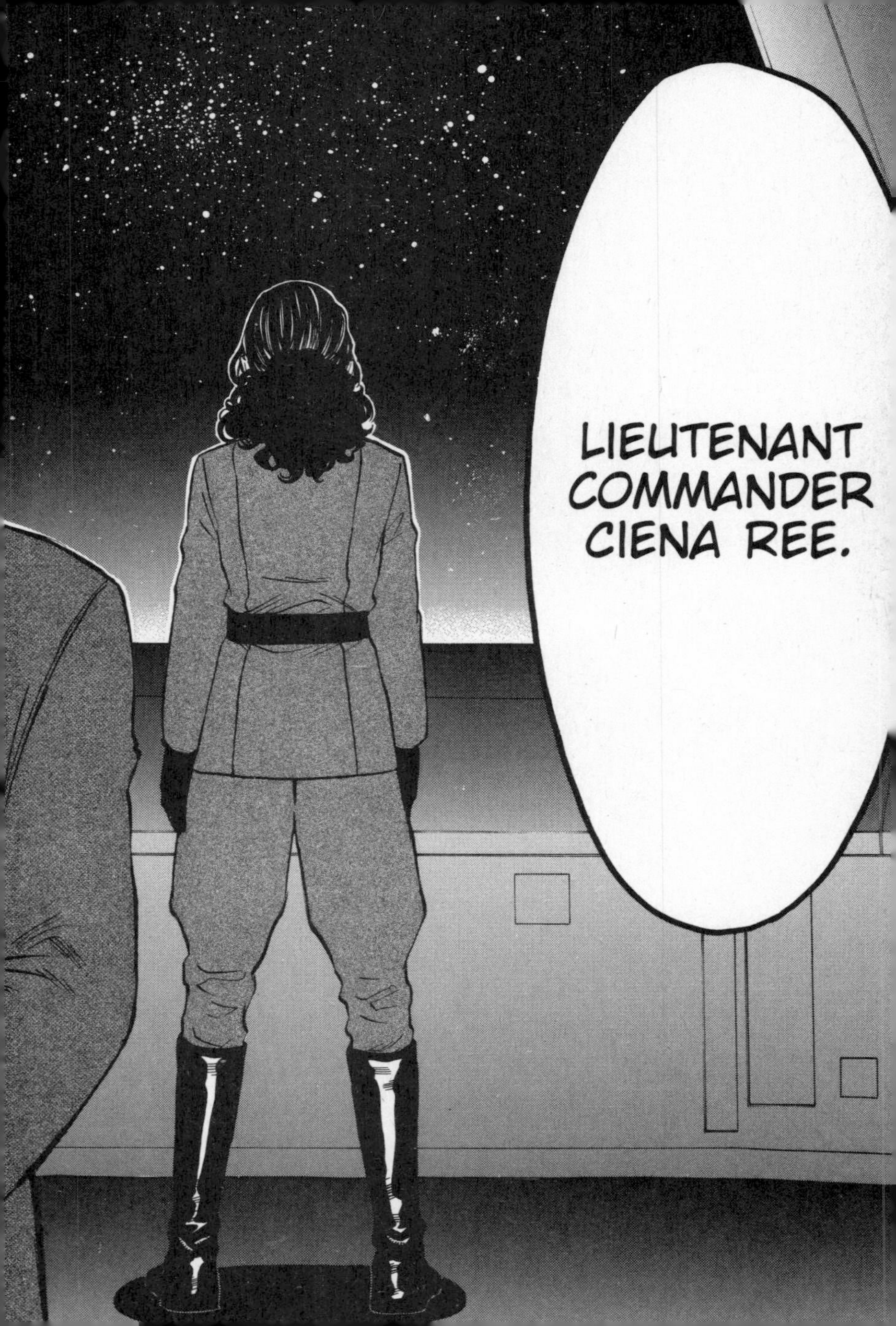
LIEUTENANT COMMANDER CIENA REE.

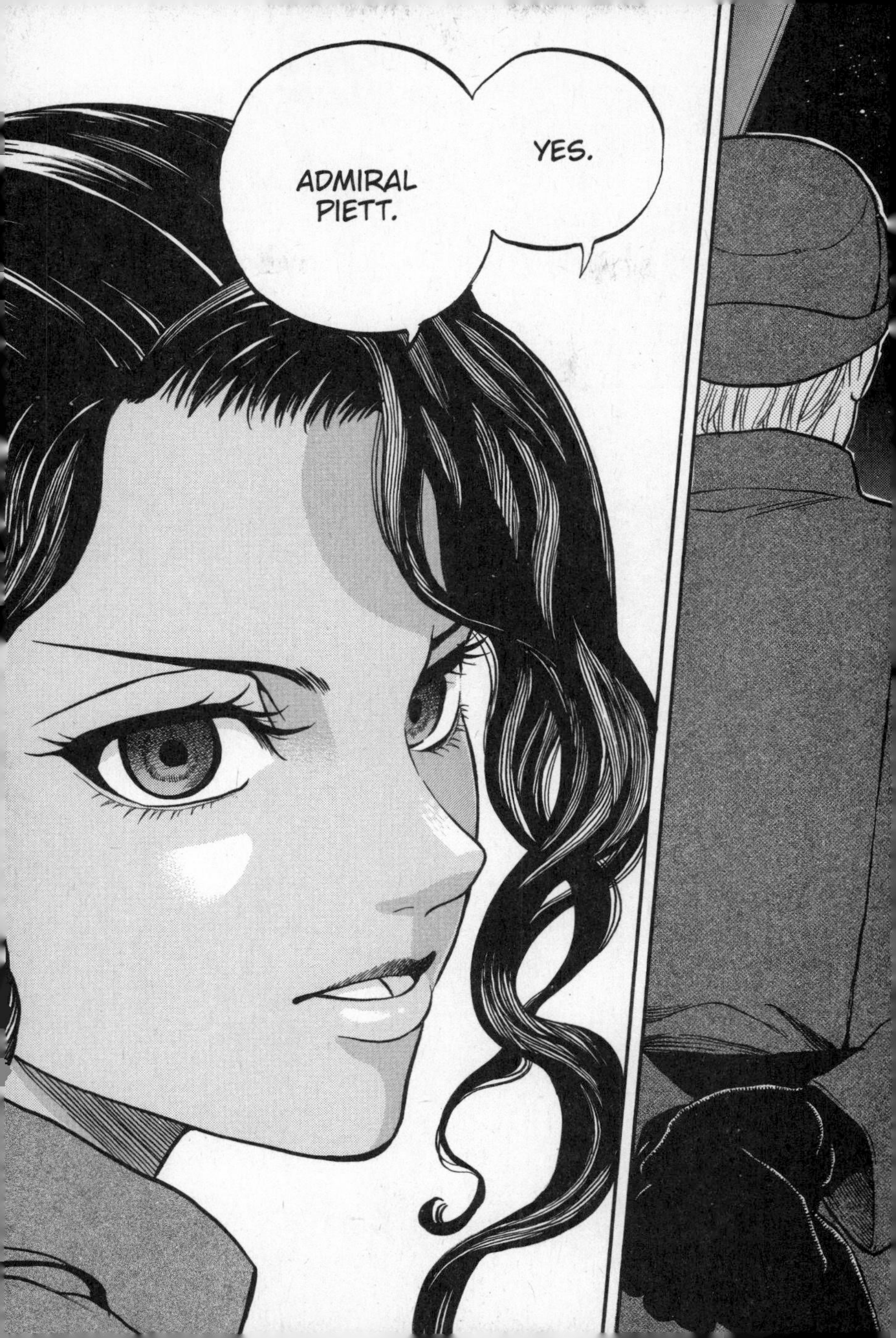
YES.
ADMIRAL PIETT.

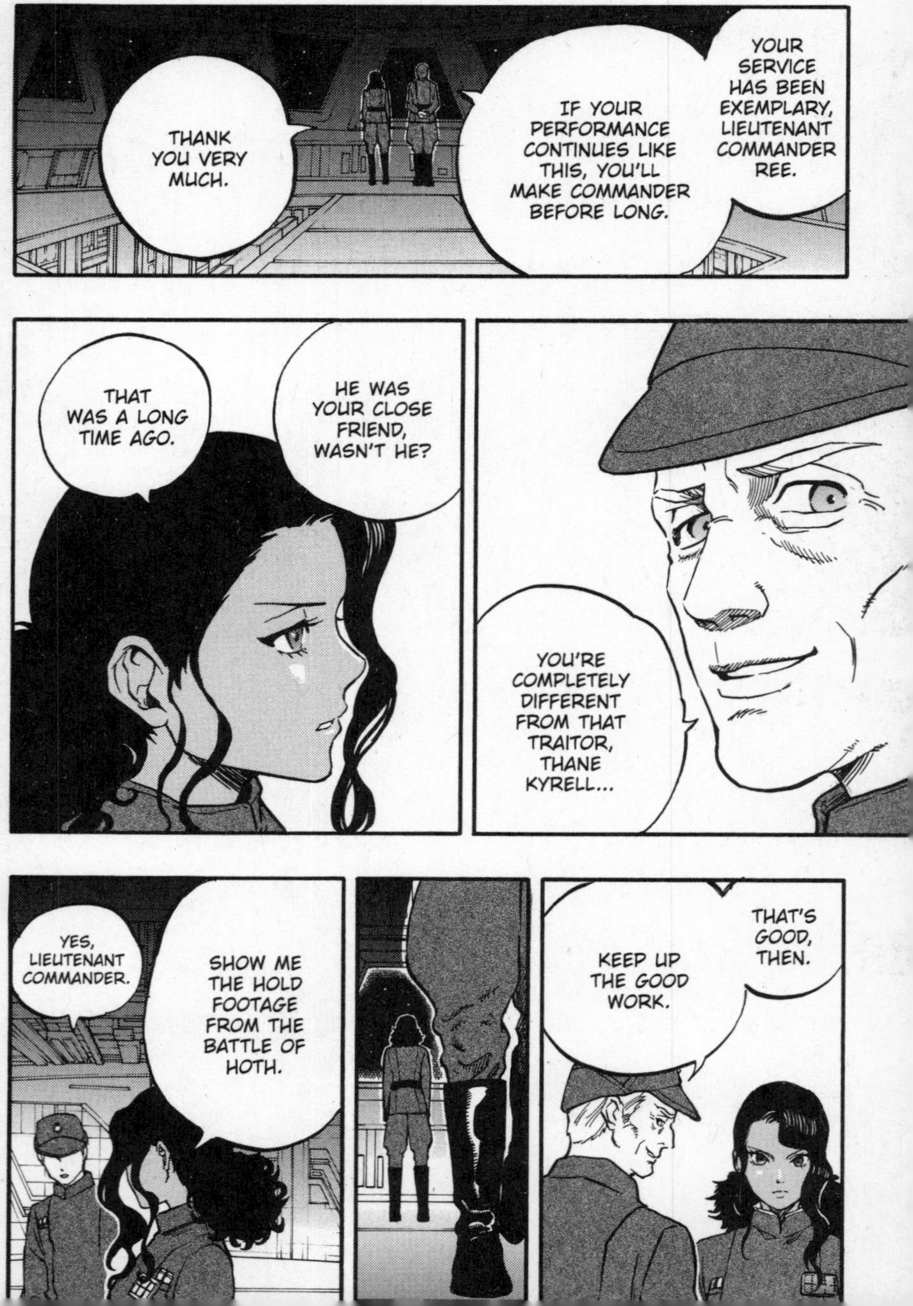
YOUR SERVICE HAS BEEN EXEMPLARY, LIEUTENANT COMMANDER REE.
IF YOUR PERFORMANCE CONTINUES LIKE THIS, YOU'LL MAKE COMMANDER BEFORE LONG.
THANK YOU VERY MUCH.
YOU'RE COMPLETELY DIFFERENT FROM THAT TRAITOR, THANE KYRELL...
HE WAS YOUR CLOSE FRIEND, WASN'T HE?
THAT WAS A LONG TIME AGO.
THAT'S GOOD, THEN.
KEEP UP THE GOOD WORK.
SHOW ME THE HOLD FOOTAGE FROM THE BATTLE OF HOTH.
YES, LIEUTENANT COMMANDER.

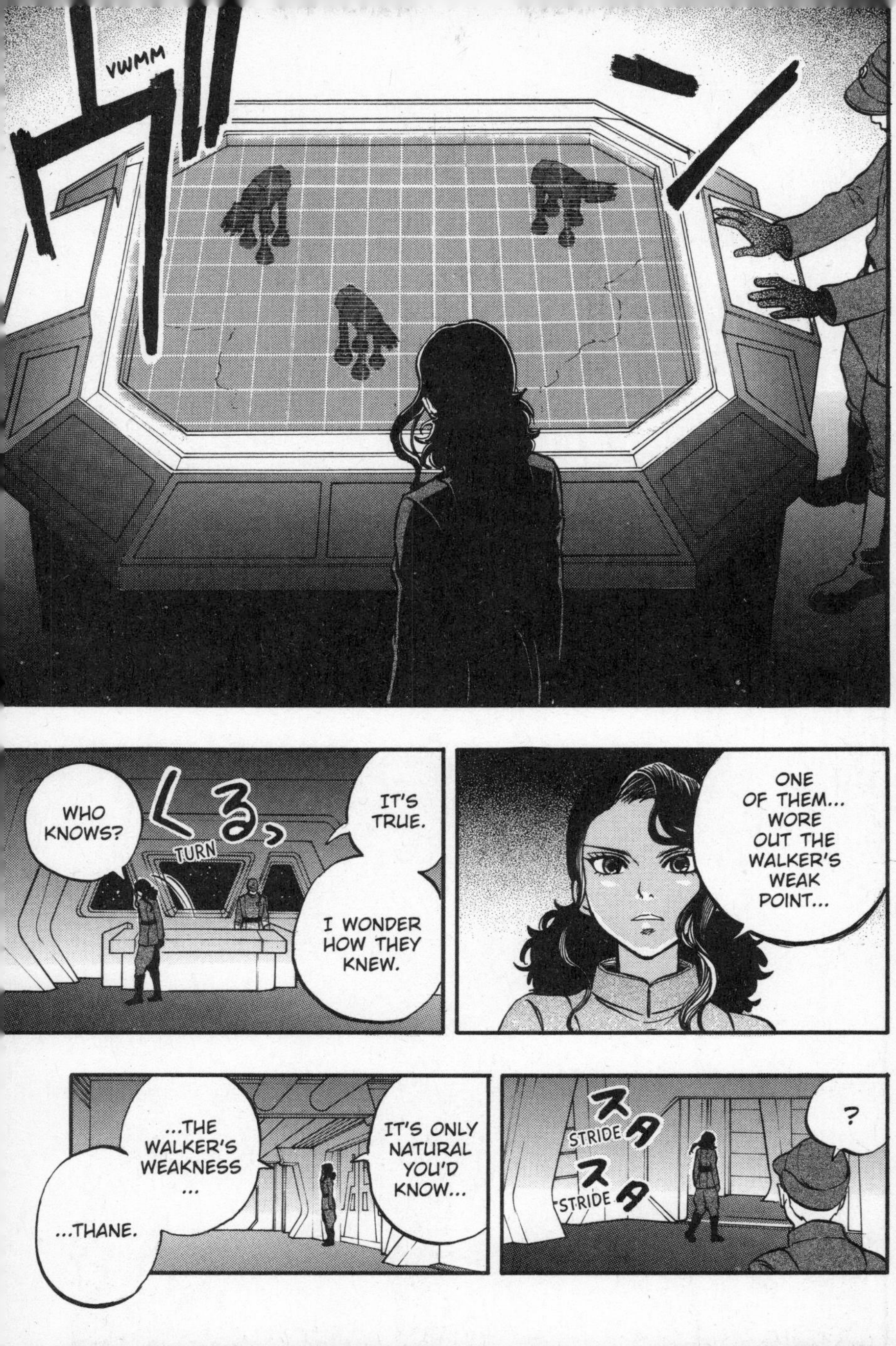
VWMM
ONE OF THEM... WORE OUT THE WALKER'S WEAK POINT...
IT'S TRUE.
I WONDER HOW THEY KNEW.
TURN
WHO KNOWS?
?
STRIDE
STRIDE
IT'S ONLY NATURAL YOU'D KNOW...
...THE WALKER'S WEAKNESS ...
...THANE.

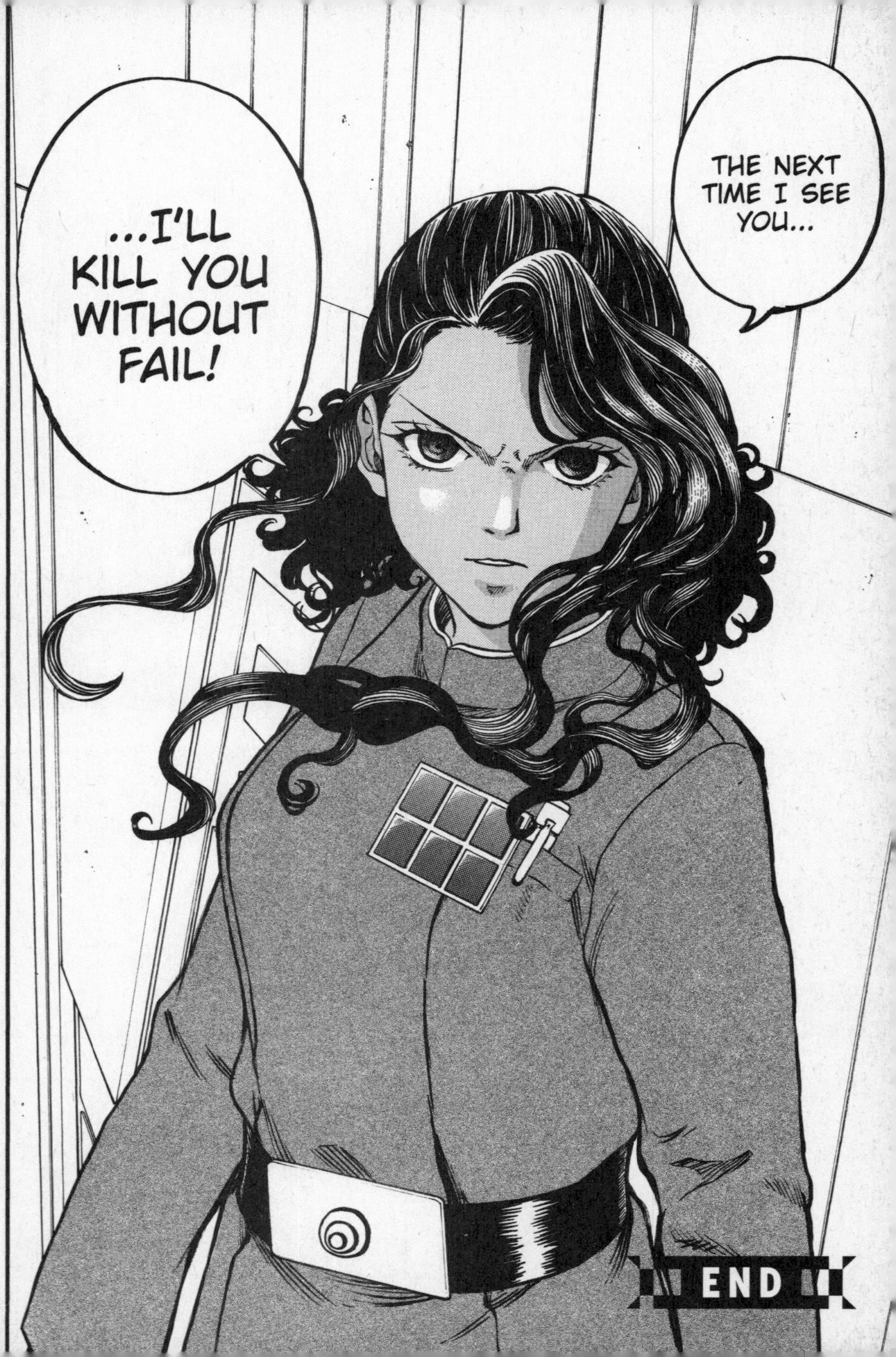
THE NEXT TIME I SEE YOU...
...I'LL KILL YOU WITHOUT FAIL!
END

STAR WARS LOST STARS
ロスト・スターズ

Chapter. 02

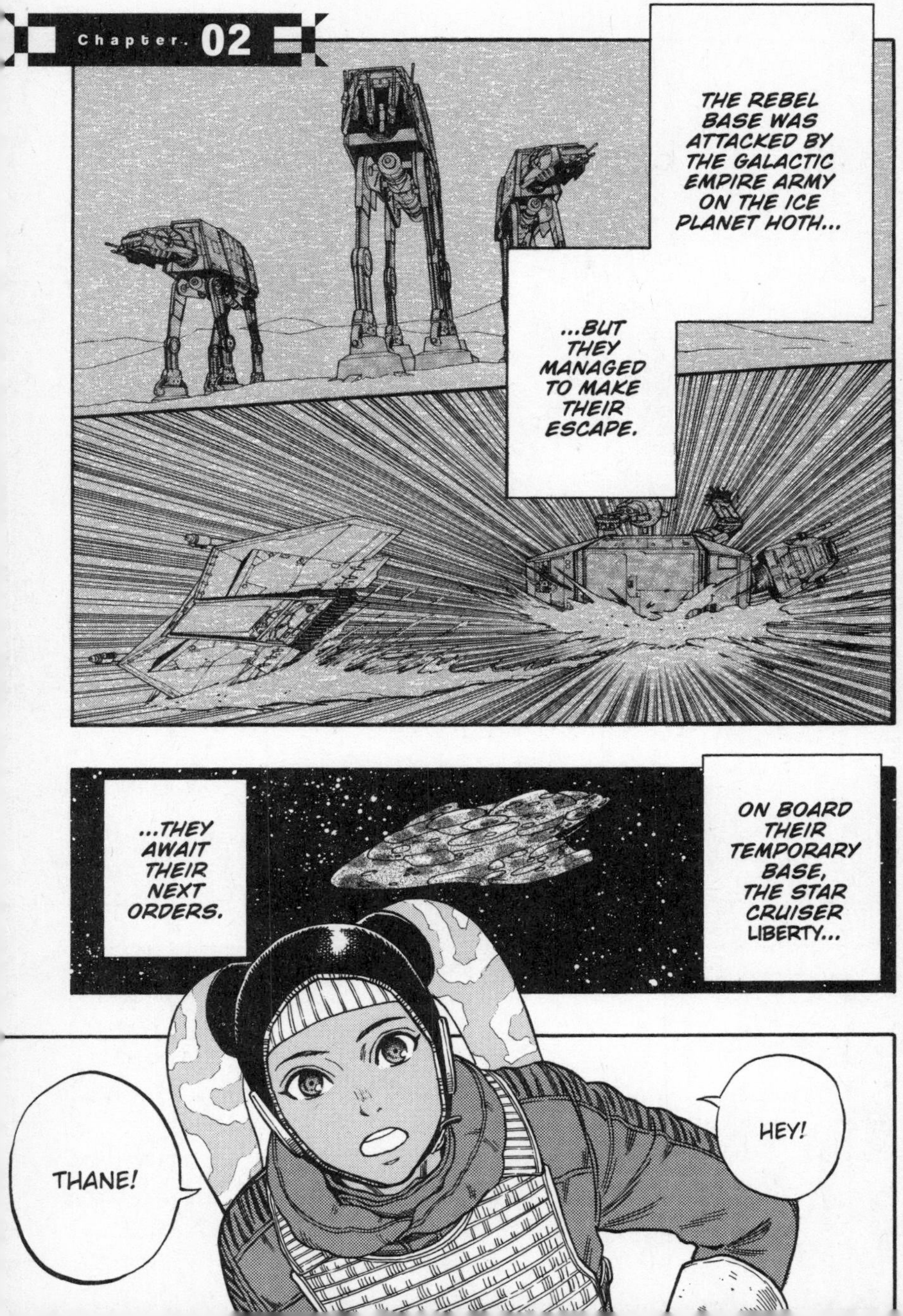
THE REBEL BASE WAS ATTACKED BY THE GALACTIC EMPIRE ARMY ON THE ICE PLANET HOTH...
...BUT THEY MANAGED TO MAKE THEIR ESCAPE.
ON BOARD THEIR TEMPORARY BASE, THE STAR CRUISER LIBERTY...
...THEY AWAIT THEIR NEXT ORDERS.
HEY!
THANE!

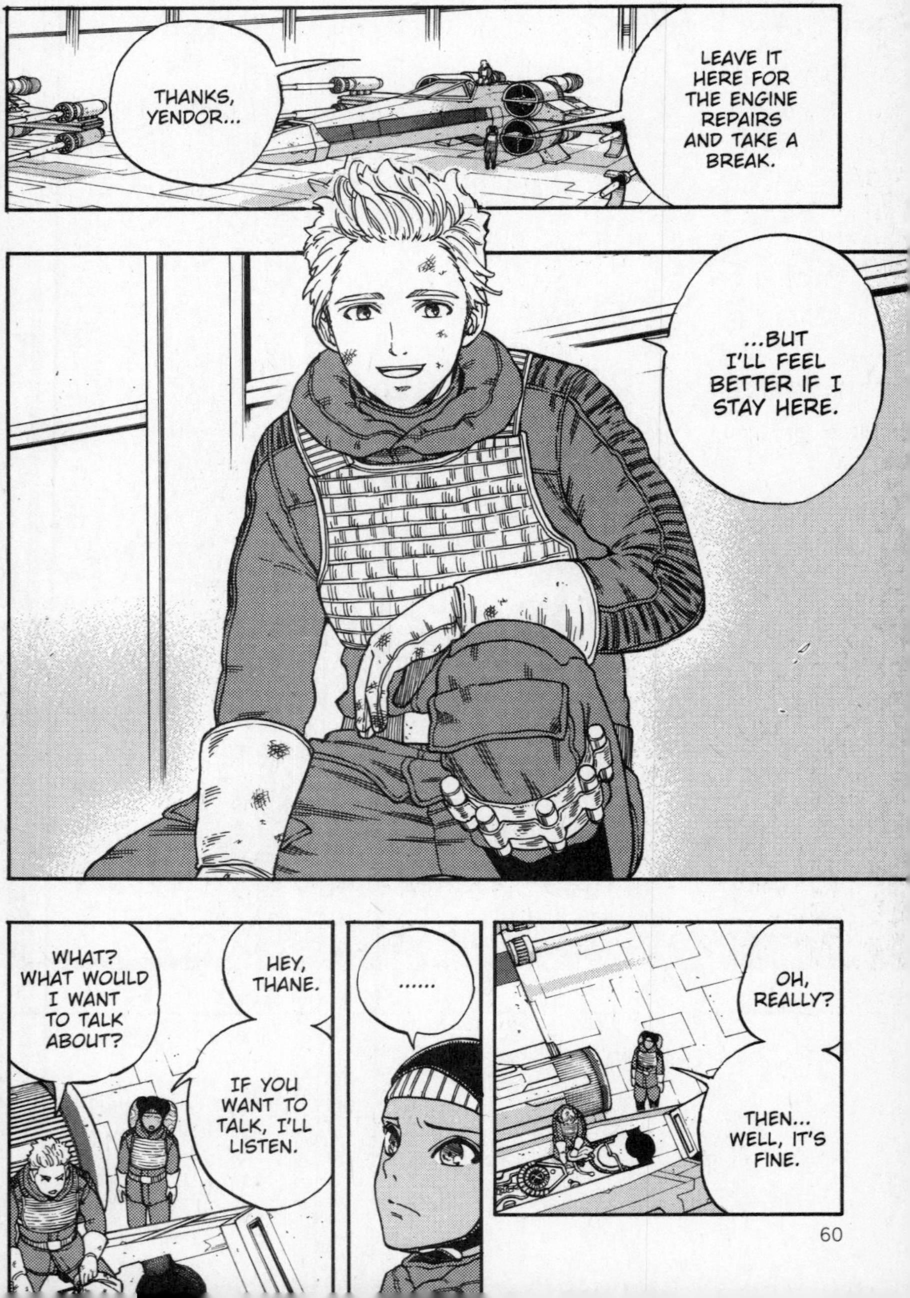
LEAVE IT HERE FOR THE ENGINE REPAIRS AND TAKE A BREAK.
THANKS, YENDOR...
...BUT I'LL FEEL BETTER IF I STAY HERE.
OH, REALLY?
THEN... WELL, IT'S FINE.
......
HEY, THANE.
IF YOU WANT TO TALK, I'LL LISTEN.
WHAT? WHAT WOULD I WANT TO TALK ABOUT?

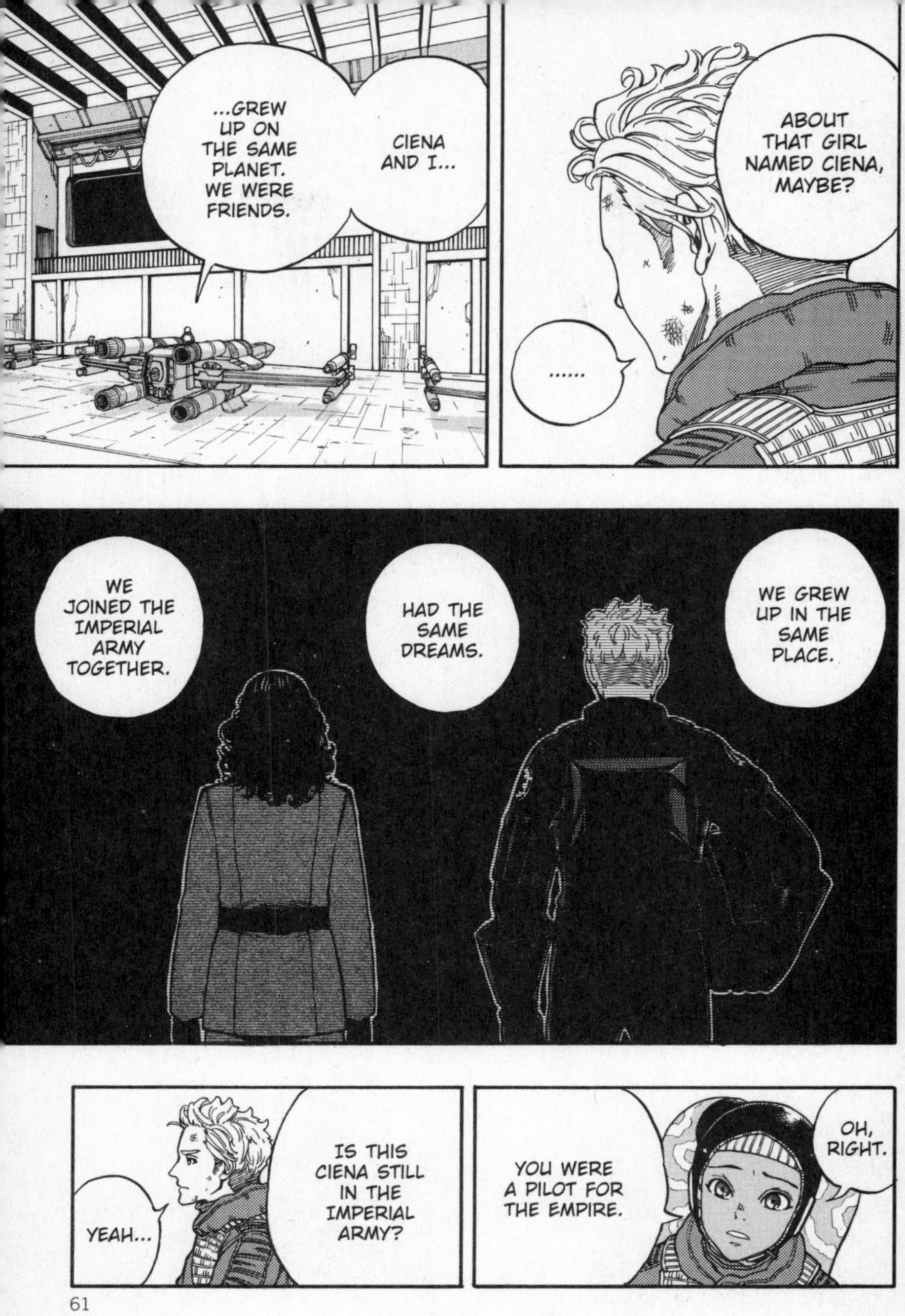
ABOUT THAT GIRL NAMED CIENA, MAYBE?
......
CIENA AND I...
...GREW UP ON THE SAME PLANET. WE WERE FRIENDS.
WE GREW UP IN THE SAME PLACE.
HAD THE SAME DREAMS.
WE JOINED THE IMPERIAL ARMY TOGETHER.
OH, RIGHT.
YOU WERE A PILOT FOR THE EMPIRE.
IS THIS CIENA STILL IN THE IMPERIAL ARMY?
YEAH...

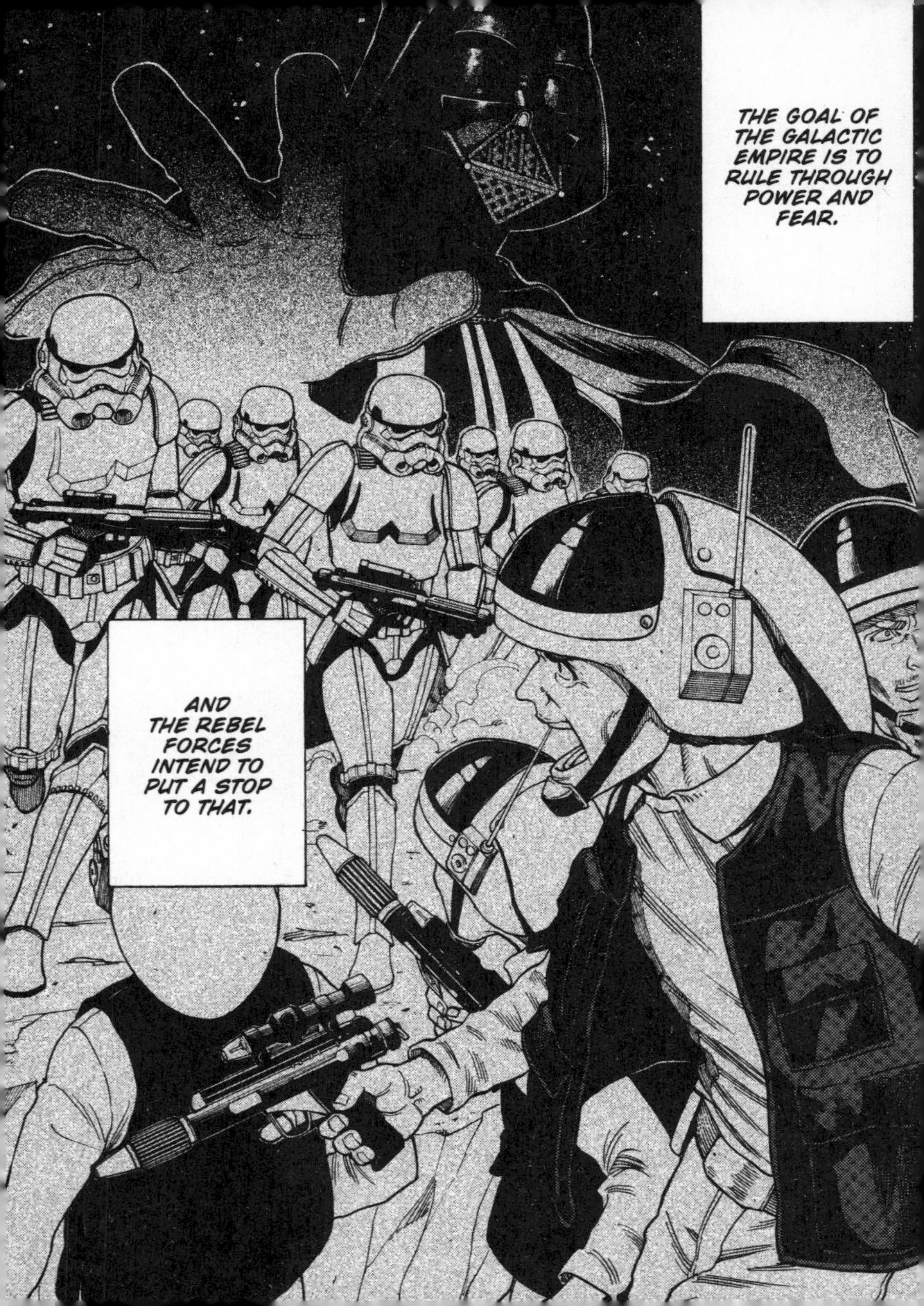
THE GOAL OF THE GALACTIC EMPIRE IS TO RULE THROUGH POWER AND FEAR.
AND THE REBEL FORCES INTEND TO PUT A STOP TO THAT.

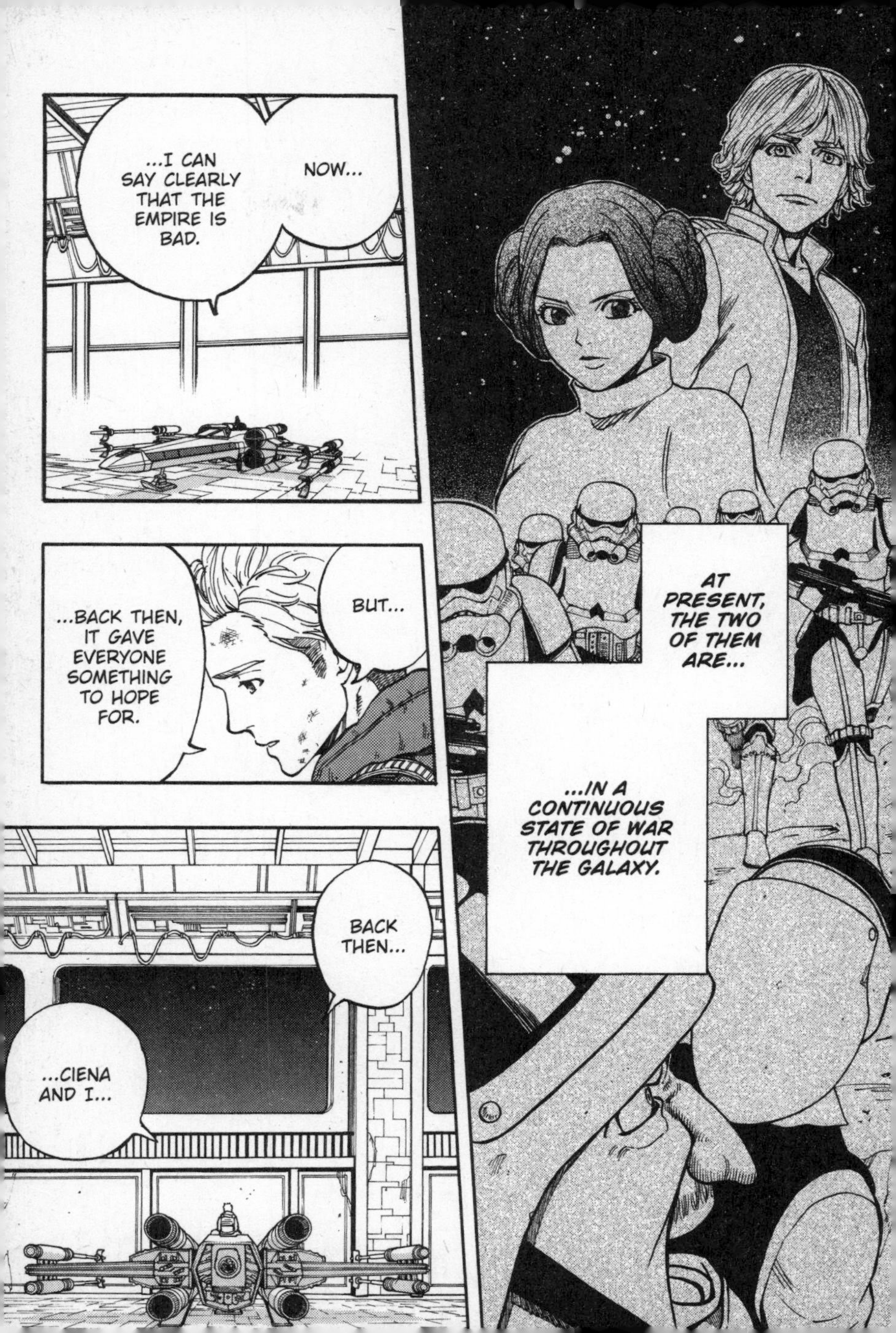
AT PRESENT, THE TWO OF THEM ARE...
...IN A CONTINUOUS STATE OF WAR THROUGHOUT THE GALAXY.
NOW...
...I CAN SAY CLEARLY THAT THE EMPIRE IS BAD.
BUT...
...BACK THEN, IT GAVE EVERYONE SOMETHING TO HOPE FOR.
BACK THEN...
...CIENA AND I...

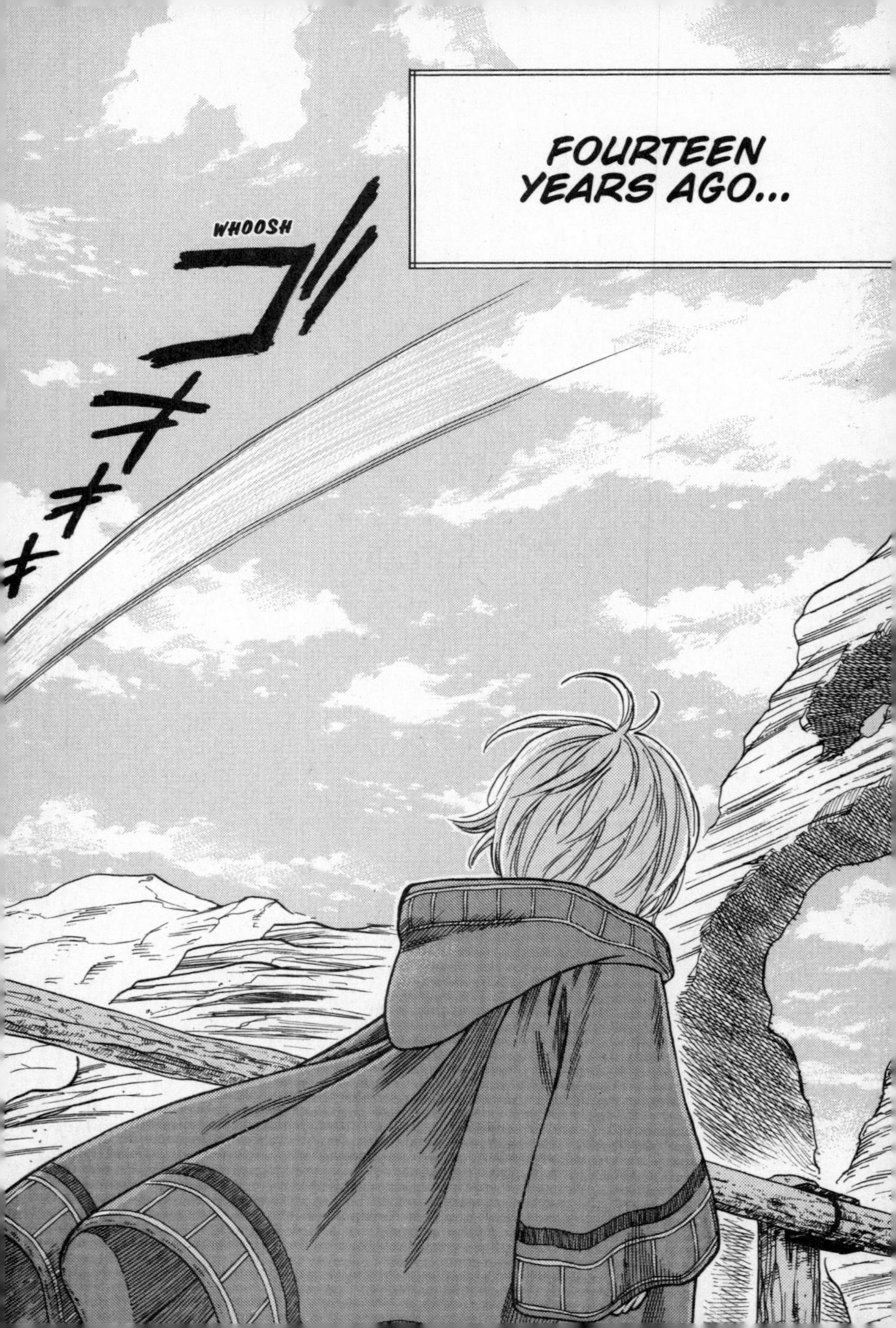
FOURTEEN
YEARS AGO...
WHOOSH

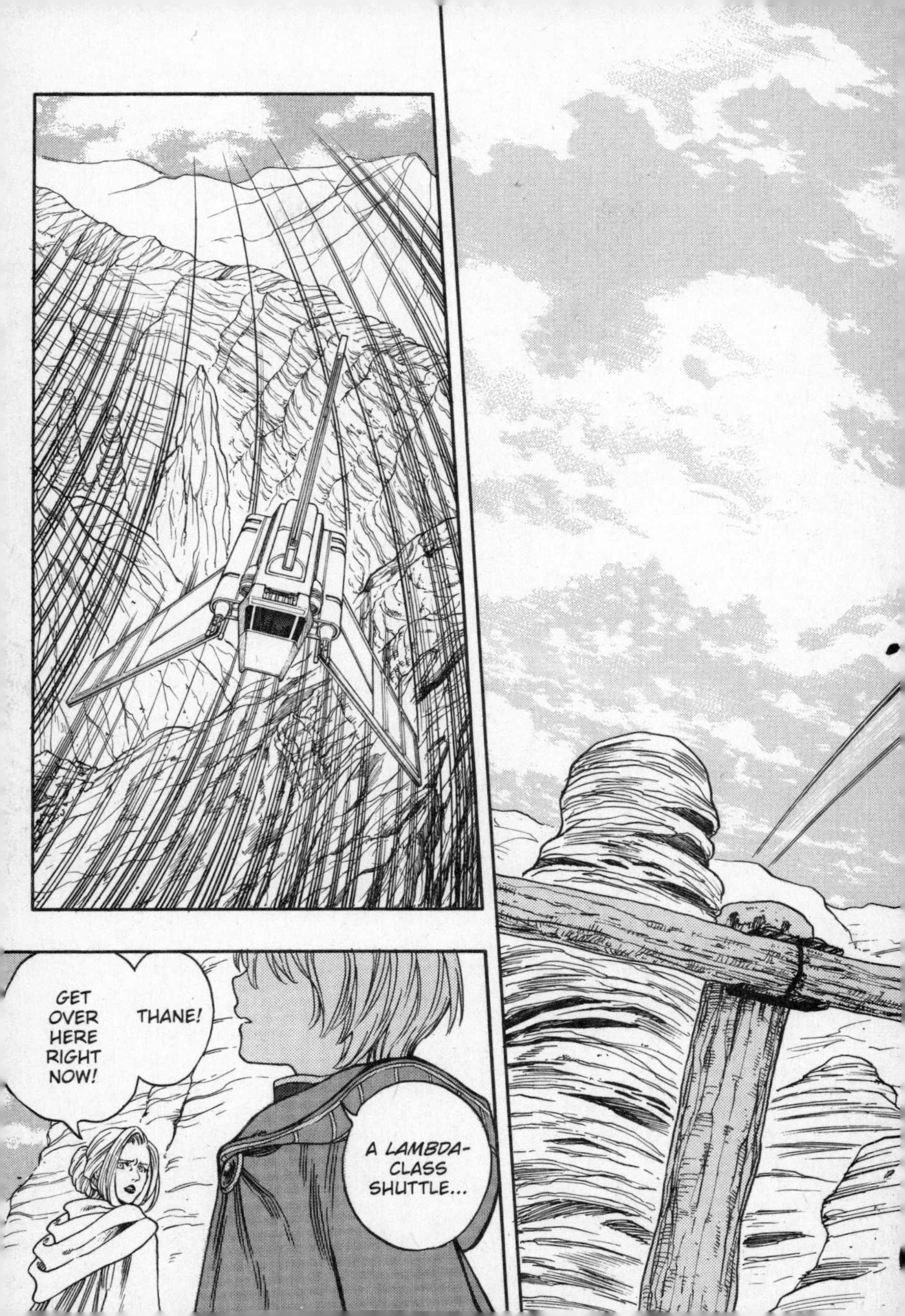
THANE!
GET OVER HERE RIGHT NOW!
A LAMBDA-CLASS SHUTTLE...

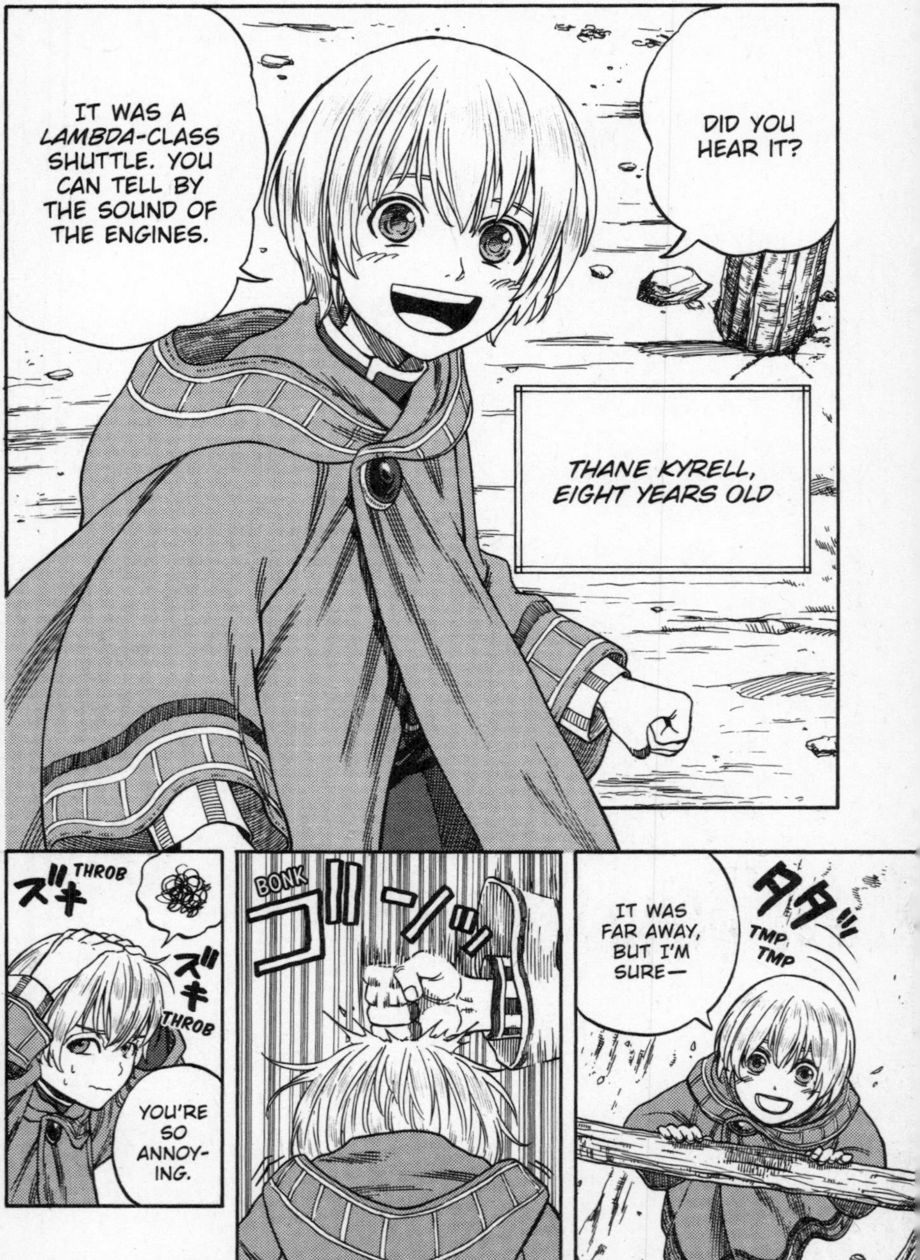
DID YOU HEAR IT?
IT WAS A *LAMBDA*-CLASS SHUTTLE. YOU CAN TELL BY THE SOUND OF THE ENGINES.
THANE KYRELL, EIGHT YEARS OLD
タタッ
TMP TMP
IT WAS FAR AWAY, BUT I'M SURE—
BONK
ゴーンッ
ズキ
THROB
ズキ
THROB
YOU'RE SO ANNOY-ING.

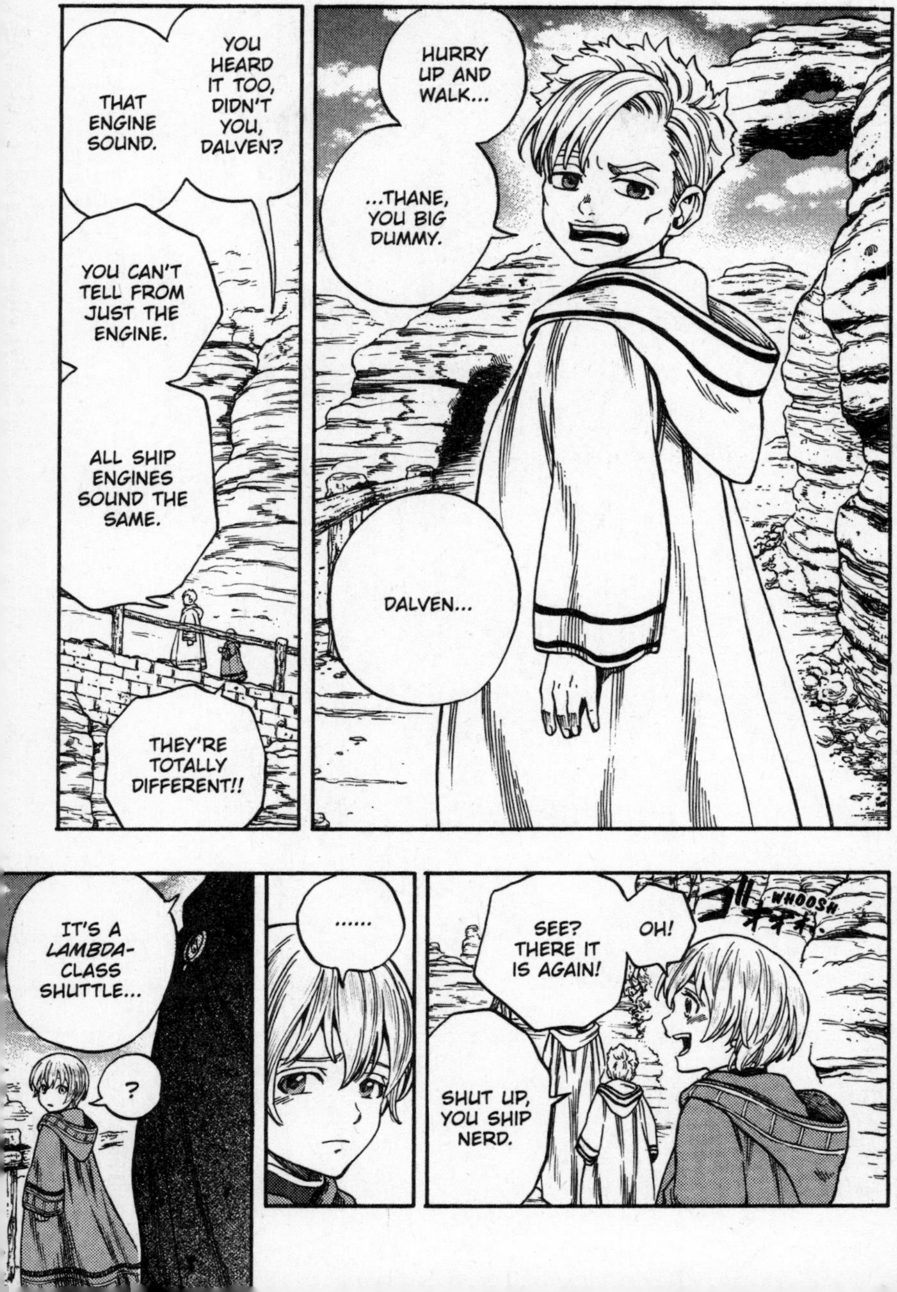
HURRY UP AND WALK...
...THANE, YOU BIG DUMMY.
DALVEN...
YOU HEARD IT TOO, DIDN'T YOU, DALVEN?
THAT ENGINE SOUND.
YOU CAN'T TELL FROM JUST THE ENGINE.
ALL SHIP ENGINES SOUND THE SAME.
THEY'RE TOTALLY DIFFERENT!!
WHOOSH
OH!
SEE? THERE IT IS AGAIN!
SHUT UP, YOU SHIP NERD.
......
IT'S A LAMBDA-CLASS SHUTTLE...
?

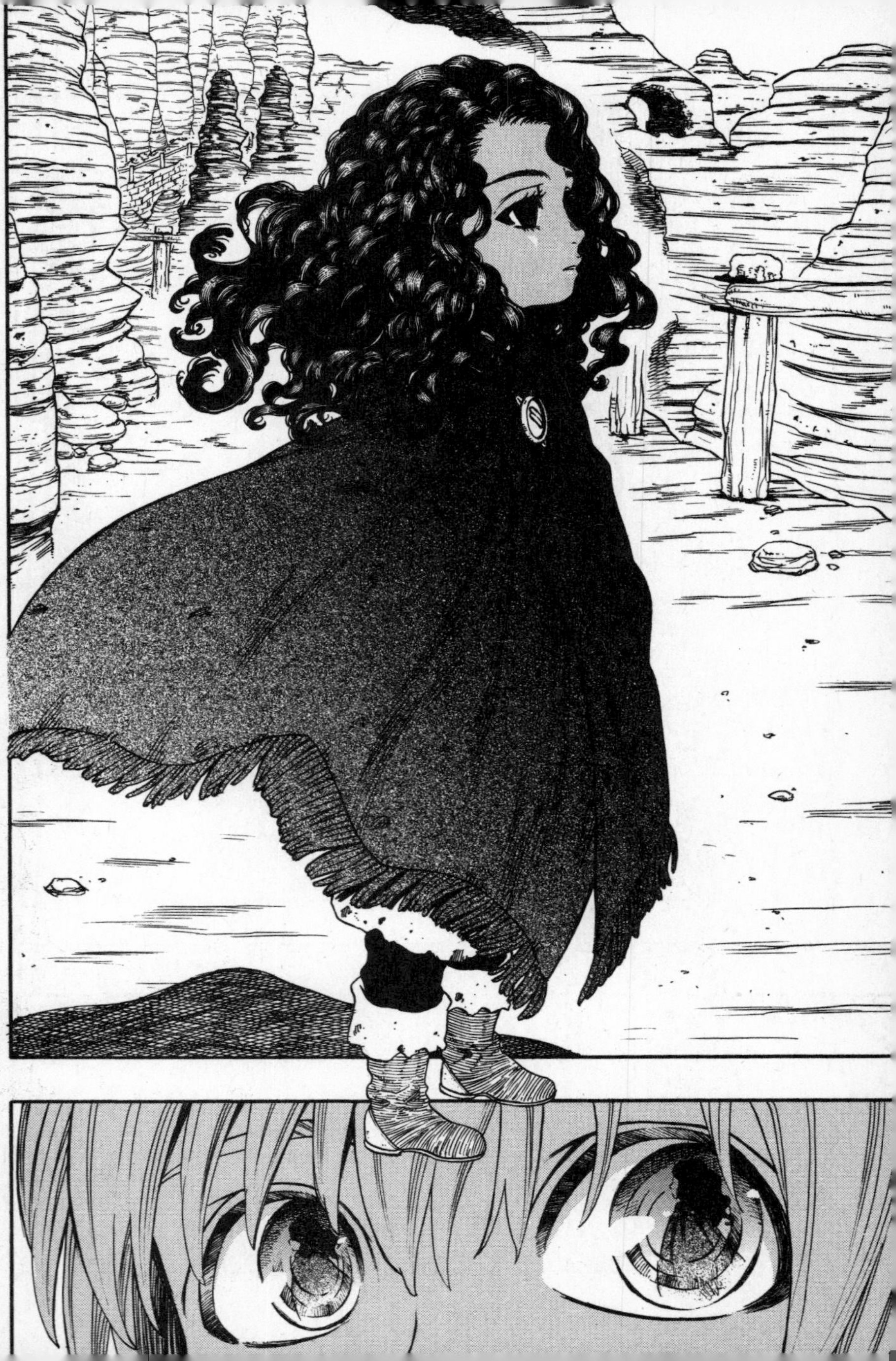

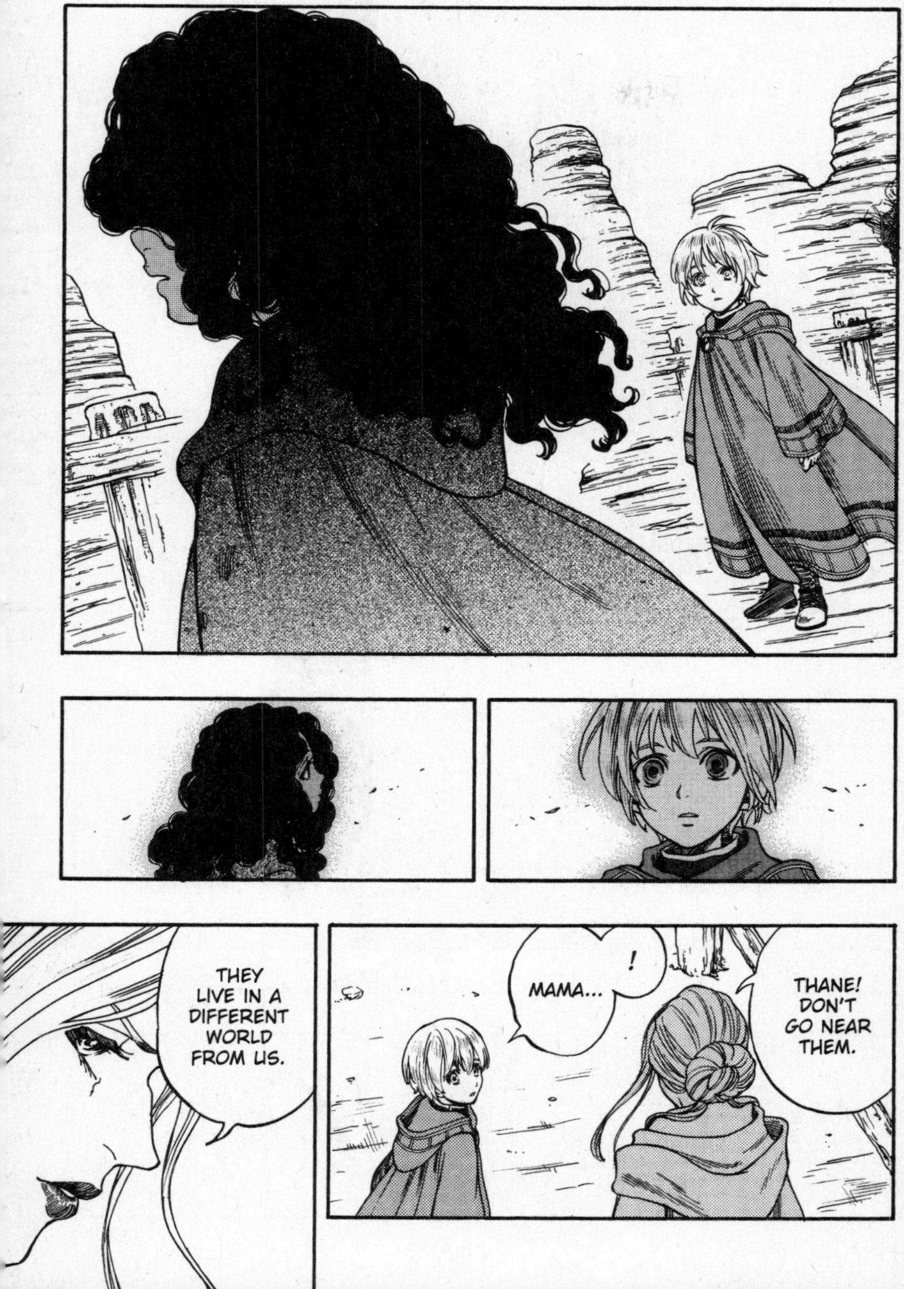
THANE! DON'T GO NEAR THEM.
!
MAMA...
THEY LIVE IN A DIFFERENT WORLD FROM US.

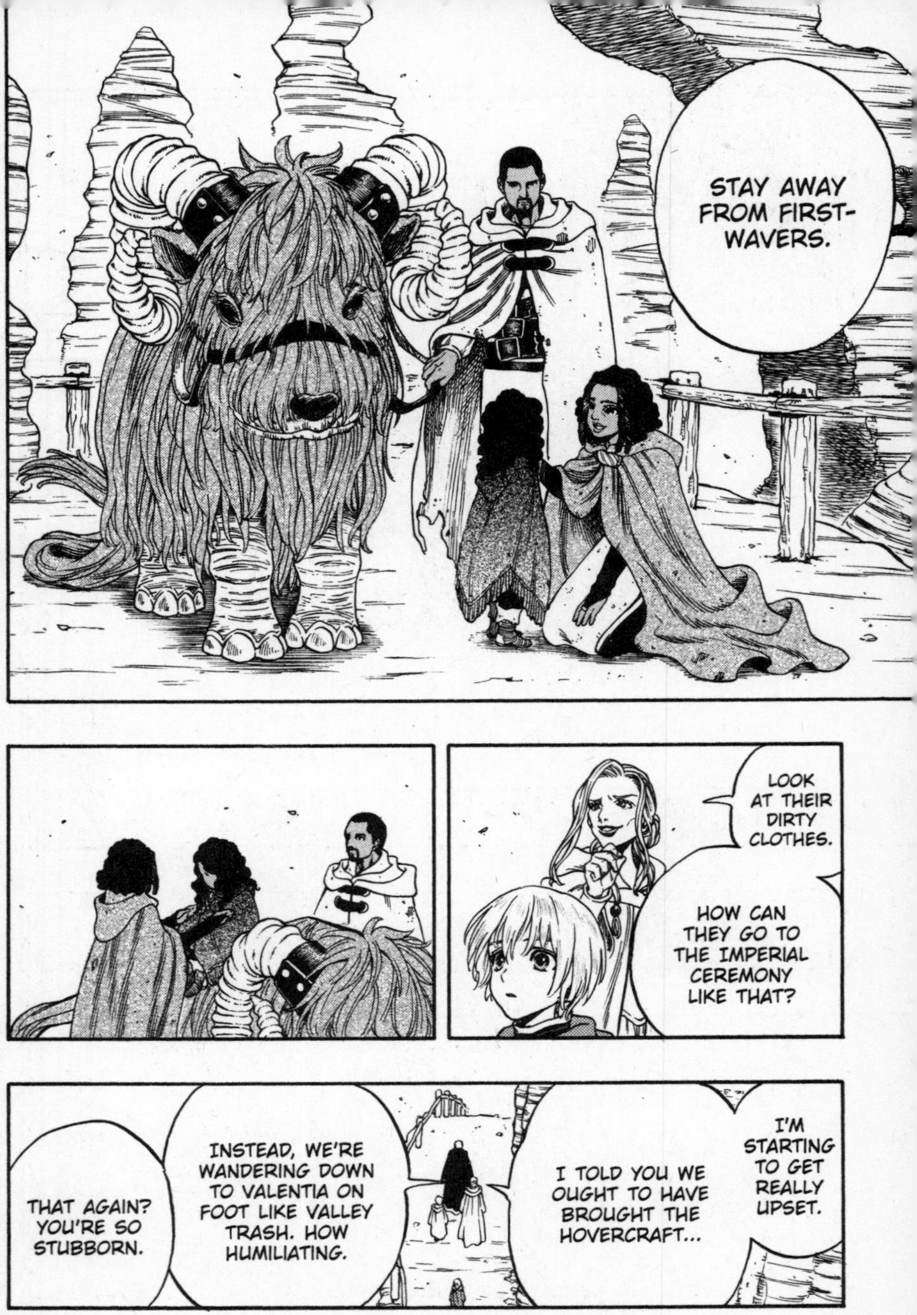
STAY AWAY FROM FIRST-WAVERS.
LOOK AT THEIR DIRTY CLOTHES.
HOW CAN THEY GO TO THE IMPERIAL CEREMONY LIKE THAT?
I'M STARTING TO GET REALLY UPSET.
I TOLD YOU WE OUGHT TO HAVE BROUGHT THE HOVERCRAFT...
INSTEAD, WE'RE WANDERING DOWN TO VALENTIA ON FOOT LIKE VALLEY TRASH. HOW HUMILIATING.
THAT AGAIN? YOU'RE SO STUBBORN.

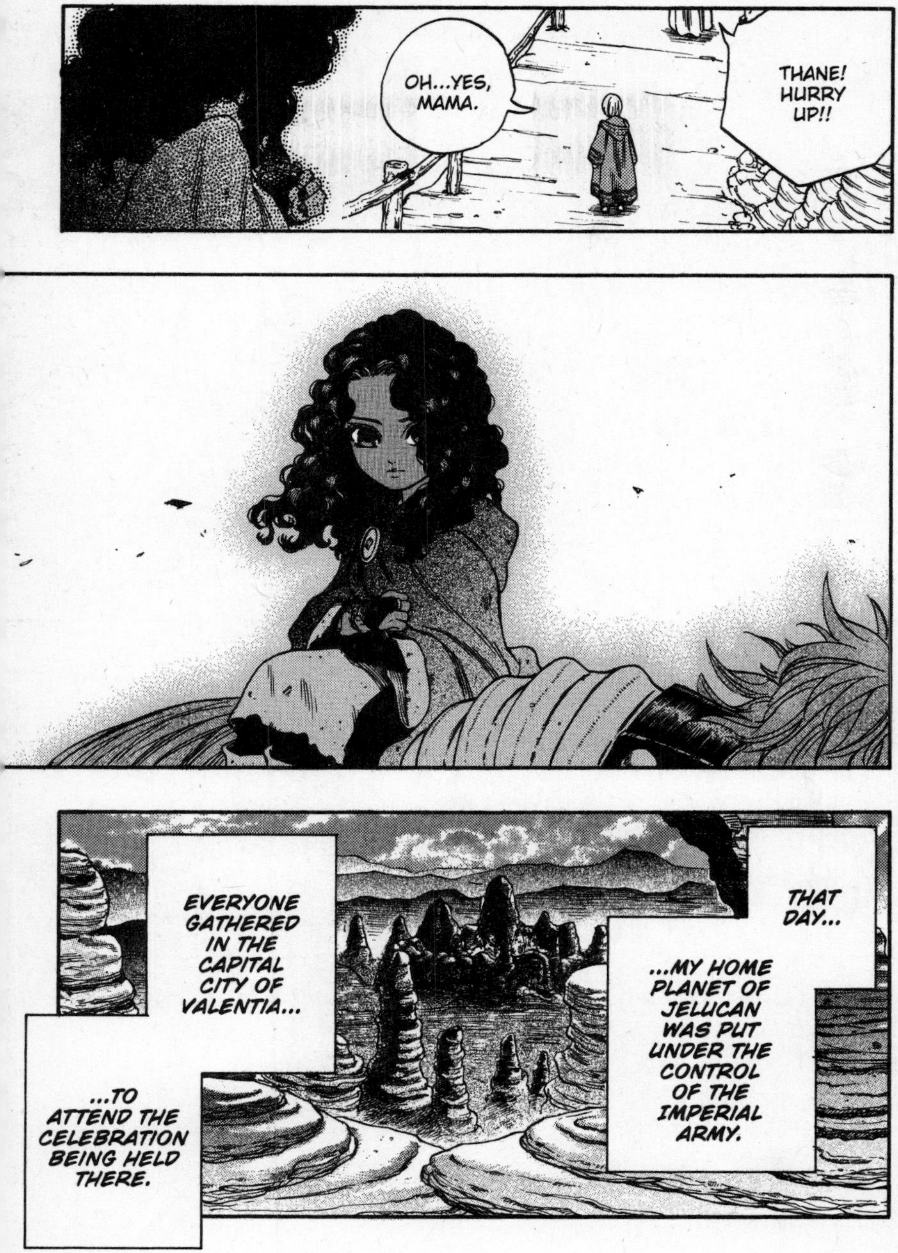
THANE! HURRY UP!!
OH...YES, MAMA.
THAT DAY...
...MY HOME PLANET OF JELICAN WAS PUT UNDER THE CONTROL OF THE IMPERIAL ARMY.
EVERYONE GATHERED IN THE CAPITAL CITY OF VALENTIA...
...TO ATTEND THE CELEBRATION BEING HELD THERE.

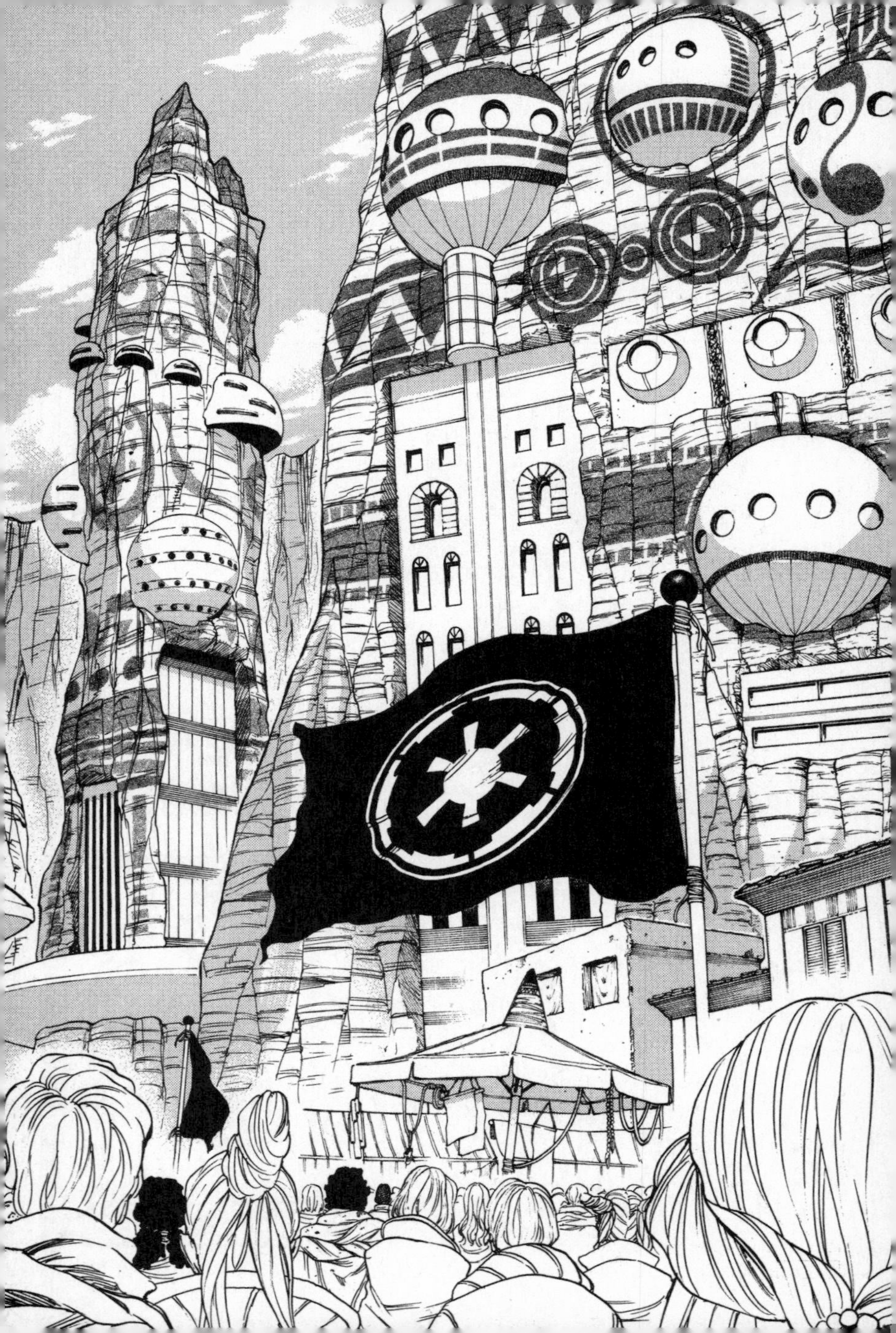

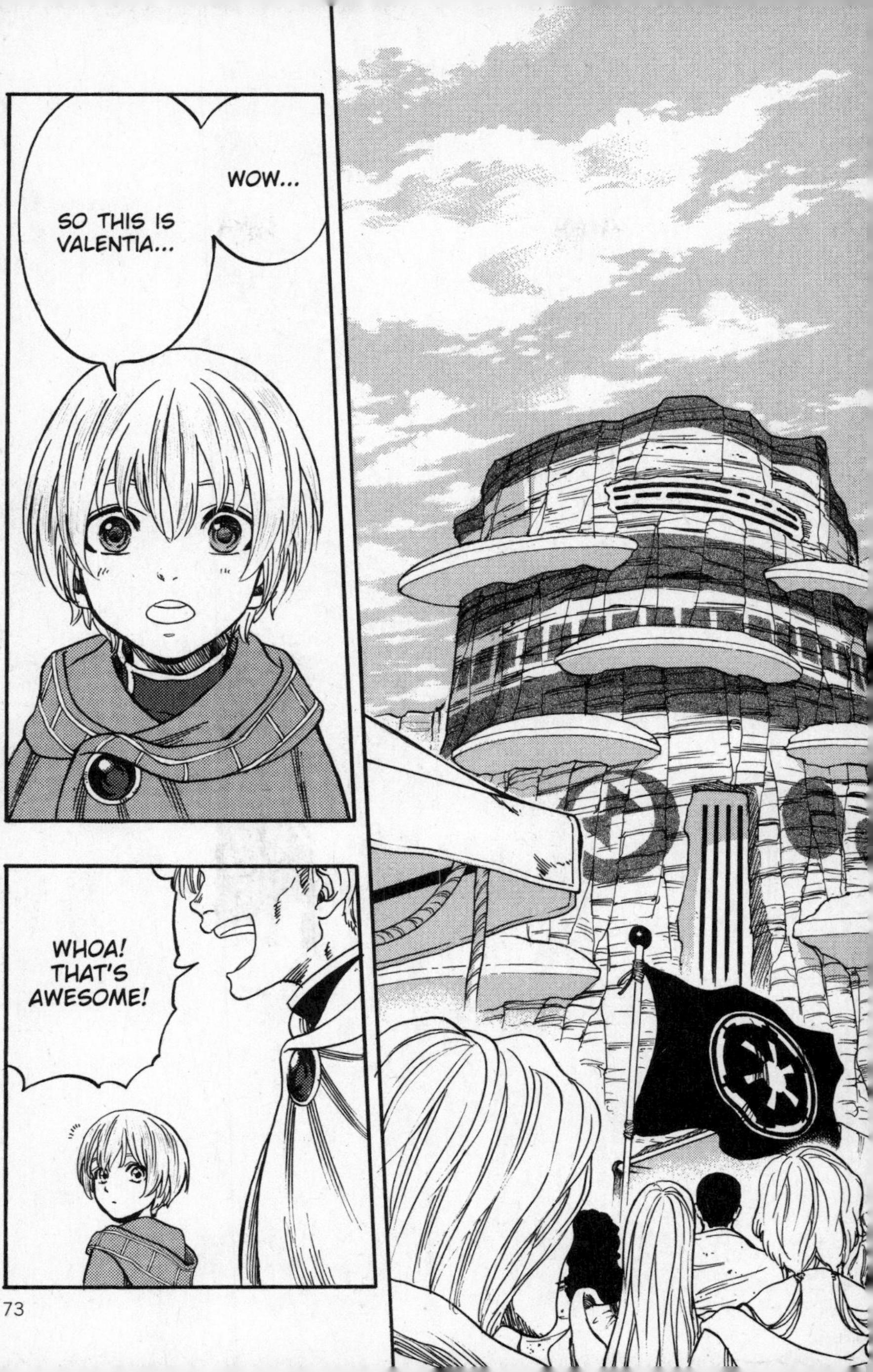
WOW...
SO THIS IS VALENTIA...
WHOA! THAT'S AWESOME!

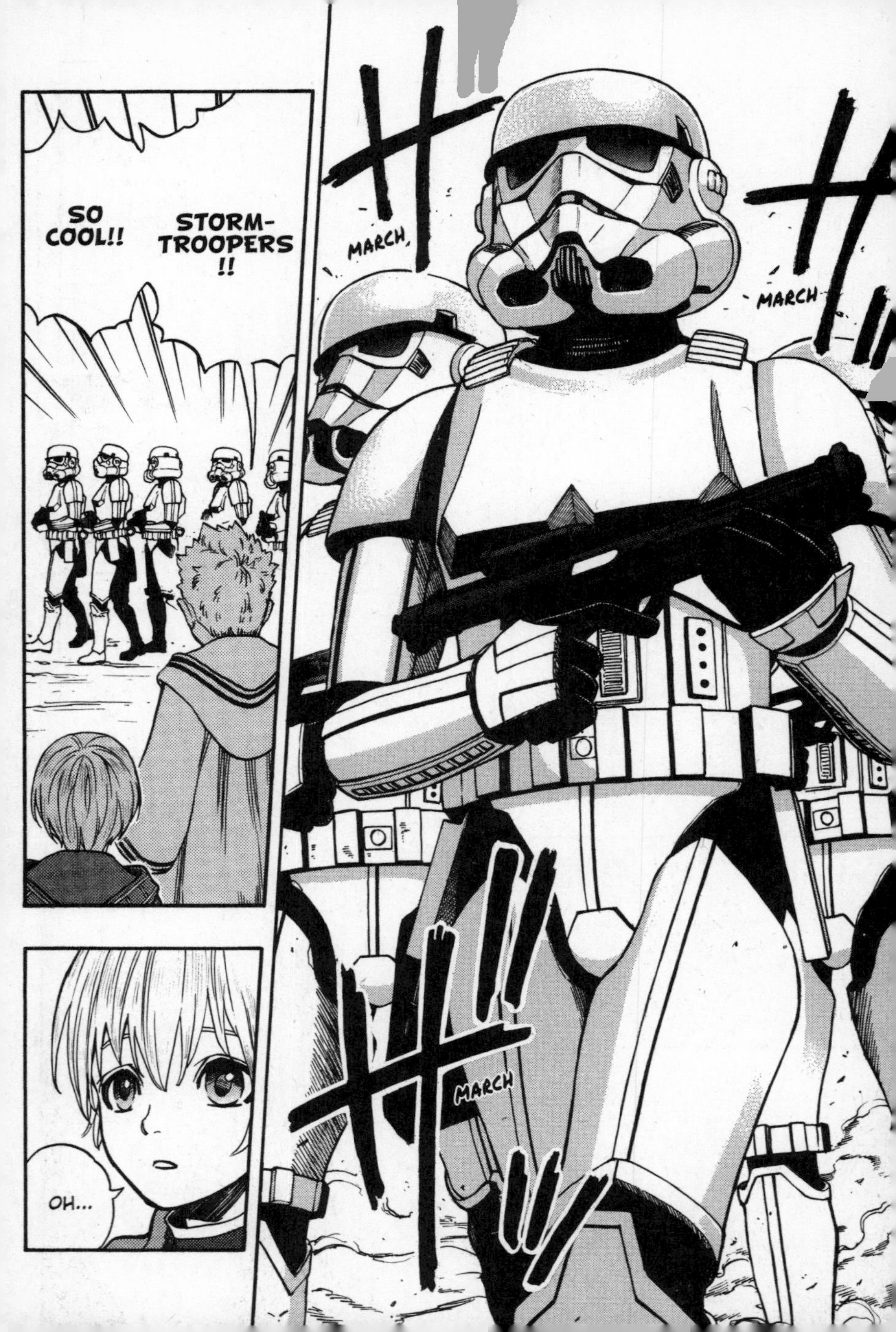
MARCH
MARCH,
MARCH
STORM-TROOPERS !!
SO COOL!!
OH...

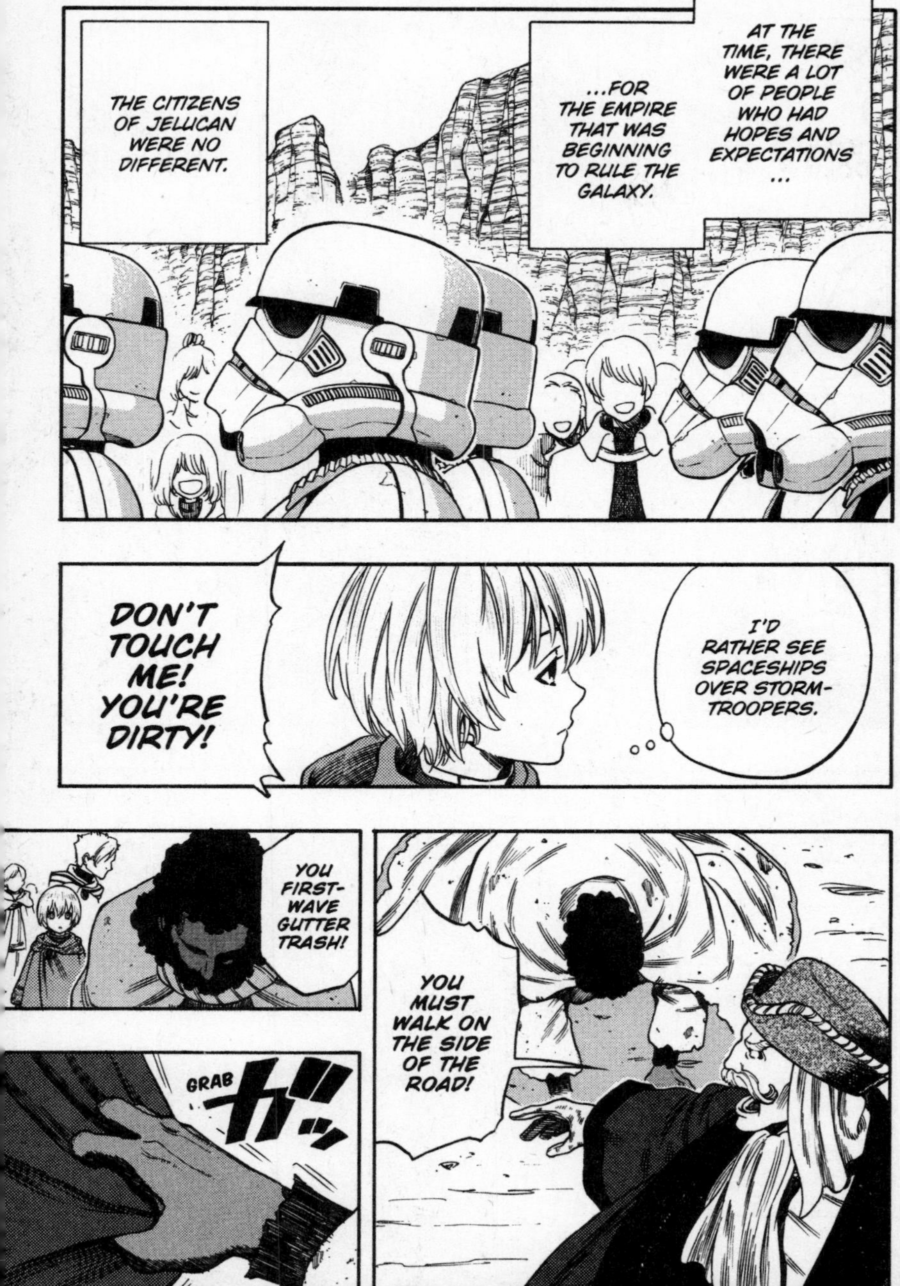
AT THE TIME, THERE WERE A LOT OF PEOPLE WHO HAD HOPES AND EXPECTATIONS ...
...FOR THE EMPIRE THAT WAS BEGINNING TO RULE THE GALAXY.
THE CITIZENS OF JELUCAN WERE NO DIFFERENT.
I'D RATHER SEE SPACESHIPS OVER STORM-TROOPERS.
DON'T TOUCH ME! YOU'RE DIRTY!
YOU MUST WALK ON THE SIDE OF THE ROAD!
YOU FIRST-WAVE GUTTER TRASH!
GRAB

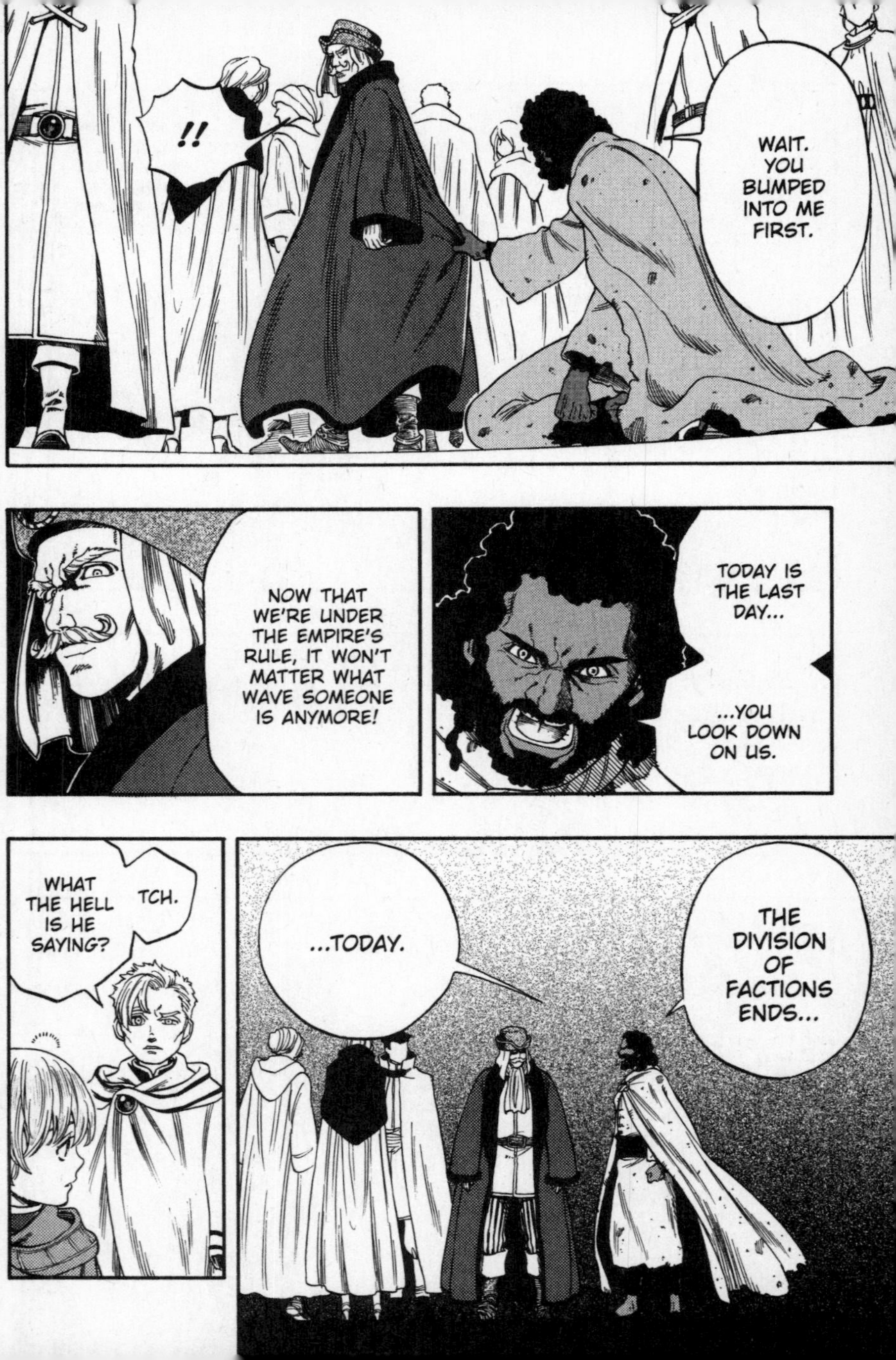
WAIT. YOU BUMPED INTO ME FIRST.
!!
TODAY IS THE LAST DAY...
...YOU LOOK DOWN ON US.
NOW THAT WE'RE UNDER THE EMPIRE'S RULE, IT WON'T MATTER WHAT WAVE SOMEONE IS ANYMORE!
THE DIVISION OF FACTIONS ENDS...
...TODAY.
TCH.
WHAT THE HELL IS HE SAYING?

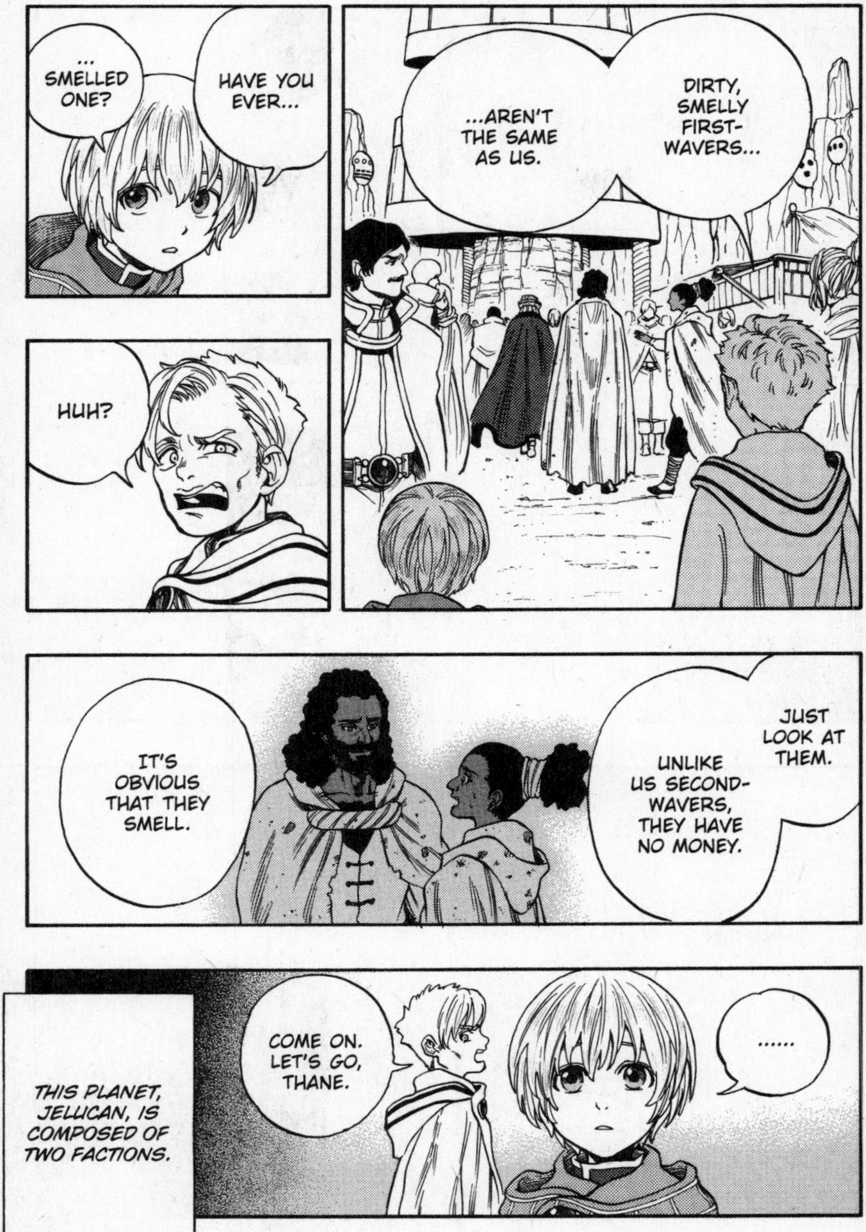
DIRTY, SMELLY FIRST-WAVERS...
...AREN'T THE SAME AS US.
HAVE YOU EVER...
... SMELLED ONE?
HUH?
JUST LOOK AT THEM.
UNLIKE US SECOND-WAVERS, THEY HAVE NO MONEY.
IT'S OBVIOUS THAT THEY SMELL.
......
COME ON. LET'S GO, THANE.
THIS PLANET, JELUCAN, IS COMPOSED OF TWO FACTIONS.

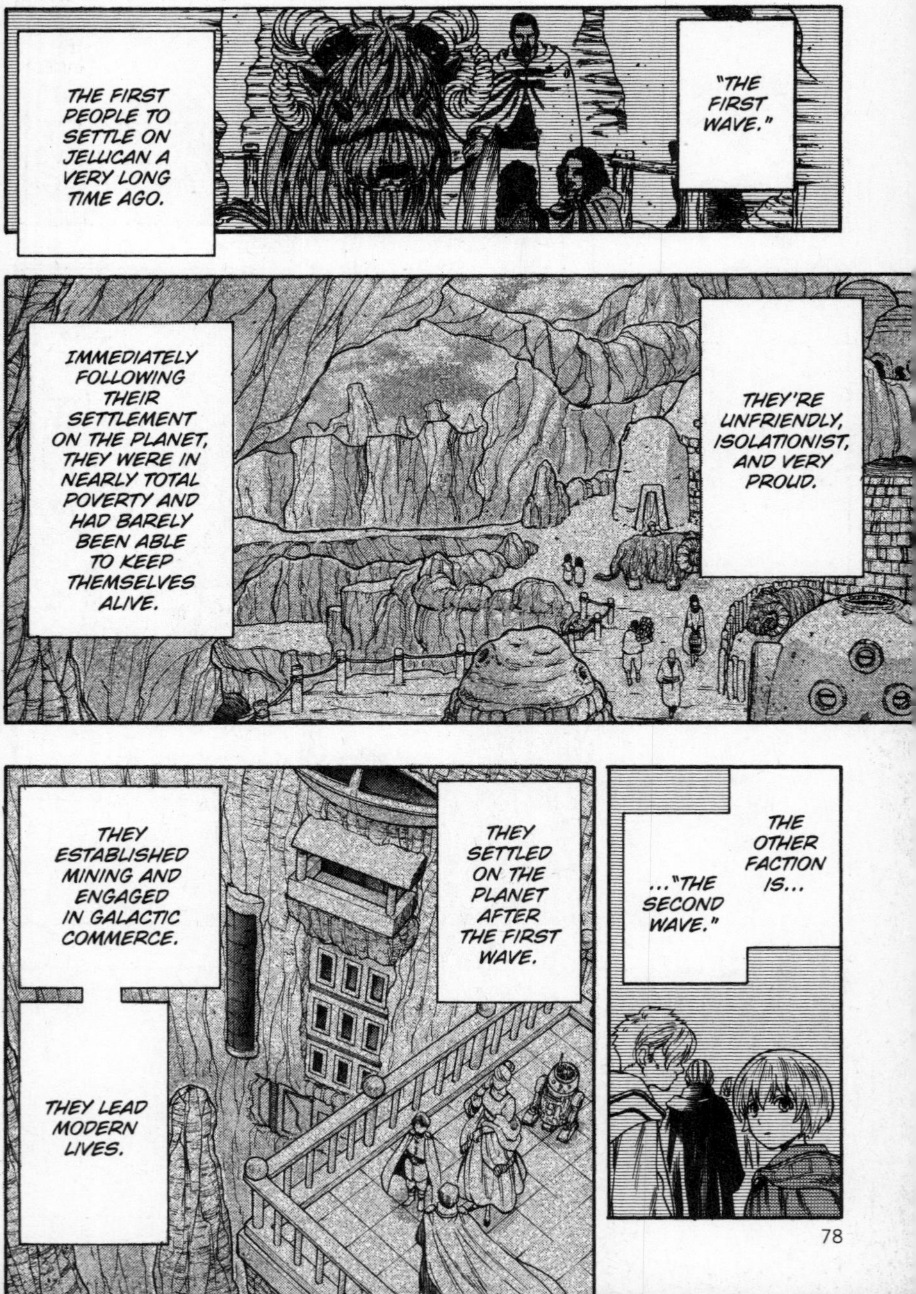
"THE FIRST WAVE."
THE FIRST PEOPLE TO SETTLE ON JELUCAN A VERY LONG TIME AGO.
THEY'RE UNFRIENDLY, ISOLATIONIST, AND VERY PROUD.
IMMEDIATELY FOLLOWING THEIR SETTLEMENT ON THE PLANET, THEY WERE IN NEARLY TOTAL POVERTY AND HAD BARELY BEEN ABLE TO KEEP THEMSELVES ALIVE.
THE OTHER FACTION IS...
..."THE SECOND WAVE."
THEY SETTLED ON THE PLANET AFTER THE FIRST WAVE.
THEY ESTABLISHED MINING AND ENGAGED IN GALACTIC COMMERCE.
THEY LEAD MODERN LIVES.

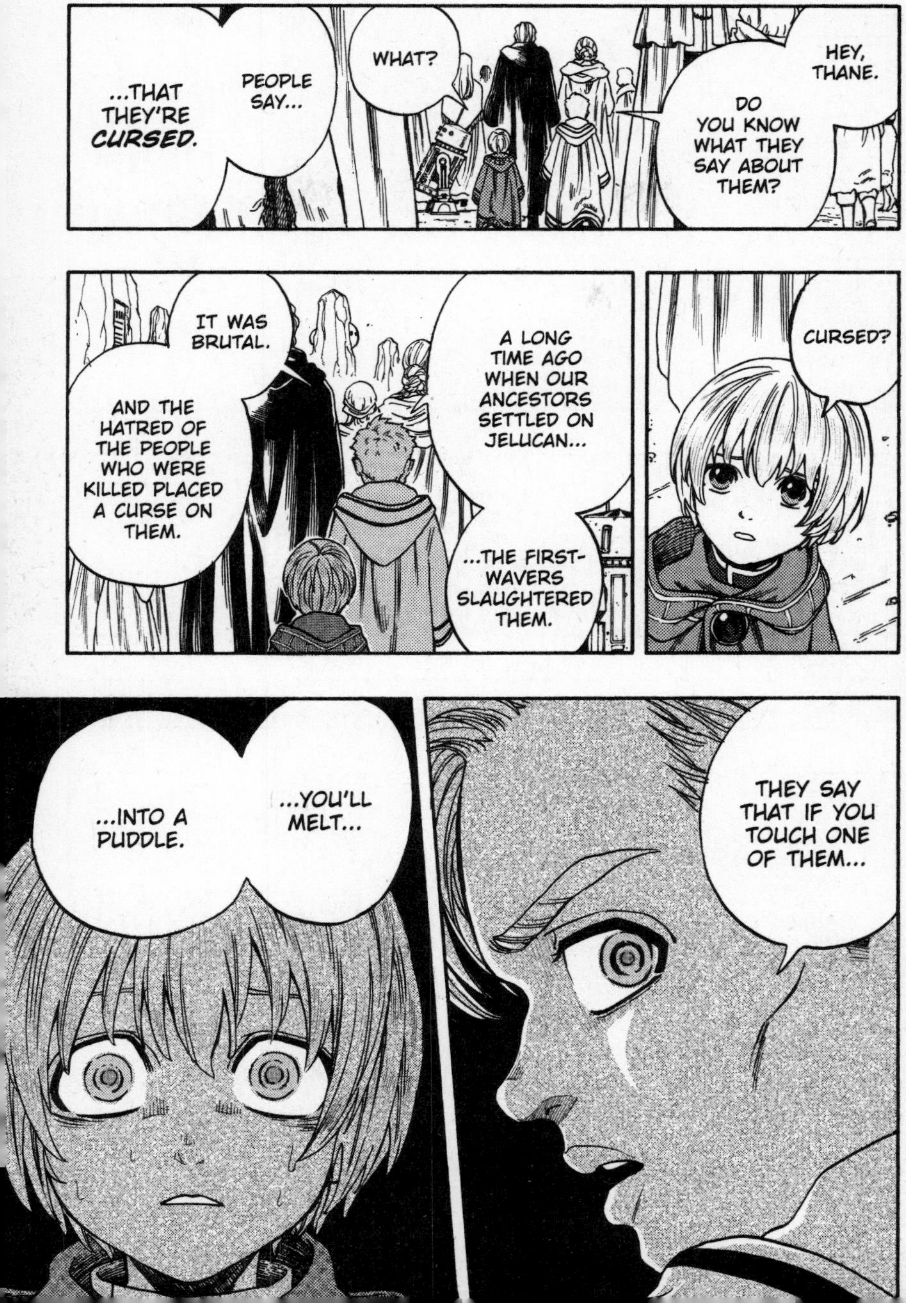
HEY, THANE.
DO YOU KNOW WHAT THEY SAY ABOUT THEM?
WHAT?
PEOPLE SAY...
...THAT THEY'RE *CURSED*.
CURSED?
A LONG TIME AGO WHEN OUR ANCESTORS SETTLED ON JELUCAN...
...THE FIRST-WAVERS SLAUGHTERED THEM.
IT WAS BRUTAL.
AND THE HATRED OF THE PEOPLE WHO WERE KILLED PLACED A CURSE ON THEM.
THEY SAY THAT IF YOU TOUCH ONE OF THEM...
...YOU'LL MELT...
...INTO A PUDDLE.

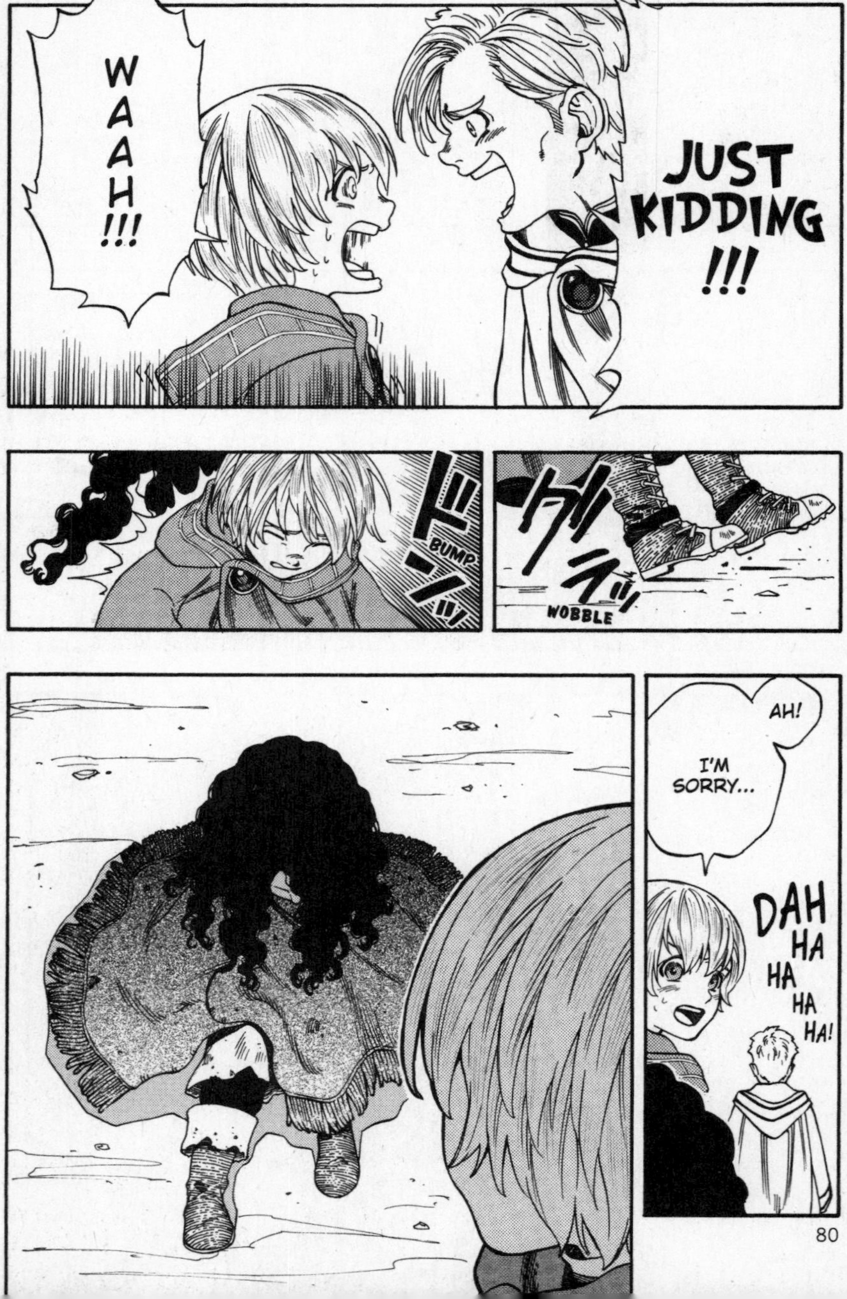
JUST KIDDING!!!
WAAAH!!!
グラッ
WOBBLE
ドンッ
BUMP
AH!
I'M SORRY...
DAH HA HA HA HA HA!

"...YOU'LL MELT INTO A PUDDLE."

"THEY SAY THAT IF YOU TOUCH ONE OF THEM...

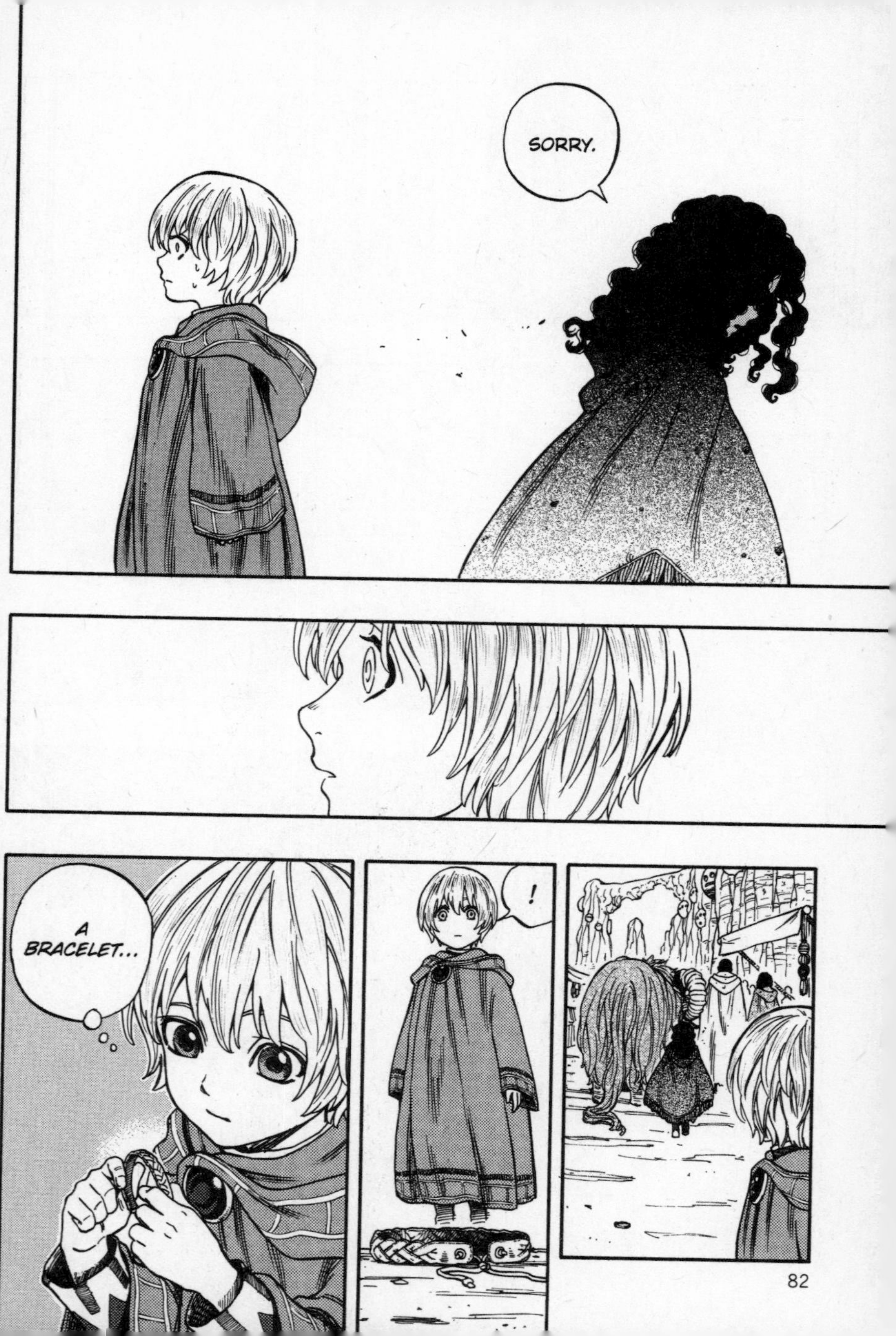
SORRY.
!
A BRACELET...

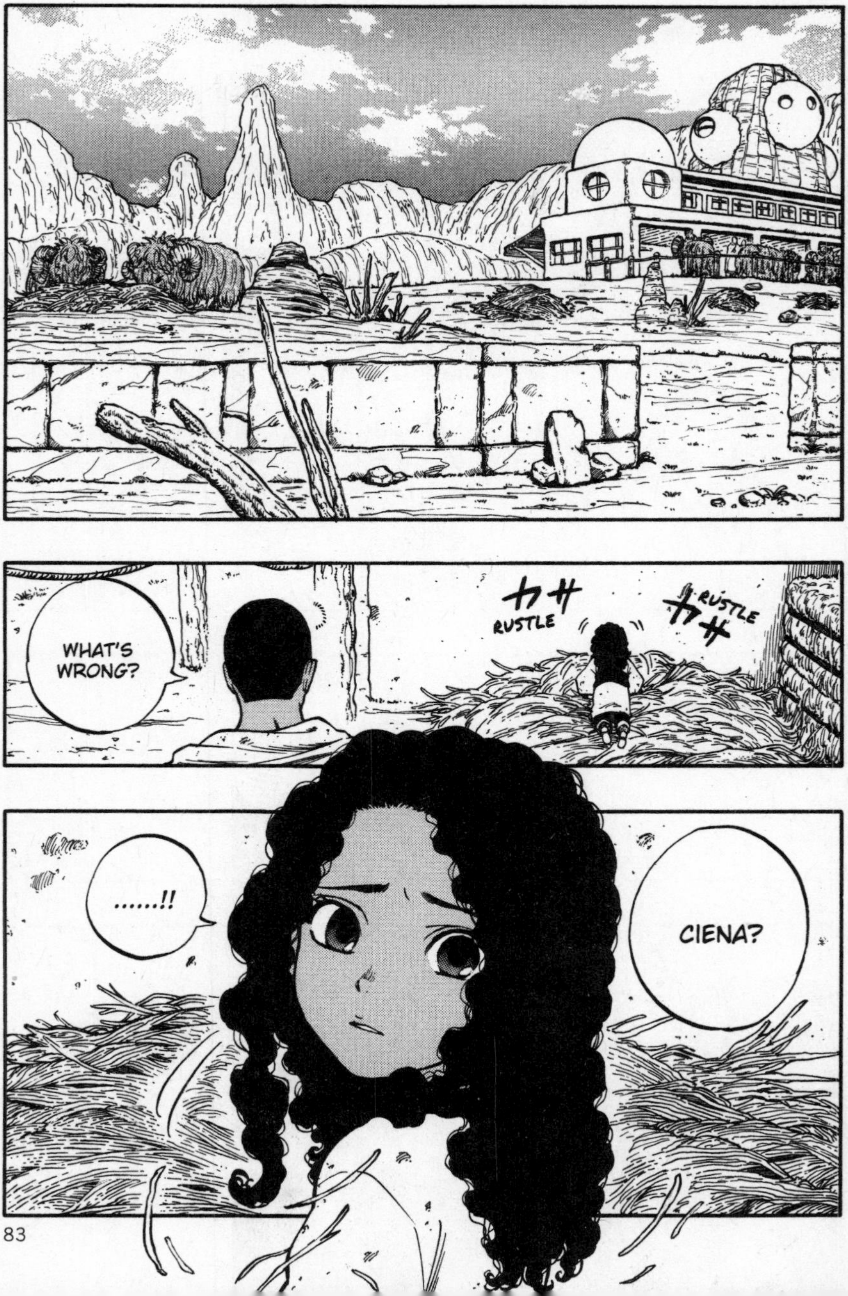
カサ RUSTLE
カサ RUSTLE
WHAT'S WRONG?
CIENA?
......!!

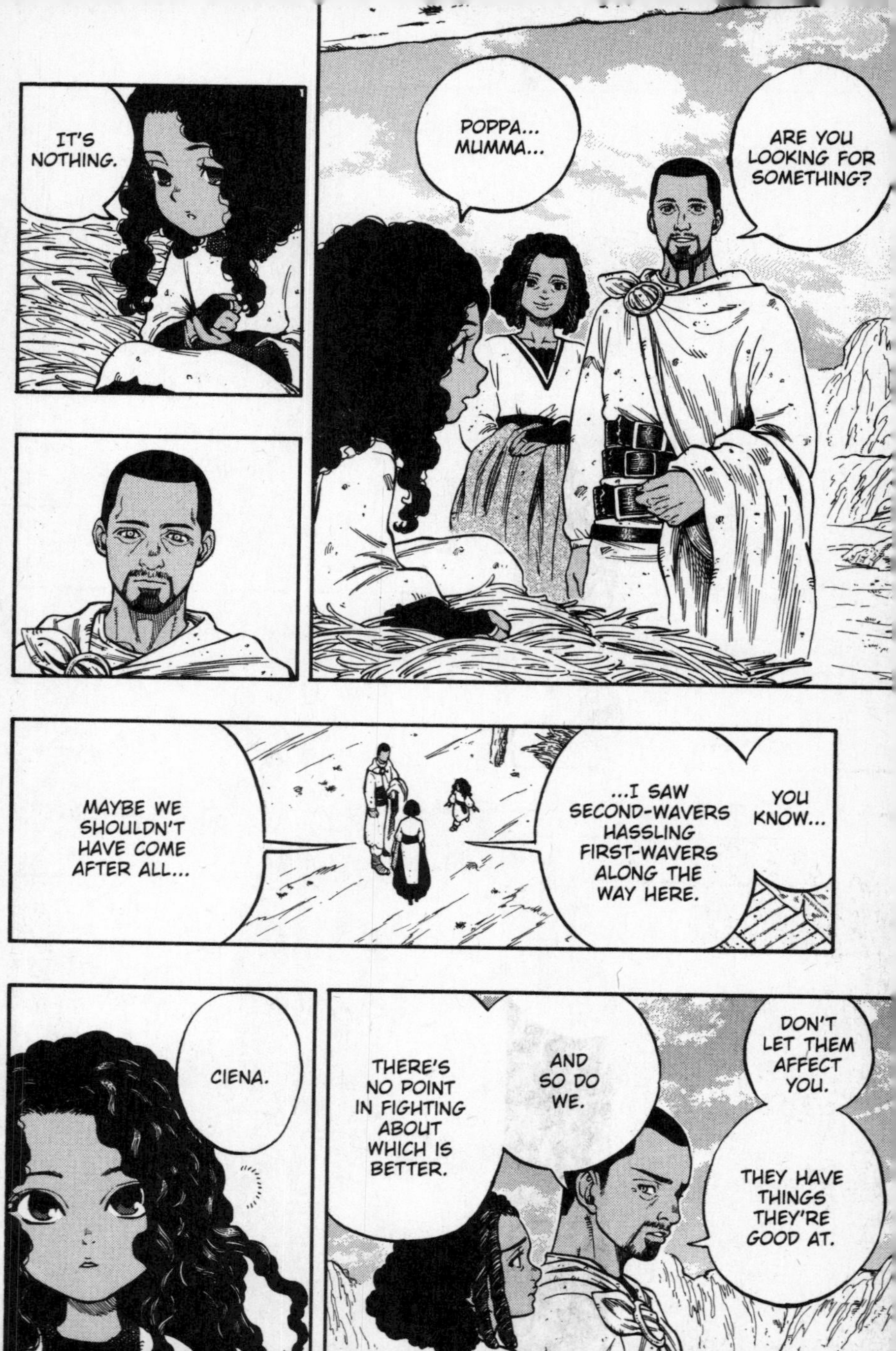
ARE YOU LOOKING FOR SOMETHING?
POPPA... MUMMA...
IT'S NOTHING.
YOU KNOW...
...I SAW SECOND-WAVERS HASSLING FIRST-WAVERS ALONG THE WAY HERE.
MAYBE WE SHOULDN'T HAVE COME AFTER ALL...
DON'T LET THEM AFFECT YOU.
THEY HAVE THINGS THEY'RE GOOD AT.
AND SO DO WE.
THERE'S NO POINT IN FIGHTING ABOUT WHICH IS BETTER.
CIENA.

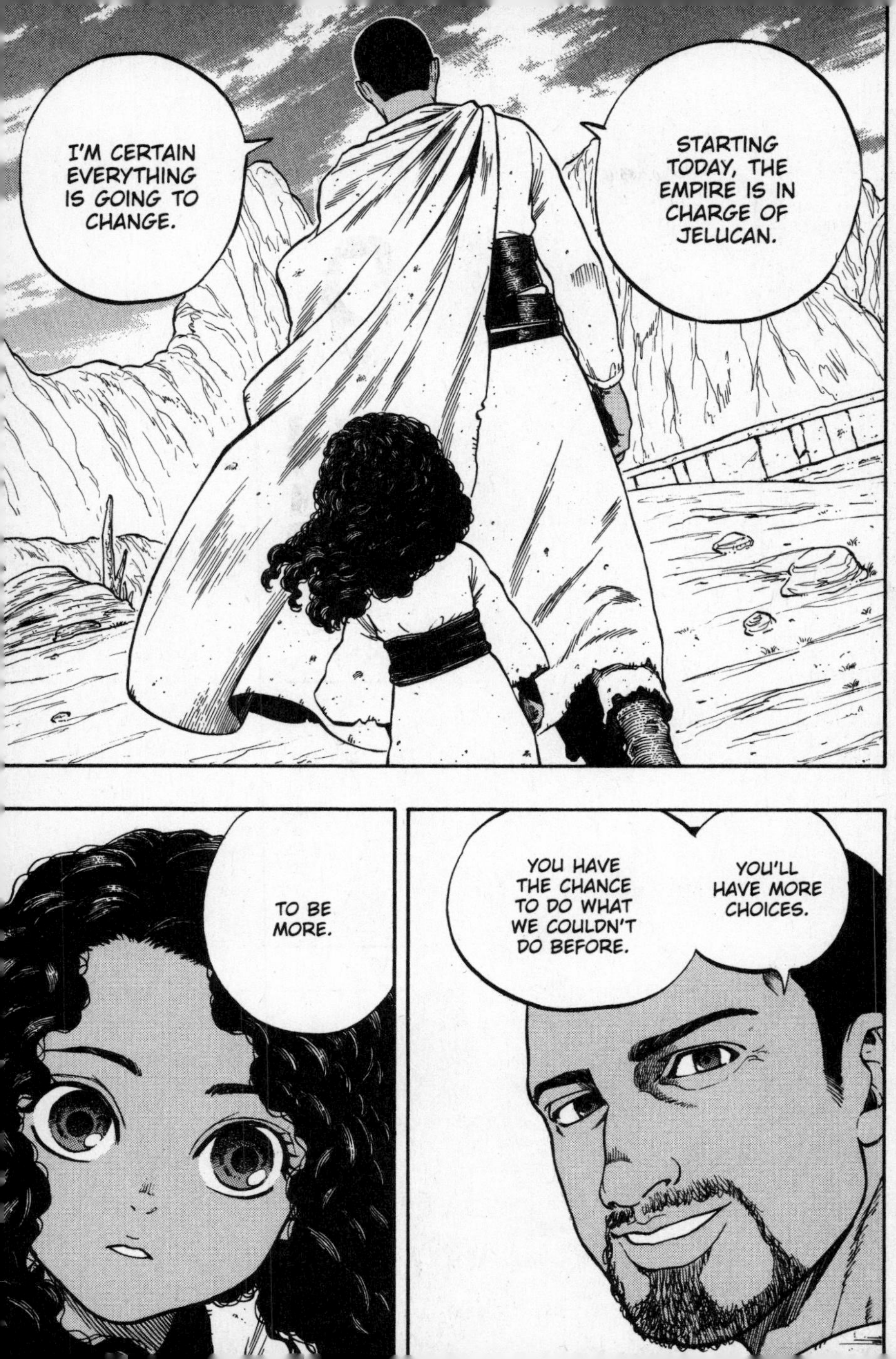
STARTING TODAY, THE EMPIRE IS IN CHARGE OF JELUCAN.
I'M CERTAIN EVERYTHING IS GOING TO CHANGE.
YOU'LL HAVE MORE CHOICES.
YOU HAVE THE CHANCE TO DO WHAT WE COULDN'T DO BEFORE.
TO BE MORE.

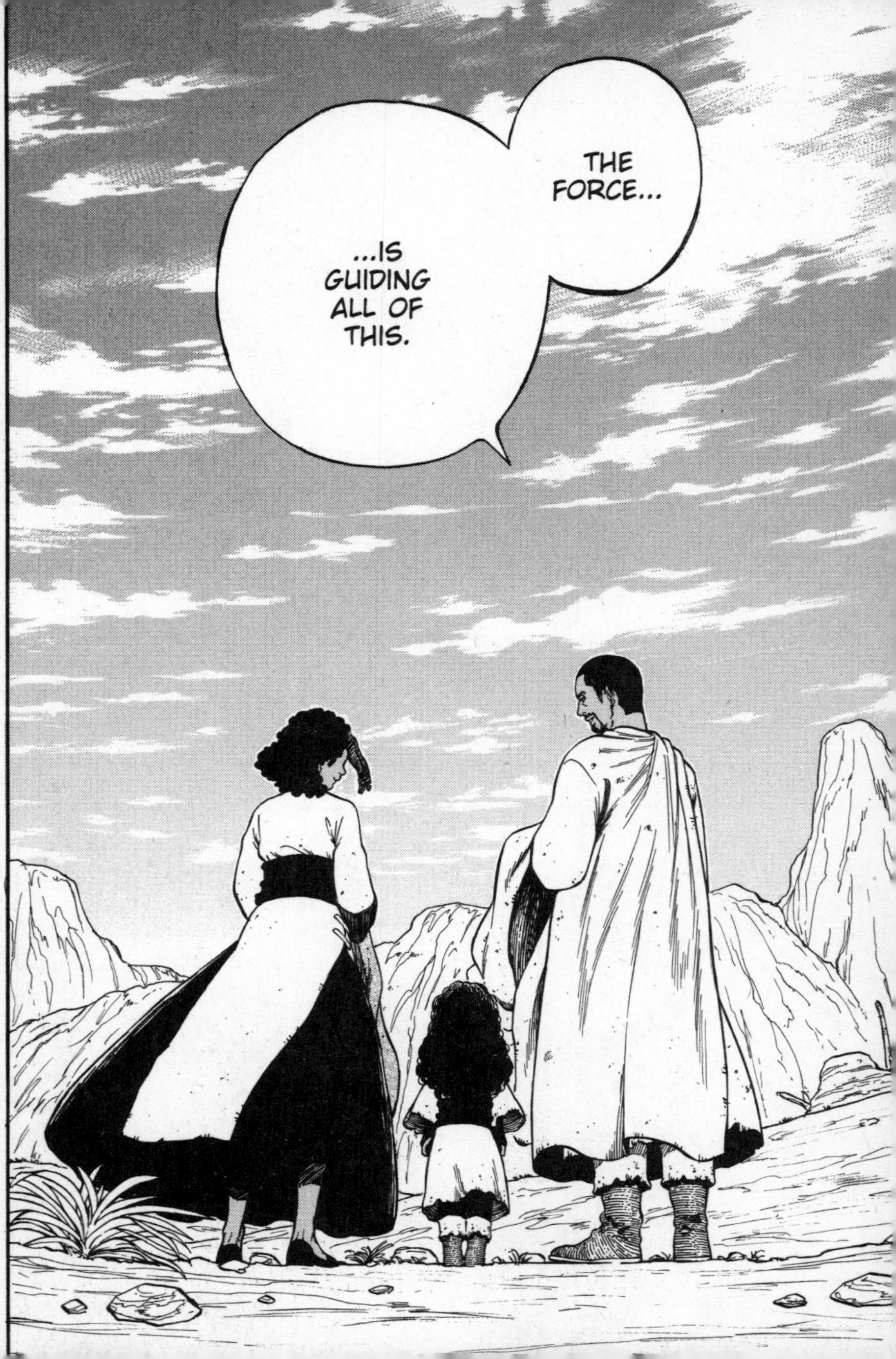
THE FORCE...
...IS GUIDING ALL OF THIS.

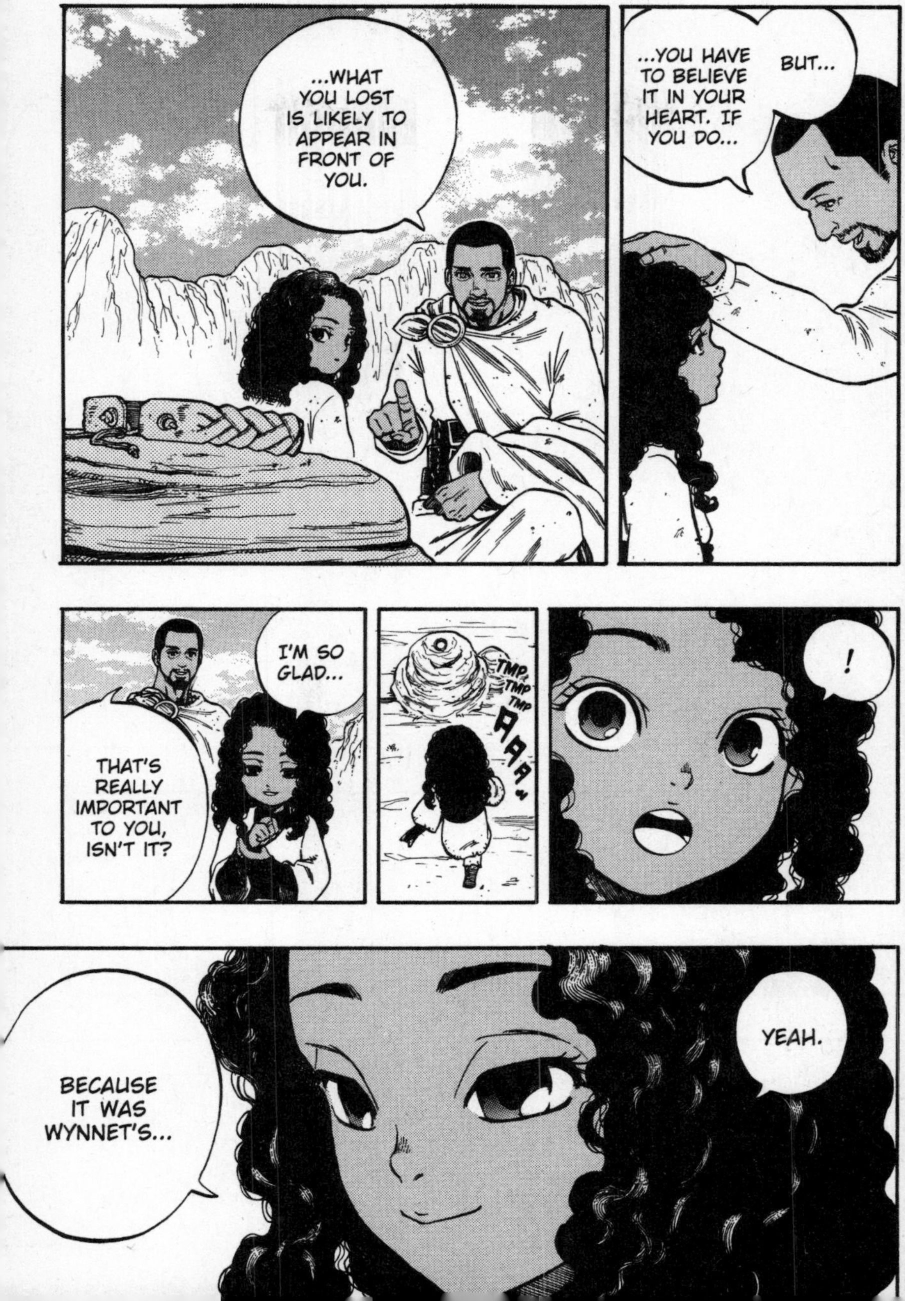
BUT...
...YOU HAVE TO BELIEVE IT IN YOUR HEART. IF YOU DO...
...WHAT YOU LOST IS LIKELY TO APPEAR IN FRONT OF YOU.
!
TMP TMP TMP
I'M SO GLAD...
THAT'S REALLY IMPORTANT TO YOU, ISN'T IT?
YEAH.
BECAUSE IT WAS WYNNET'S...

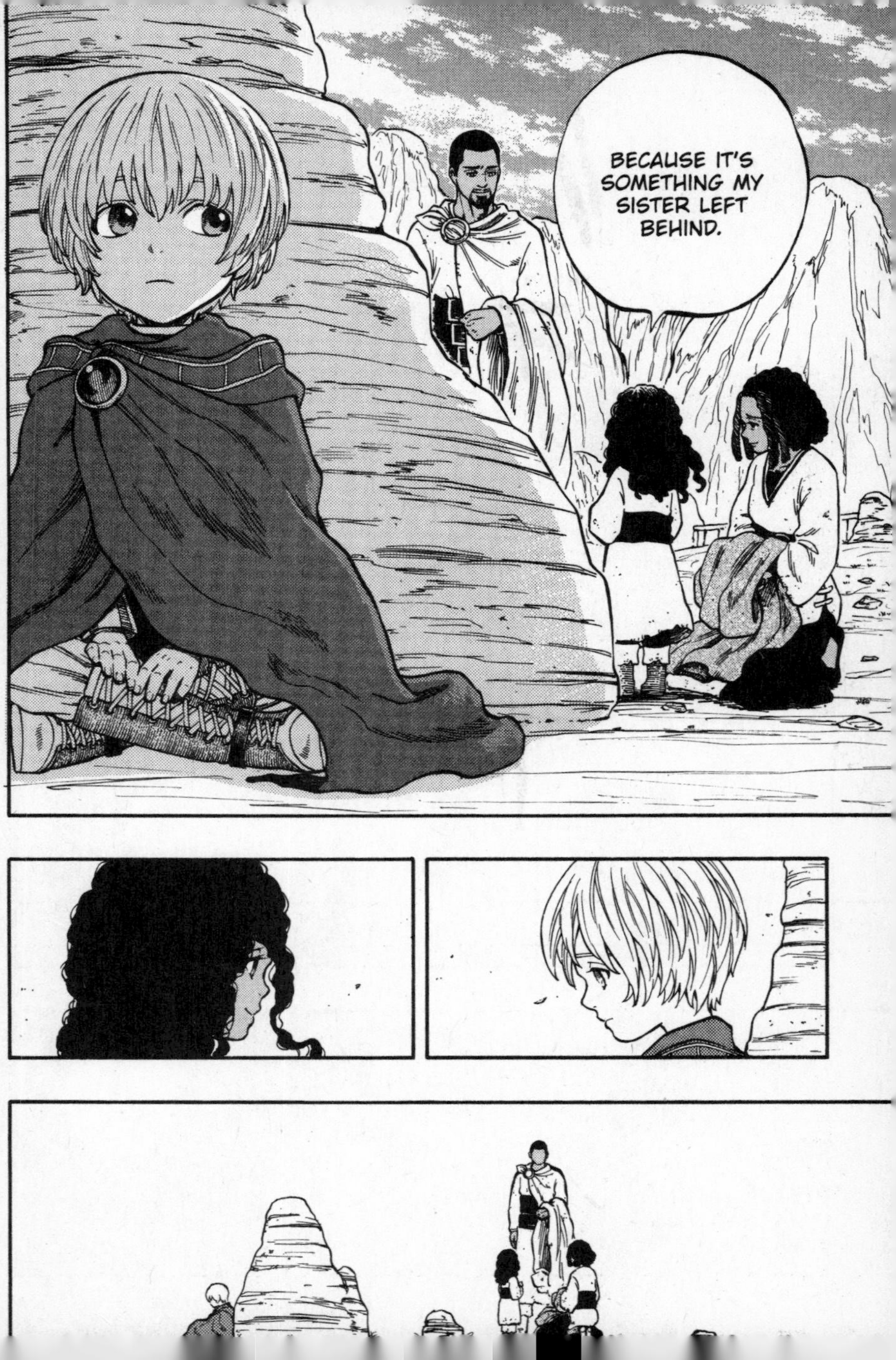
BECAUSE IT'S SOMETHING MY SISTER LEFT BEHIND.

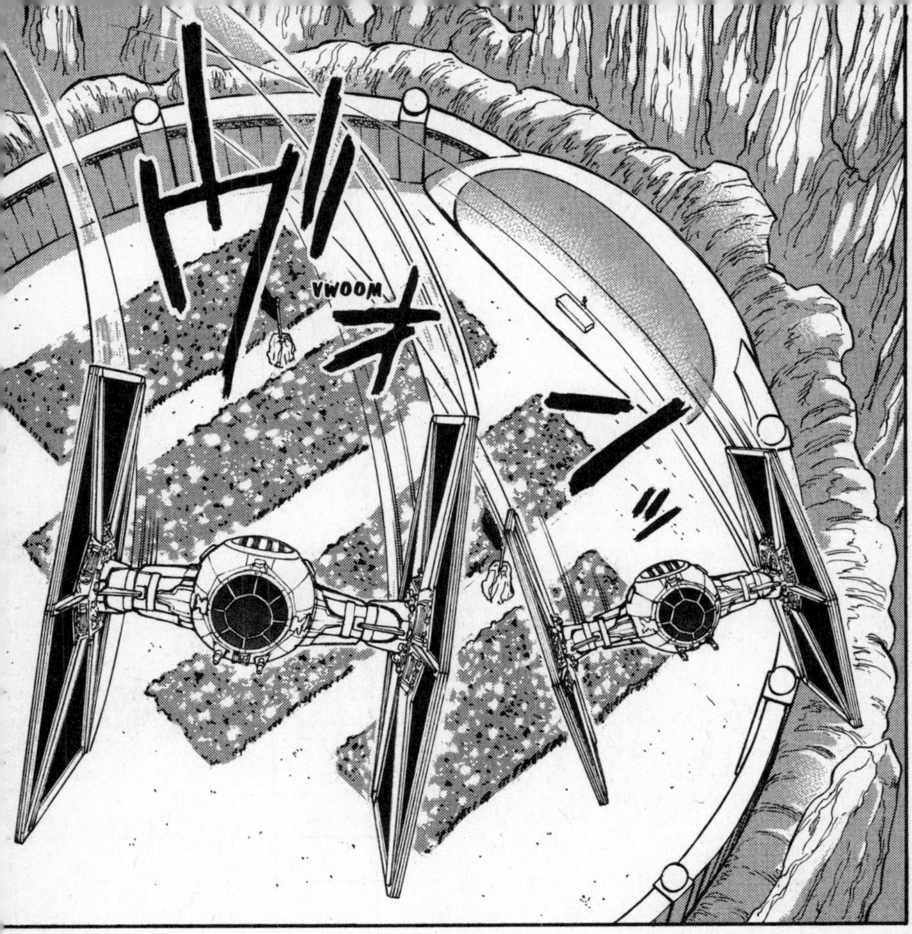
VWOOM
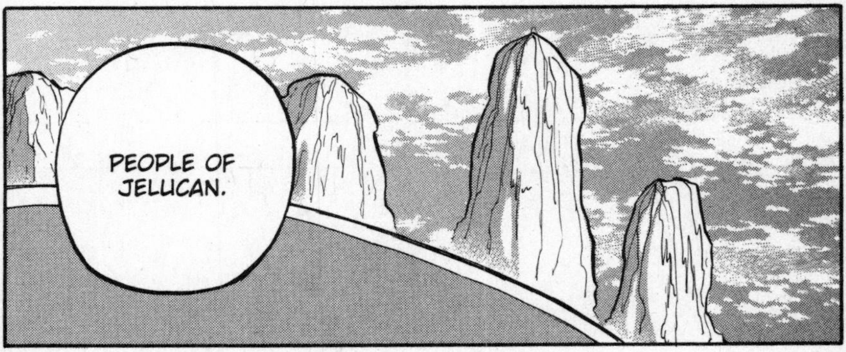
PEOPLE OF JELUCAN.

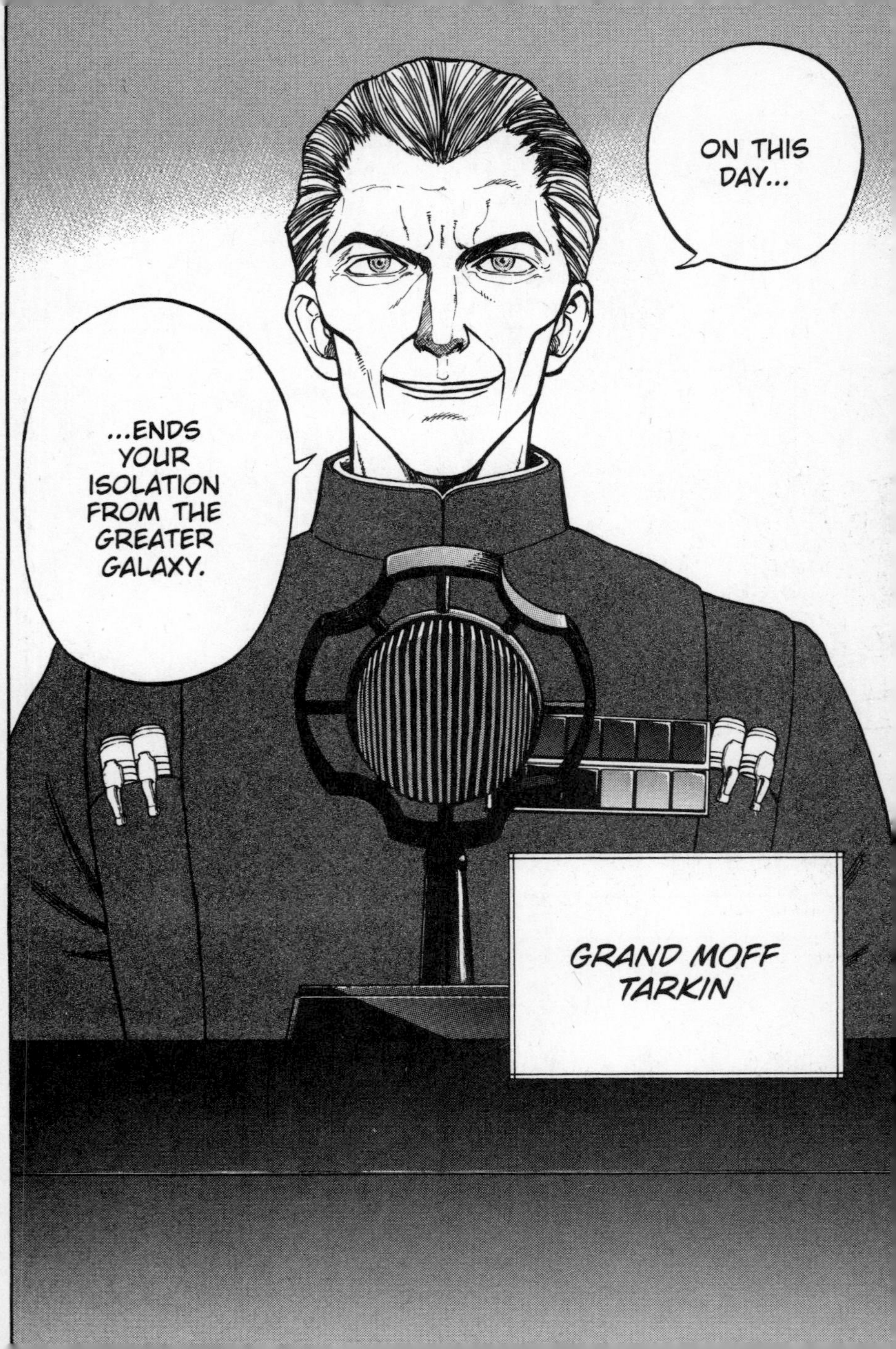
ON THIS DAY...
...ENDS YOUR ISOLATION FROM THE GREATER GALAXY.
GRAND MOFF TARKIN

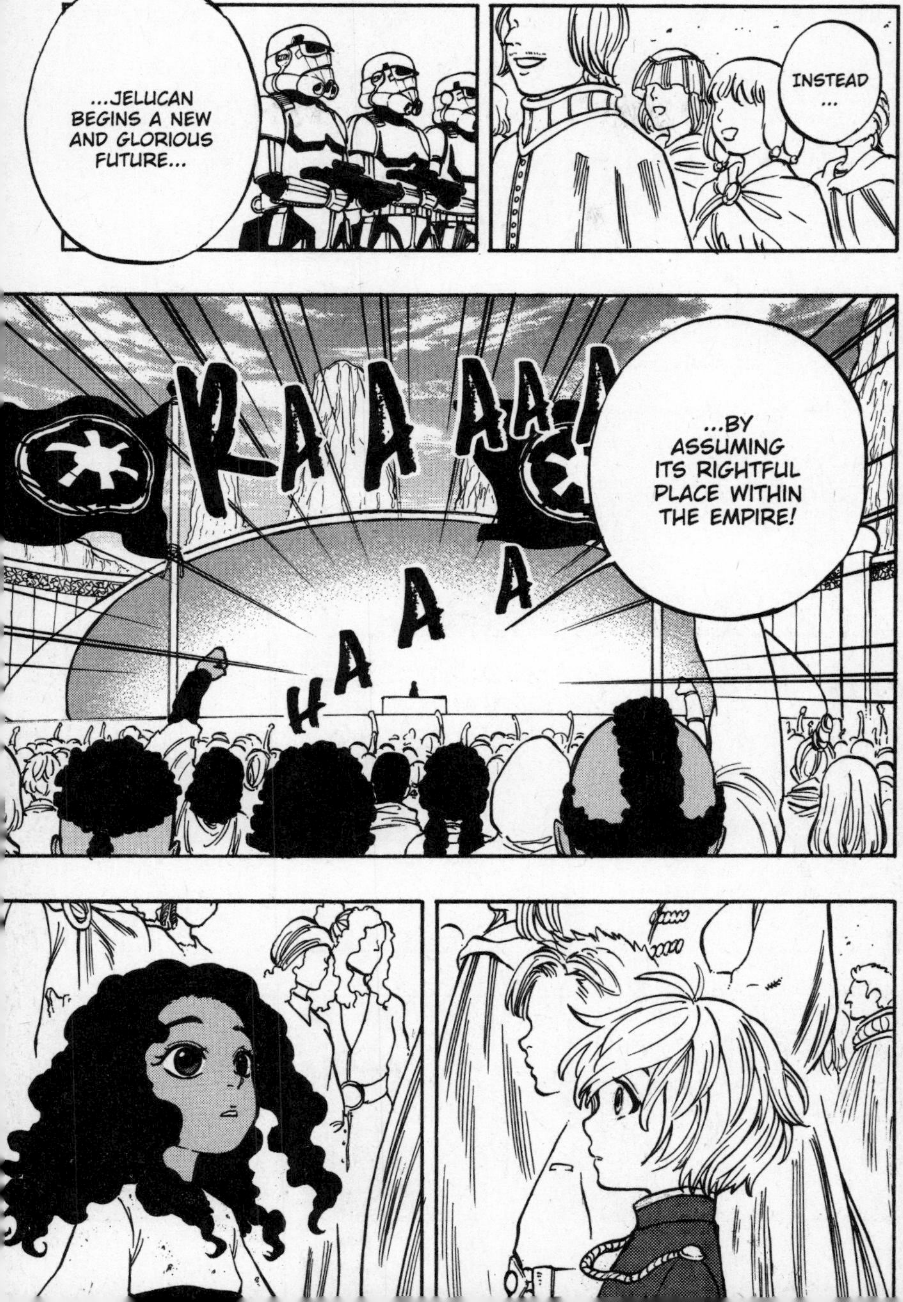
INSTEAD
...
...JELUCAN BEGINS A NEW AND GLORIOUS FUTURE...
...BY ASSUMING ITS RIGHTFUL PLACE WITHIN THE EMPIRE!
KAAAAA
HAAAA

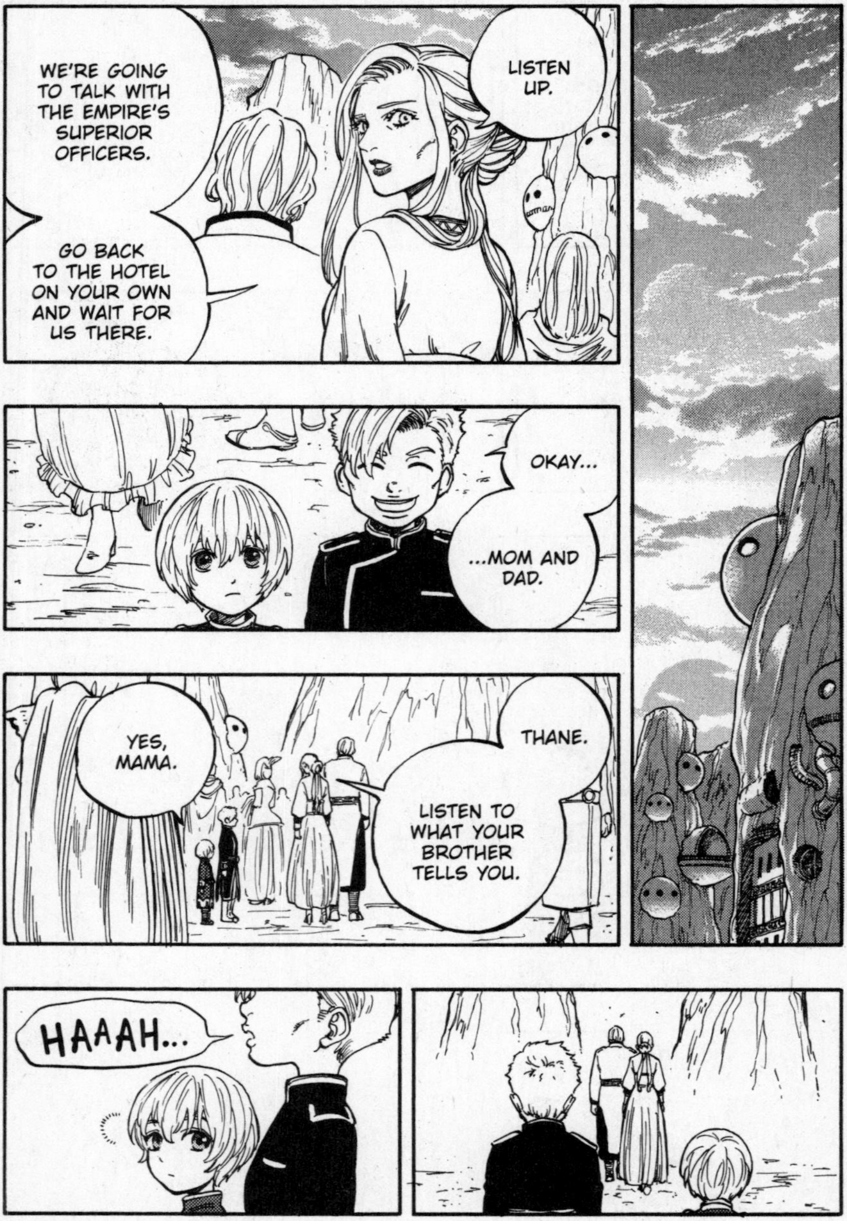
LISTEN UP.
WE'RE GOING TO TALK WITH THE EMPIRE'S SUPERIOR OFFICERS.
GO BACK TO THE HOTEL ON YOUR OWN AND WAIT FOR US THERE.
OKAY...
...MOM AND DAD.
THANE.
LISTEN TO WHAT YOUR BROTHER TELLS YOU.
YES, MAMA.
HAAAH...

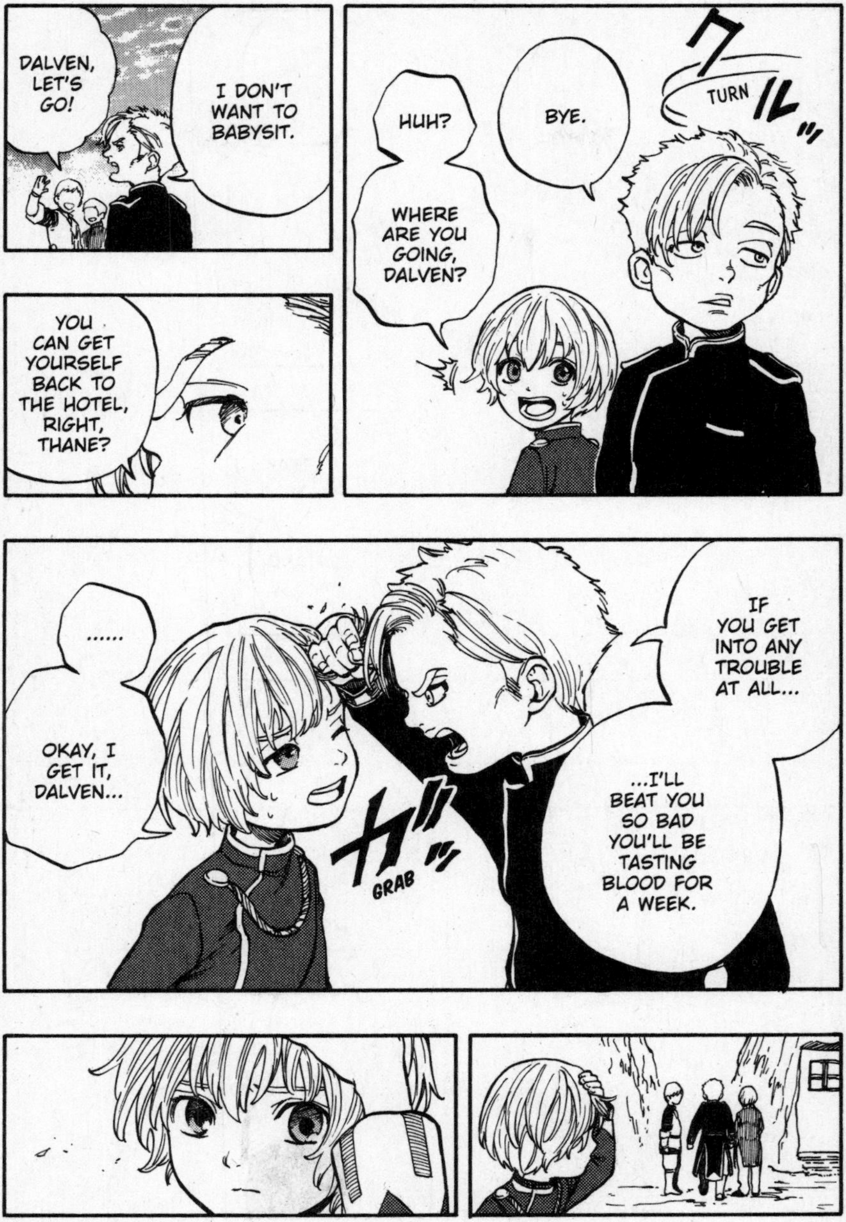
TURN
BYE.
HUH?
WHERE ARE YOU GOING, DALVEN?
I DON'T WANT TO BABYSIT.
DALVEN, LET'S GO!
YOU CAN GET YOURSELF BACK TO THE HOTEL, RIGHT, THANE?
IF YOU GET INTO ANY TROUBLE AT ALL...
...I'LL BEAT YOU SO BAD YOU'LL BE TASTING BLOOD FOR A WEEK.
GRAB
......
OKAY, I GET IT, DALVEN...

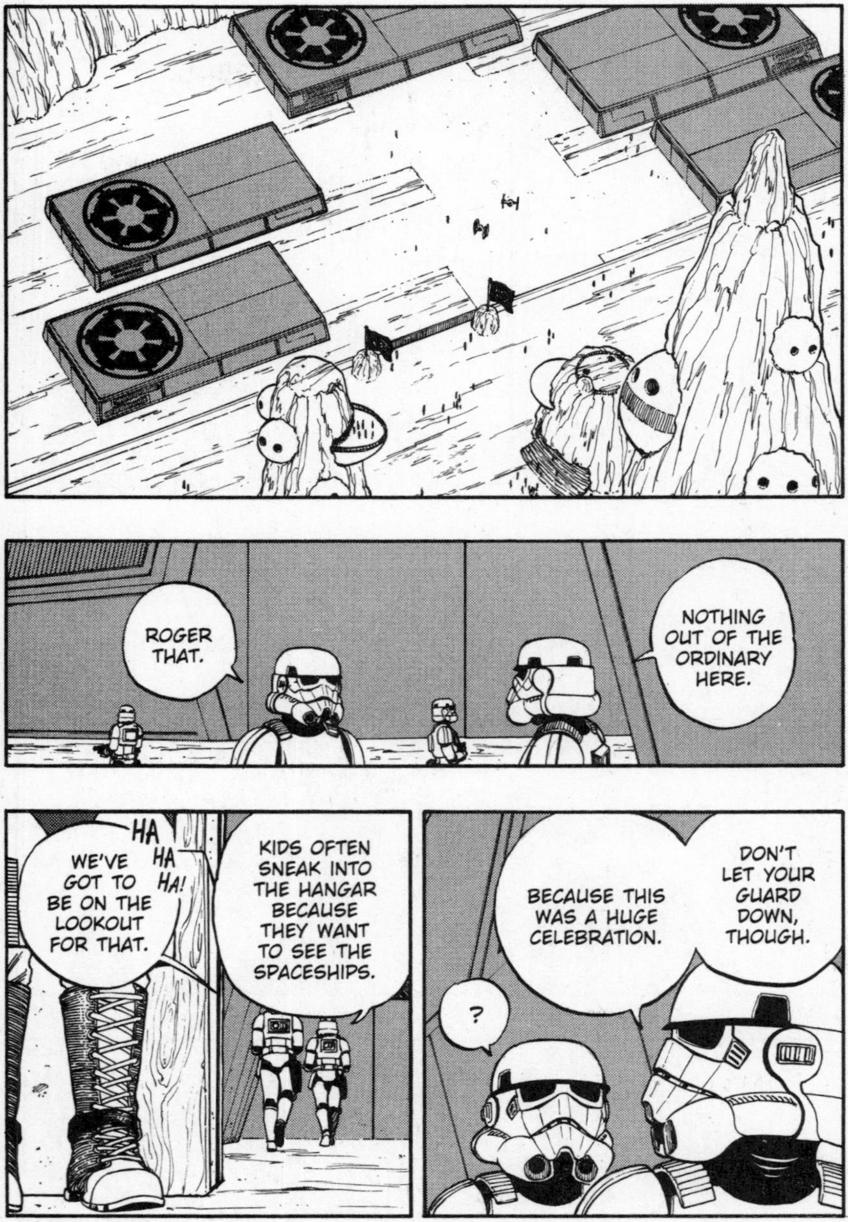

NOTHING OUT OF THE ORDINARY HERE.
ROGER THAT.
DON'T LET YOUR GUARD DOWN, THOUGH.
BECAUSE THIS WAS A HUGE CELEBRATION.
?
KIDS OFTEN SNEAK INTO THE HANGAR BECAUSE THEY WANT TO SEE THE SPACESHIPS.
HA HA HA!
WE'VE GOT TO BE ON THE LOOKOUT FOR THAT.

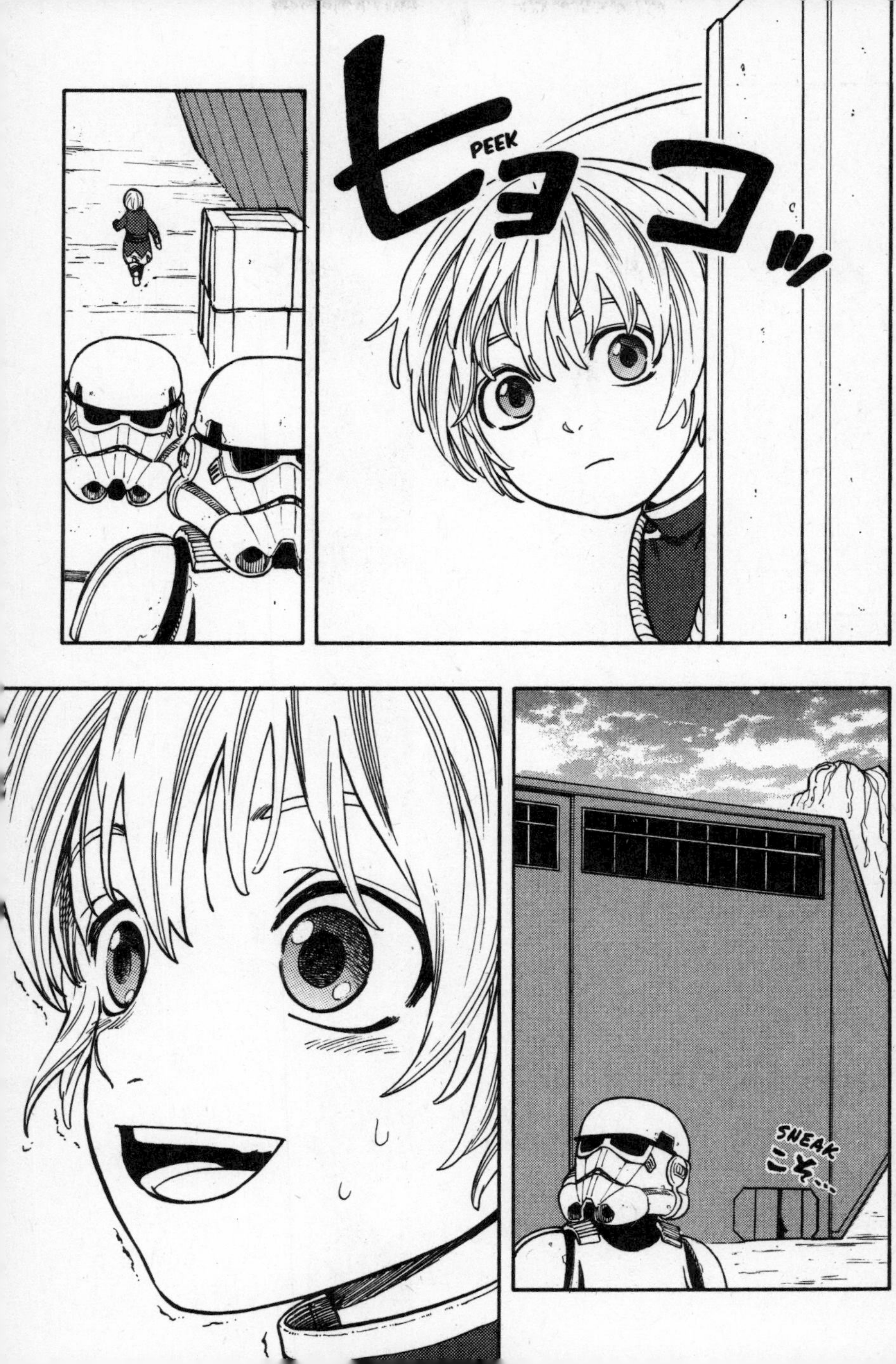
ヒョコッ
PEEK
SNEAK
こそ…

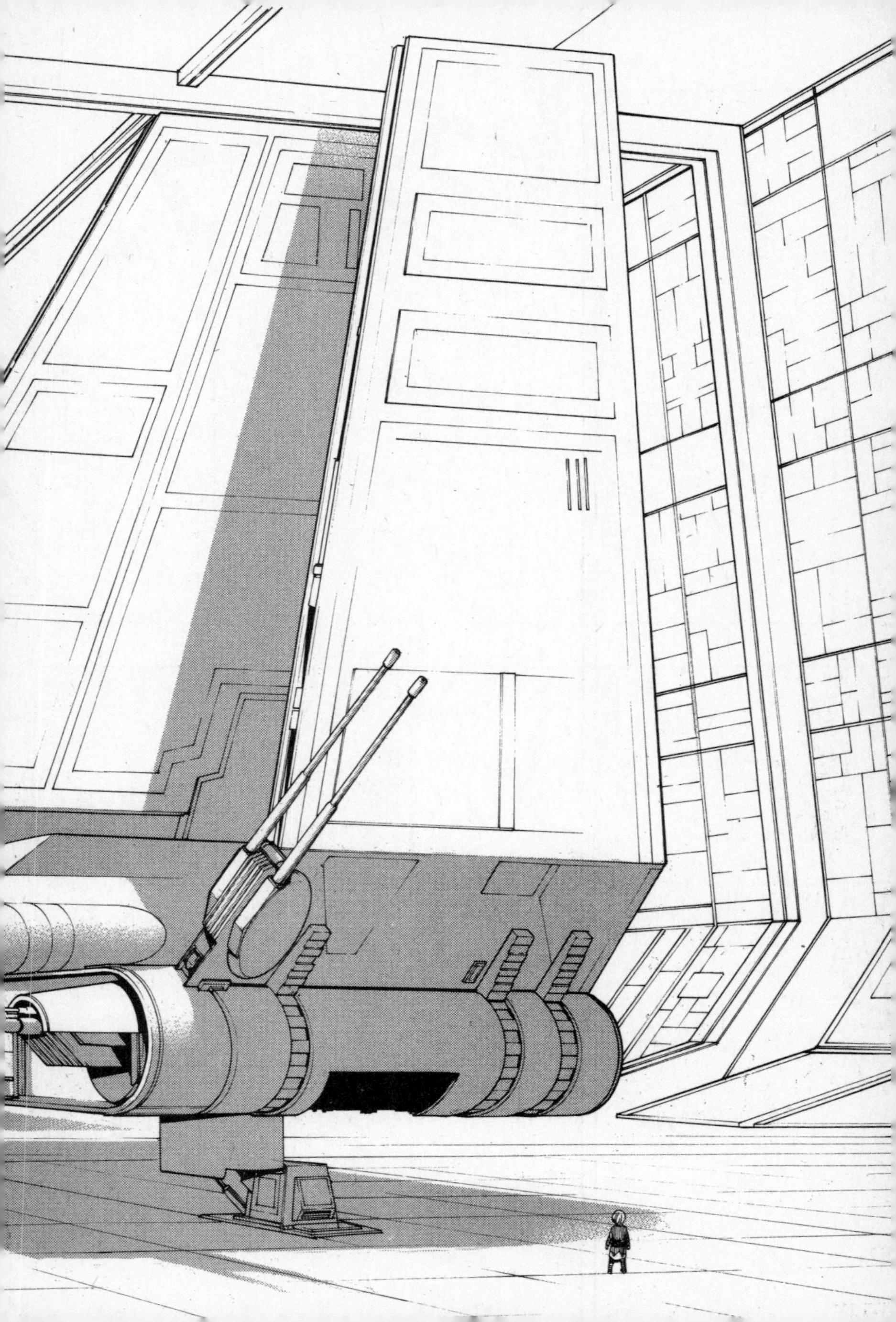

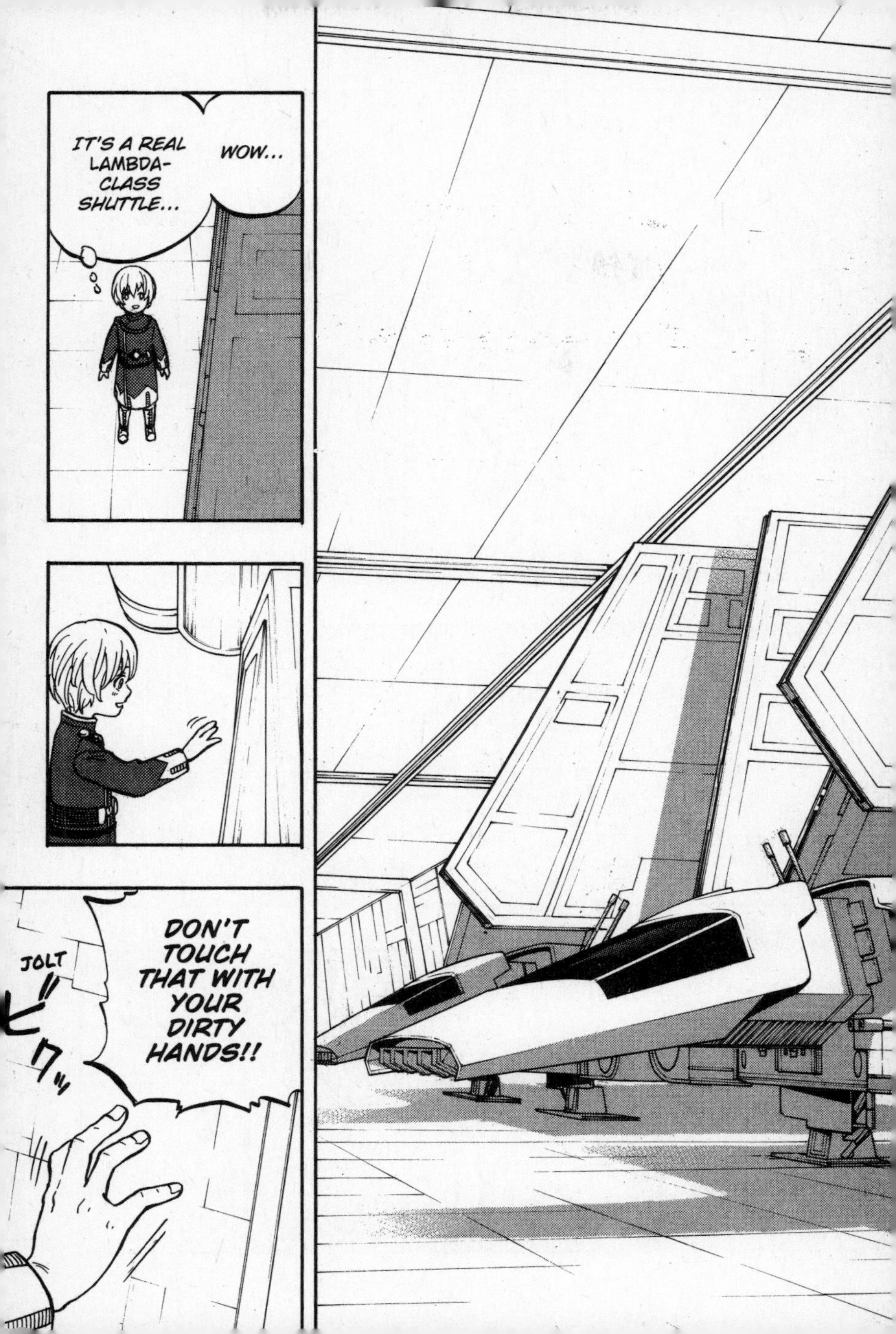
WOW...
IT'S A REAL LAMBDA-CLASS SHUTTLE...
DON'T TOUCH THAT WITH YOUR DIRTY HANDS!!
JOLT
ビクッ

......?

MY HANDS AREN'T DIRTY.

OH...I'M SORRY...!

THEY'VE GOTTA BE DIRTY!!

HUNH !?

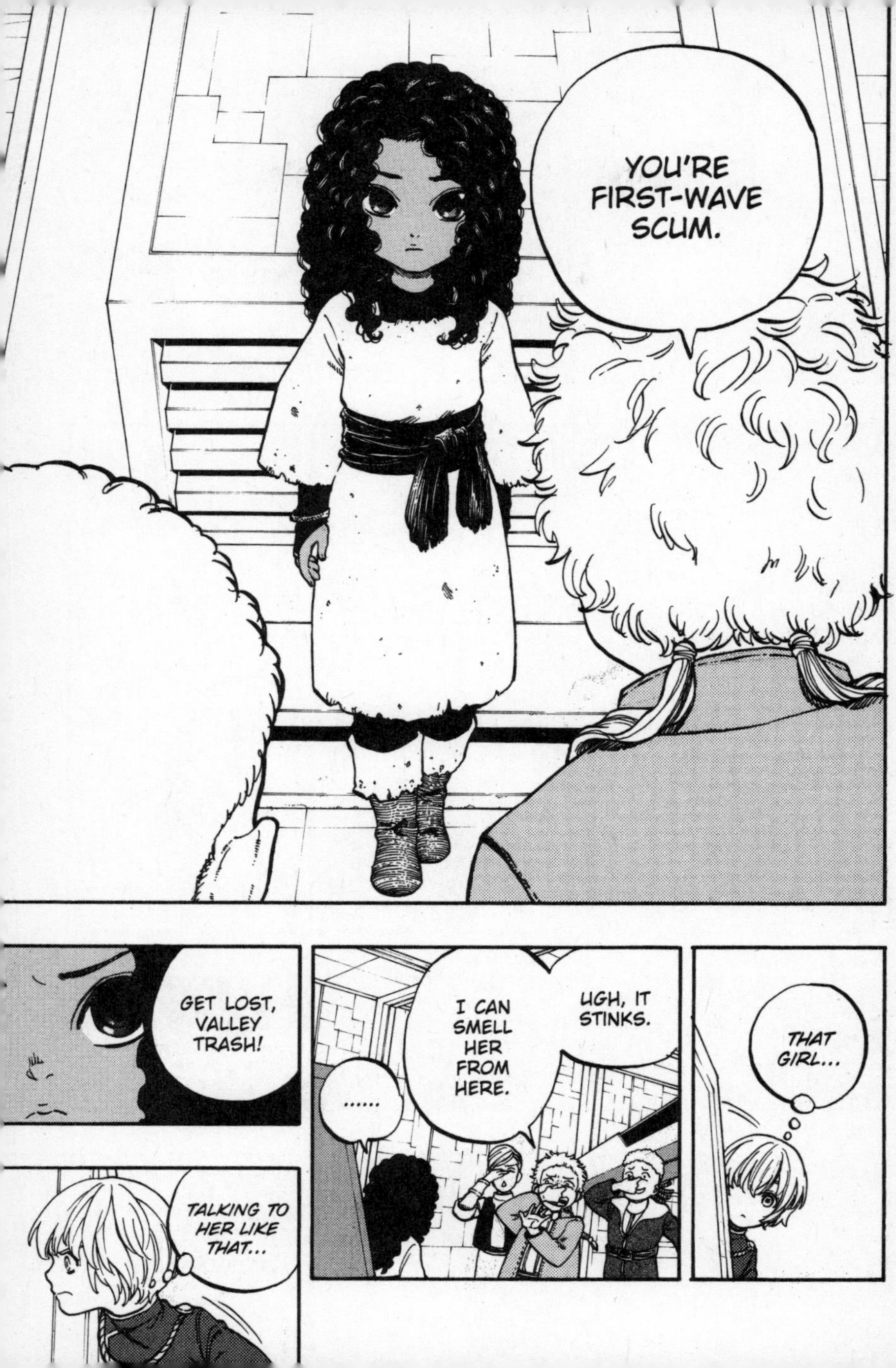
YOU'RE FIRST-WAVE SCUM.
THAT GIRL...
UGH, IT STINKS.
I CAN SMELL HER FROM HERE.
......
GET LOST, VALLEY TRASH!
TALKING TO HER LIKE THAT...

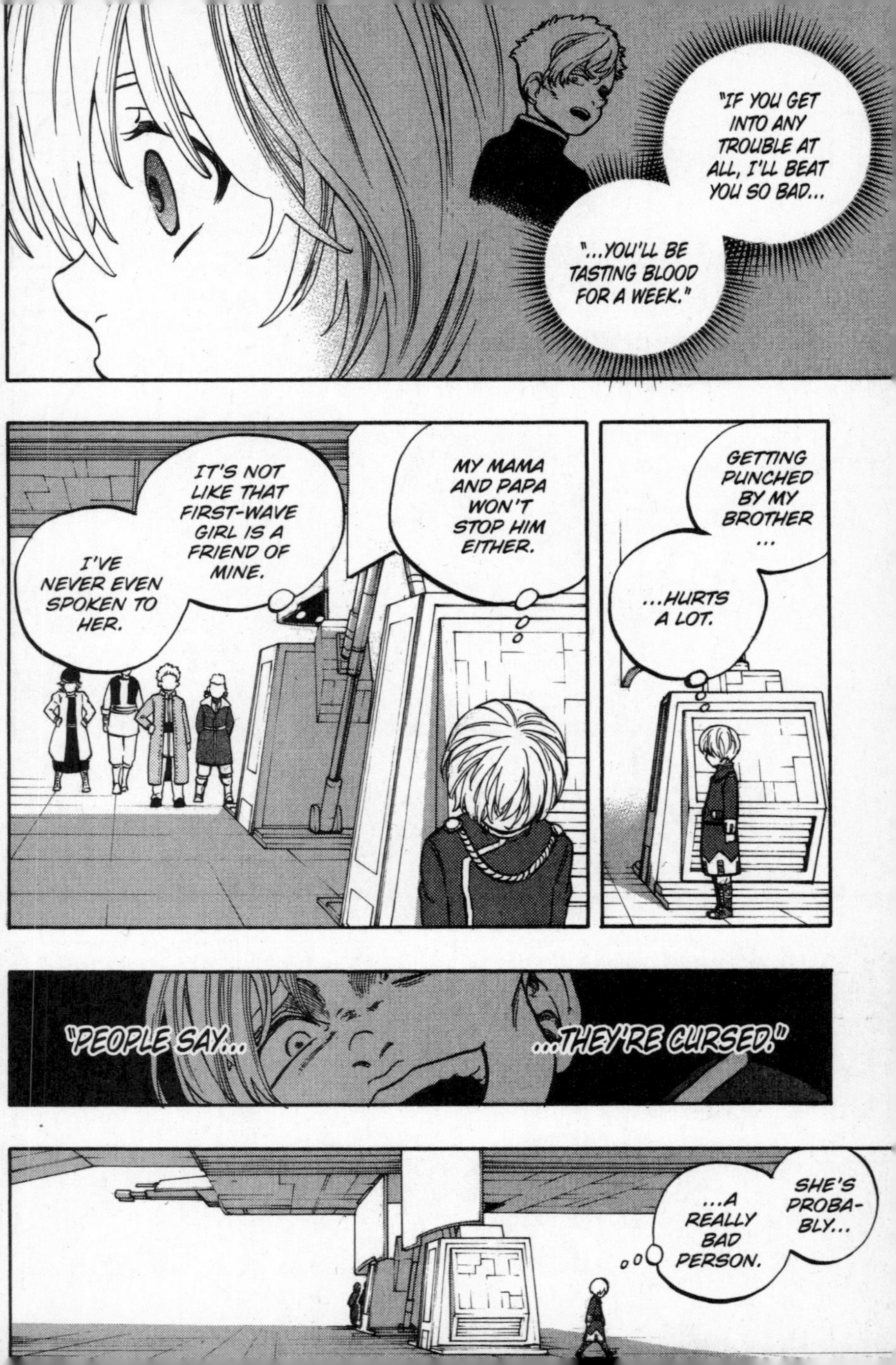
"IF YOU GET INTO ANY TROUBLE AT ALL, I'LL BEAT YOU SO BAD...
"...YOU'LL BE TASTING BLOOD FOR A WEEK."
GETTING PUNCHED BY MY BROTHER ...
...HURTS A LOT.
MY MAMA AND PAPA WON'T STOP HIM EITHER.
IT'S NOT LIKE THAT FIRST-WAVE GIRL IS A FRIEND OF MINE.
I'VE NEVER EVEN SPOKEN TO HER.
"PEOPLE SAY...
...THEY'RE CURSED."
SHE'S PROBA-BLY...
...A REALLY BAD PERSON.

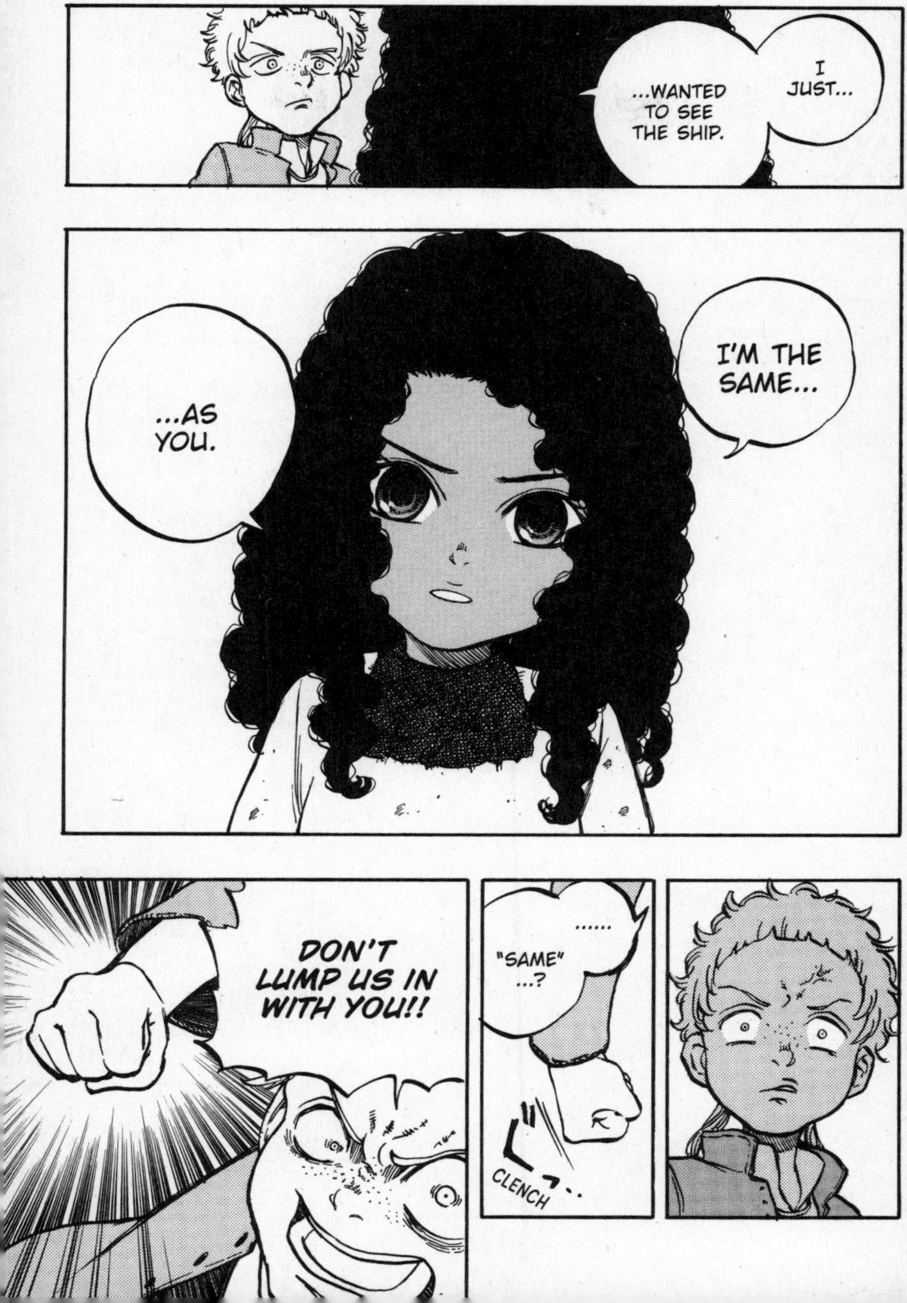
I JUST...
...WANTED TO SEE THE SHIP.
I'M THE SAME...
...AS YOU.
......
"SAME" ...?
CLENCH
DON'T LUMP US IN WITH YOU!!

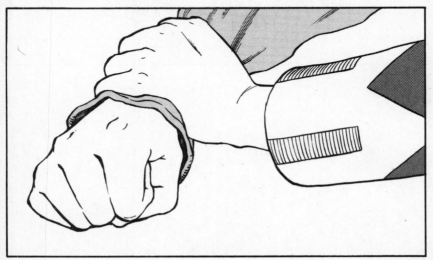

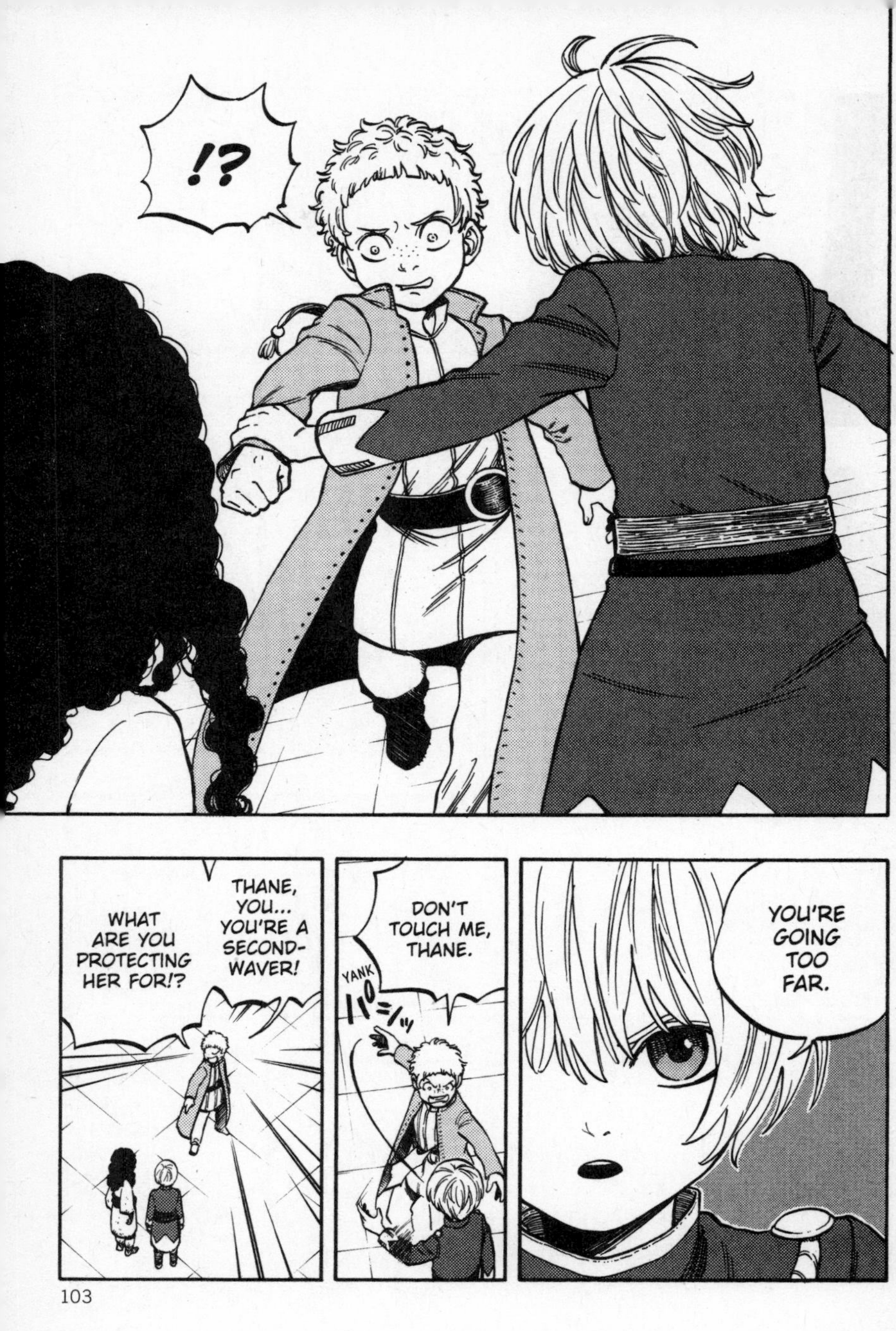
!?
YOU'RE GOING TOO FAR.
DON'T TOUCH ME, THANE.
YANK
THANE, YOU... YOU'RE A SECOND-WAVER!
WHAT ARE YOU PROTECTING HER FOR!?

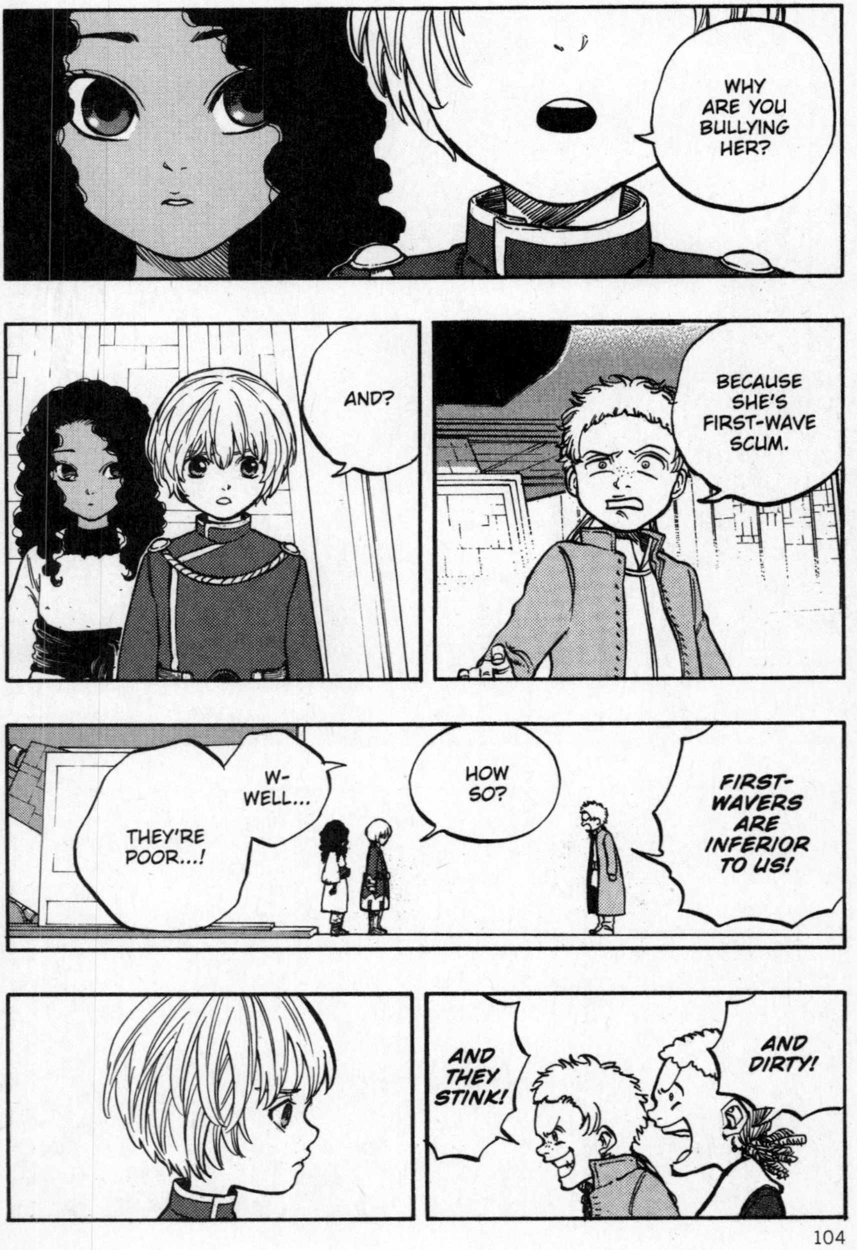
WHY ARE YOU BULLYING HER?
BECAUSE SHE'S FIRST-WAVE SCUM.
AND?
FIRST-WAVERS ARE INFERIOR TO US!
HOW SO?
W-WELL...
THEY'RE POOR...!
AND DIRTY!
AND THEY STINK!

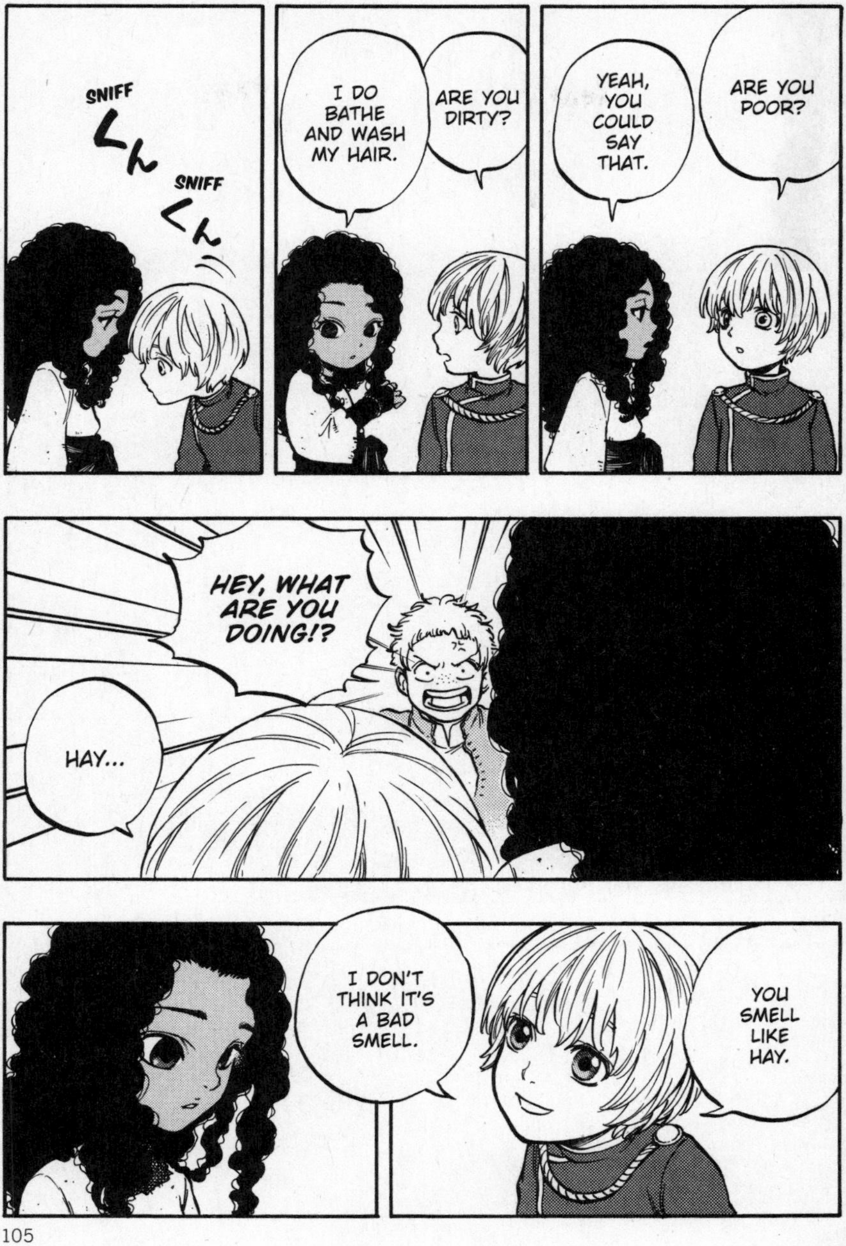

ARE YOU POOR?
YEAH, YOU COULD SAY THAT.
ARE YOU DIRTY?
I DO BATHE AND WASH MY HAIR.
SNIFF
くん
SNIFF
くん
HEY, WHAT ARE YOU DOING!?
HAY...
YOU SMELL LIKE HAY.
I DON'T THINK IT'S A BAD SMELL.

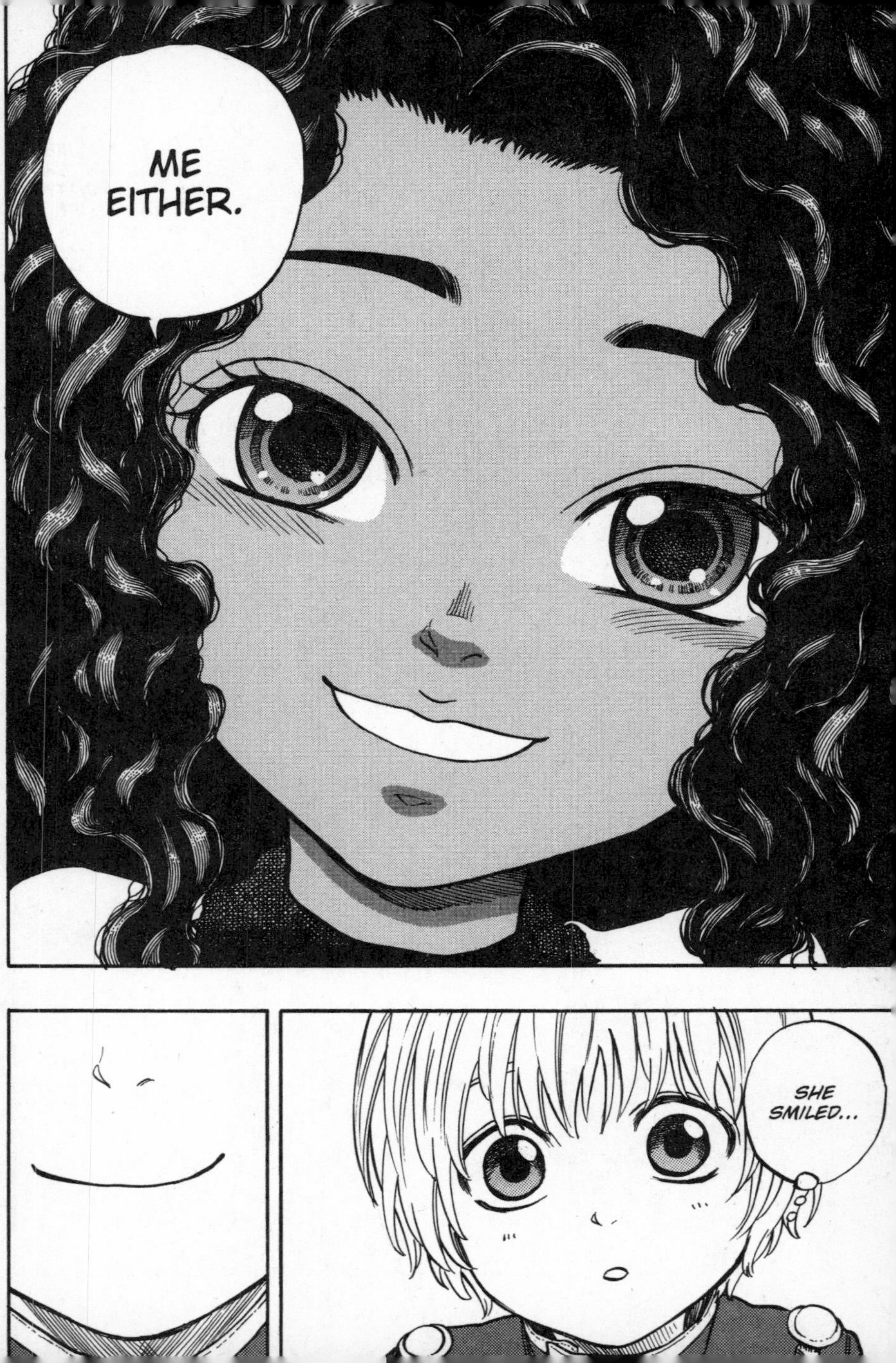
ME EITHER.
SHE SMILED...

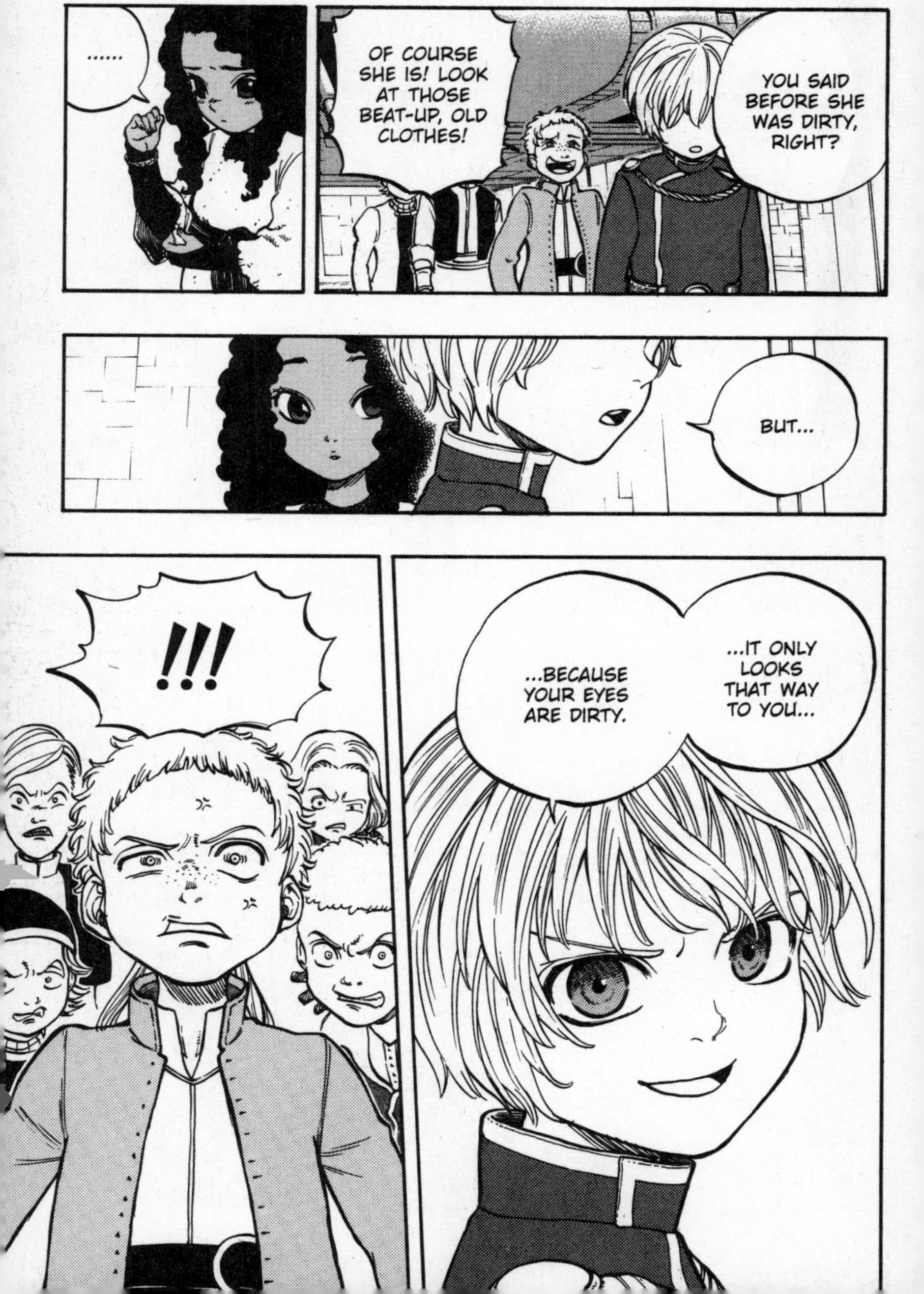
YOU SAID BEFORE SHE WAS DIRTY, RIGHT?
OF COURSE SHE IS! LOOK AT THOSE BEAT-UP, OLD CLOTHES!
......
BUT...
...IT ONLY LOOKS THAT WAY TO YOU...
...BECAUSE YOUR EYES ARE DIRTY.
!!!

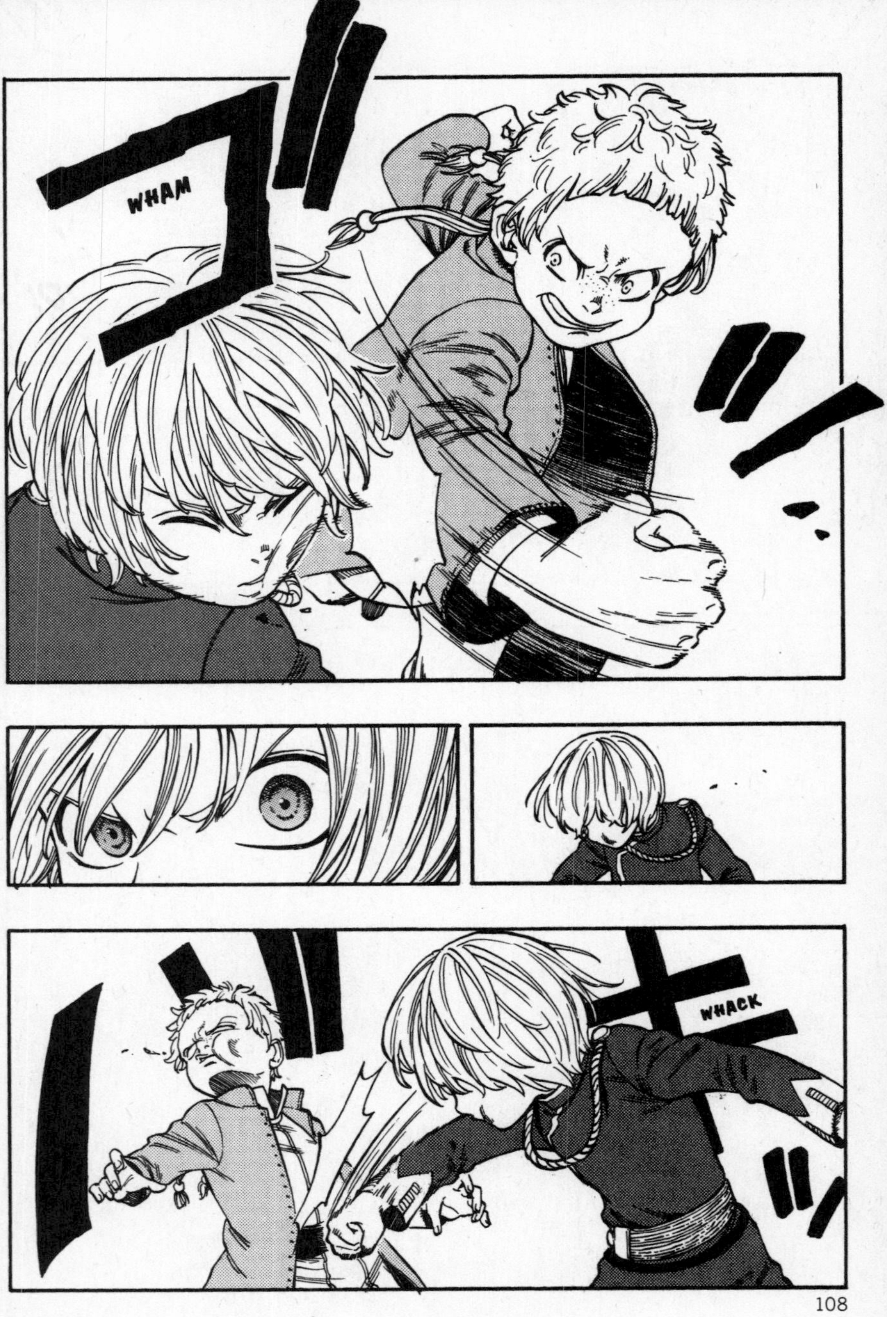
WHAM
WHACK

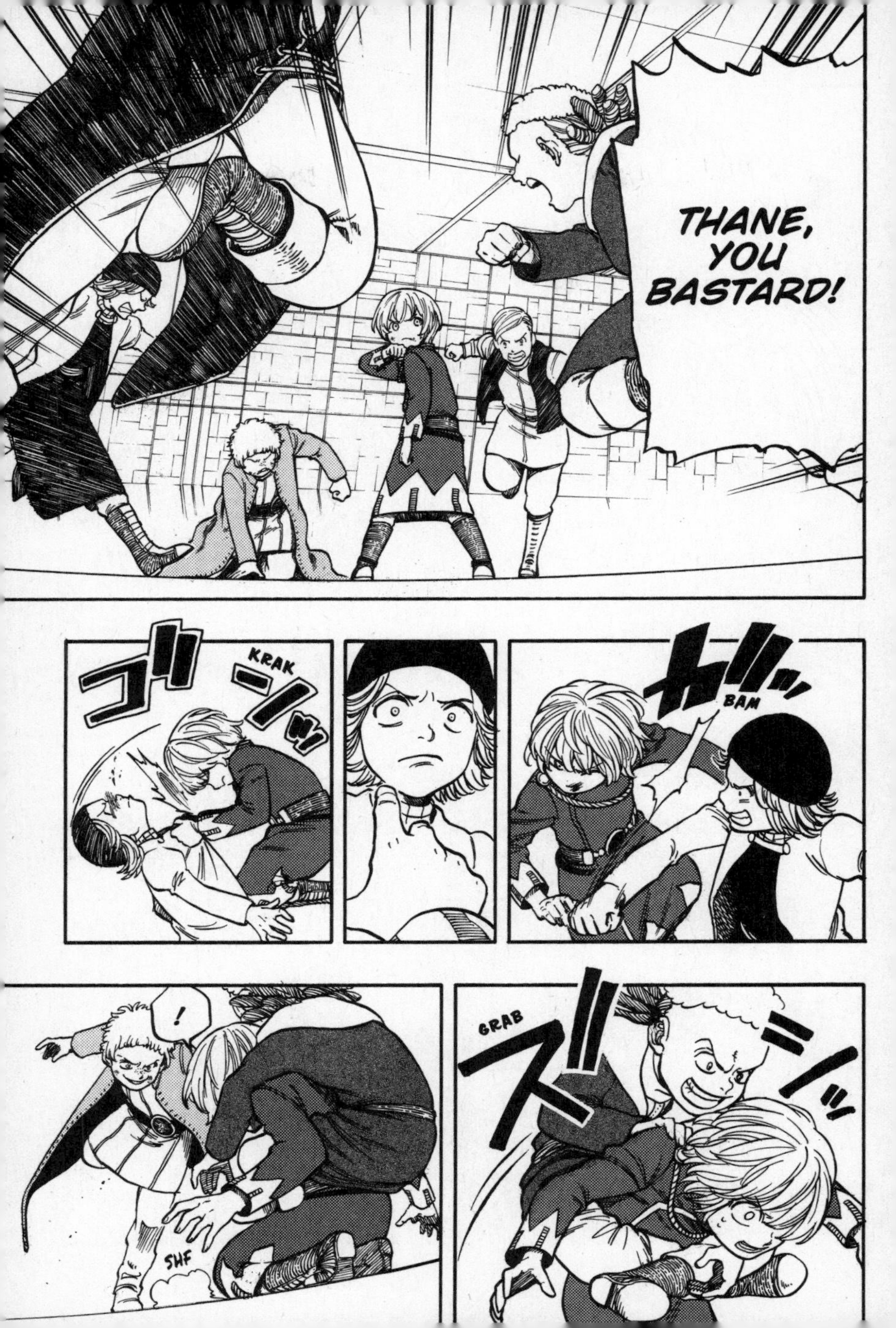
THANE, YOU BASTARD!
BAM
KRAK
GRAB
!
SHF

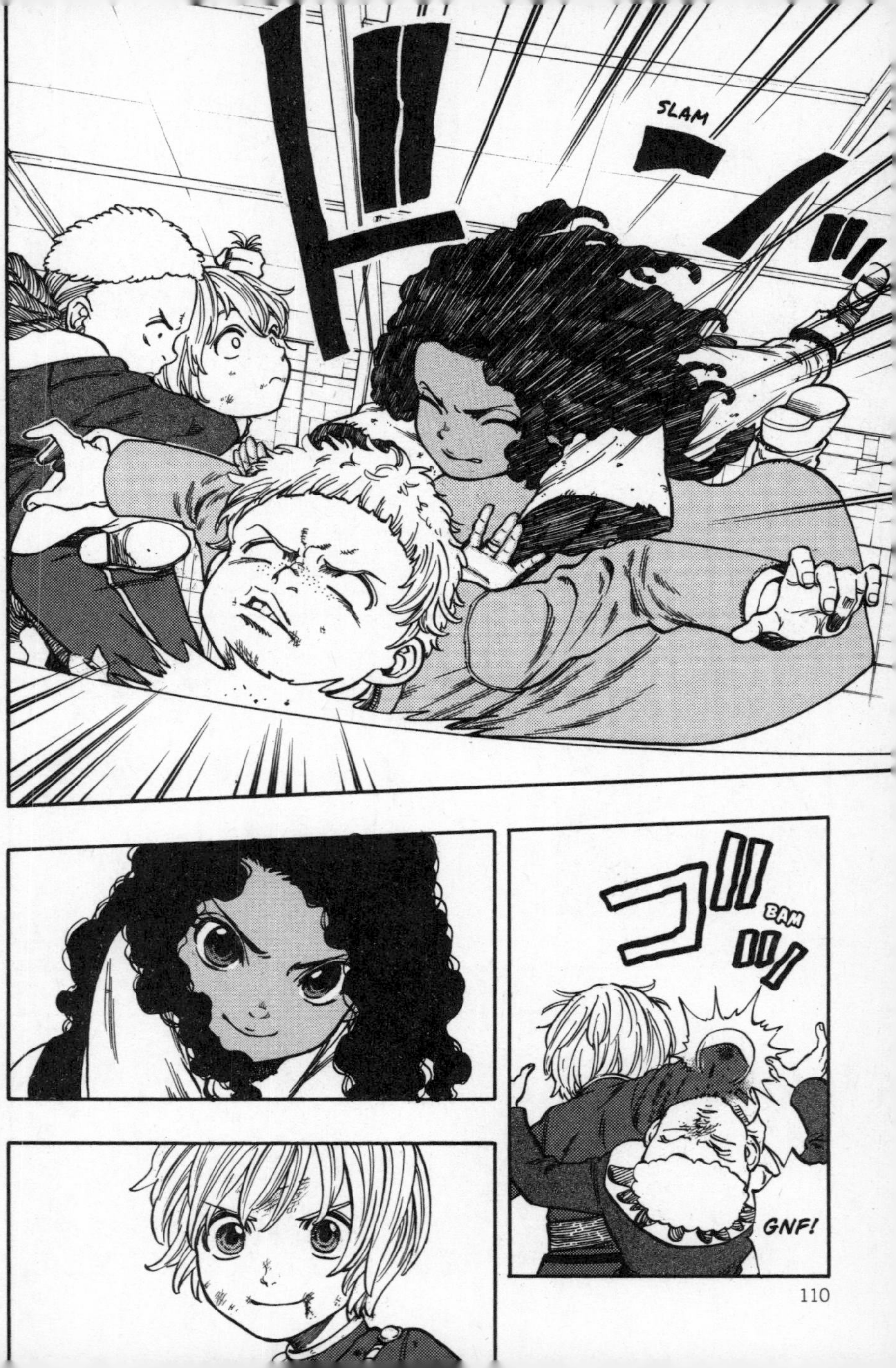
SLAM
BAM
GNF!

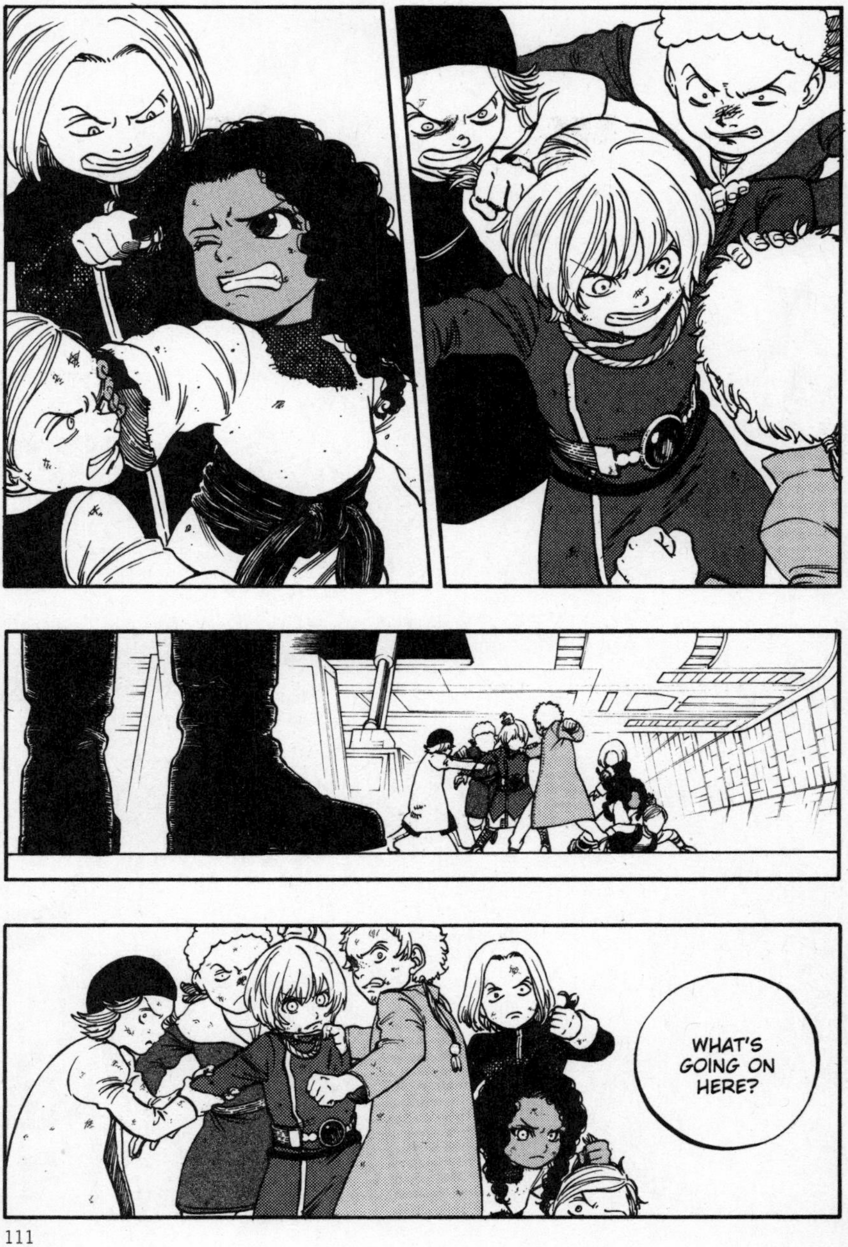
WHAT'S GOING ON HERE?

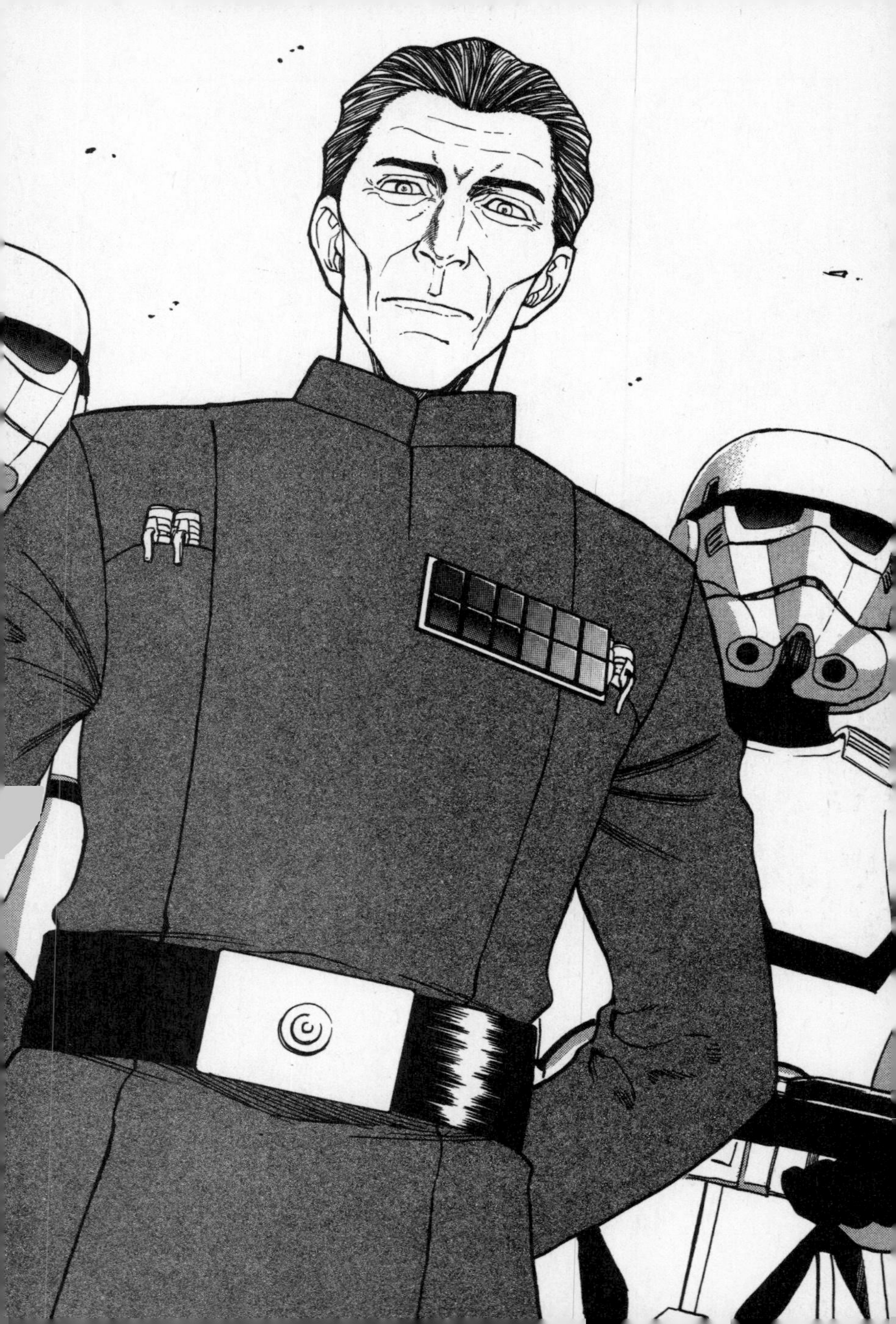

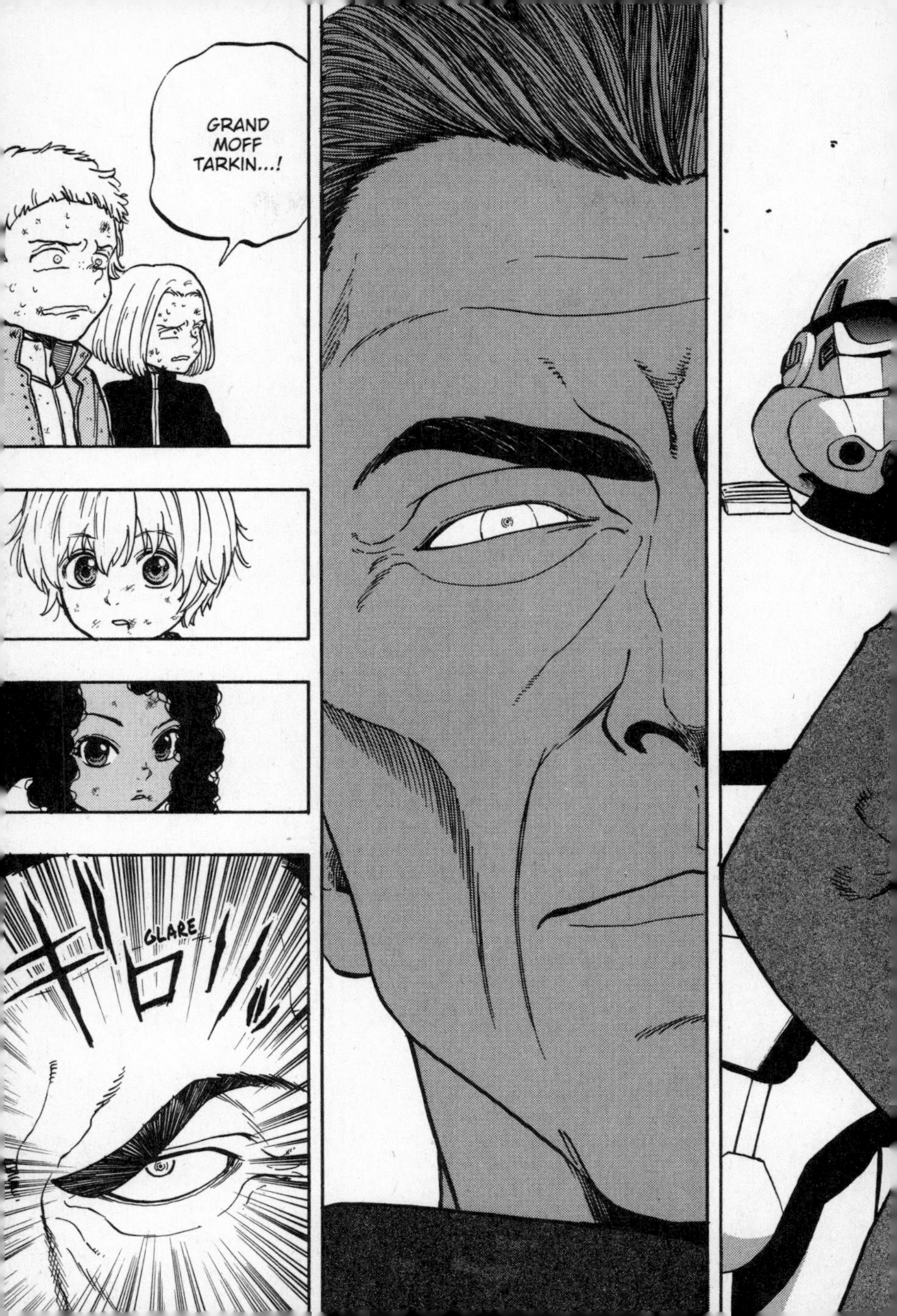
GRAND MOFF TARKIN...!
GLARE

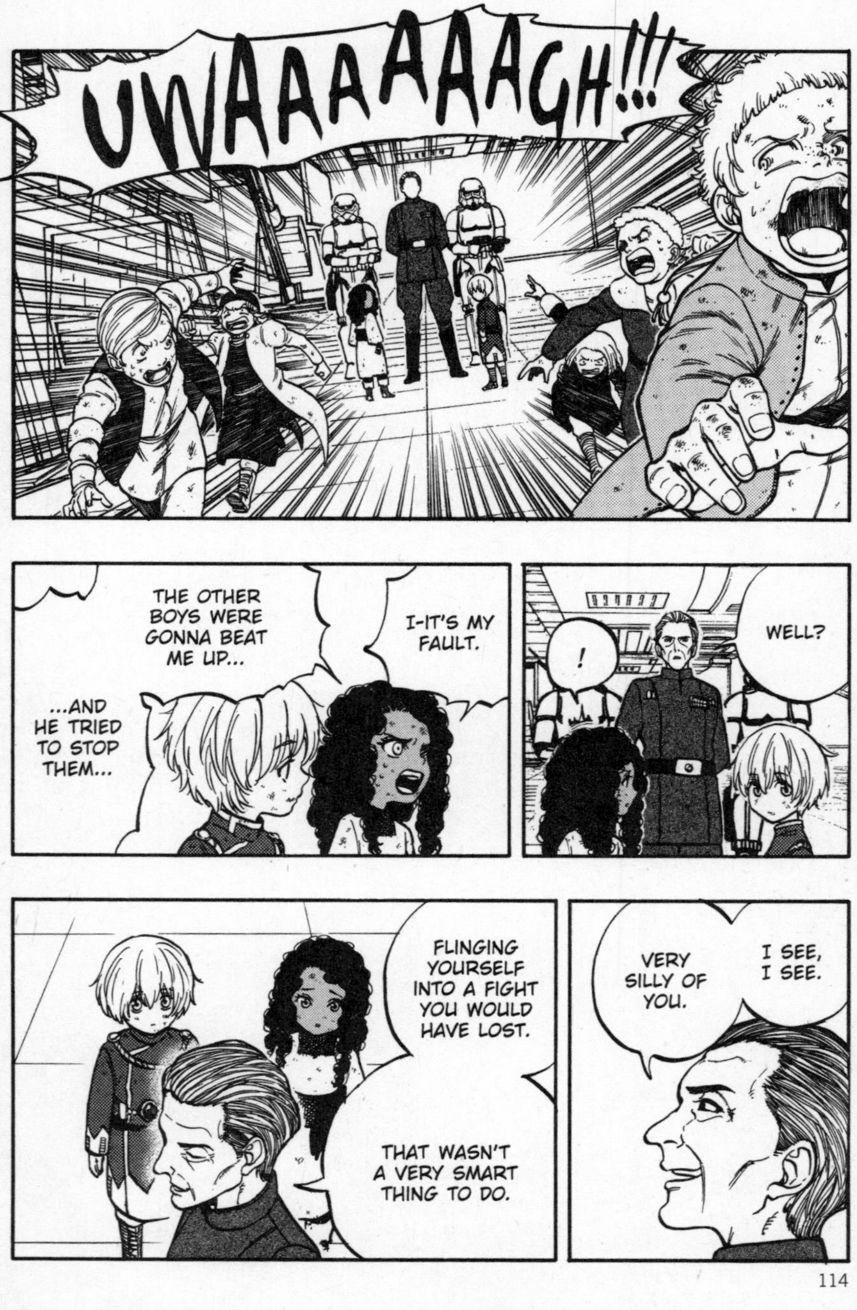
UWAAAAAAAGH!!!
WELL?
!
I-IT'S MY FAULT.
THE OTHER BOYS WERE GONNA BEAT ME UP...
...AND HE TRIED TO STOP THEM...
I SEE, I SEE.
VERY SILLY OF YOU.
FLINGING YOURSELF INTO A FIGHT YOU WOULD HAVE LOST.
THAT WASN'T A VERY SMART THING TO DO.

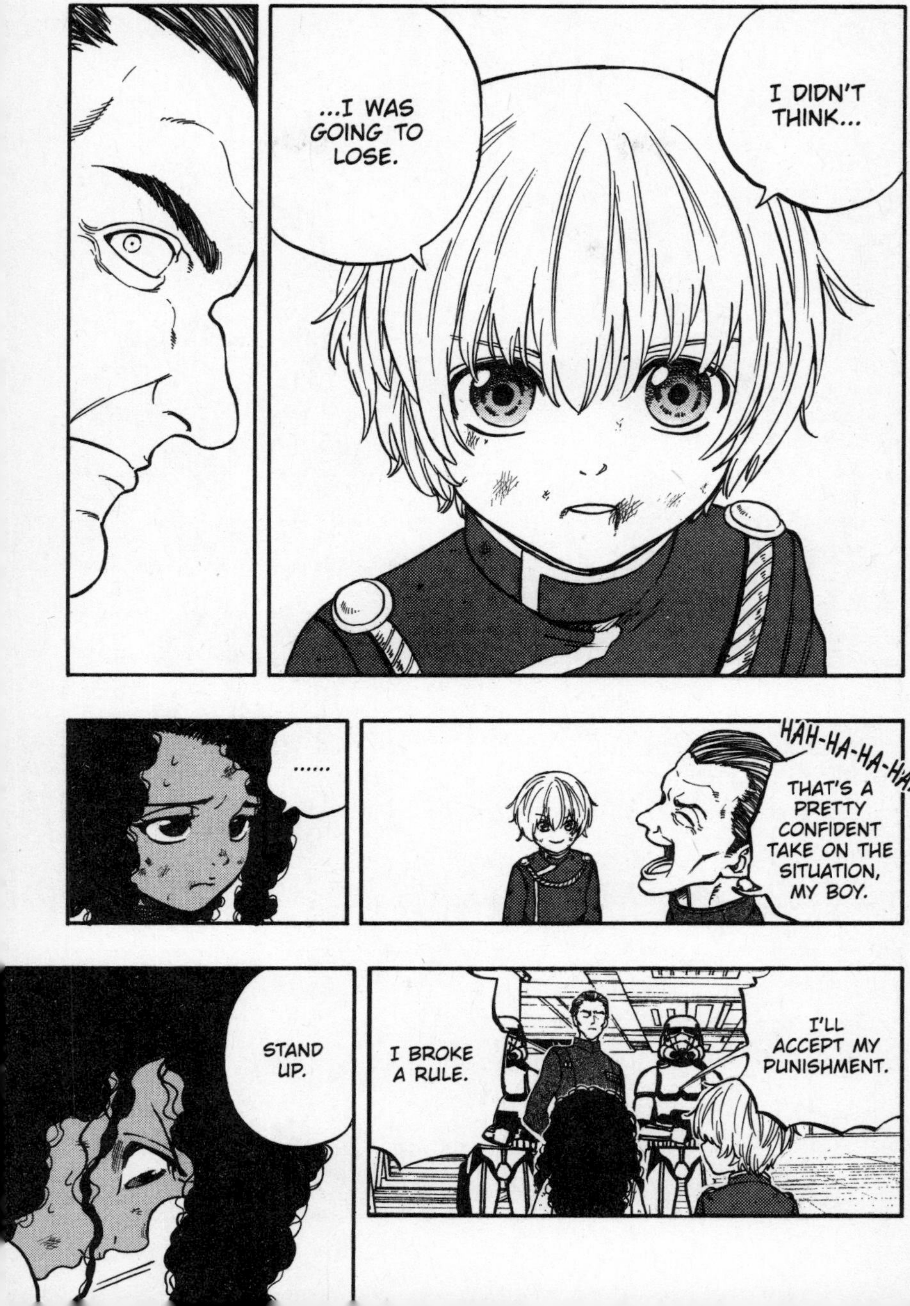
I DIDN'T THINK...
...I WAS GOING TO LOSE.
HAH-HA-HA-HA!
THAT'S A PRETTY CONFIDENT TAKE ON THE SITUATION, MY BOY.
......
I'LL ACCEPT MY PUNISHMENT.
I BROKE A RULE.
STAND UP.

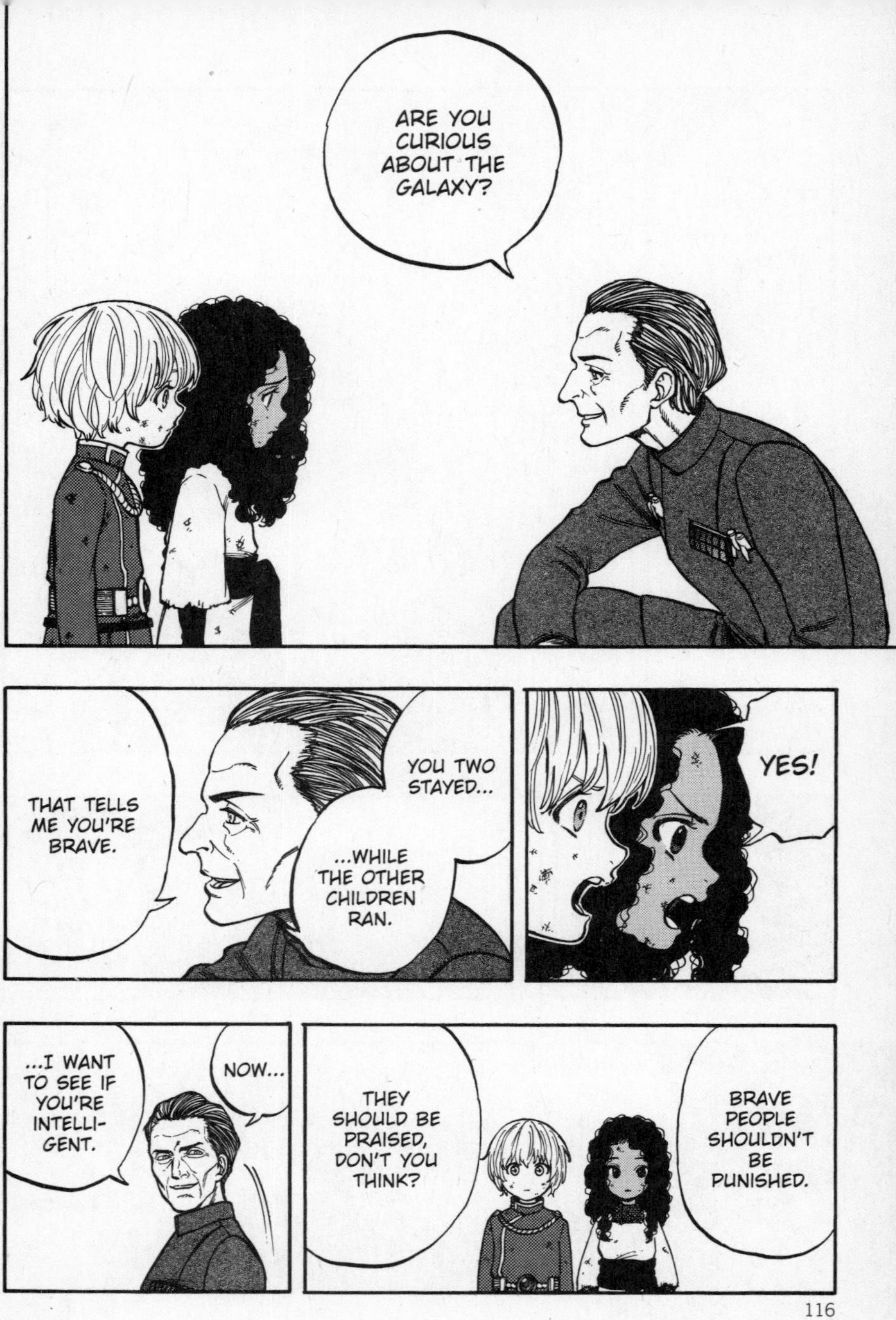
ARE YOU CURIOUS ABOUT THE GALAXY?
YES!
YOU TWO STAYED...
...WHILE THE OTHER CHILDREN RAN.
THAT TELLS ME YOU'RE BRAVE.
BRAVE PEOPLE SHOULDN'T BE PUNISHED.
THEY SHOULD BE PRAISED, DON'T YOU THINK?
NOW...
...I WANT TO SEE IF YOU'RE INTELLI-GENT.

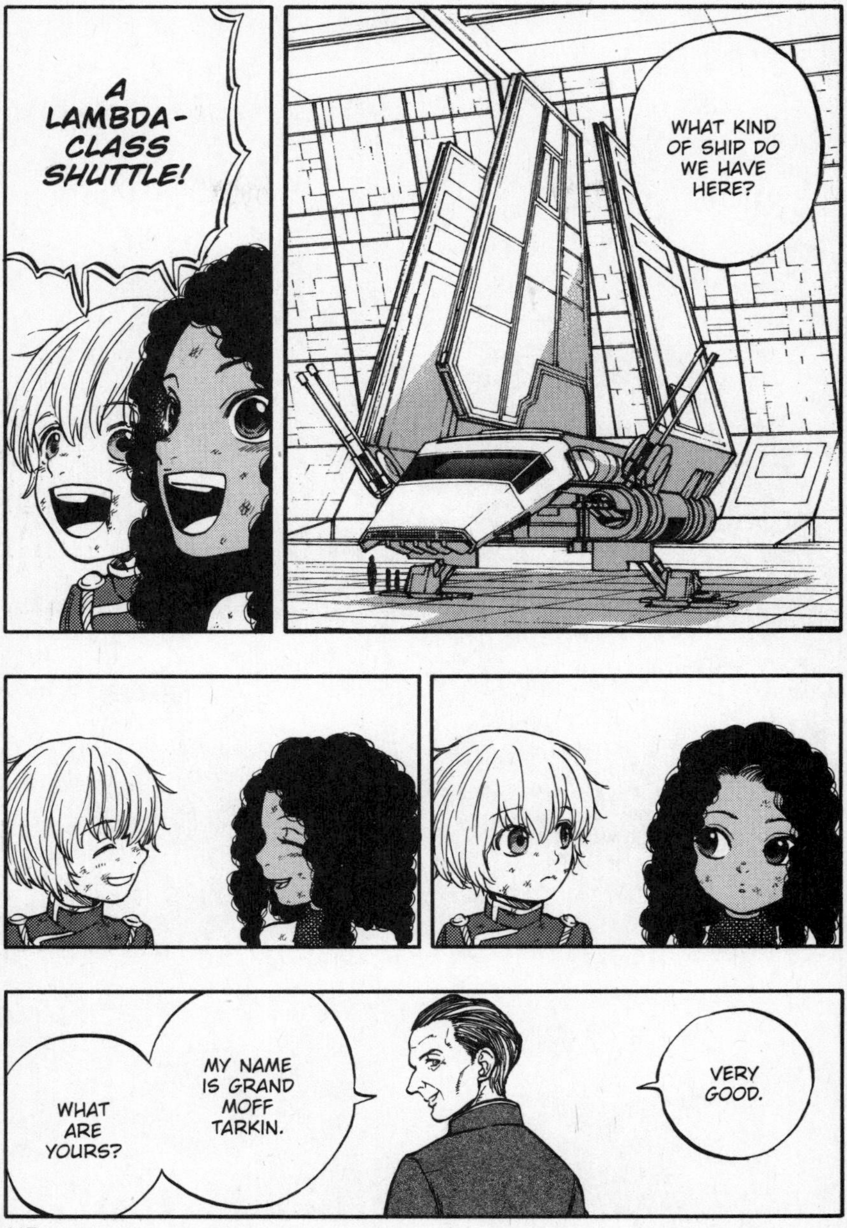
WHAT KIND OF SHIP DO WE HAVE HERE?
A LAMBDA-CLASS SHUTTLE!
VERY GOOD.
MY NAME IS GRAND MOFF TARKIN.
WHAT ARE YOURS?

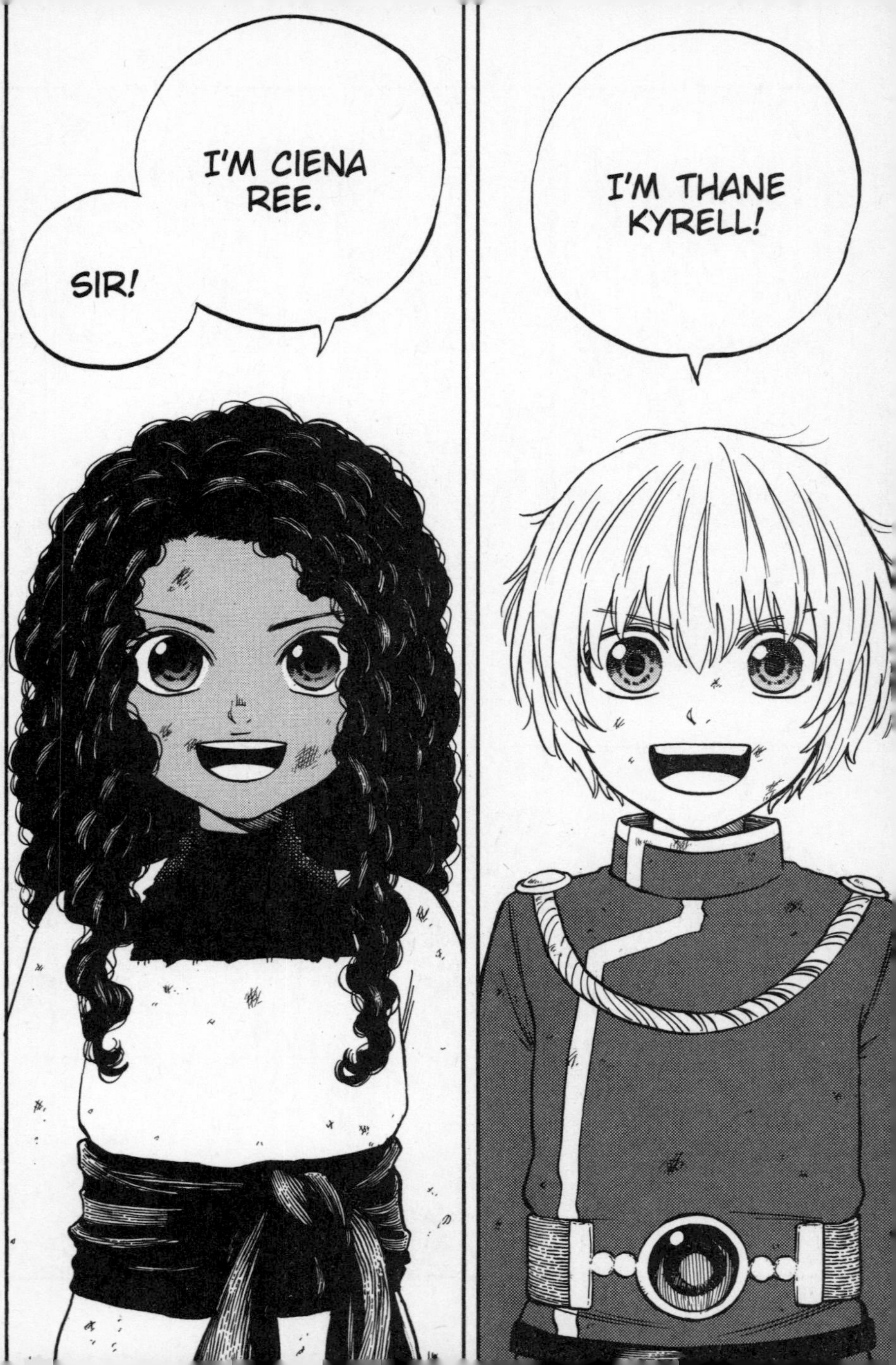
I'M THANE KYRELL!
I'M CIENA REE.
SIR!

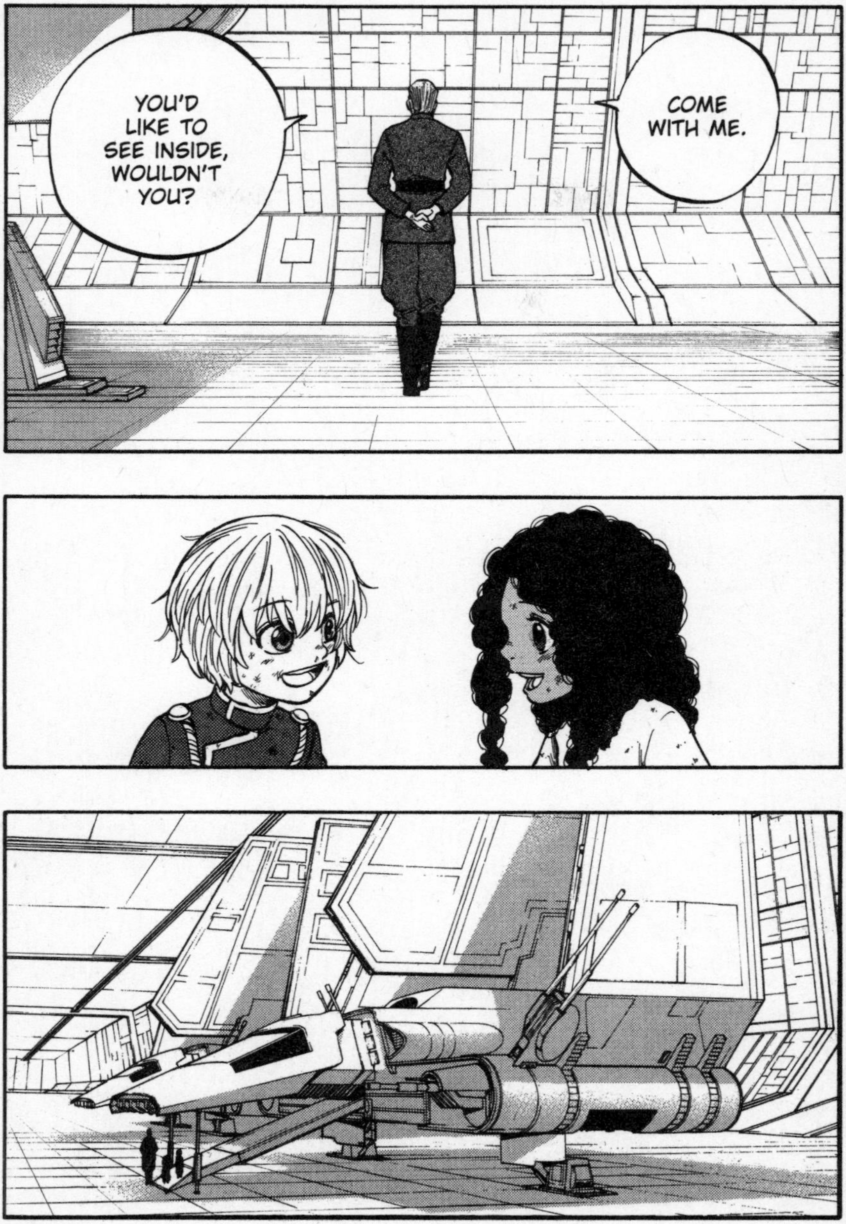
YOU'D LIKE TO SEE INSIDE, WOULDN'T YOU?
COME WITH ME.

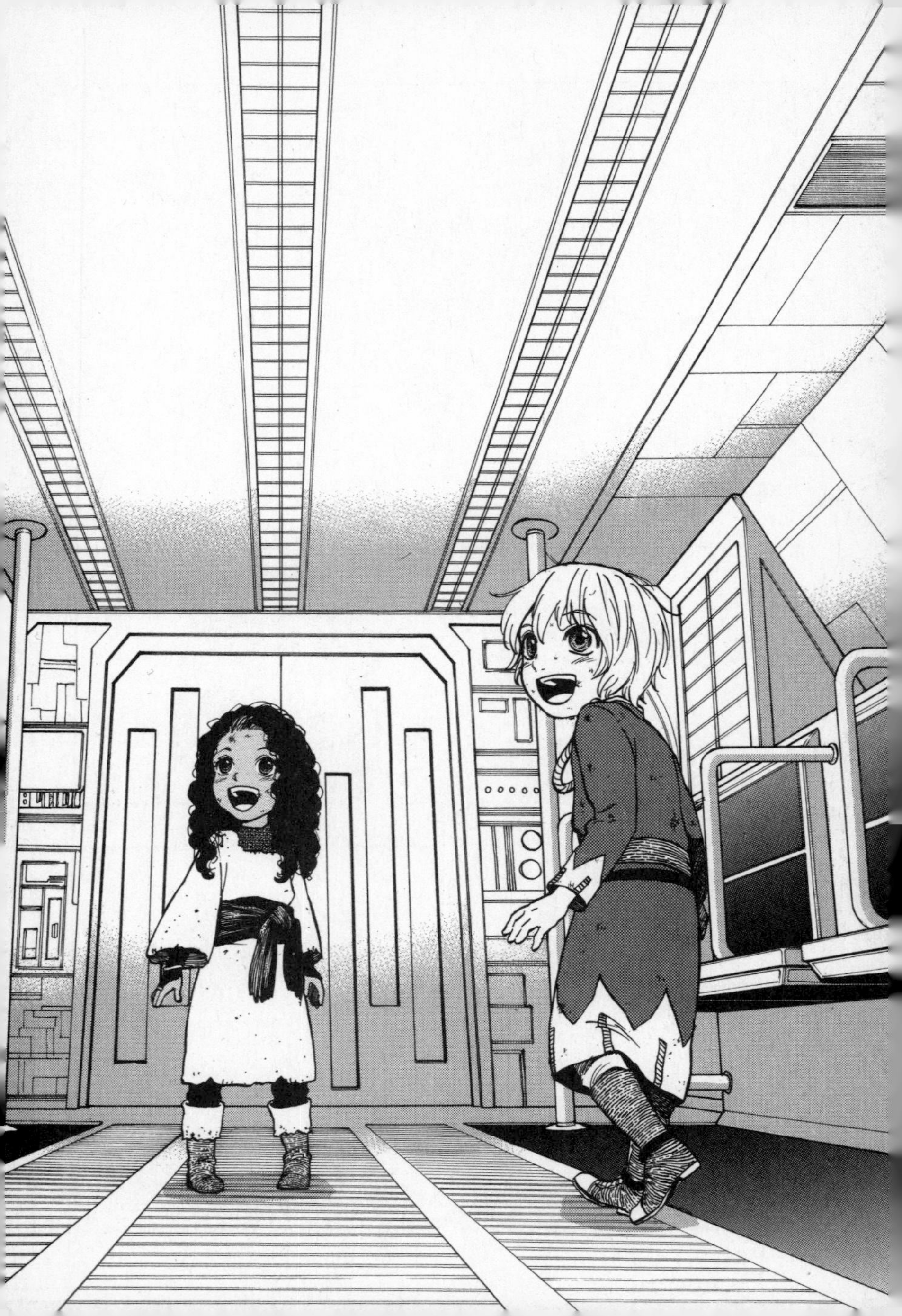

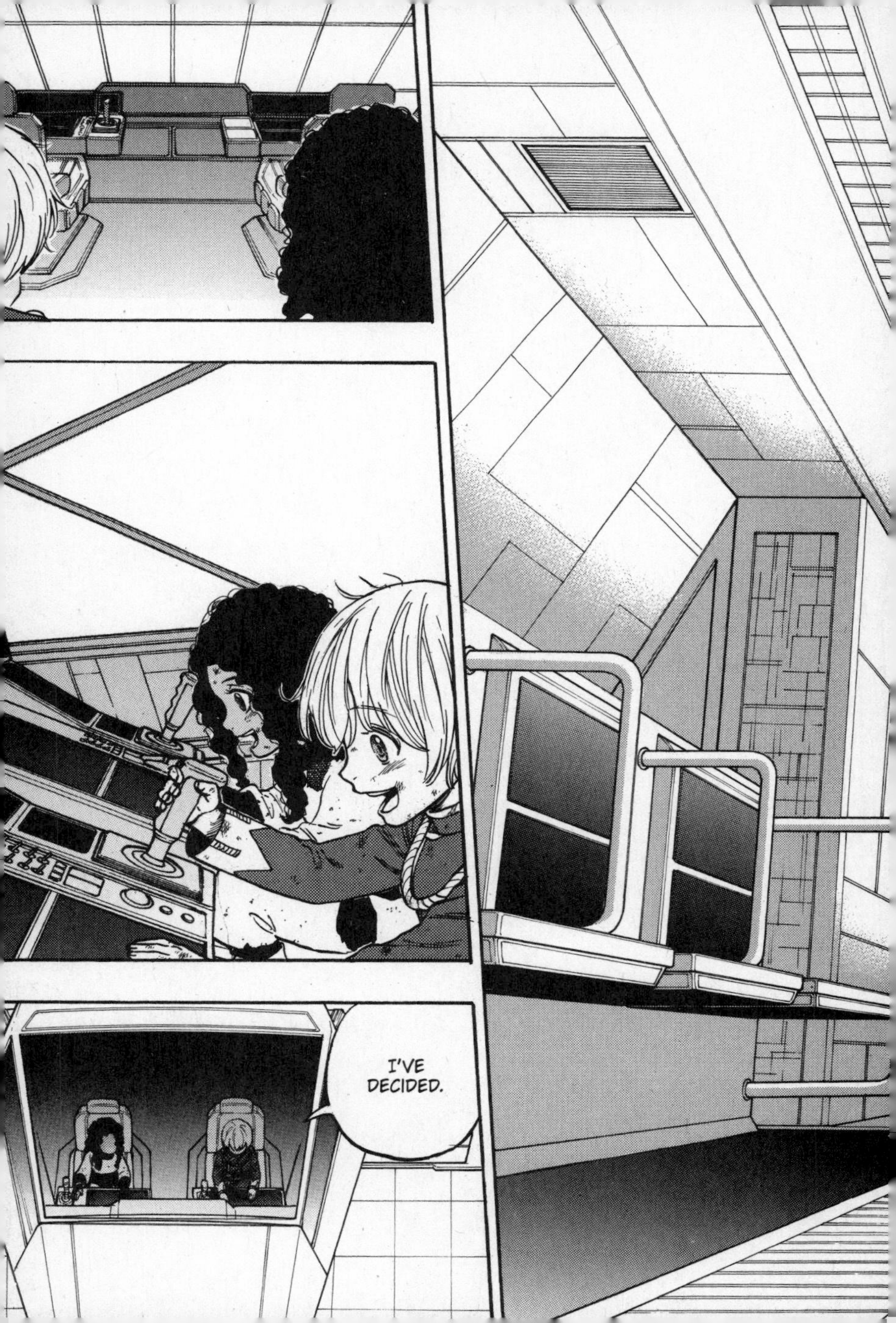
I'VE DECIDED.

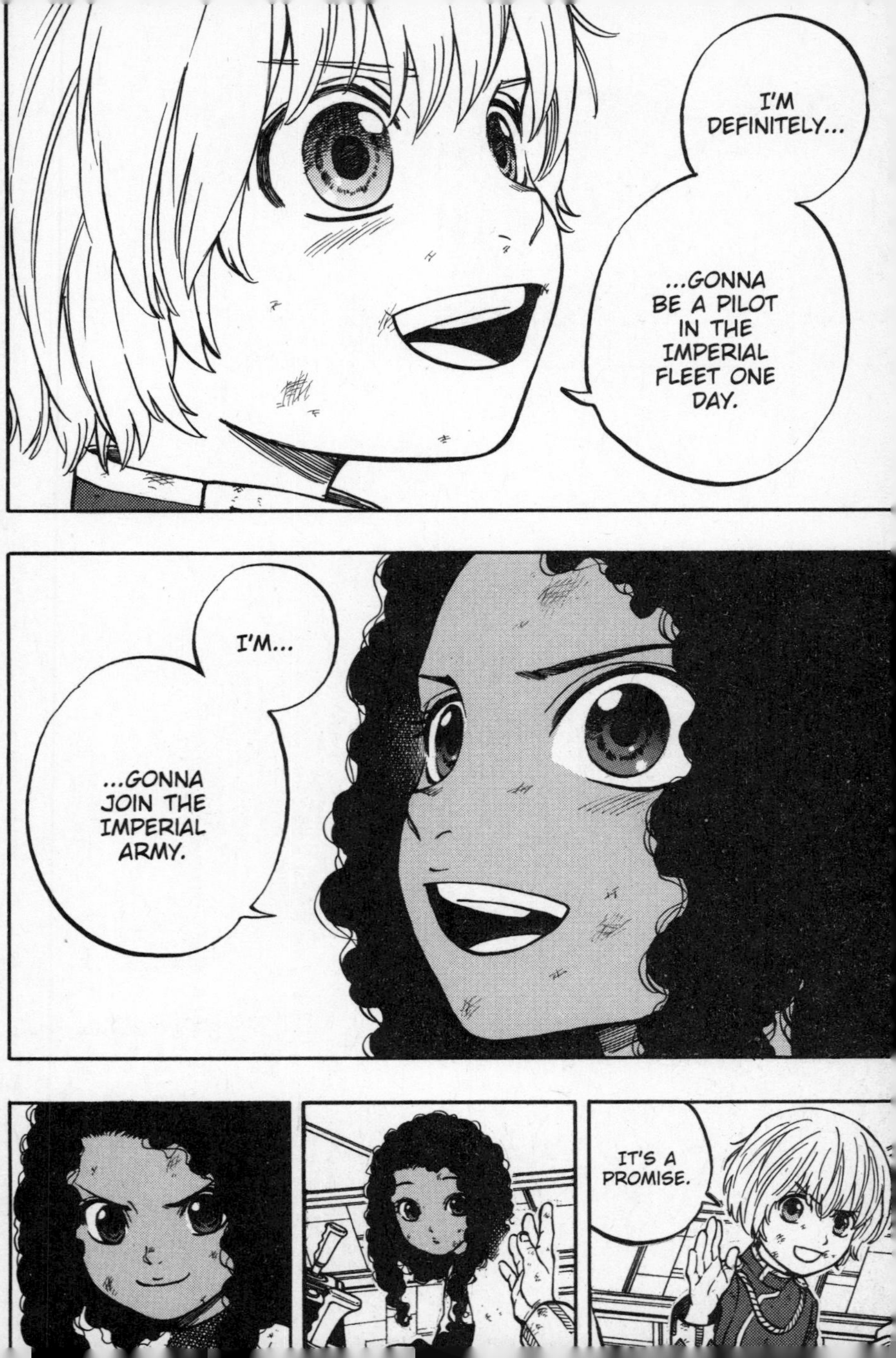
I'M DEFINITELY...
...GONNA BE A PILOT IN THE IMPERIAL FLEET ONE DAY.
I'M...
...GONNA JOIN THE IMPERIAL ARMY.
IT'S A PROMISE.

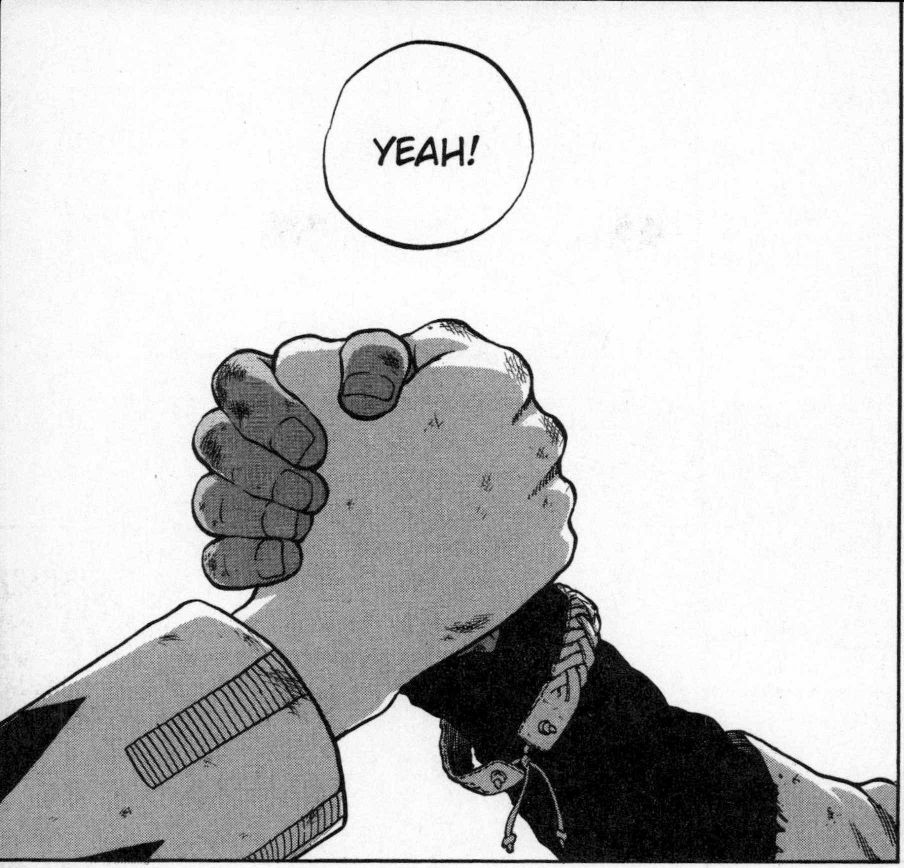
YEAH!

EIGHT YEARS LATER

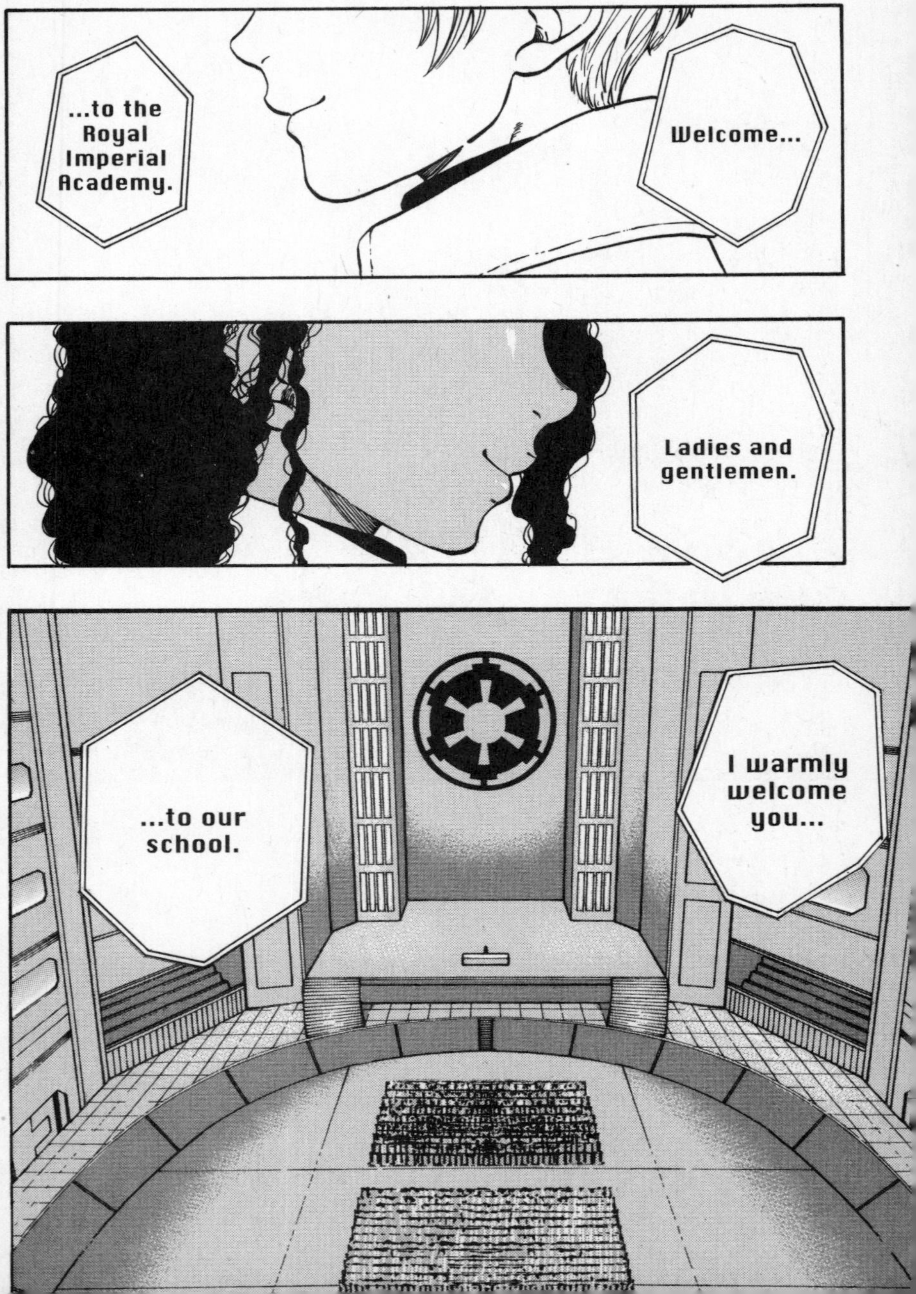
Welcome...
...to the Royal Imperial Academy.
Ladies and gentlemen.
I warmly welcome you...
...to our school.

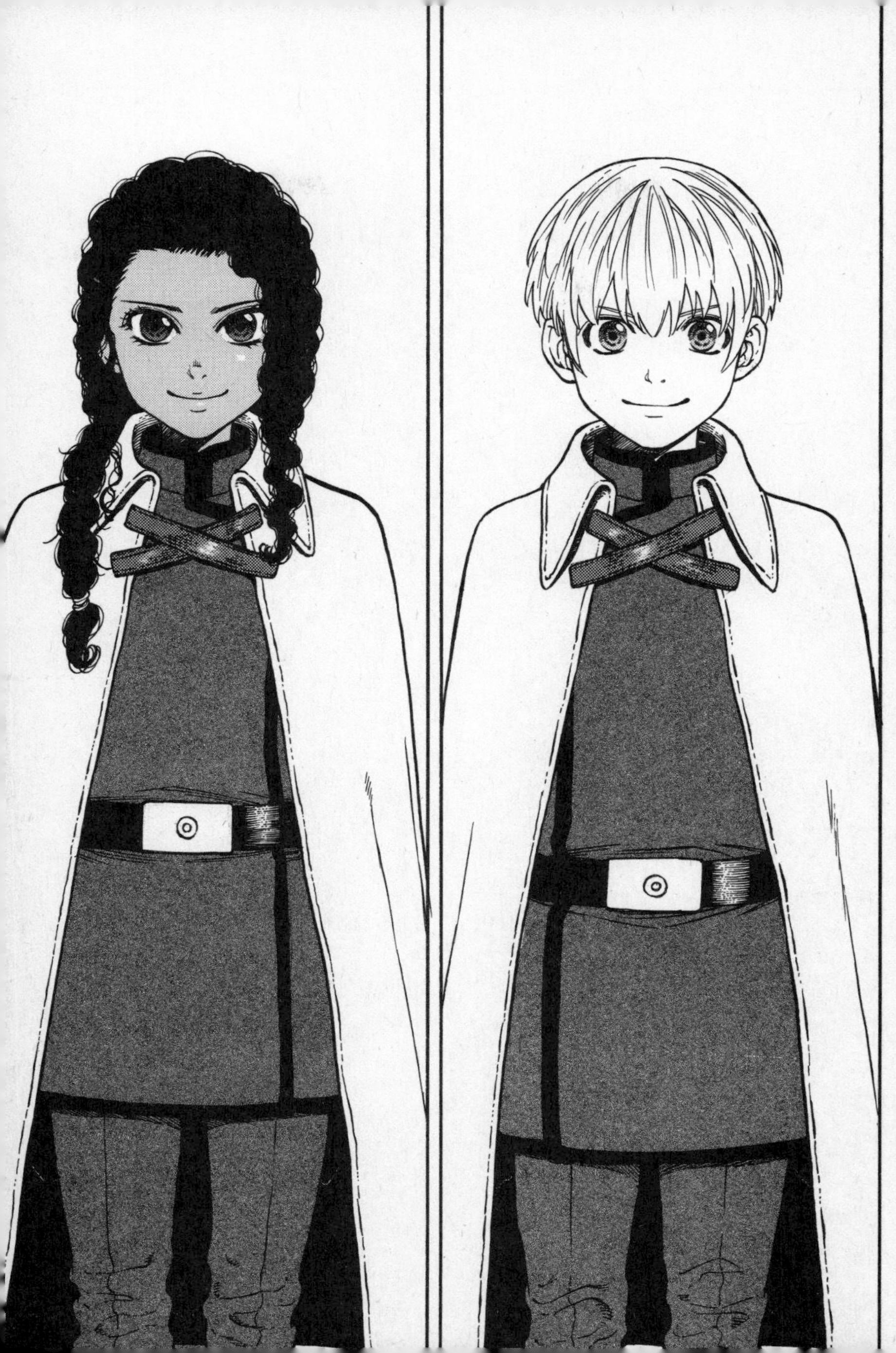

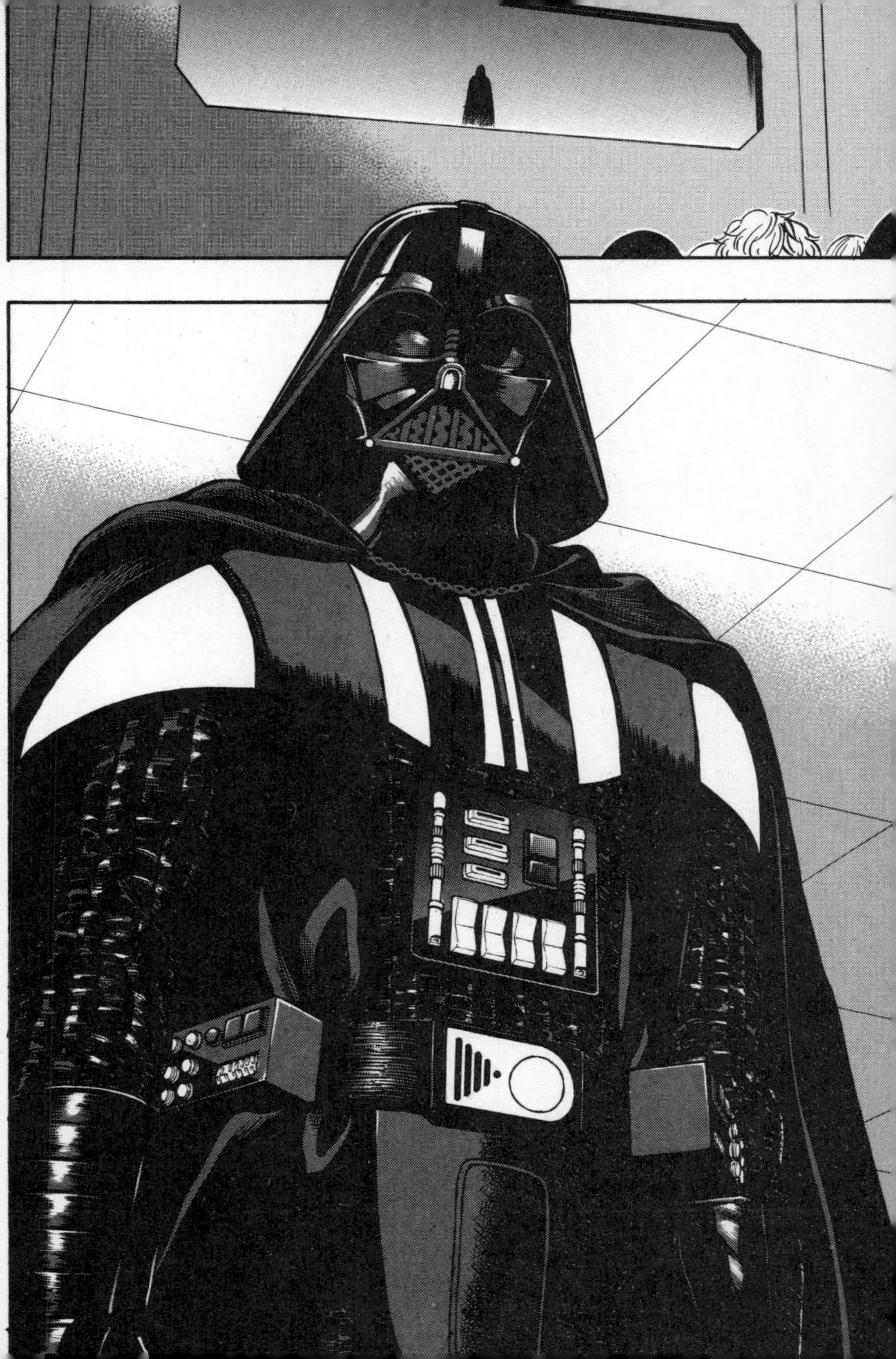

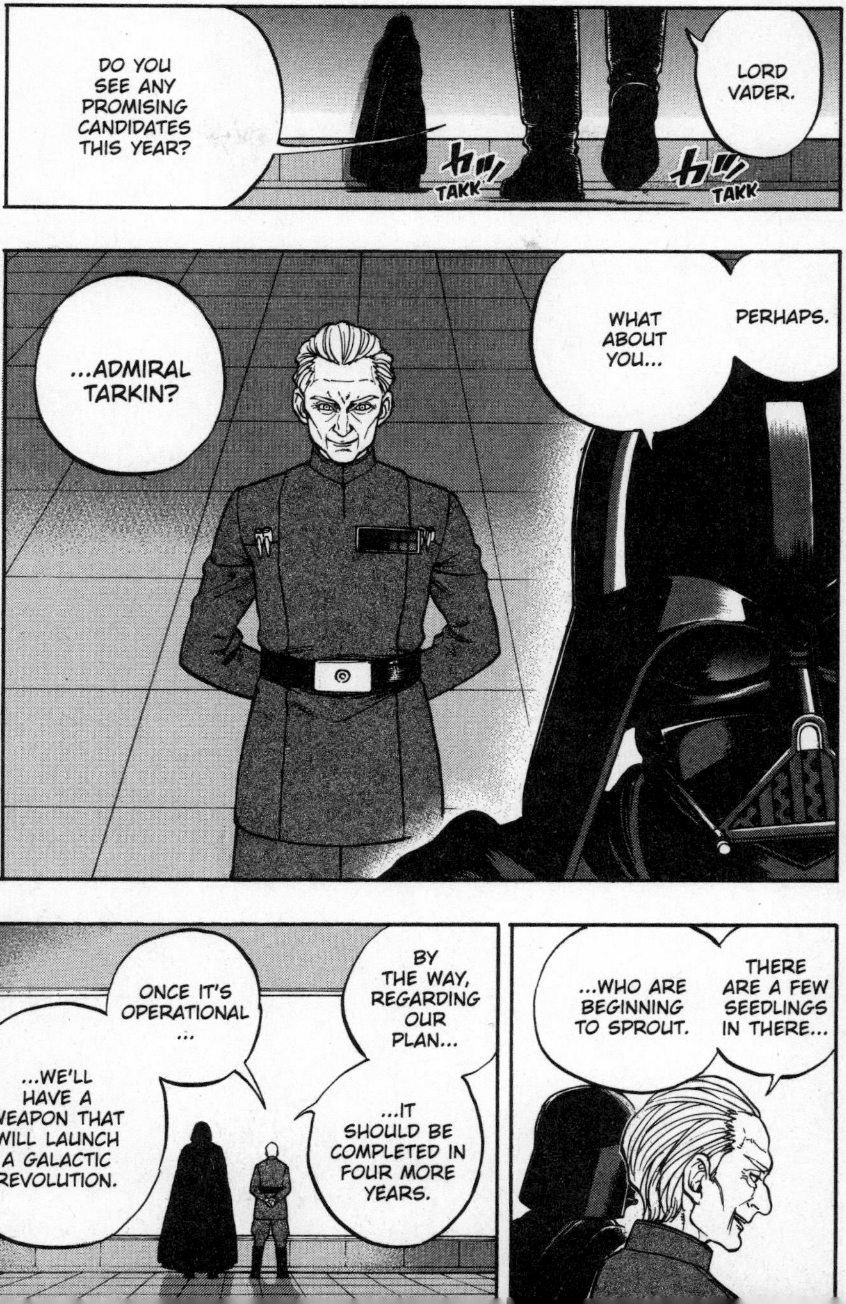
LORD VADER.
DO YOU SEE ANY PROMISING CANDIDATES THIS YEAR?
TAKK
TAKK
PERHAPS.
WHAT ABOUT YOU...
...ADMIRAL TARKIN?
THERE ARE A FEW SEEDLINGS IN THERE...
...WHO ARE BEGINNING TO SPROUT.
BY THE WAY, REGARDING OUR PLAN...
...IT SHOULD BE COMPLETED IN FOUR MORE YEARS.
ONCE IT'S OPERATIONAL...
...WE'LL HAVE A WEAPON THAT WILL LAUNCH A GALACTIC REVOLUTION.

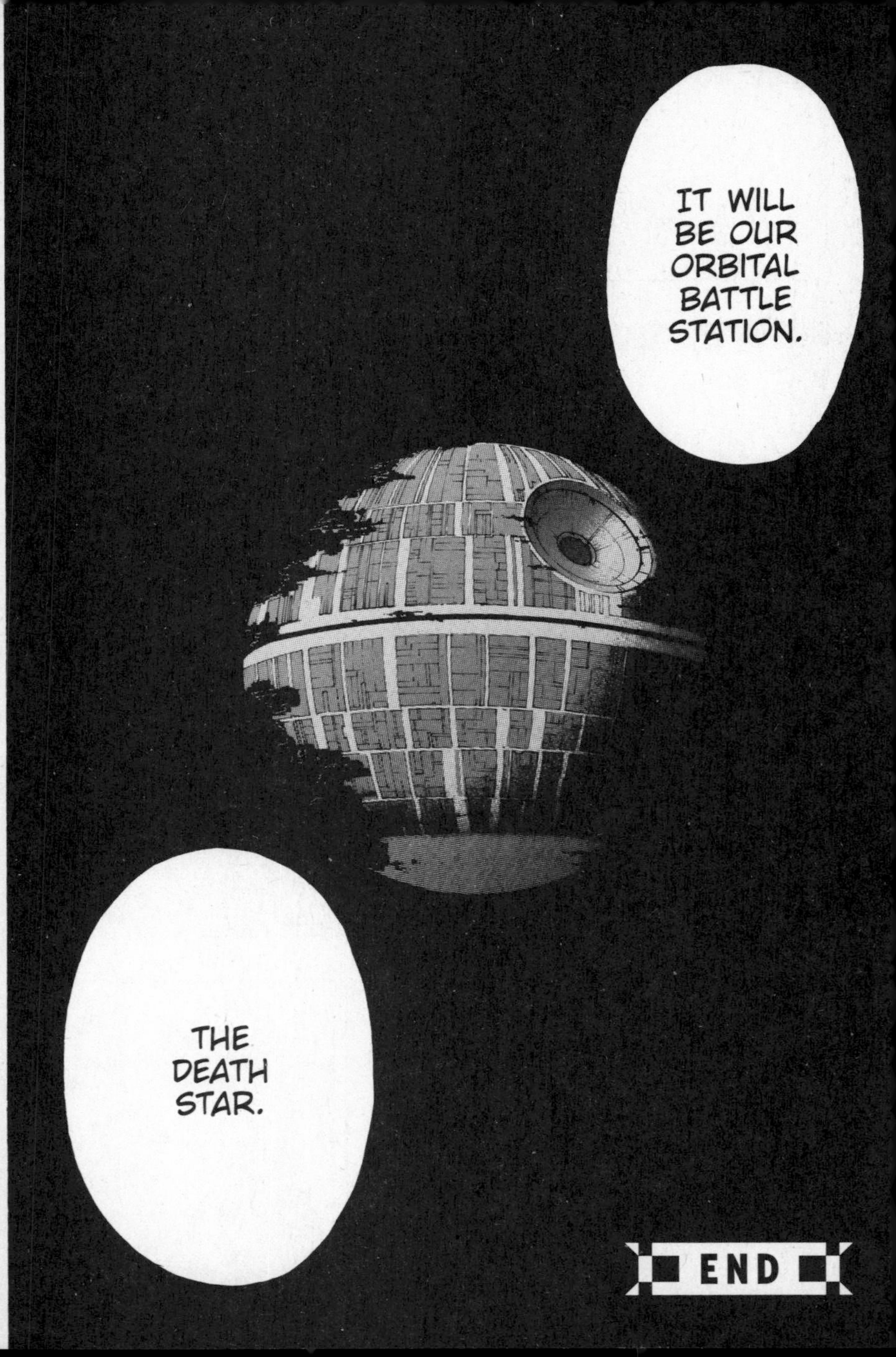
IT WILL BE OUR ORBITAL BATTLE STATION.
THE DEATH STAR.
END

STAR WARS
LOST STARS

STAR WARS
LOST STARS
ロスト・スターズ

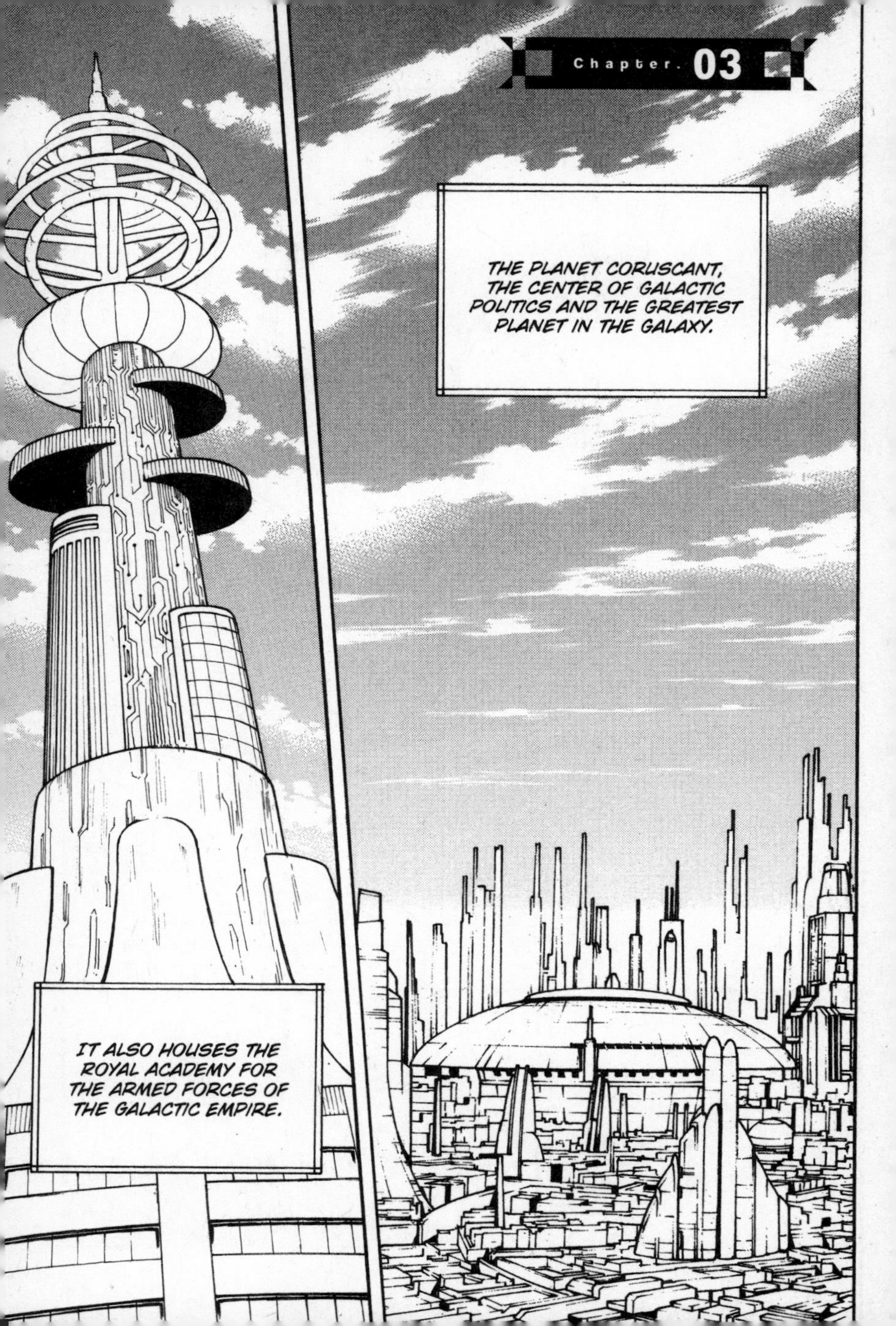
Chapter. 03
THE PLANET CORUSCANT, THE CENTER OF GALACTIC POLITICS AND THE GREATEST PLANET IN THE GALAXY.
IT ALSO HOUSES THE ROYAL ACADEMY FOR THE ARMED FORCES OF THE GALACTIC EMPIRE.

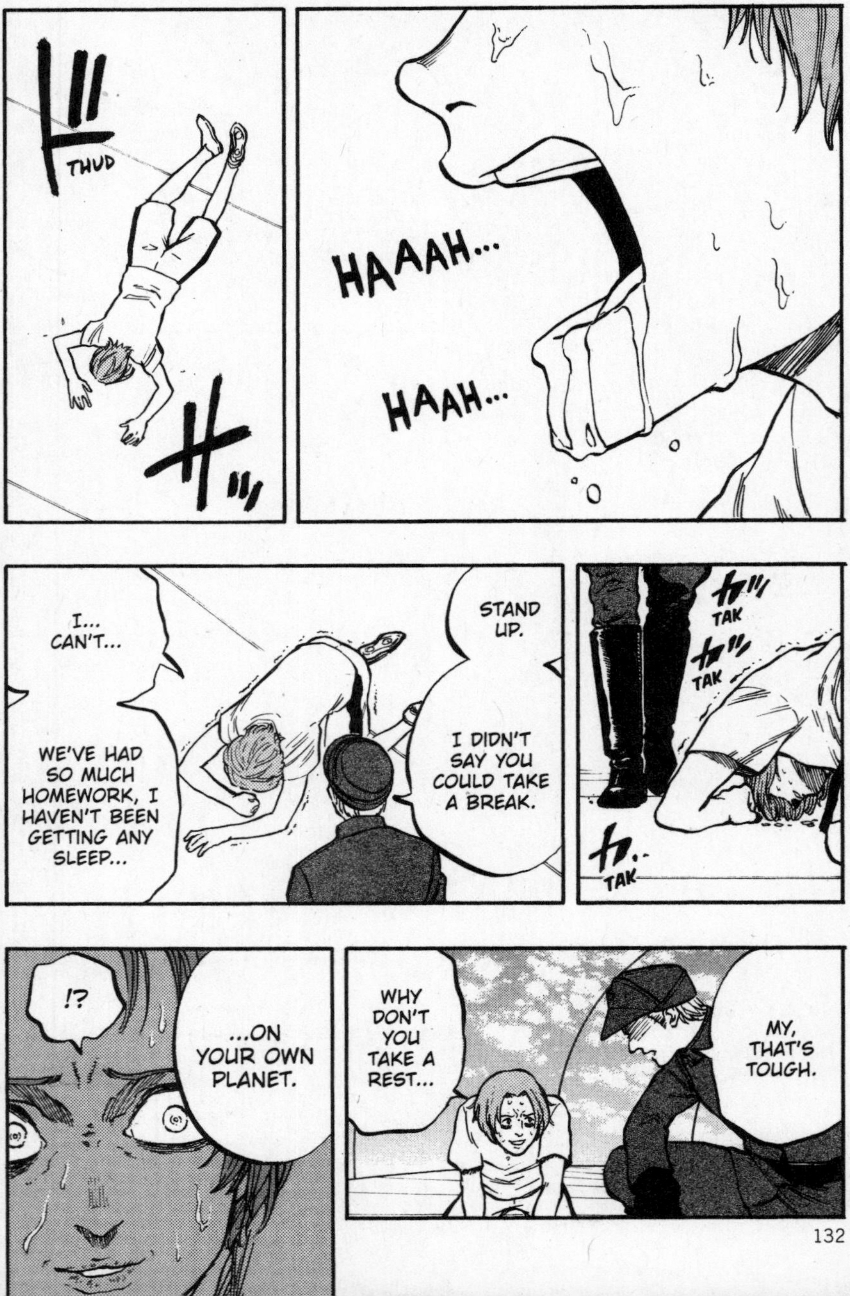
HAAAH...
HAAH...
THUD
TAK
TAK
TAK
STAND UP.
I DIDN'T SAY YOU COULD TAKE A BREAK.
I... CAN'T...
WE'VE HAD SO MUCH HOMEWORK, I HAVEN'T BEEN GETTING ANY SLEEP...
MY, THAT'S TOUGH.
WHY DON'T YOU TAKE A REST...
...ON YOUR OWN PLANET.
!?

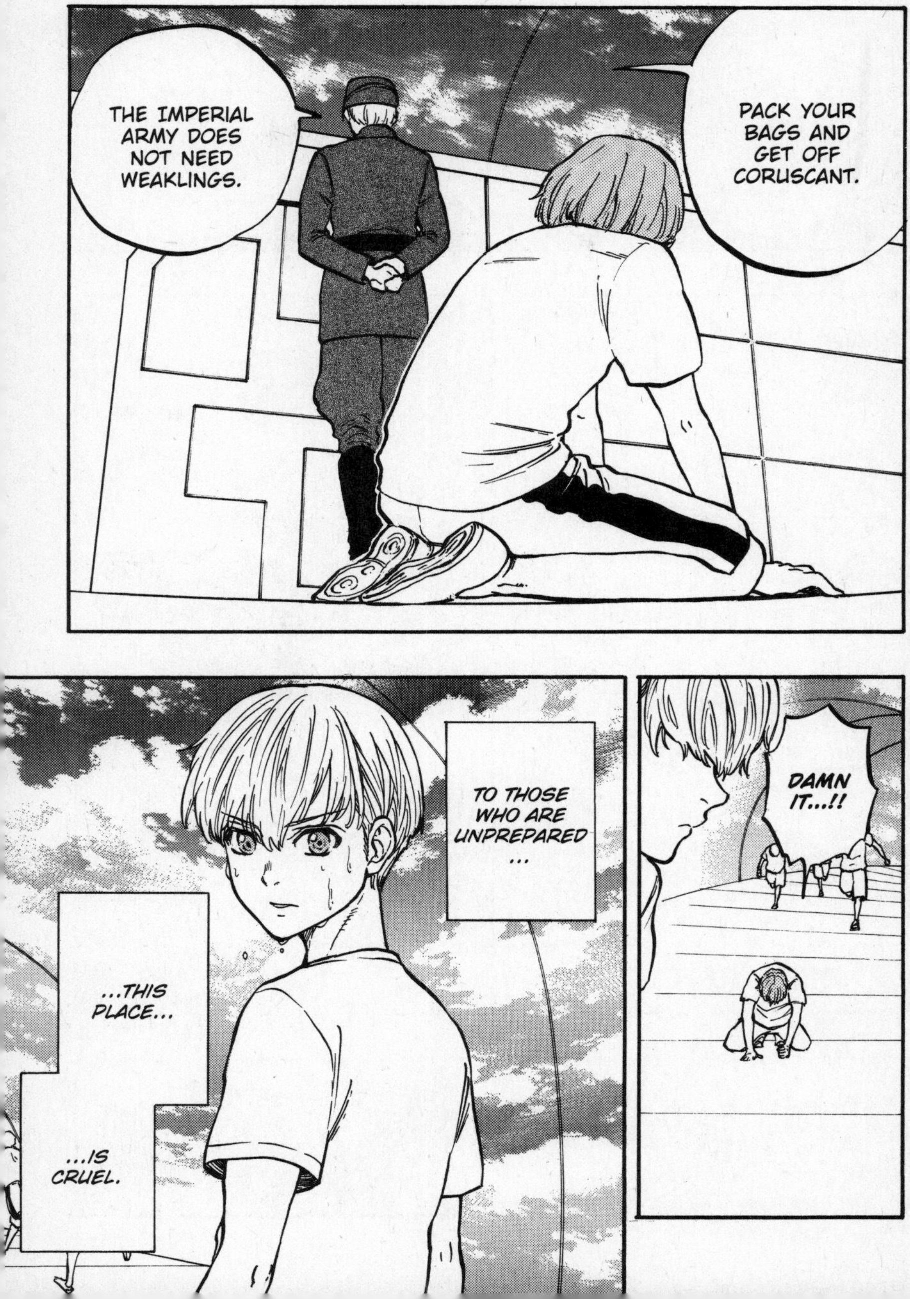
PACK YOUR BAGS AND GET OFF CORUSCANT.
THE IMPERIAL ARMY DOES NOT NEED WEAKLINGS.
DAMN IT...!!
TO THOSE WHO ARE UNPREPARED...
...THIS PLACE...
...IS CRUEL.

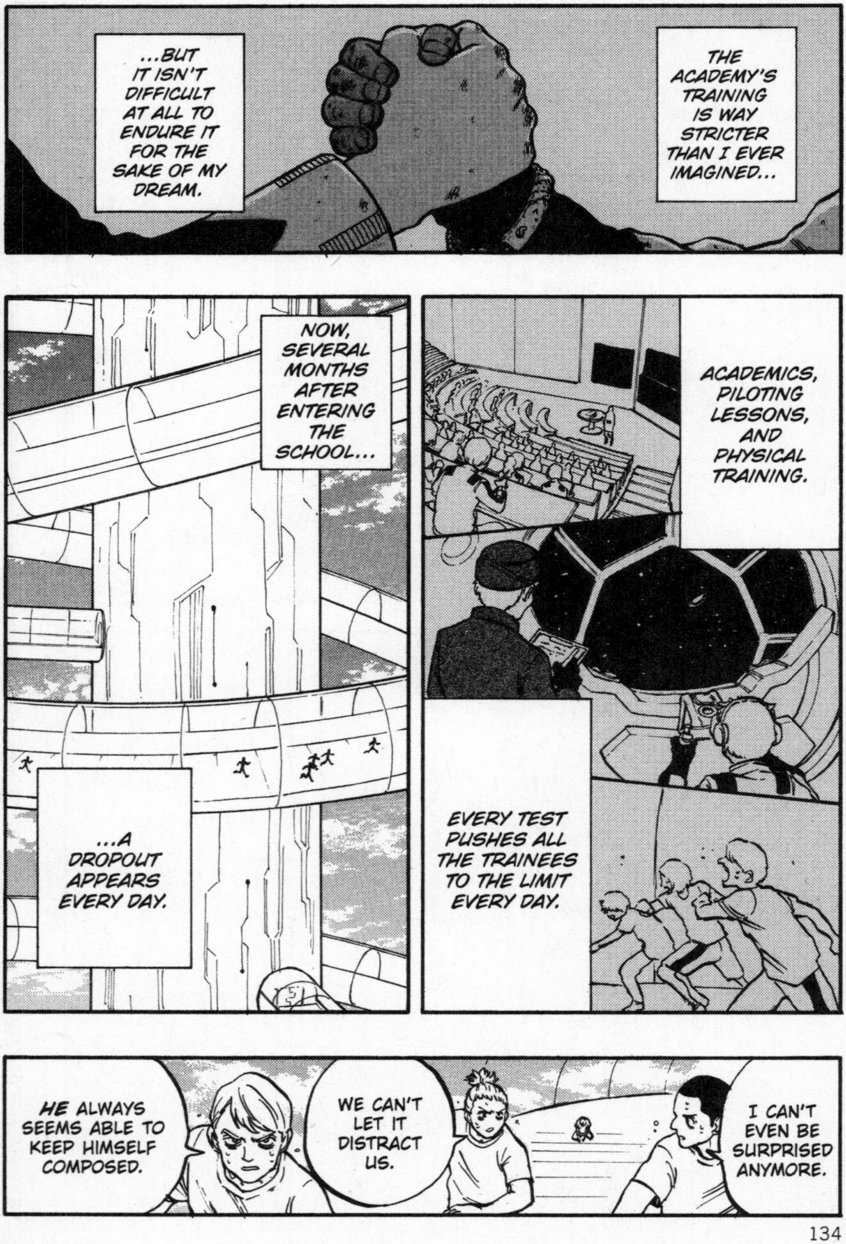
THE ACADEMY'S TRAINING IS WAY STRICTER THAN I EVER IMAGINED...
...BUT IT ISN'T DIFFICULT AT ALL TO ENDURE IT FOR THE SAKE OF MY DREAM.
ACADEMICS, PILOTING LESSONS, AND PHYSICAL TRAINING.
EVERY TEST PUSHES ALL THE TRAINEES TO THE LIMIT EVERY DAY.
NOW, SEVERAL MONTHS AFTER ENTERING THE SCHOOL...
...A DROPOUT APPEARS EVERY DAY.
I CAN'T EVEN BE SURPRISED ANYMORE.
WE CAN'T LET IT DISTRACT US.
HE ALWAYS SEEMS ABLE TO KEEP HIMSELF COMPOSED.

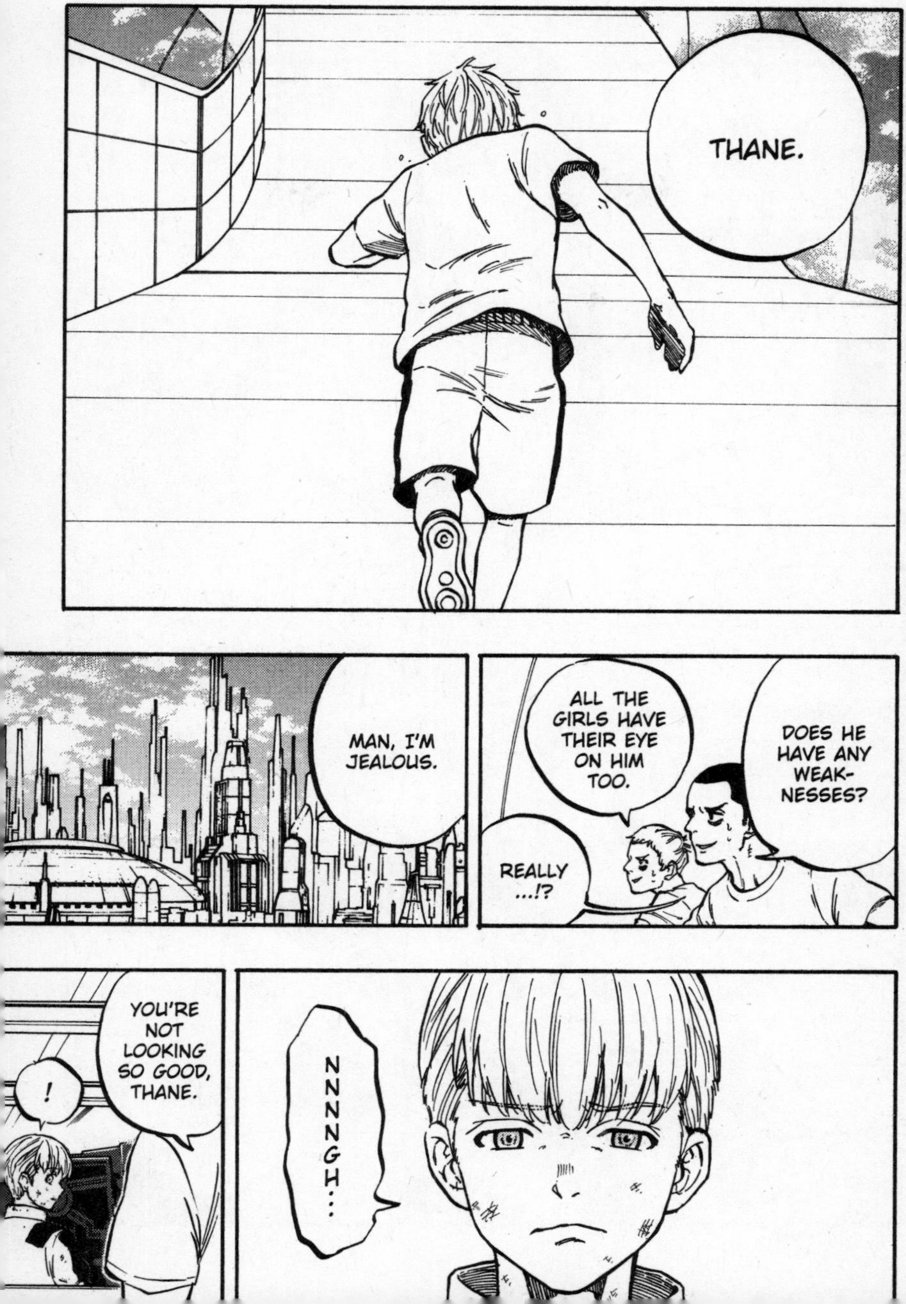
THANE.
DOES HE HAVE ANY WEAK-NESSES?
ALL THE GIRLS HAVE THEIR EYE ON HIM TOO.
REALLY ...!?
MAN, I'M JEALOUS.
NNNNGH...
YOU'RE NOT LOOKING SO GOOD, THANE.
!

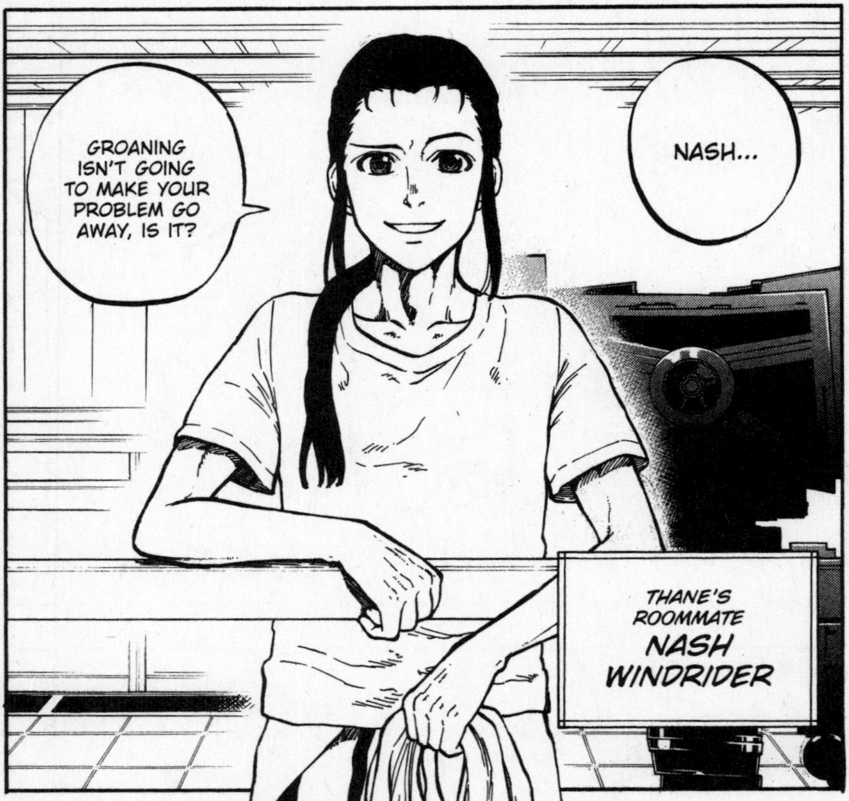
NASH...
GROANING ISN'T GOING TO MAKE YOUR PROBLEM GO AWAY, IS IT?
THANE'S ROOMMATE NASH WINDRIDER
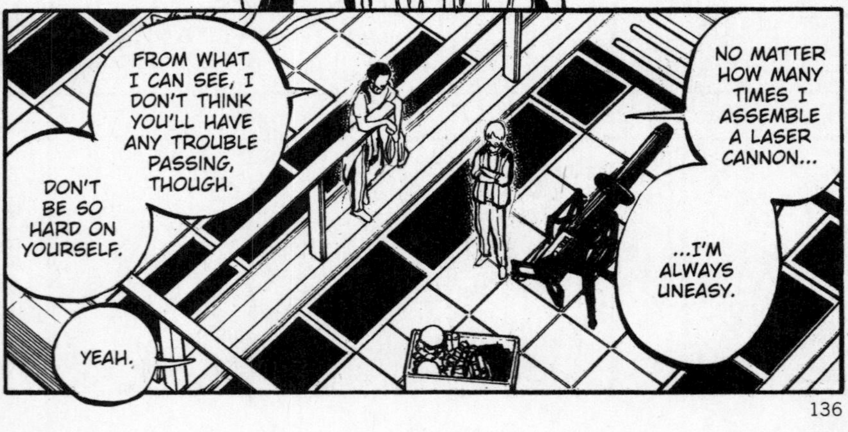
NO MATTER HOW MANY TIMES I ASSEMBLE A LASER CANNON...
...I'M ALWAYS UNEASY.
FROM WHAT I CAN SEE, I DON'T THINK YOU'LL HAVE ANY TROUBLE PASSING, THOUGH.
DON'T BE SO HARD ON YOURSELF.
YEAH.

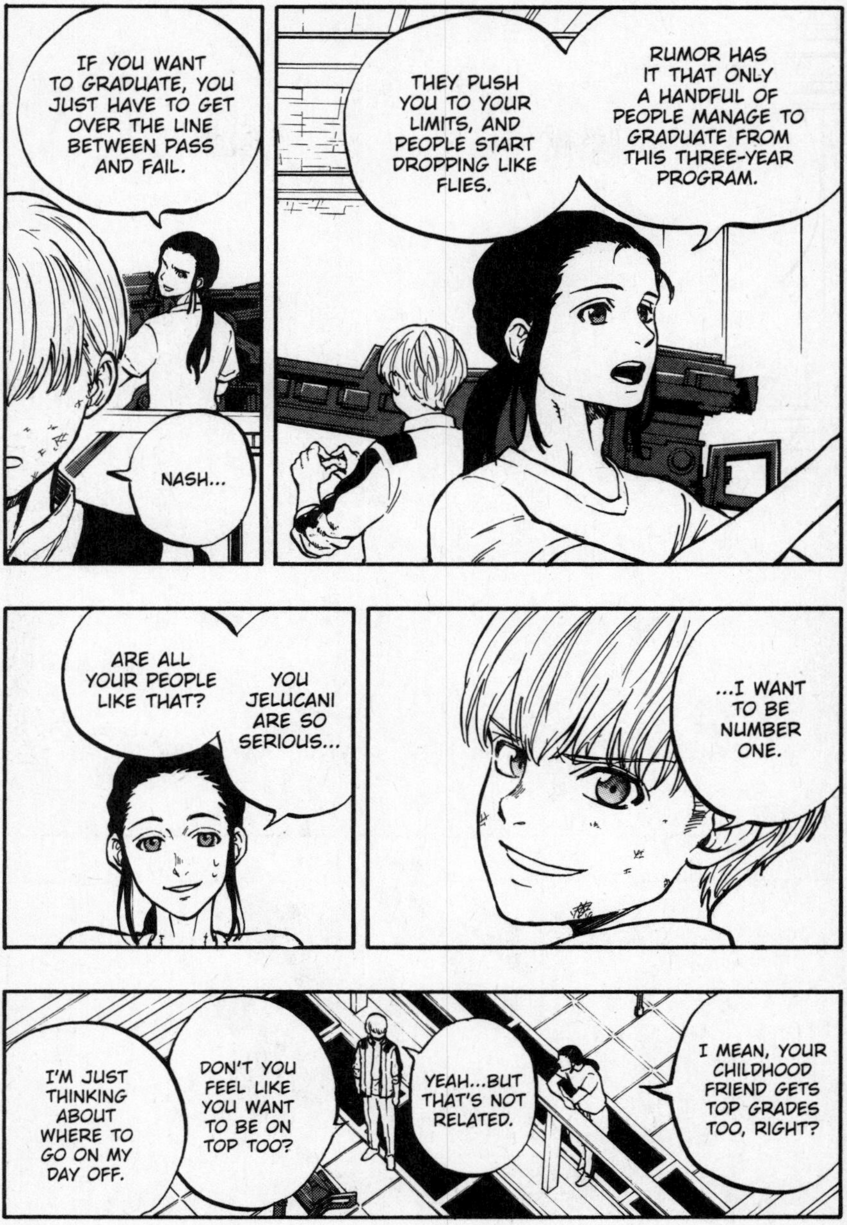
RUMOR HAS IT THAT ONLY A HANDFUL OF PEOPLE MANAGE TO GRADUATE FROM THIS THREE-YEAR PROGRAM.
THEY PUSH YOU TO YOUR LIMITS, AND PEOPLE START DROPPING LIKE FLIES.
IF YOU WANT TO GRADUATE, YOU JUST HAVE TO GET OVER THE LINE BETWEEN PASS AND FAIL.
NASH...
...I WANT TO BE NUMBER ONE.
YOU JELUCANI ARE SO SERIOUS...
ARE ALL YOUR PEOPLE LIKE THAT?
I MEAN, YOUR CHILDHOOD FRIEND GETS TOP GRADES TOO, RIGHT?
YEAH...BUT THAT'S NOT RELATED.
DON'T YOU FEEL LIKE YOU WANT TO BE ON TOP TOO?
I'M JUST THINKING ABOUT WHERE TO GO ON MY DAY OFF.

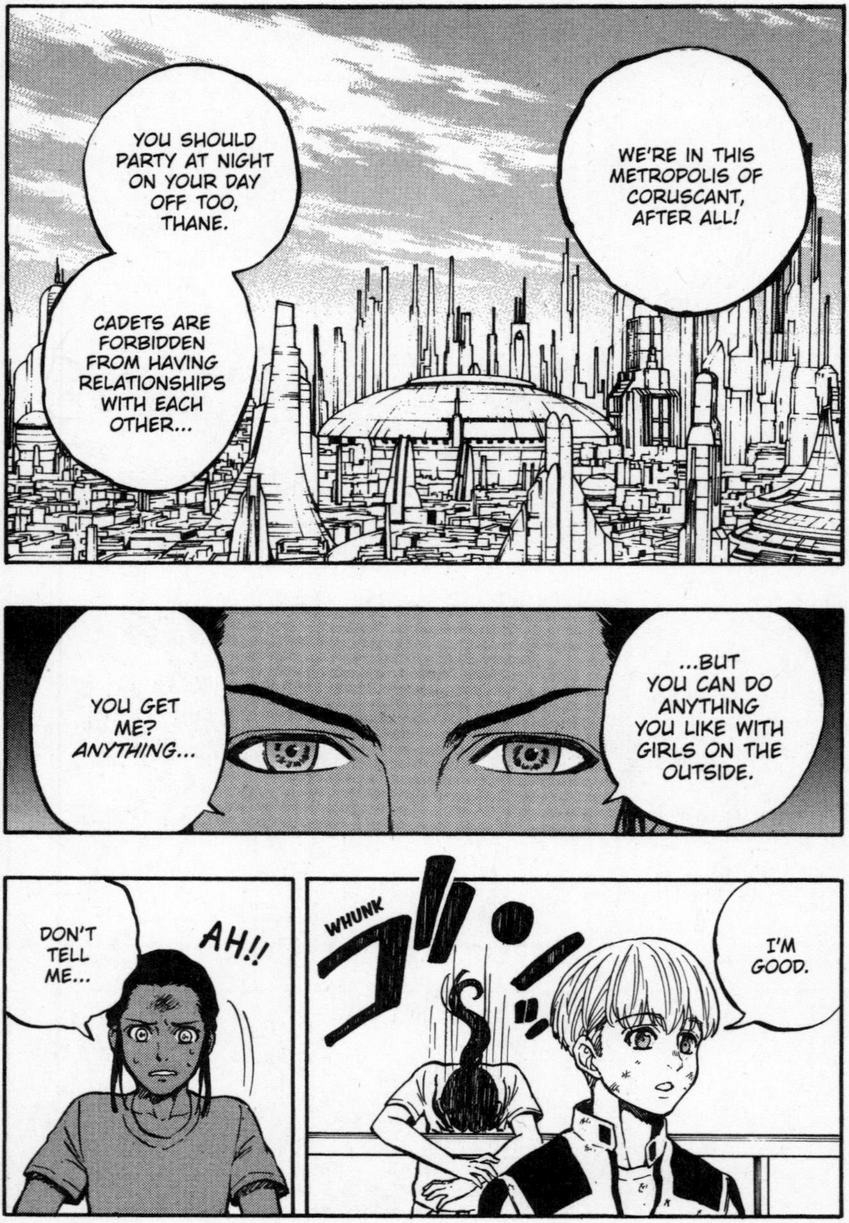
WE'RE IN THIS METROPOLIS OF CORUSCANT, AFTER ALL!
YOU SHOULD PARTY AT NIGHT ON YOUR DAY OFF TOO, THANE.
CADETS ARE FORBIDDEN FROM HAVING RELATIONSHIPS WITH EACH OTHER...
...BUT YOU CAN DO ANYTHING YOU LIKE WITH GIRLS ON THE OUTSIDE.
YOU GET ME? ANYTHING...
I'M GOOD.
WHUNK
AH!!
DON'T TELL ME...

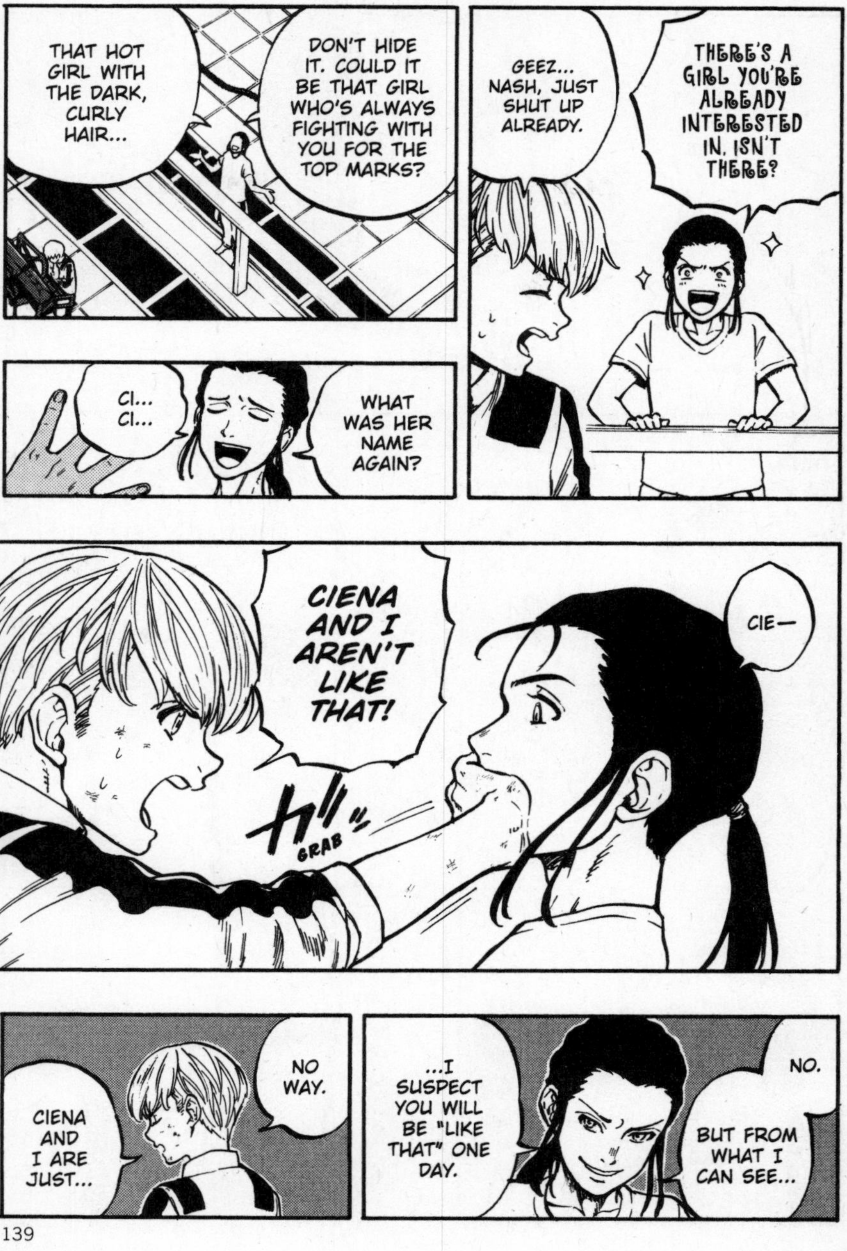
THERE'S A GIRL YOU'RE ALREADY INTERESTED IN, ISN'T THERE?
GEEZ... NASH, JUST SHUT UP ALREADY.
DON'T HIDE IT. COULD IT BE THAT GIRL WHO'S ALWAYS FIGHTING WITH YOU FOR THE TOP MARKS?
THAT HOT GIRL WITH THE DARK, CURLY HAIR...
WHAT WAS HER NAME AGAIN?
CI... CI...
CIE—
CIENA AND I AREN'T LIKE THAT!
GRAB
NO.
BUT FROM WHAT I CAN SEE...
...I SUSPECT YOU WILL BE "LIKE THAT" ONE DAY.
NO WAY.
CIENA AND I ARE JUST...

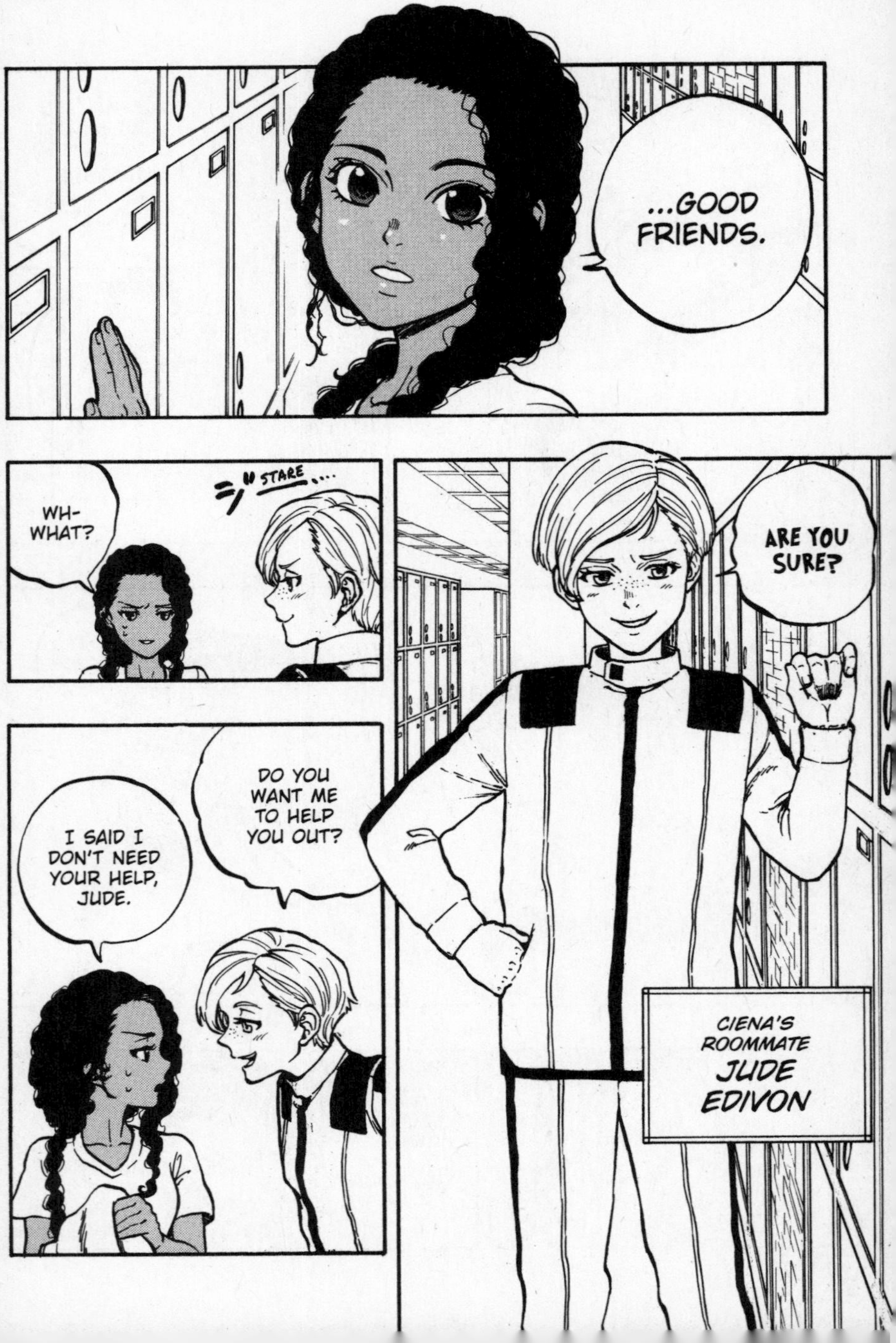
...GOOD FRIENDS.
ARE YOU SURE?
CIENA'S ROOMMATE JUDE EDIVON
STARE....
WH- WHAT?
DO YOU WANT ME TO HELP YOU OUT?
I SAID I DON'T NEED YOUR HELP, JUDE.

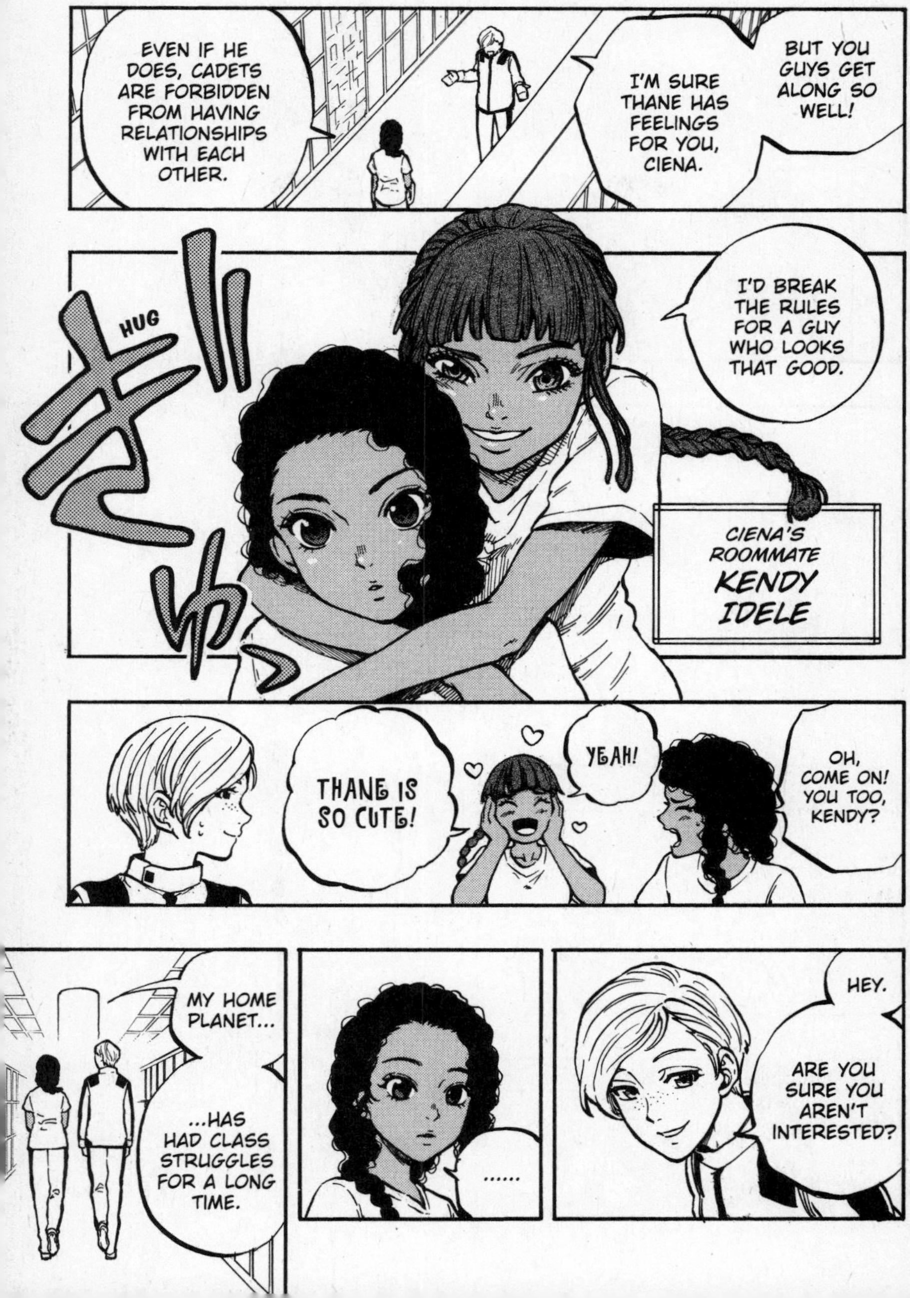
BUT YOU GUYS GET ALONG SO WELL!
I'M SURE THANE HAS FEELINGS FOR YOU, CIENA.
EVEN IF HE DOES, CADETS ARE FORBIDDEN FROM HAVING RELATIONSHIPS WITH EACH OTHER.
I'D BREAK THE RULES FOR A GUY WHO LOOKS THAT GOOD.
CIENA'S ROOMMATE KENDY IDELE
HUG
ぎゅ
OH, COME ON! YOU TOO, KENDY?
YEAH!
THANE IS SO CUTE!
HEY.
ARE YOU SURE YOU AREN'T INTERESTED?
......
MY HOME PLANET...
...HAS HAD CLASS STRUGGLES FOR A LONG TIME.

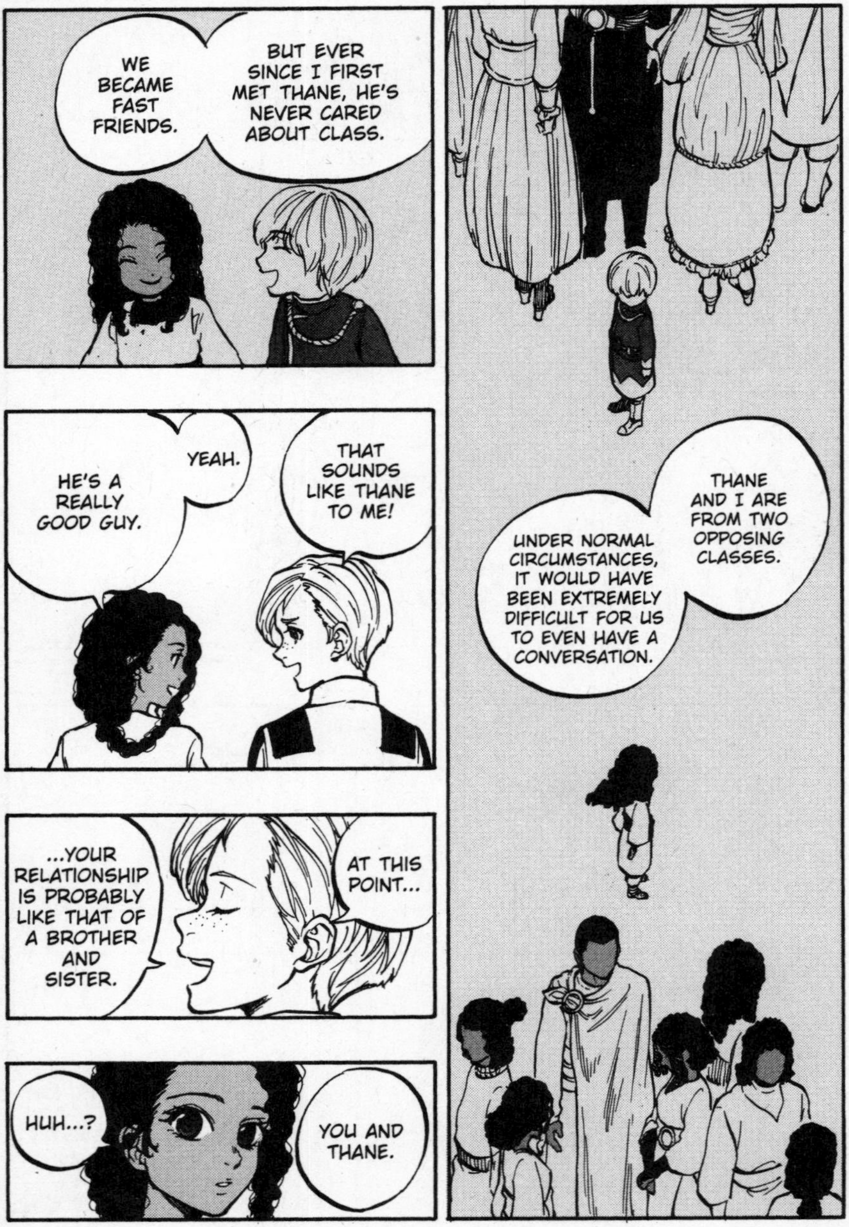
THANE AND I ARE FROM TWO OPPOSING CLASSES.
UNDER NORMAL CIRCUMSTANCES, IT WOULD HAVE BEEN EXTREMELY DIFFICULT FOR US TO EVEN HAVE A CONVERSATION.
BUT EVER SINCE I FIRST MET THANE, HE'S NEVER CARED ABOUT CLASS.
WE BECAME FAST FRIENDS.
THAT SOUNDS LIKE THANE TO ME!
YEAH.
HE'S A REALLY GOOD GUY.
AT THIS POINT...
...YOUR RELATIONSHIP IS PROBABLY LIKE THAT OF A BROTHER AND SISTER.
YOU AND THANE.
HUH...?

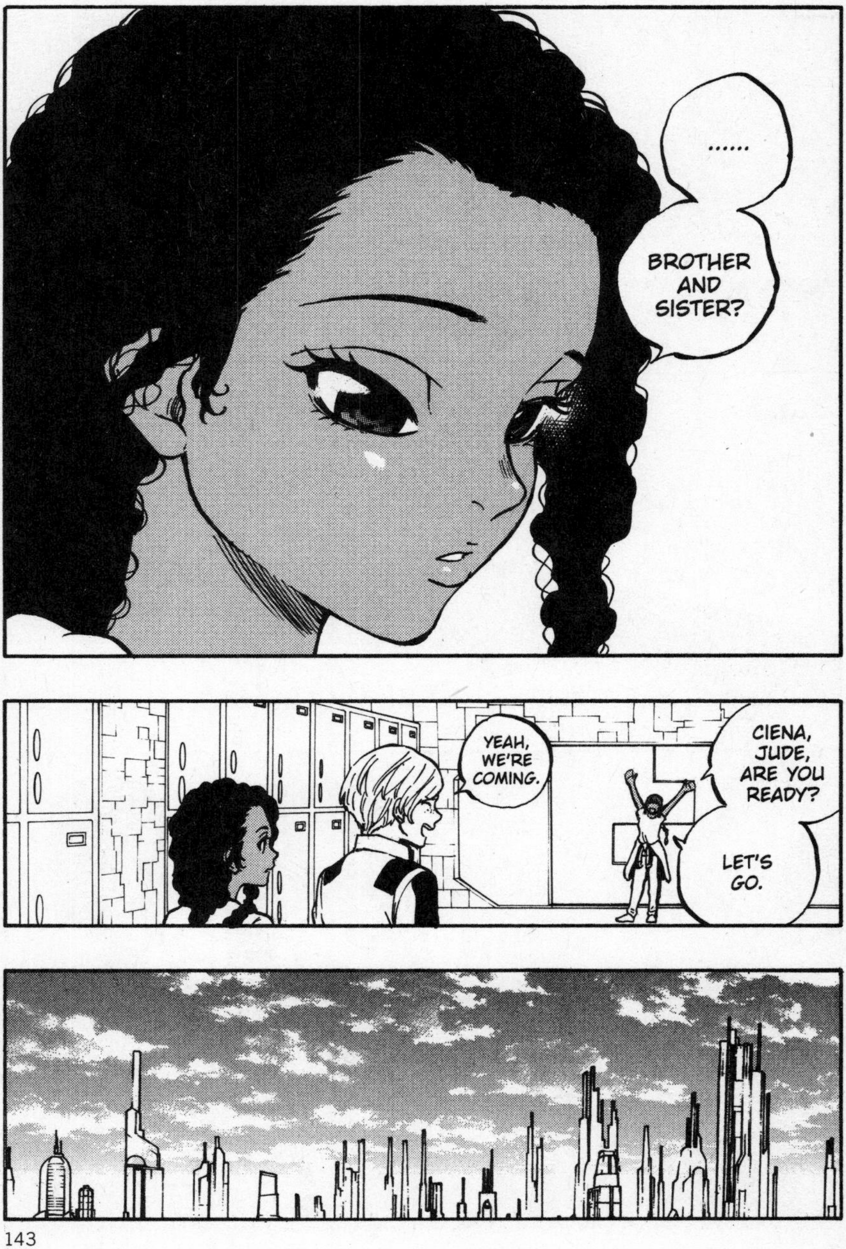
......
BROTHER AND SISTER?
CIENA, JUDE, ARE YOU READY?
LET'S GO.
YEAH, WE'RE COMING.

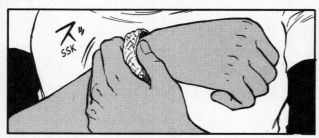

スッ
SSK

"HEY, CIENA.

"IS THAT SOME KIND OF GOOD LUCK CHARM?"

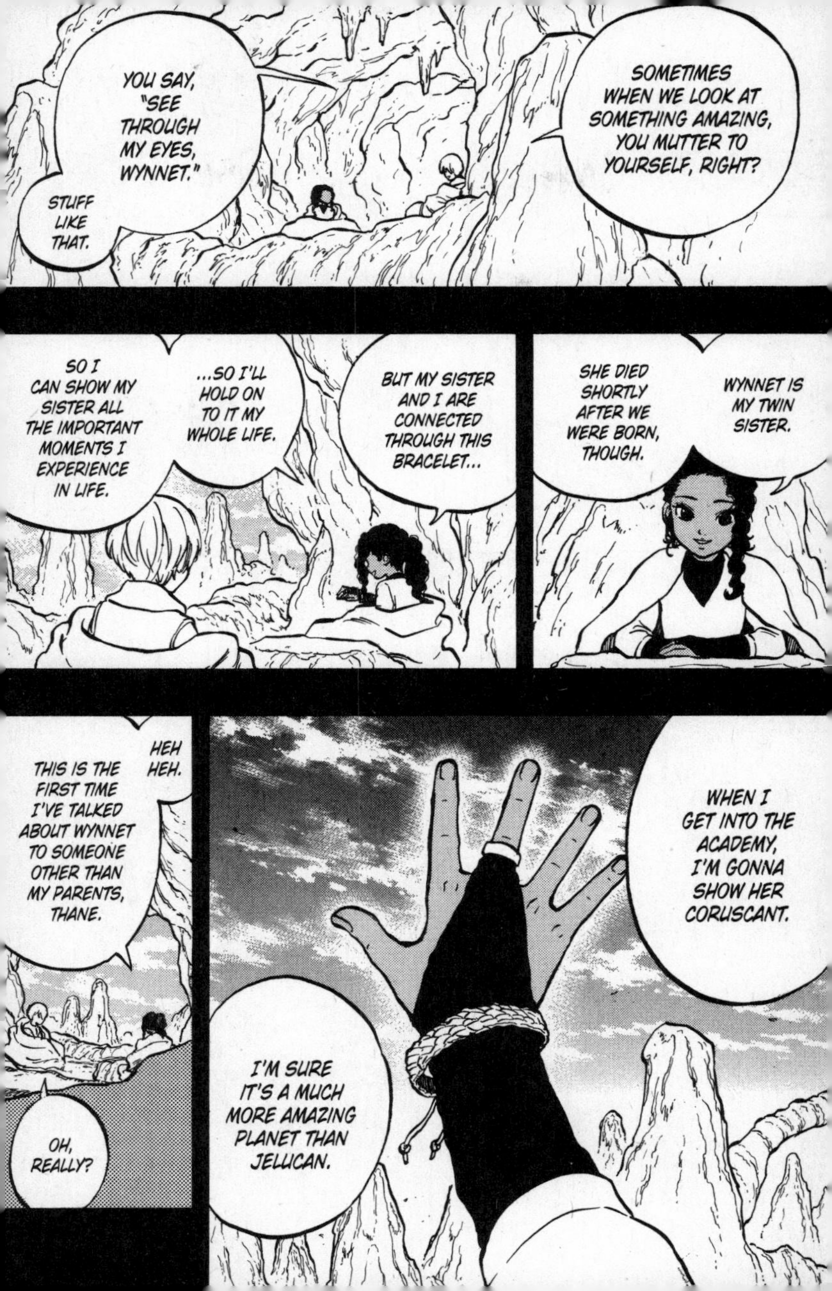
SOMETIMES WHEN WE LOOK AT SOMETHING AMAZING, YOU MUTTER TO YOURSELF, RIGHT?
YOU SAY, "SEE THROUGH MY EYES, WYNNET."
STUFF LIKE THAT.
WYNNET IS MY TWIN SISTER.
SHE DIED SHORTLY AFTER WE WERE BORN, THOUGH.
BUT MY SISTER AND I ARE CONNECTED THROUGH THIS BRACELET...
...SO I'LL HOLD ON TO IT MY WHOLE LIFE.
SO I CAN SHOW MY SISTER ALL THE IMPORTANT MOMENTS I EXPERIENCE IN LIFE.
WHEN I GET INTO THE ACADEMY, I'M GONNA SHOW HER CORUSCANT.
I'M SURE IT'S A MUCH MORE AMAZING PLANET THAN JELUCAN.
HEH HEH.
THIS IS THE FIRST TIME I'VE TALKED ABOUT WYNNET TO SOMEONE OTHER THAN MY PARENTS, THANE.
OH, REALLY?

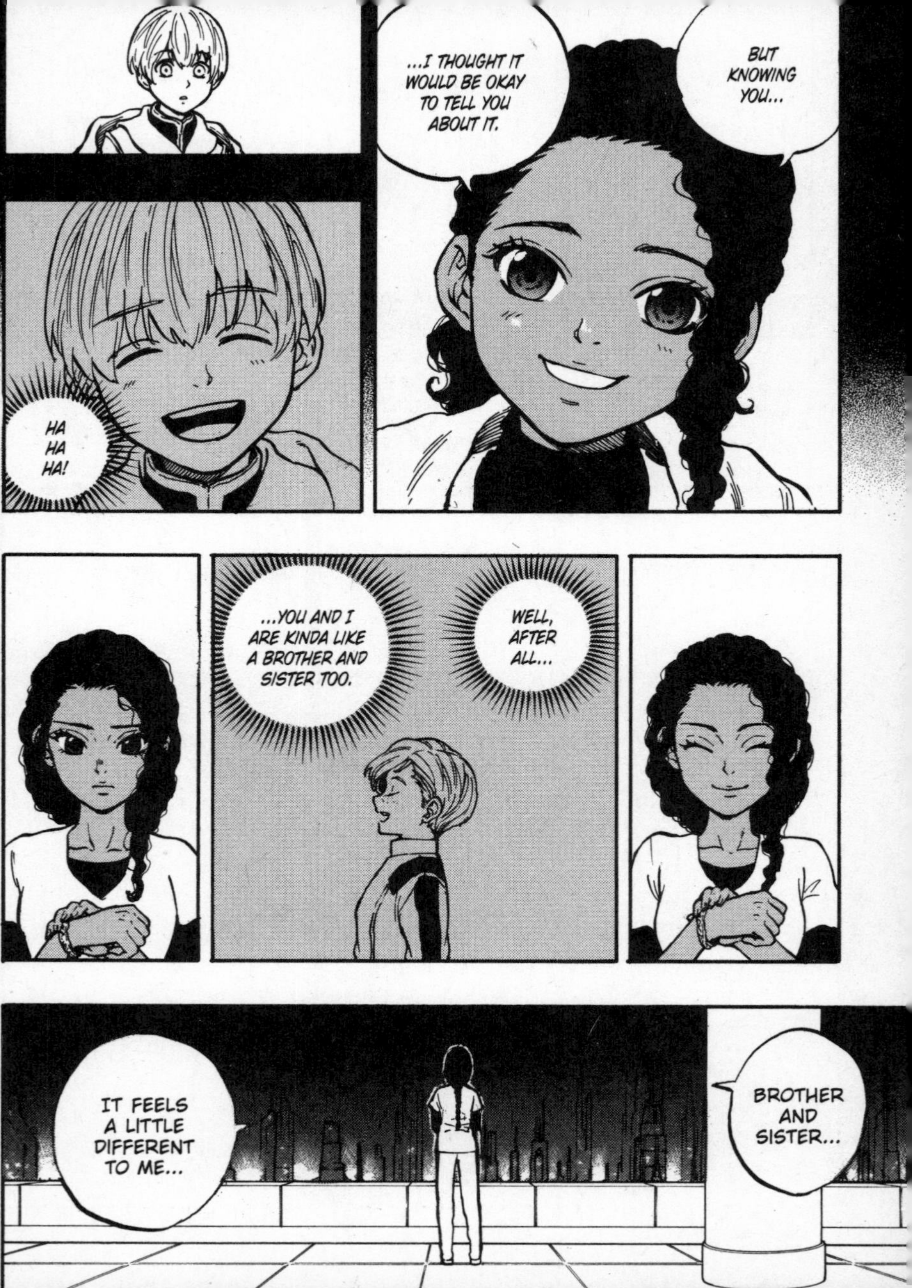
BUT KNOWING YOU...
...I THOUGHT IT WOULD BE OKAY TO TELL YOU ABOUT IT.
HA HA HA!
WELL, AFTER ALL...
...YOU AND I ARE KINDA LIKE A BROTHER AND SISTER TOO.
BROTHER AND SISTER...
IT FEELS A LITTLE DIFFERENT TO ME...

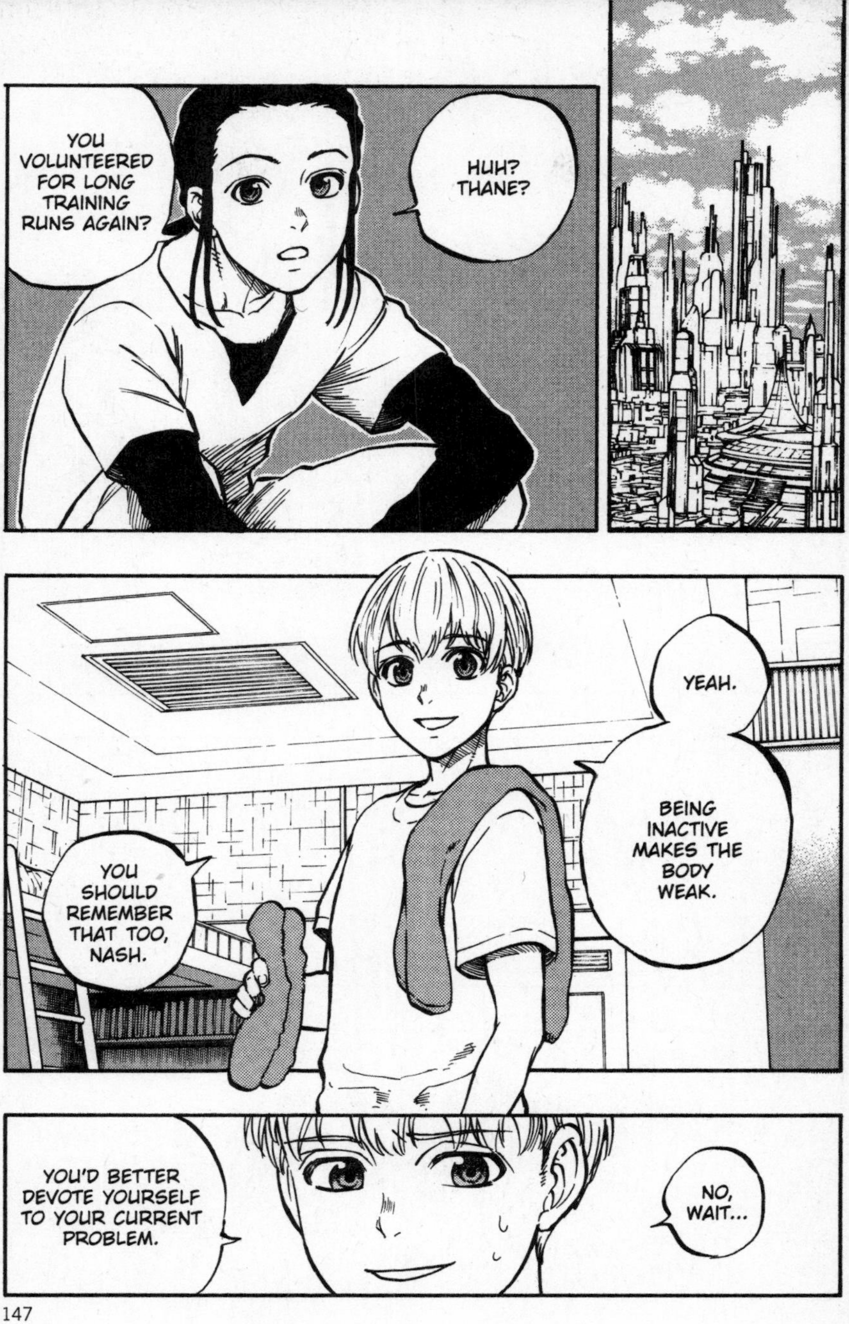
HUH? THANE?
YOU VOLUNTEERED FOR LONG TRAINING RUNS AGAIN?
YEAH.
BEING INACTIVE MAKES THE BODY WEAK.
YOU SHOULD REMEMBER THAT TOO, NASH.
NO, WAIT...
YOU'D BETTER DEVOTE YOURSELF TO YOUR CURRENT PROBLEM.

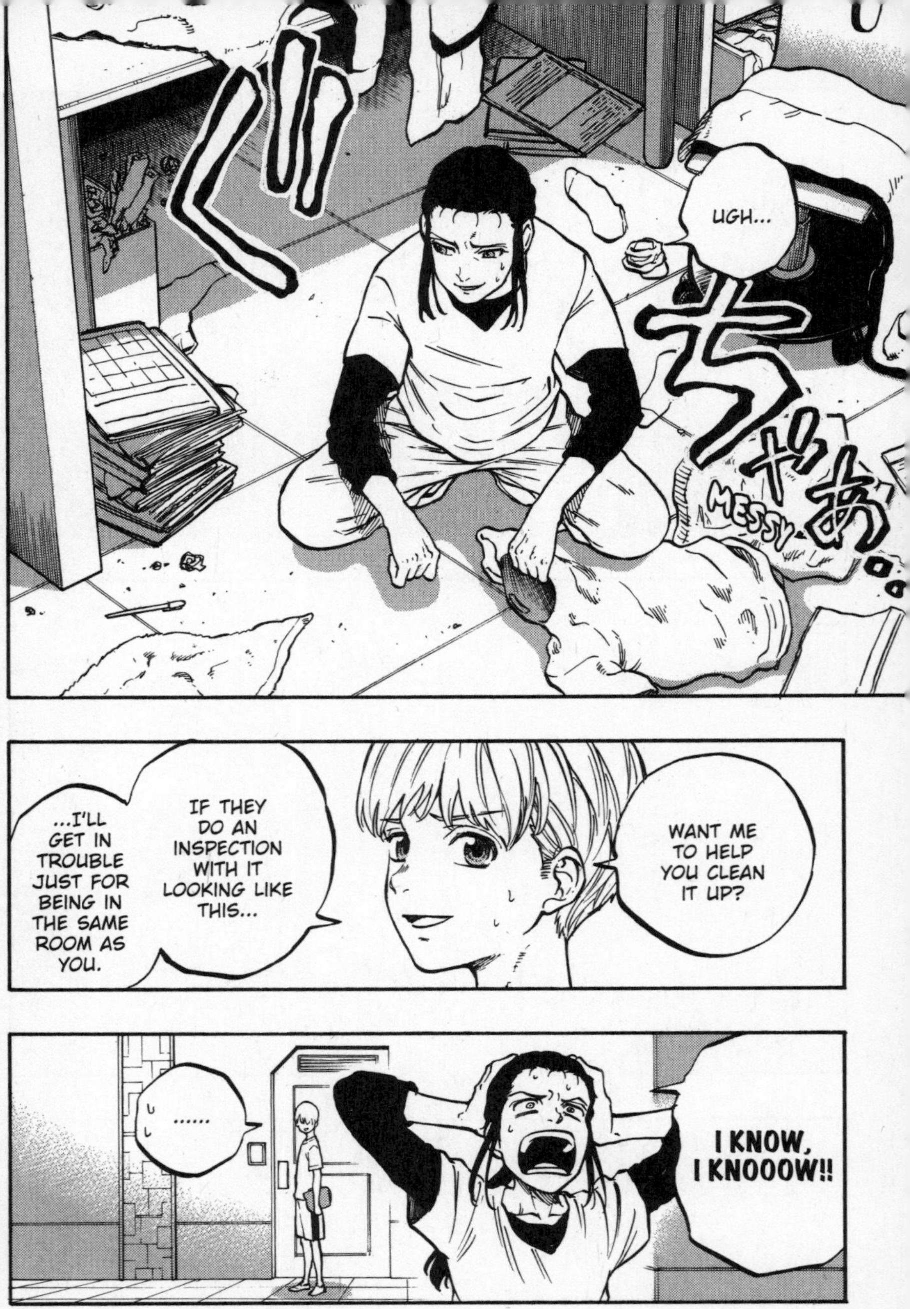
UGH...
MESSY
WANT ME TO HELP YOU CLEAN IT UP?
IF THEY DO AN INSPECTION WITH IT LOOKING LIKE THIS...
...I'LL GET IN TROUBLE JUST FOR BEING IN THE SAME ROOM AS YOU.
I KNOW, I KNOOOW!!
......

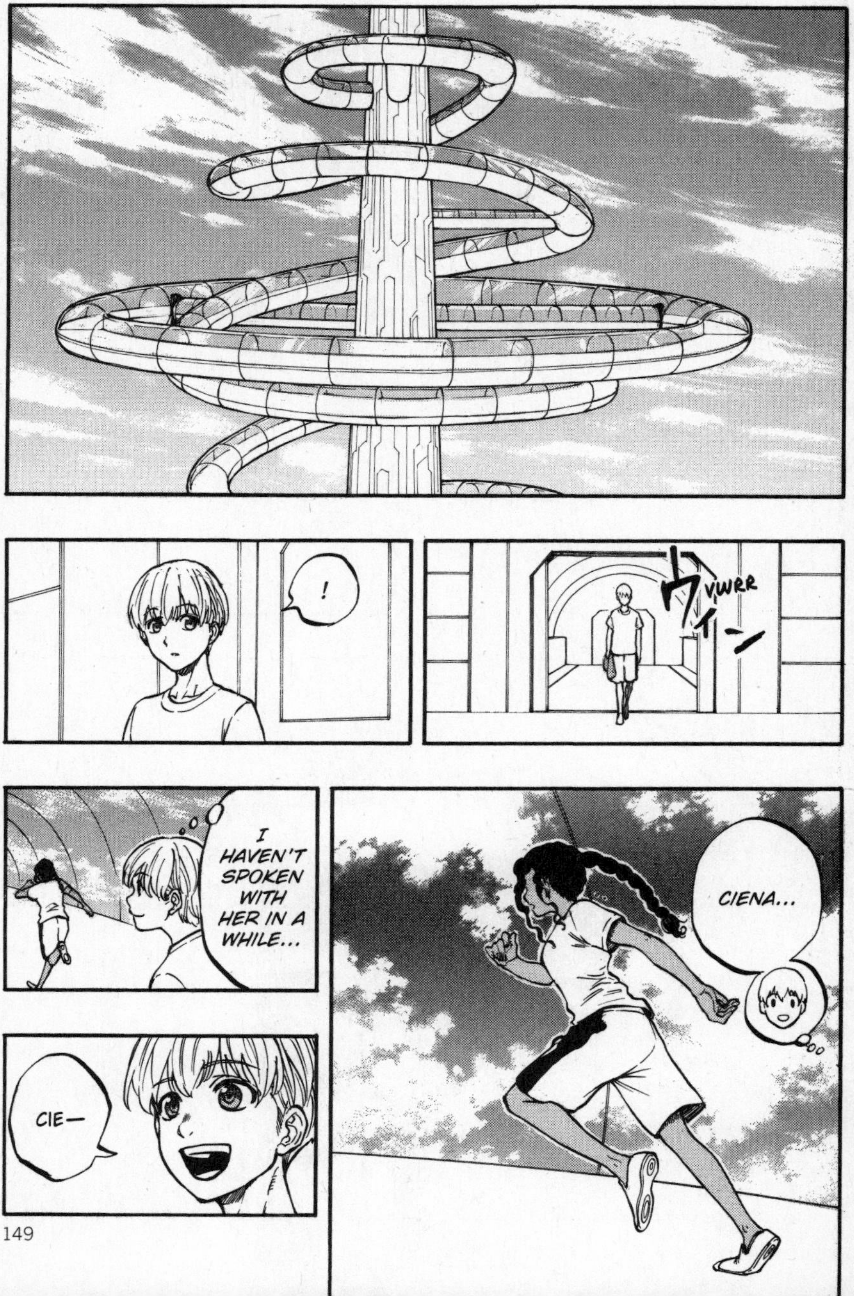
VWRR
!
CIENA...
I HAVEN'T SPOKEN WITH HER IN A WHILE...
CIE—

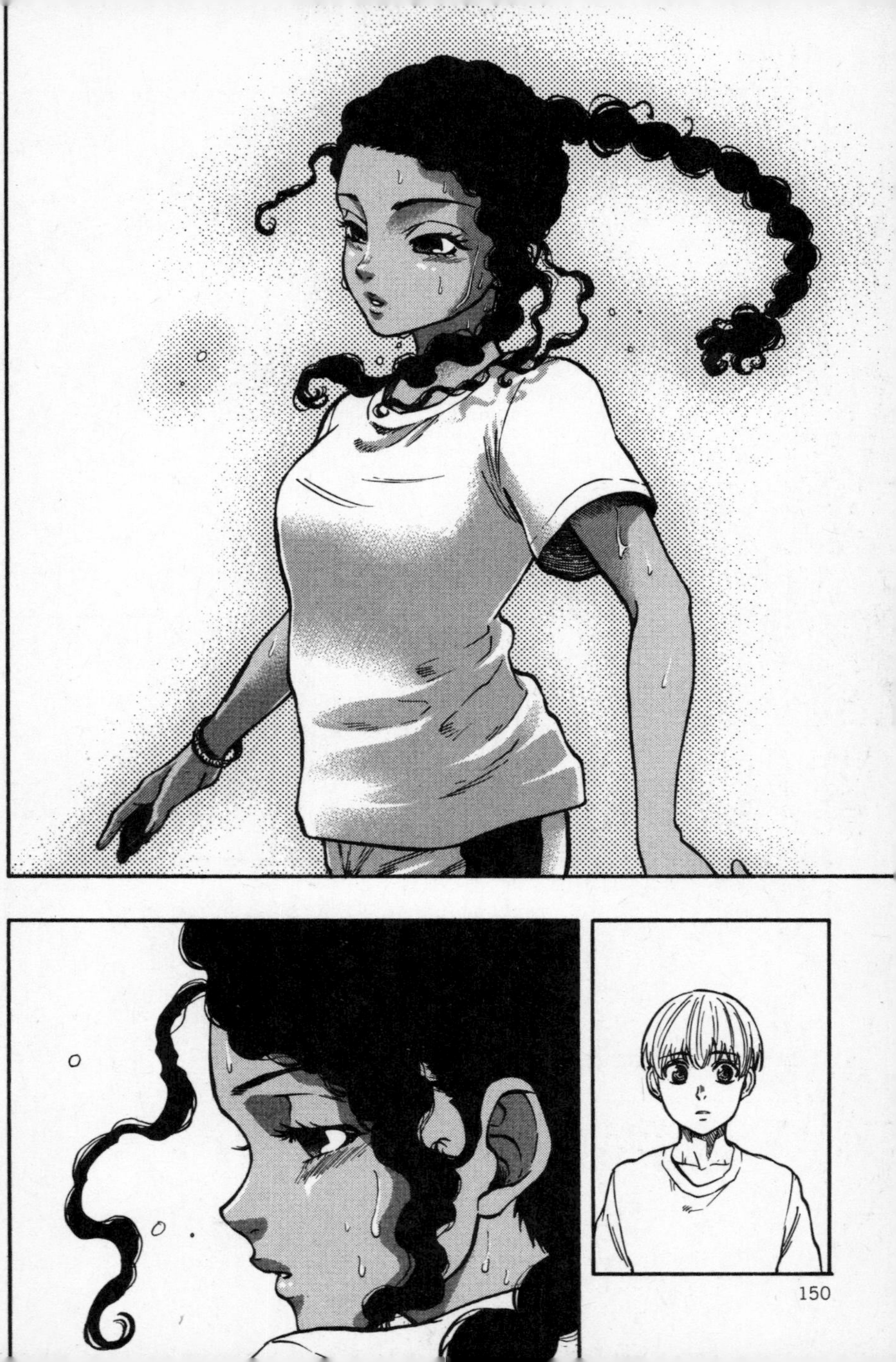

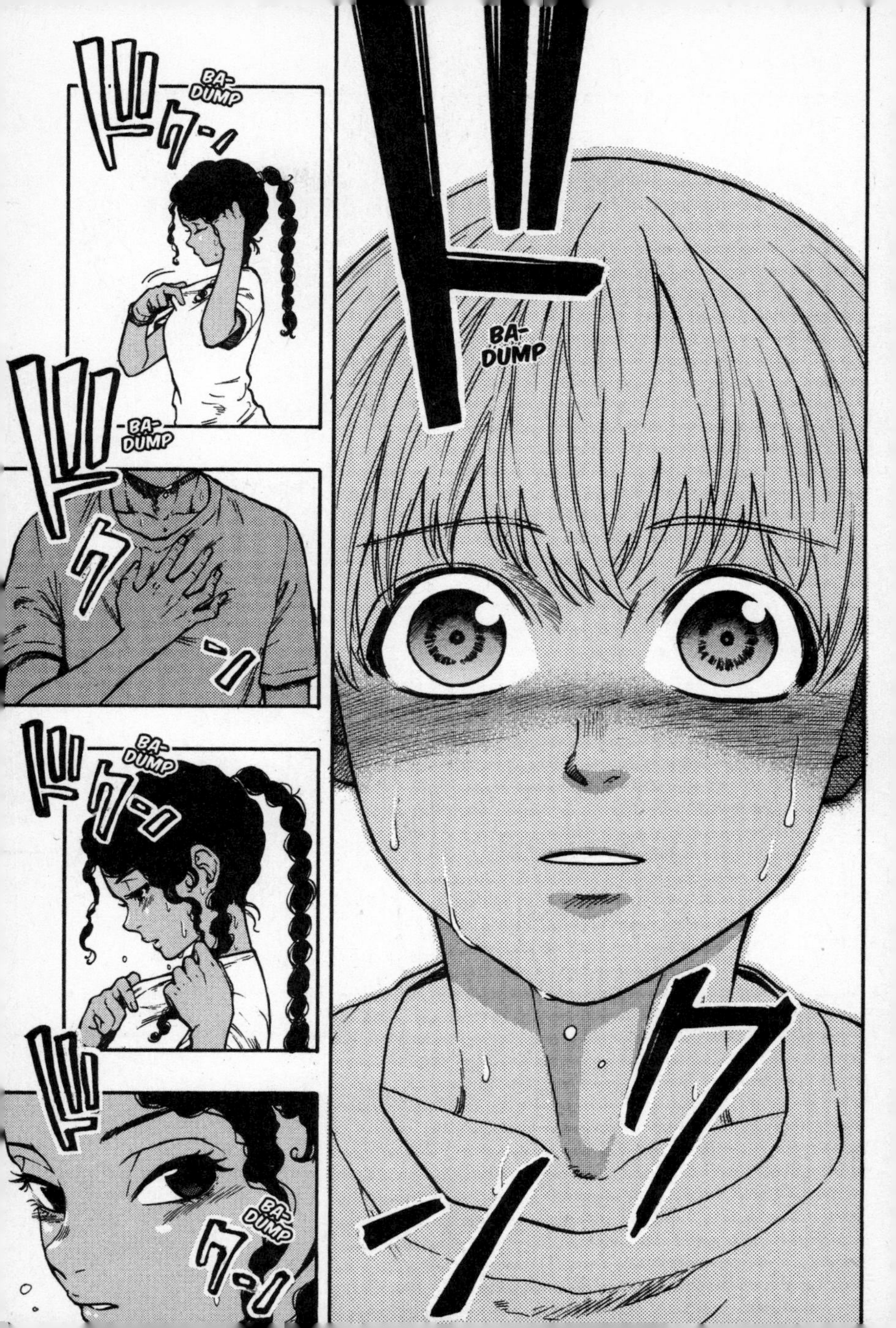
BA-DUMP
BA-DUMP
BA-DUMP
BA-DUMP
BA-DUMP

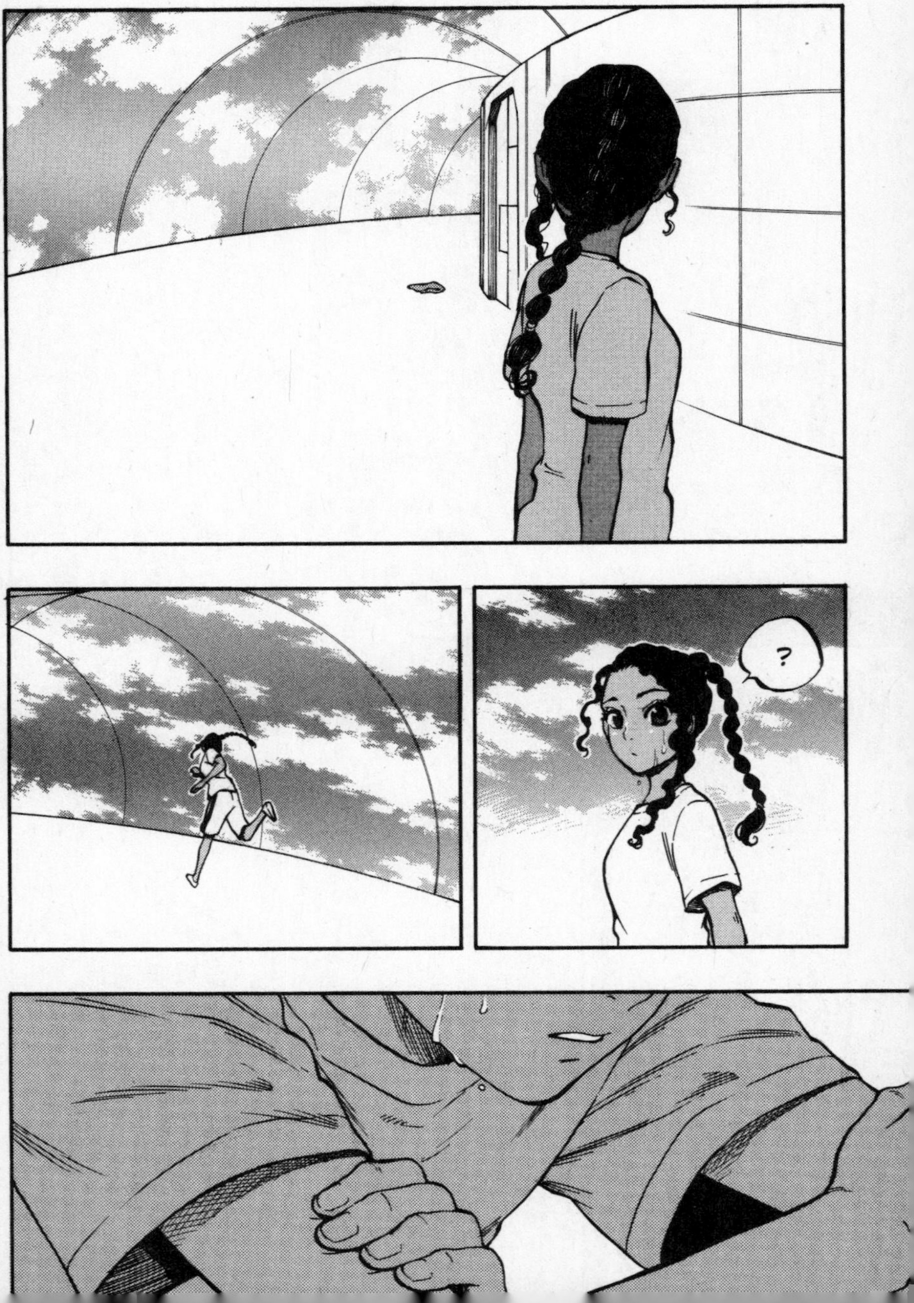
?

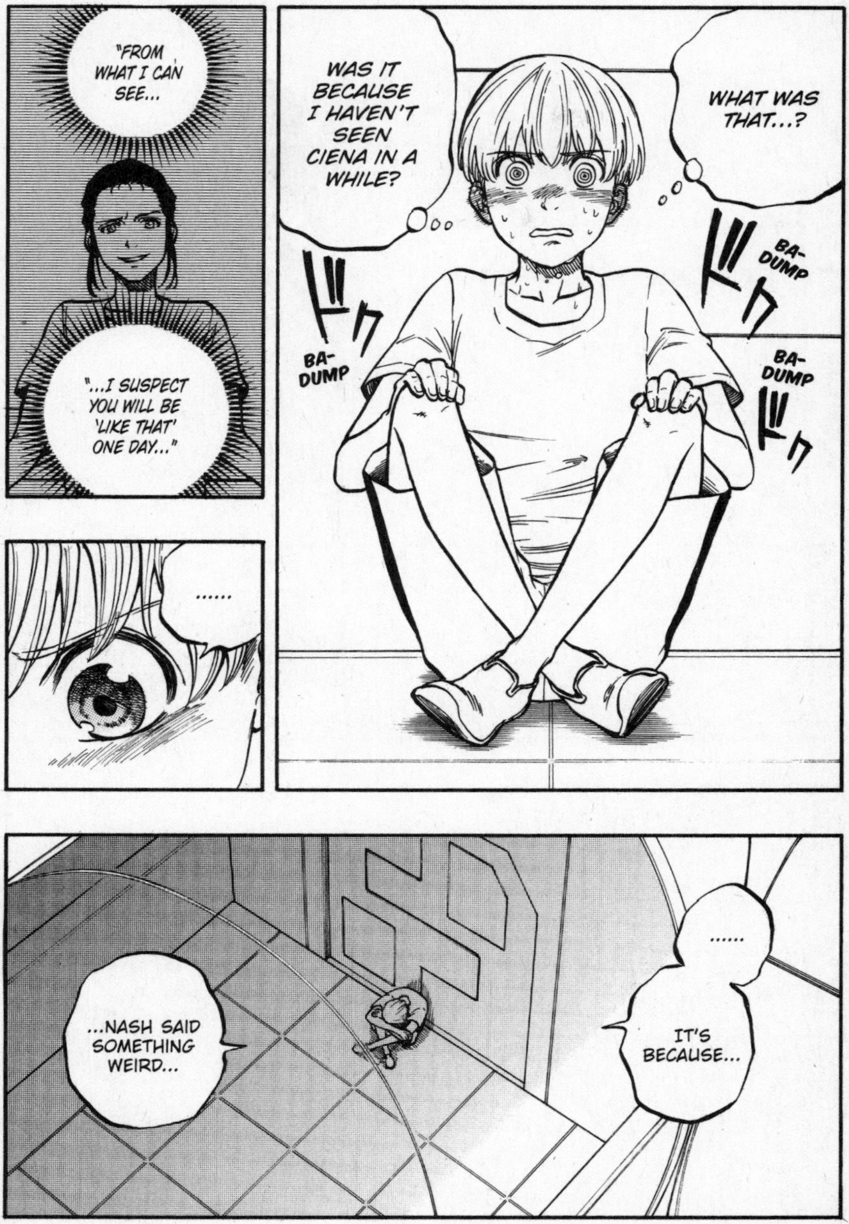
WHAT WAS THAT...?
WAS IT BECAUSE I HAVEN'T SEEN CIENA IN A WHILE?
ドク
BA-DUMP
ドク
BA-DUMP
BA-DUMP
ドク
"FROM WHAT I CAN SEE...
"...I SUSPECT YOU WILL BE 'LIKE THAT' ONE DAY..."
......
......
IT'S BECAUSE...
...NASH SAID SOMETHING WEIRD...

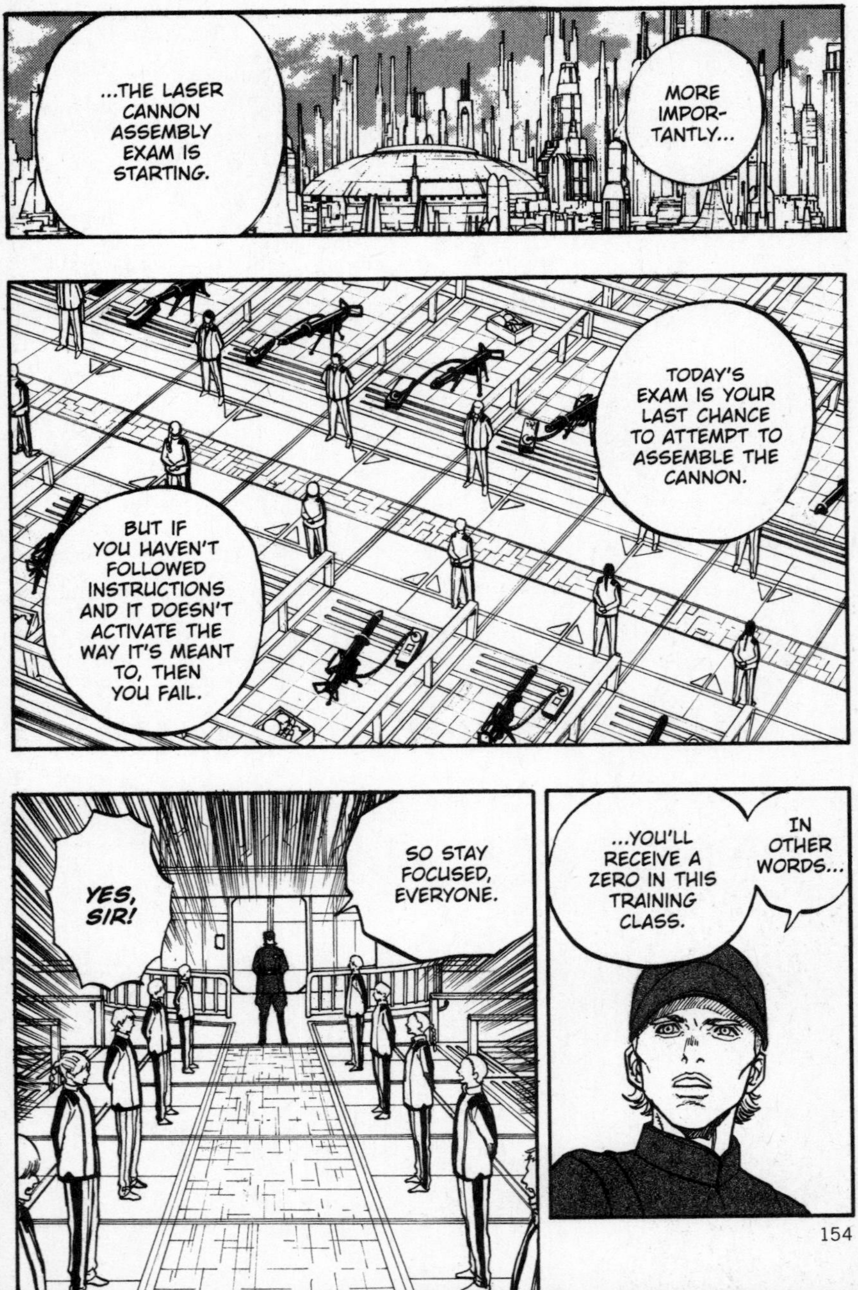
MORE IMPORTANTLY...
...THE LASER CANNON ASSEMBLY EXAM IS STARTING.
TODAY'S EXAM IS YOUR LAST CHANCE TO ATTEMPT TO ASSEMBLE THE CANNON.
BUT IF YOU HAVEN'T FOLLOWED INSTRUCTIONS AND IT DOESN'T ACTIVATE THE WAY IT'S MEANT TO, THEN YOU FAIL.
IN OTHER WORDS...
...YOU'LL RECEIVE A ZERO IN THIS TRAINING CLASS.
SO STAY FOCUSED, EVERYONE.
YES, SIR!

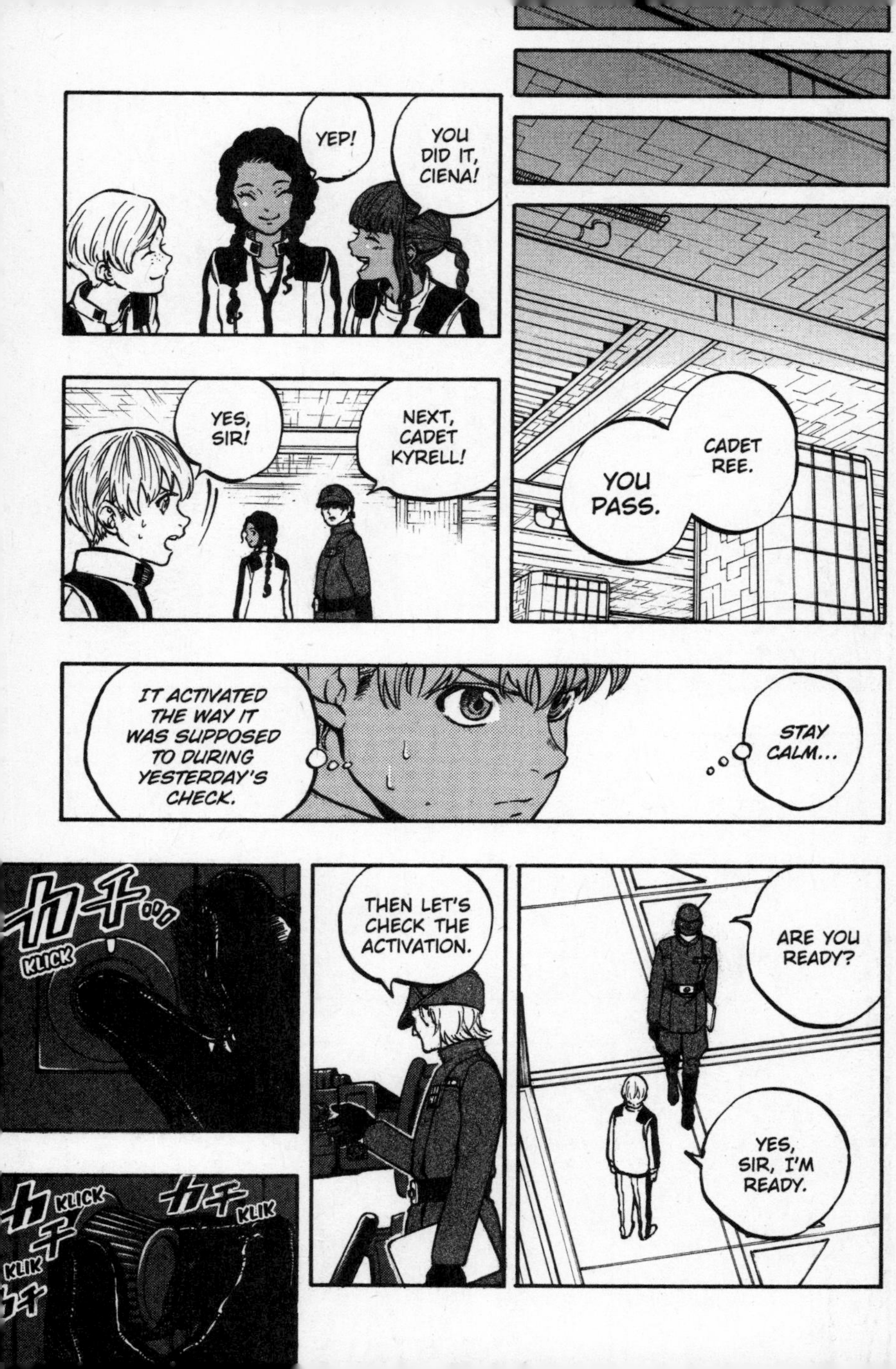
CADET REE.
YOU PASS.
YOU DID IT, CIENA!
YEP!
NEXT, CADET KYRELL!
YES, SIR!
STAY CALM...
IT ACTIVATED THE WAY IT WAS SUPPOSED TO DURING YESTERDAY'S CHECK.
ARE YOU READY?
YES, SIR, I'M READY.
THEN LET'S CHECK THE ACTIVATION.
カチ。。。
KLICK
カチ
KLIK
カチ
KLICK
KLIK
カチ

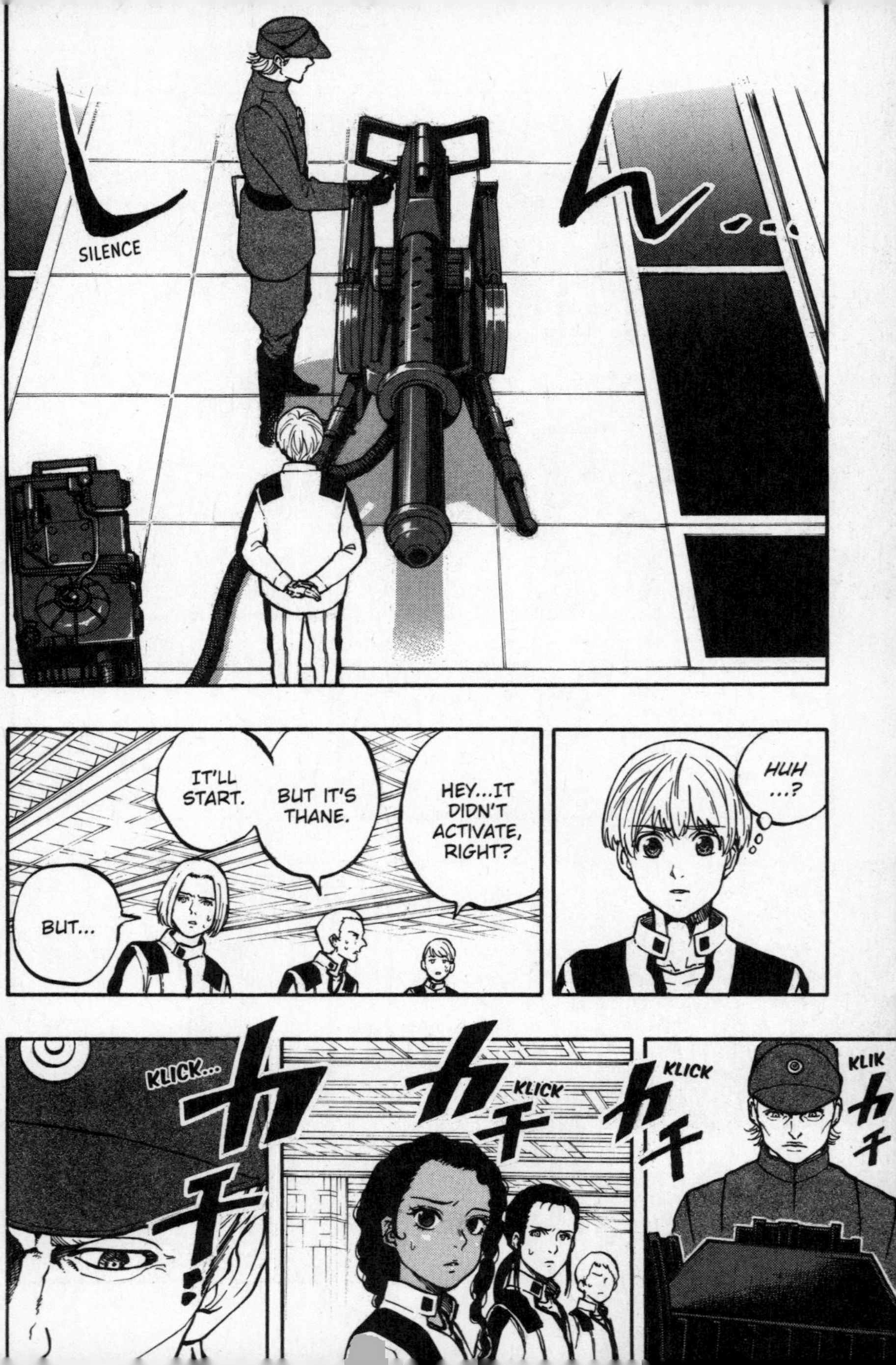
しーん...
SILENCE
HUH ...?
HEY...IT DIDN'T ACTIVATE, RIGHT?
BUT IT'S THANE.
IT'LL START.
BUT...
KLIK
カチ
KLICK
カチ
KLICK
カチ
KLICK...
カチ

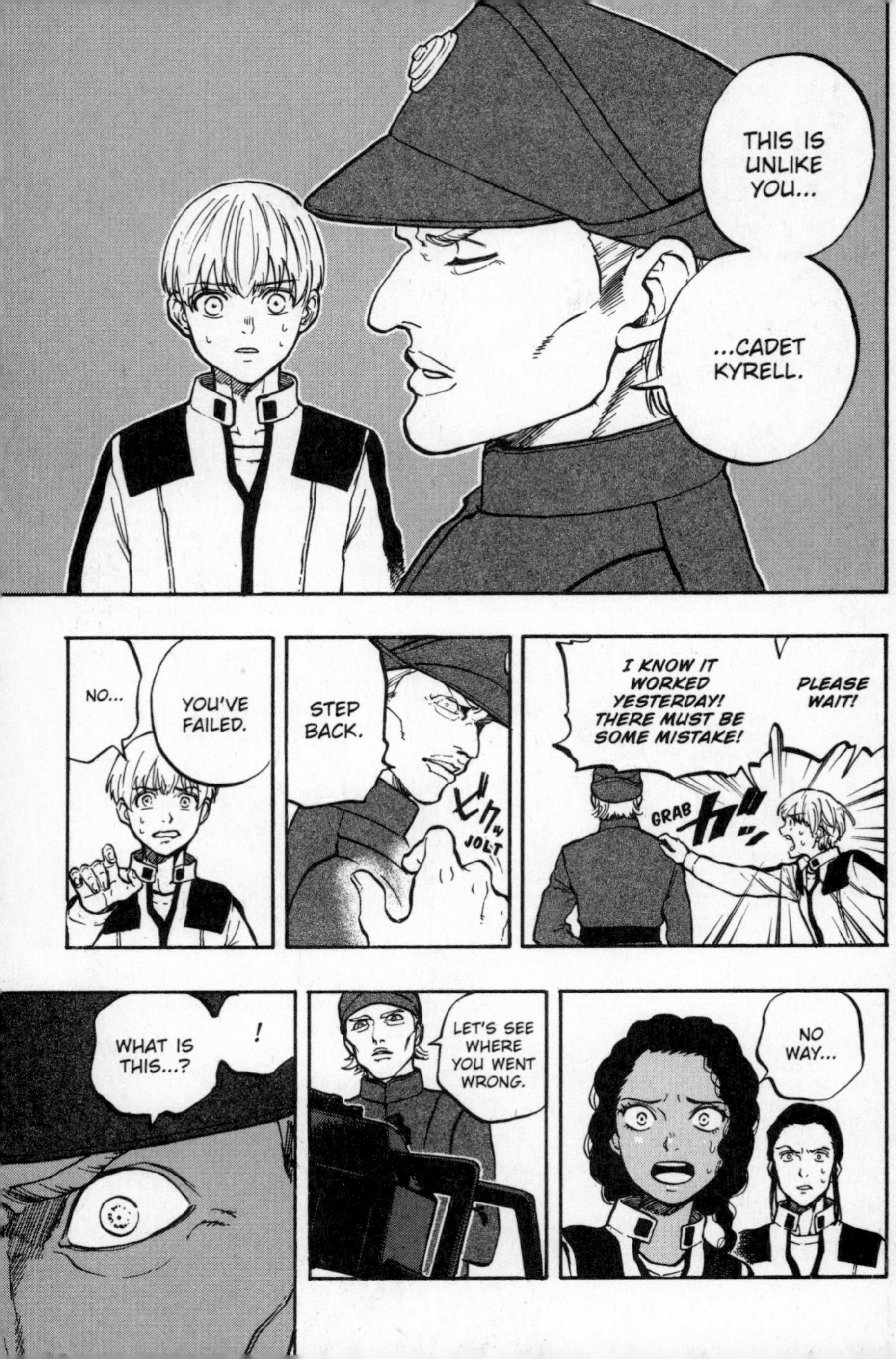
THIS IS UNLIKE YOU...
...CADET KYRELL.
PLEASE WAIT!
I KNOW IT WORKED YESTERDAY! THERE MUST BE SOME MISTAKE!
GRAB
STEP BACK.
JOLT
YOU'VE FAILED.
NO...
NO WAY...
LET'S SEE WHERE YOU WENT WRONG.
!
WHAT IS THIS...?

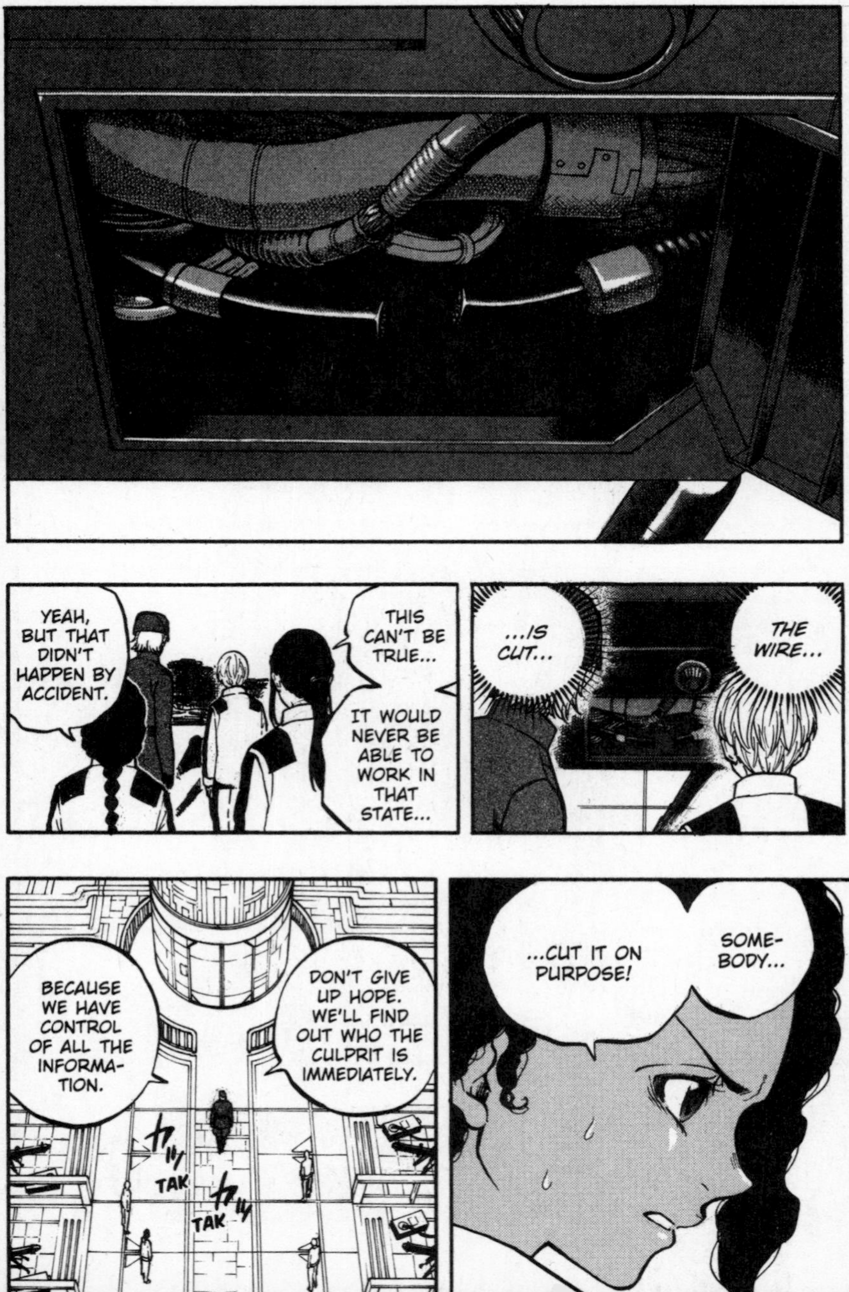
THE WIRE...
...IS CUT...
THIS CAN'T BE TRUE...
IT WOULD NEVER BE ABLE TO WORK IN THAT STATE...
YEAH, BUT THAT DIDN'T HAPPEN BY ACCIDENT.
SOME-BODY...
...CUT IT ON PURPOSE!
DON'T GIVE UP HOPE. WE'LL FIND OUT WHO THE CULPRIT IS IMMEDIATELY.
BECAUSE WE HAVE CONTROL OF ALL THE INFORMA-TION.
TAK
TAK

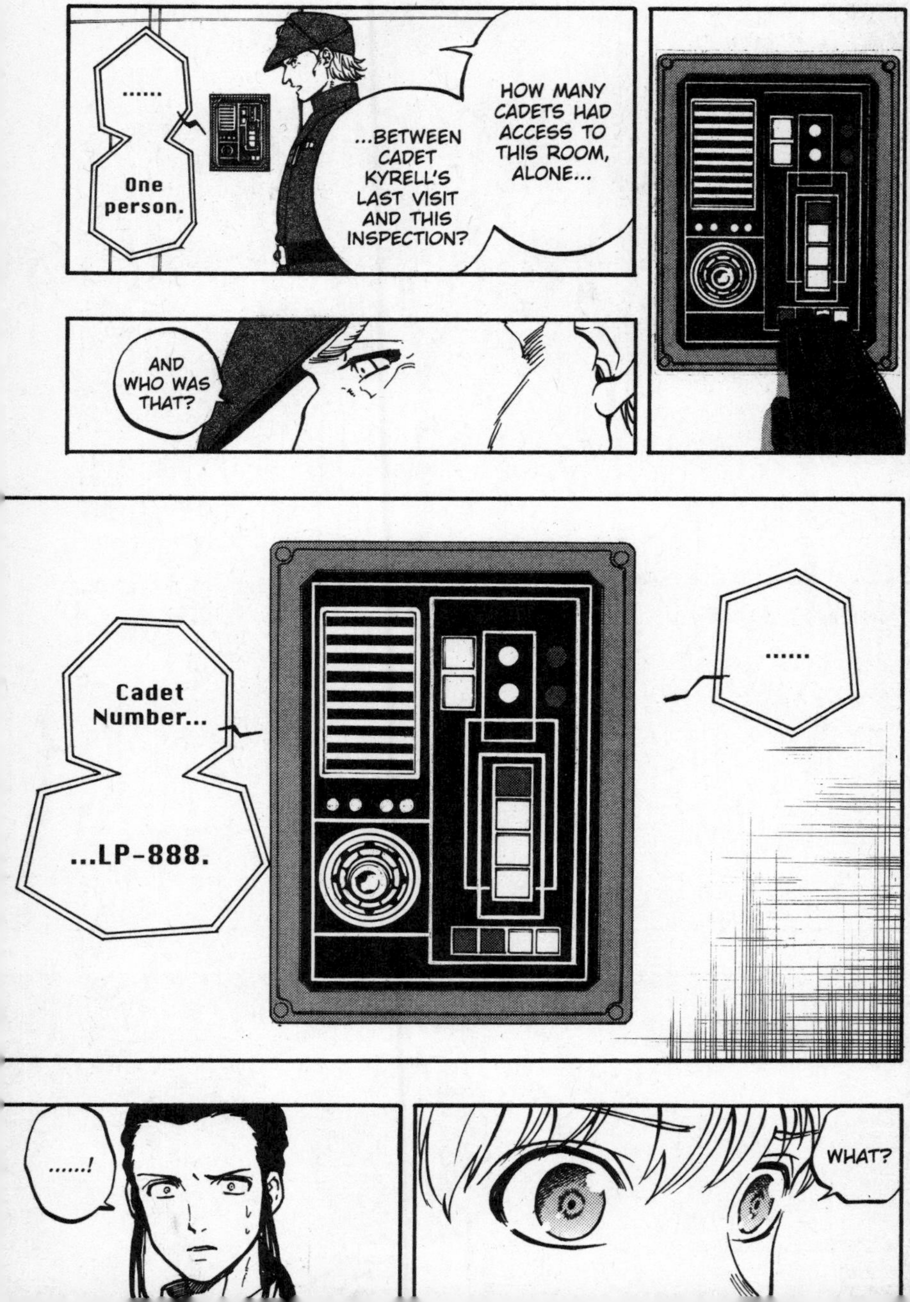
HOW MANY CADETS HAD ACCESS TO THIS ROOM, ALONE...
...BETWEEN CADET KYRELL'S LAST VISIT AND THIS INSPECTION?
......
One person.
AND WHO WAS THAT?
......
Cadet Number...
...LP-888.
WHAT?
......!

It was
Cadet
Ciena
Ree.

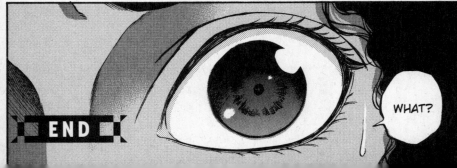

END

WHAT?

STAR WARS
LOST STARS

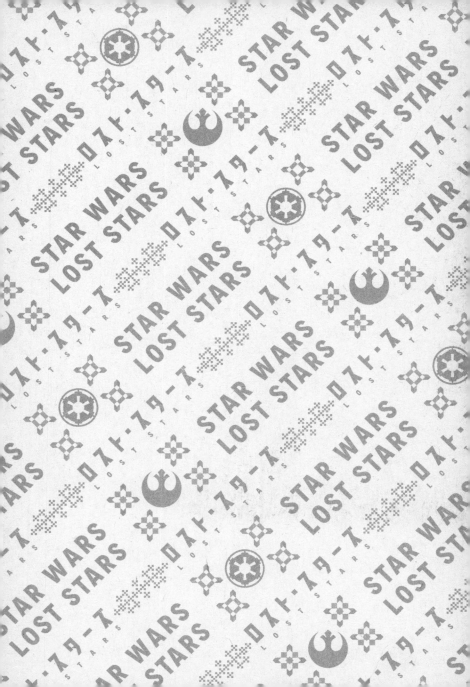

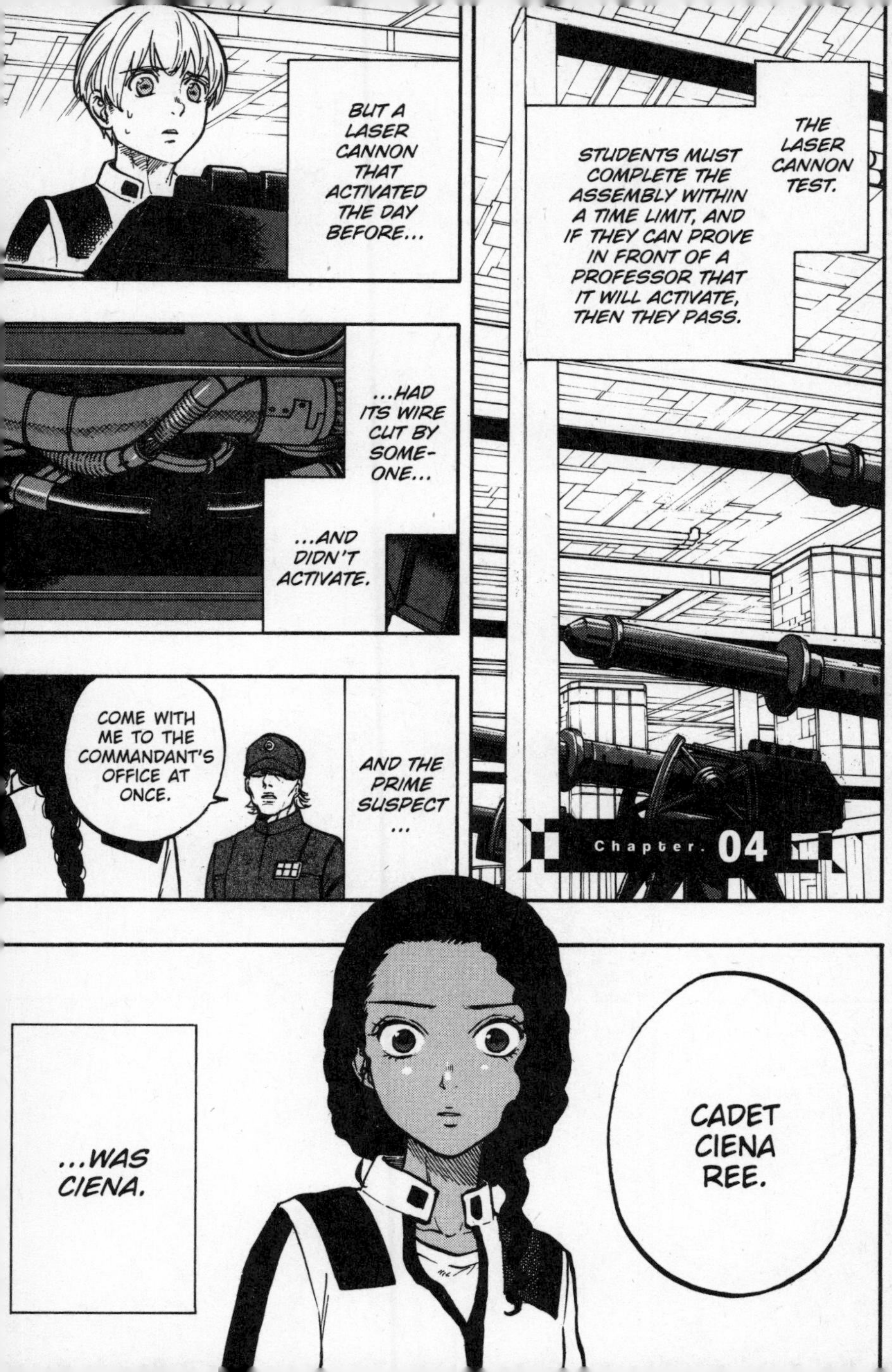
THE LASER CANNON TEST.
STUDENTS MUST COMPLETE THE ASSEMBLY WITHIN A TIME LIMIT, AND IF THEY CAN PROVE IN FRONT OF A PROFESSOR THAT IT WILL ACTIVATE, THEN THEY PASS.
Chapter. 04
BUT A LASER CANNON THAT ACTIVATED THE DAY BEFORE...
...HAD ITS WIRE CUT BY SOME-ONE...
...AND DIDN'T ACTIVATE.
AND THE PRIME SUSPECT...
COME WITH ME TO THE COMMANDANT'S OFFICE AT ONCE.
CADET CIENA REE.
...WAS CIENA.

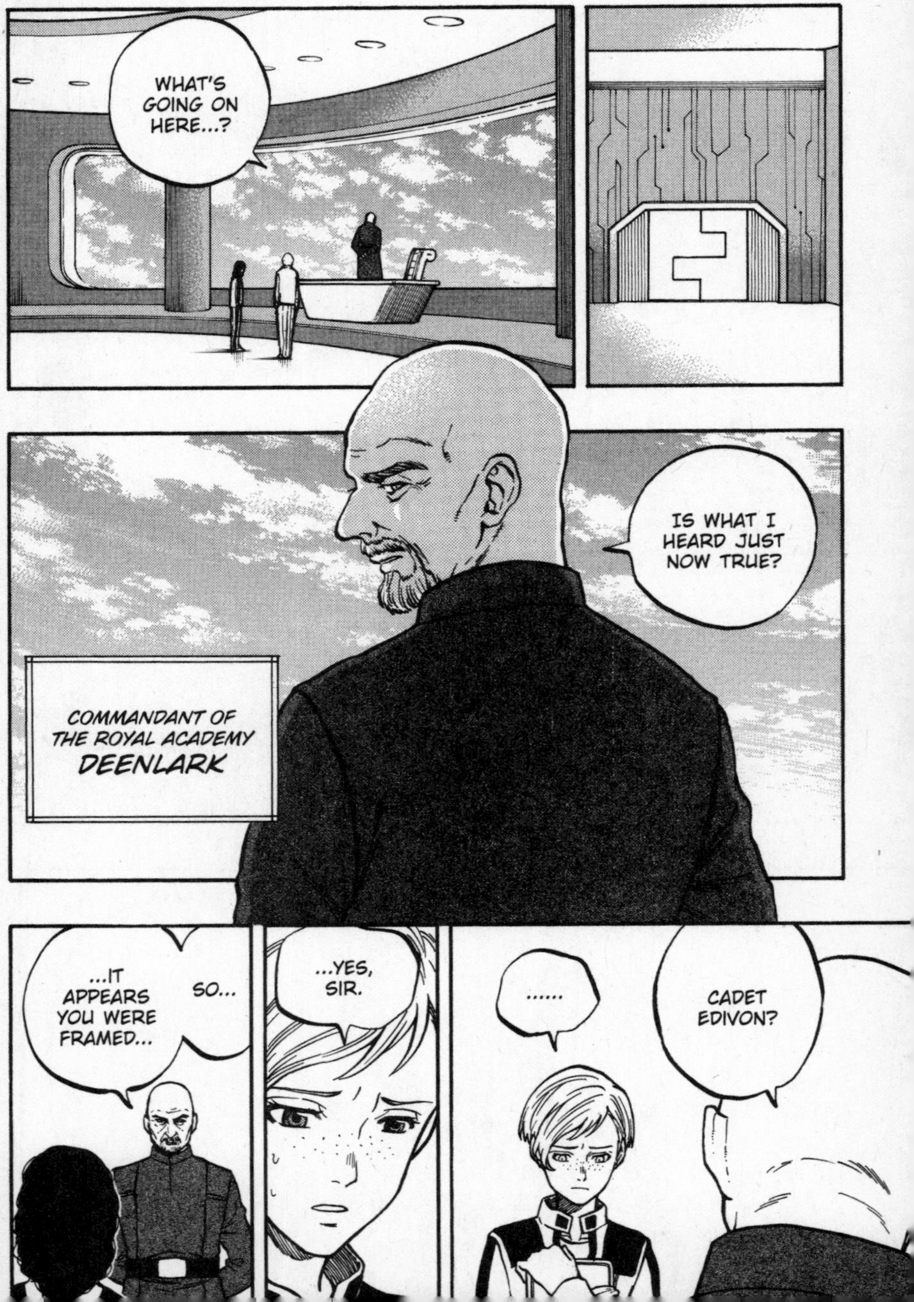
WHAT'S GOING ON HERE...?
IS WHAT I HEARD JUST NOW TRUE?
COMMANDANT OF THE ROYAL ACADEMY
DEENLARK
CADET EDIVON?
......
...YES, SIR.
SO...
...IT APPEARS YOU WERE FRAMED...

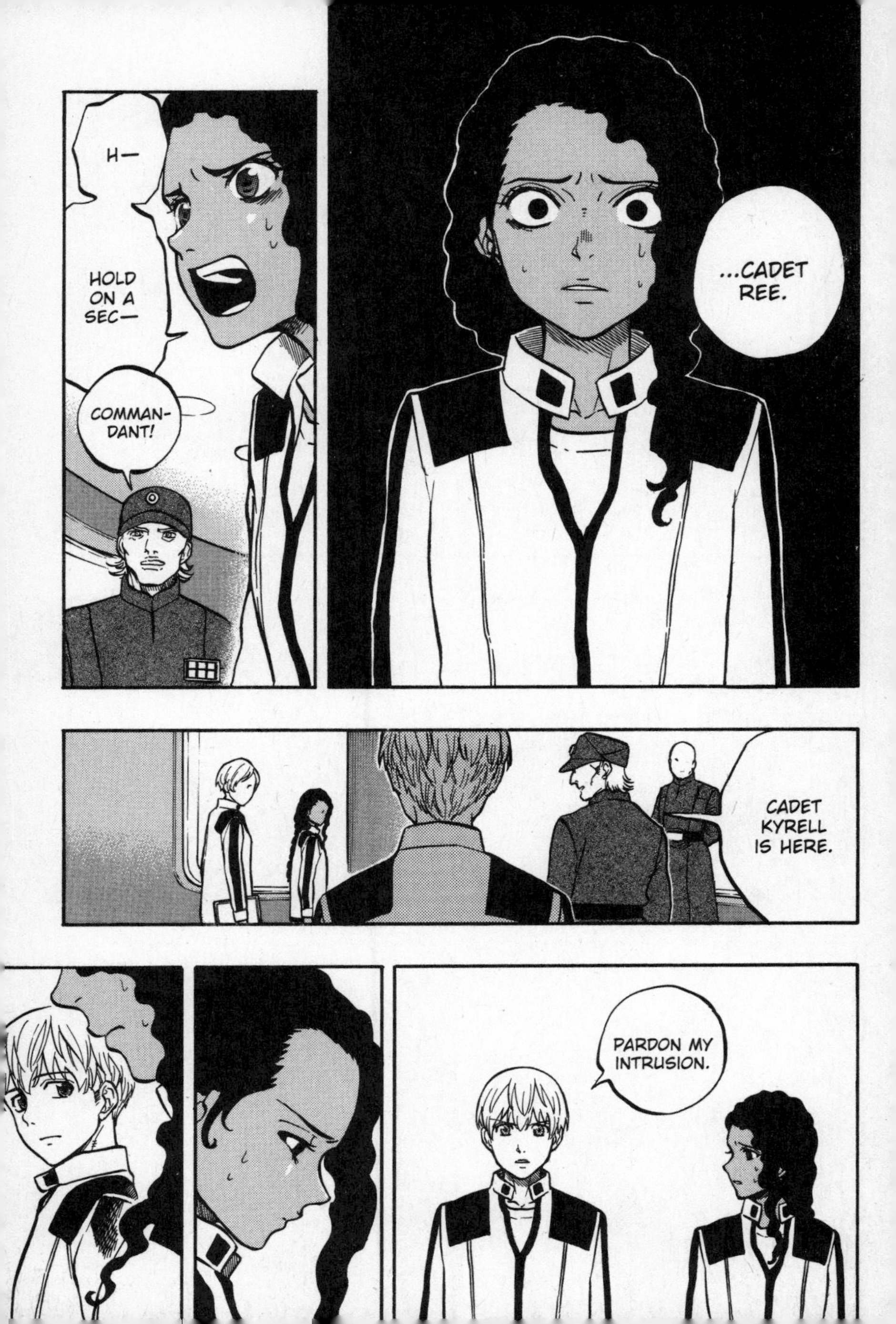
...CADET REE.
H—
HOLD ON A SEC—
COMMANDANT!
CADET KYRELL IS HERE.
PARDON MY INTRUSION.

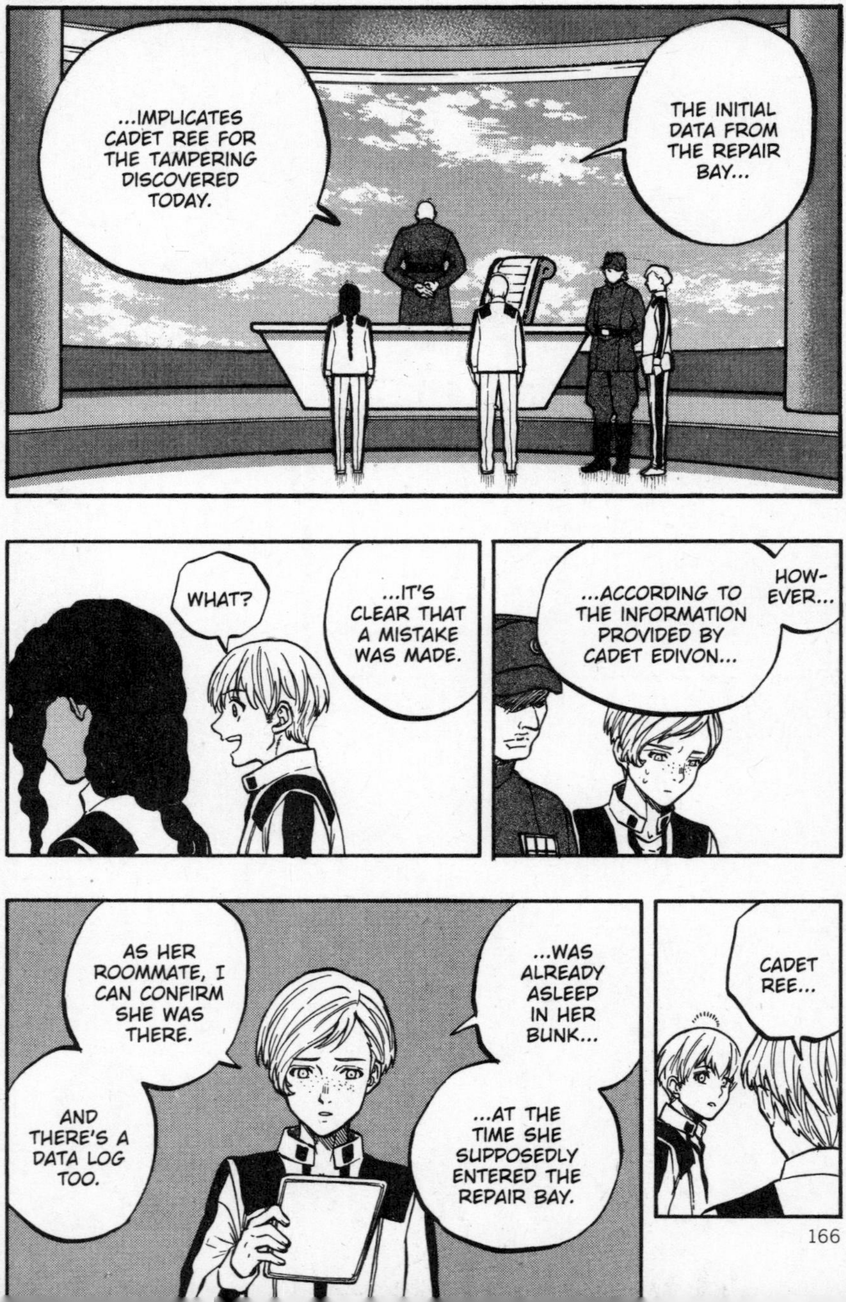
THE INITIAL DATA FROM THE REPAIR BAY...
...IMPLICATES CADET REE FOR THE TAMPERING DISCOVERED TODAY.
HOW-EVER...
...ACCORDING TO THE INFORMATION PROVIDED BY CADET EDIVON...
...IT'S CLEAR THAT A MISTAKE WAS MADE.
WHAT?
CADET REE...
...WAS ALREADY ASLEEP IN HER BUNK...
...AT THE TIME SHE SUPPOSEDLY ENTERED THE REPAIR BAY.
AS HER ROOMMATE, I CAN CONFIRM SHE WAS THERE.
AND THERE'S A DATA LOG TOO.

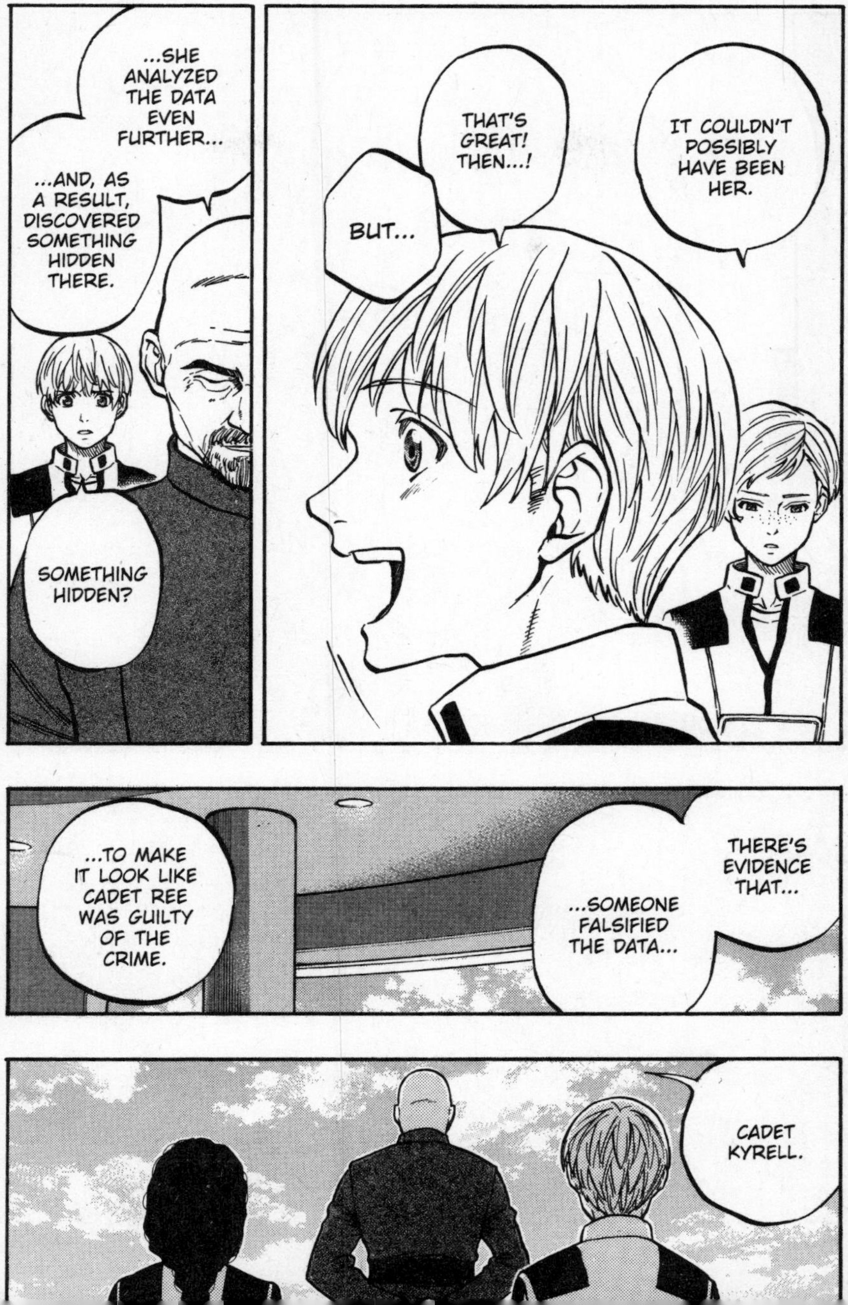
IT COULDN'T POSSIBLY HAVE BEEN HER.
THAT'S GREAT! THEN...!
BUT...
...SHE ANALYZED THE DATA EVEN FURTHER...
...AND, AS A RESULT, DISCOVERED SOMETHING HIDDEN THERE.
SOMETHING HIDDEN?
THERE'S EVIDENCE THAT...
...SOMEONE FALSIFIED THE DATA...
...TO MAKE IT LOOK LIKE CADET REE WAS GUILTY OF THE CRIME.
CADET KYRELL.

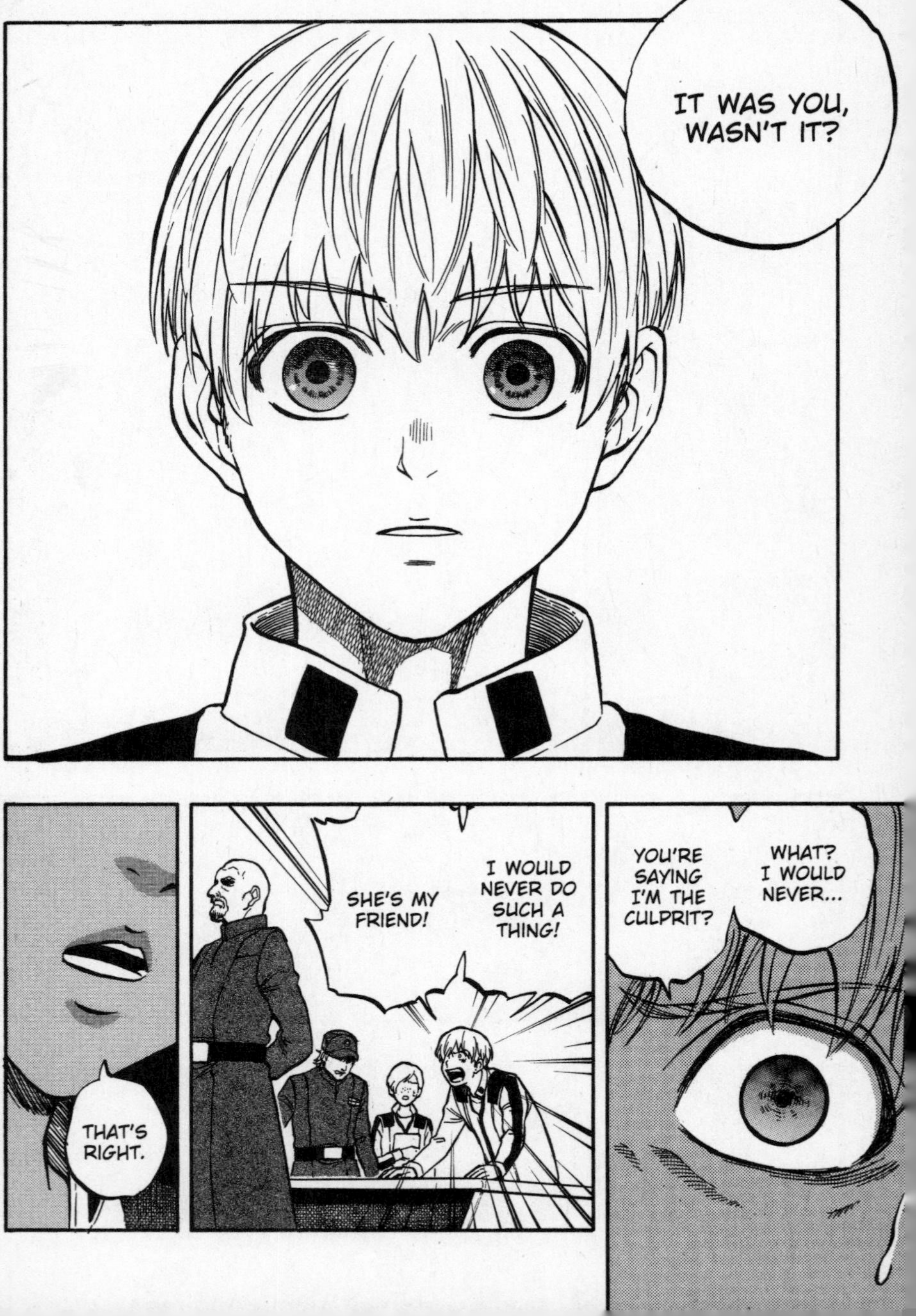
IT WAS YOU, WASN'T IT?
WHAT? I WOULD NEVER...
YOU'RE SAYING I'M THE CULPRIT?
I WOULD NEVER DO SUCH A THING!
SHE'S MY FRIEND!
THAT'S RIGHT.

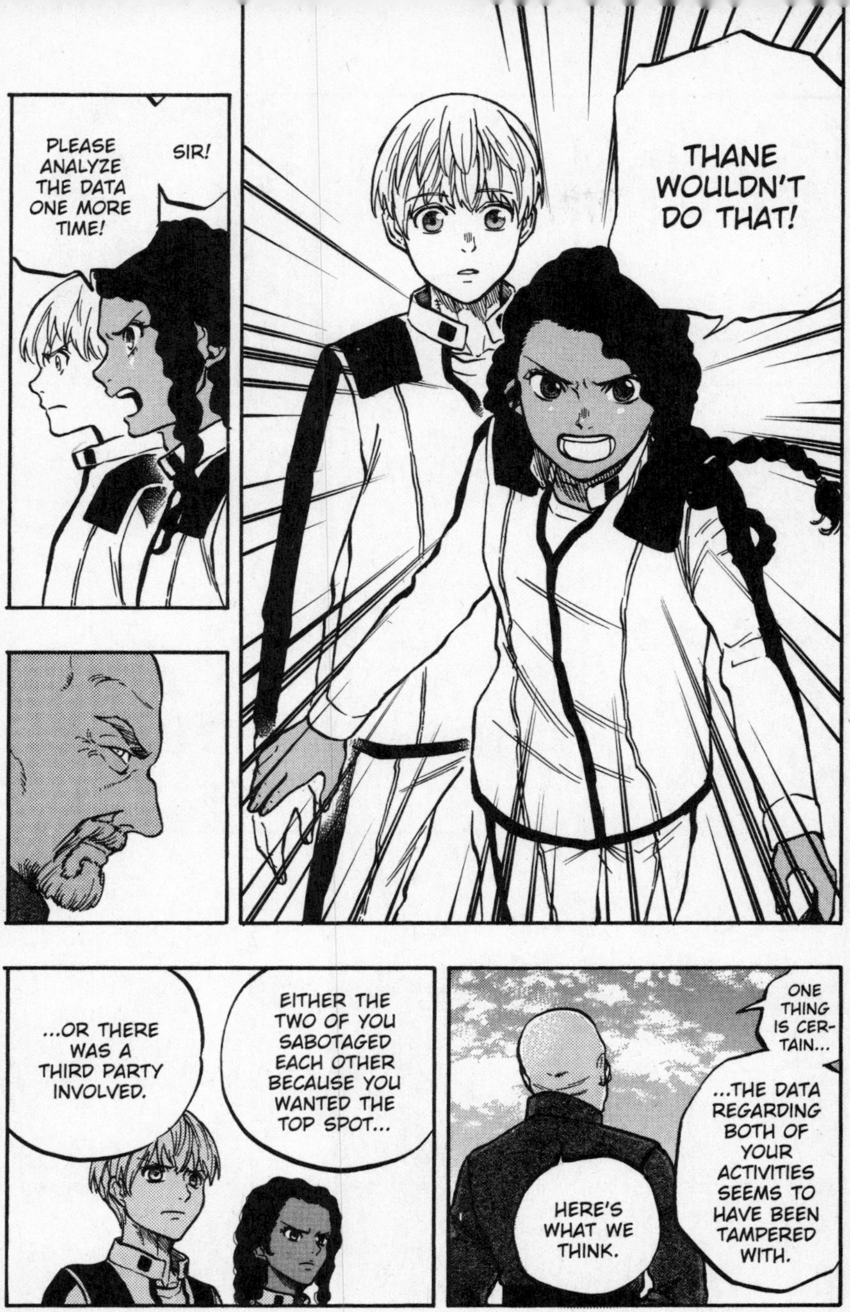
THANE WOULDN'T DO THAT!
SIR!
PLEASE ANALYZE THE DATA ONE MORE TIME!
ONE THING IS CER-TAIN...
...THE DATA REGARDING BOTH OF YOUR ACTIVITIES SEEMS TO HAVE BEEN TAMPERED WITH.
HERE'S WHAT WE THINK.
EITHER THE TWO OF YOU SABOTAGED EACH OTHER BECAUSE YOU WANTED THE TOP SPOT...
...OR THERE WAS A THIRD PARTY INVOLVED.

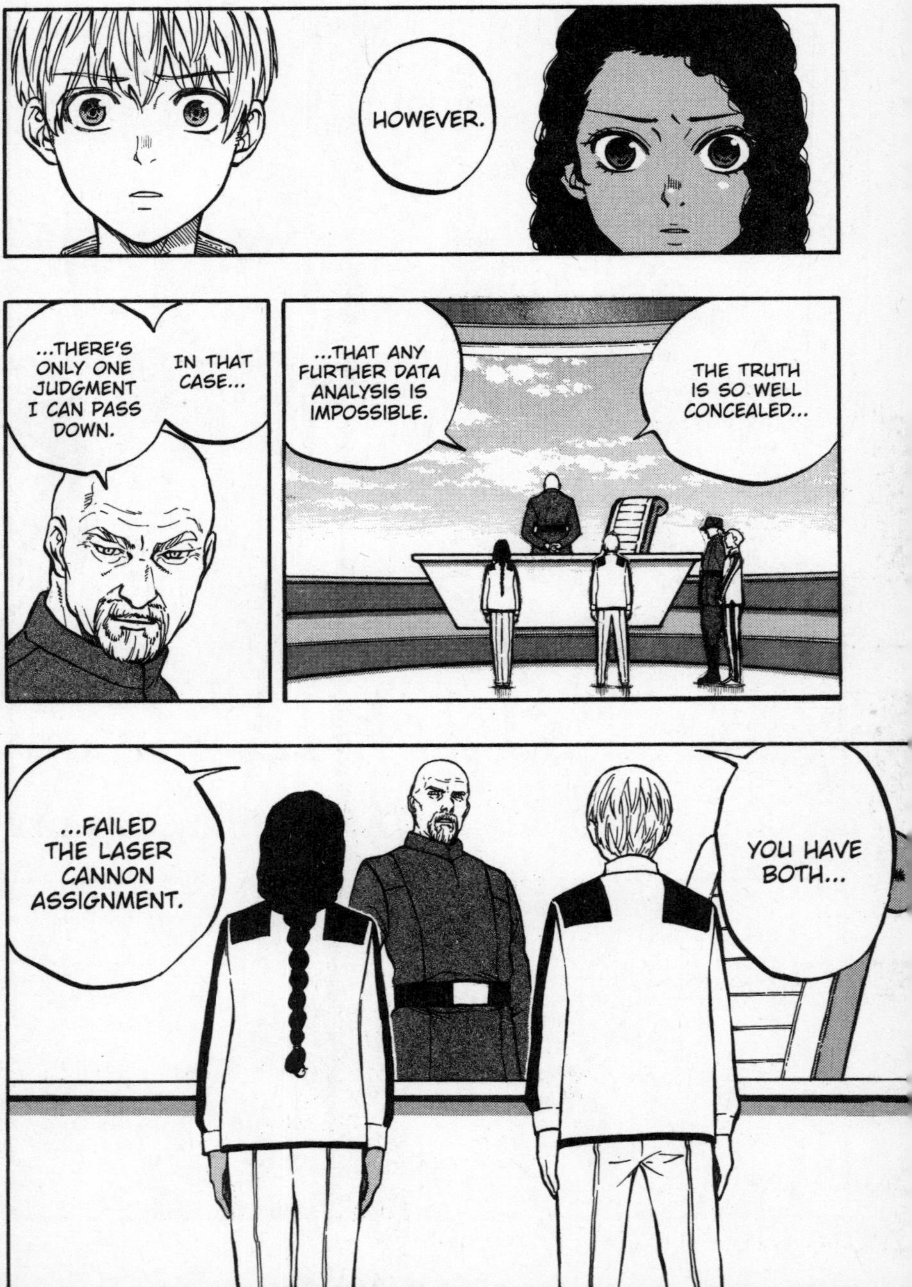
HOWEVER.
THE TRUTH IS SO WELL CONCEALED...
...THAT ANY FURTHER DATA ANALYSIS IS IMPOSSIBLE.
IN THAT CASE...
...THERE'S ONLY ONE JUDGMENT I CAN PASS DOWN.
YOU HAVE BOTH...
...FAILED THE LASER CANNON ASSIGNMENT.

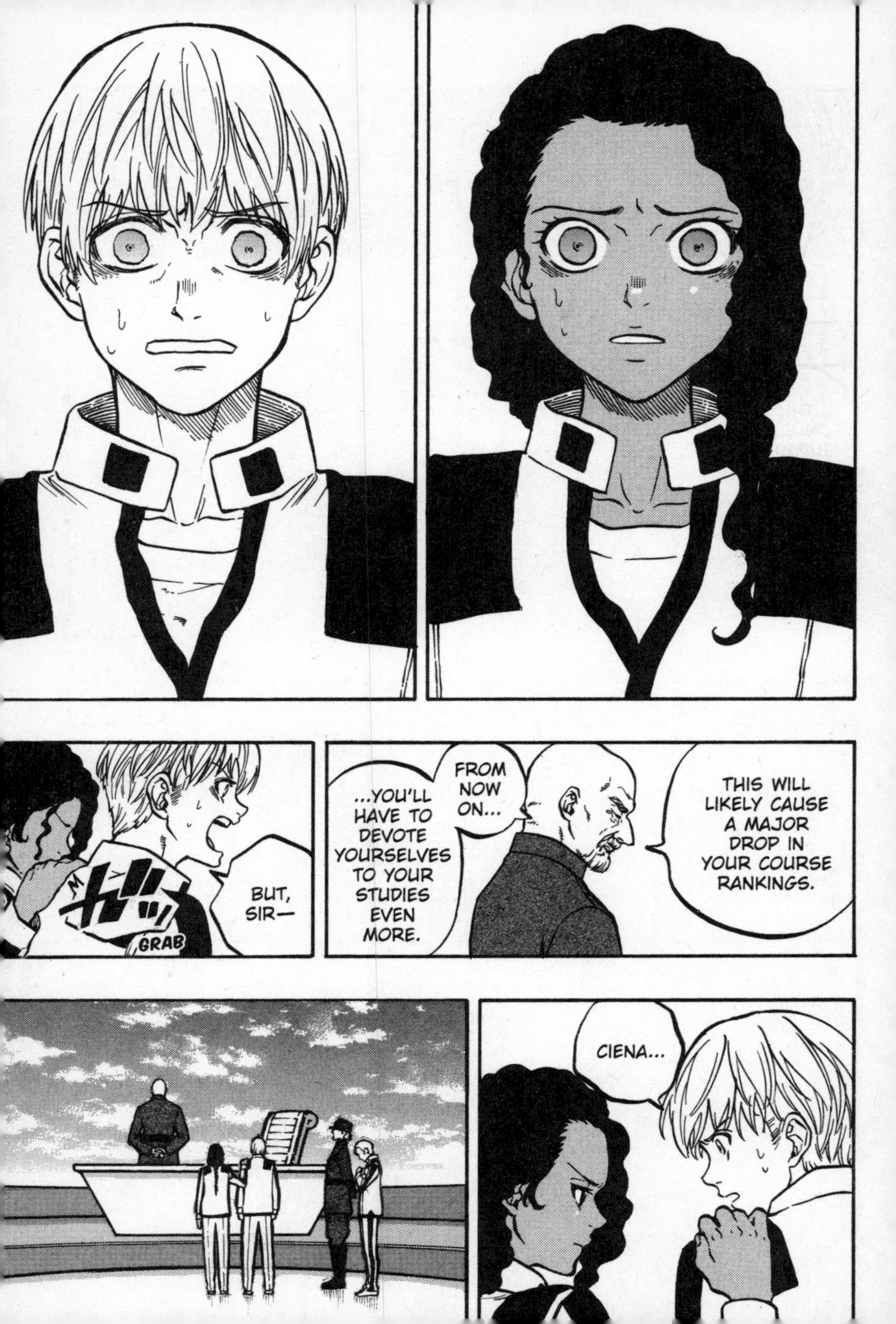
THIS WILL LIKELY CAUSE A MAJOR DROP IN YOUR COURSE RANKINGS.
FROM NOW ON...
...YOU'LL HAVE TO DEVOTE YOURSELVES TO YOUR STUDIES EVEN MORE.
BUT, SIR—
GRAB
CIENA...

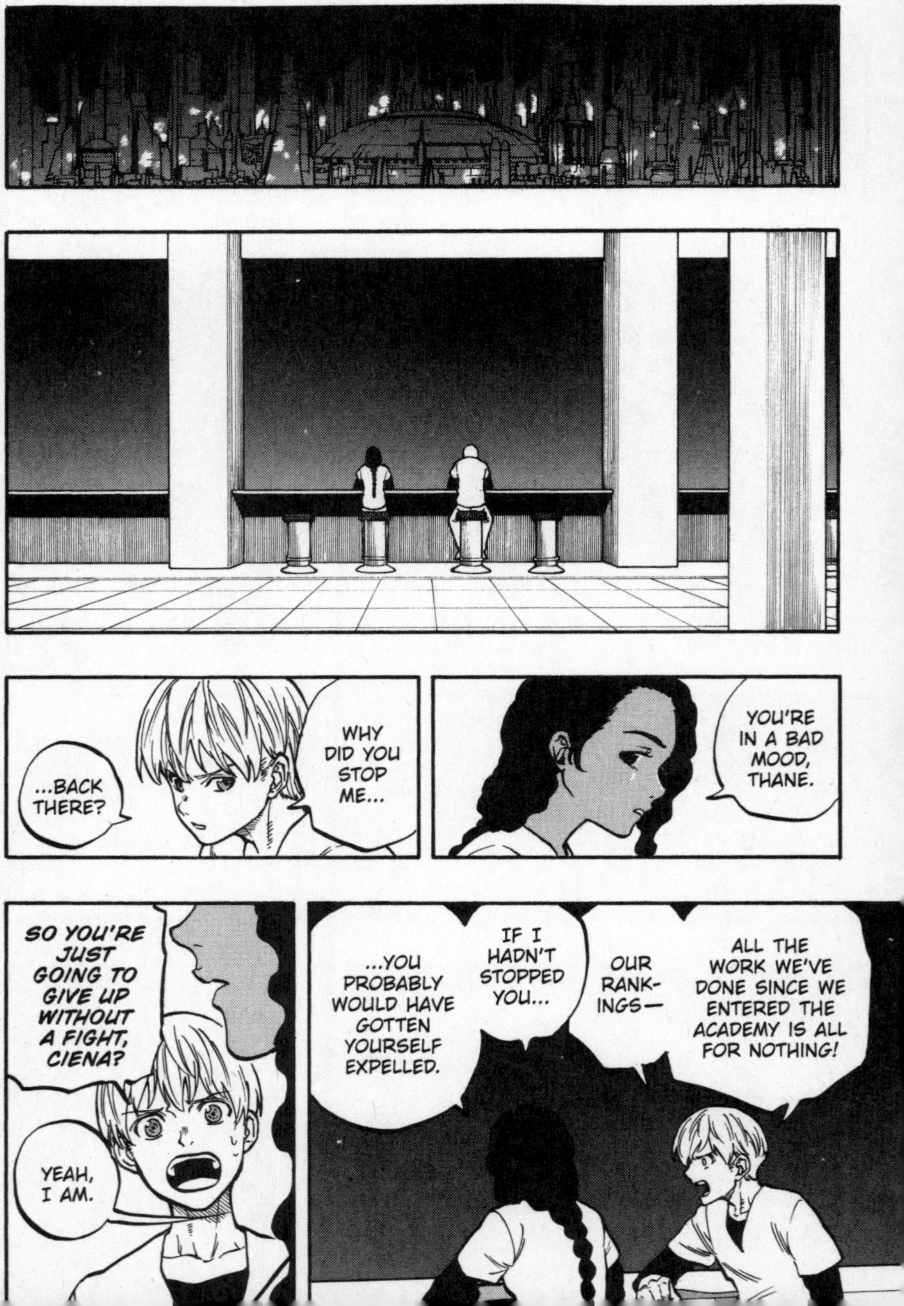
YOU'RE IN A BAD MOOD, THANE.
WHY DID YOU STOP ME...
...BACK THERE?
ALL THE WORK WE'VE DONE SINCE WE ENTERED THE ACADEMY IS ALL FOR NOTHING!
OUR RANK-INGS—
IF I HADN'T STOPPED YOU...
...YOU PROBABLY WOULD HAVE GOTTEN YOURSELF EXPELLED.
SO YOU'RE JUST GOING TO GIVE UP WITHOUT A FIGHT, CIENA?
YEAH, I AM.

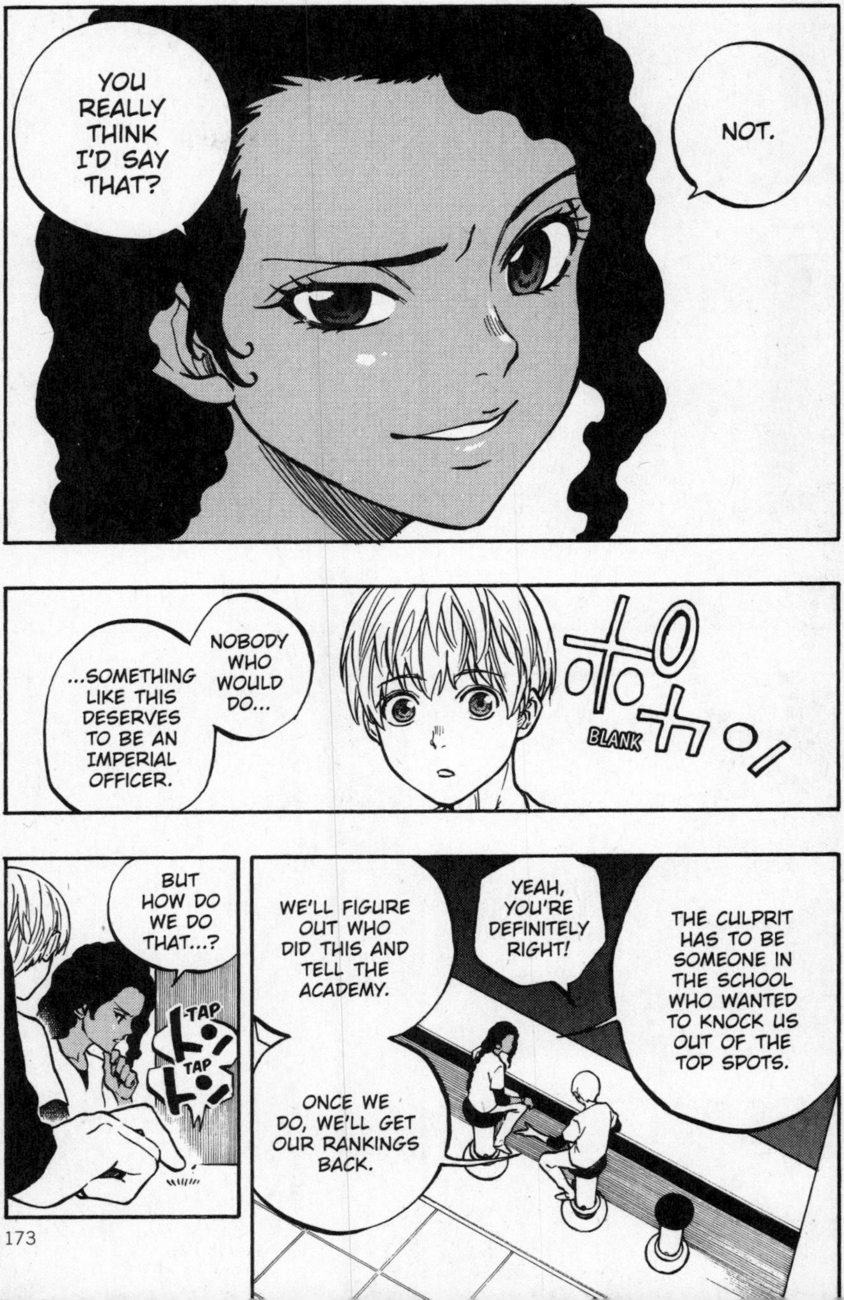
NOT.
YOU REALLY THINK I'D SAY THAT?
BLANK
NOBODY WHO WOULD DO...
...SOMETHING LIKE THIS DESERVES TO BE AN IMPERIAL OFFICER.
THE CULPRIT HAS TO BE SOMEONE IN THE SCHOOL WHO WANTED TO KNOCK US OUT OF THE TOP SPOTS.
YEAH, YOU'RE DEFINITELY RIGHT!
WE'LL FIGURE OUT WHO DID THIS AND TELL THE ACADEMY.
ONCE WE DO, WE'LL GET OUR RANKINGS BACK.
BUT HOW DO WE DO THAT...?
TAP
TAP

I MIGHT BE ABLE TO HELP YOU.

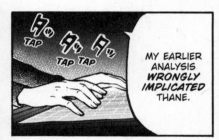

TAP

TAP TAP TAP

MY EARLIER ANALYSIS *WRONGLY IMPLICATED* THANE.

IT'S MY SKILLS THAT SHOULD REALLY BE UNDER FIRE RIGHT NOW.

IT WASN'T YOUR FAULT.

WHAT IS IT?

THAT'S WEIRD.

......

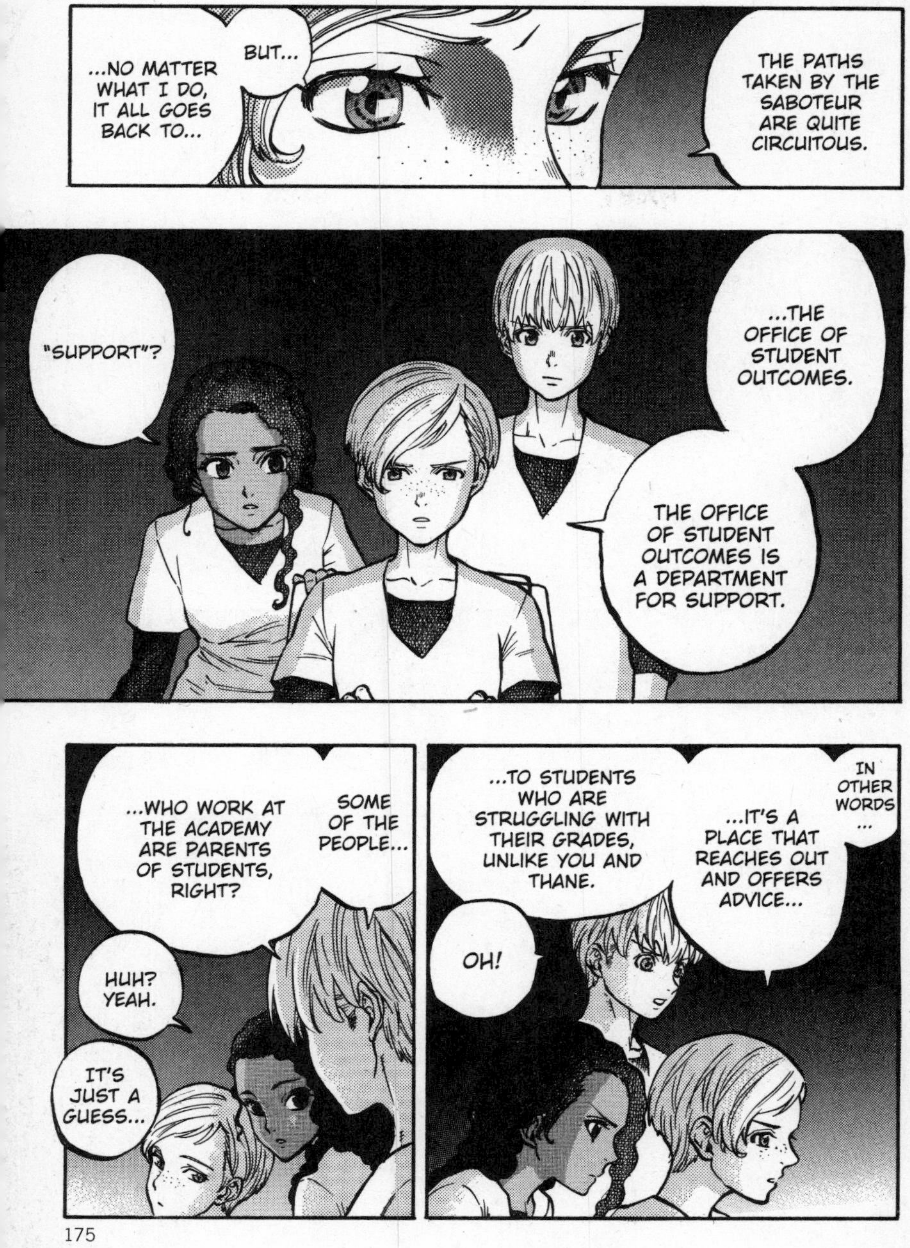
THE PATHS TAKEN BY THE SABOTEUR ARE QUITE CIRCUITOUS.
BUT...
...NO MATTER WHAT I DO, IT ALL GOES BACK TO...
...THE OFFICE OF STUDENT OUTCOMES.
THE OFFICE OF STUDENT OUTCOMES IS A DEPARTMENT FOR SUPPORT.
"SUPPORT"?
IN OTHER WORDS...
...IT'S A PLACE THAT REACHES OUT AND OFFERS ADVICE...
...TO STUDENTS WHO ARE STRUGGLING WITH THEIR GRADES, UNLIKE YOU AND THANE.
OH!
SOME OF THE PEOPLE...
...WHO WORK AT THE ACADEMY ARE PARENTS OF STUDENTS, RIGHT?
HUH? YEAH.
IT'S JUST A GUESS...

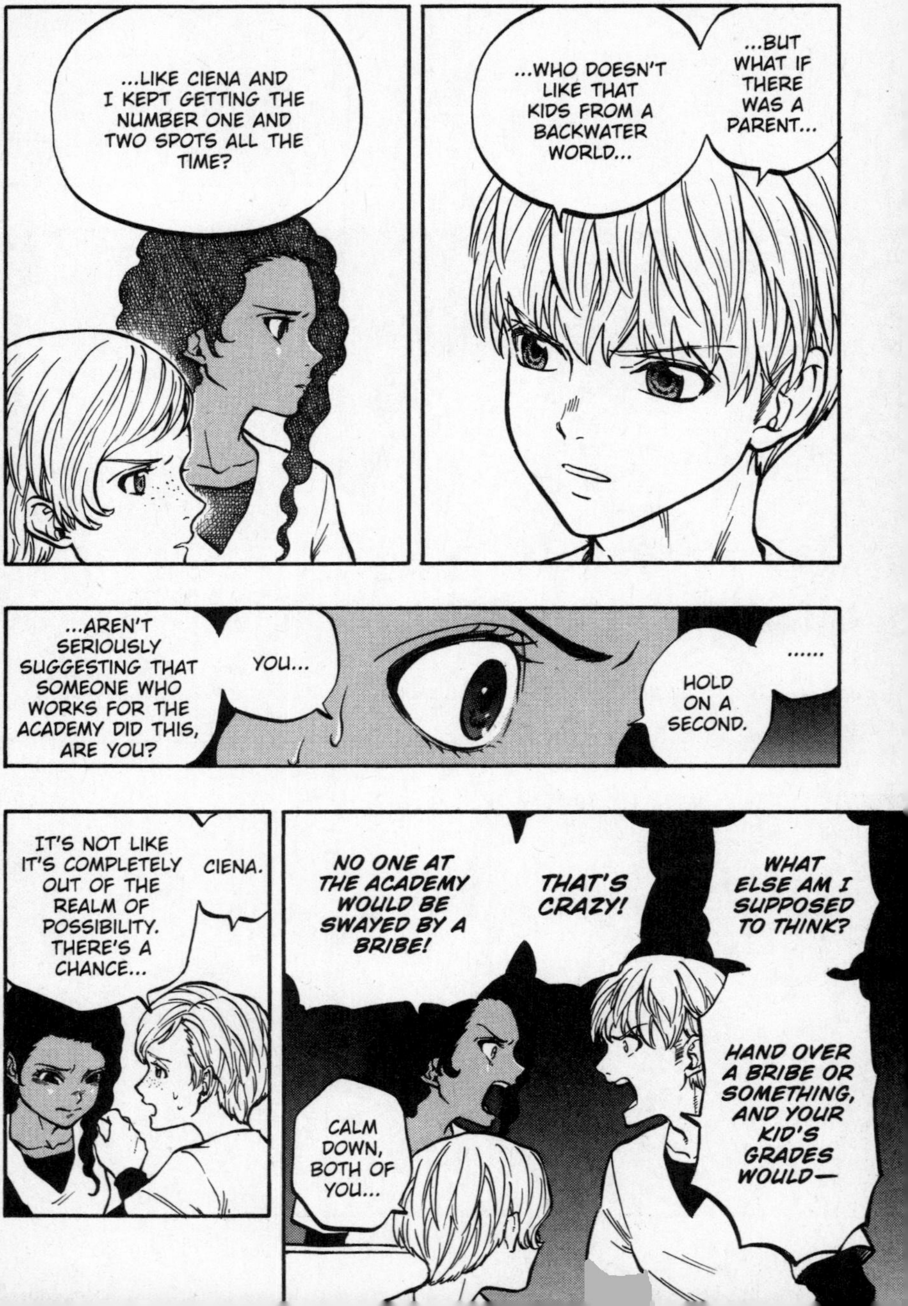
...BUT WHAT IF THERE WAS A PARENT...
...WHO DOESN'T LIKE THAT KIDS FROM A BACKWATER WORLD...
...LIKE CIENA AND I KEPT GETTING THE NUMBER ONE AND TWO SPOTS ALL THE TIME?
......
HOLD ON A SECOND.
YOU...
...AREN'T SERIOUSLY SUGGESTING THAT SOMEONE WHO WORKS FOR THE ACADEMY DID THIS, ARE YOU?
WHAT ELSE AM I SUPPOSED TO THINK?
THAT'S CRAZY!
NO ONE AT THE ACADEMY WOULD BE SWAYED BY A BRIBE!
HAND OVER A BRIBE OR SOMETHING, AND YOUR KID'S GRADES WOULD—
CALM DOWN, BOTH OF YOU...
CIENA.
IT'S NOT LIKE IT'S COMPLETELY OUT OF THE REALM OF POSSIBILITY. THERE'S A CHANCE...

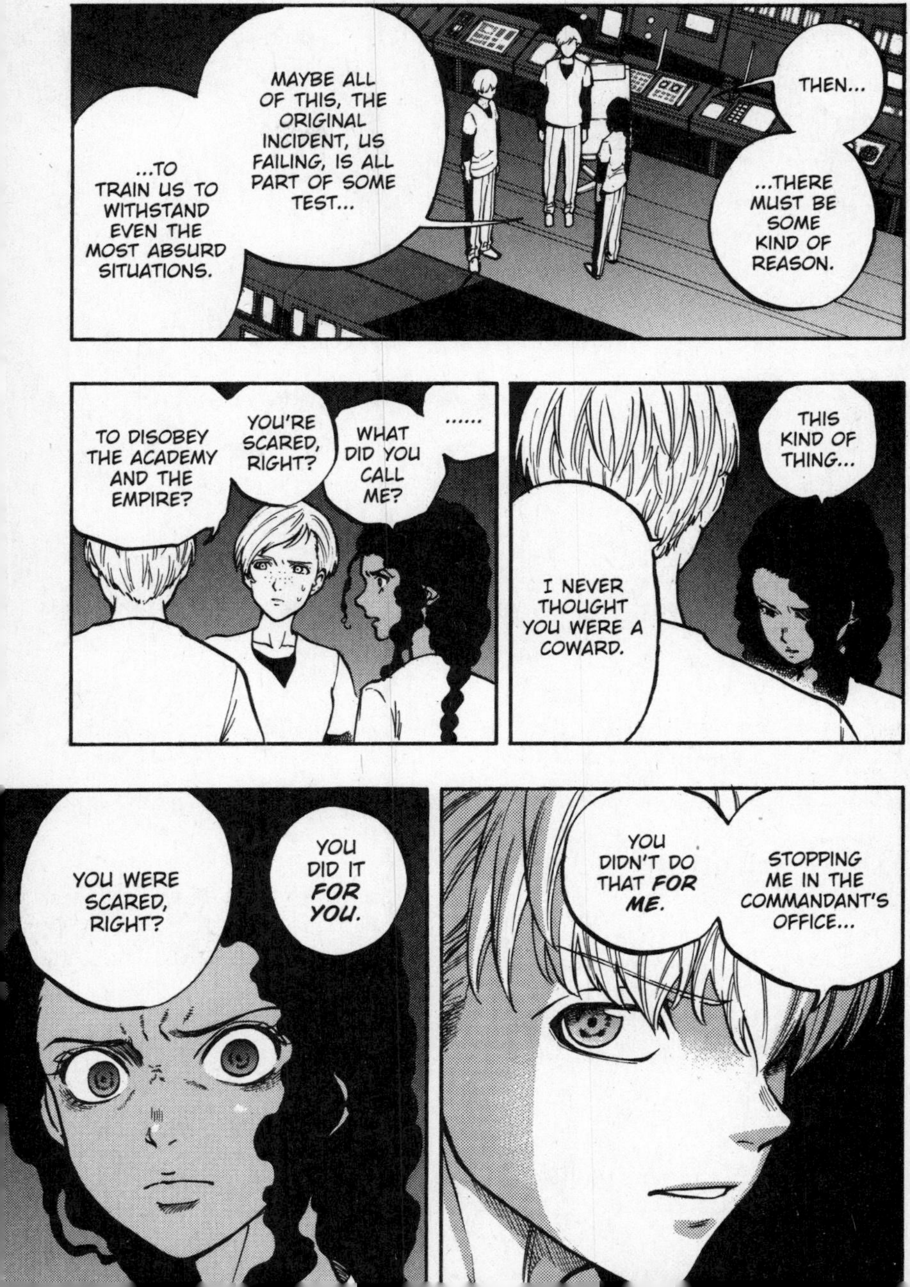
THEN...
...THERE MUST BE SOME KIND OF REASON.
MAYBE ALL OF THIS, THE ORIGINAL INCIDENT, US FAILING, IS ALL PART OF SOME TEST...
...TO TRAIN US TO WITHSTAND EVEN THE MOST ABSURD SITUATIONS.
THIS KIND OF THING...
I NEVER THOUGHT YOU WERE A COWARD.
......
WHAT DID YOU CALL ME?
YOU'RE SCARED, RIGHT?
TO DISOBEY THE ACADEMY AND THE EMPIRE?
STOPPING ME IN THE COMMANDANT'S OFFICE...
YOU DIDN'T DO THAT *FOR ME*.
YOU DID IT *FOR YOU*.
YOU WERE SCARED, RIGHT?

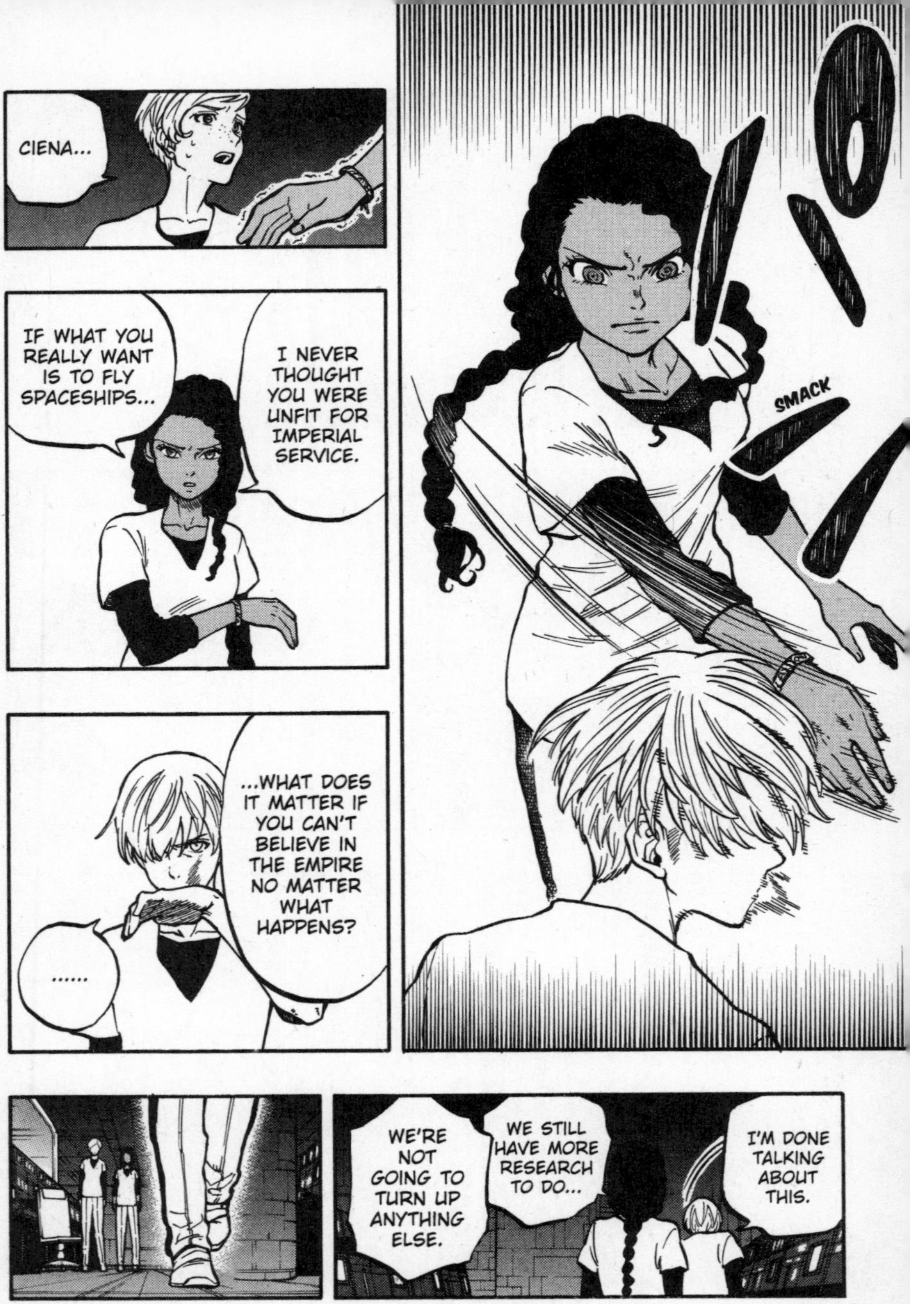
SMACK
CIENA...
I NEVER THOUGHT YOU WERE UNFIT FOR IMPERIAL SERVICE.
IF WHAT YOU REALLY WANT IS TO FLY SPACESHIPS...
...WHAT DOES IT MATTER IF YOU CAN'T BELIEVE IN THE EMPIRE NO MATTER WHAT HAPPENS?
......
I'M DONE TALKING ABOUT THIS.
WE STILL HAVE MORE RESEARCH TO DO...
WE'RE NOT GOING TO TURN UP ANYTHING ELSE.

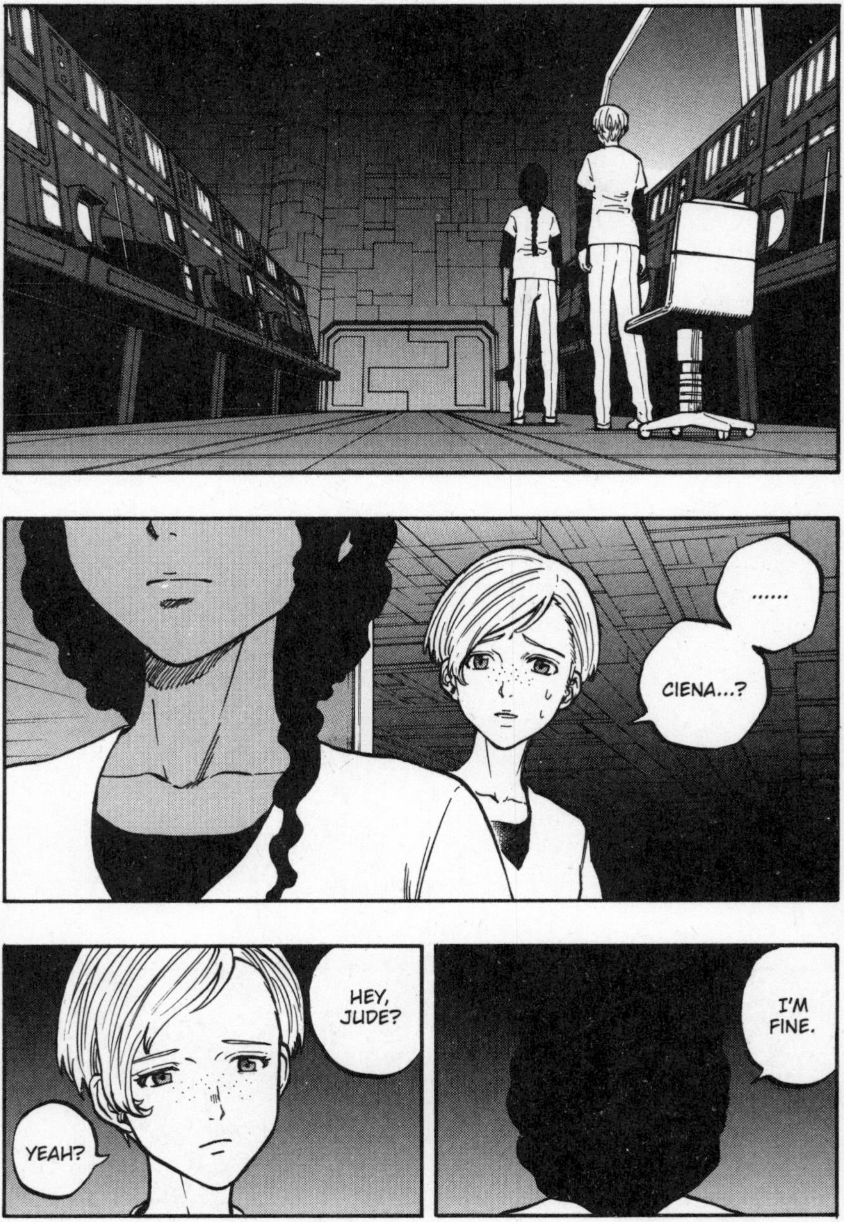
......
CIENA...?
I'M FINE.
HEY, JUDE?
YEAH?

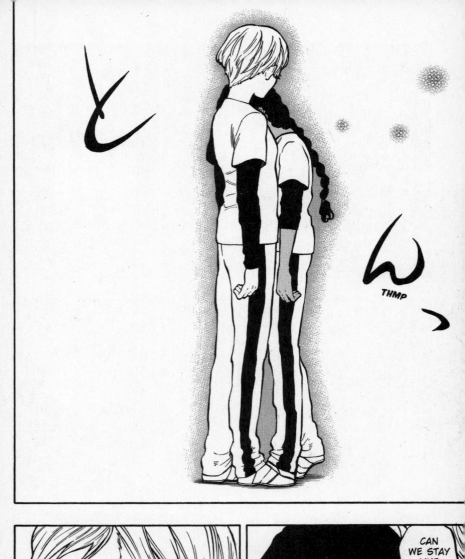

THMP

CAN
WE STAY
LIKE
THIS...

...FOR
JUST A
LITTLE
WHILE?

SURE...

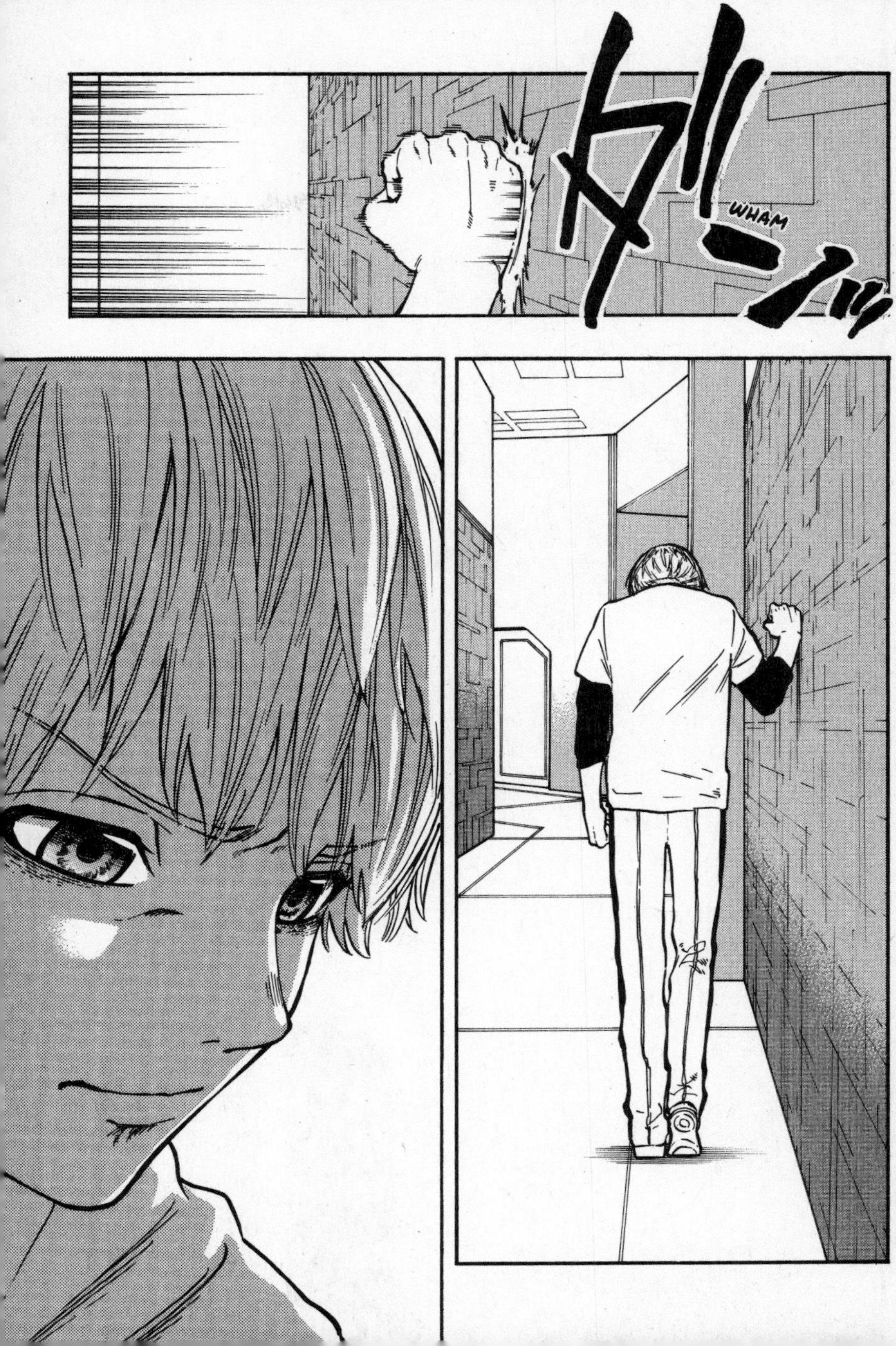
ダン
WHAM

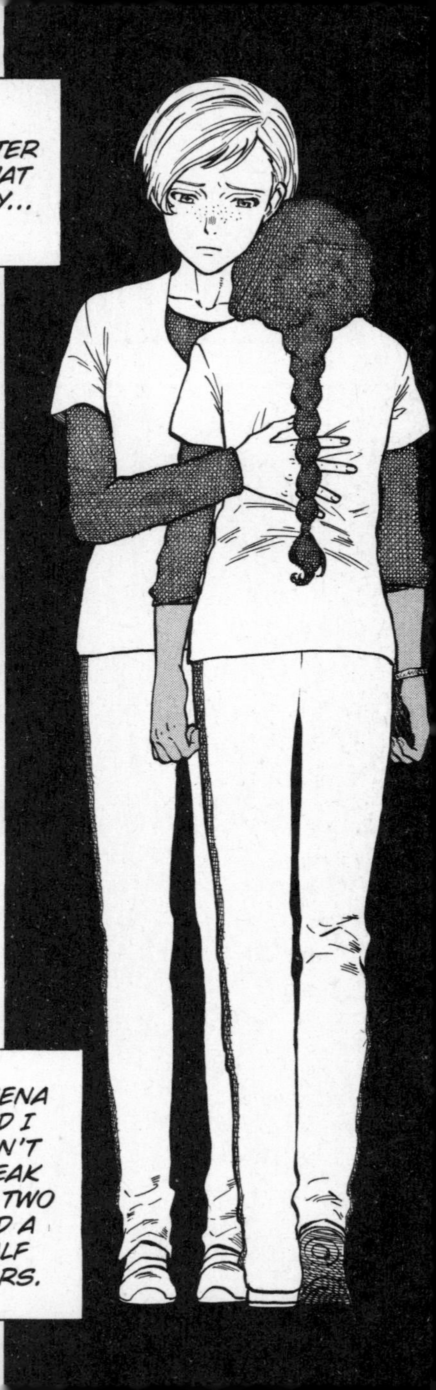
AFTER THAT DAY...
...CIENA AND I DIDN'T SPEAK FOR TWO AND A HALF YEARS.
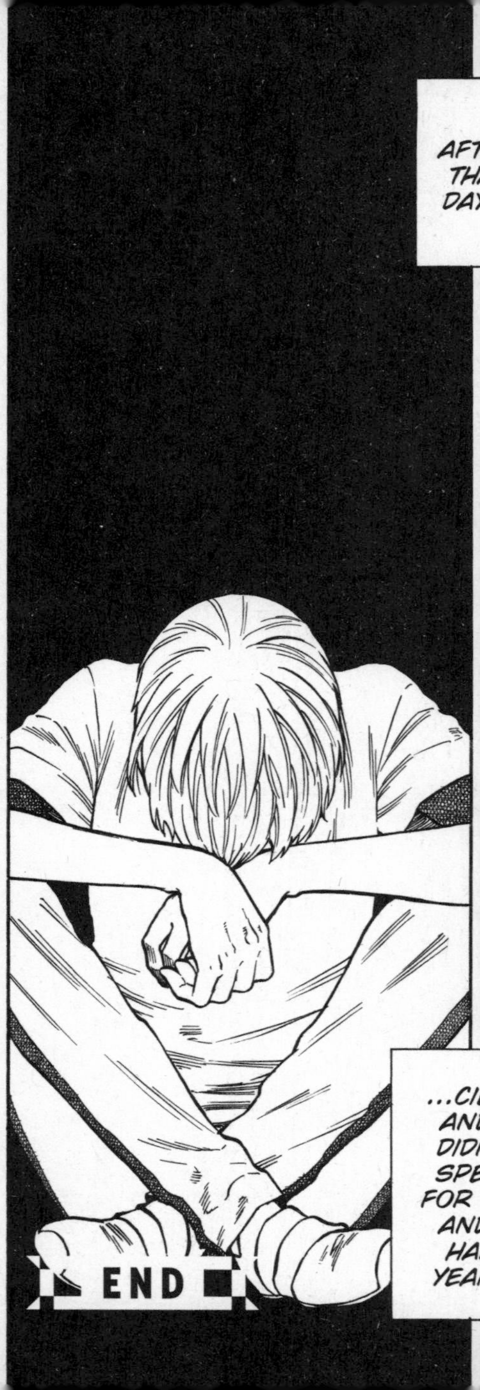
END

STAR WARS
LOST STARS

STAR WARS
LOST STARS

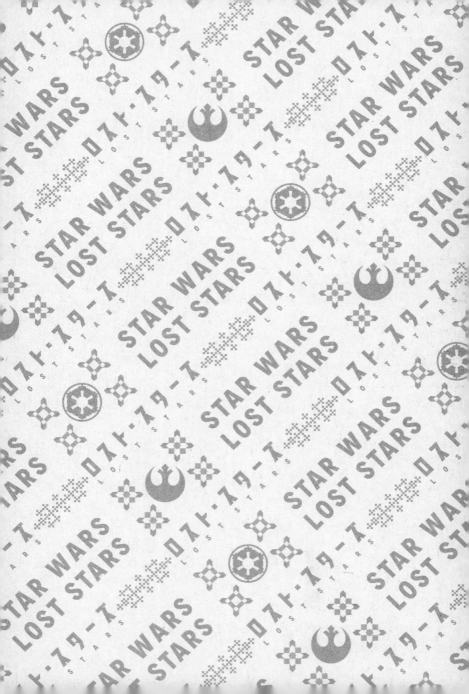

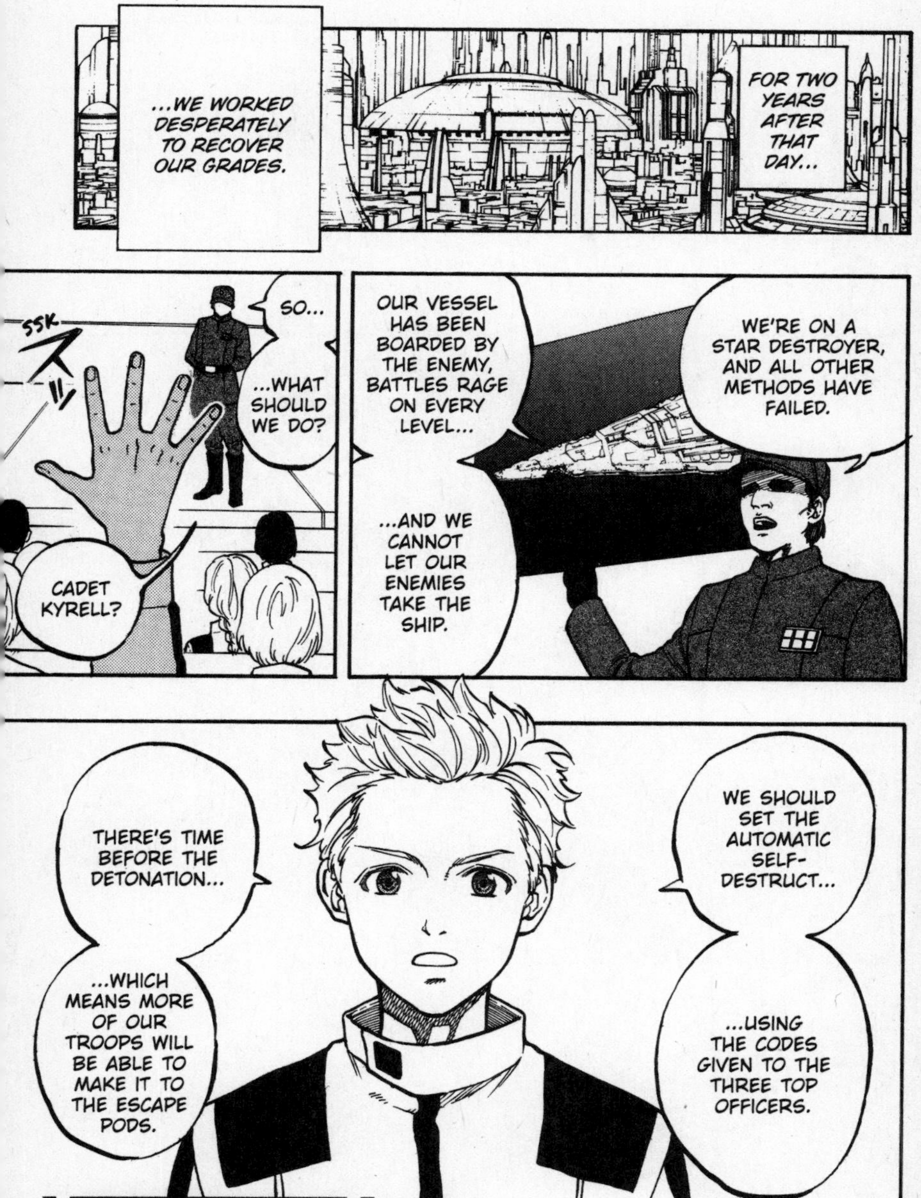
FOR TWO YEARS AFTER THAT DAY...
...WE WORKED DESPERATELY TO RECOVER OUR GRADES.
WE'RE ON A STAR DESTROYER, AND ALL OTHER METHODS HAVE FAILED.
OUR VESSEL HAS BEEN BOARDED BY THE ENEMY, BATTLES RAGE ON EVERY LEVEL...
...AND WE CANNOT LET OUR ENEMIES TAKE THE SHIP.
SO...
...WHAT SHOULD WE DO?
SSK
CADET KYRELL?
WE SHOULD SET THE AUTOMATIC SELF-DESTRUCT...
...USING THE CODES GIVEN TO THE THREE TOP OFFICERS.
THERE'S TIME BEFORE THE DETONATION...
...WHICH MEANS MORE OF OUR TROOPS WILL BE ABLE TO MAKE IT TO THE ESCAPE PODS.
Chapter. 05

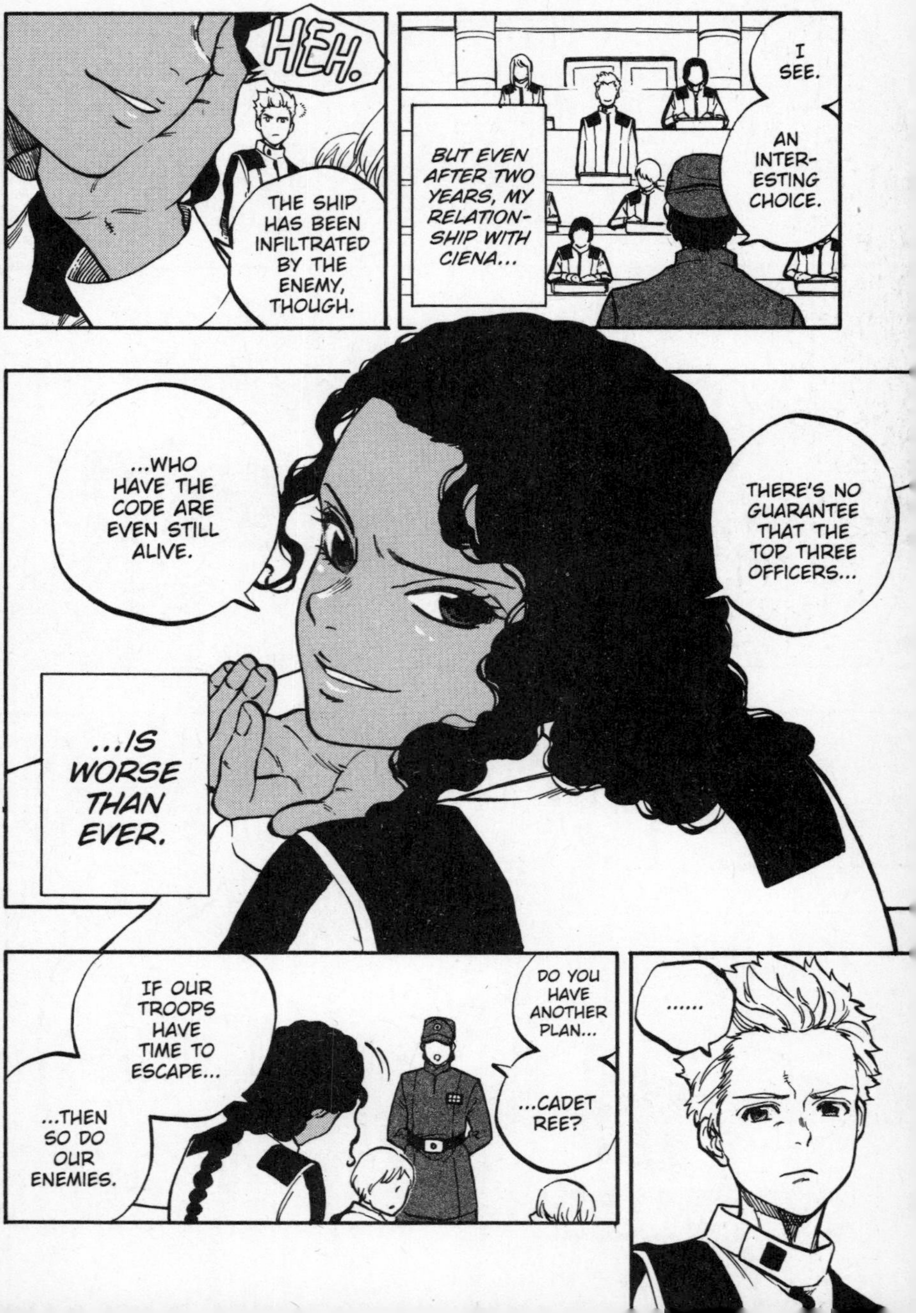
I SEE.
AN INTERESTING CHOICE.
BUT EVEN AFTER TWO YEARS, MY RELATIONSHIP WITH CIENA...
HEH.
THE SHIP HAS BEEN INFILTRATED BY THE ENEMY, THOUGH.
THERE'S NO GUARANTEE THAT THE TOP THREE OFFICERS...
...WHO HAVE THE CODE ARE EVEN STILL ALIVE.
...IS WORSE THAN EVER.
......
DO YOU HAVE ANOTHER PLAN...
...CADET REE?
IF OUR TROOPS HAVE TIME TO ESCAPE...
...THEN SO DO OUR ENEMIES.

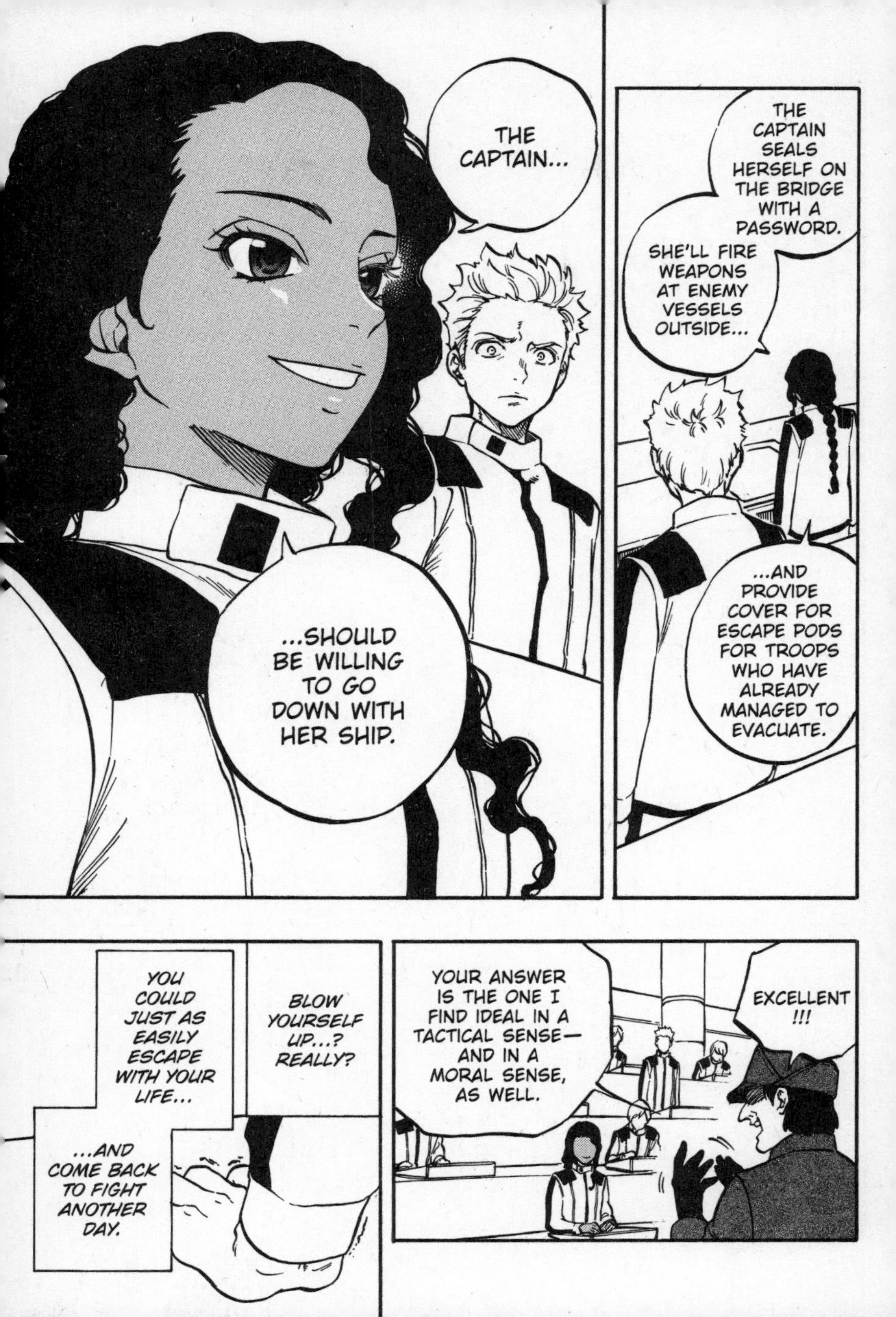
THE CAPTAIN SEALS HERSELF ON THE BRIDGE WITH A PASSWORD.
SHE'LL FIRE WEAPONS AT ENEMY VESSELS OUTSIDE...
...AND PROVIDE COVER FOR ESCAPE PODS FOR TROOPS WHO HAVE ALREADY MANAGED TO EVACUATE.
THE CAPTAIN...
...SHOULD BE WILLING TO GO DOWN WITH HER SHIP.
EXCELLENT !!!
YOUR ANSWER IS THE ONE I FIND IDEAL IN A TACTICAL SENSE—AND IN A MORAL SENSE, AS WELL.
BLOW YOURSELF UP...? REALLY?
YOU COULD JUST AS EASILY ESCAPE WITH YOUR LIFE...
...AND COME BACK TO FIGHT ANOTHER DAY.

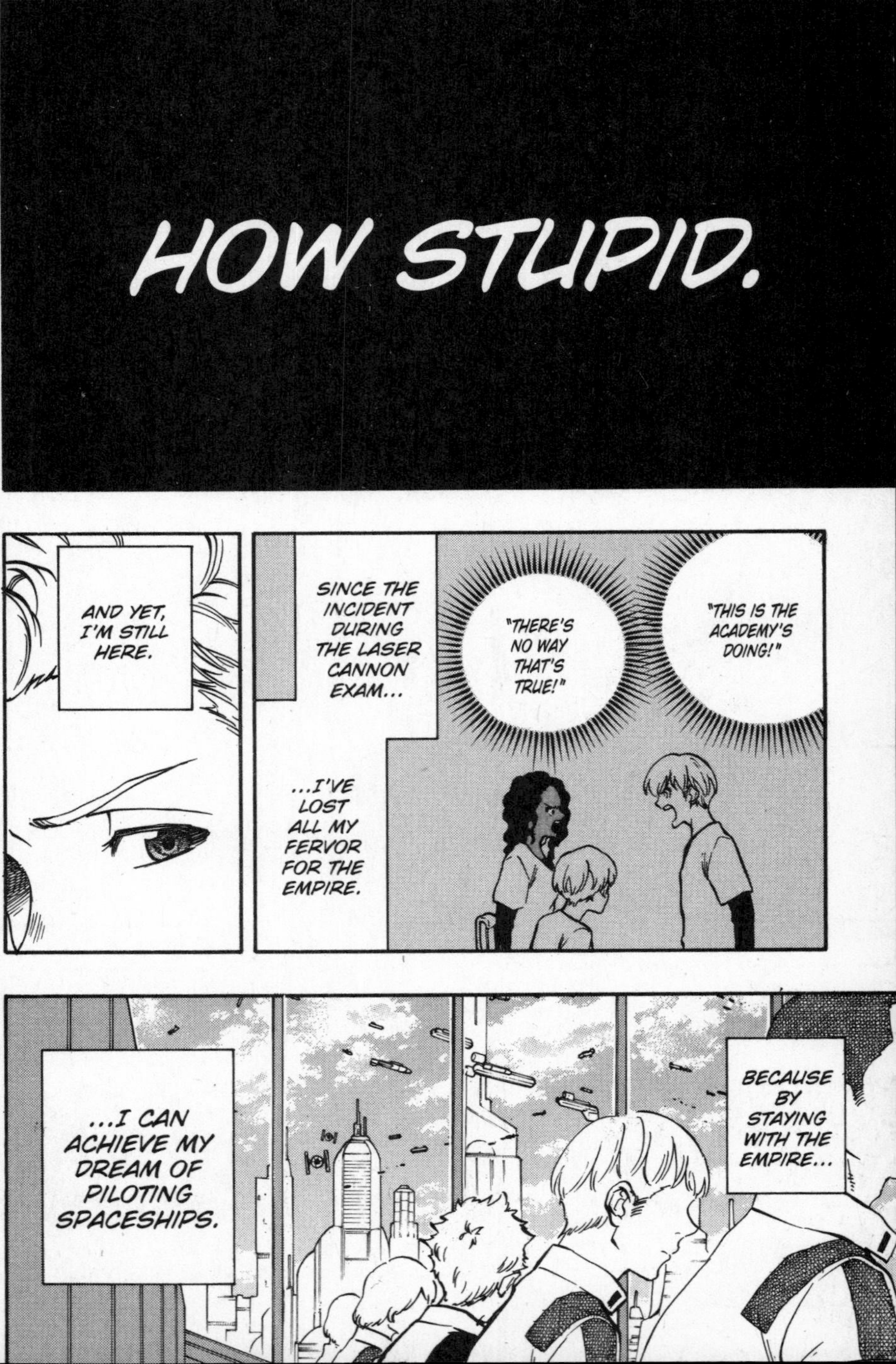
HOW STUPID.
"THIS IS THE ACADEMY'S DOING!"
"THERE'S NO WAY THAT'S TRUE!"
SINCE THE INCIDENT DURING THE LASER CANNON EXAM...
...I'VE LOST ALL MY FERVOR FOR THE EMPIRE.
AND YET, I'M STILL HERE.
BECAUSE BY STAYING WITH THE EMPIRE...
...I CAN ACHIEVE MY DREAM OF PILOTING SPACESHIPS.

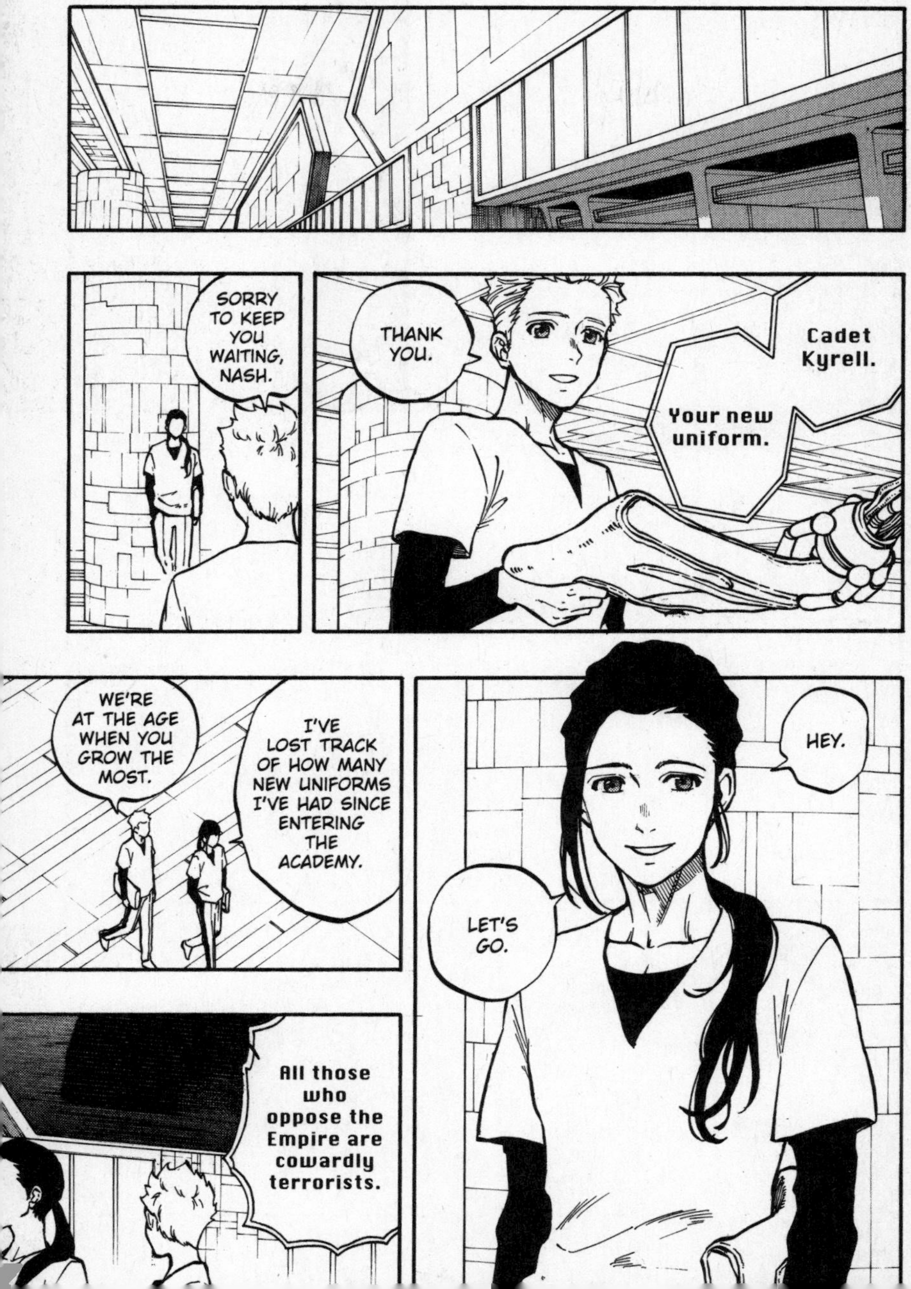
Cadet Kyrell.
Your new uniform.
THANK YOU.
SORRY TO KEEP YOU WAITING, NASH.
HEY.
LET'S GO.
I'VE LOST TRACK OF HOW MANY NEW UNIFORMS I'VE HAD SINCE ENTERING THE ACADEMY.
WE'RE AT THE AGE WHEN YOU GROW THE MOST.
All those who oppose the Empire are cowardly terrorists.

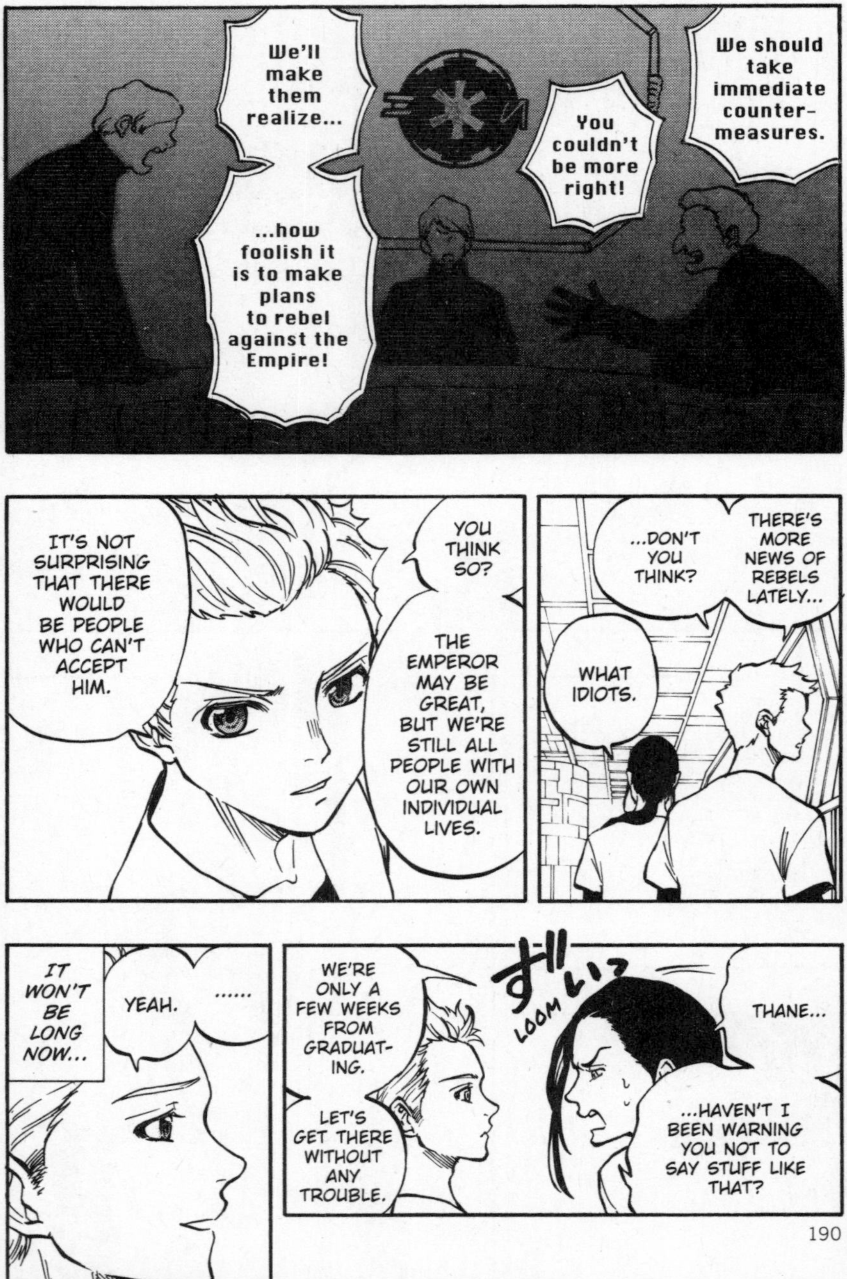
We should take immediate counter-measures.
You couldn't be more right!
We'll make them realize...
...how foolish it is to make plans to rebel against the Empire!
THERE'S MORE NEWS OF REBELS LATELY...
...DON'T YOU THINK?
WHAT IDIOTS.
YOU THINK SO?
THE EMPEROR MAY BE GREAT, BUT WE'RE STILL ALL PEOPLE WITH OUR OWN INDIVIDUAL LIVES.
IT'S NOT SURPRISING THAT THERE WOULD BE PEOPLE WHO CAN'T ACCEPT HIM.
THANE...
ずいっ
LOOM
...HAVEN'T I BEEN WARNING YOU NOT TO SAY STUFF LIKE THAT?
WE'RE ONLY A FEW WEEKS FROM GRADUATING.
LET'S GET THERE WITHOUT ANY TROUBLE.
......
YEAH.
IT WON'T BE LONG NOW...

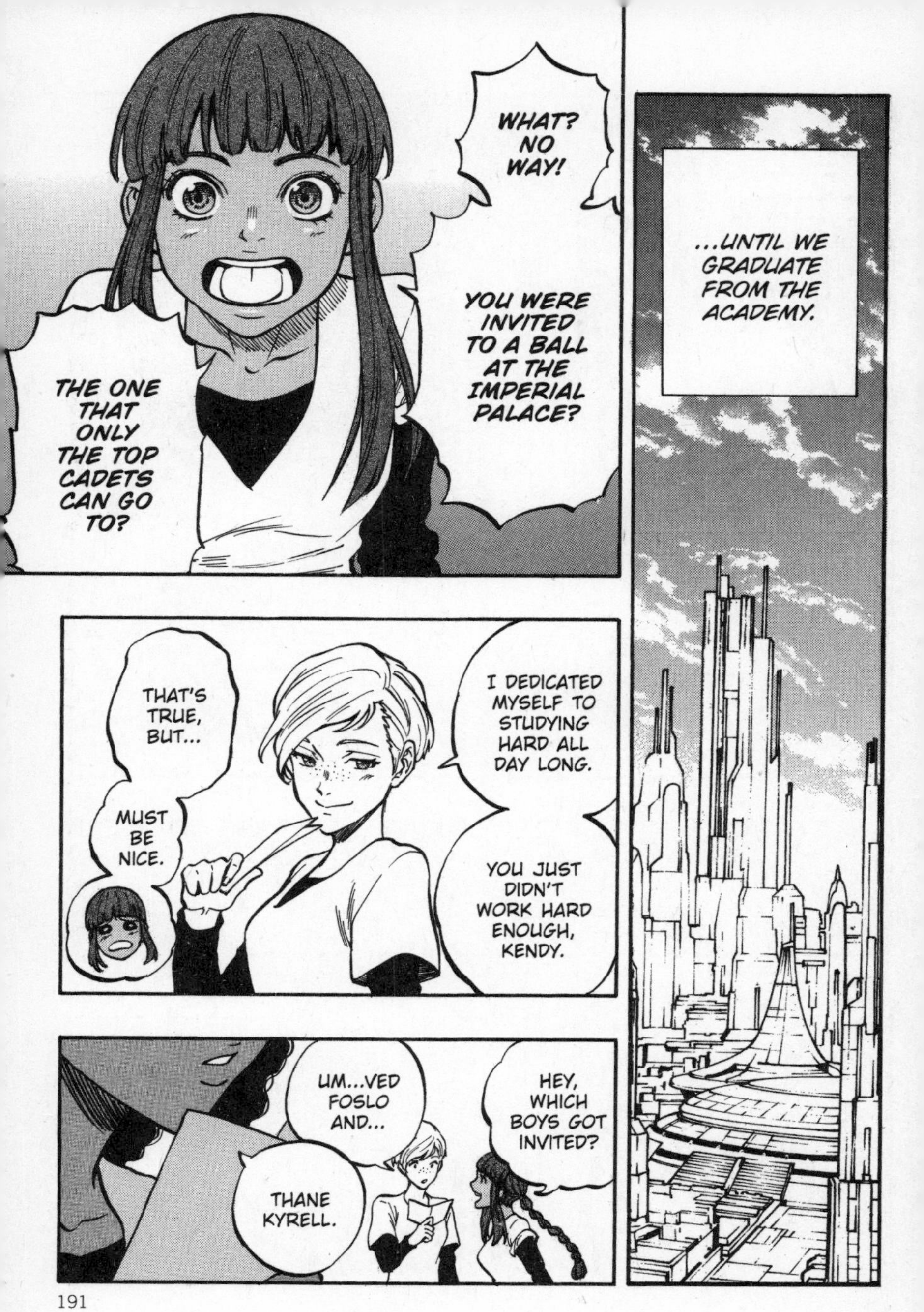
...UNTIL WE GRADUATE FROM THE ACADEMY.
WHAT? NO WAY!
YOU WERE INVITED TO A BALL AT THE IMPERIAL PALACE?
THE ONE THAT ONLY THE TOP CADETS CAN GO TO?
I DEDICATED MYSELF TO STUDYING HARD ALL DAY LONG.
YOU JUST DIDN'T WORK HARD ENOUGH, KENDY.
THAT'S TRUE, BUT...
MUST BE NICE.
HEY, WHICH BOYS GOT INVITED?
UM...VED FOSLO AND...
THANE KYRELL.

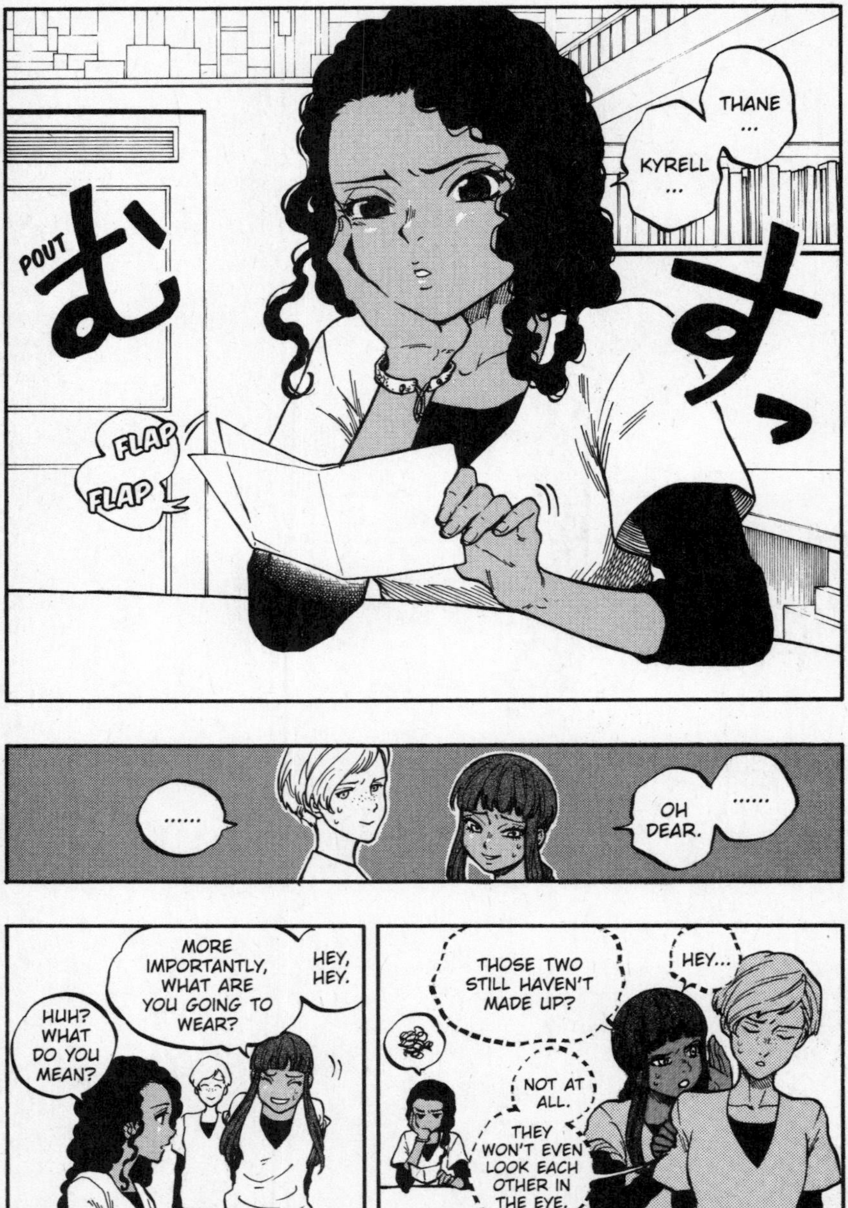
THANE ...
KYRELL ...
むすっ
POUT
FLAP FLAP
......
OH DEAR.
......
HEY...
THOSE TWO STILL HAVEN'T MADE UP?
NOT AT ALL.
THEY WON'T EVEN LOOK EACH OTHER IN THE EYE.
HEY, HEY.
MORE IMPORTANTLY, WHAT ARE YOU GOING TO WEAR?
HUH? WHAT DO YOU MEAN?

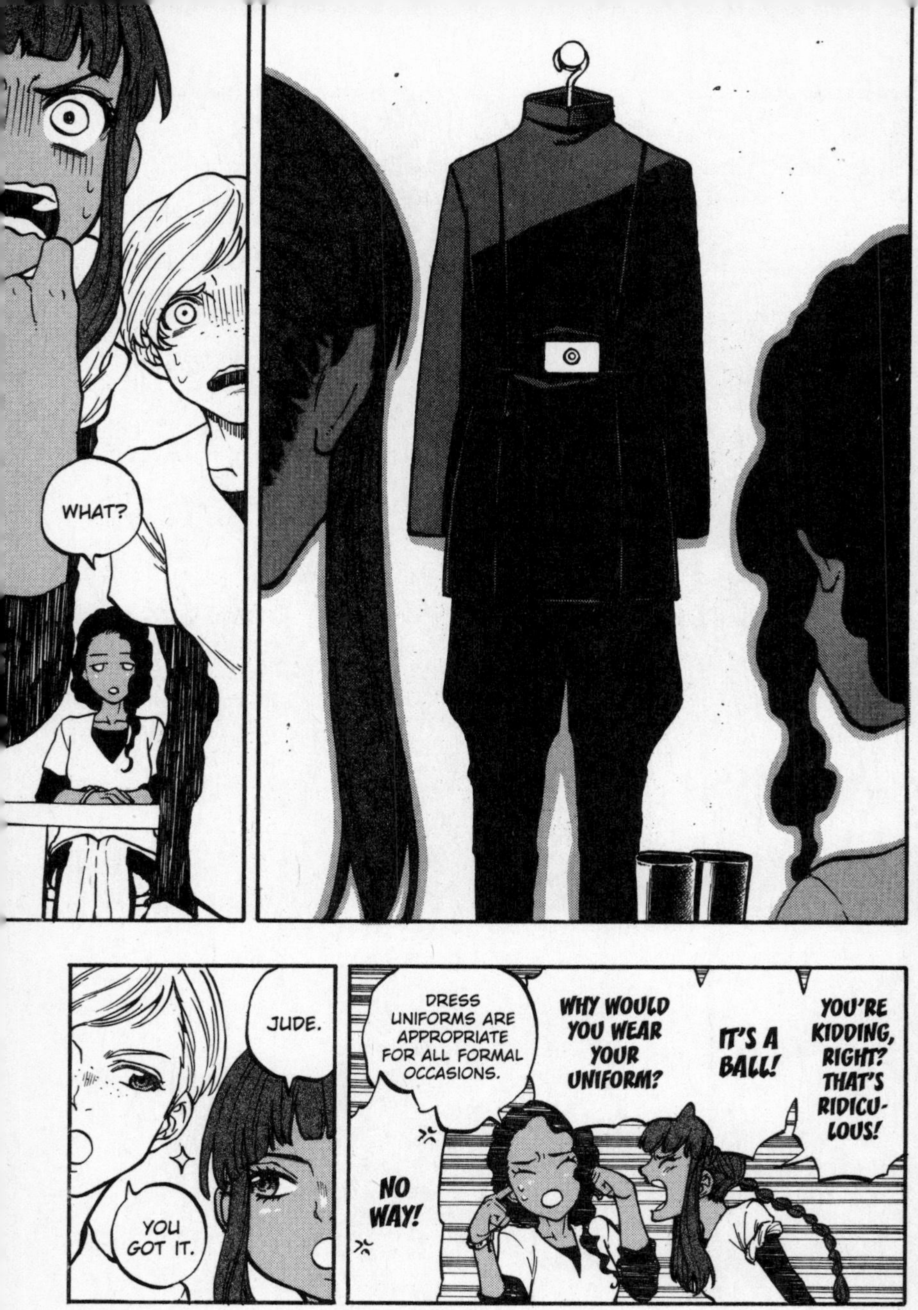
WHAT?
YOU'RE KIDDING, RIGHT? THAT'S RIDICU-LOUS!
IT'S A BALL!
WHY WOULD YOU WEAR YOUR UNIFORM?
DRESS UNIFORMS ARE APPROPRIATE FOR ALL FORMAL OCCASIONS.
NO WAY!
JUDE.
YOU GOT IT.

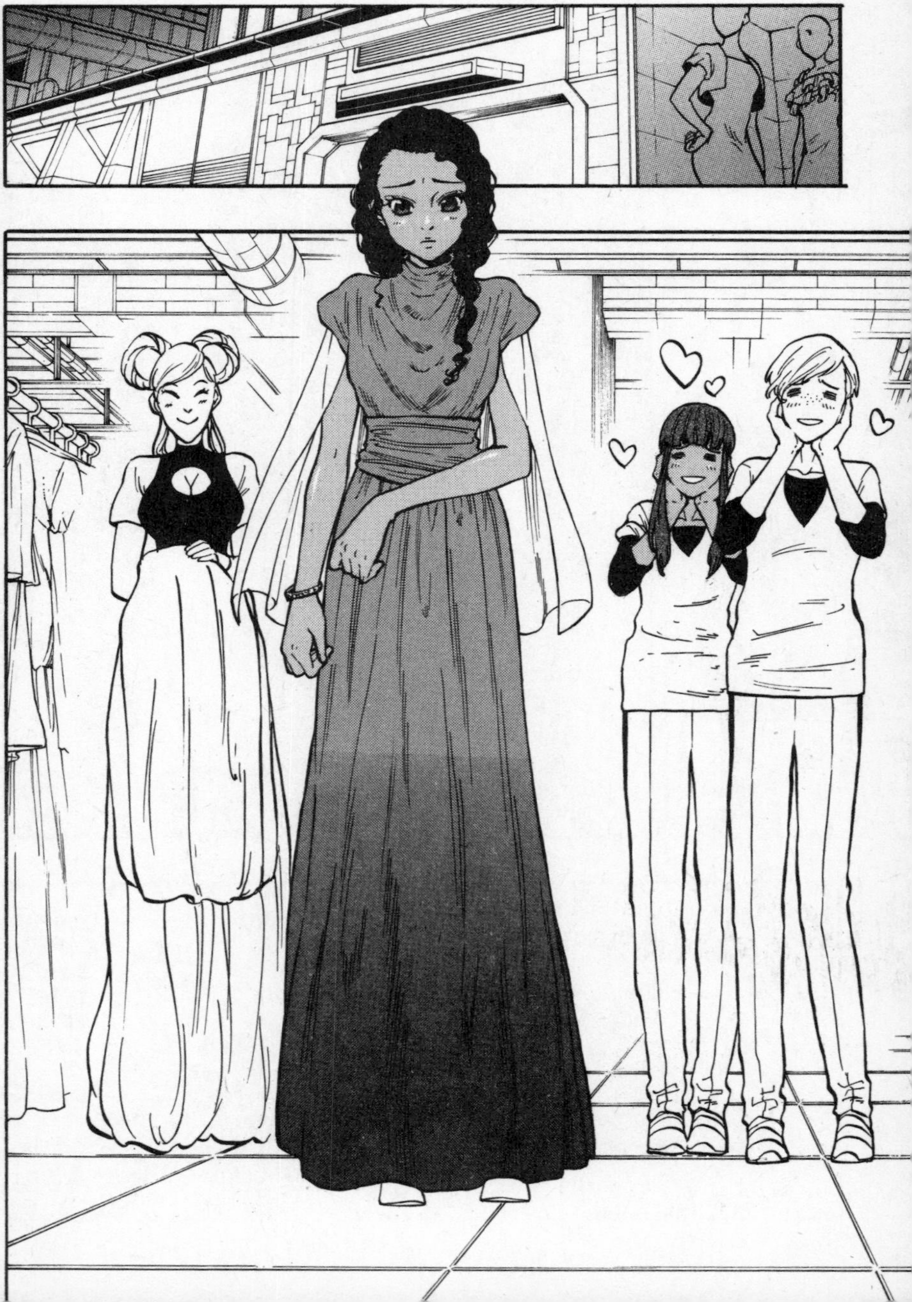

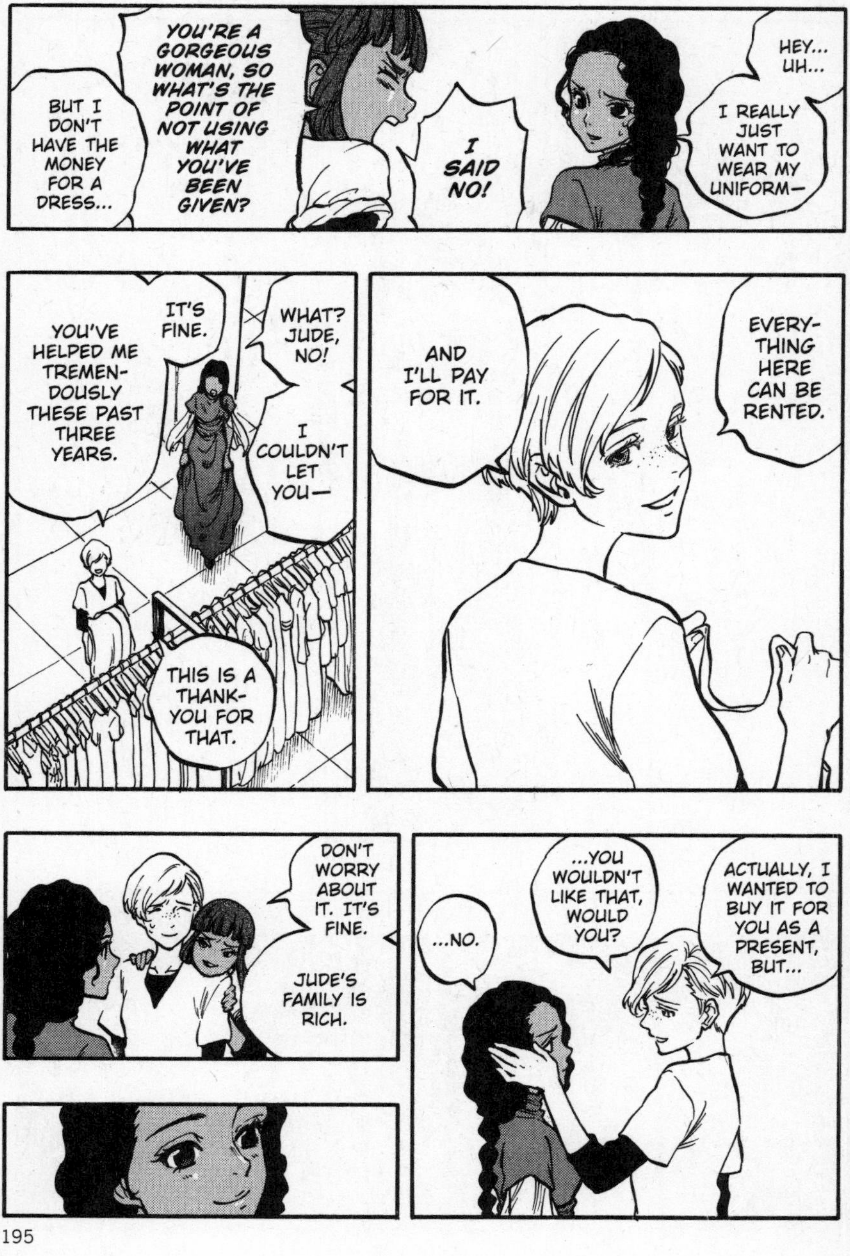
HEY... UH...
I REALLY JUST WANT TO WEAR MY UNIFORM—
I SAID NO!
YOU'RE A GORGEOUS WOMAN, SO WHAT'S THE POINT OF NOT USING WHAT YOU'VE BEEN GIVEN?
BUT I DON'T HAVE THE MONEY FOR A DRESS...
EVERY-THING HERE CAN BE RENTED.
AND I'LL PAY FOR IT.
WHAT? JUDE, NO!
I COULDN'T LET YOU—
IT'S FINE.
YOU'VE HELPED ME TREMEN-DOUSLY THESE PAST THREE YEARS.
THIS IS A THANK-YOU FOR THAT.
ACTUALLY, I WANTED TO BUY IT FOR YOU AS A PRESENT, BUT...
...YOU WOULDN'T LIKE THAT, WOULD YOU?
...NO.
DON'T WORRY ABOUT IT. IT'S FINE.
JUDE'S FAMILY IS RICH.

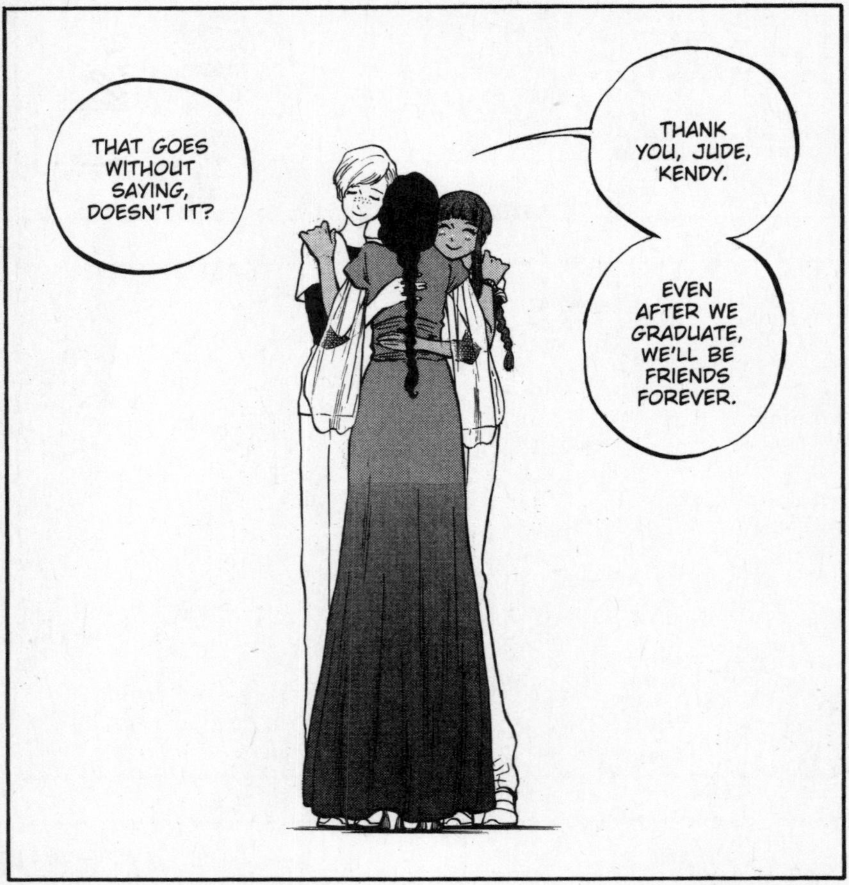
THANK YOU, JUDE, KENDY.
EVEN AFTER WE GRADUATE, WE'LL BE FRIENDS FOREVER.
THAT GOES WITHOUT SAYING, DOESN'T IT?

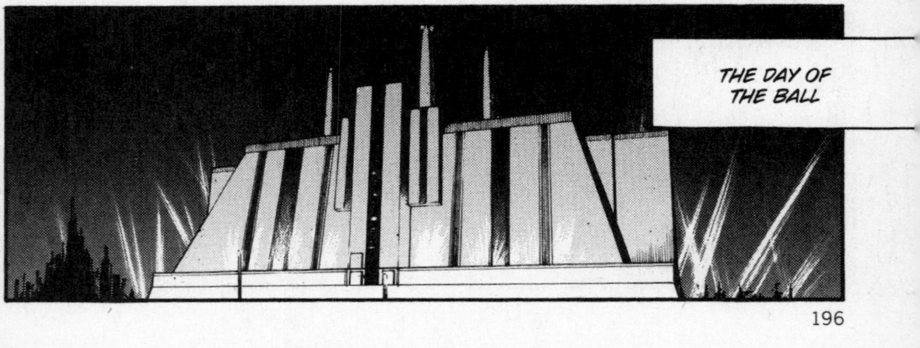
THE DAY OF THE BALL

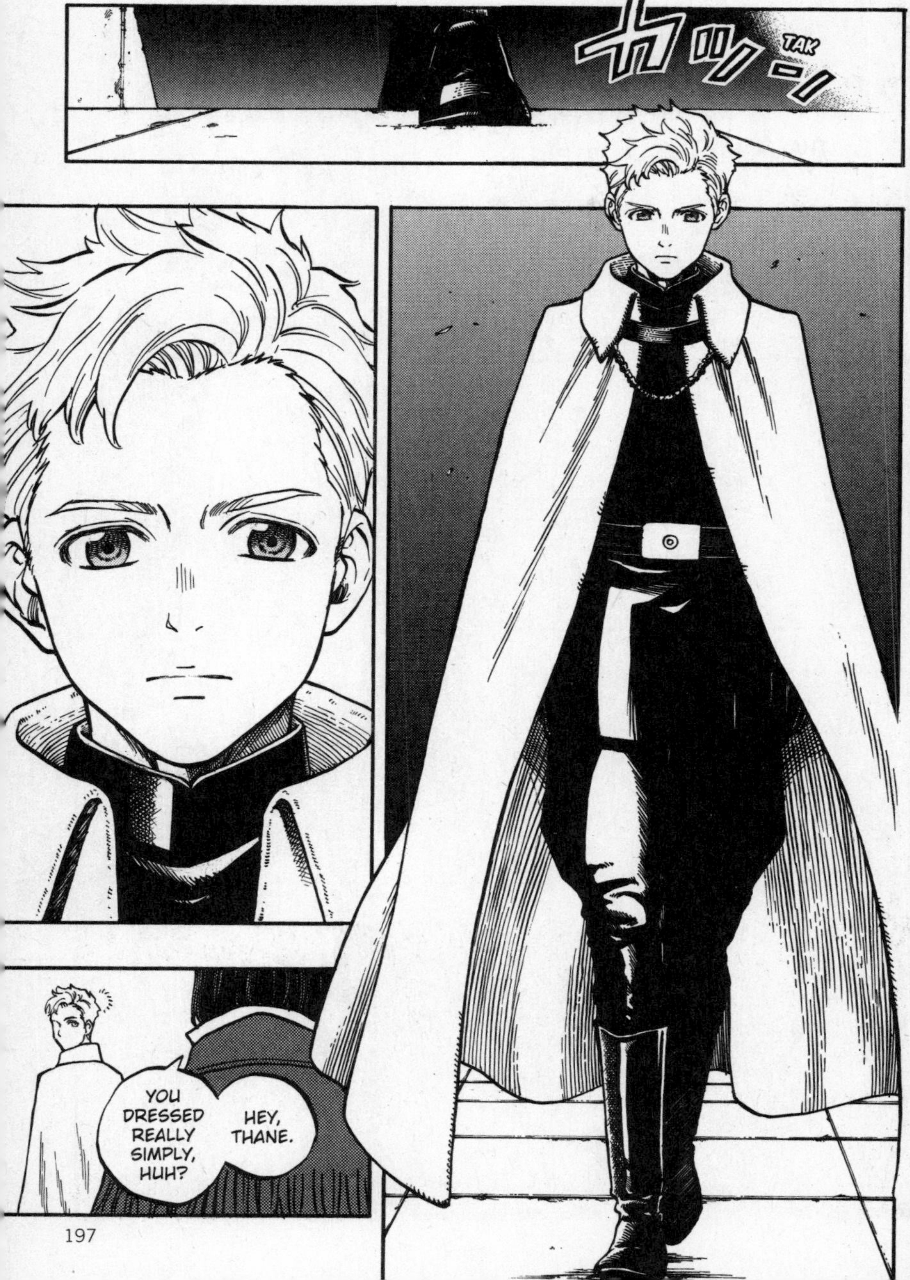
TAK
HEY, THANE.
YOU DRESSED REALLY SIMPLY, HUH?

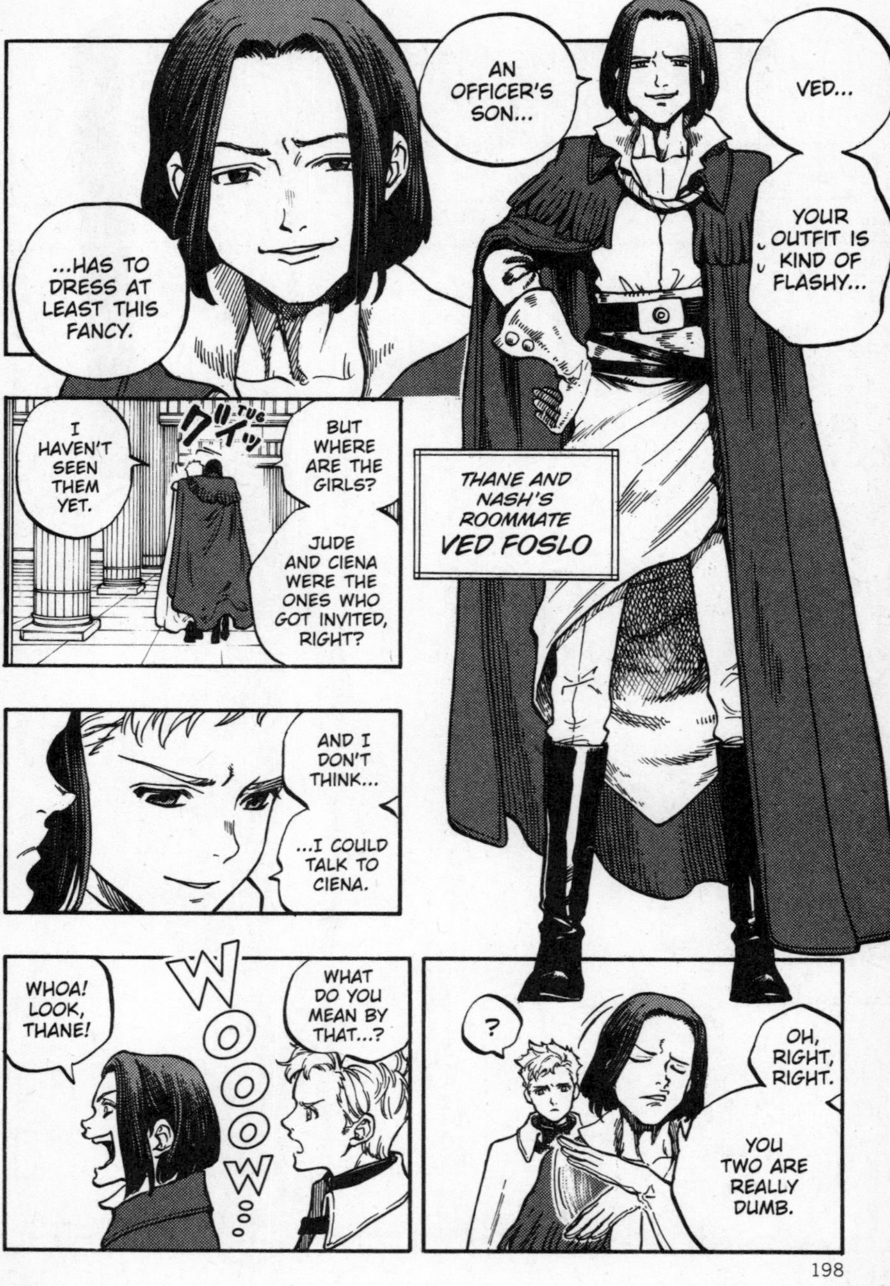
VED...
YOUR OUTFIT IS KIND OF FLASHY...
AN OFFICER'S SON...
...HAS TO DRESS AT LEAST THIS FANCY.
THANE AND NASH'S ROOMMATE VED FOSLO
グイッ TUG
BUT WHERE ARE THE GIRLS?
JUDE AND CIENA WERE THE ONES WHO GOT INVITED, RIGHT?
I HAVEN'T SEEN THEM YET.
AND I DON'T THINK...
...I COULD TALK TO CIENA.
?
OH, RIGHT, RIGHT.
YOU TWO ARE REALLY DUMB.
WHAT DO YOU MEAN BY THAT...?
WOOOOW...
WHOA! LOOK, THANE!

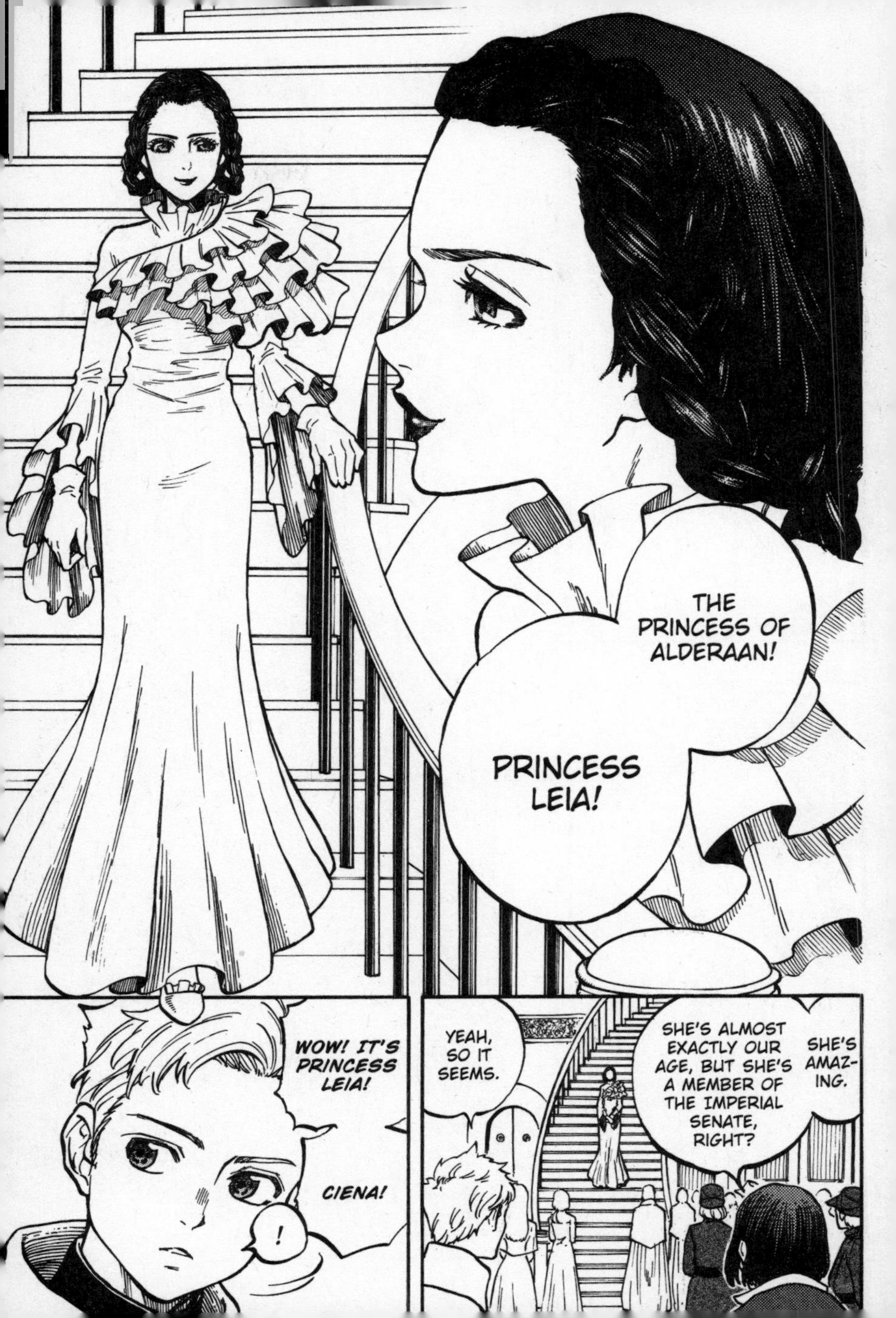
THE PRINCESS OF ALDERAAN!
PRINCESS LEIA!
SHE'S AMAZ-ING.
SHE'S ALMOST EXACTLY OUR AGE, BUT SHE'S A MEMBER OF THE IMPERIAL SENATE, RIGHT?
YEAH, SO IT SEEMS.
WOW! IT'S PRINCESS LEIA!
CIENA!
!

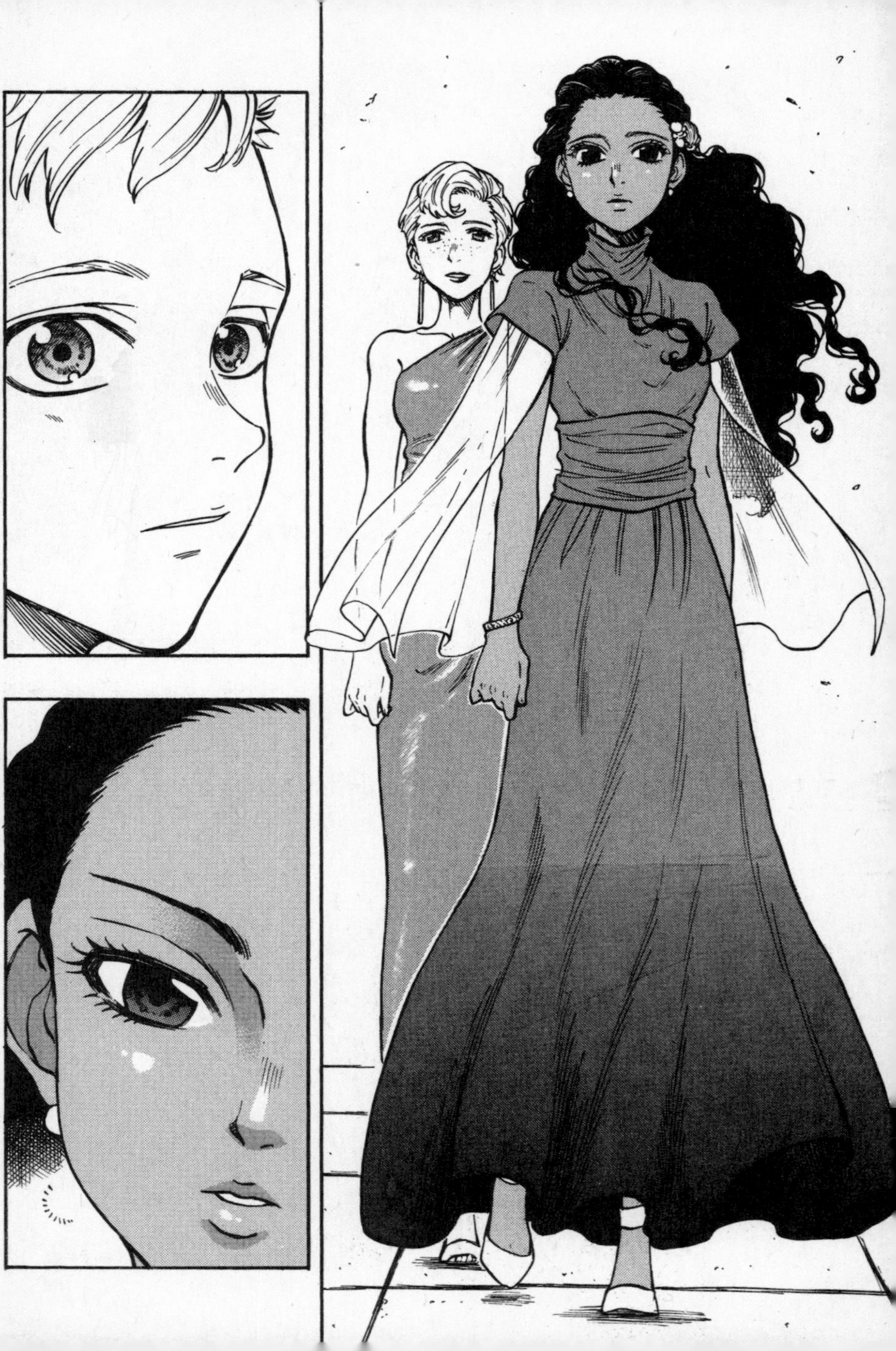

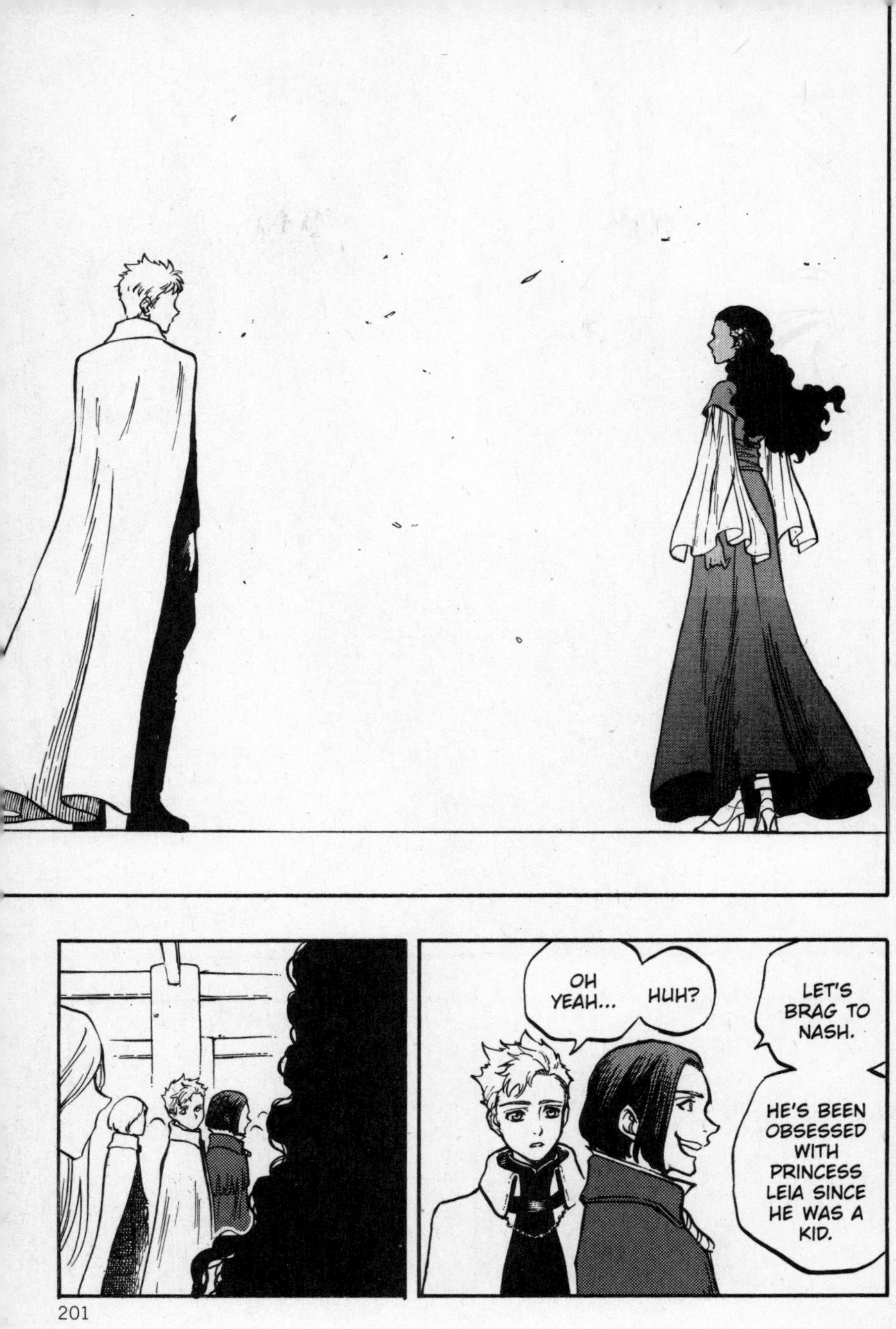
LET'S BRAG TO NASH.
HE'S BEEN OBSESSED WITH PRINCESS LEIA SINCE HE WAS A KID.
OH YEAH... HUH?

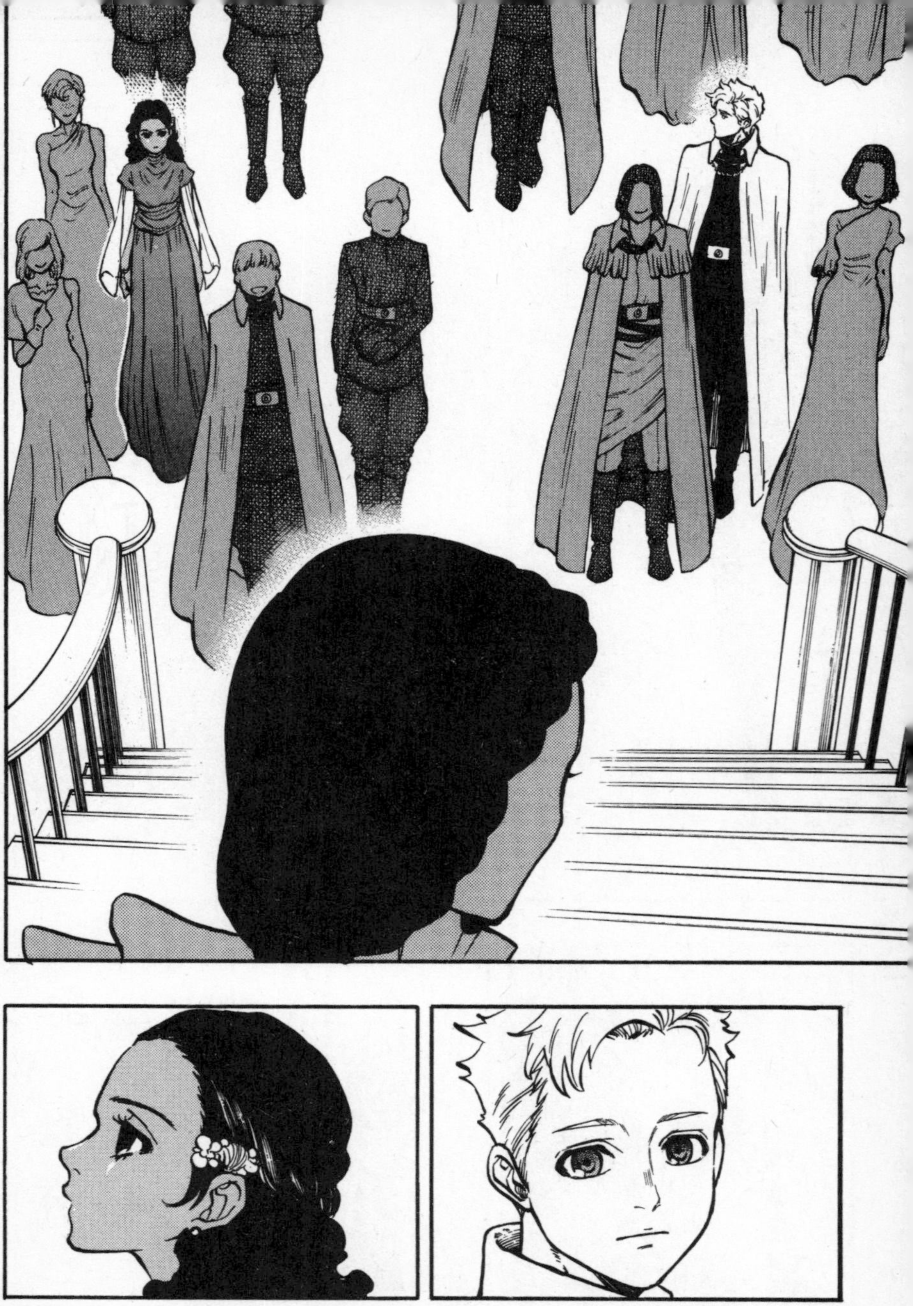

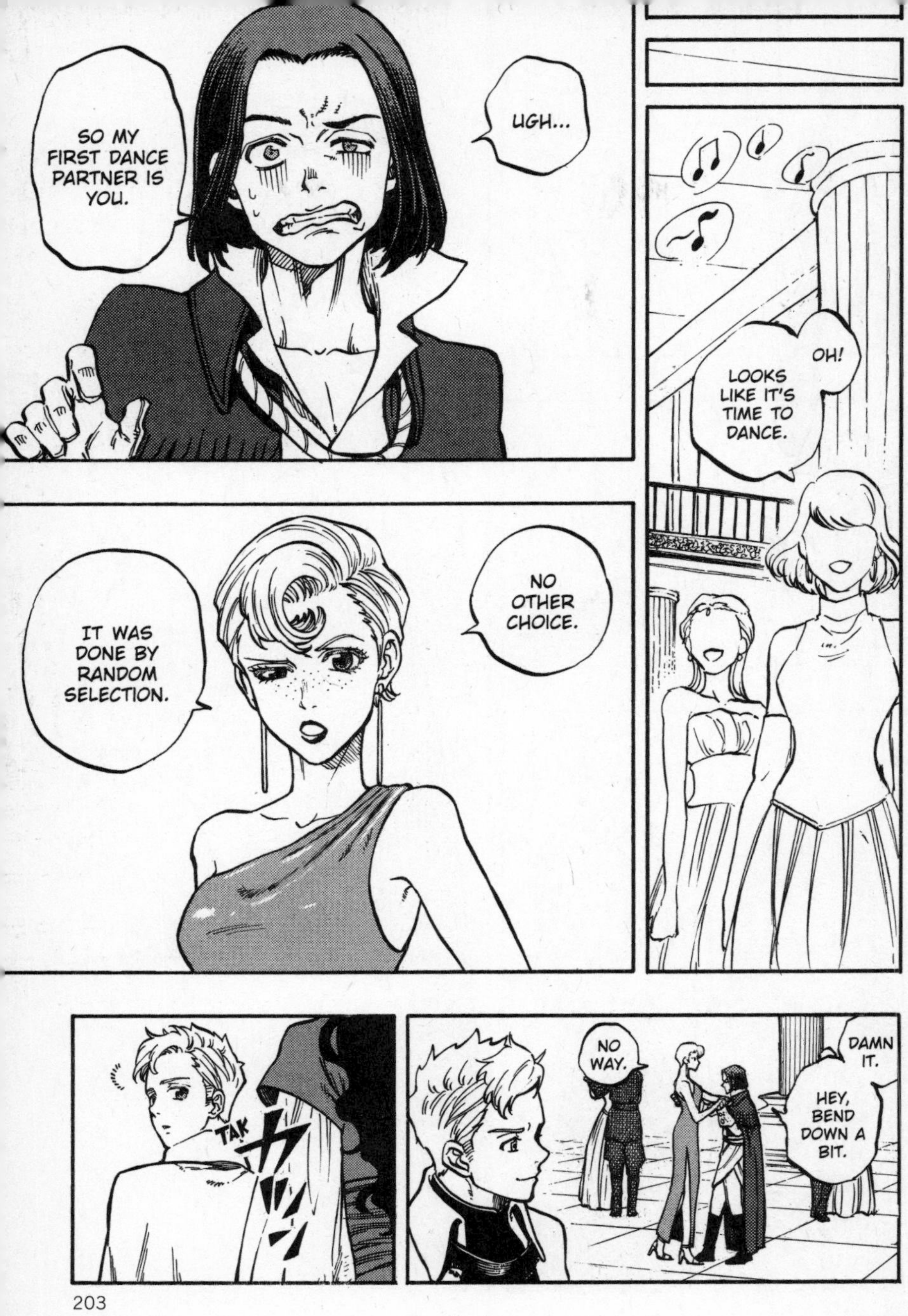
OH!
LOOKS LIKE IT'S TIME TO DANCE.
UGH...
SO MY FIRST DANCE PARTNER IS YOU.
NO OTHER CHOICE.
IT WAS DONE BY RANDOM SELECTION.
DAMN IT.
HEY, BEND DOWN A BIT.
NO WAY.
TAK

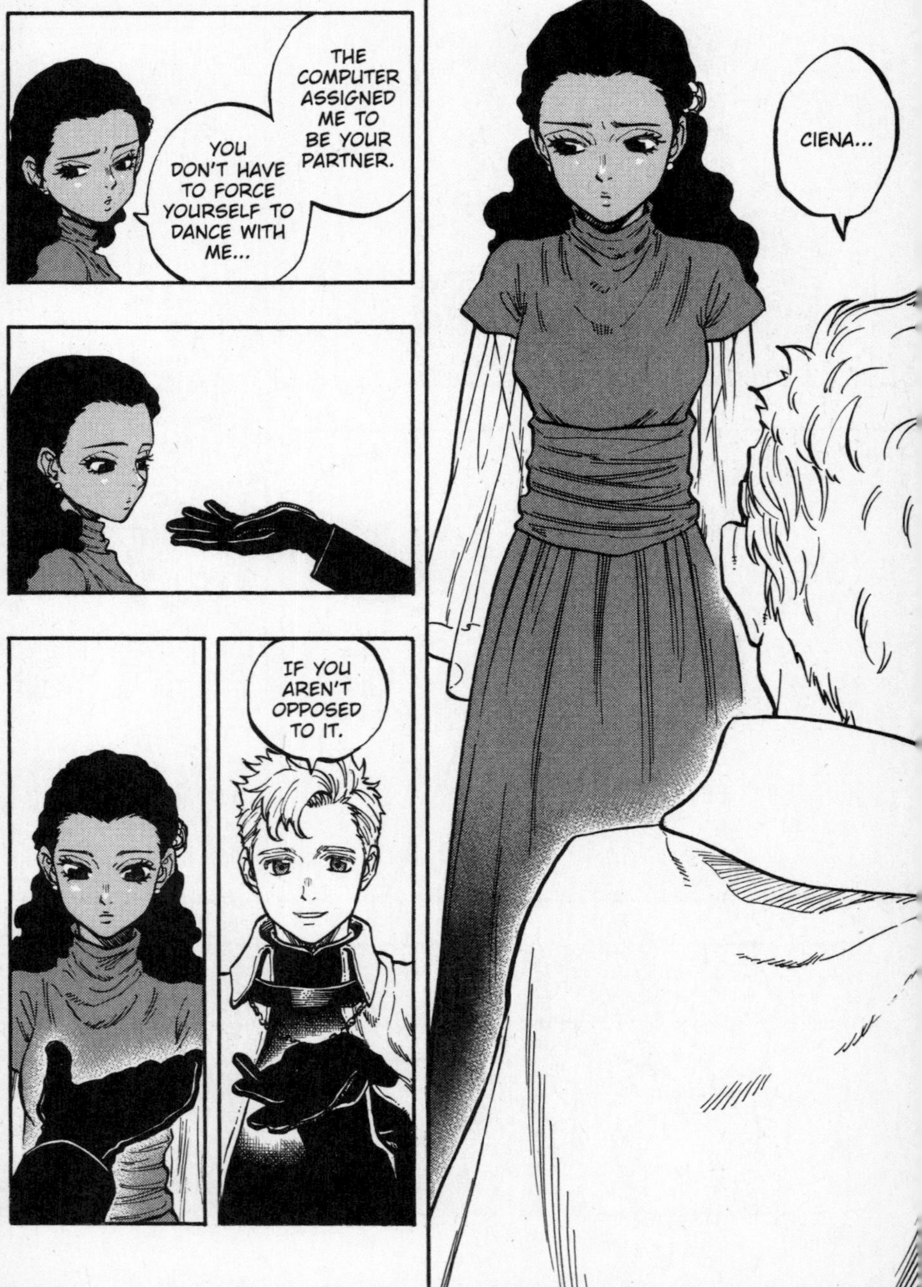
CIENA...
THE COMPUTER ASSIGNED ME TO BE YOUR PARTNER.
YOU DON'T HAVE TO FORCE YOURSELF TO DANCE WITH ME...
IF YOU AREN'T OPPOSED TO IT.

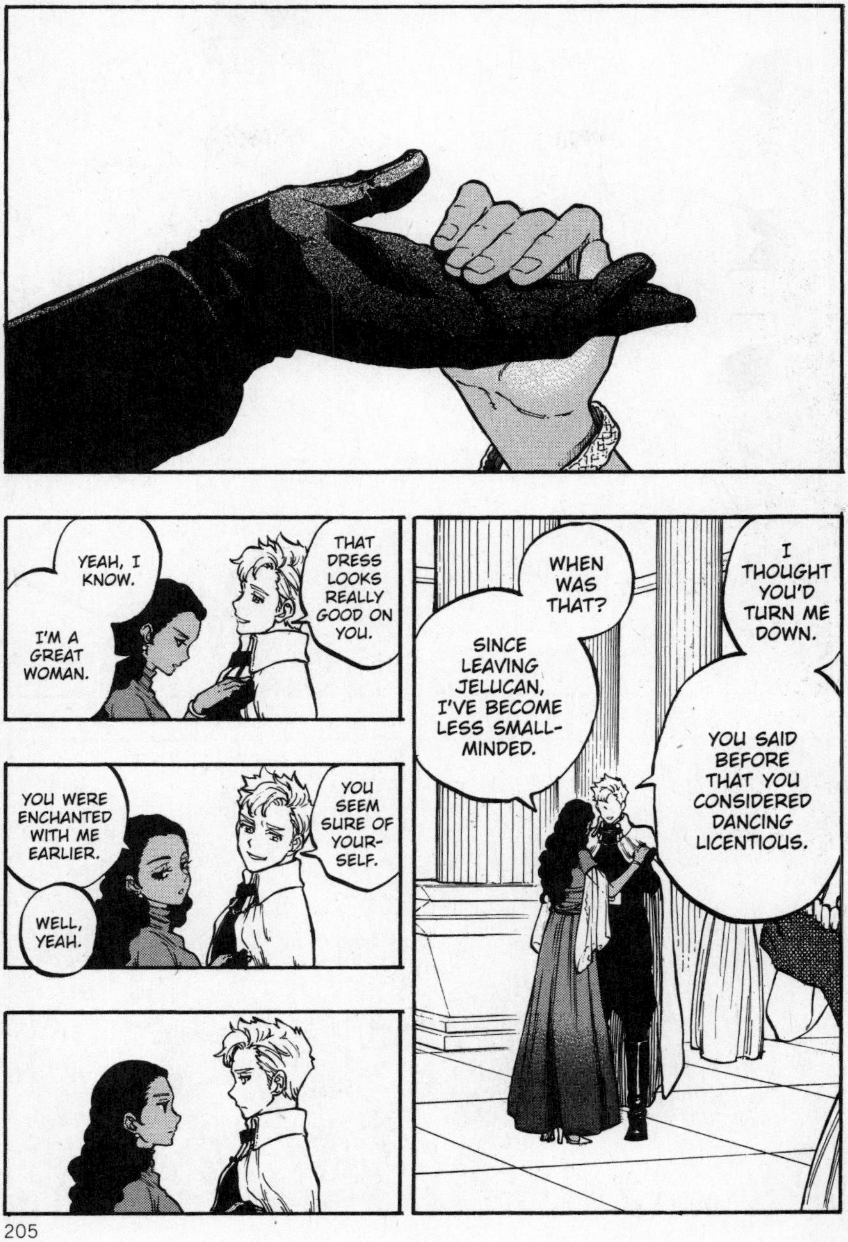
I THOUGHT YOU'D TURN ME DOWN.
WHEN WAS THAT?
YOU SAID BEFORE THAT YOU CONSIDERED DANCING LICENTIOUS.
SINCE LEAVING JELUCAN, I'VE BECOME LESS SMALL-MINDED.
THAT DRESS LOOKS REALLY GOOD ON YOU.
YEAH, I KNOW.
I'M A GREAT WOMAN.
YOU SEEM SURE OF YOUR-SELF.
YOU WERE ENCHANTED WITH ME EARLIER.
WELL, YEAH.

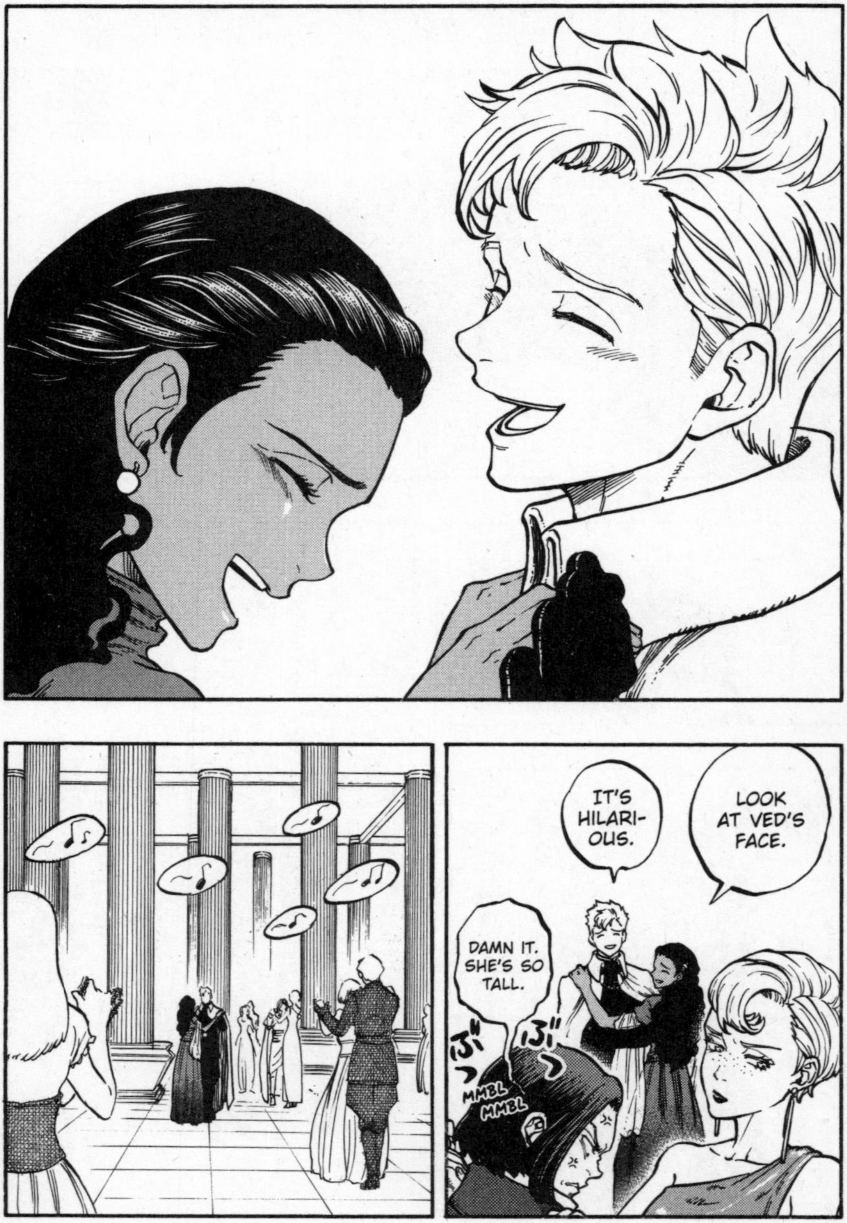
LOOK AT VED'S FACE.
IT'S HILARI- OUS.
DAMN IT. SHE'S SO TALL.
ぶつ
ぶつ
MMBL MMBL

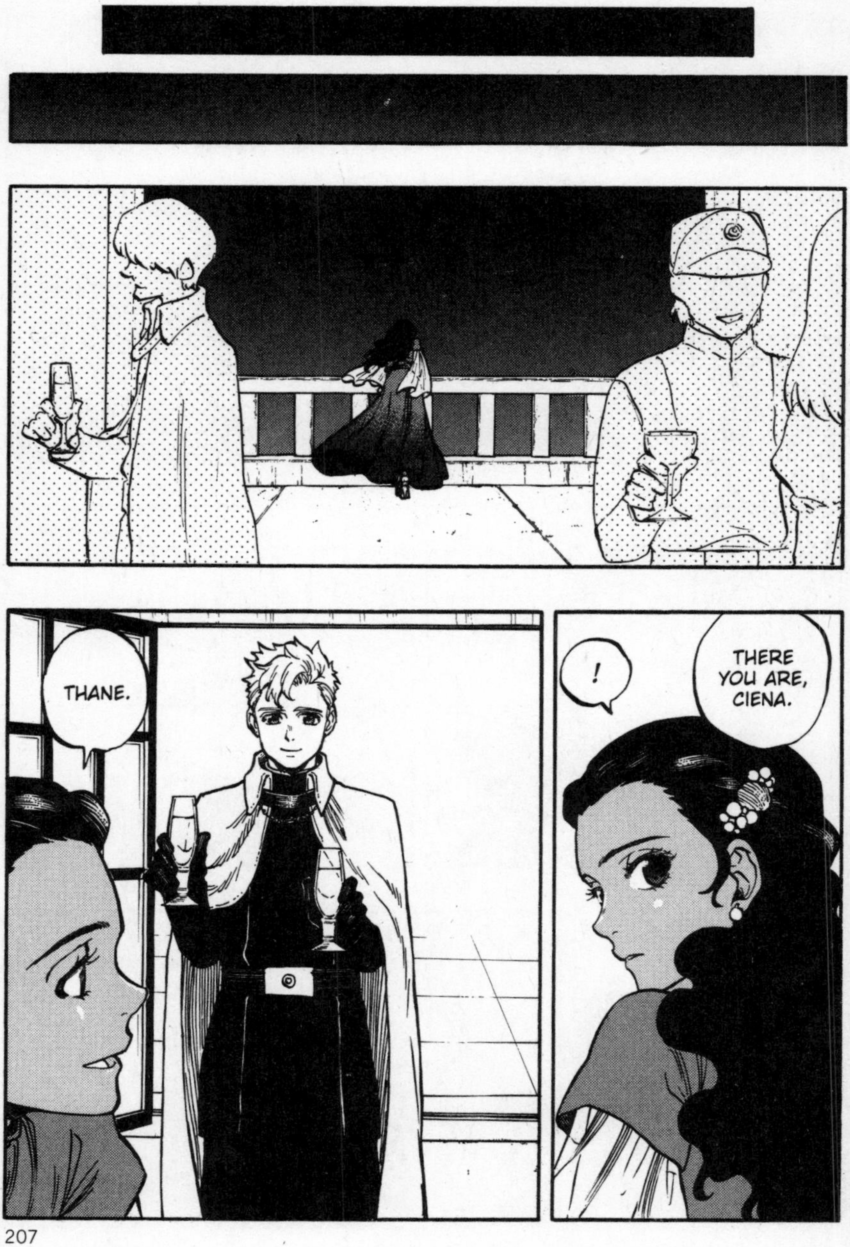
THERE YOU ARE, CIENA.
!
THANE.

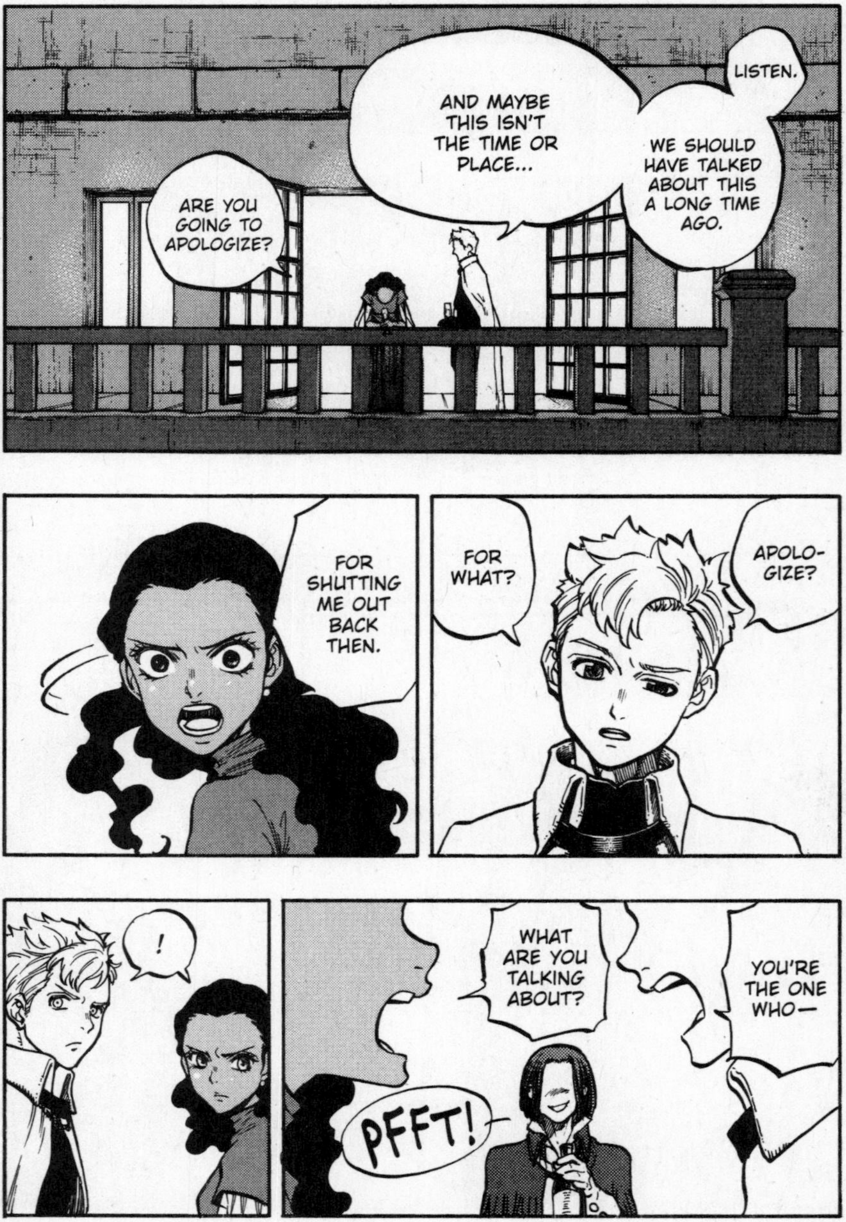
LISTEN.
WE SHOULD HAVE TALKED ABOUT THIS A LONG TIME AGO.
AND MAYBE THIS ISN'T THE TIME OR PLACE...
ARE YOU GOING TO APOLOGIZE?
APOLO-GIZE?
FOR WHAT?
FOR SHUTTING ME OUT BACK THEN.
YOU'RE THE ONE WHO—
WHAT ARE YOU TALKING ABOUT?
PFFT!
!

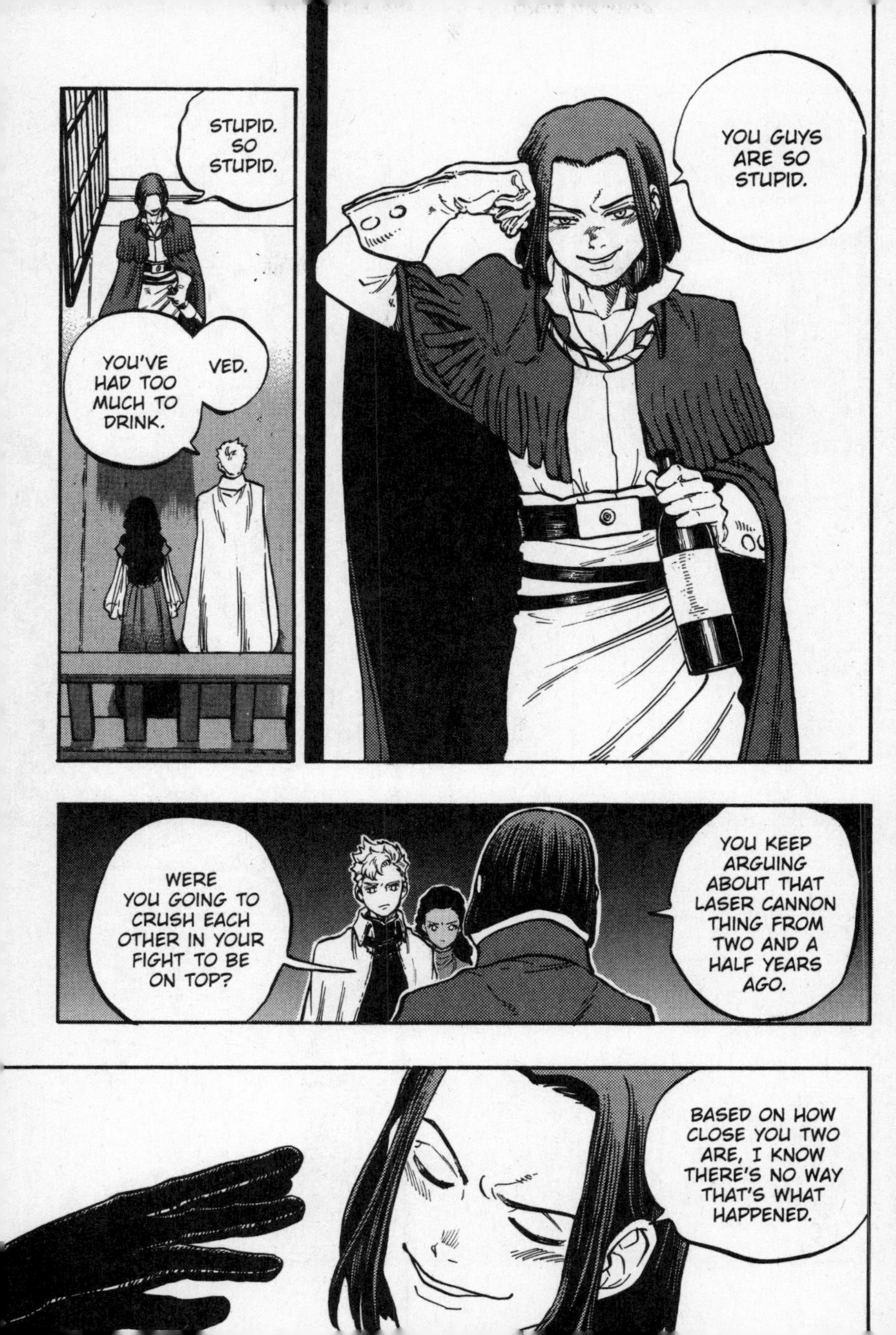
YOU GUYS ARE SO STUPID.
STUPID. SO STUPID.
VED.
YOU'VE HAD TOO MUCH TO DRINK.
YOU KEEP ARGUING ABOUT THAT LASER CANNON THING FROM TWO AND A HALF YEARS AGO.
WERE YOU GOING TO CRUSH EACH OTHER IN YOUR FIGHT TO BE ON TOP?
BASED ON HOW CLOSE YOU TWO ARE, I KNOW THERE'S NO WAY THAT'S WHAT HAPPENED.

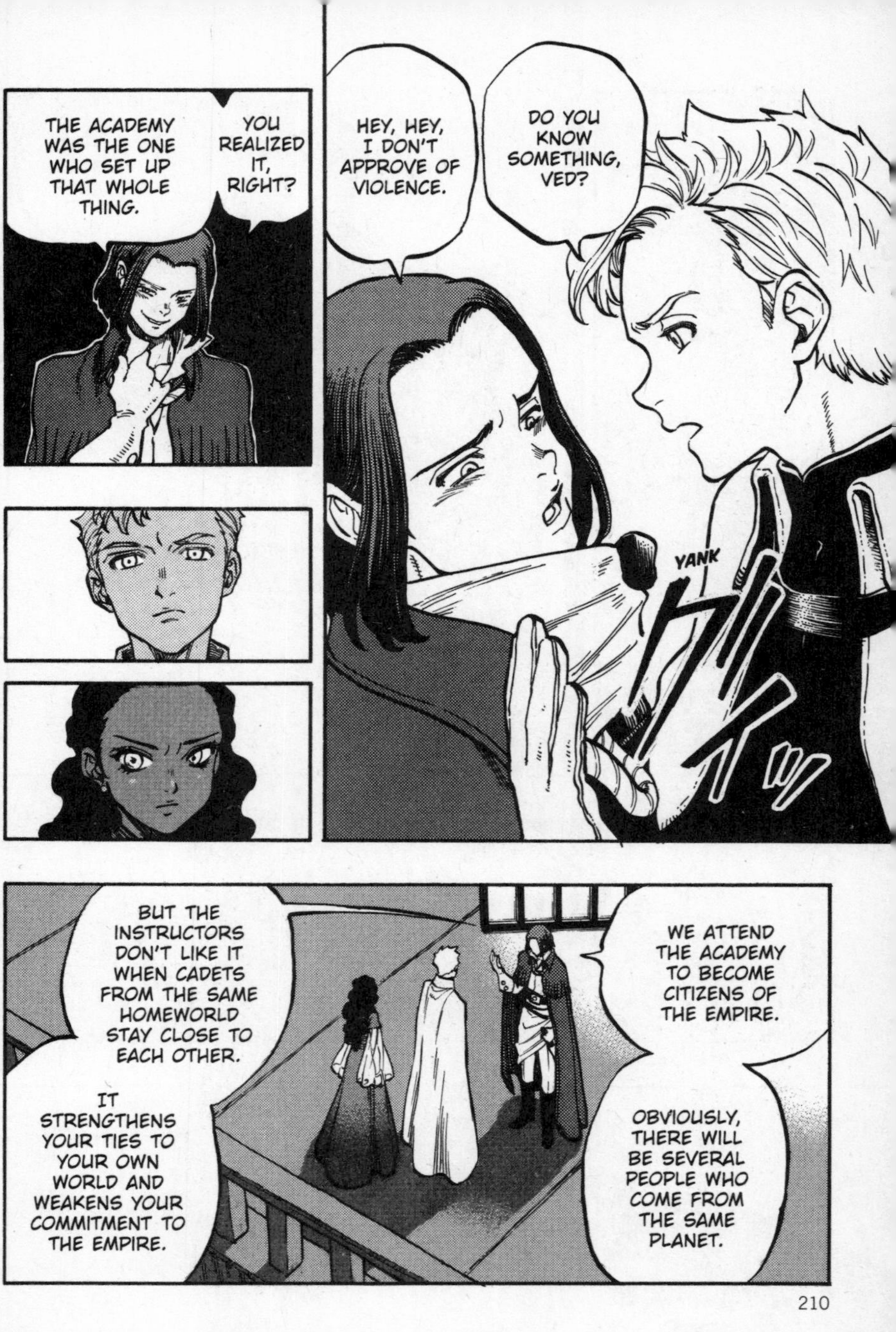
DO YOU KNOW SOMETHING, VED?
HEY, HEY, I DON'T APPROVE OF VIOLENCE.
YANK
YOU REALIZED IT, RIGHT?
THE ACADEMY WAS THE ONE WHO SET UP THAT WHOLE THING.
WE ATTEND THE ACADEMY TO BECOME CITIZENS OF THE EMPIRE.
OBVIOUSLY, THERE WILL BE SEVERAL PEOPLE WHO COME FROM THE SAME PLANET.
BUT THE INSTRUCTORS DON'T LIKE IT WHEN CADETS FROM THE SAME HOMEWORLD STAY CLOSE TO EACH OTHER.
IT STRENGTHENS YOUR TIES TO YOUR OWN WORLD AND WEAKENS YOUR COMMITMENT TO THE EMPIRE.

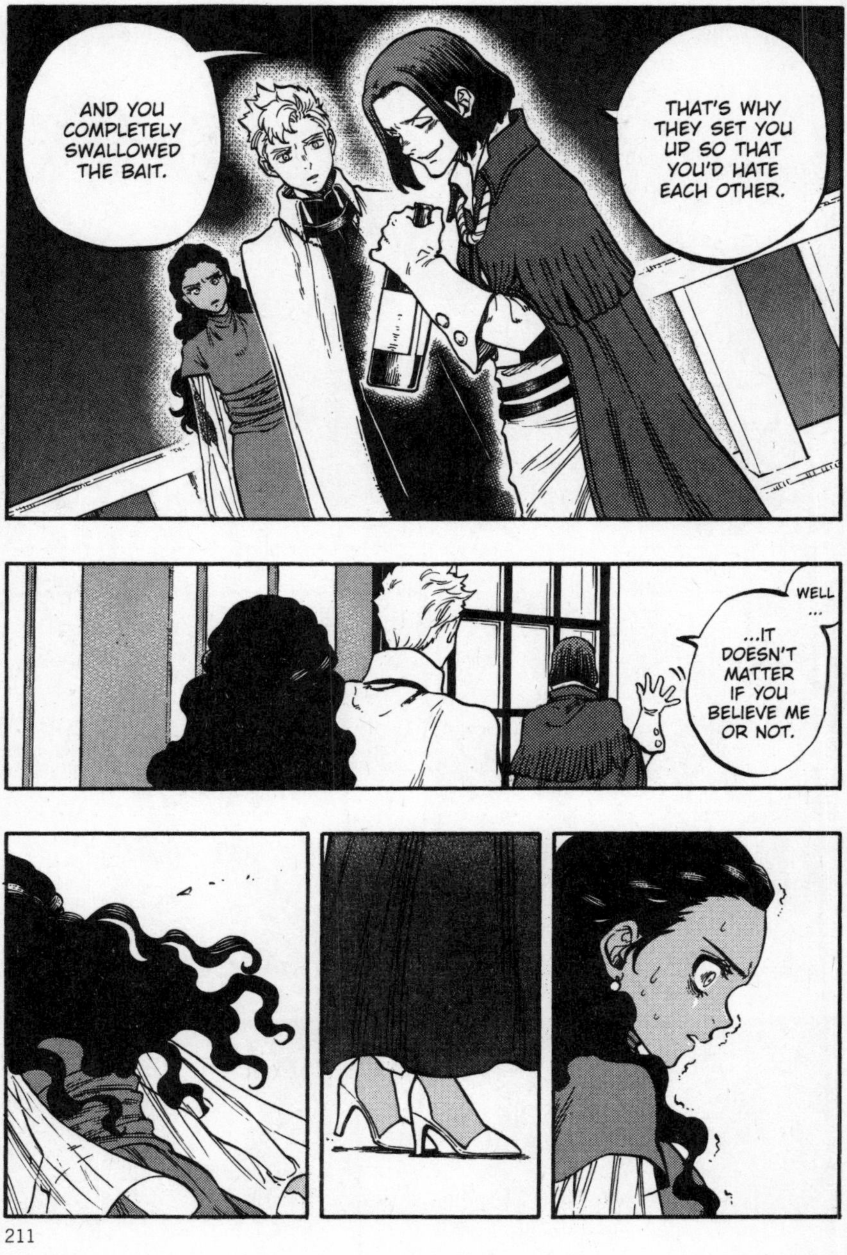
THAT'S WHY THEY SET YOU UP SO THAT YOU'D HATE EACH OTHER.
AND YOU COMPLETELY SWALLOWED THE BAIT.
WELL ...
...IT DOESN'T MATTER IF YOU BELIEVE ME OR NOT.

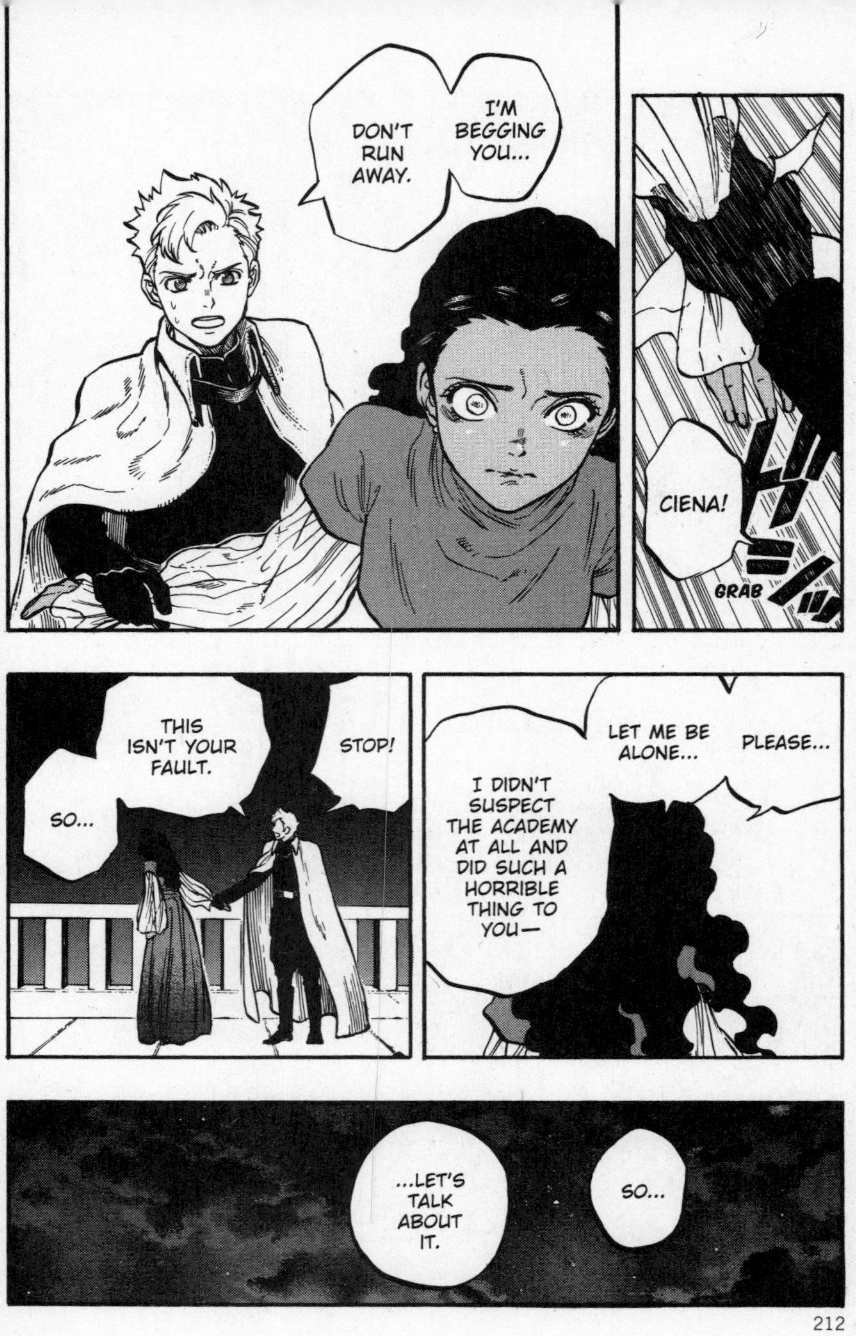
CIENA!
GRAB
I'M BEGGING YOU...
DON'T RUN AWAY.
PLEASE...
LET ME BE ALONE...
I DIDN'T SUSPECT THE ACADEMY AT ALL AND DID SUCH A HORRIBLE THING TO YOU—
STOP!
THIS ISN'T YOUR FAULT.
SO...
SO...
...LET'S TALK ABOUT IT.

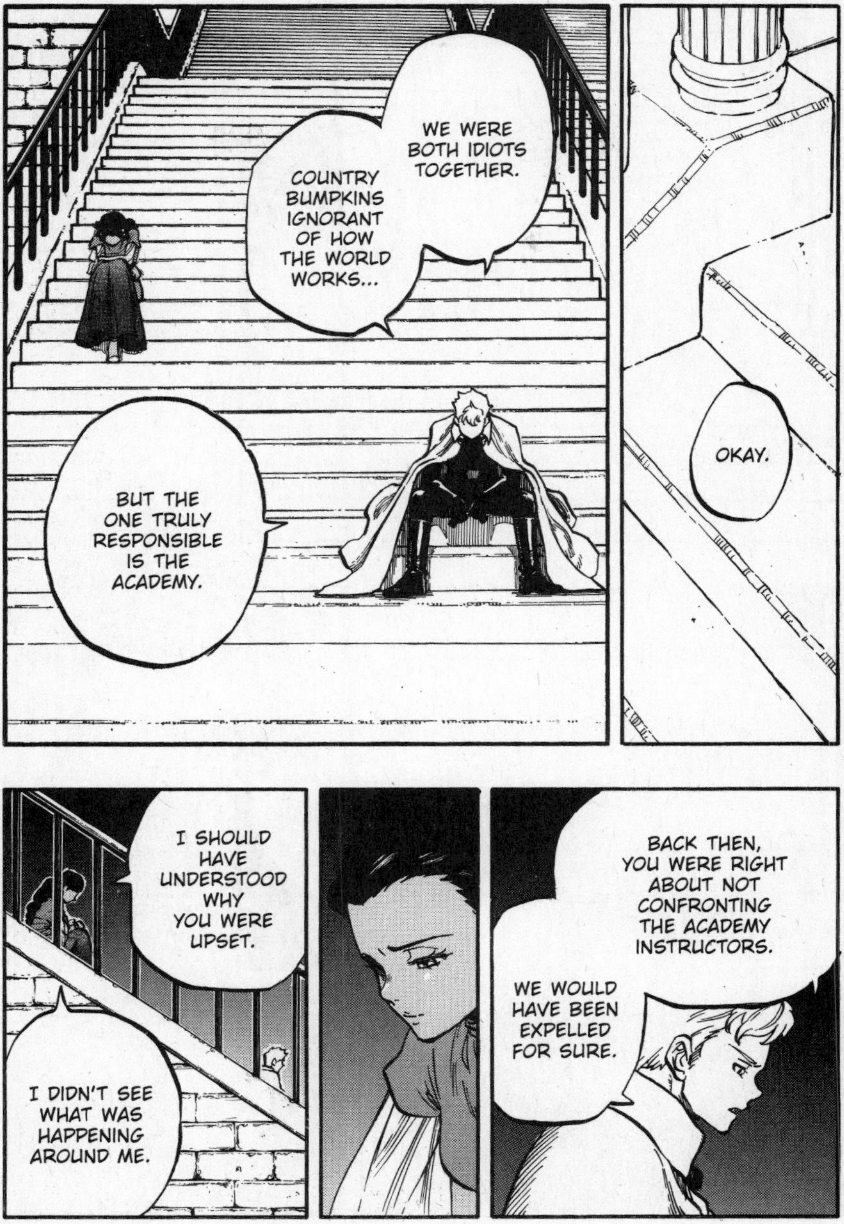
OKAY.
WE WERE BOTH IDIOTS TOGETHER.
COUNTRY BUMPKINS IGNORANT OF HOW THE WORLD WORKS...
BUT THE ONE TRULY RESPONSIBLE IS THE ACADEMY.
BACK THEN, YOU WERE RIGHT ABOUT NOT CONFRONTING THE ACADEMY INSTRUCTORS.
WE WOULD HAVE BEEN EXPELLED FOR SURE.
I SHOULD HAVE UNDERSTOOD WHY YOU WERE UPSET.
I DIDN'T SEE WHAT WAS HAPPENING AROUND ME.

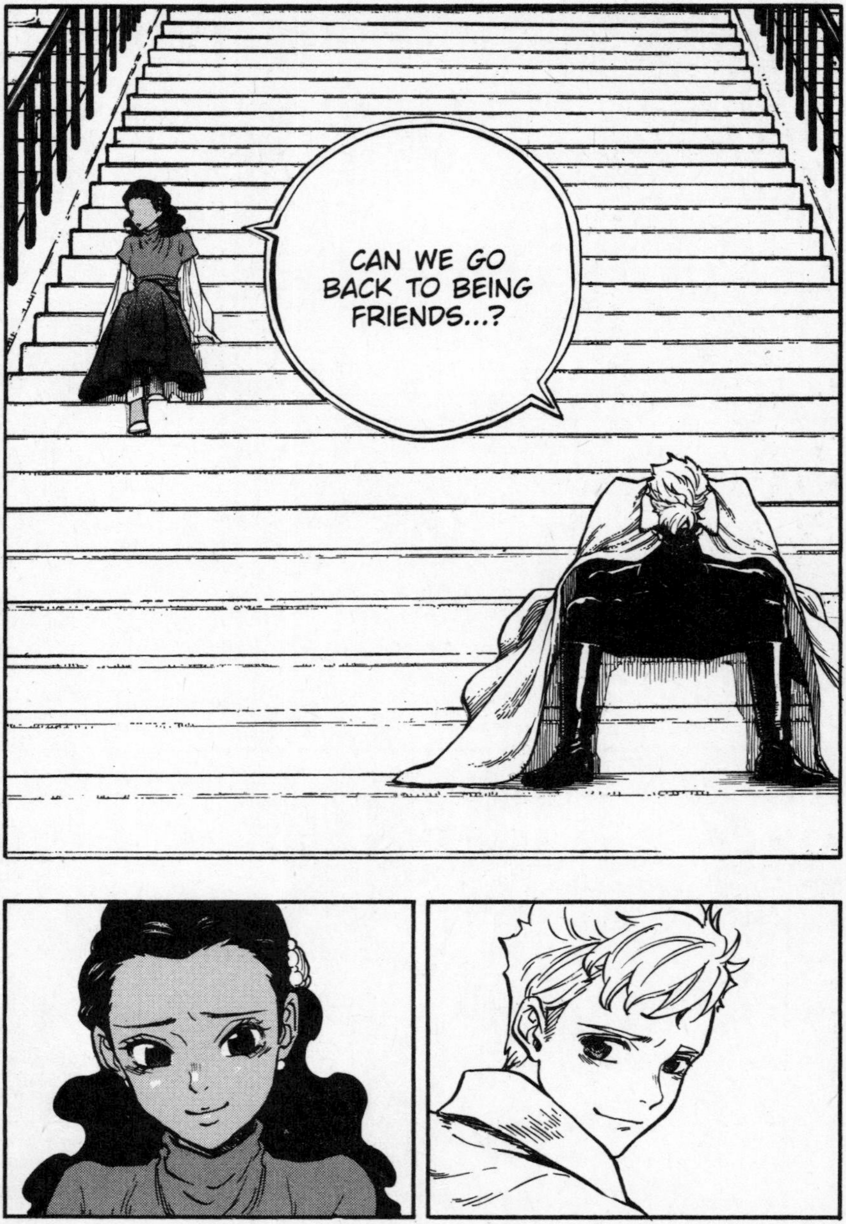
CAN WE GO BACK TO BEING FRIENDS...?

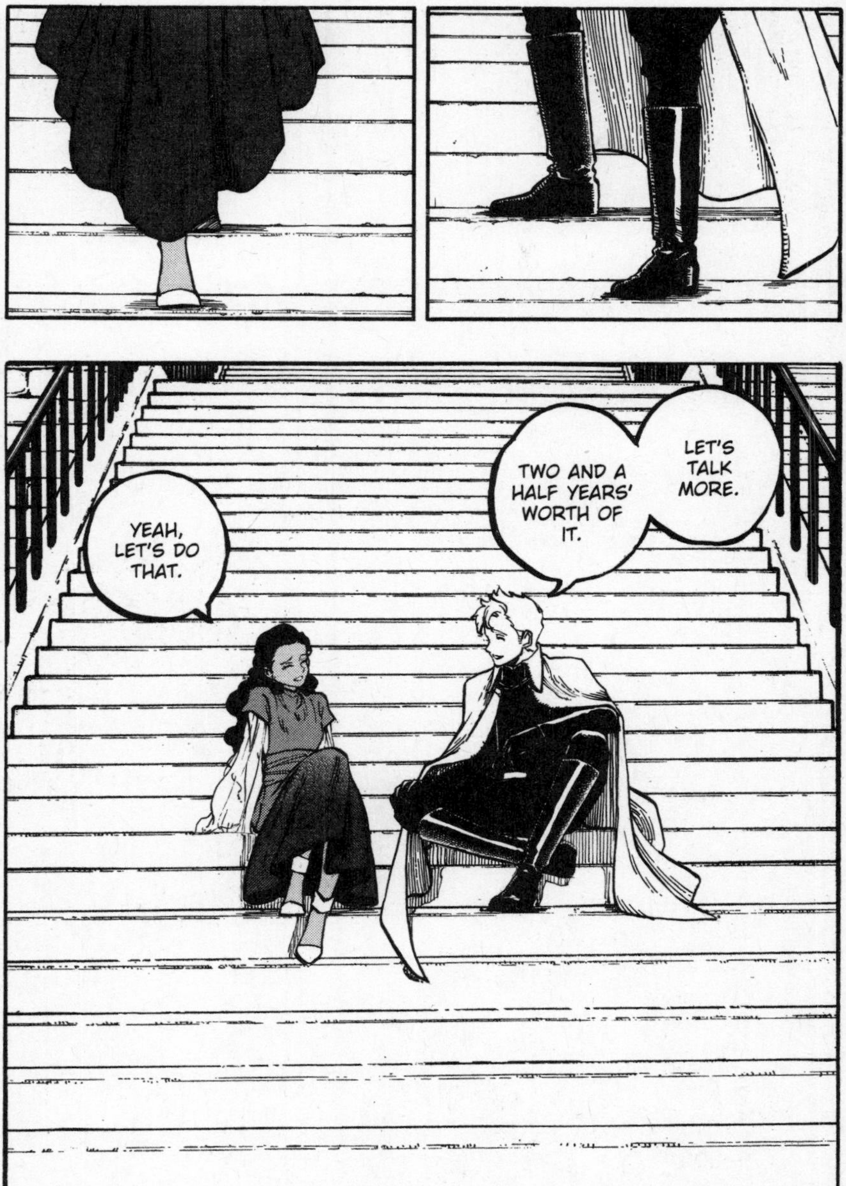
LET'S TALK MORE.
TWO AND A HALF YEARS' WORTH OF IT.
YEAH, LET'S DO THAT.

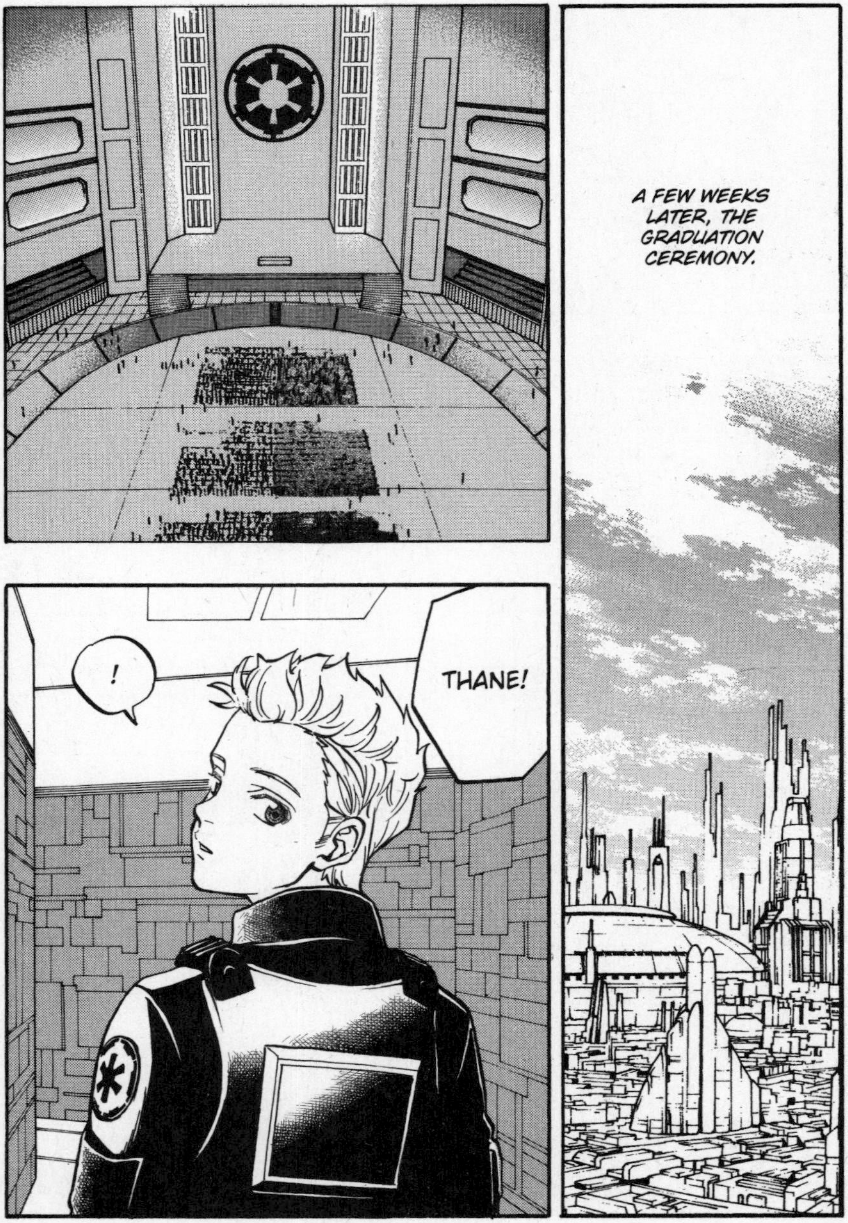
A FEW WEEKS LATER, THE GRADUATION CEREMONY.
THANE!
!

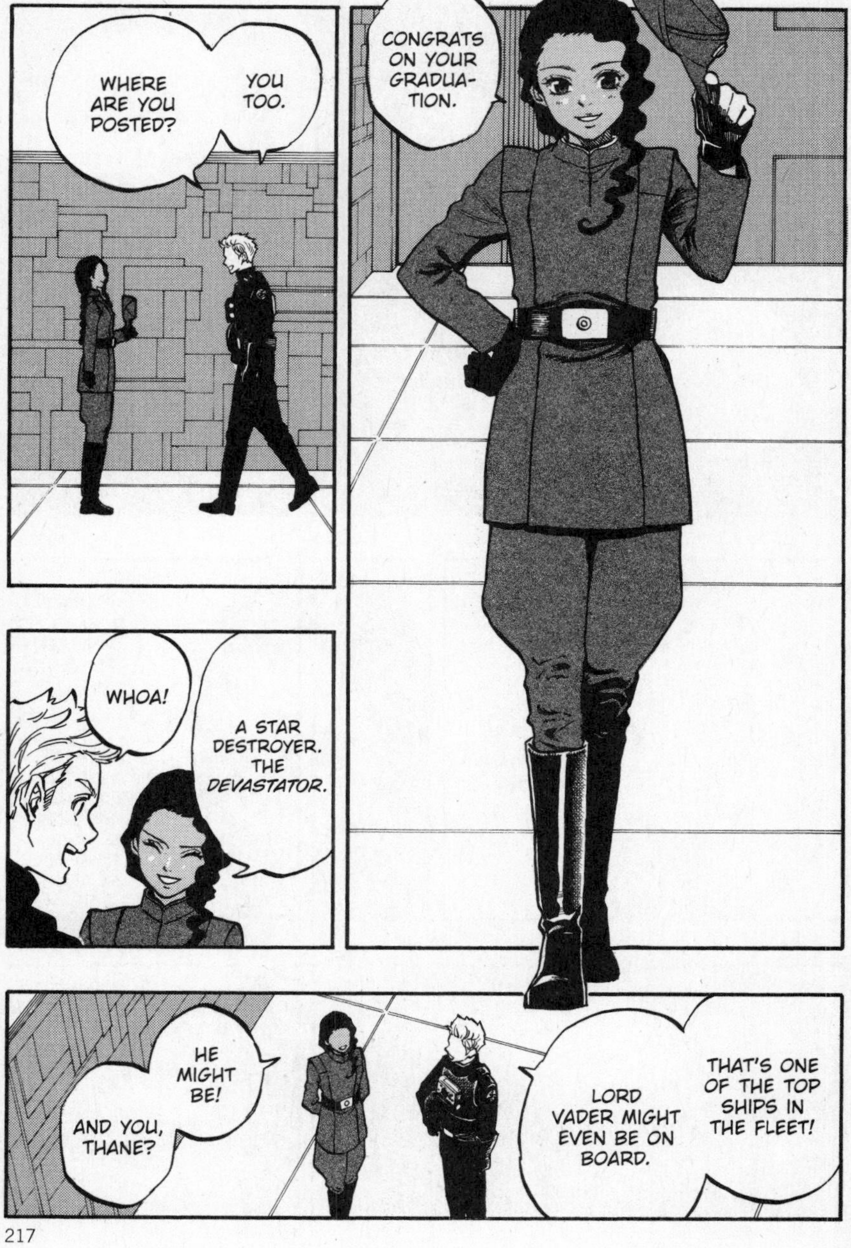
CONGRATS ON YOUR GRADUATION.
YOU TOO.
WHERE ARE YOU POSTED?
A STAR DESTROYER. THE *DEVASTATOR*.
WHOA!
THAT'S ONE OF THE TOP SHIPS IN THE FLEET!
LORD VADER MIGHT EVEN BE ON BOARD.
HE MIGHT BE!
AND YOU, THANE?

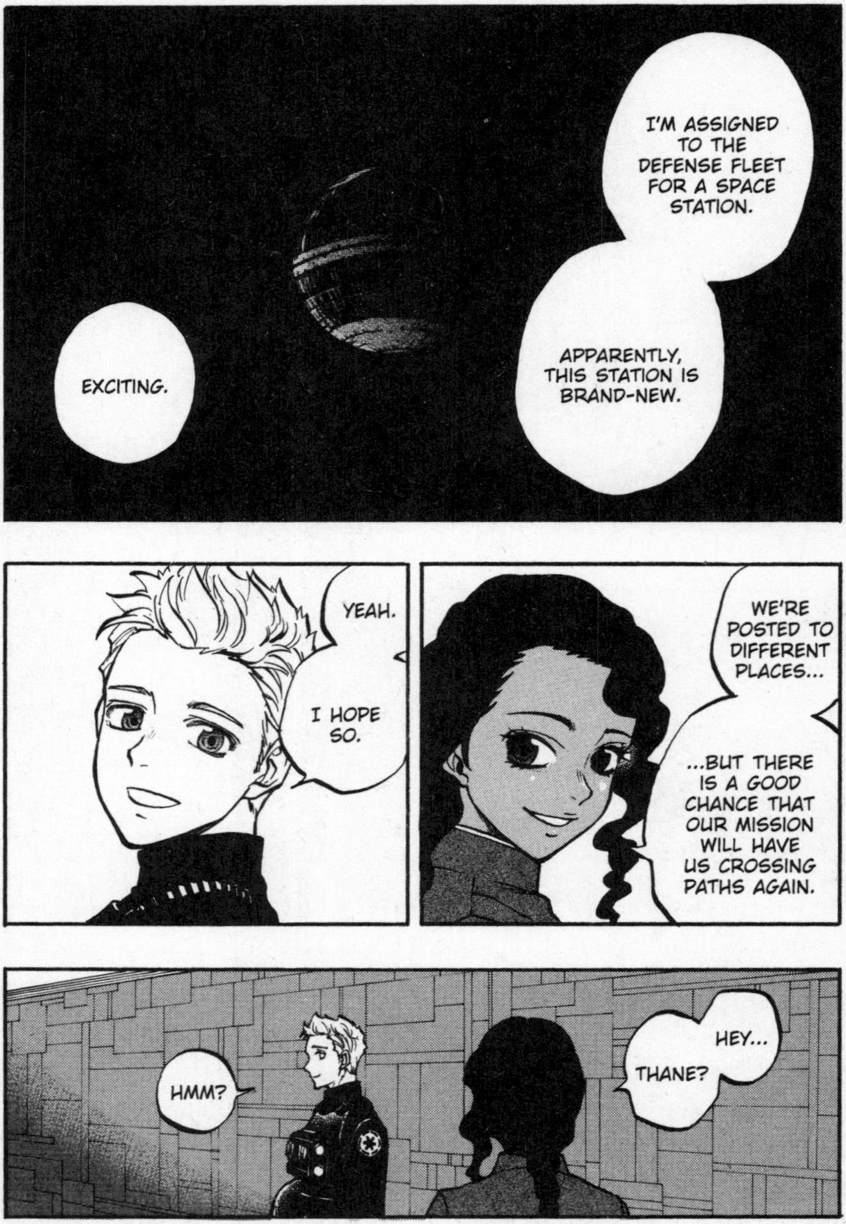
I'M ASSIGNED TO THE DEFENSE FLEET FOR A SPACE STATION.
APPARENTLY, THIS STATION IS BRAND-NEW.
EXCITING.
WE'RE POSTED TO DIFFERENT PLACES...
...BUT THERE IS A GOOD CHANCE THAT OUR MISSION WILL HAVE US CROSSING PATHS AGAIN.
YEAH.
I HOPE SO.
HEY... THANE?
HMM?

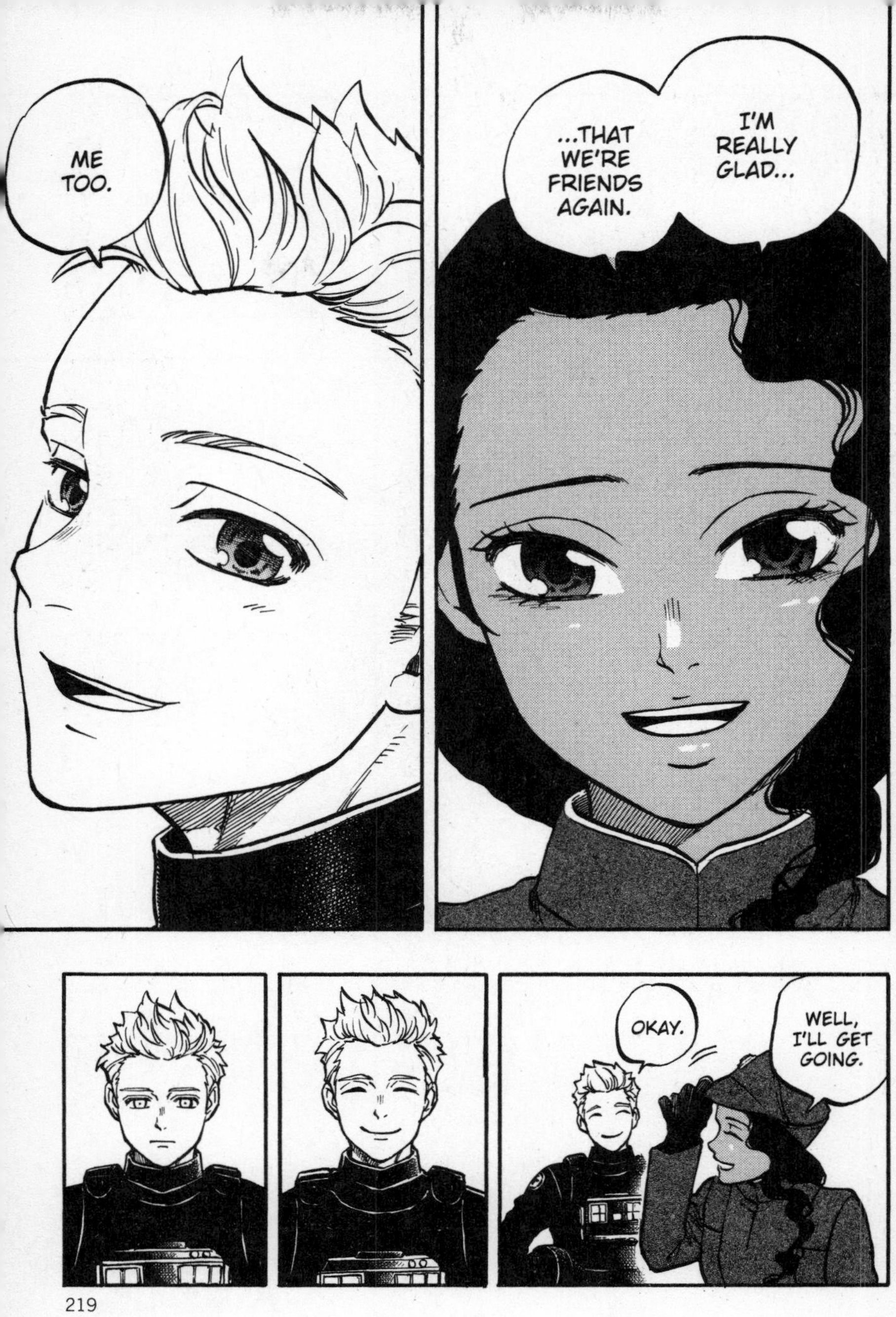
I'M REALLY GLAD...
...THAT WE'RE FRIENDS AGAIN.
ME TOO.
WELL, I'LL GET GOING.
OKAY.

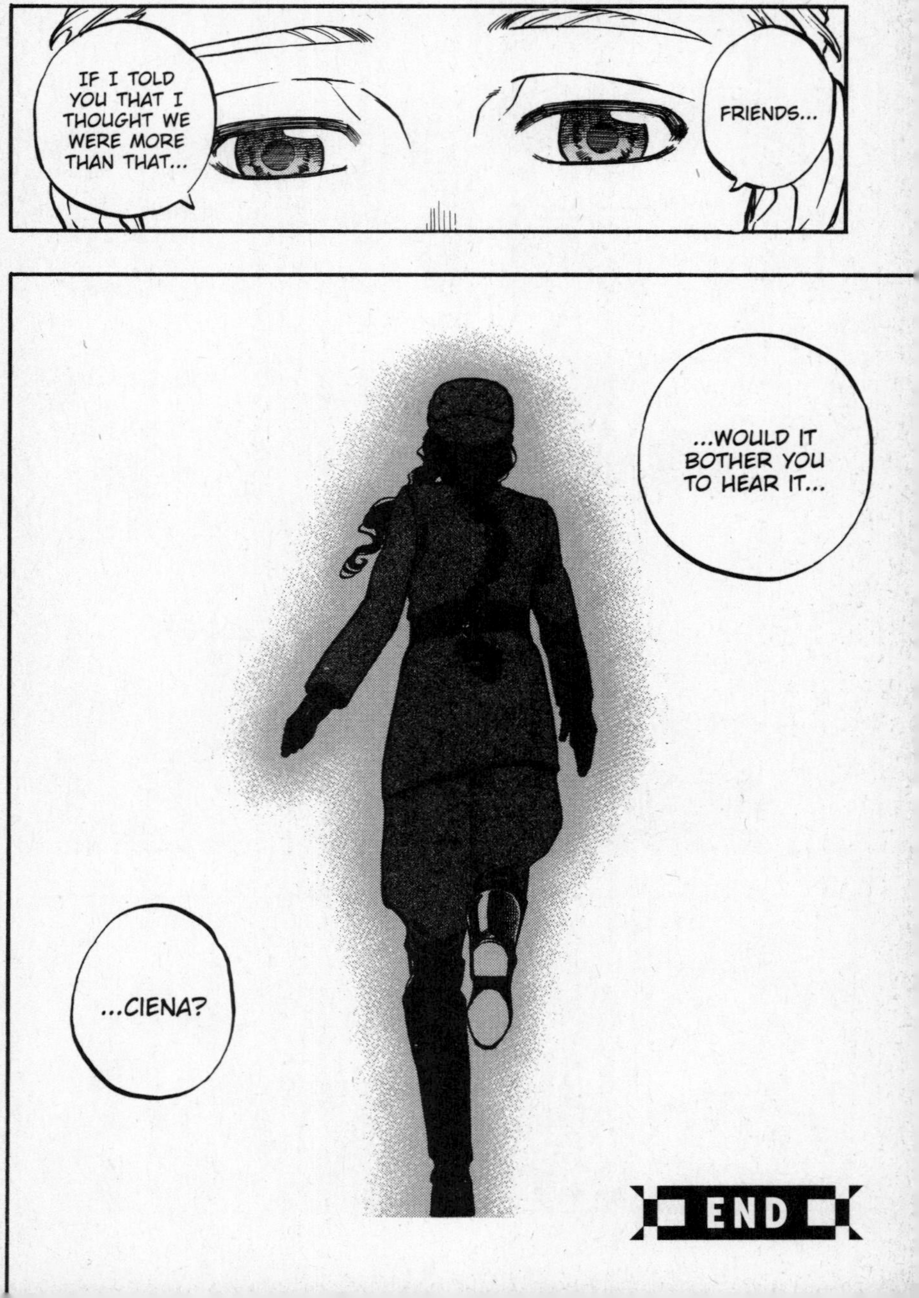
FRIENDS...
IF I TOLD YOU THAT I THOUGHT WE WERE MORE THAN THAT...
...WOULD IT BOTHER YOU TO HEAR IT...
...CIENA?
END

STAR WARS
LOST STARS
ロスト・スターズ

STAR WARS
LOST STARS
ロスト・スターズ

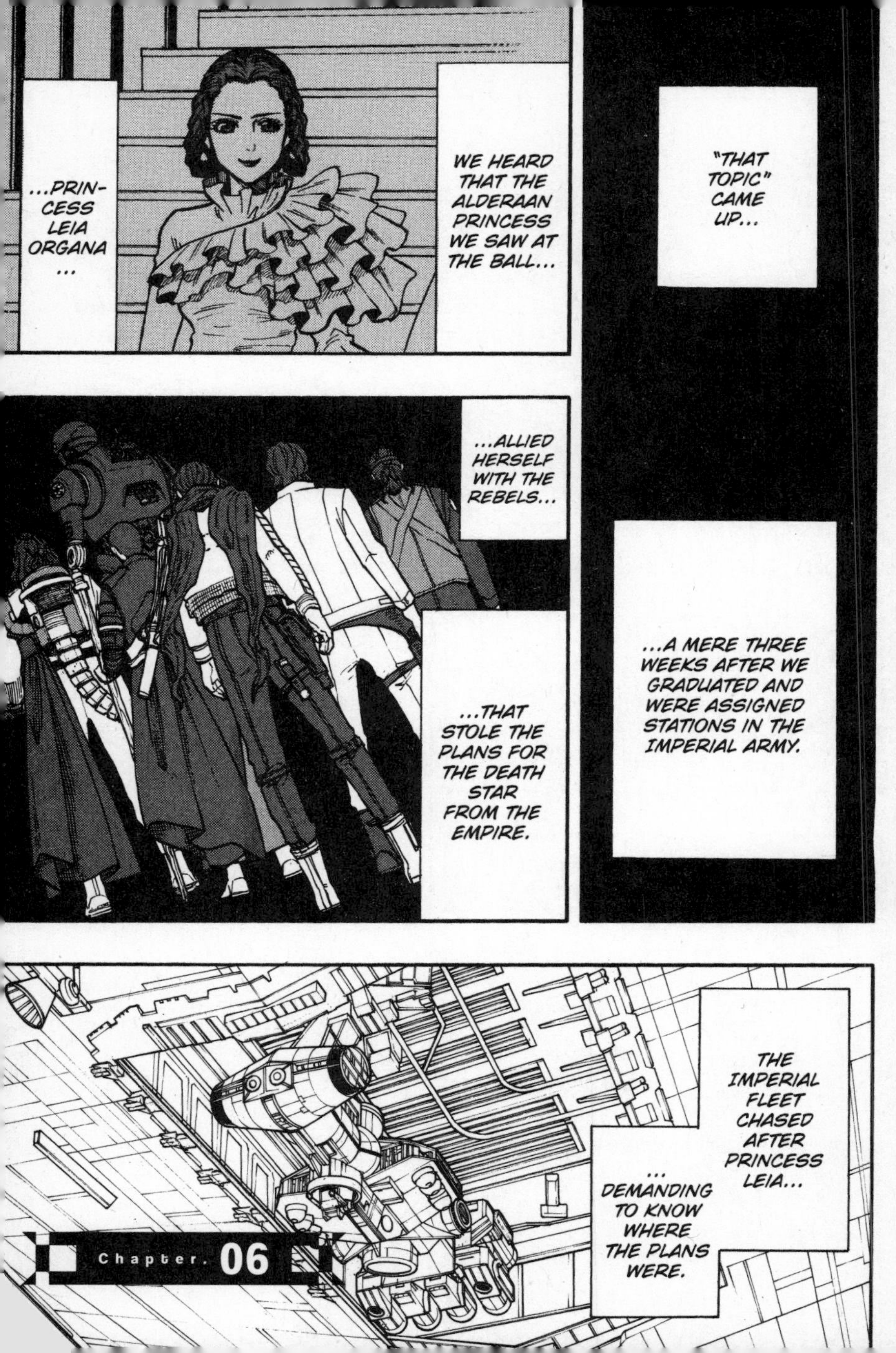
"THAT TOPIC" CAME UP...
...A MERE THREE WEEKS AFTER WE GRADUATED AND WERE ASSIGNED STATIONS IN THE IMPERIAL ARMY.
WE HEARD THAT THE ALDERAAN PRINCESS WE SAW AT THE BALL...
...PRIN-CESS LEIA ORGANA...
...ALLIED HERSELF WITH THE REBELS...
...THAT STOLE THE PLANS FOR THE DEATH STAR FROM THE EMPIRE.
THE IMPERIAL FLEET CHASED AFTER PRINCESS LEIA...
...DEMANDING TO KNOW WHERE THE PLANS WERE.
Chapter. 06

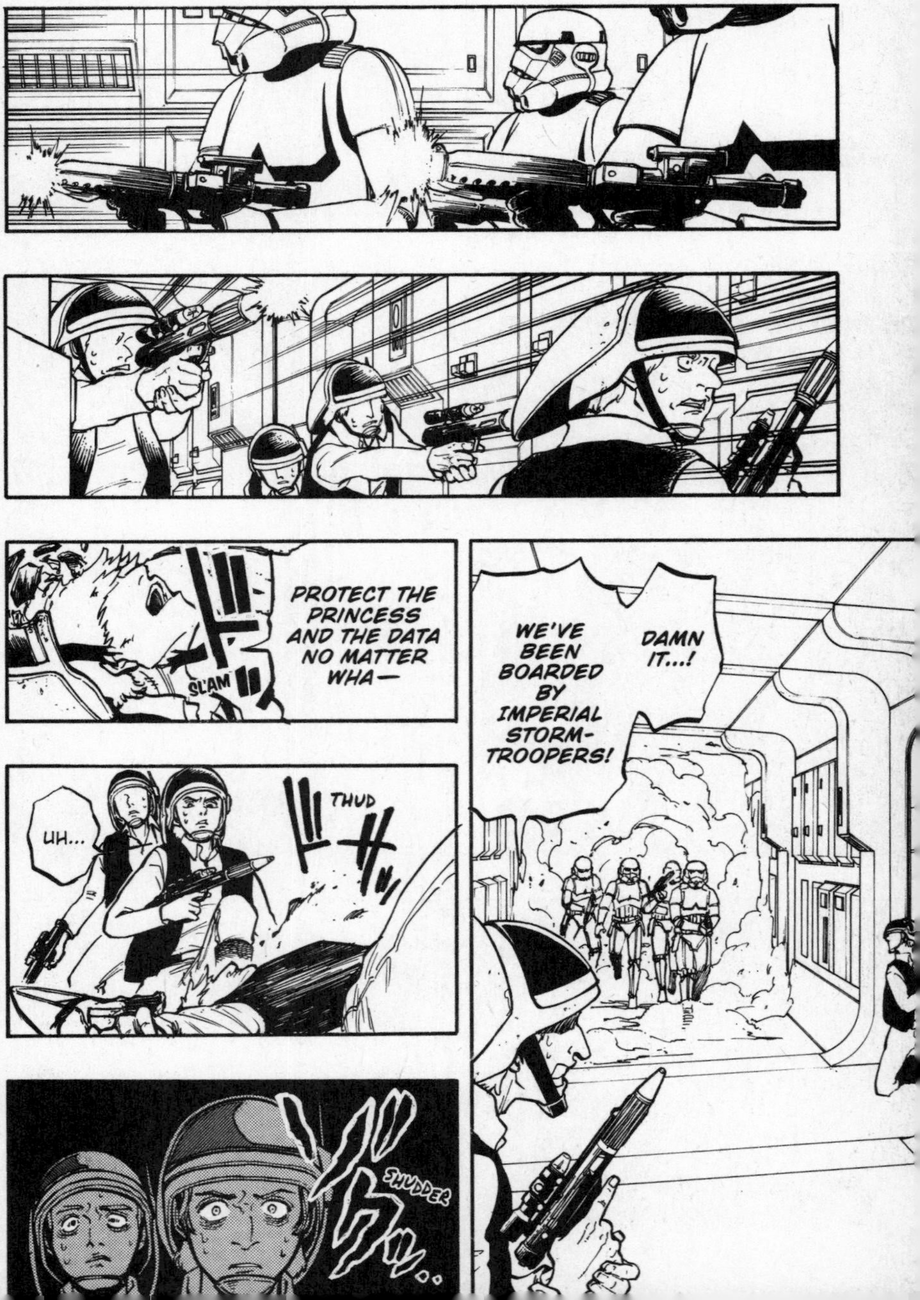
DAMN IT...!
WE'VE BEEN BOARDED BY IMPERIAL STORM-TROOPERS!
PROTECT THE PRINCESS AND THE DATA NO MATTER WHA—
SLAM
THUD
UH...
SHUDDER

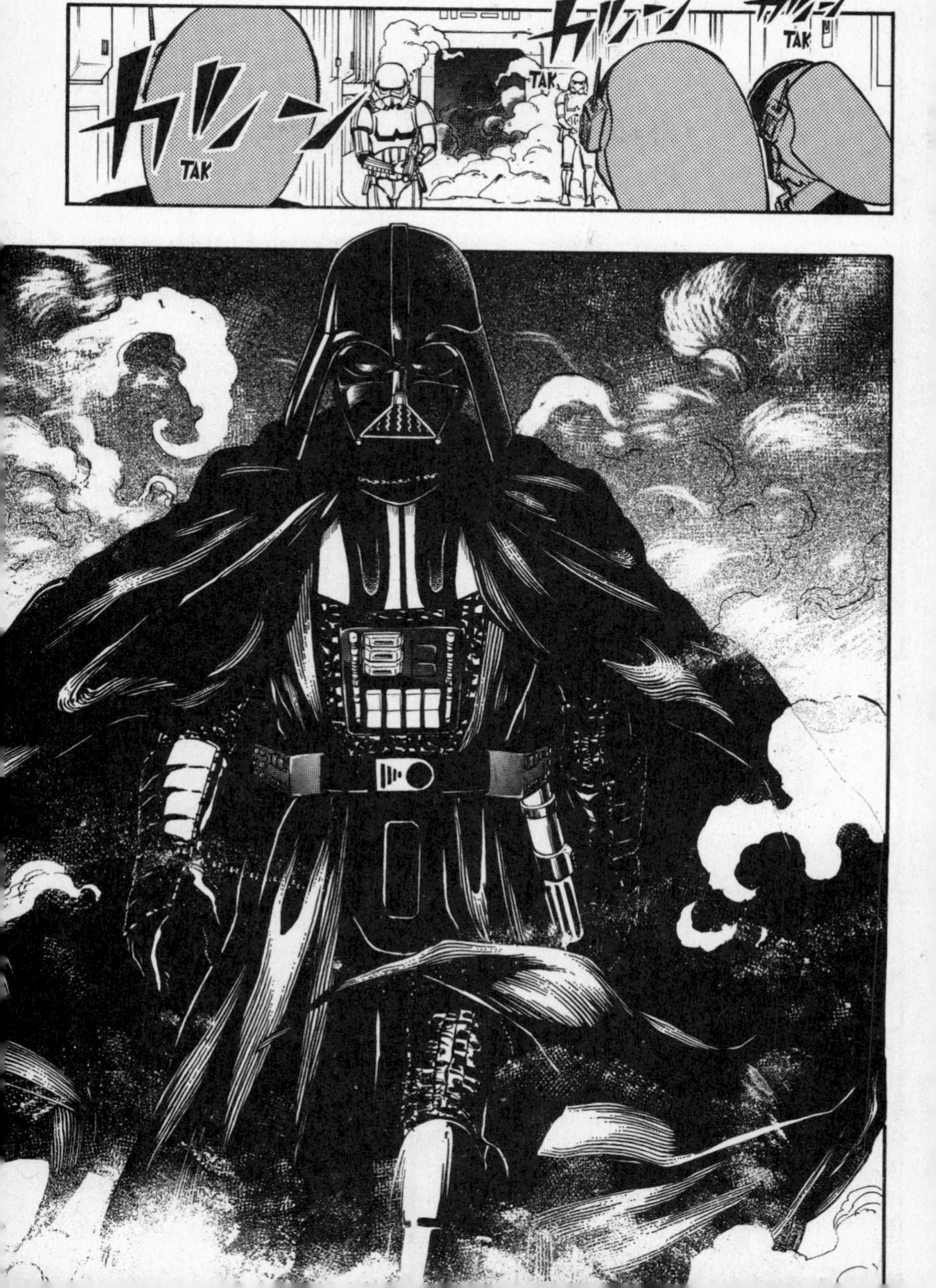

カツーン
TAK
カツーン
TAK
カツーン
TAK

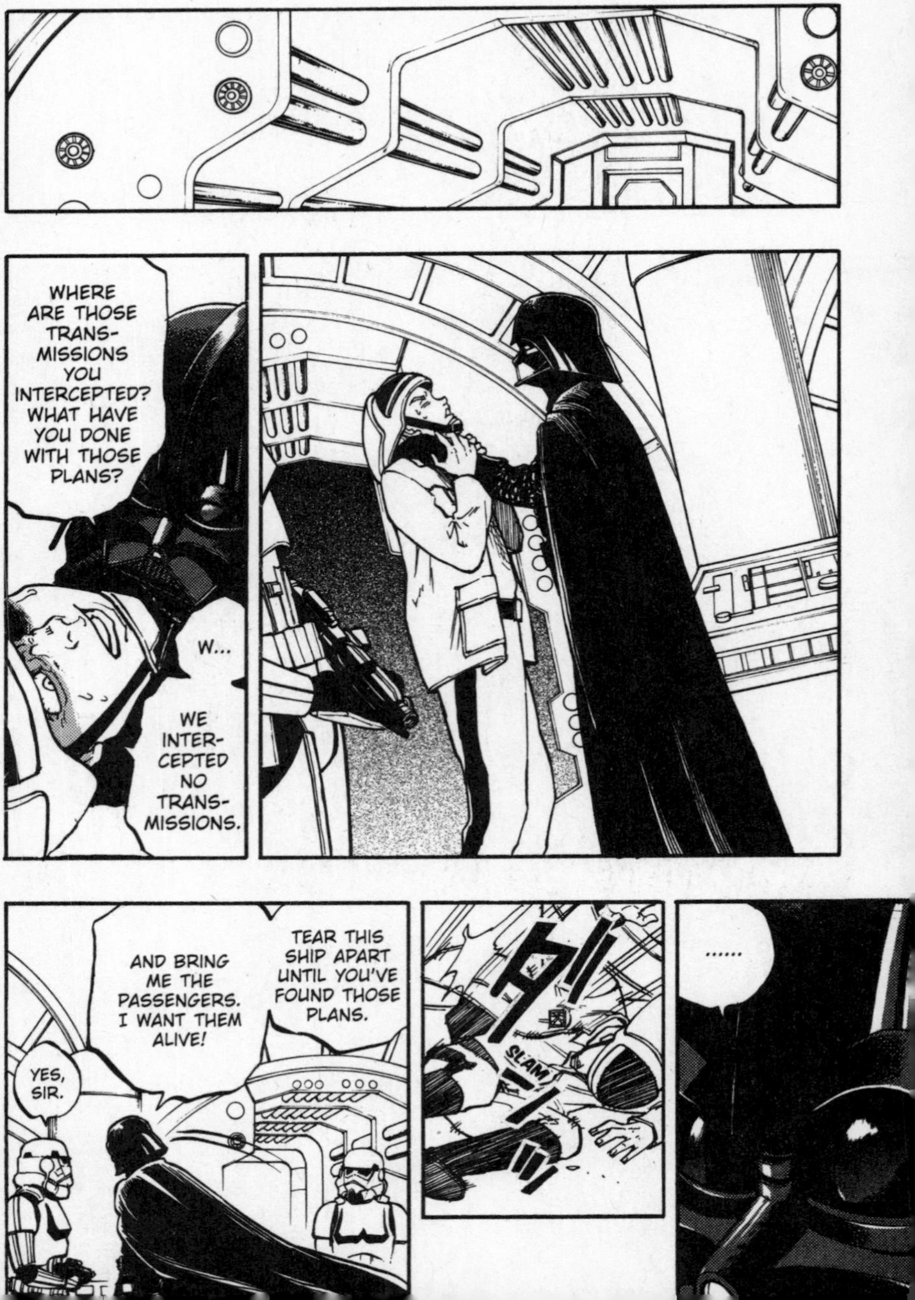
WHERE ARE THOSE TRANS-MISSIONS YOU INTERCEPTED? WHAT HAVE YOU DONE WITH THOSE PLANS?
W...
WE INTER-CEPTED NO TRANS-MISSIONS.
......
SLAM
TEAR THIS SHIP APART UNTIL YOU'VE FOUND THOSE PLANS.
AND BRING ME THE PASSENGERS. I WANT THEM ALIVE!
YES, SIR.

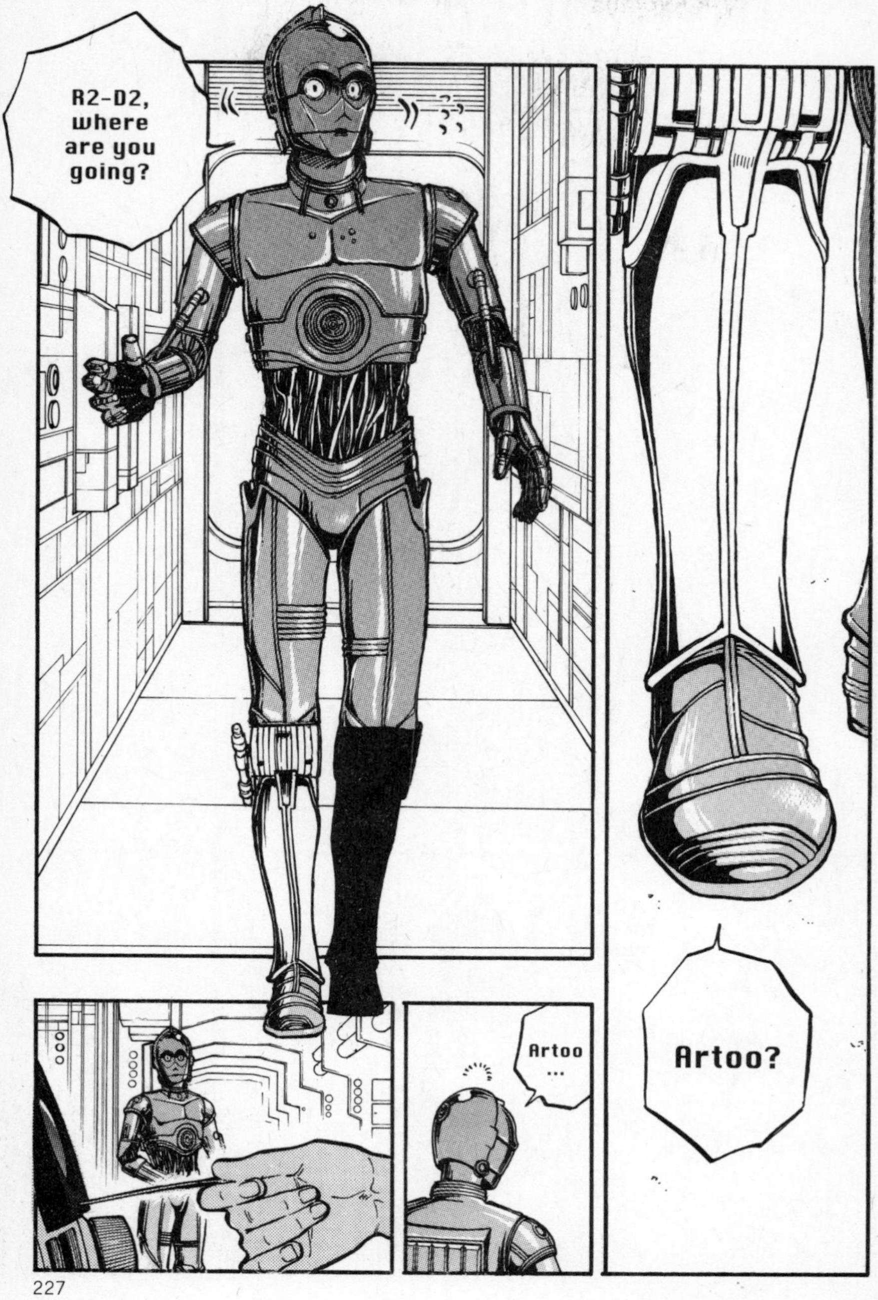
Artoo?
R2-D2, where are you going?
Artoo ...

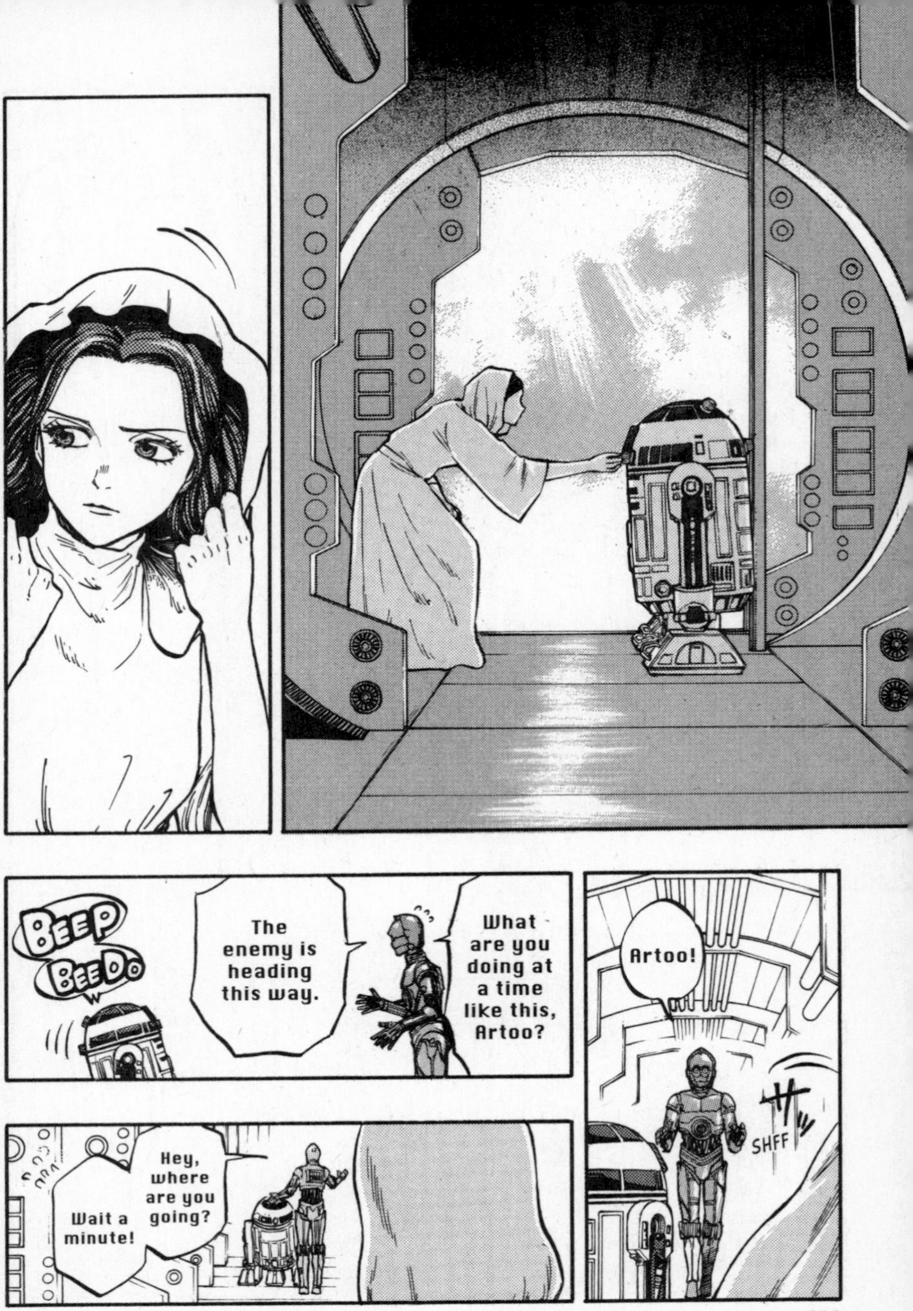
Artoo!
SHFF
What are you doing at a time like this, Artoo?
The enemy is heading this way.
BEEP BEEDO
Hey, where are you going?
Wait a minute!

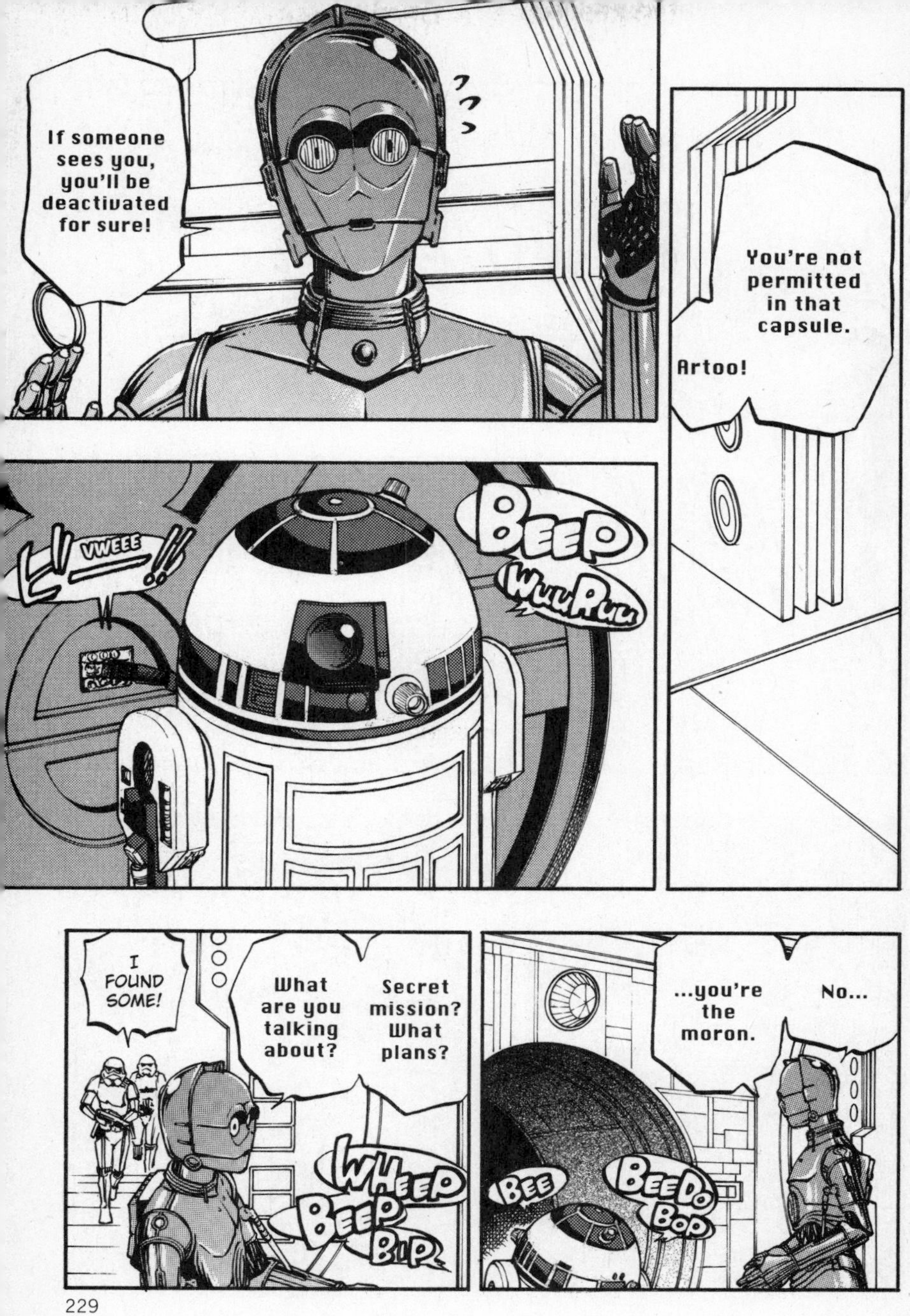
You're not permitted in that capsule.
Artoo!
If someone sees you, you'll be deactivated for sure!
BEEP
WuuRuu
VWEEE
No...
...you're the moron.
BEEDO BOP
BEE
Secret mission? What plans?
What are you talking about?
I FOUND SOME!
WHEEP
BEEP BIP

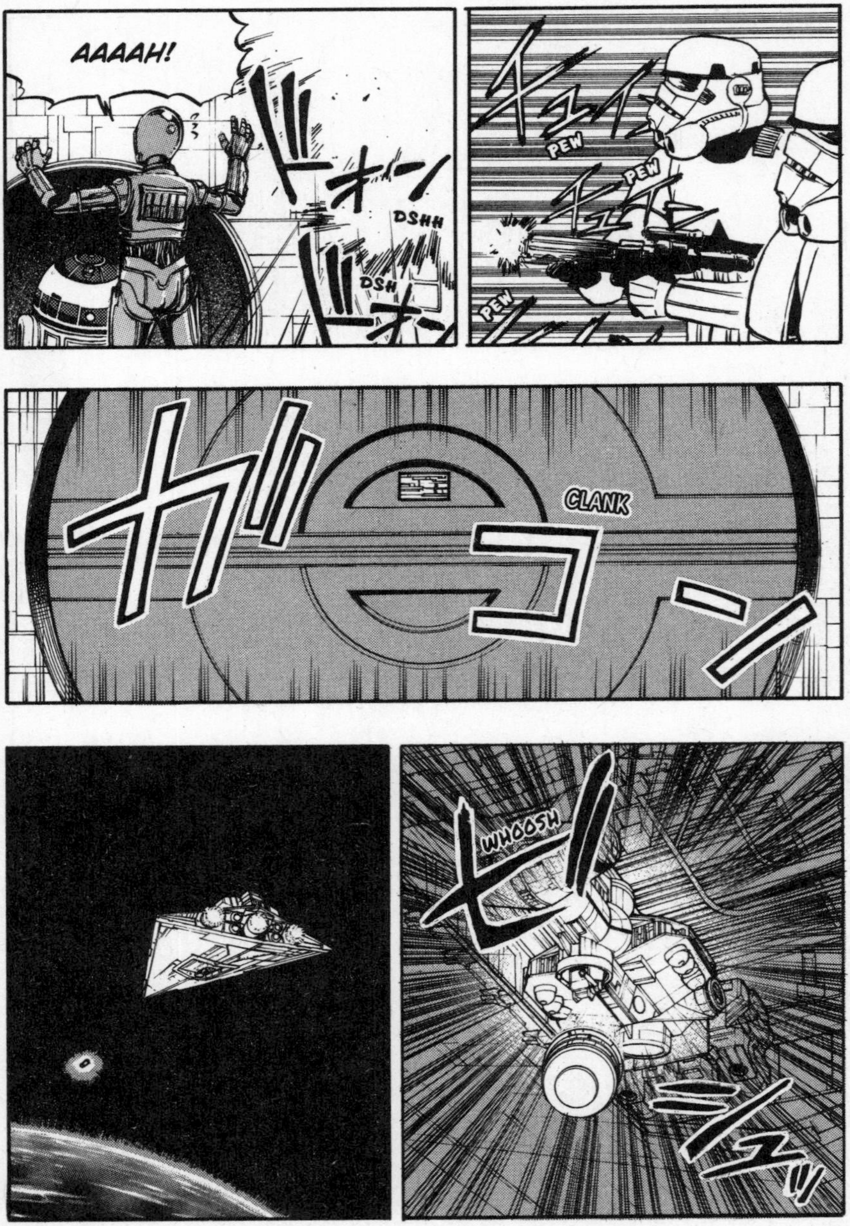
PEW
PEW
PEW
AAAAH!
DSHH
DSH
CLANK
WHOOSH

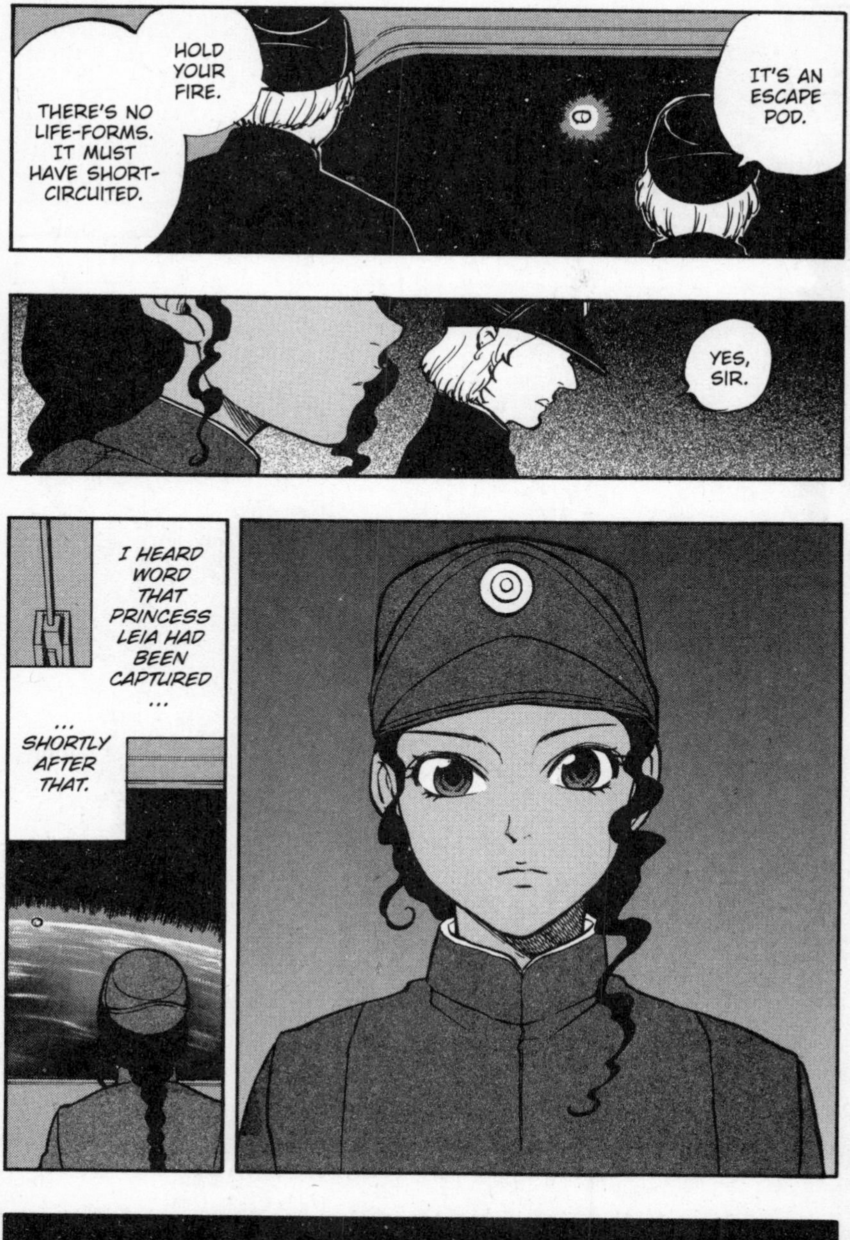
IT'S AN ESCAPE POD.
HOLD YOUR FIRE.
THERE'S NO LIFE-FORMS. IT MUST HAVE SHORT-CIRCUITED.
YES, SIR.
I HEARD WORD THAT PRINCESS LEIA HAD BEEN CAPTURED ...
... SHORTLY AFTER THAT.

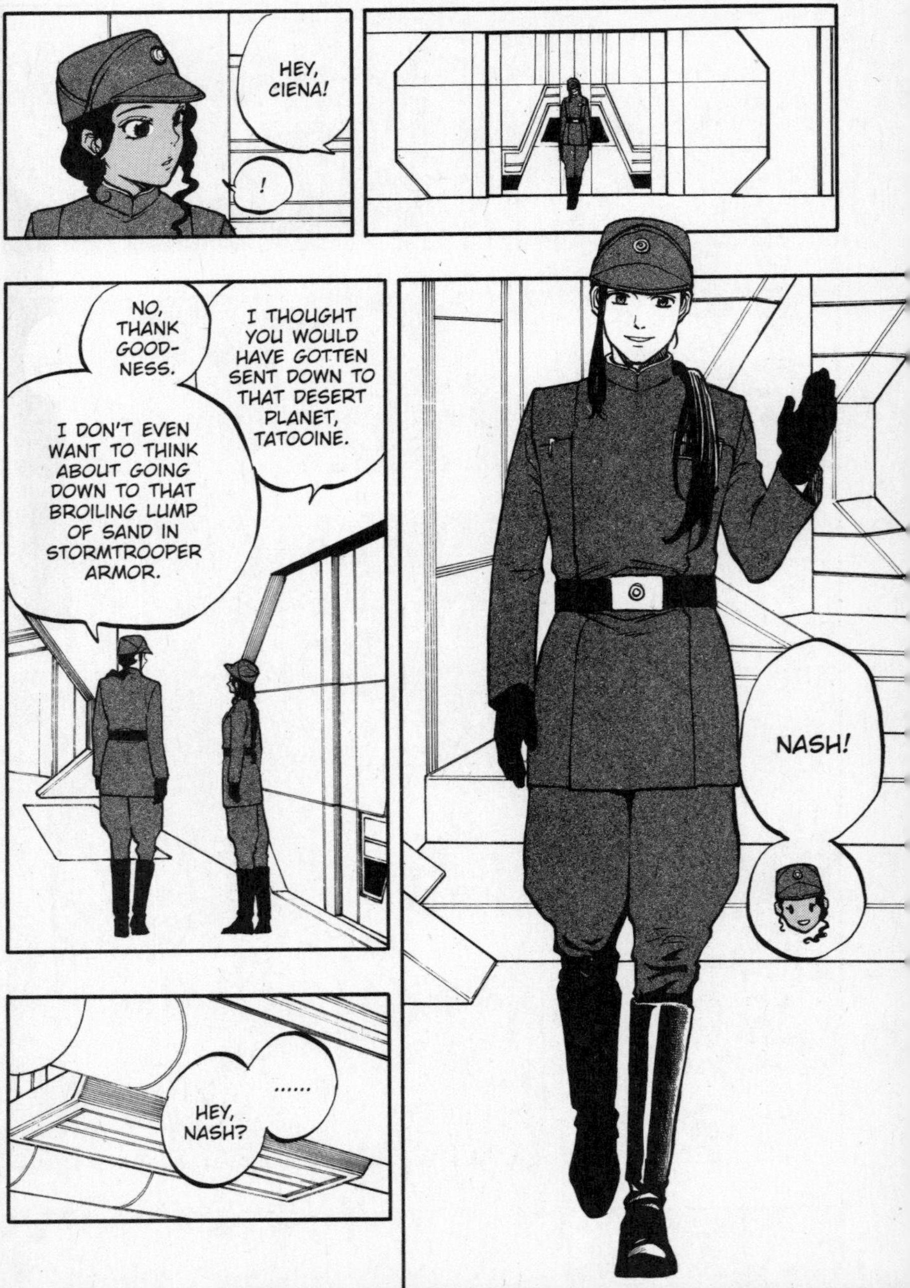
HEY, CIENA!
!
NASH!
I THOUGHT YOU WOULD HAVE GOTTEN SENT DOWN TO THAT DESERT PLANET, TATOOINE.
NO, THANK GOOD-NESS.
I DON'T EVEN WANT TO THINK ABOUT GOING DOWN TO THAT BROILING LUMP OF SAND IN STORMTROOPER ARMOR.
......
HEY, NASH?

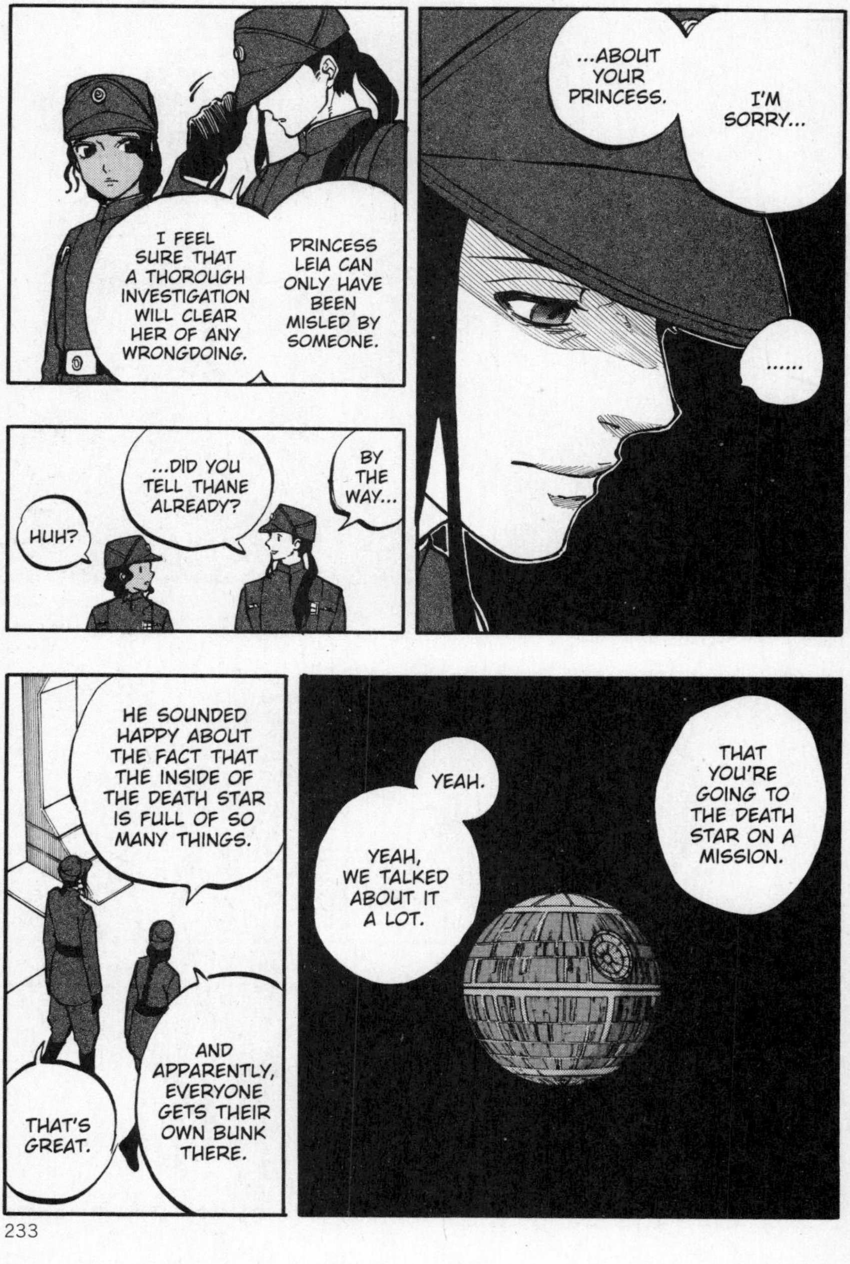
I'M SORRY...
...ABOUT YOUR PRINCESS.
......
PRINCESS LEIA CAN ONLY HAVE BEEN MISLED BY SOMEONE.
I FEEL SURE THAT A THOROUGH INVESTIGATION WILL CLEAR HER OF ANY WRONGDOING.
BY THE WAY...
...DID YOU TELL THANE ALREADY?
HUH?
THAT YOU'RE GOING TO THE DEATH STAR ON A MISSION.
YEAH.
YEAH, WE TALKED ABOUT IT A LOT.
HE SOUNDED HAPPY ABOUT THE FACT THAT THE INSIDE OF THE DEATH STAR IS FULL OF SO MANY THINGS.
AND APPARENTLY, EVERYONE GETS THEIR OWN BUNK THERE.
THAT'S GREAT.

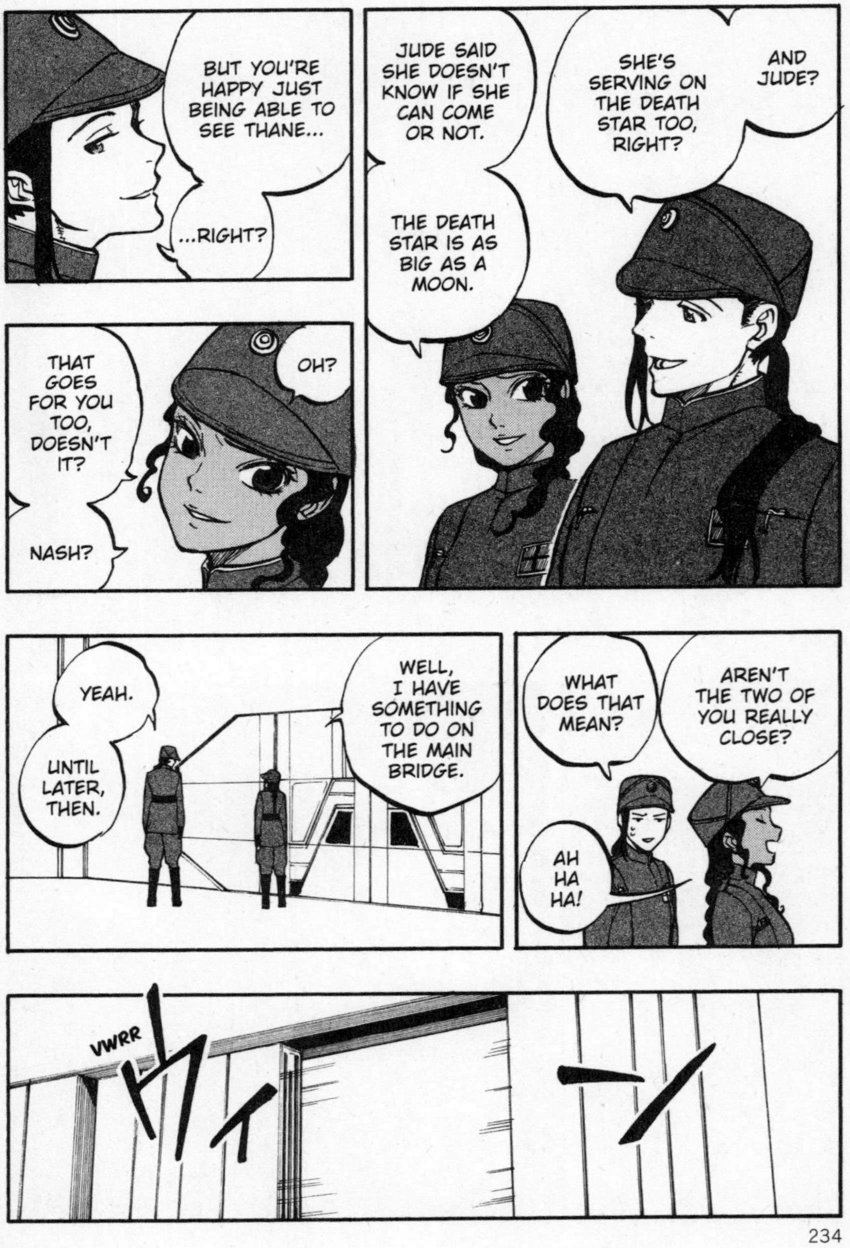
AND JUDE?
SHE'S SERVING ON THE DEATH STAR TOO, RIGHT?
JUDE SAID SHE DOESN'T KNOW IF SHE CAN COME OR NOT.
THE DEATH STAR IS AS BIG AS A MOON.
BUT YOU'RE HAPPY JUST BEING ABLE TO SEE THANE...
...RIGHT?
OH?
THAT GOES FOR YOU TOO, DOESN'T IT?
NASH?
AREN'T THE TWO OF YOU REALLY CLOSE?
WHAT DOES THAT MEAN?
AH HA HA!
WELL, I HAVE SOMETHING TO DO ON THE MAIN BRIDGE.
YEAH.
UNTIL LATER, THEN.
VWRR

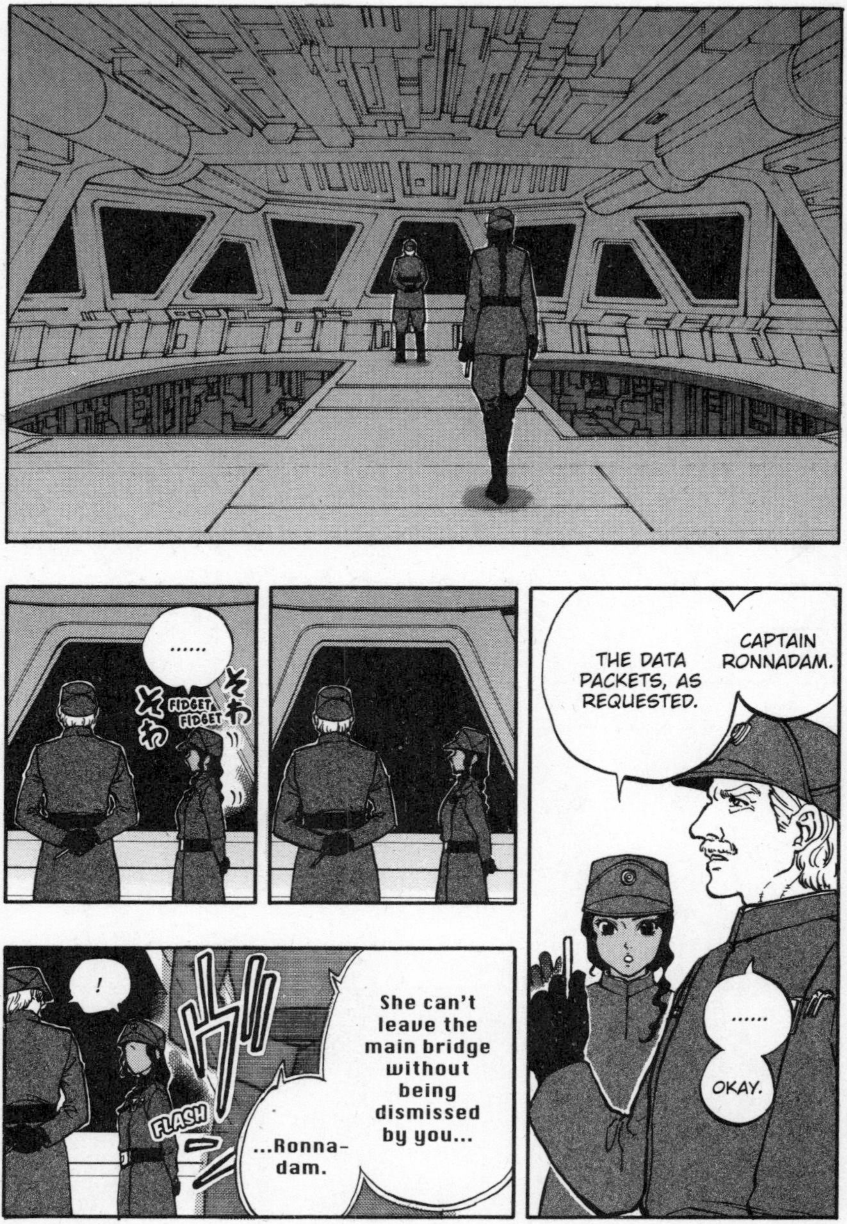
CAPTAIN RONNADAM.
THE DATA PACKETS, AS REQUESTED.
......
OKAY.
......
そわ そわ
FIDGET FIDGET
She can't leave the main bridge without being dismissed by you...
...Ronna-dam.
FLASH
!

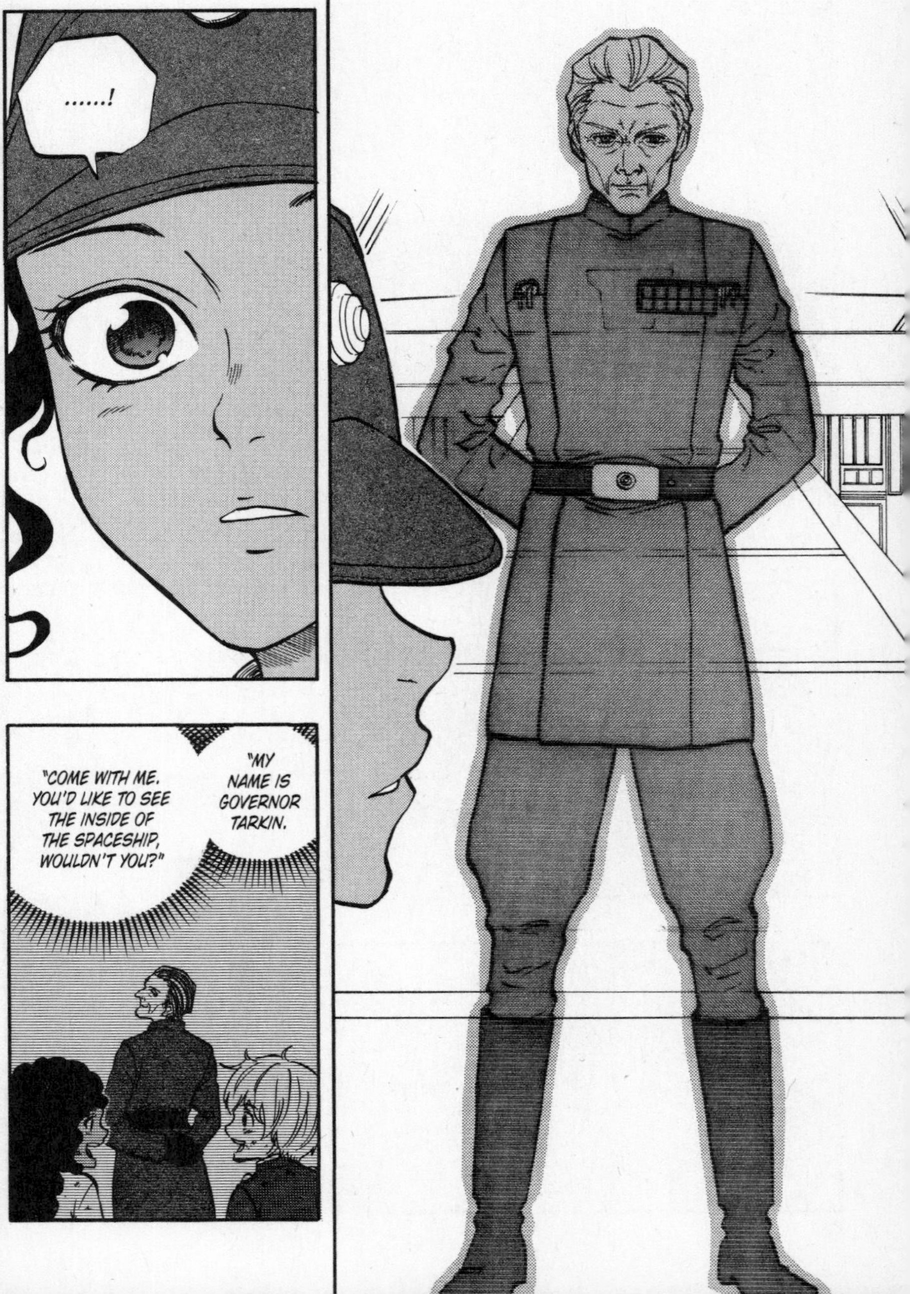
......!
"MY NAME IS GOVERNOR TARKIN.
"COME WITH ME. YOU'D LIKE TO SEE THE INSIDE OF THE SPACESHIP, WOULDN'T YOU?"

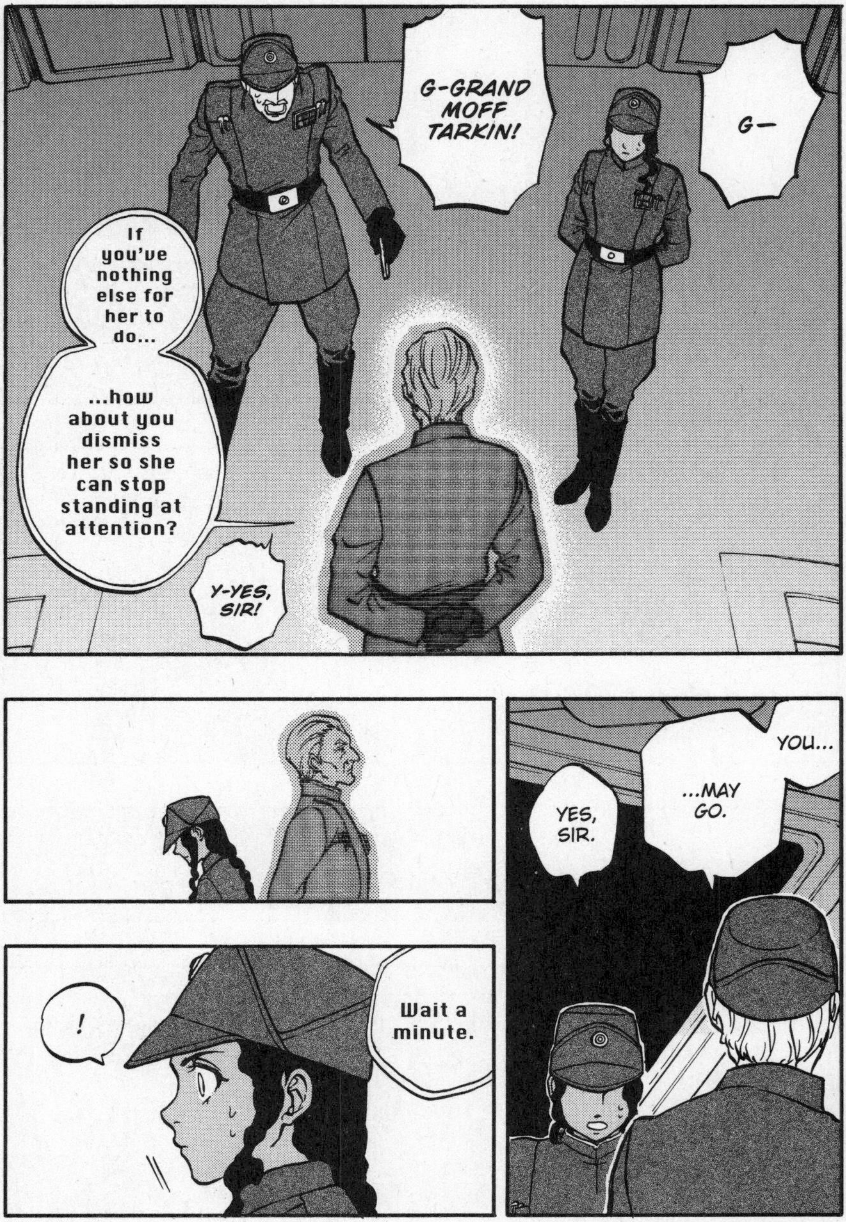
G—
G-GRAND MOFF TARKIN!
If you've nothing else for her to do...
...how about you dismiss her so she can stop standing at attention?
Y-YES, SIR!
YOU...
...MAY GO.
YES, SIR.
Wait a minute.
!

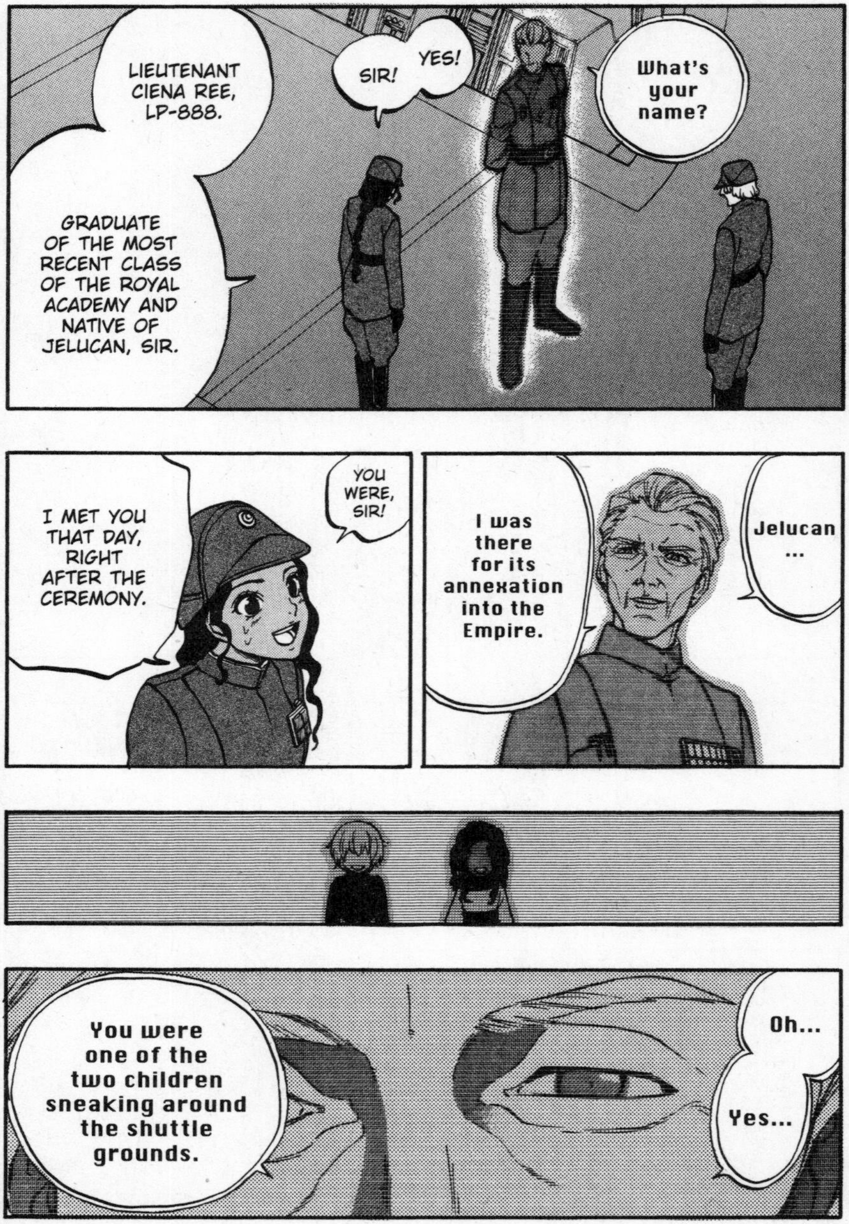
What's your name?
YES!
SIR!
LIEUTENANT CIENA REE, LP-888.
GRADUATE OF THE MOST RECENT CLASS OF THE ROYAL ACADEMY AND NATIVE OF JELUCAN, SIR.
Jelucan ...
I was there for its annexation into the Empire.
YOU WERE, SIR!
I MET YOU THAT DAY, RIGHT AFTER THE CEREMONY.
Oh...
Yes...
You were one of the two children sneaking around the shuttle grounds.

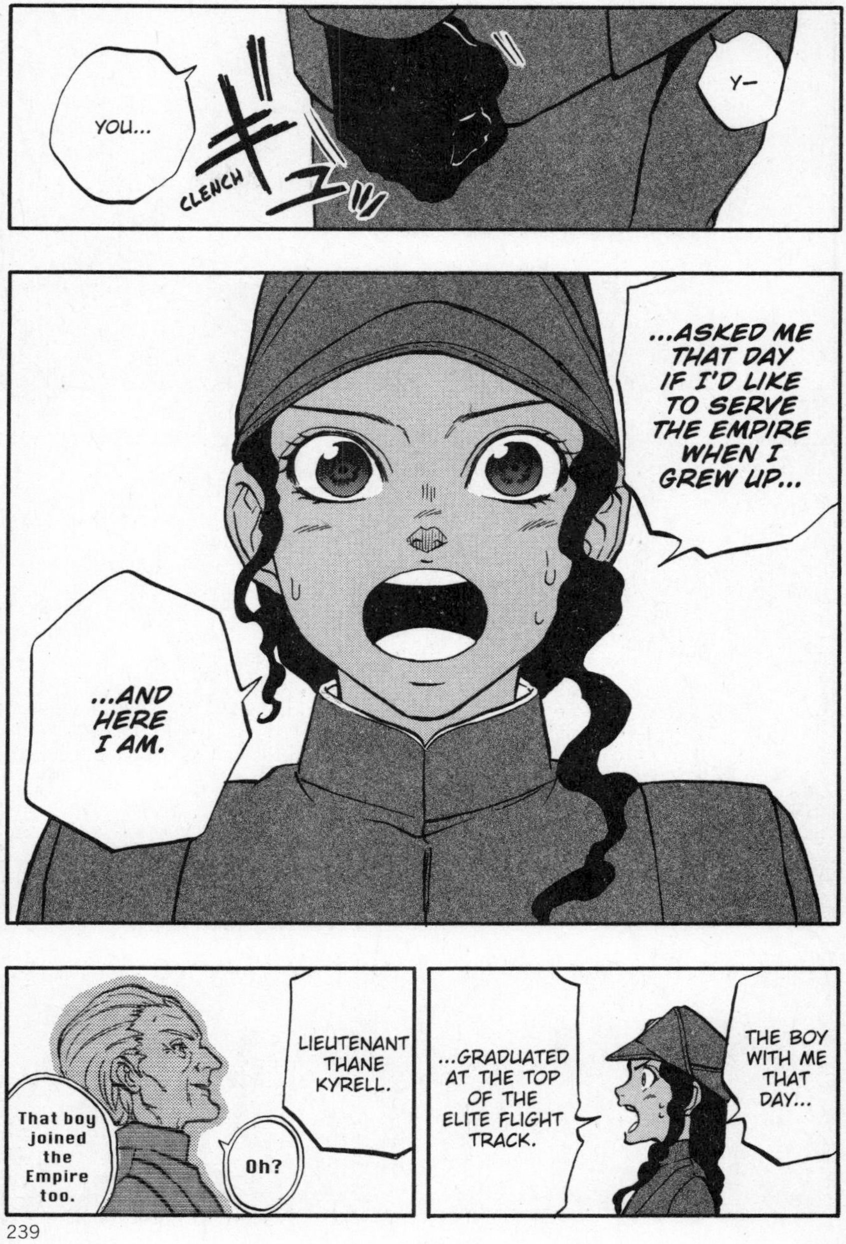
Y—
YOU...
ギュッ
CLENCH
...ASKED ME THAT DAY IF I'D LIKE TO SERVE THE EMPIRE WHEN I GREW UP...
...AND HERE I AM.
THE BOY WITH ME THAT DAY...
...GRADUATED AT THE TOP OF THE ELITE FLIGHT TRACK.
LIEUTENANT THANE KYRELL.
Oh?
That boy joined the Empire too.

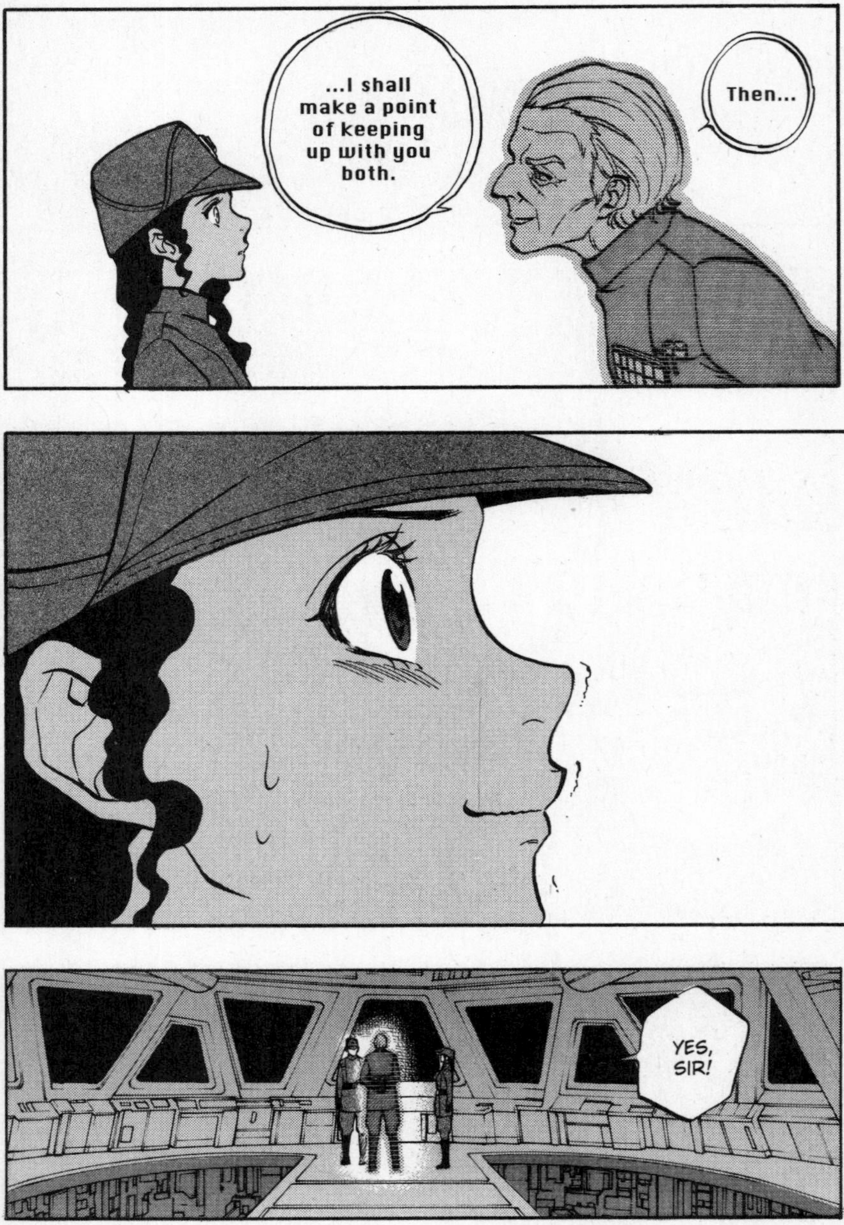
Then...
...I shall make a point of keeping up with you both.
YES, SIR!

SPACE STATION
DEATH STAR

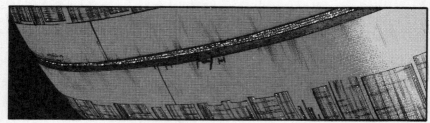

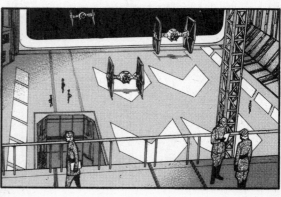

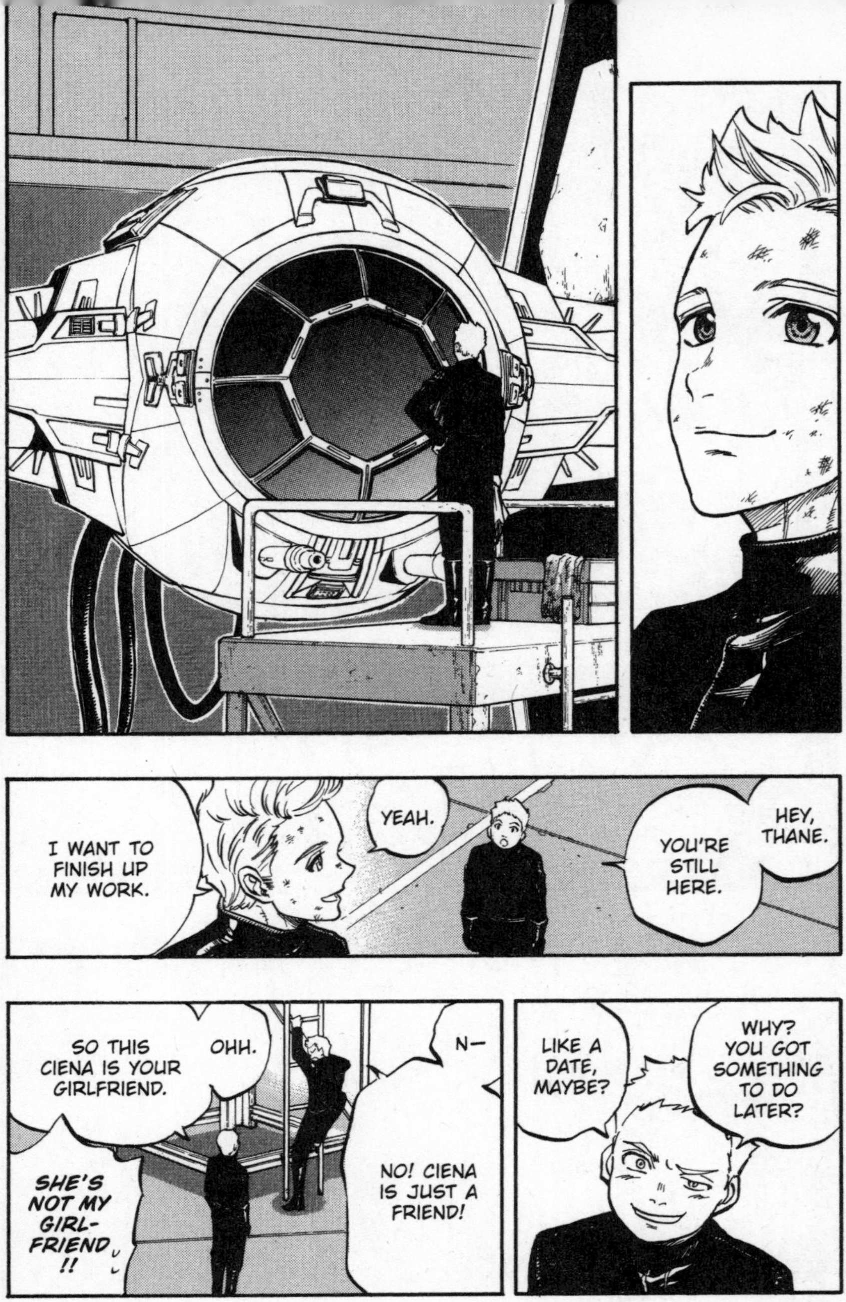
HEY, THANE.
YOU'RE STILL HERE.
YEAH.
I WANT TO FINISH UP MY WORK.
WHY? YOU GOT SOMETHING TO DO LATER?
LIKE A DATE, MAYBE?
N—
OHH.
SO THIS CIENA IS YOUR GIRLFRIEND.
NO! CIENA IS JUST A FRIEND!
SHE'S NOT MY GIRL-FRIEND!!

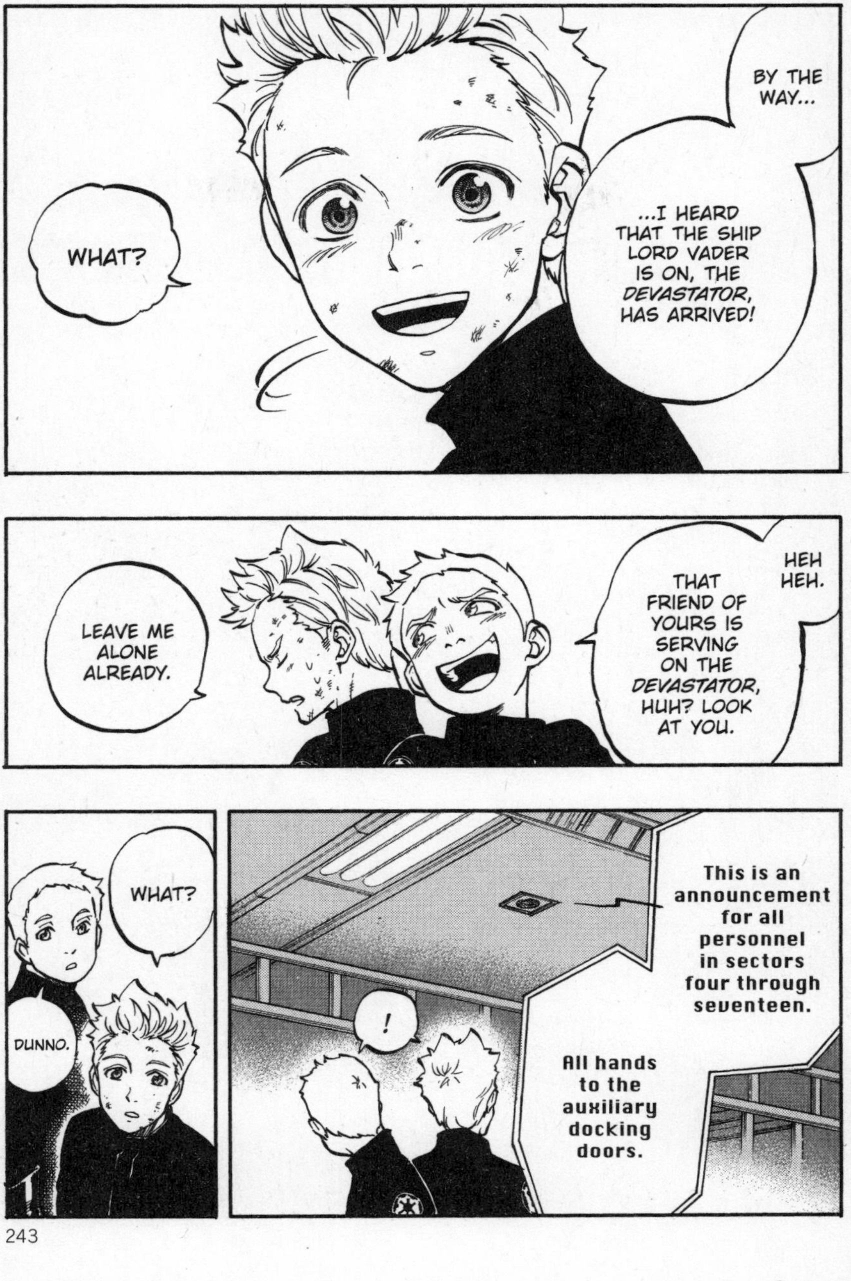
BY THE WAY...
...I HEARD THAT THE SHIP LORD VADER IS ON, THE *DEVASTATOR*, HAS ARRIVED!
WHAT?
HEH HEH.
THAT FRIEND OF YOURS IS SERVING ON THE *DEVASTATOR*, HUH? LOOK AT YOU.
LEAVE ME ALONE ALREADY.
This is an announcement for all personnel in sectors four through seventeen.
All hands to the auxiliary docking doors.
!
WHAT?
DUNNO.

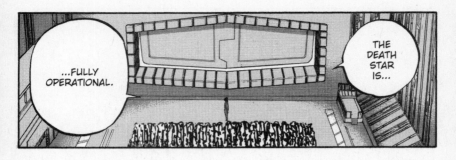

THE DEATH STAR IS...
...FULLY OPERATIONAL.
AND IT IS THE WILL OF THE EMPEROR THAT WE DEMONSTRATE ITS POWER...
...TO THE ENTIRE GALAXY!
RMBL
WHAT'S ABOUT TO HAPPEN?
RUMBLE
IT FEELS LIKE THE MAIN ENGINES ARE AT WORK.
RUMBLE
RMBL
MAYBE THE DEATH STAR TRAVELED NEAR SOME PLANET SO THEY CAN SHOW IT OFF?
OH, I GET IT.

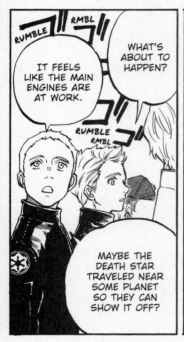

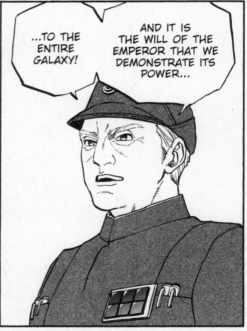

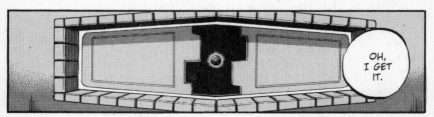

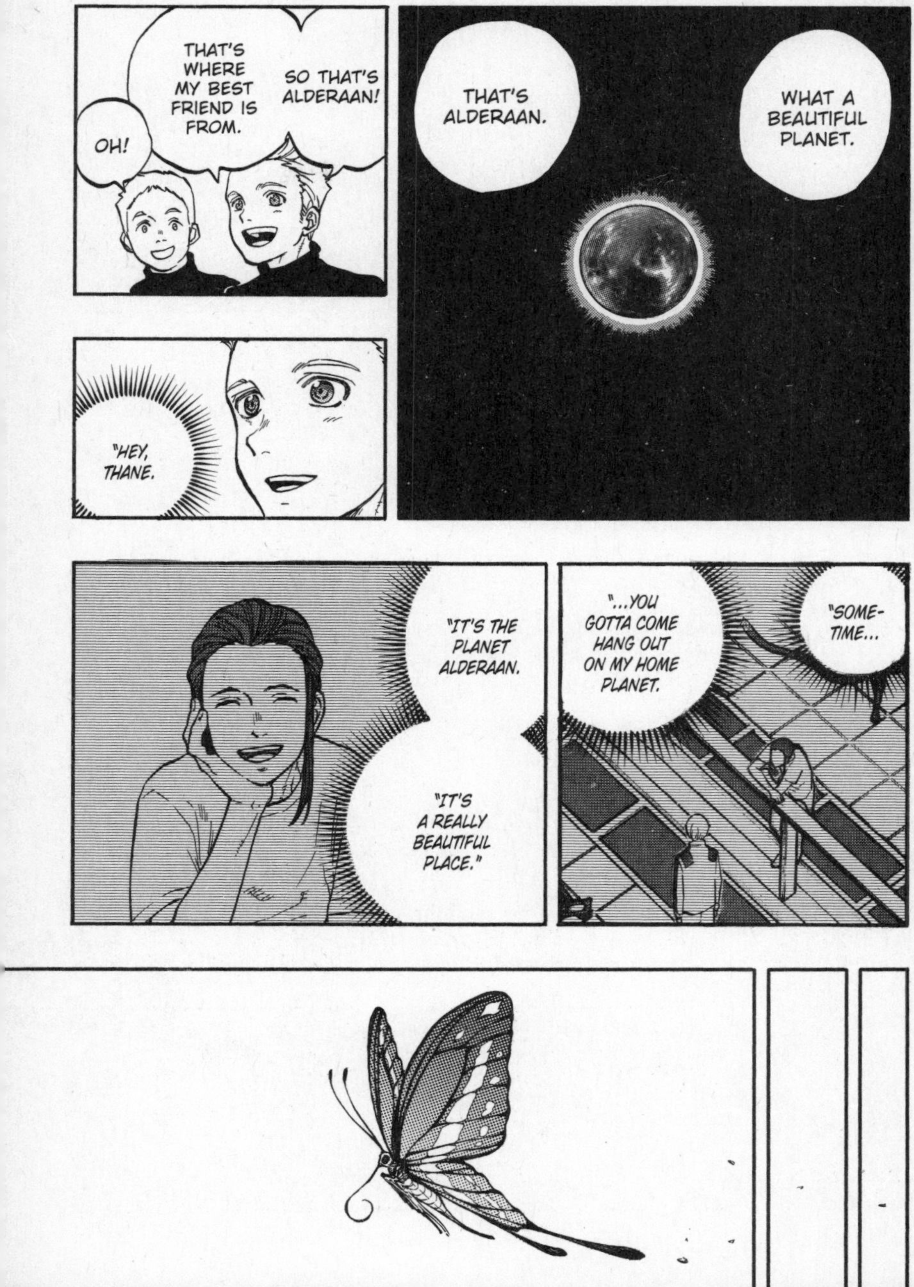
WHAT A BEAUTIFUL PLANET.
THAT'S ALDERAAN.
SO THAT'S ALDERAAN!
THAT'S WHERE MY BEST FRIEND IS FROM.
OH!
"HEY, THANE.
"SOME-TIME...
"...YOU GOTTA COME HANG OUT ON MY HOME PLANET.
"IT'S THE PLANET ALDERAAN.
"IT'S A REALLY BEAUTIFUL PLACE."

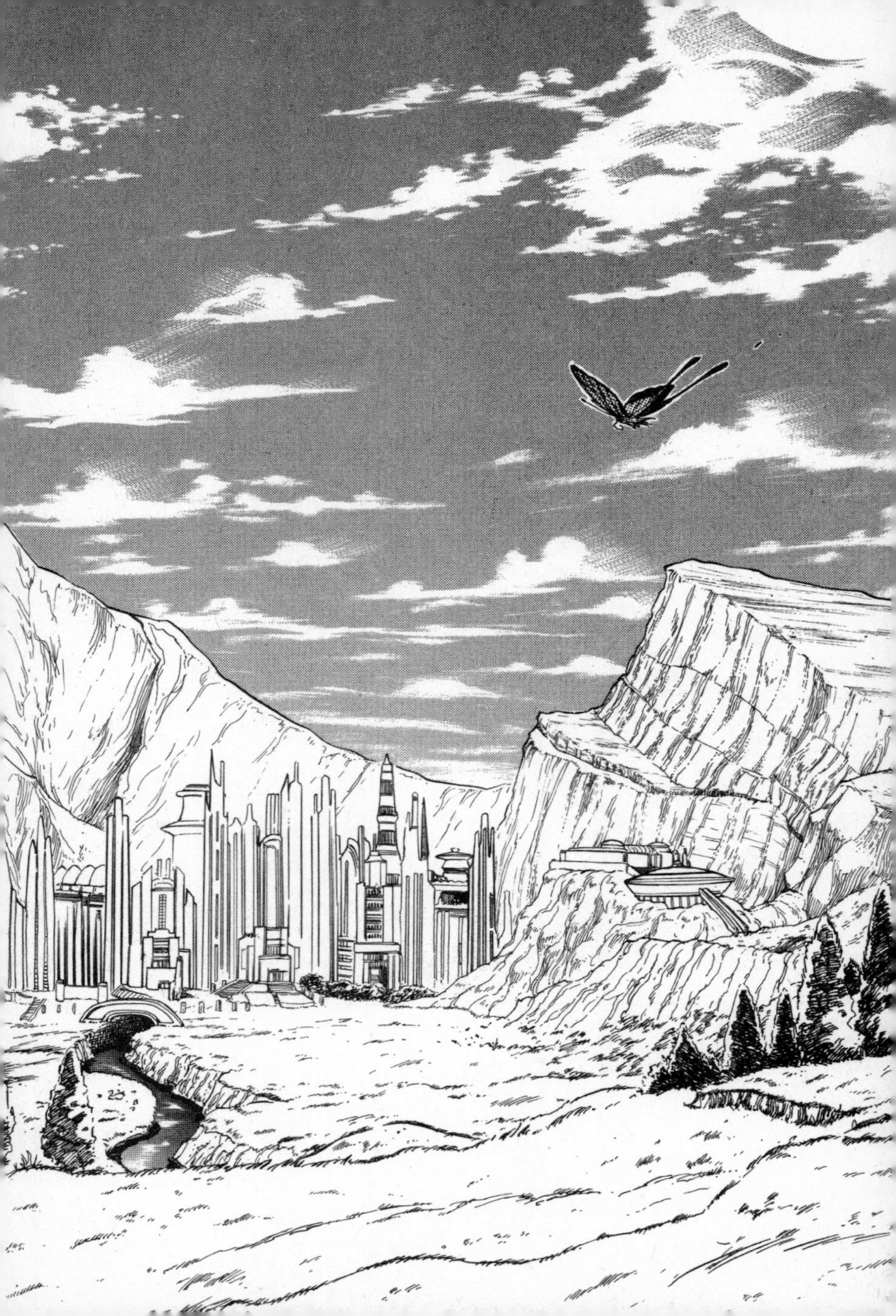

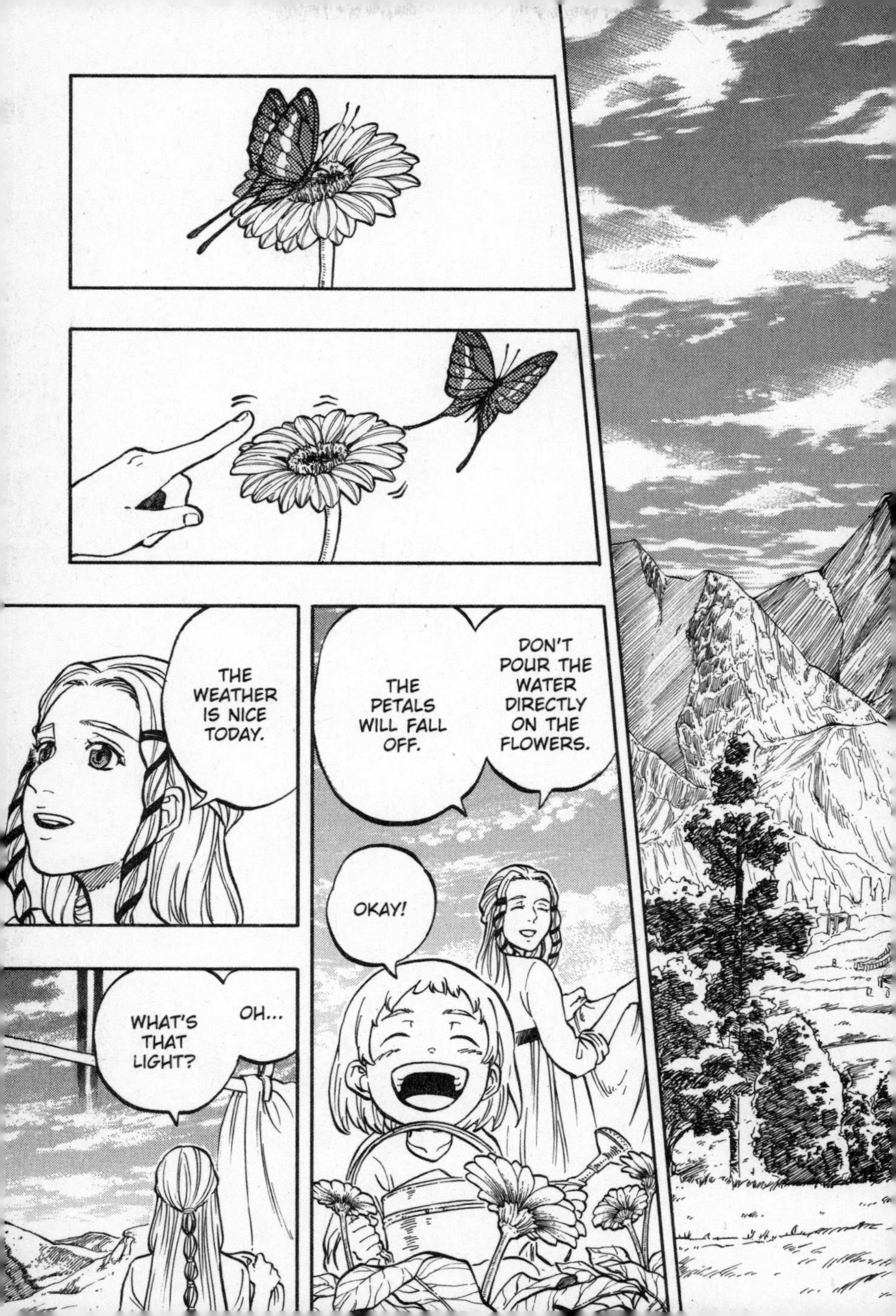
DON'T POUR THE WATER DIRECTLY ON THE FLOWERS.
THE PETALS WILL FALL OFF.
OKAY!
THE WEATHER IS NICE TODAY.
OH...
WHAT'S THAT LIGHT?

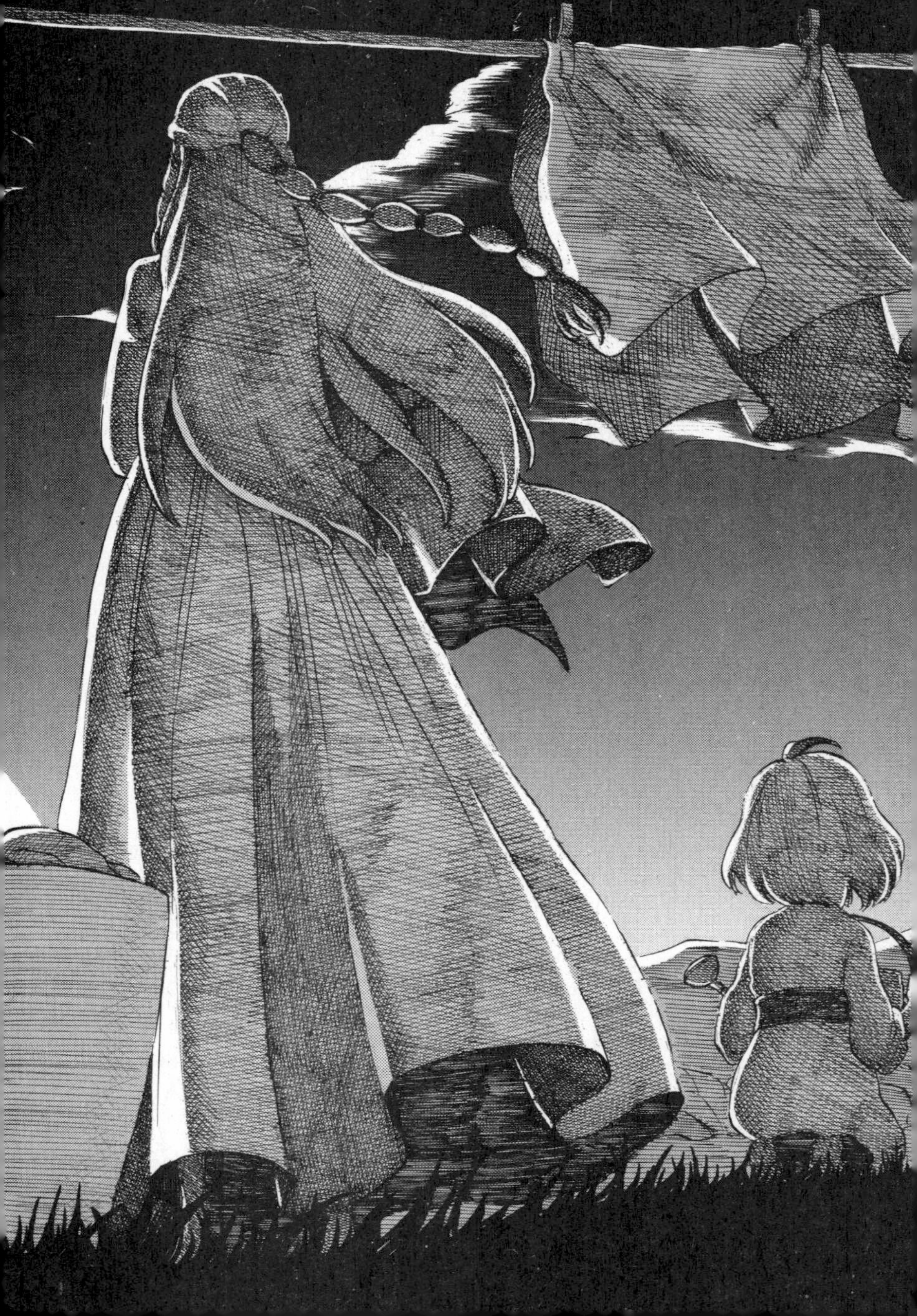

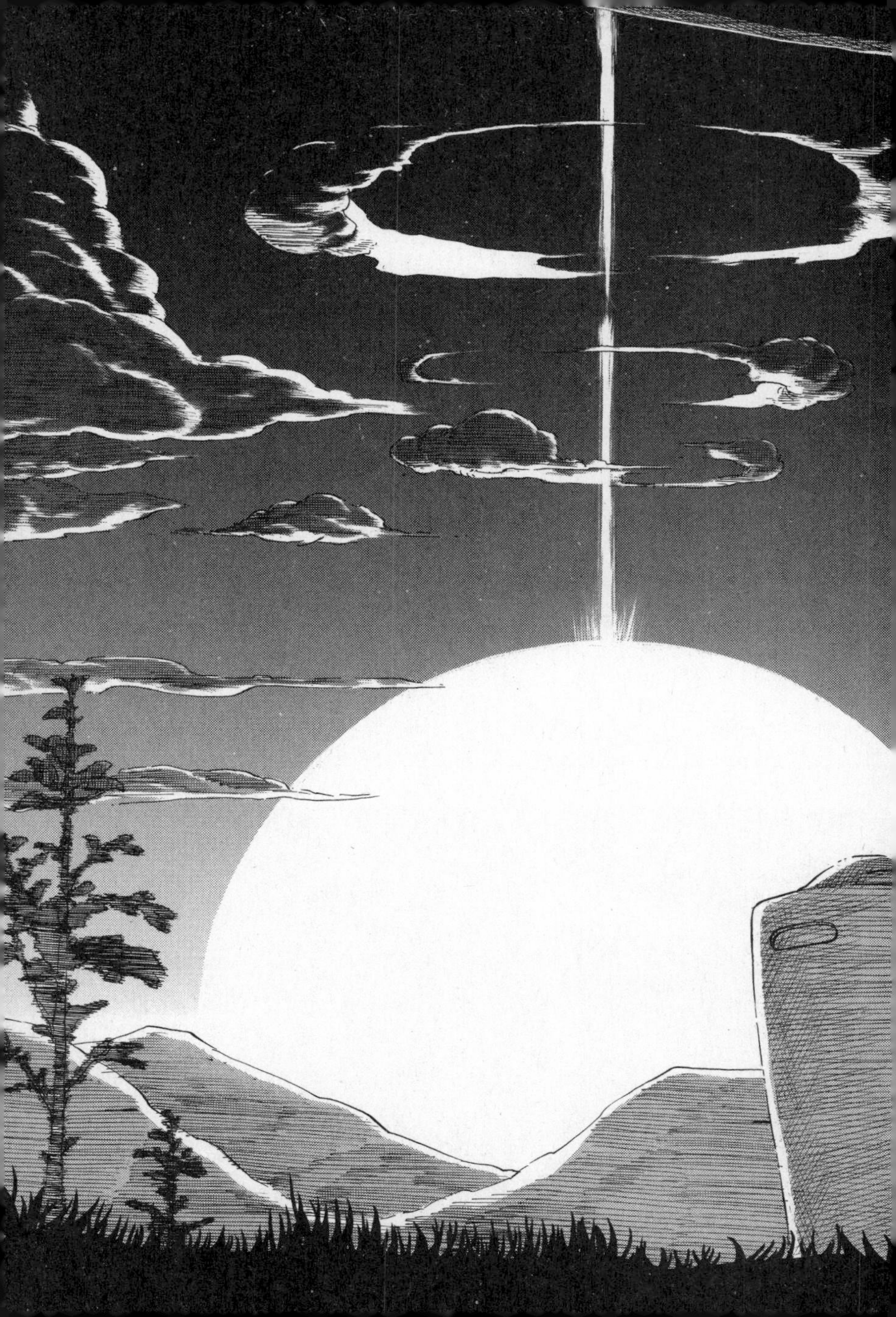

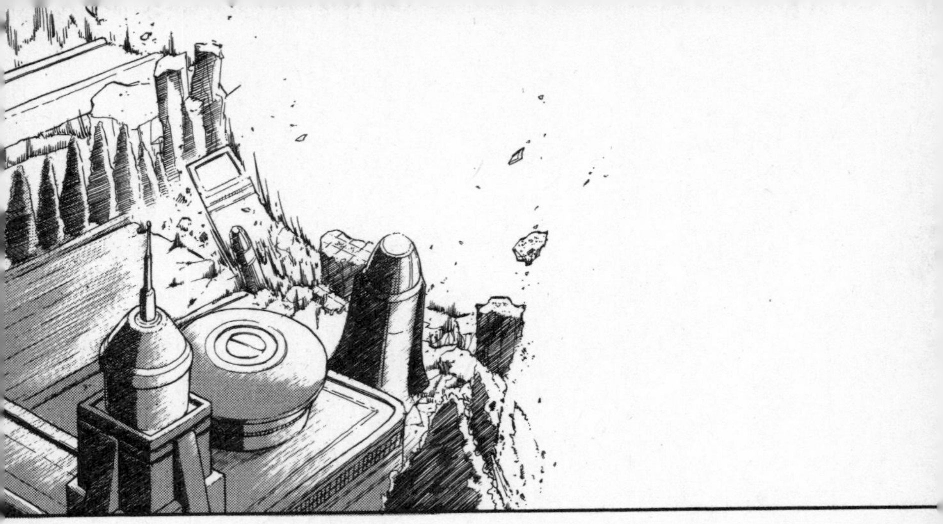

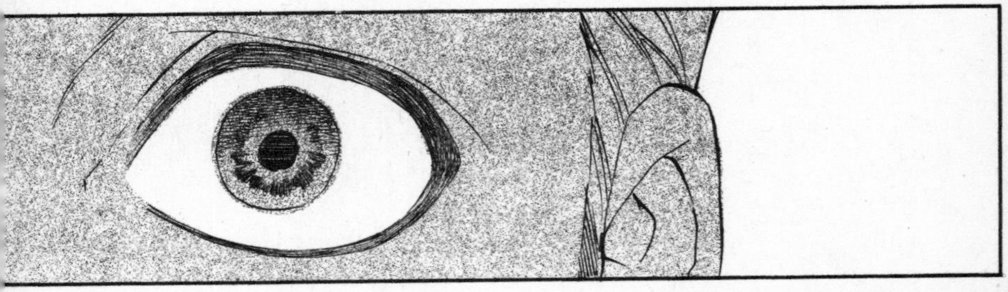

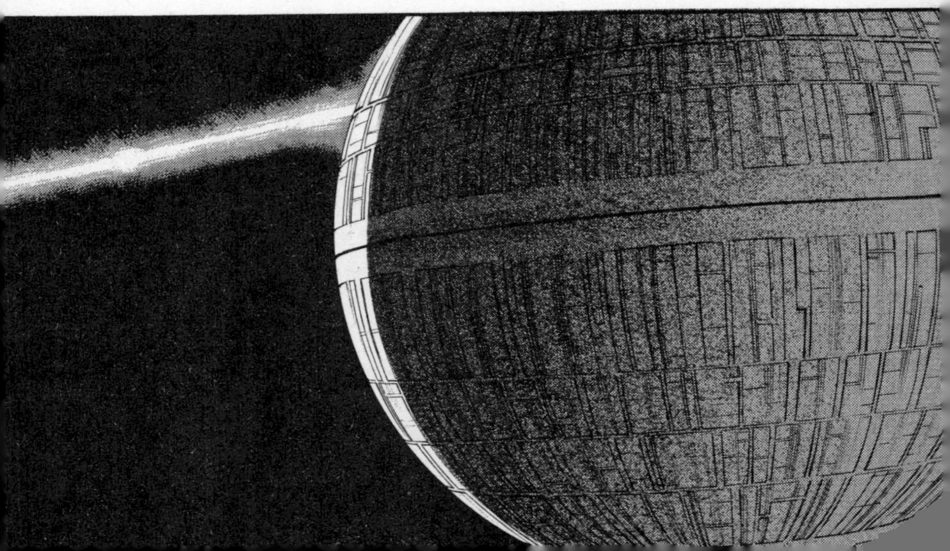

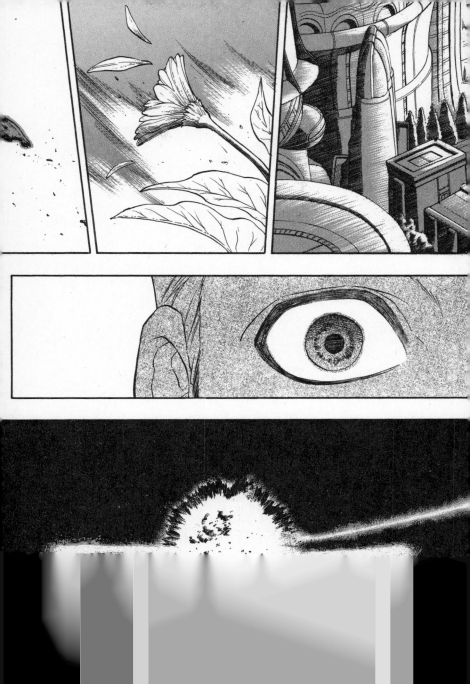

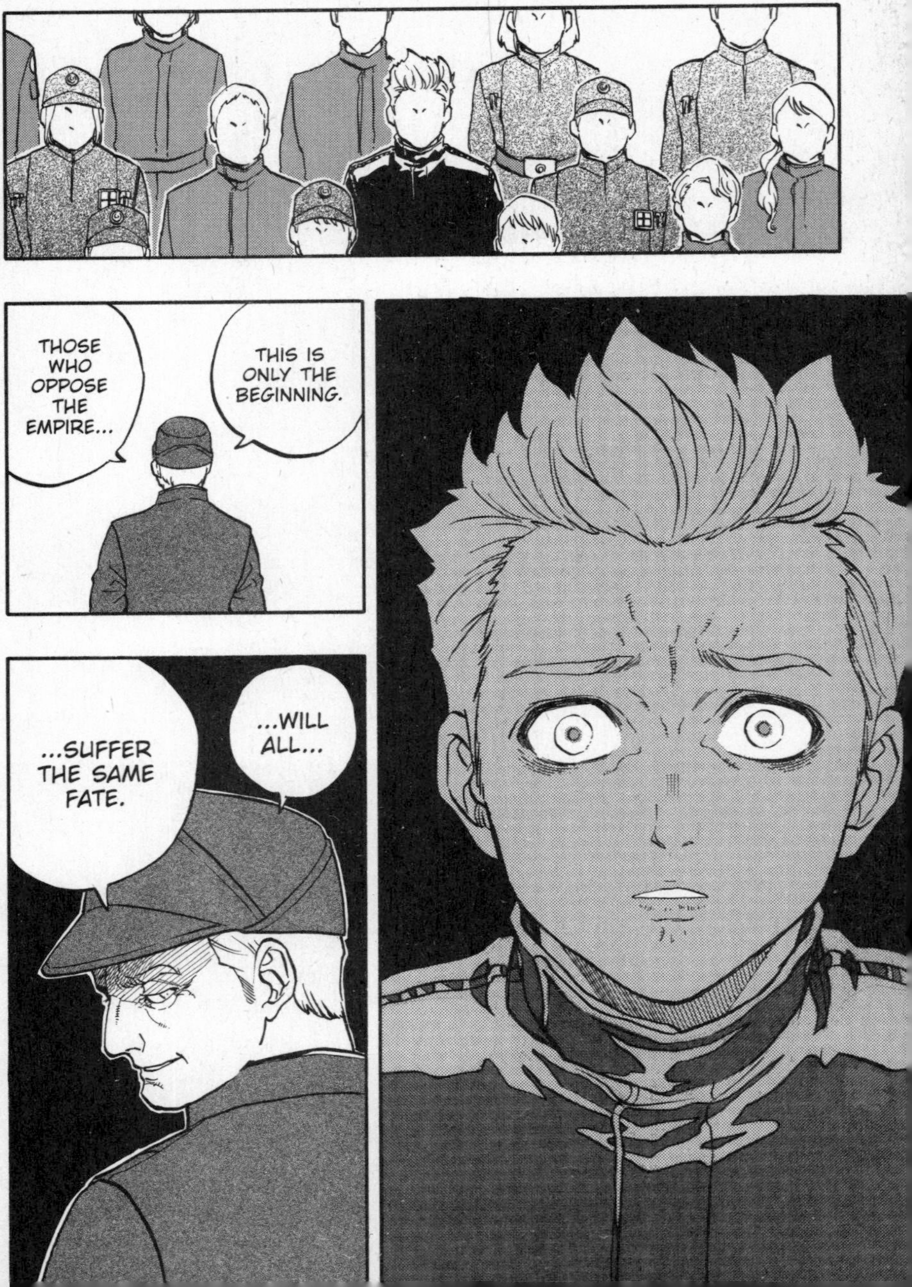
THIS IS ONLY THE BEGINNING.
THOSE WHO OPPOSE THE EMPIRE...
...WILL ALL...
...SUFFER THE SAME FATE.

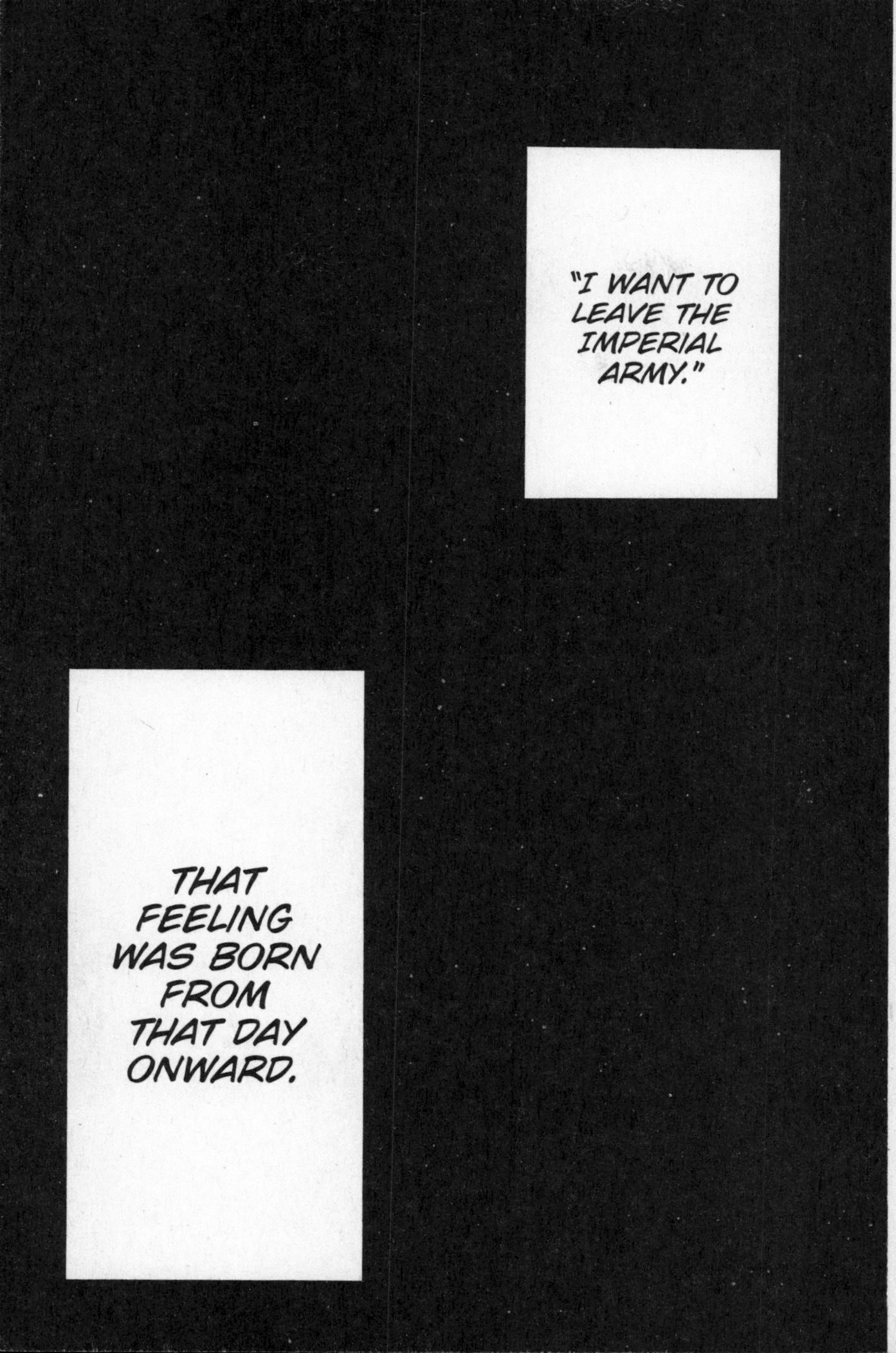
"I WANT TO LEAVE THE IMPERIAL ARMY."
THAT FEELING WAS BORN FROM THAT DAY ONWARD.

STAR

WARS

LOST

STARS

VOLUME. 1

I N D

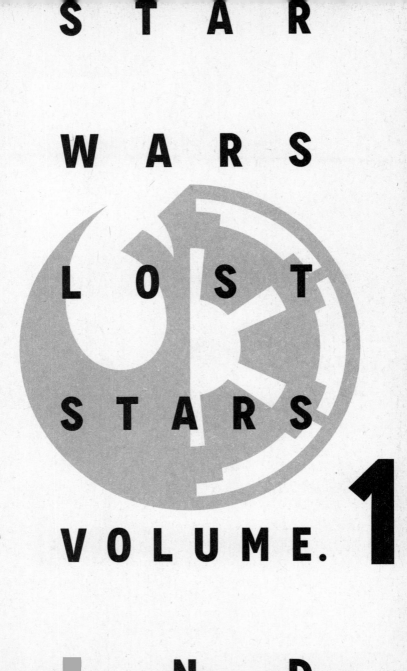

STAR WARS LOST STARS, VOLUME 2
COMING SOON

STAR WARS
LOST STARS
ロスト・スターズ